# HEIR
## —OF—
# NOVRON

Saldur smiled and then struck her hard across the face. The chains binding Arista's wrists snapped taut as she tried to protect herself. He listened to her crying softly for a moment and then said, "You're a smart girl—too smart for your own good—but you're not *that* smart. Hilfred may have helped you escape arrest. He might even have hidden you for those weeks we searched. But he couldn't have gotten you into the palace or found this prison. Hilfred died wearing the uniform of a fourth-floor guard. You must have had help from someone on the staff to get that, and I want to know who it was."

"There was no one. It was just me and Hilfred."

Saldur slapped her again. Arista cried out, her body shaking, jangling the chains.

"Don't lie to me," he said while raising his hand again.

Arista spoke quickly to stay the blow. "I told you. It was just me. I got a job working in the palace as a chambermaid. I stole the uniform."

"I know all about you posing as Ella the scrub girl. But you couldn't have gotten the uniform without help. It had to be someone in a position of authority. I must know who the traitor is. Now tell me. Who was helping you?"

When she said nothing, he struck her twice more.

Arista cringed. "Stop it!"

"Tell me," Saldur growled.

"No, you'll hurt her!" she blurted.

*"Her?"*

# By Michael J. Sullivan

*The Riyria Revelations*

Theft of Swords

Rise of Empire

Heir of Novron

# HEIR
## — OF —
# NOVRON

## MICHAEL J. SULLIVAN

### THE RIYRIA
### REVELATIONS
#### VOLUME 3

www.orbitbooks.net

ORBIT

First published in Great Britain in 2012 by Orbit

Copyright © 2012 by Michael J. Sullivan
(*Wintertide* © 2010)
Map by Michael J. Sullivan

Excerpt from *Seven Princes* by John R. Fultz
Copyright © 2012 by John R. Fultz

A CIP catalogue record for this book
is available from the British Library.

ISBN 978-0-356-50108-6

Printed and bound by CPI Group
(UK) Ltd, Croydon, CR0 4YY

Papers used by Orbit are from well-managed forests
and other responsible sources.

MIX
Paper from
responsible sources
FSC® C104740

Orbit
An imprint of
Little, Brown Book Group
100 Victoria Embankment
London EC4Y 0DY

An Hachette UK Company
www.hachette.co.uk

www.orbitbooks.net

*This book is entirely dedicated to my wife, Robin Sullivan.*

*Some have asked how it is I write such strong women without resorting to putting swords in their hands. It is because of her.*

*She is Arista*
*She is Thrace*
*She is Modina*
*She is Amilia*
*And she is my Gwen.*

*This series has been a tribute to her.*

*This is your book, Robin.*


*I hope you don't mind that I put down in words*
*How wonderful life is while you're in the world.*
—ELTON JOHN, BERNIE TAUPIN

# CONTENTS

## BOOK V

## Known Regions of the World of Elan

*Estrendor: Northern wastes*
*Erivan Empire: Elvenlands*
*Apeladorn: Nations of man*
*Ba Ran Archipelago: Islands of goblins*
*Westerlands: Western wastes*
*Dacca: Isle of south men*

## Nations of Apeladorn

*Avryn: Central wealthy kingdoms*
*Trent: Northern mountainous kingdoms*
*Calis: Southeastern tropical region ruled by warlords*
*Delgos: Southern republic*

## Kingdoms of Avryn

*Ghent: Ecclesiastical holding of the Nyphron Church*
*Melengar: Small but old and respected kingdom*
*Warric: Most powerful of the kingdoms of Avryn*
*Dunmore: Youngest and least sophisticated kingdom*
*Alburn: Forested kingdom*
*Rhenydd: Poor kingdom*
*Maranon: Producer of food. Once part of Delgos, which was lost when Delgos became a republic*
*Galeannon: Lawless kingdom of barren hills, the site of several great battles*

## The Gods

*Erebus: Father of the gods*
*Ferrol: Eldest son, god of elves*
*Drome: Second son, god of dwarves*
*Maribor: Third son, god of men*
*Muriel: Only daughter, goddess of nature*
*Uberlin: Son of Muriel and Erebus, god of darkness*

## Political Parties

*Imperialists: Those wishing to unite mankind under a single leader who is the direct descendant of the demigod Novron*
*Nationalists: Those wishing to be ruled by a leader chosen by the people*
*Royalists: Those wishing to perpetuate rule by individual, independent monarchs*

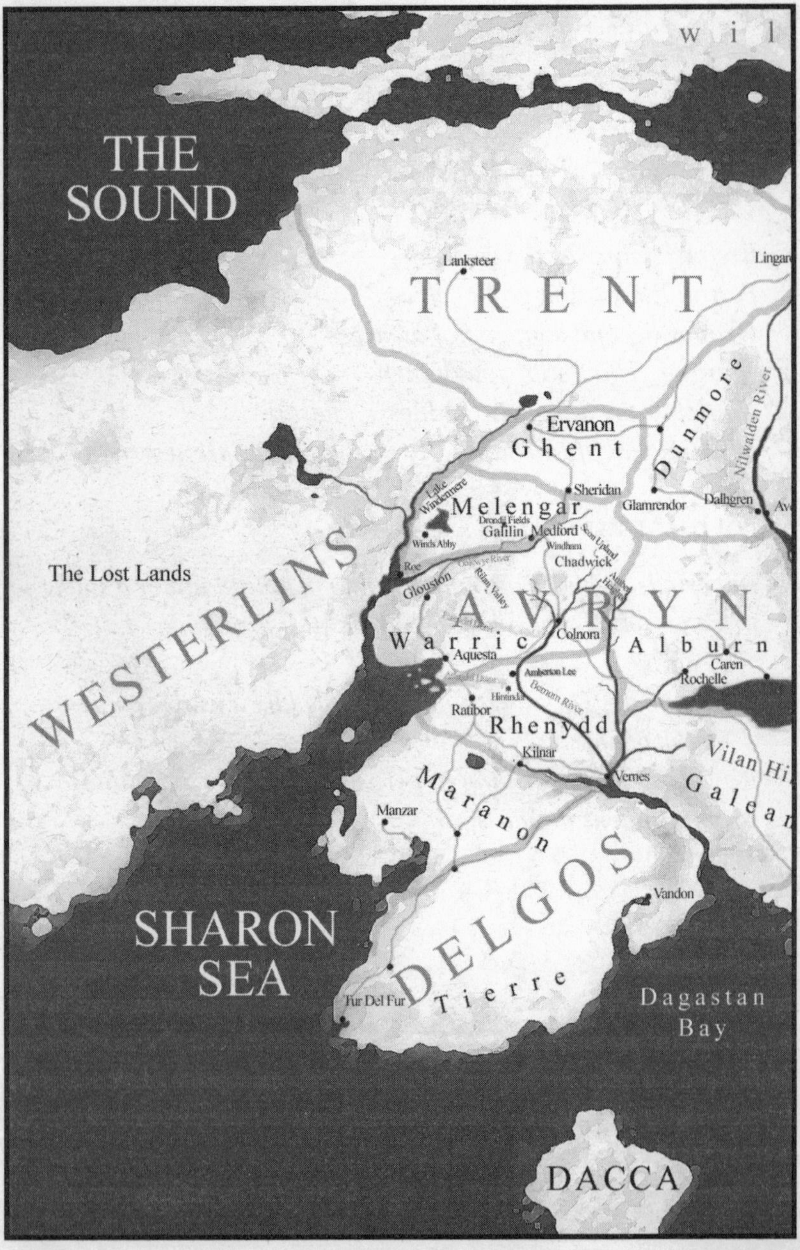
THE SOUND
TRENT
Lankstee
Ervanon
Ghent
Dunmore
Nilwalden River
Sheridan
Glamrendor
Dalhgren
Melengar
Medford
Galilin
Winds Abby
Chadwick
The Lost Lands
WESTERLINS
Roe
Glouston
AVRYN
Warric
Colnora
Alburn
Aquesta
Caren
Rochelle
Amberton Lee
Ratibor
Rhenydd
Kilnar
Vernes
Maranon
Manzar
Galean
DELGOS
Vandon
SHARON SEA
Tierre
Fur Del Fur
Dagastan Bay
DACCA

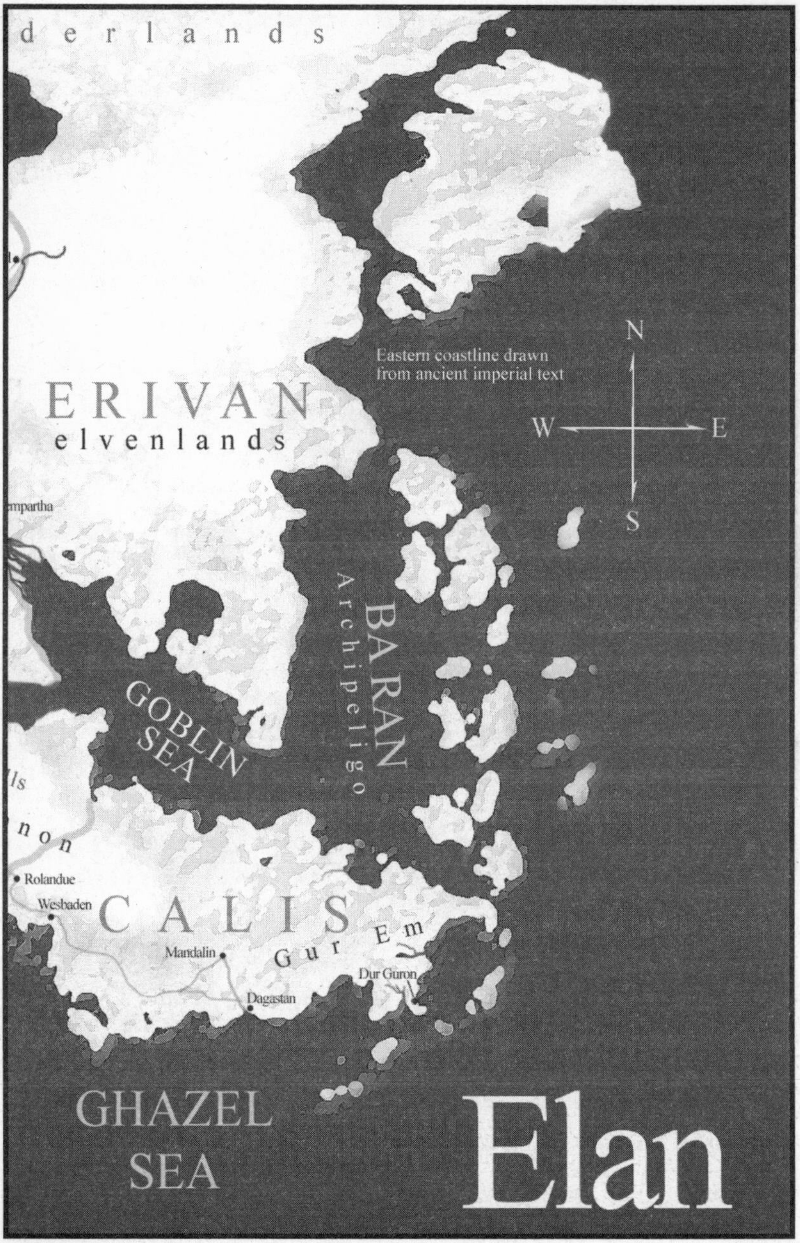

d e r l a n d s
Eastern coastline drawn
from ancient imperial text
N
W
E
S
ERIVAN
elvenlands
mpartha
BARAN
Archipeligo
GOBLIN
SEA
lls
n o n
Rolandue
Wesbaden
CALIS
Mandalin
Gur Em
Dur Guron
Dagastan
GHAZEL
SEA
Elan

# BOOK V

# WINTERTIDE

# Chapter 1

# Aquesta

Some people are skilled, and some are lucky, but at that moment Mince realized he was neither. Failing to cut the merchant's purse strings, he froze with one hand still cupping the bag. He knew the pickpocket's creed allowed for only a single touch, and he had dutifully slipped into the crowd after two earlier attempts. A third failure meant they would bar him from another meal. Mince was too hungry to let go.

With his hands still under the merchant's cloak, he waited. The man remained oblivious.

*Should I try again?*

The thought was insane, but his empty stomach won the battle over reason. In a moment of desperation, Mince pushed caution aside. The leather seemed oddly thick. Sawing back and forth, he felt the purse come loose, but something was not right. It took only an instant for Mince to realize his mistake. Instead of purse strings, he had sliced through the merchant's belt. Like a hissing snake, the leather strap slithered off the fat man's belly, dragged to the cobblestones by the weight of his weapons.

Mince did not breathe or move as the entire span of his ten disappointing years flashed by.

*Run!* the voice inside his head screamed as he realized there was a heartbeat, perhaps two, before his victim—

The merchant turned.

He was a large, soft man with saddlebag cheeks reddened by the cold. His eyes widened when he noticed the purse in Mince's hand. "Hey, you!" The man reached for his dagger, and surprise filled his face when he found it missing. Groping for his other weapon, he spotted them both lying in the street.

Mince heeded the voice of his smarter self and bolted. Common sense told him the best way to escape a rampaging giant was to head for the smallest crack. He plunged beneath an ale cart outside The Blue Swan Inn and slid to the far side. Scrambling to his feet, he raced for the alley, clutching the knife and purse to his chest. The recent snow hampered his flight, and his small feet lost traction rounding a corner.

"Thief! Stop!" The shouts were not nearly as close as he had expected.

Mince continued to run. Finally reaching the stable, he ducked between the rails of the fence framing the manure pile. Exhausted, he crouched with his back against the far wall. The boy shoved the knife into his belt and stuffed the purse down his shirt, leaving a noticeable bulge. Panting amidst the steaming piles, he struggled to hear anything over the pounding in his ears.

"There you are!" Elbright shouted, skidding in the snow and catching himself on the fence. "What an idiot. You just stood there—waiting for the fat oaf to turn around. You're a moron, Mince. That's it—that's all there is to it. I honestly don't know why I bother trying to teach you."

Mince and the other boys referred to thirteen-year-old Elbright as the Old Man. In their small band only he wore an actual cloak, which was dingy gray and secured with a tarnished metal broach. Elbright was the smartest and most accomplished of their crew, and Mince hated to disappoint him.

Laughing, Brand arrived only moments later and joined Elbright at the fence.

"It's not funny," Elbright said.

"But—he—" Brand could not finish as laughter consumed him.

Like the other two, Brand was dirty, thin, and dressed in mismatched clothing of varying sizes. His pants were too long and snow gathered in the folds of the rolled-up bottoms. Only his tunic fit properly. Made from green brocade and trimmed with fine supple leather, it fastened down the front with intricately carved wooden toggles. A year younger than the Old Man, he was a tad taller and a bit broader. In the unspoken hierarchy of their gang, Brand came second—the muscle to Elbright's brains. Kine, the remaining member of their group, ranked third, because he was the best pickpocket. This left Mince unquestionably at the bottom. His size matched his position, as he stood barely four feet tall and weighed little more than a wet cat.

"Stop it, will ya?" the Old Man snapped. "I'm trying to teach the kid a thing or two. He could have gotten himself killed. It was stupid—plain and simple."

"I thought it was brilliant." Brand paused to wipe his eyes. "I mean, sure it was dumb, but spectacular just the same. The way Mince just stood there blinking as the guy goes for his blades. But they ain't there 'cuz the little imbecile done cut the git's whole bloody belt off! Then..." Brand struggled against another bout of laughter. "The best part is that just after Mince runs, the fat bastard goes to chase him, and his breeches fall down. The guy toppled like a ruddy tree. *Wham*. Right into the gutter. By Mar, that was hilarious."

Elbright tried to remain stern, but Brand's recounting soon had them all laughing.

"Okay, okay, quit it." Elbright regained control and went straight to business. "Let's see the take."

Mince fished out the purse and handed it over with a wide grin. "Feels heavy," he proudly stated.

Elbright drew open the top and scowled after examining the contents. "Just coppers."

Brand and Elbright exchanged disappointed frowns and Mince's momentary elation melted. "It felt heavy," he repeated, mainly to himself.

"What now?" Brand asked. "Do we give him another go?"

Elbright shook his head. "No, and all of us will have to avoid Church Square for a while. Too many people saw Mince. We'll move closer to the gates. We can watch for new arrivals and hope to get lucky."

"Do ya want—" Mince started.

"No. Give me back my knife. Brand is up next."

The boys jogged toward the palace walls, following the trail that morning patrols had made in the fresh snow. They circled east and entered Imperial Square. People from all over Avryn were arriving for Wintertide, and the central plaza bustled with likely prospects.

"There," Elbright said, pointing toward the city gate. "Those two. See 'em? One tall, the other shorter."

"They're a sorry-looking pair," Mince said.

"Exhausted," Brand agreed.

"Probably been riding all night in the storm," Elbright said with a hungry smile. "Go on, Brand, do the old helpful stableboy routine. Now, Mince, watch how this is done. It might be your only hope, as you've got no talent for purse cutting."

❧

Royce and Hadrian entered Imperial Square on ice-laden horses. Defending against the cold, the two appeared as ghosts shrouded in snowy blankets. Despite wearing all they had, they were ill-equipped for the winter roads, much less the mountain passes that lay between Ratibor and Aquesta. The all-night snowstorm had only added to their hardship. As the two drew their horses to a stop, Royce noticed Hadrian breathing into his cupped hands. Neither of them had winter gloves. Hadrian had wrapped his fingers in torn strips from his blanket, while Royce opted for pulling his hands into the shelter of his sleeves. The sight of his own handless arms disturbed Royce as they reminded him of the old wizard. The two had learned the details of his murder while passing through Ratibor. Assassinated late one night, Esrahaddon had been silenced forever.

They had meant to get gloves, but as soon as they had arrived in Ratibor, they saw announcements proclaiming the Nationalist leader's upcoming execution. The empire planned to publicly burn Degan Gaunt in the imperial capital of Aquesta as part of the Wintertide celebrations. After Hadrian and Royce had spent months traversing high seas and dark jungles seeking Gaunt, to have found his whereabouts tacked up to every tavern door in the city was as much a blow as a blessing. Fearing some new calamity might arise to stop them from finally reaching him, they left early the next morning, long before the trade shops opened.

Unwrapping his scarf, Royce drew back his hood and looked around. The snow-covered palace took up the entire southern side of the square, while shops and vendors dominated the rest. Furriers displayed trimmed capes and hats. Shoemakers cajoled passers-by, offering to oil their boots.

Bakers tempted travelers with snowflake-shaped cookies and white-powdered pastries. And colorful banners were everywhere announcing the upcoming festival.

Royce had just dismounted when a boy ran up. "Take your horses, sirs? One night in a stable for just a silver each. I'll brush them down myself and see they get good oats too."

Dismounting and pulling back his own hood, Hadrian smiled at the boy. "Will you sing them a lullaby at night?"

"Certainly, sir," the boy replied without losing a beat. "It will cost you two coppers more, but I do have a very fine voice, I does."

"Any stable in the city will quarter a horse for five coppers," Royce challenged.

"Not this month, sir. Wintertide pricing started three days back. Stables and rooms fill up fast. Especially this year. You're lucky you got here early. In another two weeks, they'll be stocking horses in the fields behind hunters' blinds. The only lodgings will be on dirt floors, where people will be stacked like cordwood for five silvers each. I know the best places and the lowest costs in the city. A silver is a good price right now. In a few days it'll cost you twice that."

Royce eyed him closely. "What's your name?"

"Brand the Bold they call me." He straightened up, adjusting the collar of his tunic.

Hadrian chuckled and asked, "Why is that?"

" 'Cuz I don't never back down from a fight, sir."

"Is that where you got your tunic?" Royce asked.

The boy looked down as if noticing the garment for the first time. "This old thing? I got five better ones at home. I'm just wearing this rag so I don't get the good ones wet in the snow."

"Well, Brand, do you think you can take these horses to The Bailey Inn at Hall and Coswall and stable them there?"

"I could indeed, sir. And a fine choice, I might add. It's run by a reputable owner charging fair prices. I was just going to suggest that very place."

Royce gave him a smirk. He turned his attention to two boys who stood at a distance, pretending not to know Brand. Royce waved for them to come over. The boys appeared hesitant, but when he repeated the gesture, they reluctantly obliged.

"What are your names?" he asked.

"Elbright, sir," the taller of the two replied. This boy was older than Brand and had a knife concealed beneath his cloak. Royce guessed he was the real leader of their group and had sent Brand over to make the play.

"Mince, sir," said the other, who looked to be the youngest and whose hair showed evidence of having recently been cut with a dull knife. The boy wore little more than rags of stained, worn wool. His shirt and pants exposed the bright pink skin of his wrists and shins. Of all his clothing, the item that fit best was a torn woven bag draped over his shoulders. The same material wrapped his feet, secured around his ankles by twine.

Hadrian checked through the gear on his horse, removed his spadone blade, and slid it into the sheath, which he wore on his back beneath his cloak.

Royce handed two silver tenents to the first boy, then, addressing all three, said, "Brand here is going to have our horses stabled at the Bailey and reserve us a room. While he's gone, you two will stay here and answer some questions."

"But, ah, sir, we can't—" Elbright started, but Royce ignored him.

"When Brand returns with a receipt from the Bailey, I will pay *each* of you a silver. If he doesn't return, if instead he runs off and sells the horses, I shall slit both of your throats and hang you on the palace gate by your feet. I'll let your blood drip into a pail, then paint a sign with it to notify the city that Brand the Bold is a horse thief. Then I'll track him down, with the help of the imperial guard and *other connections* I have in this city, and see he gets the same treatment." Royce glared at the boy. "Do we understand each other, Brand?"

The three boys stared at him with mouths agape.

"By Mar! Not a very trusting fellow, are ya, sir?" Mince said.

Royce grinned ominously. "Make the reservation under the names of Grim and Baldwin. Run along now, Brand, but do hurry back. You don't want your friends to worry."

Brand led the horses away while the other two boys watched him go. Elbright gave a little shake of his head when Brand looked back.

"Now, boys, why don't you tell us what is planned for this year's festivities?"

"Well…" Elbright started, "I suspect this will be the most memorable Wintertide in a hundred years on account of the empress's marriage and all."

"Marriage?" Hadrian asked.

"Yes, sir. I thought everyone knew about that. Invitations went out months ago, and all the rich folk, even kings and queens, have been coming from all over."

"Who's she marrying?" Royce asked.

"*Lard* Ethelred," Mince said.

Elbright lowered his voice. "Shut it, Mince."

"He's a snake."

Elbright growled and cuffed him on the ear. "Talk like that will get you dead." Turning back to Royce and Hadrian, he said, "Mince has a bit of a crush on the empress. He's not too pleased with the old king, on account of him marrying her and all."

"She's like a goddess, she is," Mince declared, misty-eyed. "I seen her once. I climbed to that roof for a better view when she gave a speech last summer. She shimmered like a star, she did. By Mar, she's beautiful. Ya can tell she's the daughter of Novron. I've never seen anyone so pretty."

"See what I mean? Mince is a bit crazy when it comes to the empress," Elbright apologized. "He's got to get used to Regent Ethelred running things again. Not that he ever really stopped, on account of the empress being sick and all."

"She was hurt by the beast she killed up north," Mince explained. "Empress Modina was dying from the poison, and healers came from all over, but no one could help. Then Regent Saldur prayed for seven days and nights without food or water. Maribor showed him that the pure heart of a servant girl named Amilia from Tarin Vale had the power to heal the empress. And she did. Lady Amilia has been nursing the empress back to health and doing a fine job." He took a breath, his eyes brightened, and a smile grew across his face.

"Mince, enough," Elbright said.

"What's all this about?" Royce asked, pointing at bleachers that were being built in the center of the square. "They aren't holding the wedding out here, are they?"

"No, the wedding will be at the cathedral. Those are for folks to watch the execution. They're gonna kill the rebel leader."

"Yeah, that piece of news we heard about," Hadrian said softly.

"Oh, so you came for the execution?"

"More or less."

"I've got our spots all picked out," Elbright said. "I'm gonna have Mince go up the night before and save us a good seat."

"Hey, why do I have to go?" Mince asked.

"Brand and I have to carry all the stuff. You're too small to help and Kine's still sick, so you need to—"

"But you have the cloak and it's gonna be cold just sitting up there."

The two boys went on arguing, but Royce could tell Hadrian was no longer listening. His friend's eyes scanned the palace gates, walls, and front entrance. Hadrian was counting guards.

ക

Rooms at the Bailey were the same as at every inn—small and drab, with worn wooden floors and musty odors. A small pile of firewood was stacked next to the hearth in each room but never enough for the whole night. Patrons were forced to buy more at exorbitant prices if they wanted to stay warm. Royce made his usual rounds, circling the block, watching for faces that appeared too many times. He returned to their room confident that no one had noticed their arrival—at least, no one who mattered.

"Room eight. Been here almost a week," Royce said.

"A week? Why so early?" Hadrian asked.

"If you were living in a monastery for ten months a year, wouldn't you show up early for Wintertide?"

Hadrian grabbed his swords and the two moved down the hall. Royce picked the lock of a weathered door and slid it open. On the far side of the room, two candles burned on a small table set with plates, glasses, and a bottle of wine. A man, dressed in velvet and silk, stood before a wall mirror, checking the tie that held back his blond hair and adjusting the high collar of his coat.

"Looks like he was expecting us," Hadrian said.

"Looks like he was expecting someone," Royce clarified.

"What the—" Startled, Albert Winslow spun around. "Would it hurt to knock?"

"What can I say?" Royce flopped on the bed. "We're scoundrels and thieves."

"Scoundrels certainly," Albert said, "but thieves? When was the last time you two stole anything?"

"Do I detect dissatisfaction?"

"I'm a viscount. I have a reputation to uphold, which takes a certain amount of income—money that I don't receive when you two are idle."

Hadrian took a seat at the table. "He's not dissatisfied. He's outright scolding us."

"Is that why you're here so early?" Royce asked. "Scouting for work?"

"Partially. I also needed to get away from the Winds Abbey. I'm becoming a laughingstock. When I contacted Lord Daref, he couldn't lay off the Viscount Monk jokes. On the other hand, Lady Mae does find my pious reclusion appealing."

"And is she the one who..." Hadrian swirled a finger at the neatly arranged table.

"Yes. I was about to fetch her. I'm going to have to cancel, aren't I?" He looked from one to the other and sighed.

"Sorry."

"I hope this job pays well. This is a new doublet and I still owe the tailor." Blowing out the candles, he took a seat across from Hadrian.

"How are things up north?" Royce asked.

Albert pursed his lips, thinking. "I'm guessing you know about Medford being taken? Imperial troops hold it and most of the provincial castles except for Drondil Fields."

Royce sat up. "No, we didn't know. How's Gwen?"

"I have no idea. I was here when I heard."

"So Alric and Arista are at Drondil Fields?" Hadrian asked.

"King Alric is but I don't think the princess was in Medford. I believe she's running Ratibor. They appointed her mayor, or so I've heard."

"No," Hadrian said. "We just came through there. She was governing after the battle but left months ago in the middle of the night. No one knows why. I just assumed she went home."

Albert shrugged. "Maybe, but I never heard anything about her going back. Probably better for her if she didn't. The Imps have Drondil Fields surrounded. Nothing is going in or out. It's only a matter of time before Alric will have to surrender."

"What about the abbey? Has the empire come knocking?" Royce asked.

Albert shook his head. "Not that I know of. But like I said, I was already here when the Imperialists crossed the Galewyr."

Royce got up and began to pace.

"Anything else?" Hadrian asked.

"Rumor has it that Tur Del Fur was invaded by goblins. But that's only a rumor, as far as I can tell."

"Not a rumor," Hadrian said.

"Oh?"

"We were there. Actually, we were responsible."

"Sounds…interesting," Albert said.

Royce stopped his pacing. "Don't get him started."

"Okay, so what brings you to Aquesta?" Albert asked. "I'm guessing it's not to celebrate Wintertide."

"We're going to break Degan Gaunt out of the palace dungeon, and we'll need you for the usual inside work," Royce said.

"Really? You do know he's going to be executed on Wintertide, don't you?"

"Yeah, that's why we need to get moving. It would be bad if we were late," Hadrian added.

"Are you crazy? The palace? At Wintertide? You've heard

about this little wedding that's going on? Security might be a tad tighter than usual. Every day I see a line of men in the courtyard, signing up to join the guard."

"Your point?" Hadrian asked.

"We should be able to use the wedding to our advantage," Royce said. "Anyone we know in town yet?"

"Genny and Leo arrived recently, I think."

"Really? That's perfect. Get in touch. They'll have rooms in the palace for sure. See if they can get you in. Then find out all you can, especially about where they're keeping Gaunt."

"I'm going to need money. I was only planning to attend a few local balls and maybe one of the feasts. If you want me inside the palace, I'll have to get better clothes. By Mar, look at my shoes. Just look at them! I can't meet the empress in these."

"Borrow from Genny and Leo for now," Royce said. "I'm going to leave for Medford tonight and return with funds to cover our expenses."

"You're going back? Tonight?" Albert asked. "You just got here, didn't you?"

The thief nodded.

"She's okay," Hadrian assured Royce. "I'm sure she got out."

"We've got nearly a month to Wintertide," Royce said. "I should be back in a week or so. In the meantime, learn what you can, and we'll formulate a plan when I return."

"Well," Albert grumbled, "at least Wintertide won't be boring."

## Chapter 2

# Into Darkness

Someone was whimpering.

It was a man's voice this time, one that Arista had heard before. Everyone cried eventually. Some people even broke down into fits of hysterics. There used to be a woman who was prone to screaming, but she had been removed some time earlier. Arista held no illusions of the woman being set free. She had heard them drag the body away. The whimpering man used to cry out but had grown quieter over the past few days. He never wailed anymore. Although not long before, she had heard him praying. Arista was surprised that he did not ask for rescue or even a quick death. All he prayed for was *her*. He asked Maribor to keep her safe, but in all his ramblings, the princess never caught the name of the man's lover.

There was no way to track the passage of time in the dark. Arista tried counting meals, but her hunger suggested they came less than once per day. Still, weeks must have passed since her capture. In all that time, she had never heard Gaunt, despite having called out to him. The only time she had heard his voice was the night she and Hilfred had failed to rescue him.

Since then, she had been confined to her cell, which contained only a pail for waste and a few handfuls of straw. The room was so small that she could touch all four walls at once, making it feel like a cage or a grave. Arista knew that Modina, the girl once known as Thrace, had been kept somewhere just like that. Perhaps even in that very cell. After she had lost everyone and everything that mattered to her, it would have been a nightmare to wake alone in the dark without explanation, cause, or reason. Not knowing where she was or how she had gotten there must have driven the girl mad.

Despite her own tragedies, at least Arista knew she was not alone in the world. Once the news of her disappearance reached him, her brother, Alric, would move the world to save her. The two had grown closer in the years since their father's death. He was no longer the privileged boy, and she was no longer the jealous, reclusive sister. They still had their arguments, but nothing would stop him from finding her. Alric would enlist the help of the Pickerings—her extended family. He might even call on Royce and Hadrian, whom Alric affectionately referred to as the royal protectors. It would not be long now.

Arista pictured Hadrian's lopsided smile. The image stung but her mind refused to let it go. Memories of the sound of his voice, the touch of his hand, and that tiny scar on his chin pulled at her heart. There had been moments of warmth, but only kindness on his part, only sympathy—compassion for a person in pain or need. To him, Arista was just *the princess*, his employer, his job, just one more desperate noble.

*How empty an existence I've led that those few I count among my best friends are two people I paid to work for me.*

She wanted to believe that Hadrian saw her as something special, that the time they had spent on the road together had endeared her to him—that it meant as much to Hadrian as it did to her. Arista hoped he considered her smarter or more capable than most. But even if he did, men did not want smart or capable. They wanted pretty. Arista was not pretty like Alenda Lanaklin or Lenare Pickering. If only Hadrian saw her the way Emery and Hilfred had.

*Then he would be dead too.*

The deep rumble of stone against stone echoed through the corridors. Footsteps sounded in the hall. Someone was coming.

Now was not the time for food. While Arista could not count the days in the darkness, she knew food never came until she feared it might never come. They fed her so little that she welcomed the thin, putrid soup, which smelled of rotten eggs.

The approaching footfalls came from two sets of shoes. The first she recognized as a guard who wore metal and made a pronounced *tink-tink*. The other wore hard heels and soles that created a distinct *click-clack*. That was not a guard, nor was it a servant. Servants wore soft shoes that made a *swish-swish* sound or no shoes at all—*slap-slap*. Only someone wealthy could afford shoes that clacked on stone. The steps were slow but not hesitant. There was confidence in the long, measured strides.

A key rattled against the assembly of her lock and then clicked.

*A visitor?*

The door to her cell opened, and a bright light made Arista wince.

A guard entered, jerked her roughly to one side, and attached a pair of iron bracelets, chaining her wrists to the wall. Leaving her sitting with her arms above her head, the guard exited but left the door open.

A moment later, Regent Saldur entered holding a lantern. "How are you this evening, Princess?" The old man shook his head sadly, making tsking noises. "Look at you, my dear. You are so thin and filthy, and where in Maribor's name did you get that dress? Not that there's much of it left, is there? Those look like new bruises too. Have the guards been raping you? No, I suppose not." Saldur lowered his voice to a whisper. "They had *extremely* strict orders not to touch Modina when she was here. I accused an innocent jailor of improperly touching her and then had him pulled apart by oxen as an example. There were no problems after that. It might seem extreme, but I couldn't have a pregnant empress, now could I? Of course, in your case I really don't care, but the guards don't know that."

"Why are you here?" she asked. Her low raspy voice sounded strange, even to her.

"I thought I would bring you some news, my dear. Kilnar and Vernes have fallen. Rhenydd is now a happy member of the empire. The farmlands of Maranon on the Delgos peninsula had a nice harvest, so we'll have plenty of supplies to feed our troops all winter. We've retaken Ratibor but had to execute quite a few traitors as examples. The peasants must learn the consequences of rebellion. They were cursing your name before we had finished."

Arista knew he was telling the truth. Not because she could read his face, which she barely saw through her matted hair, but because Saldur had no reason to lie. "What do you want?"

"Two things, really. I want you to realize that the New Empire has risen and nothing can stand in its way. Your life, Arista, is over. You will be executed in a matter of weeks. And your dreams are already dead. You need to bury them alongside the sad little graves of Hilfred and Emery."

Arista stiffened.

"Surprised? We learned all about Emery when we retook Ratibor. You really do have such a way with men. First you got him killed and then Hilfred as well. You must make black widows jealous."

"And the second?" She noticed his momentary confusion. "The other reason we're having this little chat?"

"Oh yes. I want to know who you were working with."

"Hilfred—you killed him for it, remember?"

Saldur smiled and then struck her hard across the face. The chains binding Arista's wrists snapped taut as she tried to protect herself. He listened to her crying softly for a moment and then said, "You're a smart girl—too smart for your own good—but you're not *that* smart. Hilfred may have helped you escape arrest. He might even have hidden you for those weeks we searched. But he couldn't have gotten you into the palace or found this prison. Hilfred died wearing the uniform of a fourth-floor guard. You must have had help from someone on the staff to get that, and I want to know who it was."

"There was no one. It was just me and Hilfred."

Saldur slapped her again. Arista cried out, her body shaking, jangling the chains.

"Don't lie to me," he said while raising his hand again.

Arista spoke quickly to stay the blow. "I told you. It was just me. I got a job working in the palace as a chambermaid. I stole the uniform."

"I know all about you posing as Ella the scrub girl. But you couldn't have gotten the uniform without help. It had to be someone in a position of authority. I must know who the traitor is. Now tell me. Who was helping you?"

When she said nothing, he struck her twice more.

Arista cringed. "Stop it!"

"Tell me," Saldur growled.

"No, you'll hurt her!" she blurted.

*"Her?"*

Realizing her mistake, Arista bit her lip.

"So it was a woman. That limits the possibilities considerably, now doesn't it?" Saldur played with a key that dangled from a small chain, spinning it around his index finger. After several minutes, the regent crouched down and placed the lantern on the floor.

"I need a name and you *will* tell me. I know you *think* you can carry her identity to your grave, but whether you hold your tongue out of loyalty to her or to spite me, you should reconsider. You might believe that a few weeks is not long to hold your tongue, but once we start, you'll wish for a quick death."

He brushed her hair aside. "Look at that face. You don't believe me, do you? Still so naive. Still such an optimistic child. As a princess, you've led such a pampered life. Do you think that living among the commoners of Ratibor and scrubbing floors here at the palace has made you strong? Do you think you have nothing else to lose and you've finally hit bottom?"

When he stroked her cheek, Arista recoiled.

"I can see by your expression that you still have some pride and a sense of nobility. You don't yet realize just how far you have to fall. Trust me, Arista, I can strip you of that courage and break your spirit. You don't want to find out just how low I can bring you."

He stroked her hair gently for a moment, then grabbed a handful. Saldur pulled hard, jerking her head back and forcing Arista to look at him. His gaze lingered on her face. "You're still pure, aren't you? Still untouched and locked in your tower in more ways than one. I suspect neither Emery nor Hilfred dared to bed a princess. Perhaps we should begin with that. I will let the guards know that they can—no—I will specifically order them to violate you. It will make both of us very popular. The men will be requesting extra duty so they can desecrate you night and day."

Saldur let go of her hair, allowing her head to drop.

"Once you are thoroughly used and your pride has evaporated, I'll send for the master inquisitor. I'm sure he will relish the opportunity to purge the evil from the infamous Witch of Melengar." Saldur moved closer and spoke softly, intimately. "The inquisitor is very imaginative, and what he can do with chains, a bucket of water, and a searing hot brand is sheer artistry. You'll scream until you lose your voice. You'll black out and wake where the nightmare left off."

Arista tried to turn away, but his wrinkled hands forced her to look at him once again. His expression was not pleased or maniacal. Saldur appeared grim—almost sad.

"You'll experience anguish that you never thought possible. Your remaining courage will evaporate into myth and memory. Your mind will abandon you, leaving behind a drooling lump of scarred flesh. Even the guards won't want you then."

Saldur leaned forward until she could feel his breath and feared he might kiss her. "If, after all that, you've still not given me what I want, I will turn my attention to that pleasant little family who took you in—the Barkers, wasn't it? I will have them arrested and brought here. The father will watch as his wife takes your place with the guards. Then she will witness her husband and sons drawn and quartered one by one. Imagine what it will do to the woman when she sees her youngest, the one you supposedly saved, die. She will blame *you*, Arista. That poor woman will curse your name, and rightly so, for it will be your silence that destroyed her life."

He gently patted Arista's burning cheek. "Don't force me to do it. Tell me the traitor's name. She is guilty of treason, but the poor Barkers are innocent. They have done nothing. Simply tell me the name of this woman and you can prevent all these horrors."

Arista found it difficult to think and fought for breath as

she started losing control. Her face throbbed from his blows, and she was sickened by the salty-metallic taste of blood in her mouth. Guilt conjured images of Emery and Hilfred, both of whom had died because of her. She could not bear to add the Barkers' blood to her hands. To have them suffer for her mistakes.

"I'll tell you," Arista finally said. "But in return I want your assurance nothing will happen to the Barkers."

Saldur looked sympathetic, and she could almost see the grandfatherly face from her youth. How he could make such despicable threats and then return to such a kindly expression was beyond her understanding.

"Of course, my dear. After all, I'm not a monster. Just give me what I want and none of those things will come to pass. Now, tell me...What is her name?"

Arista hesitated. Saldur lost his smile once again—her time was up. She swallowed and said, "There *was* someone who hid me, gave me food, and even helped to find Gaunt. She's been a true friend, so kind and selfless. I can't believe I am betraying her to you now."

"Her *name*?" Saldur pressed.

Tears ran from Arista's eyes as she looked up. "Her name is...is...Edith Mon."

# CHAPTER 3

## SIR BRECKTON

Archibald Ballentyne, the Earl of Chadwick, stared out the windows of the imperial throne room. Behind him, Saldur shuffled parchments at a table while Ethelred warmed a throne not yet his own. A handful of servants occasionally drifted in and out, as did the imperial chancellor, who briefly spoke with one regent or the other. No one ever spoke to Archibald or asked for his counsel.

In just a few short years, Regent Saldur had risen from Bishop of Medford to the architect of the New Empire. Ethelred was about to trade his king's crown of Warric for the imperial scepter of all Avryn. Even the commoner Merrick Marius had managed to secure a noble fief, wealth, and a title.

*What do I have to show for all my contributions? Where is my crown? My wife? My glory?*

The answers Archibald knew all too well. He would wear no crown. Ethelred would wed his wife. And as for his glory, the man who had stolen that was just entering the hall. Archibald heard the boots pounding against the polished marble floor. The sound of the man's stride was unmistakable — uncompromising, straightforward, brash.

Turning around, Archibald saw Sir Breckton Belstrad's

floor-length blue cape sweeping behind the knight. Holding his helm in the crook of one arm and wearing a metal breastplate, he looked as if he were just returning from battle. Sir Breckton was tall, his shoulders broad, his chin chiseled. He was a leader of men, victorious in battle, and Archibald hated him.

"Sir Breckton, welcome to Aquesta," Ethelred called as the knight crossed the room.

Breckton ignored him, and Saldur as well, walking directly to Archibald's side, where he stomped dramatically and dropped to one knee. "Your Lordship," he said.

"Yes, yes, get up." The Earl of Chadwick waved a hand at him.

"As always, I am at your service, my lord."

"Sir Breckton?" Ethelred addressed the knight again.

Breckton showed no sign of acknowledgment and continued to speak with his liege. "You called, my lord? What is it you wish of me?"

"Actually, I summoned you on behalf of Regent Ethelred. He wishes to speak with you."

The knight stood. "As you wish, my lord."

Breckton turned and crossed the distance to the throne. His sword slapped against his side, and his boots pounded against the stone. He stopped at the base of the steps and offered only a shallow bow.

Ethelred scowled, but only briefly. "Sir Breckton, at long last. I've sent summons for you six times over the past several weeks. Have the messages not reached you?"

"They have, Your Lordship."

"But you did not respond," Ethelred said.

"No, Your Lordship."

"Why?"

"My lord, the Earl of Chadwick, commanded me to take Melengar. I was following his orders," Breckton replied.

"So the crucial demands of battle prevented you from breaking away until now." Ethelred nodded.

"No, Your Lordship. Only the fall of Drondil Fields remains and the siege is well tended. Victory is assured and does not require my attention."

"Then I don't understand. Why didn't you come when I ordered you to appear before me?"

"I do not serve you, Your Lordship. I serve the Earl of Chadwick."

Archibald's disdain for Breckton did not diminish his delight at seeing Ethelred verbally slapped.

"May I remind you, sir knight, that I will be emperor in just a few weeks?"

"You may, Your Lordship."

Ethelred looked confused. This brought a smile to Archibald's face. He enjoyed seeing someone else trying to deal with Breckton and knew exactly how the regent felt. Was Breckton granting Ethelred permission to remind the knight, or had he just insinuated the regent might not be emperor? Either way, the comment was rude yet spoken so plainly and respectfully that it appeared innocent of any ill intent. Breckton was like that—politely confounding and pointedly confusing. He had a way of making Archibald feel stupid, and that was just one of the many reasons he despised the arrogant man.

"I see this is going to continue to be an issue," Ethelred said. "It demonstrates the point of this meeting. As emperor, I will require good men to help me reign. You have proven yourself a capable leader, and as such, I want you to serve me directly. I am prepared to offer you the office and title of grand marshal of all imperial forces. In addition, I'll grant you the province of Melengar."

Archibald staggered. "Melengar is mine! Or will be when it is taken. It was promised to me."

"Yes, Archie, but times change. I need a strong man in the north, defending my border." Ethelred looked at Breckton. "I will appoint you the Marquis of Melengar. All too fitting, given that you were responsible for taking it."

"This is outrageous!" Archibald shouted, stomping his foot. "We had a deal. You have the imperial crown and Saldur has the imperial miter. What do I get? What is the reward for all my sweat and sacrifice? Without me, you wouldn't have Melengar to bestow to anyone!"

"Don't make a fool of yourself, Archie," Saldur said gently. "You must have known we could never entrust such an important realm to you. You are too young, too inexperienced, too... weak."

There was silence as Archibald fumed.

"Well?" Ethelred turned his attention back to Breckton. "Marquis of Melengar? Grand marshal of the imperial host? What say you?"

Sir Breckton showed no emotion. "I serve the Earl of Chadwick, just as my father and grandfather before me. It does not appear he wishes this. If there is nothing else, I must return to my charge in Melengar." Sir Breckton pivoted sharply and strode back to Archibald, where he knelt once more.

Ethelred stared after him in shock.

"Don't leave Aquesta just yet," Archibald told the knight. "I may have need of you here."

"As you wish, my lord." Breckton stood and briskly departed.

They were silent as they listened to the knight's footfalls echo and fade. Ethelred's face turned scarlet and he clenched his fists. Saldur stared after Breckton with his usual irritated glare.

"It seems you didn't take into account the man's unwavering sense of loyalty when you made your plans," Archibald railed. "But then, how could you, seeing as how you obviously don't understand the meaning of the word yourself? You should have consulted me first. I would have told you what the result would be. But you couldn't do that, could you? No, because it was *me* you were plotting to stab in the back!"

"Calm down, Archie," Saldur said.

"Stop calling me that. My name is Archibald!" Spit flew from his lips. "You're both so smug and arrogant, but I'm no pawn. One word from me and Breckton will turn his army and march on Aquesta." The earl pointed toward the still open door. "They're loyal to him, you know—every last one of the miserable cretins. They will do whatever he says, and as you can see, he worships me."

He clenched his fists and advanced, maddened that his soft heels did not have the same audible impact as Breckton's.

"I could get King Alric to throw his support behind me as well. I could return his precious Melengar in exchange for the rest of Avryn. I could beat you at your own little game. I'd have the Northern Imperial Army in my right hand and what remains of the Royalists in my left. I could crush both of you in less than a month. So don't tell me to calm down, *Sauly*! I've had it with your condescending tone and your holier-than-thou attitude. You're as much a worm as Ethelred. You're both in this together, weaving your webs and plotting against me. You just may have caught your own selves in your sticky trap this time!"

He headed for the door.

"Archi—I mean, Archibald!" Ethelred called after him.

The earl did not pause as he swept past Chancellor Biddings, who was just outside the throne room and gave the earl a concerned look. Servants scattered before Archibald as he marched in a fury through the doorway to the inner ward. Bursting into the brilliant sunshine reflected by the courtyard's snow, he discovered he was unsure where to go from there. After a few moments, Archibald decided that it did not matter. It felt good just to move, to burn off energy, to get away. He considered calling for his horse. A long ride over hard ground seemed like just the thing he needed, but it was cold out. Archibald did not want to end up miles from shelter freezing, tired, and hungry. Instead, he settled for pacing back and forth, creating a shallow trench in the new snow.

Frustration turned to pleasure as he recalled his little speech. He liked the look it had put on both of their faces. They had not expected such a bold response from him. The delight ate up most of the burning anger, and the pacing dissipated the rest. Taking a seat on an upturned bucket, he stomped the snow from his boots.

*Would Breckton turn his forces against Aquesta? Could I become the new emperor and have Modina for my own with just a single order?*

The answer formed almost as quickly as the question had. The thought was an appealing dream but nothing more. Breckton would never agree and would refuse the order. For all the knight's loyal bravado, everything that man did was subservient to some inscrutable code.

The entire House of Belstrad had been that way. Archibald recalled his father complaining about their ethics. The Ballentynes believed that knights should take orders without question in exchange for wealth and power. The Belstrads believed differently. They clung to an outdated ideal that the ruler—appointed by Maribor—must act within His will to earn a knight's loyalty. Archibald was certain Breckton would not consider civil war to be Maribor's will. Apparently, nothing Archibald ever really wanted fit that category.

Still, he had rocked the regents on their heels, and they

would treat him better. He would finally have respect now that they realized just how important he was. The regents would have no clue that he could not deliver on his threats, so they would try to placate him with a larger prize. In the end, Archibald would have Melengar and perhaps more.

# CHAPTER 4

# WEDDING PLANS

The Duchess of Rochelle was a large woman in more than just girth. Her husband matched her, as they were both rotund people with thick necks, short pudgy fingers, and cheeks that jiggled when they laughed, which in the case of the lady was often and loud. They were like bookends to each other. A male and female version, cut from the same cloth in every way except temperament. While the duke was quiet, Lady Genevieve was anything but.

Amilia always knew when the duchess was coming, as the lady heralded her own arrival with a trumpetlike voice that echoed through the palace halls. She greeted everyone, regardless of class, with a hearty "Hullo! How *are* you?" in her brassy voice, which boomed off the dull stone. She would hug servants, guards, and even the huntsman's hound if he crossed her path.

Amilia had met the duke and duchess when they first arrived. Saldur was there and had made the mistake of trying to explain why an audience with the empress was not possible. Amilia had been able to excuse herself, but she was certain Saldur had not been so lucky and probably was delayed for hours. Since then, Amilia had been avoiding the duchess, as the woman was not one to take no for an answer, and she did not want to repeat Saldur's mistake. After three days Amilia's luck finally ran out, when she was leaving the chapel.

"Amilia, darling!" the duchess shouted, rushing forward with her elegant gown billowing behind her. When she reached Amilia, two huge arms surrounded the imperial secretary in a crushing embrace. "I've been looking for you everywhere. Every time I inquire, I'm told you are busy. They must work you to death!"

The duchess released her grip. "You poor thing. Let me look at you." She took Amilia's hands and spread her arms wide. "Oh my, how lovely you are. But, darling, please tell me this is a washday and your servants are behind. No, don't bother. I am certain that is the case. Still, I hope you won't mind if I have Lois, my seamstress, whip you up something. I do so love giving gifts and it's Wintertide, after all. By the look of you, it will hardly take any material or time. Lois will be thrilled."

Lady Genevieve took Amilia's arm and walked her down the hall. "You really are a treasure, you know, but I can tell they treat you poorly. What can you expect with men like Ethelred and Saldur running the show? Everything will be fine, though, now that I'm here."

They rounded a corner and Amilia was amazed by the woman's ability to talk so quickly without seeming to take a breath.

"Oh! I just loved the invitation you sent me, and yes, I know it was all your doing. It's *all* been your doing, hasn't it? They have you planning the whole wedding, don't they? No wonder you are so busy. How insensitive. How cruel! But don't worry. As I said, I'm here to help you. I've fashioned many weddings in my day and they've all been wonderful. What you need is an experienced planner—a wizard of wonder. We aristocrats expect panache and dazzle at these events and we hate to be disappointed. Being that this is the wedding of the empress, it must be larger, grander, and more amazing than anything that has come before. Nothing less will suffice."

She stopped suddenly and peered at Amilia. "Do you have doves to release? You must have them. You simply must!"

Amilia thought to reply, but the concern fled the duchess's face before she had a chance. Lady Genevieve was walking once more, pulling Amilia along. "Oh, I don't want to frighten you, darling. There is still plenty of time, given the proper help, of course. I am here now, and Modina will be thrilled at what we will achieve together. It will simply astound her."

"I—"

"How many white horses have you arranged for? Not nearly enough, I'm sure. Never mind, it will all come together. You'll see. Speaking of horses, I insist you accompany me on the hawking. I won't stand for you riding with anyone else. You'll love Leopold—he's quiet, just like you are, but a real pumpkin. Do you know what I mean? It doesn't look like you do—but no matter. You two will get on marvelously. Do you have a bird?"

"A bird?" Amilia managed to squeeze in.

"I'll let you use Murderess. She is one of my own goshawks."

"But—"

"No worries, my dear. There's nothing to it. The bird does all the work. All you need to do is just sit on your horse and look pretty—which you will in the new dress Lois will make. Blue would be a good color and will go wonderfully with your eyes. I suppose I will have to arrange a horse as well. We can't have you trudging through the snow and ruining the gown, now can we? I just know Saldur never thinks of such things. He appointed you secretary to the empress, but does he realize the need for clothing? A horse? Jewelry?"

The duchess paused again, still gripping her arm like a cider press. "Oh, my darling, I just realized you aren't wearing any—jewelry, that is. Don't be embarrassed. I understand perfectly. Otto is a fabulous jeweler. He can set a sapphire pendant in the blink of an eye. Won't that look stunning with your new blue gown? Thank Maribor I brought my full retinue. Lord knows the local artisans could never keep up with me. When you think about it, who can?" She laughed, and Amilia wondered just how much longer she could go on.

With another pull, they were off again. "I tend to be a bit much, don't I? It's the way I am. I can't help it. My husband stopped trying to turn me into a proper wife years ago. Of course, now he knows that my exuberance is what he loves most about me. 'Never a dull moment or a moment's peace,' he always says. Speaking of men, have you chosen a champion to carry your favor in the joust?"

"N-no."

"You haven't? But, darling, knights just adore fighting for pretty, young things like you. I'll bet you've driven them mad by waiting so long."

There was a pause, which startled Amilia into speech. "Ah, I didn't know I was supposed to."

"Ha hah!" Lady Genevieve laughed delightedly. "You *are* a marvel, darling. Simply fabulous! Ethelred tells me you're new to the gentry—elevated by Maribor himself. Isn't that delightful? Maribor's Chosen One watching over Maribor's Heir. How amazing!"

They turned the corner into the west wing, where a handful of chambermaids scattered like pigeons before a carriage. "You're a living legend, dear Amilia. Why, every knight in the kingdom will clamor for your favor. There will be none more sought after except the empress herself, but of course, no one would dare insult Ethelred by asking for *her* favor just weeks before his wedding! No one wants to make an enemy of a new emperor. That makes you the darling of the festival. You can have your pick of any eligible bachelor. Dukes, princes, earls, counts, and barons are all hoping for the chance to capture your attention or win the honor of sitting next to you at the feast with a victory on the field of Highcourt."

"I wasn't planning on going to either," Amilia stated.

The mere idea of noblemen chasing her was beyond frightening. While courtly love might be honorable and romantic for princesses and countesses, no noble ever practiced gentleness with a common woman. Serving girls who caught the eye of any noble—whether a knight or a king—could be taken against their will. Amilia had never been attacked, but she had wiped tears and bound wounds for more friends than she cared to count. Although she now possessed the title of *lady* before her name, everyone knew her background, and Amilia feared her flimsy title would be a poor shield against a lust-driven noble.

"Nonsense, you must attend the feasts. Besides, it's your duty. Your absence could very well start a riot! You don't want to be the cause of an insurrection in the weeks leading to your empress's wedding, do you?"

"Ah, no, of course—"

"Good, so it's all settled. Now you just need to pick someone. Do you have a favorite?"

"I don't know any of them."

"None? Good gracious, darling! Do they keep you a prisoner? What about Sir Elgar or Sir Murthas? Prince Rudolf is competing, and he is a fine choice with an excellent future. Of course, there is also Sir Breckton. You couldn't find a better choice than that. I know he *does* have the reputation of being a bit stuffy. It is true, of course. But after his victory in Melengar, he's the hero of the hour—and quite dashing." The duchess wiggled her eyebrows. "Yes, Breckton would be a perfect choice. Why, the ladies of several courts have been fawning over him for years."

A look of concern crossed Lady Genevieve's face. "Hmm... that does bring up a good point. You'll probably need to be careful. While you are certainly the object of every knight's affections, that means you're also the target of every lady's jealousy."

The duchess threw a meaty arm around Amilia's neck and pulled her close, as if she were going to whisper in her ear, but her voice did not drop a bit in volume. "Trust me, these women are dangerous. Courtly love isn't a game to them. You're new to politics, so I am telling you this for your own good. These are daughters of kings, dukes, and earls, and they are used to getting what they want. When they don't, they can be vengeful. They know all about your background. I am certain that many have sent spies to visit your family, trying to dig up any dirt they can. If they can't find any, trust me, they will invent some."

Lady Genevieve tugged her around another corner, this time toward the northern postern and up the steps to the third floor.

"I don't understand what you mean."

"It's quite simple, my dear. On the one hand, they think belittling you should be easy because of your common roots. But, on the other, you've never made any pretense of being otherwise, which negates their effort. It's difficult to demean someone for something they're not embarrassed of, now isn't it? Still, you must turn a deaf ear to any jibes told at your expense. You may hear name-calling, like swine herder and such. Which, of course, you're not. You must remember you're the daughter of a carriage maker and a fine one at that. Why, absolutely everyone who is anyone is beating a path to your father's door. They all want to ride in a coach crafted by the father of the Chosen One of Maribor."

"You know about my father? My family? Are they all right?" Amilia stopped so suddenly that the duchess walked four steps before realizing she had lost her.

Amilia had long feared her family was dead from starvation or illness. They had had so little. She had left home two years earlier to remove an extra mouth from the table, with the intent of sending money home, but she had not counted on Edith Mon.

The head maid had declared Amilia's old clothes unfit and demanded she pay for new ones. This forced Amilia to borrow against her salary. Broken or chipped plates also added to her bill, and in the first few months, there were many. With Edith, there was always something to keep Amilia penniless. Eventually the head maid even began fining her for disobedience or misbehavior, keeping Amilia in constant debt.

How she had hated Edith. The old ogre had been so cruel that there had been nights when Amilia had gone to sleep wishing the woman would die. She fantasized that a carriage would hit her or that she would choke on a bone. Now that Edith was gone, she almost regretted those thoughts. Charged with treason, Edith had been executed less than a week earlier, with all the palace staff required to watch.

In more than two years, Amilia had been unable to save even a single copper to send home and had heard nothing from her family. While the empress had been trapped in her catatonic daze, the regents had sequestered the palace staff to prevent others from learning about her condition. During that time, Amilia had been as much a prisoner as Modina. Writing letters home had been useless. The palace rumor mill maintained that all letters were burned by order of the regents. After Modina recovered, Amilia continued to write, but she never received a single reply. There had been reports of an epidemic near her home, and she feared her family was dead. Amilia had given up all hope of ever seeing them again—until now.

"Of course they're all right, darling. They are more than all right. Your family is the toast of Tarin Vale. From the moment the empress spoke your name during her speech on the balcony, people have flocked to the hamlet to kiss the hand of the woman who bore you and to beg words of wisdom from the man who raised you."

As they reached the third-floor guest chambers, Amilia's eyes began to water. "Tell me about them. Please. I must know."

"Well, let's see. Your father expanded his workshop, and it now takes up an entire block. He's received hundreds of orders from all over Avryn. Artisans from as far away as Ghent beg for the chance to work as his apprentices, and he's hired dozens. The townsfolk have elected him to city council. There is even talk of making him mayor come spring."

"And my mother?" Amilia asked with a quivering lip. "How is she?"

"She's just marvelous, darling. Your father bought the grandest house in town and filled it with servants, leaving her plenty of time for leisure. She started a modest salon for the local artisan women. They mostly eat cake and gossip. Even your brothers are prospering. They supervise your father's workers and have their pick of the women for wives. So you see, my dear, I think it is safe to say your family is doing *very* well indeed."

Tears ran down Amilia's face.

"Oh, darling! What is wrong? Wentworth!" she called out as they reached her quarters. A dozen servants paused in their tasks to look up. "Give me your handkerchief, and get a glass of water immediately!"

The duchess directed Amilia to sit on a settee, and Genevieve dabbed the girl's tears away with surprising delicacy.

"I'm sorry," Amilia said softly. "I just—"

"Nonsense! I'm the one who should apologize. I had no idea such news would upset you." She spoke in a soft motherly voice. Then, turning in the direction the servant had gone, the duchess roared, "Where's that water!"

"I'm all right—really," Amilia assured her. "I just haven't seen my family in so long and I was afraid..."

Lady Genevieve smiled and embraced Amilia. The duchess whispered in her ear, "Dear, I've heard it said that people come from far and wide to ask your family how *you* saved the empress. Their reported response is that they know nothing about that, but what they can say with complete certainty is that you saved them."

Amilia shook with emotion at the words.

Lady Genevieve picked up the handkerchief. "Where's that water!" she bellowed once more. When it arrived, the duchess thrust the cool glass into Amilia's hands. She drank while the big woman brushed back her hair.

"There now, that's better," Lady Genevieve purred.

"Thank you."

"Not at all, darling. Do you feel up to finding out why I brought you here?"

"Yes, I think so."

They were in the duchess's formal reception area, part of the four-room suite that Lady Genevieve had redecorated, transforming the dull stone shell into a warm, rich parlor. Thick woolen drapes of red and gold covered every inch of wall. Facades made the arrow slits appear large and opulent. An intricately carved cherry mantel fronted the previously bare stone fireplace. Layers of carpets covered the entire room, making the floor soft and cozy. Not a stick of the original furniture remained. Everything was new and lovelier than anything Amilia had ever seen before.

A dozen servants, all dressed in reds and golds, returned to work. One individual, however, stood out. He was a tall, well-tailored man in a delightful outfit of silver and gold brocade. On his head he wore a whimsical, yet elegant, hat that displayed a long, billowing plume.

"Viscount," the duchess called, waving the man over. "Amilia, darling, I want you to meet Viscount Albert Winslow."

"Enchanted indeed." He removed his hat and swept it elaborately in a reverent bow.

"Albert is perhaps the foremost expert on organizing grand events. I hired him to mastermind my Summersrule Festival, and it was utterly amazing. I tell you, the man is a genius."

"You are far too kind, my lady," Winslow said softly with a warm smile.

"How you managed to fill the moat with leaping dolphins is beyond me. And the streamers that filled the sky—why, I've never seen such a thing. It was pure magic!"

"I'm pleased to have pleased you, my lady."

"Amilia, you simply must use Albert. Don't worry about the cost. I insist on paying for his services."

"Nonsense, good ladies. I couldn't conceive of taking payment for such a noble and worthwhile endeavor. My time is yours, and I'll do whatever I can out of devotion to you both and, of course, for Her Eminence."

"There now!" Lady Genevieve exclaimed. "The man is as chivalrous as a paladin. You *must* take him up on his offer, darling!"

They both stared at Amilia until she found herself nodding.

"I am delighted to be of service, my lady. When can I meet with your staff?"

"Ah…" Amilia hesitated. "There's only me and Nimbus. *Oh, Nimbus!* I'm sorry but I was on my way to meet with him when you—I mean—when we met. I'm supposed to be selecting entertainment for the feasts and I'm terribly late."

"Well, you should hurry off, then," Lady Genevieve said. "Take Albert with you. He can begin there. Now run along. There is no need to thank me, my dear. Your success will be my reward."

꿎

Amilia noticed that Viscount Winslow was less formal when away from the duchess. He greeted each performer warmly, and those not selected were dismissed with respect and good humor. He knew exactly what was required, and the auditions proceeded quickly under his guidance. All told, they selected twenty acts: one for each of the pre-wedding feasts, three for the Eve's Eve banquet, and five for the wedding reception. The viscount even picked four more, just in case of illness or injury.

Amilia was grateful for the viscount's help. As much as she had grown to rely on Nimbus, he had no experience with event planning. Originally, the courtier had been hired as the empress's tutor, but it had been quite some time since he had educated Modina on poise or protocol. Such skills were not required, as Modina never left her room. Instead, Nimbus became the secretary to the secretary, Amilia's right hand. He knew how to get things done in a royal court, whereas Amilia had no clue.

From his years of service to the nobles in Rhenydd, Nimbus had mastered the subtle language of manipulation. He tried to explain the nuances of this skill to Amilia, but she was a poor student. From time to time he corrected her for doing foolish things, such as bowing to the chamberlain, thanking a steward, or standing in the presence of others, which forced them to remain on their feet. Almost every success she had in the palace was because of Nimbus's coaching. A more ambitious man would resent her taking the credit, but Nimbus always offered his counsel in a kind and helpful manner.

Sometimes when Amilia caught herself doing something particularly stupid, or when she blushed from embarrassment, she noticed Nimbus spilling something on himself or tripping on a carpet. Once he even fell halfway down a flight of stairs. For a long while, Amilia thought he was extremely clumsy, but recently she had begun to suspect Nimbus might be the most agile person she had ever met.

The hour was late and Amilia hurried toward the empress's chamber. Gone were the days when she spent nearly every minute in Modina's company. Her responsibilities kept her busy, but she never retired without checking in on the empress, who was still her closest friend.

Rounding a corner, she bumped headlong into a man.

"I'm sorry!" she exclaimed, feeling more than a little foolish for walking with her head down.

"Oh no, my lady," the man replied. "It is I who must apologize for standing as a roadblock. Please, forgive me."

Amilia did not recognize him, but there were many new faces at the palace these days. He was tall and stood straight with his shoulders squared. His face was closely shaved and his hair neatly trimmed. By his bearing and clothing, she could tell he was a noble. He was dressed well, but unlike those of many of the Wintertide guests, his outfit was subdued.

"It's just that I am a bit confused," he said, looking around.

"Are you lost?" she asked.

He nodded. "I know my way in forests and fields. I can pinpoint my whereabouts by the use of moon and stars, but for the life of me, I am a total imbecile when trapped within walls of stone."

"That's okay, I used to get lost in here all the time. Where are you going?"

"I've been staying in the knights' wing at my lord's request, but I stepped outside for a walk and can't find my way back to my quarters."

"You're a soldier, then?"

"Yes, forgive me. My stupidity is without end." He stepped back and bowed formally. "Sir Breckton of Chadwick, son of Lord Belstrad, at your service, my lady."

"Oh! *You're* Sir Breckton?"

Appearances never impressed Amilia, but Breckton was perfect. He was exactly what she expected a knight should be: handsome, refined, strong, and—just as Lady Genevieve had described—dashing. For the first time since coming to the palace, she wished she were pretty.

"Indeed, I am. You've heard of me, then ... For good or ill?"

"Good, most certainly. Why, just—" She stopped herself and felt her face blush.

Concern furrowed his brow. "Have I done something to make you uncomfortable? I am terribly sorry if I—"

"No, no, not at all. I'm just being silly. To be honest, I never heard of you until today, and then ..."

"Then?"

"It's embarrassing," she admitted, feeling even more flustered by his attention.

The knight's expression turned serious. "My lady, if someone has dishonored me, or harmed you through the use of my name—"

"Oh no! Nothing as terrible as all that. It was the Duchess of Rochelle, and she said ..."

"Yes?"

Amilia cringed. "She said I should ask you to carry my favor in the joust."

"Oh, I see." He looked relieved. "I'm sorry to disappoint you, but I am not—"

"I know. I know," she interrupted, preferring not to hear the words. "I would have told her so myself if she ever stopped talking—the woman is a whirlwind. The idea of a knight—any knight—carrying *my* favor is absurd."

Sir Breckton appeared puzzled. "Why is that?"

"Look at me!" She took a step back so he could get a full view. "I'm not pretty, and as we both now know, I'm the opposite of graceful. I'm not of noble blood, having been born a poor carriage maker's daughter. I don't think I could hope for the huntsman's dog to sit beside me at the feast, much less have a renowned knight such as yourself riding on my behalf."

Breckton's eyebrows rose abruptly. "Carriage maker's daughter? *You* are *her*? Lady Amilia of Tarin Vale?"

"Oh yes, I'm sorry." She placed her hand to her forehead and rolled her eyes. "See? I have all the etiquette of a mule. Yes, I am Amilia."

Breckton studied her for a long moment. At last he spoke. "You're the maid who saved the empress?"

"Disappointing, I know." She waited for him to laugh and insist she could not possibly be the Chosen One of Maribor. While Modina's public declaration had helped protect Amilia, it had also made her uncomfortable. For a girl who had spent her whole life trying to hide from attention, being famous was difficult. Worse yet, she was a fraud. The story about a divine intervention selecting her to save the empress was a lie, a political fabrication—Saldur's way of manipulating the situation to his advantage.

To her surprise, the knight did not laugh. He merely asked,

"And you think no knight will carry your favor because you are of common blood?"

"Well, that and about a dozen other reasons. I hear the whispers sometimes."

Sir Breckton dropped to one knee and bowed his head. "Please, Lady Amilia, I beseech you. Give me the honor of carrying your token into the joust."

She just stood there.

The knight looked up. "I've offended you, haven't I? I am too bold! Forgive my impudence. I had no intention to participate in the joust, as I deem such contests the unnecessary endangerment of good men's lives for vanity and foolish entertainment. Now, however, after meeting you, I realize I must compete, for more is at stake. The honor of any lady should be defended and you are no ordinary lady, but rather the Chosen One of Maribor. For you, I would slay a thousand men to bring justice to those blackguards who would soil your good name! My sword and lance are yours, dear lady, if you will but grant me your favor."

Dumbstruck, Amilia did not realize she had agreed until after walking away. She was numb and could not stop smiling for the rest of her trip up the stairs.

～

As Amilia reached Modina's room, her spirits were still soaring. It had been a good day, perhaps the best of her life. She had discovered her family was alive and thriving. The wedding was proceeding under the command of an experienced and gracious man. And a handsome knight had knelt before her and asked for her token. Amilia grasped the latch, excited to share the good news with Modina, but all was forgotten the moment the door swung open.

As usual, Modina sat before the window, dressed in her thin white nightgown, staring out at the brilliance of the snow in the moonlight. Next to her was a full-length intricately carved oval mirror mounted with brass fittings on a beautiful wooden swivel.

"Where did *that* come from?" Amilia asked, shocked.

The empress did not answer.

"How did it get here?"

Modina glanced at the mirror. "It's pretty, isn't it? A pity they brought such a nice one. I suppose they wanted to please me."

Amilia approached the mirror and ran her fingers along the polished edge. "How long have you had it?"

"They brought it in this morning."

"I'm surprised it survived the day." Amilia turned her back on the mirror to face the empress.

"I'm in no hurry, Amilia. I still have some weeks yet."

"So you've decided to wait for your wedding?"

"Yes. At first I didn't think it would matter, but then I realized it could reflect badly on you. If I wait, it will appear to be Ethelred's fault. Everyone will assume I couldn't stand the thought of him touching me."

"Is that the reason?"

"No, I have no feelings about him or anything. Well, except for you. But you'll be all right." Modina turned to look at Amilia. "I can't even cry anymore. I never even wept when they captured Arista...not a single tear. I watched the whole thing from this window. I saw Saldur and the seret go in and knew what that meant. They came back out, but she never has. She's down there right now in that horrible dark place. Just like I once was. When she was here, I had a purpose, but now there is nothing left. It's time for this ghost to fade away. I have served the regents' purpose by helping them build the empire. I've given you a better life, and not even Saldur will harm you now. I tried to help Arista, but I failed. Now it's time for me to leave."

Amilia knelt down next to Modina, gently drew back the hair from her face, and kissed her cheek. "Don't speak that way. You were happy once, weren't you? You can be again."

Modina shook her head. "A girl named Thrace was happy. She lived with the family she loved in a small village near a river. Surrounded by friends, she played in the woods and fields. That girl believed in a better tomorrow. She looked forward to gifts Maribor would bring. Only instead of gifts, he sent darkness and horror."

"Modina, there is always room for hope. Please, you must believe."

"There was one day, when you were getting the clerk to order some cloth, that I saw a man from my past. He was hope. He saved Thrace once. For a moment, one very brief moment, I thought he had come to save me too, only he didn't. When he walked away, I knew he was just a memory from a time when I was alive."

Amilia's hands found Modina's and cradled them as she might hold a dying bird. Amilia was having trouble breathing. As her lower lip began to tremble, she looked back at the mirror. "You're right. It *is* a shame they brought such a pretty one." She put her arms around Modina and began to cry.

## Chapter 5

# Footprints in the Snow

Several miles from Medford, Royce saw the smoke and prepared himself for the worst. Crossing the Galewyr used to mean entering the bustling streets of the capital, but on that day, as he raced across the bridge, he found only a charred expanse of blackened posts and scorched stone. The city he had known was gone.

Royce never called anywhere *home*. To him the word meant a mythical place, like paradise or fairyland, but Wayward Street had been the closest thing he had ever found. A recent snowfall covered the city like a sheet that nature had drawn over a corpse. Not a building remained undamaged, and many were nothing but charcoal and ash. The castle's gates were shattered, portions of the walls collapsed. Even the trees in Gentry Square were gone.

Medford House, in the Lower Quarter, was a pile of smoldering beams. Nothing remained across the street except a gutted foundation and a burned sign displaying the hint of a rose in blistered paint.

He dismounted and moved to the rubble of the House. Where Gwen's office used to be, he caught a glimpse of pale fingers beneath a collapsed wall. His legs turned weak and his feet foolish as he stumbled over the wreckage. Smoke caught in his throat, and he drew up the scarf to cover his nose and mouth. Reaching the edge of the wall, he bent, trying to lift it. The edge broke away, but it was enough to reveal what was underneath.

An empty cream-colored glove.

Royce stepped back from the smoke. Sitting on the blackened porch, he noticed he was shaking. He was unaccustomed to being scared. Over the years, he had given up caring if he lived or died, figuring that a quick demise spared him the pain of living in a world so miserly that it begrudged an orphan boy a life. He had always been ready for death, gambling with it, waging bets against it. Royce had been satisfied in the knowledge that his risks were sound because he had nothing of value to lose — nothing to fear.

Gwen had changed everything.

He was an idiot and never should have left her alone.

*Why did I wait?*

They could have been safe in Avempartha, where only he held the key. The New Empire could beat themselves senseless against its walls and never reach him or his family.

A block away, a noisy flock of crows took flight. Royce stood and listened, hearing voices on the wind. Noticing his horse wandering down the street, he cursed himself for not tying her up. By the time he caught the reins, he spotted a patrol of imperial soldiers passing the charred ruins of Mason Grumon's place.

"Halt!" the leader shouted.

Royce leapt on his mare and kicked her just as he heard a dull *thwack*. His horse lurched, then collapsed with a bolt lodged deep in her flank. Royce jumped free before being crushed. He tumbled in the snow and came up on his feet with his dagger, Alverstone, drawn. Six soldiers hurried toward him. Only one had a crossbow, and he was busy ratcheting the string for his next shot.

Royce turned and ran.

He slipped into an alley filled with debris and vaulted over the shattered remains of The Rose and Thorn. Crossing the sewer near the inn's stable, he was surprised to find the plank bridge still there. Shouts rose behind him, but they were distant and muffled by the snow. The old feed store was still standing, and with a leap, he caught the windowsill on the second story. If they tracked him through the alley, the soldiers would be briefly baffled by his disappearance. That was all the head start Royce needed. He pulled himself to the roof, crossed it, and climbed down the far side. He took one last moment to obscure his tracks before heading west.

∽

Royce stood at the edge of the forest, trying to decide between the road and the more direct route, through the trees. Snow started to fall again, and the wind swept the flakes at an angle. The white curtain muted colors, turning the world a hazy gray. The thief flexed his hands. He had lost feeling in his fingers again. In his haste to find Gwen, he had once more neglected to purchase winter gloves. He pulled his hood tight and wrapped the scarf around his face. The northwest gale tore at his cloak, cracking the edges like a whip. He hooked it in his belt several times but eventually gave up—the wind insisted.

The distance to the Winds Abbey was a long day's ride in summer, a day and a half in winter, but Royce had no idea how long it would take him on foot through snow. Without proper gear, it was likely he would not make it at all. Almost everything he had was lost with his horse, including his blanket, food, and water. He did not even have the means to start a fire. The prudent choice would be the road. The walking would be easier, and he would at least have the chance of encountering other travelers. Still, it was the longer route. He chose the shortcut through the forest. He hoped Gwen had kept her promise and gone to the monastery, but there was only one way to be certain and his need to see her had grown desperate.

As night fell, the stars shone brightly above a glistening world of white. Struggling to navigate around logs and rocks hidden beneath the snow, Royce halted when he came upon a fresh line of tracks—footprints. He listened but heard only the wind blowing through the snow-burdened trees.

With an agile jump he leapt on a partially fallen tree and nimbly sprinted up its length until he was several feet off the ground. Royce scanned the tracks in the snow below him. They were only as deep as his own, too shallow for a man weighed down by even light armor.

*Who can possibly be traveling on foot here tonight besides me?*

Given that the footprints were headed the direction he was going, and Royce wanted to keep the owner in front of him, he followed. The going was less difficult and Royce was thankful for the ease in his route.

When he reached the top of a ridge, the tracks veered right, apparently circling back the way he had come.

"Sorry to see you go," Royce muttered. His breath puffed out in a moonlit fog.

As he climbed down the slope, he recalled this ravine from the trip he had taken three years earlier with Hadrian and Prince Alric. Then, as now, finding a clear route had been difficult and he struggled to work his way to the valley below. The snow made travel a challenge, and once he reached level ground, he found it deep with drifts. He had not made more than a hundred feet of headway before encountering the footprints once more. Again he followed them, and found the way easier.

Reaching the far side of the valley, he faced the steep slope back up. The footprints turned to the right. This time Royce paused. Slightly to the left he could see an easy route. A V-shaped ravine, cleared and leveled by runoff, was inviting. He considered going that way but noticed that directly in front of him, carved in the bark of a spruce tree, was an arrow-shaped marker pointing to the right. The trailblazer's footprints were sprinkled with wood chips.

"So you want me to keep following you," Royce whispered to himself. "That's only marginally more disturbing than you knowing I'm following you at all."

He glanced around. There was no one he could see. The only movement was the falling snow. The stillness was both eerie and peaceful, as if the wood waited for him to decide.

His legs were weak, his feet and hands numb. Royce had never liked invitations, but he guessed following the prints would once again be the easier route. He looked up at the slope and sighed. After following the tracks only a few hundred feet more, he spotted a pair of fur mittens dangling from the branch of a tree. Royce slipped them on and found they were still warm.

"Okay, that's creepy," Royce said aloud. He raised his voice and added, "I'd love a skin of water, a hot steak with onions, and perhaps some fresh-baked bread with butter."

All around him was the tranquil silence of a dark wood in falling snow. Royce shrugged and continued onward. The trail eventually hooked left, but by then the steep bluff was little more than a mild incline. Royce half expected to find a dinner waiting for him when he reached the crest, but the hilltop was bare. In the distance was a light, and the footprints headed straight toward it.

Royce ticked through the possibilities and concluded nothing. There was no chance imperial soldiers were leading him through the forest, and he was too far from Windermere for it to be monks. Dozens of legends spoke of fairies and ghosts inhabiting the woods of western Melengar, but none mentioned denizens that left footprints and warm mittens.

No matter how he ran the scenarios, he could find no way to justify an impending trap. Still, Royce gripped the handle of Alverstone and trudged forward. As he closed the distance, he saw that the light came from a small house built high in the limbs of a large oak tree. Below the tree house, a ring of thick evergreens surrounded a livestock pen, where a dark horse pawed the snow beside a wooden lean-to.

"Hello?" Royce called.

"Climb up," a voice yelled down. "If you're not too tired."

"Who are you?"

"I'm a friend. An old friend—or rather, you're mine."

"What's your name...*friend*?" Royce stared up at the opening on the underside of the tree house.

"Ryn."

"Now see, that's a bit odd, as I have few friends, and none of them is called Ryn."

"I never told you my name before. Now, are you going to come up and have some food or simply steal my horse and ride off? Personally, I suggest a bite to eat first."

Royce looked at the horse for a long moment before grabbing the knotted rope dangling along the side of the tree trunk and pulling himself up. Reaching the floor of the house, he peeked inside. The space was larger than he had expected, was oven warm, and smelled of meat stew. Branches reached out in all directions, each one rubbed smooth as a banister.

Pots and scarves hung from the limbs, and several layers of mats and blankets hid the wooden floor.

In a chair crafted from branches, a slim figure smoked a pipe. "Welcome, Mr. Royce," Ryn said with a smile.

He wore crudely stitched clothes made from rough, treated hides. On his head was a hat that looked like an old flopped sack. Even with his ears hidden, his slanted eyes and high cheekbones betrayed his elven heritage.

On the other side of the room, a woman and a small boy chopped mushrooms and placed them in a battered pot suspended in a small fireplace made of what looked to be river stones. They too were *mir*—a half-breed mix of human and elf—like Royce himself. Neither said a word, but they glanced over at him from time to time while adding vegetables to the pot.

"You know my name?" Royce asked.

"Of course. It isn't a name I could easily forget. Please, come in. My home is yours."

"How do you know me?" Royce pulled up his legs and closed the door.

"Three autumns ago, just after Amrath's murder, you were at The Silver Pitcher."

Royce thought back. *The hat!*

"They were sick." Ryn tilted his head toward his family. "Fever—the both of them. We were out of food and I spent my last coin on some old bread and a turnip from Mr. Hall. I knew it wouldn't be enough, but there was nothing else I could do."

"You were the elf that they accused of thieving. They pulled your hat off."

Ryn nodded. He puffed on his pipe and said, "You and your friend were organizing a group of men to save the Prince of Melengar. You asked me to join. You promised a reward—a fair share."

Royce shrugged. "We needed anyone willing to help."

"I didn't believe you. Who of my kind would? No one ever gave fair shares of anything to an elf, but I was desperate. When it was over, Drake refused to pay me, just as I expected. But you kept your word and forced him to give me an equal share—*and a horse*. You threatened to kill the whole lot of them if they didn't." He allowed himself a little smile. "Drake handed over the gelding with full tack and never even checked it. I think he just wanted to get rid of me. I left before they could change their minds. I was miles away before I finally got a chance to look in the saddlebags. Fruits, nuts, meat, cheese, a pint of whiskey, a skin of cider, those would've been treasure enough. But I also found warm blankets, fine clothes, a hand axe, flint and steel, a knife—and *the purse*. There were gold tenents in that bag—twenty-two of them."

"Gold tenents? You got Baron Trumbul's horse?"

Ryn nodded. "There was more than enough gold to buy medicine, and with the horse I got back in time. I prayed I would be able to thank you before I died, and today I got my chance. I saw you in the city but could do nothing there. I am so glad I persuaded you to visit."

"The mittens were a nice touch."

"Please sit and be my guest for dinner."

Royce hung his scarf alongside his cloak on one of the branches and set his boots to warm near the fire. The four ate together with little conversation.

After she had taken his empty bowl, Ryn's wife spoke for the first time. "You look tired, Mr. Royce. Can we make you a bed for the night?"

"No. Sorry. I can't stay," Royce said while getting up, pleased to feel his feet again.

"You're in a hurry?" Ryn asked.

"You could say that."

"In that case, you will take my horse, Hivenlyn," Ryn said.

An hour earlier, Royce would have stolen a horse from anyone he had happened upon, so he was surprised to hear himself say, "No. I mean, thanks, but no."

"I insist. I named him Hivenlyn because of you. It means *unexpected gift* in Elvish. So you see, you must take him. He knows every path in this wood and will get you safely wherever you need to go." Ryn nodded toward the boy, who nimbly slipped out the trapdoor.

"You need that horse," Royce said.

"I'm not the one trudging through the forest in the middle of the night without a pack. I lived without a horse for many years. Right now, you need him more than I do. Or can you honestly say you have no use for a mount?"

"Okay, I'll *borrow* him. I am riding to the Winds Abbey. I'll let them know he is your animal. You can claim him there." Royce bundled up and descended the rope. At the bottom, Ryn's son stood with the readied horse.

Ryn climbed down as well. "Hivenlyn is yours now. If you have no further need, give him to someone who does."

"You're crazy," Royce said, shaking his head in disbelief. "But I don't have time to argue." He mounted and looked back at Ryn, standing in the snow beneath his little home. "Listen...I'm not...I'm just not used to people...you know..."

"Ride safe and be well, my friend."

Royce nodded and turned Hivenlyn toward the road.

✑

He traveled all night, following the road and fighting a fresh storm that rose against him. The wind blew bitter, pulling his cloak away and causing him to shiver. He pushed the horse hard, but Hivenlyn was a fine animal and did not falter.

At sunrise they took a short rest in the shelter of fir trees. Royce ate the hard round of mushroom-stuffed bread Ryn's wife had provided and gave Hivenlyn a bit of one end. "Sorry about the pace," he told the horse. "But I'll make sure you get a warm stall and plenty to eat when we arrive." Royce failed to mention that the deal depended on his finding Gwen safe. Anything less, and he would not care about the needs of the horse. He would not care about anything.

The storm continued to rage all through that day. Gale-swept snow blew across the road, forming patterns that resembled ghostly snakes. During the entire trip, Royce did not come across a single traveler, and the day passed by in a blinding haze of white.

As darkness fell, the two finally reached the summit of Monastery Hill. The abbey, silent and still, appeared from behind a veil of falling snow. The quiet of the compound was disturbing, too similar to that visit he had made three years earlier after the Imperialists had burned the church to the ground with dozens of monks locked inside. Panic threatened to overtake Royce as he raced up the stone steps and pulled on the expansive doors. He entered, moving quickly down the length of the east range. He just needed a face, any face, someone he could ask about Gwen. Not a single monk in the abbey could have missed the arrival of a band of prostitutes.

The corridor was dark, as was the hall leading to the cloister. He opened the door to the refectory and found it vacant. The empty dining tables were matched by empty benches. As Royce listened to the hollow echo of his own footsteps, the sense of doom that had driven him through the snow caused him to sprint to the church. Reaching the two-story double doors, he feared that, just as once before, he would find them chained shut. Taking hold of the latches, he pulled hard.

The soft sound of singing washed over him as Royce gazed

down a long nave filled with monks. The massive doors boomed as they slammed against the walls. The singing halted and dozens of heads turned.

"Royce?" a voice said. A woman's voice—her voice.

The forest of brown-clad monks shifted, and he spotted Gwen among them, dressed in an emerald gown. By the time she reached the aisle, he was throwing his arms around her and squeezing until she gasped.

"Master Melborn, please," the abbot said. "We are in the middle of vespers."

## CHAPTER 6

# THE PALACE

Hadrian drew the drapes and lit a candle on the small table before asking Albert, "What have you discovered?" In the past Royce had always run the meetings, and Hadrian found himself trying to remember all the little things he would do to ensure secrecy.

They were in Hadrian's room at the Bailey, and this was their first meeting since Royce had left. Albert was staying at the palace now, and Hadrian wanted to keep Albert's visits infrequent. A guest of the empress might patronize a seedy inn for entertainment, but too many visits could appear suspicious.

"Genny introduced me to the empress's secretary," Albert said. He was dressed in a heavy cloak, which hid his lavish attire beneath simple wool. "The girl cried tears of joy when Genny told her the news about her family. I think it's safe to say that Lady Amilia loves the duchess and at least trusts me. You should have seen Genny. She was marvelous. And her chambers are exquisite!"

"What about Leo?" Hadrian asked.

"He's quiet as always but playing along. If Genny is all right with it, so is he. Besides, he's always hated Ethelred."

The two sat at the table. The dim, flickering light revealed not much more than their faces. For over a week Hadrian had tried to find out what he could in town, but he was not getting very far. He did not have the head for planning that Royce did.

"And you know how Genny loves intrigue," Albert added. "Anyway, she got me appointed as the official wedding planner."

"That's perfect. Have you learned anything useful?"

"I asked Lady Amilia about places that could be used to temporarily house performers. I told her it's common practice to utilize empty cells, since tavern space is hard to come by."

"Nice."

"Thanks, but it didn't help. According to her, the palace doesn't have a dungeon, just a prison tower."

"Prison tower sounds good."

"It's empty."

"Empty? Are you sure? Have you checked?"

Albert shook his head. "Off-limits."

"Why would it be off-limits if it's empty?"

The viscount shrugged. "No idea, but Lady Amilia assures me it is. Said she was up there herself. Besides, I've watched it the last few nights, and I'm pretty sure she's right. I've never seen a light. Although, I did see a Seret Knight go in once."

"Any other ideas?"

Albert drummed his fingers on the tabletop, thinking for a moment. "The only other restricted area is the fifth floor, which I've determined is where the empress resides."

"Have you seen her?" Hadrian leaned forward. "Have you managed to speak with her?"

"No. As far as I can tell, Modina never leaves her room. She has all her meals brought to her. Amilia insists the empress is busy administrating the empire and is still weak. Apparently, the combination leaves her unable to receive guests. This has been a source of irritation recently. All the visiting dignitaries want an audience with the empress—but all are denied."

"Someone has to see her."

"Lady Amilia certainly does. There is also a chamber-maid…" Albert fished inside his tunic, pulling out a wadded bundle of parchments, which he unfolded on the table. "Yes, here it is. The chambermaid is named Anna, and the door guard is…" He shuffled through his notes. "Gerald. Anna is the daughter of a mercer from Colnora. As for Gerald, his full name is Gerald Baniff. He's from Chadwick. Family friend of the Belstrads." Albert took a moment to flip through a few more pages. "Was once personal aide to Sir Breckton. A com-mendation for bravery won him the position of honor guard to the empress."

"What about the regents?"

"I assume they *could* see her, but as far as I can tell, they don't. At least, no one I've talked to reports ever having seen them on the fifth floor."

"How can she govern if she never takes a meeting with Ethelred or Saldur?" Hadrian asked.

"I think it's obvious. The regents are running the empire."

Hadrian slumped back in his seat with a scowl. "So she's a puppet."

Albert shrugged. "Maybe. Is this significant?"

"Royce and I knew her—before she became the empress. I thought maybe she might help us."

"Doesn't look like she has any real power."

"Does anyone know this?"

"Some of the nobles may suspect, although most appear colossally unaware."

"They can't all be *that* gullible."

"You have to keep in mind that many of these people are extremely religious and dedicated Imperialists. They accept the story of her being the heir descended from Maribor. From what I've determined, the vast majority of the peasant class feels the same way. The servants and even palace guards view her with a kind of awe. The rarity of her appearances has only reinforced this notion. It's a politician's dream. Since she's hardly seen, no one attaches any mistake to her and instead they blame the regents."

"So no one other than Amilia, the guard, and the chamber-maid sees her?"

"Looks that way. Oh, wait." Albert paused. "Nimbus also apparently has access."

"*Nimbus?*" Hadrian asked.

"Yes, he is a courtier from Vernes. I met him several years ago at some gala or ball. No one of account, as I remember, but generally a decent fellow. He's actually the one that introduced Lord Daref and me to Ballentyne, which led to that pair of stolen letter jobs you did for the Earl of Chadwick and Alenda Lanaklin. Nimbus is a thin, funny guy, prone to wearing loud clothes and a powdered wig. Always carries a little leather satchel over his shoulder—rumor is he carries makeup in it. Smarter than he appears certainly. Very alert—he listens to everything. He was hired by Lady Amilia and works as her assistant."

"So what is the likelihood *you* could see the empress?"

"Slim, I suspect. Why? I just told you there's not much chance she can help, or do you think they're keeping Gaunt in Modina's room?"

"No." Hadrian rubbed a hand over the surface of the table amidst the flickering shadows. "I'd just like to—I don't know—to see if she's all right, I guess. I sort of promised her father I'd watch out for her—make sure she was okay, you know?"

"She's the empress," Albert stated. "Or hasn't he heard?"

"He's dead."

"Oh." Albert paused.

"I just would feel better if I could talk to her."

"Are we after Gaunt or the empress?"

Hadrian scowled. "Well, it doesn't look like we're very close to finding where Gaunt is being held."

"I think I've pushed things about as far as I can. I'm a wedding planner, not a guard, and people get suspicious if I start asking about prisoners."

"I really didn't think it would be this hard to find him."

Albert sighed. "I'll try again," he said, standing and pulling the drawstrings on his cloak.

"Hold on a second. When we first arrived, didn't you mention that the palace was recruiting new guards?"

"Yeah, they're expecting huge crowds. Why?"

Hadrian didn't reply right away, staring into the single candle and massaging his callused palms. "I thought I might try my hand at being a man-at-arms again."

Albert smiled. "I think you're a tad overqualified."

"Then I ought to get the job."

⤙

Hadrian waited in line among the weak-shouldered, bent-backed, would-be soldiers. They shifted their weight from foot to foot and blew into cupped hands to warm their fingers. The line of men stretched from the main gate to the barracks' office within the palace courtyard. Being the only man with his own weapons and a decent cloak, Hadrian felt out of place and forced himself to stoop and shuffle when he walked.

Heaps of snow packed the inner walls of the well-shoveled courtyard. Outside the barracks, a fire burned in a pit, where the yard guards would occasionally pause to warm their hands or get a cup of something steaming hot. Servant boys made routine trips back and forth to the well or the woodpile, hauling buckets of water or slings of split logs.

"Name?" a gruff soldier asked as Hadrian entered the dim barracks and stood before a rickety desk.

Three men in thick leather sat behind it. Beside them was a small clerk, whom Hadrian had seen once before in the palace. A disagreeable sort with a balding head and ink-stained fingers, he sat with a roll of parchment, pen, and ink.

"You have a name?" the man in the center asked.

"Baldwin," Hadrian said. The clerk scratched the parchment. The end of his feathered quill whipped about like the tail of an irritated squirrel.

"Baldwin, eh? Where have you fought?"

"All over, really."

"Why aren't you in the imperial army? Ya a deserter?"

Hadrian allowed himself a smile, which the soldier did not return. "You could say that. I left the Nationalists."

This caught the ear of everyone at the table and a few men standing in line. The clerk stopped scribbling and looked up.

"For some reason they stopped paying me," Hadrian added with a shrug.

A slight smile pulled at the edges of the soldier's lips. "Not terribly loyal, are you?"

"I'm as loyal as they come…as long as you pay me."

This brought a chuckle from the soldier, and he looked to the others. The older man to his right nodded. "Put him on the line. It doesn't require much loyalty to work a crowd."

The clerk began writing again and Hadrian was handed a wooden token.

"Take that back outside and give it to Sergeant Millet, near the fire. He'll get you set up. Name?" he called to the next in line as Hadrian headed back out into the blinding white.

Unable to see clearly for a moment, Hadrian blinked. As his eyes adjusted, he saw Sentinel Luis Guy ride through the front gate, leading five Seret Knights. The two men spotted each other at the same instant. Hadrian had not seen Guy since the death of Fanen Pickering in Dahlgren. And while he hoped to one day repay Guy for Fanen's death, this was perhaps the worst possible time to cross paths.

For a heartbeat, neither moved. Then Guy slowly leaned and spoke to the man beside him, his eyes never straying from Hadrian.

"Now!" Guy growled when the knight hesitated.

Hadrian could not think of a worse place to be caught. He had no easy exit—no window to leap through or door to close. Between him and the gate were twenty-six men, still in line, who would jump at the chance to prove their mettle by helping the palace guard. Despite their numbers, Hadrian was the least concerned by the guard hopefuls, as none of them were armed. The bigger problem was the ten palace guards dressed for battle. At the sound of the first clash of swords, the barracks would empty, adding more men. Hadrian conservatively estimated he would need to kill or cripple at least eighteen people just to reach the exit. Guy and his five seret would be at the top of that list. The serets' horses would also need to be dispatched for him to have any chance of escaping through the city streets. The final obstacle would be the crossbowmen on the wall. Among the eight, he guessed at least two would be skilled enough to hit him in the back as he ran out through the gate.

"Just—don't—move," Guy said with his hands spread out in front of him. He looked as if he were trying to catch a wild horse, and did not advance, dismount, or draw his sword.

Just then the portcullis dropped.

"There's no escape," Guy assured him.

From a nearby door, a handful of guards trotted toward Hadrian with their swords drawn.

"Stop!" Guy ordered, raising his hand abruptly. "Don't go near him. Just fan out."

The men waiting in line looked from the soldiers to Hadrian and then backed away.

"I know what you're thinking, Mr. Blackwater," Guy said in an almost friendly tone. "But we *truly* have you outnumbered *this* time."

✨

Hadrian stood in an elegantly furnished office on the fourth floor of the palace. Regent Saldur sat behind his desk, fidgeting with a small bejeweled letter opener shaped like a dagger. The ex-bishop looked slightly older and a bit heavier than the last time Hadrian had seen him. Luis Guy stood off to the right, his eyes locked on Hadrian. He was dressed in the traditional black armor and scarlet cape of his position, his sword hanging in its sheath. Guy's stance was straight and attentive, and he kept his hands gripped behind his back. Hadrian did not recognize the last man in the room. The stranger, dressed in an elegant garnache, sat near a chessboard, casually rolling one of the pieces back and forth between his fingers.

"Mr. Blackwater," Saldur addressed Hadrian, "I've heard some pretty incredible things about you. Please, won't you sit?"

"Will I really be staying that long?"

"Yes, I am afraid so. No matter how this turns out, you'll be staying."

Hadrian looked at the chair but chose to remain standing.

The old man leaned back in his seat and placed the tips of his fingers together. "You're probably wondering why you're here instead of locked in the north tower, or at least why we haven't shackled your wrists and ankles. You can thank Sentinel Guy for that. He has told us an incredible story about you. Aside from murdering Seret Knights—"

"The only murder that day was Fanen Pickering," Hadrian said. "The seret attacked us."

"Well, who's to say who did what when? Still, the death of a seret demands a severe penalty. I'm afraid it's customarily an executable offense. However, Sentinel Guy insists that you are a Teshlor—the only Teshlor—and *that* is an unusual extenuating circumstance.

"Now, if I recall my history lessons correctly, there was only one Teshlor to escape the destruction of the Old Empire—Jerish Grelad, who had taken the Heir of Novron into hiding. Legend claims that the Teshlor skills were passed down from generation to generation to protect the bloodline of the emperor.

"The Pickerings and the Killdares are each said to have discovered just a single one of the Teshlor disciplines. These jealously guarded secrets have made those families renowned for their fighting skills. A fully trained Teshlor would be...well... invincible in any one-on-one competition of arms. Am I correct?"

Hadrian said nothing.

"In any case, let's assume for the moment that Guy is not mistaken. If this is so, your presence presents us with an interesting opportunity, which can provide a uniquely mutual benefit. Given this, we felt it might encourage you to listen if we treated you with a degree of respect. By leaving you free—"

The door burst open and Regent Ethelred entered. The stocky, barrel-chested man was dressed in elaborate regal vestments of velvet and silk. He too looked older, and the former king's once-trim physique sported a bulge around the middle. Gray invaded his mustache and beard in patches and left white lines in his black hair. After pulling his cape inside, he slammed the door shut.

"So this is the fellow, I take it?" he said in a booming voice as he appraised Hadrian. "Don't I know you?"

Seeing no reason to lie, Hadrian replied, "I once served in your army."

"That's right!" Ethelred said, throwing up his hands in a large animated gesture. "You were a good fighter too. You held the line at...at..." He snapped his fingers repeatedly.

"At the Gravin River Ford."

"Of course!" He slapped his thigh. "Damn nice piece of work that was. I promoted you, didn't I? Made you a captain or something. What happened?"

"I left."

"Pity. You're a fine soldier." Ethelred clapped Hadrian on the shoulder.

"Of course he is, Lanis. That's the whole point," Saldur reminded him.

Ethelred chuckled, then said, "Too true, too true. So, has he accepted?"

"We haven't asked him yet."

"Asked me what?"

"Hadrian, we have a little problem," Ethelred began. As he spoke, he paced back and forth between Saldur's desk and the door. He kept the fingers of his left hand tucked in his belt behind his back while using his right to assist him in speaking, like a conductor uses a baton. "His name is Archibald Ballentyne. He's a sniveling little weasel. All of the Ballentynes have been worthless, pitiful excuses for men, but he's also the Earl of Chadwick. So, by virtue of his birth, he rules over a province that is worthless in all ways except one. Chadwick is the home to Lord Belstrad, whose eldest son, Sir Breckton, is very likely the best knight in Avryn. When I say *best*, I mean that in every sense of the word. His skill at arms is unmatched, as are his talent for tactics and his aptitude for leadership. Unfortunately, he's also loyal to a fault. He serves Archie Ballentyne and *only* Archie."

Ethelred crossed the room and took a seat by hopping onto Saldur's desk, causing the old man to flinch.

"I wanted Breckton as *my* general, but he refuses to obey the chain of command and won't listen to anyone except Archie. I can't waste time filtering all my orders through that pissant. So we offered Breckton a prime bit of land and a title to abandon Ballentyne, but the fool wasn't interested."

"The war is over, or soon will be," Hadrian pointed out. "You don't need Breckton anymore."

"That is exactly correct," Saldur said.

There was something in the detached way he spoke that chilled Hadrian.

"Even without a war we still need strong men to enforce order," Ethelred explained. Picking up a glass figurine from Saldur's desk, he began passing it from hand to hand.

Saldur's jaw clenched as his eyes tracked each toss.

"When Breckton turned us down, Archie threatened to use his knight and the Royalists against us. Can you believe that? He said he would march on Aquesta! He thinks he can challenge me! The little sod—" Ethelred slammed the figurine down on the desk, shattering it. "Oh—sorry, Sauly."

Saldur sighed but said nothing.

"Anyway," Ethelred went on, dusting off his hands so that bits of glass rained on the desk. "Who could have guessed a knight would turn down an offer to rise to the rank of marquis and command a whole kingdom as his fief? The piss-proud pillock! And what's he doing it for? Loyalty to Archie Ballentyne. Who hates him. Always has. It's ridiculous."

"Which brings us to why you're here, Mr. Blackwater," Saldur said. He used a lace handkerchief to gingerly sweep the broken glass off his desk into a wastebasket. "As much as I would like to take credit for it, this is all Guy's idea." Saldur nodded toward the sentinel.

Guy never changed his wooden stance, remaining at attention as if it were his natural state.

"Finding you in our courtyard, Guy realized that you can solve our little problem with Sir Breckton."

"I'm not following," Hadrian said.

Saldur rolled his eyes. "We can't allow Breckton to reach his army at Drondil Fields. We would be forever at the mercy of Archie. He could dictate any terms so long as Breckton controlled the loyalty of the army."

Hadrian's confusion continued. "And…?"

Ethelred chuckled. "Poor Sauly, you deal too much in subtlety. This man is a fighter, not a strategist. He needs it spelled out." Turning to Hadrian, he said, "Breckton is a capable warrior and we had no hope of finding anyone who could defeat him until Guy pointed out that you are the perfect man for the job. To be blunt, we want you to kill Sir Breckton."

"The Wintertide tournament will start in just a few days," Saldur continued. "Breckton is competing in the joust and we want you to battle him and win. His lance will be blunted, while yours will have a war point hidden beneath a porcelain shell. When he dies, our problem will be solved."

"And exactly why would I agree?"

"Like the good regent explained," Guy said, "killing seret is an executable offense."

"Plus," Ethelred put in, "as a token of our appreciation, we will sweeten the deal by paying you one hundred solid gold tenents. What do you say?"

Hadrian knew he could never murder Breckton. While he had never met the man, he was familiar with Breckton's younger brother Wesley, who had served with Royce and Hadrian on the *Emerald Storm*. The young man had died in battle, fighting beside them at the Palace of the Four Winds. His sacrificial charge had saved their lives. No man had ever proven himself more worthy of loyalty, and if Breckton was half the man his younger brother was, Hadrian owed him at least one life.

"What can he say?" Saldur answered for him. "He has no choice."

"I wouldn't say that," Hadrian replied. "You're right. I am a trained Teshlor, and while you've been talking, I've calculated eight different ways to kill everyone in this room. Three using nothing more than that little letter opener Regent Saldur has been playing with." He let his arms fall loose and shifted his stance. This immediately set Ethelred and Guy, the two fighters, on the defensive.

"Hold on now." Saldur's voice wavered and his face showed strain. "Before you make any rash decisions, consider that the window is too small to fit through, and the men in the corridor will not let you leave. If you really are as good as you say, you might take a great many of them with you, but even you cannot defeat them all."

"You might be right. We'll soon find out."

"Are you insane? You're choosing death?" Saldur erupted in frustration. "We are offering you gold and a pardon. What benefit is there in refusing?"

"Well, he does plan on killing all of you." The man with the chess piece spoke for the first time. "A good trade, really—forfeiting one knight to eliminate a knight, a bishop, and a king. But you offered the man the wrong incentive. Give him the princess."

"Give—what?" Saldur looked puzzled. "Who? Arista?"

"You have another princess I'm not aware of?"

"Arista?" Hadrian asked. "The Princess of Melengar is here?"

"Yes, and they plan to execute her on Wintertide," the man answered.

Saldur looked confused. "Why would he care—"

"Because Hadrian Blackwater and his partner, Royce Melborn, better known as Riyria, have been working as the royal protectors of Melengar. They've been instrumental in nearly every success either Alric or his sister has had over the last few years. I suspect they might even be friends with the royal family now. Well—as much as nobles will permit friendship with commoners."

Hadrian tried to keep his face neutral and his breathing balanced.

*They have Arista? How did they capture her? Was she hurt? How long have they been holding her? Who is this man?*

"You see, Your Grace, Mr. Blackwater is a romantic at heart. He likes his honor upheld and his quests worthy. Killing an innocent knight, particularly one as distinguished as Breckton, would be…well…wrong. Saving a damsel in distress, on the other hand, is an entirely different proposition."

"Would that be a problem?" Ethelred asked Saldur.

The regent thought a moment. "The girl has proven resourceful and given us more than her fair share of trouble but… Medford is destroyed, the Nationalists are disbanded, and Drondil Fields won't last much longer. I can't see any way she could pose a serious threat to the empire."

"Well," Ethelred said, addressing Hadrian, "do we have a deal?"

Hadrian scrutinized the man at the chessboard. While he had never seen his face before, he felt as though he should recognize him.

"No," Hadrian said at length. "I want Degan Gaunt too."

"You see? He is the guardian!" Guy proclaimed. "Or he wishes to be. Obviously Esrahaddon told him Gaunt is the heir."

Ethelred looked concerned. "That's out of the question. We've been after the Heir of Novron for years. We can't let him go."

"Not just years—centuries," Saldur corrected. He stared at Hadrian, his mouth slightly open, the tip of his tongue playing with his front teeth. "Esrahaddon is dead. You confirmed that, Guy?"

The sentinel nodded. "I had his body dug up and then burned."

"And how much does Gaunt know? I've heard you've had several *little chats* with him."

Guy shook his head. "Not much, from what I've been able to determine. He insists Esrahaddon didn't even tell him he's the heir."

"But Hadrian will tell him," Ethelred protested.

"So?" Saldur replied. "What does that matter? The two of them can travel the countryside, proclaiming Gaunt's heritage from the mountaintops. Who will listen? Modina serves us well. The people love and accept her as the unquestionable true Heir of Novron. She slew the Gilarabrywn, after all. If they try to convince people that Gaunt is the heir, they'll get no support from the peasants or nobles. The concern was never Degan, per se, but rather what Esrahaddon could do by using him as a puppet. Right? With the wizard gone, Gaunt is no real threat."

"I'm not certain the Patriarch will approve," Guy said.

"The Patriarch isn't here having a standoff with a Teshlor, is he?"

"And what about Gaunt's children, or grandchildren? Decades from now, they may attempt to regain their birthright. We have to concern ourselves with that."

"Why worry about problems that may never occur? We're at a bit of an impasse, gentlemen. Why don't we deal with our present issues and let the future take care of itself? What do you say, Lanis?"

Ethelred nodded.

Saldur turned to Hadrian. "If you *succeed in killing* Sir Breckton in the joust, we will release Degan Gaunt and Princess Arista into your custody on the condition that you leave Avryn and promise not to return. Do we have a deal?"

"Yes."

"Excellent."

"So I'm free to go?"

"Actually, no," Saldur said. "You must understand our desire to keep this little arrangement between us. I'm afraid we're going to have to insist that you stay in the palace until after your joust with Breckton. While you're here, you will be under constant observation. If you attempt to escape or pass information, we will interpret that as a refusal on your part, and Princess Arista and Degan Gaunt will be burned at the stake.

"Breckton's death has to be seen as a Wintertide accident at best or the actions of an overambitious knight at worst. There can be no suspicions of a conspiracy. Commoners aren't permitted to participate in the tournament, so we'll need to transform you into a knight. You will stay in the knights' quarters, participate in the games, attend feasts, and mingle with the aristocracy, as all knights do this time of year. We will assign a tutor to help you convince everyone that you're noble so there will be no suspicions of wrongdoing. As of this moment, your only way out of this palace is to kill Sir Breckton."

## CHAPTER 7

# DEEPER INTO DARKNESS

*D*rip, *drip, drip.*

Arista scratched her wrists, feeling the marks raised by the heavy iron during the regent's interrogation. The itching had only recently started. With what little they fed her, she was surprised her body could heal itself at all. Lying about Edith Mon had been a gamble, and she had worried Saldur would return to her cell with the inquisitor, but three bowls of gruel had arrived since his visit, which led her to conclude he had believed her story.

*Whirl...splash!*

There it was again.

The sound was faint and distant, echoing as if traveling through a long, hollow tube.

*Creak, click, creak, click, creak, click.*

The noise certainly came from a machine, a torture device of some kind. Perhaps it was a mechanical winch used to tear people to pieces or a turning wheel that submerged victims in putrid waters. Saldur had been wrong about her courage. Arista never had any doubt she would break if subjected to torture.

The stone door to the prison rumbled as it opened.

Footsteps echoed through the corridors. Once more, someone was coming when it was not time for food.

*Clip-clap, clip-clap.*

The shoes were different and not as rich as Saldur's, but they were not poor either. The gait was decidedly military, but these feet were not shod in metal. They did not come for her. Instead, the footfalls passed by, stopping just past her cell. Keys jangled and a cell door opened.

"Morning, Gaunt," said a voice she found distantly familiar and vaguely unpleasant, like the memory of a bad dream.

"What do you want, Guy?" Gaunt said.

*It's him!*

"You and I need to have another talk," Guy said.

"I barely survived our last one."

"What did Esrahaddon tell you about the Horn of Gylindora?"

Arista lifted her head and inched nearer the door.

"I don't know how many ways I can say it. He told me nothing."

"See, this is why you suffer in our little meetings. You need to be more cooperative. I can't help you if you won't help us. We need to find that horn and we need it now!"

"Why don't you just ask Esrahaddon?"

"He's dead."

There was a long pause.

"Think. Surely he mentioned it to you. Time is running out. We had a team, but they are long overdue, and I doubt they're coming back. We need that horn. In all your time together, do you really expect me to believe he never mentioned it?"

"No, he never said anything about a damn horn!"

"Either you're becoming better at lying, or you've been telling the truth all along. I just can't imagine he wouldn't tell you *anything* unless... Everyone is so certain, but I've had a nagging suspicion for some time now."

"What's that for?" Gaunt asked, his voice nervous—frightened.

"Let's call it a hunch. Now hold still."

Gaunt grunted, then cried out. "What are you doing?"

"You wouldn't understand even if I told you."

There was another pause.

"I knew it!" Guy exclaimed. "This explains so much. While it doesn't help either of us, at least it makes sense. The regents were fools to kill Esrahaddon."

"I don't understand. What are you talking about?"

"Nothing, Gaunt. I believe you. He didn't tell you anything. Why would he? The Patriarch will not be pleased. You won't be questioned anymore. You can await your execution in peace."

The door closed again and the footfalls left the dungeon.

Esrahaddon's dying words came back to Arista.

*Find the Horn of Gylindora—need the heir to find it— buried with Novron in Percepliquis. Hurry—at Wintertide the* Uli Vermar *ends. They will come—without the horn everyone dies.*

These words had brought Arista to Aquesta in the first place and were the reason she had risked her and Hilfred's lives trying to save Gaunt. Now she once more tried to understand just what Esrahaddon had meant by them.

❧

*Drip, drip, drip.*

The protruding bones of Arista's hips, knees, and shoulders ached from bearing her weight on the stone. Her fingernails had become brittle and broken. Too exhausted to stand or sit upright, Arista struggled even to turn over. Despite her weakness, she found it difficult to sleep, and lay awake for hours, glaring into the dark. The stone Arista lay on sucked the warmth from her body. Shivering in a ball, she pushed herself up in the dark and struggled to gather the scattered bits of straw. Running her fingers over the rough-hewn granite, she swept together the old, brittle thatch and mounded it as best she could into a lumpy bed.

Arista lay there imagining food. Not simply eating or touching it, but immersing herself. In her daydreams, she bathed in cream and swam in apple juice. All her senses contributed and she longed for even the smell of bread or the feel of butter on her tongue. Arista was tortured with thoughts of roasted pig dripping with fruit glaze, beef served in a thick, dark gravy, and mountains of chicken, quail, and duck. Envisioning feasts stretching across long tables made her mouth water. Arista ate several meals a day in her mind. Even the vegetables, the common diet of peasants, were welcomed. Carrots, onions, and parsnips hovered in her mind like unappreciated treasures—and what she would give for a turnip.

*Drip, drip, drip.*

In the dark there was so much to regret and so much time to do so.

What a mess she had made of a life that had started out filled with so much happiness. She recalled the days when her mother had been Queen of Melengar and music filled the halls. There had been the beautiful dress stitched from expensive Calian silk that she had received on her twelfth birthday. How the light had shimmered across its surface as she twirled before her mother's swan mirror. The same year, her father had given her a Maranon-bred pony. Lenare had been so jealous watching as Arista chased Alric and Mauvin over the Galilin hills on horseback. She loved riding and feeling the wind in her hair. Those had been such good days. In her memory, they were always sunny and warm.

Her world had changed forever the night the castle caught on fire. Her father had just appointed her uncle Braga as the Lord Chancellor of Melengar and celebrations ran late. Her mother tucked her into bed that night. Arista did not sleep in the tower then. She had a room across the hall from her parents, but she would never sleep in the royal wing again.

In the middle of that night, she had awoken to a boy pulling her from bed. Frightened and confused, she jerked away, kicking and scratching as he tried to grab hold.

"Please, Your Highness, you must come with me," the boy begged.

Outside her window, the elm tree burned like a torch, and her room flickered with its light. She heard a muffled roar from somewhere deep in the castle, and Arista found herself coughing from smoke.

*Fire!*

Screaming in terror, she cowered back to the imagined safety of her bed. The boy gripped her hard and dragged her toward him.

"The castle is burning. We have to get out of here," he said.

*Where is my mother? Where are Father and Alric? And who is this boy?*

While she fought against him, the boy lifted her in his arms and rushed from the room. The corridor was a tunnel of flames formed by the burning tapestries. Carrying her down the stairs and through several doors, he stumbled and finally collapsed in the courtyard. The cool evening air filled Arista's lungs as she gasped for breath.

Her father was not in the castle that night. After settling a dispute between two drunken friends, he had escorted them home. By sheer luck, Alric was also not there. He and Mauvin

Pickering had secretly slipped out to go *night hunting*, what they used to call frog catching. Arista's mother was the only royal who failed to escape.

Hilfred, the boy who had saved Arista, had tried to rescue the queen as well. After seeing the princess to safety, he went back into the flames and nearly died in the attempt. For months following the fire, Hilfred suffered the effects of burns, was beset by nightmares, and had coughing fits so intense that he spat blood. Despite all the agony he endured on her behalf, Arista never thanked him. All she knew was that her mother was dead, and from that day on everything had changed.

In the wake of the fire, Arista moved to the tower, as it was the only part of the castle that did not smell of smoke. Her father ordered her mother's furniture—those few items that had survived the fire—to be moved there. Arista would often cry while sitting before the swan mirror, remembering how her mother used to brush her hair. One day her father saw her and asked what was wrong. She blurted out, "All the brushes are gone." From that day forward, her father brought her a new brush after each trip he took. No two were ever alike. They were all gone now—the brushes, her father, even the dressing table with the swan mirror.

*Drip, drip, drip.*

Arista wondered if Maribor decreed she should be alone. Why else had she, a princess nearly twenty-eight years old, never had a proper suitor? Even poor, ugly daughters of fishmongers fared better. Perhaps her loneliness was her own fault, the result of her deplorable nature. In the dark, the answer was clearly visible—no one wanted her.

Emery had thought he loved Arista, but he had never really known her. Impressed by her wild ideas of taking Ratibor from the Imperialists, he had been swayed by the romantic notion of a noble fighting alongside a band of commoners. What Emery had fallen in love with was a myth. As for Hilfred, he had worshiped Arista as *his princess*. She was not a person but an icon on a pedestal. That they had died before learning the truth was a mercy to both men.

Only Hadrian had escaped being deceived. Arista was certain he saw her merely as a source of income. He likely hated her for being a privileged aristocrat living in a castle while he scraped by. All commoners were nice to nobility when in their presence—but in private, their true feelings showed. Hadrian probably snickered, proclaiming her too repulsive for even her own kind to love. With or without magic, she was still a witch. She deserved being alone. She deserved to die. She deserved to burn.

*Drip, drip, drip.*

A pain in her side caused her to turn over slowly. Sometimes she lost feeling in her feet for hours, and her fingers often tingled. After settling onto her back, she heard a skittering sound.

The rat had returned. Arista did not know where it came from or where it went in the darkness, but she always knew when it was near. She could not understand why it came around, as she ate all the food delivered. After consuming every drop of soup, she licked and even chewed on the bowl. Still, the rat visited frequently. Sometimes its nose touched her feet and kicking would send it scurrying away. In the past, she had tried to catch it, but it was smart and fast. Now Arista was too weak even to make an attempt.

Arista heard the rat moving along the wall of the cell. Its nose and whiskers lightly touched her exposed toes. She no longer had the energy to kick, so she let it smell her. After sniffing a few more times, the rat bit her toe.

Arista screamed in pain. She kicked but missed. Still, the

rat scurried off. Lying in the darkness, she shivered and cried in fear and misery.

"A — ris — ta?" Degan asked, sounding horse. "What is it?"

"A rat bit me," she said, once again shocked by her own rasping voice.

"Jasper does that if —" Gaunt coughed and hacked. After a moment, he spoke again. "If he thinks you're dead or too weak to fight."

"Jasper?"

"I call him that, but I've also named the stones in my cell."

"I only counted mine," Arista said.

"Two hundred and thirty-four," Degan replied instantly.

"I have two hundred and twenty-eight."

"Did you count the cracked ones as two?"

"No."

The princess lay there, listening to her own breathing, and felt the weight of her hands on her chest as it rose and fell. She started to drift into and out of sleep when Degan spoke again.

"Arista? Are you really a witch? Can you do magic?"

"Yes," she said. "But not in here."

Arista did not expect him to believe her and had been doubting her own powers after being cut off from them for so long. Runes lined the walls of the prison. They were the same markings that had prevented Esrahaddon from casting spells while incarcerated in Gutaria, but her stay would not last a thousand years as his had. Gutaria's runes halted the passage of time as well as preventing the practice of magic, and the ache in her stomach reminded Arista all too often that time was not suspended here.

Only since the Battle of Ratibor had Arista begun to understand the true nature of magic, or the Art, as Esrahaddon had called it. When touching the strings of reality, she felt no sense of boundaries — only complexity. With time and understanding, anything might be possible and everything achievable. She was certain that were it not for the runes disconnecting her from the natural world, she could break open the ground and rip the palace apart.

"Were you born a witch?"

"I learned magic from Esrahaddon."

"You knew him?"

"Yes."

"Do you know how he died?"

"He was murdered by an assassin."

"Oh. Did he ever talk about me? Did he tell you why he was helping me?" he asked anxiously.

"He never told you?"

"No. I didn't—" He broke into another fit of coughs. "I didn't have much of an army when we met, but then everything changed. He got men to join and follow me. I never had to do much of anything. Esrahaddon did all the planning and told me what to say. It was nice while it lasted. I had plenty to eat, and folks saluted and called me sir. I even had a horse and a tent the size of a house. I should have known all that was too good to last. I should have realized he was setting me up. I'm just curious why. What did I ever do to him?" His voice was weak, coming in gasps by the end of his speech.

"Degan, do you have a necklace? A small silver medallion?"

"Yeah—well, I did." He paused a long while, and when he spoke again, his voice was better. "My mother gave it to me before I left home—my good luck charm. They took it when they put me in here. Why do you ask?"

"Because you are the Heir of Novron. That necklace was created by Esrahaddon nearly nine hundred years ago. There were two of them, one for the heir and one for the guardian trained to defend him. For generations they protected the wearers from magic and hid their identities. Esrahaddon taught me a spell that could find who wore them. I was the one who helped him find you. He's been trying to restore you to the throne."

Degan was quiet for some time. "If I have a guardian, where is he? I could use one right now."

The waves of self-loathing washed over her again. "His name is Hadrian. Oh, Degan, it's all my fault. He doesn't know where you are. Esrahaddon and I were going to find you and tell him, but I messed it all up. After Esrahaddon's death, I thought I could get you out on my own. I failed."

"Yeah, well, it's only my life—nothing important." There was a pause, then, "Arista?"

"Yes?"

"What about that thing Guy mentioned? That *horn*? Did Esrahaddon ever mention it to you? If we can tell them something about it, maybe they won't kill us."

Arista felt the hair on her arms stand up.

*Is this a trick? Is he working for them?*

Weak and exhausted, she could not think clearly. In the darkness she felt vulnerable and disoriented—exactly what they wanted.

*Is it even Gaunt at all? Or did they discover I was coming and plant someone from the start? Or did they switch the real Gaunt while I slept? Is it the same voice?*

She tried to remember.

"Arista?" he called out again.

She opened her mouth to reply but paused and thought of something else to say. "It's hard to recall. My head's fuzzy, and I'm trying to piece the conversation together. He talked about the horn the same day I met your sister. I remember he introduced her...and then...Oh, how did it go again? He said, 'Arista, this is...this is...' Oh, it's just beyond my memory. Help me out, Degan. I feel like a fool. Can you remind me what your sister's name is?"

Silence.

Arista waited. She listened and thought she heard movement somewhere beyond her cell, but she was not sure.

"Degan?" she ventured after several minutes had passed. "Don't you know your own sister's name?"

"Why do you want to know her name?" Degan asked. His tone was lower, colder.

"I just forgot it, is all. I thought you could help me remember the conversation."

He was quiet for so long that she thought he might not speak again. Finally, he said, "What did they offer you to find out about her?"

"What do you mean?"

"Maybe you're Arista Essendon, or maybe you're an Imperialist trying to get secrets from me."

"How do I know any different about you?" she asked.

"You supposedly came to free me, and now you doubt who I am?"

"I came to free Degan Gaunt, but who are *you*?"

"I won't tell you the name of my sister."

"In that case, I think I will sleep." She meant it as a bluff, but as the silence continued, she dozed off.

# Chapter 8

# Sir Hadrian

Hadrian sat on the edge of his bunk, perplexed by the tabard. A single red diagonal stripe decorated each side. Depending on how he wore it, the stripe started from either his right or his left shoulder, and he could not figure out which was correct.

As he finally made a decision and placed it over his head, there was a quiet knock, followed by the timid opening of his door. A man's face, accentuated by a beaklike nose and topped by a foppish powdered wig, peered inside. "Excuse me, I'm looking for Sir Hadrian."

"Congratulations, you found him," Hadrian replied.

The man entered, followed closely by a boy, who remained near the door. Thin and brittle-looking, the man was dressed in bright satin knee breeches and an elaborate ruffled tunic. Even without the outlandish clothing, he would still be comical. Encased in buckled shoes, his feet seemed disproportionally large, and all his limbs were gangly. The teenage lad behind him wore the more conventional attire of a simple brown tunic and hose.

"My name is Nimbus of Vernes, and I am imperial tutor to the empress. Regent Saldur thought you might need some guidance on court protocol and instruction in knightly virtues, so he asked me to assist you."

"Pleased to meet you," Hadrian said. He stood and offered his hand. At first Nimbus appeared confused, but then he reached out and shook.

Motioning toward the tabard Hadrian wore, he nodded. "I can see why I was called upon."

Hadrian glanced down and shrugged. "Well, I figured I had a fifty-fifty chance." Removing the garment, he turned the tunic around. "Is that better?"

Nimbus struggled to suppress a laugh, holding a lace handkerchief to his lips. The boy was not so restrained and snorted, then laughed out loud. This made Nimbus lose his own battle, and finally Hadrian found himself laughing as well.

"I'm sorry. That was most inappropriate of me," Nimbus apologized, getting a hold of himself. "I beg your forgiveness."

"It's no problem. Just tell me what I'm doing wrong."

"Well, to start with, that particular garment is used only for sparring, and no self-respecting knight would wear such a thing at court."

Hadrian shrugged. "Oh, okay, good to know. It was the only thing I saw. Any ideas?"

Nimbus walked to a drape behind the bunk and flung it aside, revealing an open wardrobe filled with tunics, jackets, coats, capes, jerkins, gambesons, vests, doublets, baldrics, belts, breeches, shirts, hose, boots, and shoes.

Hadrian looked at the wardrobe and frowned. "So how was I supposed to know all that was there?"

"Why don't we begin by getting you properly dressed?" Nimbus suggested, and motioned for Hadrian to pick something.

He reached toward a pair of wool pants, but a cough from Nimbus stopped him.

"No?" Hadrian asked.

Nimbus shook his head.

"Okay, what do *you* think I should be wearing?"

Nimbus considered the wardrobe for several minutes, picking out various pieces, comparing them, putting one back, and then choosing another. He finally selected a white shirt, a gold doublet, purple hose, and shiny black shoes with brass buckles. He laid them out on the bunk.

"You're joking," Hadrian said, staring at the array. "That's your best choice? I'm not sure gold and purple are for me. Besides, what's wrong with the wool pants?"

"Those are for hunting and, like the tabard, not appropriate for dress at court. Gold and purple complement each other. They announce you are a man that makes no excuses."

Hadrian held up the clothes with a grimace. "They're loud. *Disturbingly* loud."

"They exude refinement and grace," Nimbus corrected. "Qualities, if you don't mind me saying, from which you could benefit. I know knights in the field dress in order to bully rabble-rousers and brigands, and under such circumstances, it's appropriate to select garments based on certain utilitarian qualities." He took an appraising look at Hadrian's attire. "But you are at the palace now, competing with a higher class of…thug. A strong arm and loud voice will not be enough. You need to sell yourself to the knights you wish to intimidate, to the ladies you wish to bed, to the lords you wish to impress, and to the commoners who will chant your name during the competitions. This last group is particularly important, as it will raise your stature with the others.

"A knight skilled in combat may stay alive, but it is the one skilled in persuasion who wins the king's daughter for his wife and retires to a vast estate. Truly successful knights can obtain multiple fiefs and enter their twilight years as wealthy as any count or earl."

Nimbus lowered his voice. "Regent Saldur mentioned that you might be a bit rough around the edges." He paused briefly. "I think we can both agree I've not been misled. It may take some doing to refine your mannerisms. So, in the meantime, I plan to overcompensate with clothing. We'll blind everyone with dazzle so they won't see the dirt on your face."

Hadrian reached for his cheek.

"That was a metaphor," Nimbus informed him. "Although now that I look at you, a bath is certainly in order."

"Bath? It's freezing outside. You're supposed to groom me, not kill me."

"You may be surprised to discover that in civilized society we bathe indoors in tubs with heated water. You might even find it enjoyable." Turning to the boy, Nimbus ordered, "Renwick, run and fetch the tub and get some others to help carry buckets. We'll also need a bristle brush, soap, oils, and—oh yes—scissors."

The lad ran off and quickly returned with a small army of boys carrying a wooden tub. They left and returned with buckets of hot water. After filling the tub, all the boys left except Renwick. He dutifully stood beside the door, ready for further requests.

Hadrian undressed and tested the water with a hesitant foot.

"Are you versed in the basic concept of bathing? Or do you need me to instruct you?" Nimbus asked.

Hadrian scowled at him. "I think I can handle it," he said, settling into the water. The tub overflowed and created a soapy mess. He grimaced. "Sorry about that."

Nimbus said nothing and turned away to give Hadrian a modicum of privacy.

The hot bath was wonderful. Hadrian had been assigned an interior chamber selected, no doubt, for its lack of windows.

There were a simple bed, two wooden stools, and a modest
table, but no fireplace, which left the chamber chilly. If he was
desperate, there was a large hearth in the common room at the
end of the hall, which also sported carpets and a chess set, but
despite the cold, Hadrian preferred to remain in the isolation
of his private room. Having not felt comfortably warm in
days, Hadrian sank lower to submerge as much of himself as
possible.

"Are these yours?" Nimbus asked, noticing Hadrian's weapons resting in the corner of the room.

"Yes, and I know they're worn and dirty *just like me.*"

Nimbus lifted the spadone, still encased in the leather baldric, with a noticeable degree of reverence. Turning it over
gingerly, he ran his fingertips along the hilt, grip, and pommel.
"This is very old," he said almost to himself. "Wrong sheath,
though." He laid the sword across the foot of the bed.

"I thought you were a courtier. What do you know about
swords?"

"You'll learn that there are many weapons at court. Survival in the maelstrom of the body politic requires being able
to size up another by what little they reveal to you."

Hadrian shrugged. "It's the same in combat."

"Court is combat," Nimbus said. "Only the skills and setting differ."

"So how would you size me up?"

"Regent Saldur told me your background is completely
confidential and that divulging anything would result in my—
not too painless—demise. The only information he provided
was that you were recently knighted. He refrained from any
detail about your station or ancestry. The regent merely mentioned you were lacking refinement and instructed me to
ensure you fit seamlessly into the Wintertide festivities."

Hadrian kept an unwavering stare on the tutor. "You didn't answer the question."

Nimbus smiled at him. "You really want to know, don't you? You aren't toying with me?"

Hadrian nodded.

The tutor turned to the page. "Renwick?"

"Yes, sir?"

"Fetch Sir Hadrian a cup of wine from the steward in the kitchen."

"There's wine in the common room, sir, and it's closer."

Nimbus gave him a stern look. "I want some privacy, Renwick."

"Oh, I see. Of course, sir."

"Very well, then," Nimbus said after the boy had left. He pursed his lips and tapped them several times with his index finger before continuing. "The truth of the matter is that you are not a knight. You haven't even served as a squire, groom, or page. I doubt you've ever set foot in a proper castle for more than a few minutes at a time. However—and this is the important point—you are indeed *noble*."

Hadrian paused in his scrubbing. "And what makes you think that?"

"You didn't know where the wardrobe was, you've never taken a bath in winter, you shook my hand when we met, and apologized for spilling your bathwater. These are most certainly not the actions of a knight raised from birth to feel and act superior to others."

Hadrian sniffed the scented soap and discarded it.

"Most telling, however, was the handshake itself. You offered it as a simple gesture of greeting. There was no agenda, no flattery, no insincerity. There also was no insecurity or sense that, by virtue of my clothes and mannerisms, I was your better. How odd, considering, as I now know, you were not *raised* a noble." Nimbus looked back at the sword resting on the bed. "It's an heirloom, isn't it?"

Picking up a bottle of oil, Hadrian pulled the cork and deemed it acceptable. He added a bit to the bristles of the brush. "I got it from my father."

The tutor ran his hand along the sheathed blade. "This is a remarkable weapon—a knight's sword—tarnished with time and travel. You don't use it as often as the others. The bastard and short sword are tools to you, but this—ah—this is something else—something revered. It lays concealed in a paltry sheath, covered in clothes not its own. It doesn't belong there. This sword belongs to another time and place. It is part of a grand and glorious world where knights were different, loftier— *virtuous*. It rests in this false scabbard because the proper one has been lost, or perhaps, it waits for a quest yet to be finished. It longs for that single moment when it can shine forth in all its brilliance. When dream and destiny meet on a clear field, then and only then will it find its purpose. When it faces that honorable cause—that one worthy and desperate challenge for which it was forged and on which so much depends—it will find peace in the crucible of struggle. For good or ill, it will ring true or break. But the wandering, the waiting, the hiding will at last be over. This sword waits for the day when it can save the kingdom and win the lady."

Hadrian sat staring, not realizing that he had dropped his brush.

Nimbus appeared to take no notice of Hadrian's reaction and sat on the bunk with a satisfied smile across his face. "Now, while I have your attention, shall we address the task to which I was assigned?"

Hadrian nodded.

"To help me judge where to start, can you tell m
already know about chivalry?" Nimbus asked.

"It's a code of conduct for knights," Hadrian
searching the bottom of the tub for the lost brush.

"Yes—well, you are essentially correct. What do you know
of its principles?"

"Be honorable, be brave, that sort of thing."

" 'That sort of thing'? Oh, I'm afraid we'll have to start
with the basics. Very well, please pay attention, and don't
forget to scrub the bottoms of your feet."

Hadrian frowned but lifted a foot.

"The knightly virtues derive themselves from a standard of
ethics passed down from the original empire. There are eight
such virtues. The first is proficiency. It is the easiest to achieve,
as it merely means skill at arms and can be obtained through
practice and observation. Judging from the wear on your
weapons, I trust you have a solid understanding of this virtue?"

"I'm able to hold my own."

Nimbus nodded. "Excellent. Next is courage, one of the
most important virtues. Courage, however, is not so cheaply
bought as by charging against overwhelming odds. It can take
many forms. For instance, the bravery to choose life over
death, especially if that means living with loss. Or the will to
risk all for a cause too noble to let perish. Courage can even
be found in surrender—if doing so will mean the survival of
something too valuable to lose.

"The third virtue of a knight is honesty. To possess honor,
a man must first strive to be honest to men, to women, to children, to great and to small, to the good and to the villainous,
but mostly to himself. A knight does not make excuses."

Hadrian made an extra effort to keep his eyes focused on
scrubbing his feet.

"Integrity is a virtue that comprises both loyalty and honor. Possessing integrity often means adhering to a pledge or principle. Loyalty to a sovereign is the mark of a goodly knight. However, integrity can also mean defending those in need who cannot help themselves. A knight should always work for the good of the king third, the betterment of the kingdom second, but always place what is right first."

"How does a knight know what is right?" Hadrian interrupted. He put down the brush, letting his foot slip back to the bottom of the tub. "I mean ... what if I'm forced to choose between two evils? Someone could get hurt no matter what I do. How do I decide?"

"True nobility lies in the heart. You must do what *you* know to be right."

"How do I know I'm not being selfish?"

"Ah, that brings us to the next virtue—faith. Faith is not simply a belief in the tenets of the church but a belief in virtue itself. A knight does not find fault. A knight believes in the good of all men, including himself. He trusts in this belief. A knight is confident in the word of others, in the merits of his lord, the worth of his commands, and in his own worth."

Hadrian nodded, though the words did not help ease his conscience.

"Generosity is the sixth virtue. A knight should show bounteousness to all, noble and commoner alike. More important than generosity of wares is a generosity of spirit. A knight believes the best of others and always extends the benefit of doubt. A knight does not accuse. He does not assume wrongdoing. Still, a knight grants no benefit to himself and always questions if he is at fault.

"Respect is the virtue concerning the good treatment of others. A knight is not thoughtless. He does not harm through recklessness. He seeks not to injure by lazy words or foolishness. A knight does not mimic the bad behavior of others. Instead, he sees it as an opportunity to demonstrate virtue by contrast."

Nimbus paused. "I don't think you need worry too much about this one either." He offered a smile before continuing.

"The final virtue is sincerity, which is elusive at best. Nobility by birthright is clear, but what is in question here is noblesse of heart and cannot be taught or learned. It must be accepted and allowed to grow. This virtue is demonstrated through bearing, not swagger; confidence, not arrogance; kindness, not pity; belief, not patronage; authenticity, not pretension.

"These are the virtues that comprise the Code of Chivalry," Nimbus concluded, "the path of goodness and truth to which men of high honor aspire. The reality, however, is often quite different."

As if on cue, the door burst open and three men tumbled inside. They were large, stocky brutes dressed in fine doublets with silk trim. The lead man sported a goatee and stood near the door, pointing at Hadrian.

"There he is!" he announced.

"Well, he certainly isn't this little sod," roared a second man, who pushed Nimbus hard in the chest and knocked the tutor back against the bunk. This man was the largest of the three and wore several days of beard growth. The insult, as well as the terrified expression on the courtier's face, brought the new arrivals to laughter.

"What's your name, twig?" the man with the goatee asked.

"I am Nimbus of Vernes," he said while attempting to stand and regain some level of dignity. "I am imperial tutor to—"

"Tutor? He's got a tutor!"

They howled in laughter again.

"Tell us, twig, what are you teaching Sir Bumpkin here? How to wash his arse? Is that your job? Have you taught him to use the chamber pot yet?"

Nimbus did not answer. He clenched his teeth and fixed his eyes on the unkempt man before him.

"I think you're getting under that ruffled collar of his," the last of them observed. He was clean-shaven and sipped wine from a goblet. "Careful, Elgar, he's made fists."

"Is that true?" Elgar looked at the tutor's hands, which were indeed tightly clenched. "Oh dear! Am I impinging on your sacred pedagogical honor? Would you like to throw a punch at me, little twig? Put me in my proper place, as it were?"

"If he takes a big enough swing, it's possible you might actually feel it," the shaved one said.

"I asked you a question, twig," Elgar pressed.

"If you don't mind, we'll continue this another time," Nimbus said to Hadrian. "It would seem you have guests."

Elgar blocked the tutor's path as he tried to leave, and shoved him again. Staggering backward, Nimbus fell onto the bed.

"Leave him alone," Hadrian ordered as he stood and grabbed a towel.

"Ah, Sir Bumpkin, in all his regal glory!" proclaimed the man with the goatee, pointing. "Well, not *that* regal and certainly not *that* glorious!"

"Who are you?" Hadrian demanded, stepping out of the tub and wrapping the towel around himself.

"I am Sir Murthas and the gent with the handsome face beside me here is Sir Gilbert. Over there, that dashing fellow holding the pleasant conversation with the twig is none other than Sir Elgar. We are the three finest knights of the realm, as you will soon discover. We wanted to welcome you to the pal-

ace, deliver you a fond tiding, and wish you luck on the field—
as luck is all you'll have."

Nimbus snorted. "They're here because they heard a bath
was ordered, and wanted to see your scars. Knowing nothing
about you, they came to see if you have any fresh bruises or
recent wounds they might take advantage of on the field. Also,
they are trying to intimidate you, as a man in a tub is at a dis-
advantage. Intimidation can frequently win a contest before it
starts."

Sir Elgar grabbed hold of Nimbus, pulling him up by his
tunic. "Talkative little bastard, aren't you?" He raised a fist
just as a sopping towel slammed into his face.

"Sorry. Elgar, is it?" Hadrian asked. "Just got done drying
my ass and noticed a smudge on your face."

Elgar threw off the towel and drew his sword. In just two
steps, the knight cut the distance to Hadrian, who stood
naked and unflinching even as Elgar raised the blade's tip
toward his throat.

"Brave bugger, I'll give you that much," Elgar said. "But
that just means you'll be an easier target along the fence. You
might want to save that water. You'll need it after I put you in
the mud." Sheathing his sword, he led his friends from the
room, nearly colliding with Renwick, who stood outside the
door holding a goblet of wine.

"You all right?" Hadrian asked, grabbing a fresh towel.

"Yes, of course," Nimbus replied in an unsteady voice. He
smoothed the material of his tunic.

"Your wine, sir," Renwick said to Hadrian.

Without pause, Nimbus took the cup and drained it. "As I
was saying, the reality can be quite different."

# CHAPTER 9

# WINDS ABBEY

Royce stood before the window of the bedroom, watching Gwen sleep and thinking about their future. He pushed the thought away and suppressed the urge to smile. Just imagining it would bring disaster. The gods—if they existed—detested happiness. Instead, he turned and looked out over the cloistered courtyard.

The previous night's storm had left everything covered in a new dress of unblemished white. The only exception was a single line of footprints that led from the dormitory to a stone bench, where a familiar figure sat wrapped in a monk's habit. He was alone, yet the movement of his hands and the bob of his head revealed he was speaking with great earnest. Across from the monk was a small tree. Planting it was one of the first things Myron had done when he had returned to the abbey after the fire. It now stood a proud eight feet tall but was so slender it drooped under the snow's weight. Royce knew there was great resiliency in a tree accustomed to bending in the wind, but he wondered if the strain could be endured. There was a breaking point for everything, after all. As if reading his thoughts, Myron rose and gave the tree a light shake. He had to stand close to do so, and much of the snow fell on his head.

The tree sprang back, and without the burden of snow, it appeared more like its former self. Myron returned to his seat and his conversation. Royce knew he was not speaking to the tree but to his boyhood friend who was buried there.

"You're up early," Gwen said from where she lay with her head on a clutched pillow. He could make out the elegant slope of her waist and rise of her hip beneath the covers. "After last night, I would have thought you'd be sleeping late."

"We went to bed early."

"But we didn't sleep," she teased.

"It was better than sleep. Besides, around here, waking after first light *is* sleeping in. Myron is already outside."

"He does that so he can talk privately." She smiled and drew back the covers invitingly. "Isn't it cold next to that window?"

"You're a bad influence," he said, lying down and wrapping his arms around her. He marveled at the softness of her skin. She drew the quilt over both of them and laid her head on his chest.

Their room was one of the bigger guest chambers, which was three times larger than any of the monks' cells. Gwen, who had left Medford a week before Breckton's invasion, had arranged to bring everything with her, even her canopied bed, carpets, and wall hangings. Looking around the room, Royce could easily imagine he was back on Wayward Street. He felt at home, but not because of the decorations. All he needed was Gwen.

"Am I corrupting you?" she asked playfully.

"Yes."

His fingers caressed her bare shoulder and ran along the swirled tattoo. "This last trip Hadrian and I went on, we went to Calis...into the jungles. We stayed in a Tenkin village, where I met an unusual woman."

"Did you? Was she beautiful?"

"Yes, very."

"Tenkin women can be exceptionally attractive."

"Yes, they can. And this one had a tattoo that—"

"Did Hadrian find the heir?"

"No—well, yes, but not how we expected. We stumbled on the news the empire is holding him in Aquesta. They're going to execute him on Wintertide. But this tattoo—"

"Execute him?" Gwen pushed herself up on one elbow, looking surprised—too surprised just to be avoiding questions. "Shouldn't you be helping Hadrian?"

"I will, although I'm not sure why. I was hardly any help on the last trip, and I didn't need to save him. So your little prophecy was wrong."

He thought it would put Gwen at ease to know her prediction of disaster had not come to pass. Instead, she pushed him away—the familiar sadness returned.

"You need to go help him," she said firmly. "I might be wrong about the timing, but I'm not wrong about Hadrian dying unless you are there to save him."

"Hadrian will be fine until I get back."

She hesitated, took a deep breath, and laid her head back down. Hiding her face against his chest, she became quiet.

"What's the matter?" Royce asked.

"I *am* a corrupting influence."

"I wouldn't worry about that," he told her. "Personally, I've always rather liked corruption."

There was a long pause, and he watched her head riding on the swells of his breath. Running his fingers through her hair, he marveled at it—at her. He touched the tattoo again.

"Royce, can we just lie here a little while?" She squeezed him, rubbing her cheek against his chest. "Can we just be still and listen to the wind and make believe it is blowing past us?"

"Isn't it?"

"No," she said, "but I want to pretend."

◦§

"There wasn't much of a fight," Magnus said.

Royce always thought the dwarf's voice sounded louder and deeper than it should for someone his size. They sat at a long table in the refectory. Now that Royce knew Gwen was safe, his appetite returned. The monks prepared an excellent meal, accompanied by the first good wine he had tasted in ages.

"Alric just ran," Magnus said while mopping up the last of an egg. For someone so small, he ate a lot and never passed up an opportunity for food. "So Breckton's army took over everything except Drondil Fields, but they'll have that soon."

"Who burned Medford?" Royce asked.

"Medford was burned?"

"When I came through there a couple days ago, it was."

The dwarf shrugged. "If I had to guess, I'd say church-led fanatics out of Chadwick or maybe Dunmore. They've been pillaging homes and hunting elves since the invasion."

Magnus finished eating and leaned back with his feet on an empty stool. Gwen sat beside Royce, clutching his arm as if she owned him. The very idea of belonging to her was so strange that he found it distracting, but he was surprised to discover he enjoyed the sensation.

"So how long are you back for?" the dwarf asked. "Got time to let me see Alver—"

"I'm leaving as soon as Myron gets done." Royce noticed a look from Gwen. "I'm sure it won't take him more than a few days."

"What's he doing?"

"Drawing a map. Myron saw a floor plan of the palace once, so he's off reproducing it. He said it's old…real old… dates back to Glenmorgan, apparently."

"When you leave," Gwen said, "take Mouse. Give Ryn's horse to Myron."

"What does Myron need with a horse?" he asked. Gwen just smiled, and Royce knew better than to question further. "Okay, but I'm warning you now. He'll spoil it rotten."

❦

Myron sat at his desk in the scriptorium carrel, arguably his favorite place in the world. The peaked desk and small stool took up most of the cramped space between the stone columns. To his left, a half-moon window overlooked the courtyard.

Outside, the world appeared frightfully cold. The wind howled past the window, leaving traces of snow in the corners of the leading. The hilltop scrub shook with winter's fury. Peering out, Myron appreciated the coziness of his tiny study. The niche in the room enveloped him like a rodent's burrow. Ofttimes Myron considered how he might like to be a mole or a shrew—not a dusky or a greater white-tooth or even a lesser white-tooth shrew, but just a common shrew, or perhaps a mole. How pleasant an existence it would be to live underground, safe and warm, in small hidden chambers. He could look out at the vast world with a sense of awe and delight in knowing there was no reason to venture forth.

He put the finishing touches on the drawing for Royce and returned to working on the final pages of *Elquin*. This was the masterwork of the fifth-dynastic poet Orintine Fallon. It was a massive tome of personal reflections on how the patterns of nature related to the patterns in life. When completed, it would be the twentieth book in Myron's quest to restore the Winds Abbey library, with a mere three hundred and fifty-two remaining—not including the five hundred and twenty-four scrolls and one thousand two hundred and thirteen individual parchments. For more than two years' work, that accomplishment might not seem impressive, but Myron scribed full-time only in the winter, as the warmer months were devoted to helping put the finishing touches on the monastery.

The new Winds Abbey was nearly completed. To most, it would appear exactly as it once was, but Myron knew better. It had the same types of windows, doors, desks, and beds, but they were not the same ones. The roof was exactly as he remembered, yet it was different—just like the people. He missed Brothers Ginlin, Heslon, and the rest. Not that Myron was unhappy with his new family. He liked the new abbot, Harkon. Brother Bendlton was a very fine cook, and Brother Zephyr was marvelous at drawing and helped Myron with many of his illuminations. They were all wonderful, but like the windows, doors, and beds, they were not the same.

"No, for the last time, no!" Royce shouted as he entered the small scriptorium, pursued by Magnus.

"Just for a day or two," Magnus pleaded. "You can spare the dagger for that long. I only want to look at it—study it. I won't damage it."

"Leave me alone."

The two made their way toward Myron, weaving between the other desks. There were two dozen in the room, but only Myron's was used with any regularity.

"Oh, Royce, I've just finished. But you might want to wait for the ink to dry."

Royce held the map to the light, scanning it critically for several minutes.

Myron became concerned. "Something wrong?"

"I can't believe how things like this are just sitting in your head. It's incredible. And you say this is a map of the palace?"

"The notation reads 'Warric Castle,'" Myron pointed out.

"That's no map," Magnus said with a scowl, looking at the parchment Royce held out of his reach.

"How would you know?" Royce asked.

"Because what you have there are construction plans. You can see the builder's marks."

Royce lowered the scroll and Magnus pointed. "See here, the builder jotted down the amount of stone needed."

Royce looked at the dwarf and then at Myron. "Is that right?"

Myron shrugged. "Could be. I only know what I saw. I have no idea what it means."

Royce turned back to Magnus. "So you understand these markings, these symbols."

"Sure, it's just basic engineering."

"Can you tell me where the dungeon is by looking at this?"

The dwarf took the plans and laid them on the floor, as the desks were too high for him to reach. He motioned for a candle and Royce brought it over. Magnus studied the map for several minutes before declaring, "Nope. No dungeon."

Royce frowned. "That doesn't make sense. I've never heard of a palace or castle that didn't have some kind of dungeon."

"Well, that's not the only strange thing about this place," Magnus said.

"What do you mean?"

"Well, there's nothing, and I mean nothing at all, below ground level. Not so much as a root cellar."

"So?"

"So you can't stack tons of stone on just dirt. It will sink. Rain will erode it. The walls will shift and collapse."

"But it hasn't," Myron said. "The records I reproduced date back hundreds of years."

"Which makes no sense. These plans show no supporting structure. No piles driven down to bedrock, no columns. There's nothing holding this place up. At least nothing drawn here."

"So what does that mean?"

"Not sure, but if I were to guess, it's 'cuz it's built on top of something else. They must have used an existing foundation."

"Knowing that and looking at this…could you give me an idea of where a dungeon is, if you were there?"

"Sure. Just need to see what it's sitting on and give a good listen to the ground around it. I found you that tunnel to Avempartha, after all."

"All right, get packed. You're coming with me to Aquesta."

"What about the dagger?"

"I promise to bequeath it to you when I die."

"I can't wait until then."

"Don't worry. At this rate, it won't be too long." Royce turned back to Myron. "Thanks for the help."

"Royce?" Myron stopped the thief as they started to leave.

"Yeah?"

Myron waited until Magnus left. "Can I ask you something about Miss DeLancy?"

Royce raised an eyebrow. "Is something wrong? Is the abbot upset with her and the girls being here?"

"Oh no, nothing like that. They have been wonderful. It's nice having sisters as well as brothers. And Miss DeLancy has a very nice voice."

"Nice voice?"

"The abbot keeps us segregated from the women, so we don't see them much. They eat at different times and sleep in separate dormitories, but the abbot invites the ladies to join in vespers. A few come, including Miss DeLancy. She always arrives with her head covered and face veiled. She's quiet, but from time to time, I notice her whispering a prayer. Each service begins with a hymn and Miss DeLancy joins in. She sings softly but I can hear her. She has a wonderful voice, haunting, beautiful but also sad like the song of a nightingale."

"Oh." Royce nodded. "Well, good. I'm glad there isn't a problem."

"I wouldn't call it a problem, but..."

"But?"

"I often see her in the mornings when I go to the Squirrel Tree to talk with Renian. Miss DeLancy sometimes takes walks in the cloister, and she always stops by to pay her respects to us when she does." Myron paused.

"And?" Royce prompted.

"Well, it's just that one morning she took my hand and looked at my palm for several minutes."

"Uh-oh," Royce muttered.

"Yes," Myron said with wide eyes.

"What did she say?"

"She told me I would be taking two trips—both sudden and unexpected. She said I would not feel up to it, but I should not be afraid."

"Of what?"

"She didn't say."

"Typical."

"Then she told me something else and was sad like when she sings."

"What was it?" Royce asked.

"She said she wanted to thank me in advance and tell me it wasn't my fault."

"She didn't explain that either, did she?"

Myron shook his head. "But it was very disturbing, the way she said it—so serious and all. Do you know what I mean?"

"All too well."

Myron sat up on his stool and took a breath. "You know her. Should I be concerned?"

"I always am."

⤜

Royce walked the courtyard in the early-morning light. He had a habit of getting up early. To avoid waking Gwen, he had slipped out to wander the abbey's grounds. Scaffolding remained here and there, but the majority of the monastery was finished. Alric had financed the reconstruction as a payment to Riyria for saving Arista when their uncle Braga had tried to kill her. Magnus oversaw its construction and seemed genuinely happy to be restoring the buildings to their former splendor, even though working with Myron frustrated the dwarf. Myron provided detailed, although unorthodox, specifications describing dimensions in the height of several butter churns, the width of a specific book, or the length of a spoon. Despite this, the buildings went up, and Royce had to admit the monk and the dwarf had done an excellent job.

That day, the ground was covered in a thick frost and the sky lightened to a bright, clear blue as Royce made his morning rounds. Myron had finished the map, and he knew he should be leaving soon, but Royce was stalling. He enjoyed lingering in bed with Gwen and taking walks with her in the courtyard. Noticing the sun rising above the buildings, he headed back inside. Gwen would be up, and having breakfast together was always the best part of their day. When he reached their room, Gwen was still in bed, her back to the door.

"Gwen? Are you feeling all right?"

She rolled over to face him and he saw the tears in her eyes.

Royce rushed to her side. "What is it, what's wrong?"

She reached out and hugged him. "Royce, I'm sorry. I wish there was more time. I wish..."

"Gwen? What—"

Someone knocked at the door and the force pushed it open. The portly abbot and a stranger stood awkwardly on the other side.

"What is it?" Royce snapped as he studied the stranger.

He was young and dressed in filthy clothes. His face showed signs of windburn and the tip of his nose looked frostbitten.

"Begging your pardon, Master Melborn," the abbot said. "This man rode in great haste from Aquesta to deliver a message to you."

Royce glanced at Gwen and stood up even as her fingers struggled to hold him. "What's the message?"

"Albert Winslow told me you would pay an extra gold tenent if I arrived quickly. I rode straight through."

"What's the message?" Royce's voice took on a chill.

"Hadrian Blackwater has been captured and is imprisoned in the imperial palace."

Royce ran a hand through his hair, barely hearing Gwen thank the man as she paid him.

✦

Brilliant sunlight illuminated the interior of the stable as Royce entered. The planks composing the stalls were still pale yellow, not yet having aged to gray. The smell of sawdust mingled pleasantly with the scents of manure, straw, and hay.

"I should have guessed you'd be here," Royce said, startling Myron, who stood inside the stall between the two horses.

"Good morning. I was blessing your horse. Not knowing which you would take, I blessed them both. Besides, someone has to do the petting. Brother James cleans the stalls very well, but he never takes time to scratch their necks or rub their noses. In *The Song of Beringer*, Sir Adwhite wrote: *Everyone deserves a little happiness*. It's true, don't you think?" Myron stroked the dark horse's nose. "I know Mouse, but who is this?"

"His name is Hivenlyn."

Myron tilted his head, working something out while moving his lips. "And was he?" the monk asked.

"Was he what?"

"An unexpected gift."

Royce smiled. "Yes—yes, he was. Oh, and he's yours now."

"Mine?"

"Yes, compliments of Gwen."

Royce saddled Mouse and attached the bags of food the abbot had prepared while Royce had said his goodbyes to Gwen. There had been too many partings over the years, each harder than the one before.

"So you are off to help Hadrian?"

"And when I get back, I'm taking Gwen and we're leaving, going away from everyone and everything. Like you said, 'Everyone deserves a little happiness,' right?"

Myron smiled. "Absolutely. Only..."

"Only what?"

The monk paused before speaking again, rubbing Mouse's neck one last time. "Happiness comes from moving toward something. When you run away, ofttimes you bring your misery with you."

"Who are you quoting now?"

"No one," Myron said. "I learned that one firsthand."

# CHAPTER 10

# THE FEAST OF NOBLES

The fourteen-day-long Wintertide festival officially began with the Feast of Nobles in the palace's great hall. Twenty-seven colorful banners hung from the ceiling, each with the emblem of a noble house of Avryn. Five were noticeably absent, leaving gaps in the procession: the blue tower on the white field of House Lanaklin of Glouston, the red diamond on the black field of House Hestle of Bernum, the white lily on the green field of House Exeter of Hanlin, the gold sword on the green field of House Pickering of Galilin, and the gold-crowned falcon on the red field of House Essendon of Melengar. In times of peace, the hall welcomed all thirty-two families in celebration. The gaps in the line of banners were a reminder of the costs of war.

The palace shimmered with the decorations of the holiday season. Wreaths and strings of garland festooned the walls and framed the windows. Elaborate chandeliers, draped in red and gold streamers, spilled light across polished marble floors. Four large stone hearths filled the great hall with a warm orange glow. And rows of tall arched windows gowned in snowflake-embroidered curtains let in the last light of the setting sun.

On a dais at the far end of the room, the head table ran along the interior wall. Like rays from the sun, three longer tables extended out from it, trimmed with fanciful centerpieces woven from holly branches and accentuated with pinecones.

As many as fifty nobles, each dressed in his or her finest garments, already filled the hall. Some stood in groups, speaking in lordly voices; others gathered in shadowed corners, whispering in hushed tones; but the majority sat conversing at the tables.

"They look pretty, don't they?" Nimbus whispered to Hadrian. "So do snakes in the right light. Treat them the same way. Keep your distance, watch their eyes, and back away if you rattle them. Do that, and you might survive."

Nimbus looked him over one last time and brushed something off Hadrian's shoulder. He wore the gold and purple outfit—and felt ridiculous.

"I wish I had my swords. Not only do I look silly, but I feel naked."

"You have your pretty jeweled dagger," Nimbus said, smiling. "This is a feast, not a tavern. A knight does not go armed before his liege. It's not only considered rude, it also suggests treason. We don't want that now, do we? Just keep your wits about you and try not to say much. The more you talk, the more ammunition you provide. And remember what I told you about table manners."

"You're not coming?" Hadrian asked.

"I will be seated with Lady Amilia at the head table. If you get in trouble, look for me. I'll do what I can. Now remember, you're at the third table, left side, fourth chair from the end. Good luck."

Nimbus slipped away and Hadrian stepped into the hall. The instant he did, he regretted it, realizing he was not certain which side was left, which table was third, or which end of the table he should count from. Heads turned at his entrance, and the looks on their faces brought back memories of the aftermath of the Battle of RaMar. On that day, carrion birds had feasted on the bodies as Hadrian had walked through the battlefield. Hoping to drive the vultures off, he had shot and killed one of them with an arrow. To his revulsion, the other birds descended on the fresher remains of their fallen comrade. The birds had cocked their heads and looked at him as if to say he had no business being there. Hadrian saw the same look in the eyes of the nobles around him now.

"And who might you be, good sir?" a lady said off to Hadrian's right.

In his single-minded effort to find his seat, and with all the chatter in the room, he paid no attention.

"It is rude to ignore a lady when she speaks to you," a man said. His voice was sharp and impossible to ignore.

Hadrian turned to see a young man and woman glaring at him. They looked to be twins, as each had blond hair and dazzling blue eyes.

"It is also dangerous," the man went on, "when she is a princess of the honorable kingdom of Alburn."

"Um...ah...forgive—" Hadrian started when the man cut him off.

"There you have it. The cause for the slight is that the knight has no tongue! You are a knight, are you not? Please tell me you are. Please tell me you were some bucolic farmer that a drunken lord jokingly dubbed after you chased a squirrel from his manor. I couldn't stand it if you were another illegitimate son of an earl or duke, who crawled from an alehouse, attempting to claim true nobility."

"Let the man try to speak," the lady said. "Surely he suffers from a malady that prevents his mind from forming words properly. It's nothing to make light of, dear brother. It is a true sickness. Perhaps he contracted it from suffering on the battlefield. I am told that placing pebbles in the mouth often helps. Would you care for some, good sir?"

"I don't need any pebbles, thank you," Hadrian replied coolly.

"Well, you certainly need *something*. I mean, you are afflicted, aren't you? Why else would you completely ignore me like that? Or do you delight in insulting a lady, whose only offense is to ask your name?"

"I didn't—I mean, I wasn't—"

"Oh dear, there he goes again," she said with a pitiful look. "Please send a servant to fetch some pebbles at once."

"I daresay," her brother began, "I don't think we have time for the pebbles. Perhaps he can simply suck on one or two of these pinecones. Would that help, do you think?"

"He doesn't have a speech problem," Sir Murthas said as he approached, thumbs hooked in his belt and a wide grin on his face.

"No?" the prince and princess asked together.

"No, indeed, he's merely ignorant. He has his own tutor, you know. When I first met Sir Hadrian—that is the lout's name, by the way—he was in the middle of a bathing lesson. Can you imagine? The poor clod doesn't even know how to wash."

"Oh, now that is troubling." The princess began cooling herself with a collapsible fan.

"Indeed. So at a loss was he at the complexities of bathing that he threw his washcloth at Sir Elgar!"

"Such *rude* behavior is inherent in him, then?" she asked.

"Listen, I—" Hadrian started, only to be cut off again.

"Careful, Beatrice," Murthas said. "You're agitating him. He might spit or drool on you. If he's that uncouth, who knows what degradations he's capable of? I'll lay money that he'll wet himself next."

Hadrian was taking a step toward Murthas when he saw Nimbus rushing toward them.

"Princess Beatrice, Prince Rudolf, and Sir Murthas, a wonderful Wintertide to you all!"

They turned to see the tutor, his arms spread wide, a joyous smile beamed across his face. "I see you've met our distinguished guest Sir Hadrian. I am certain he is far too modest to tell the tale of his recent knighting on the field of battle. A shame, as it is a wonderful and exciting story. Prince Rudolf, I know you'd enjoy hearing it, and in return you can tell of *your own* heroic battles. Oh, I am sorry, I forgot—you've never actually seen a real battle, have you?"

The prince stiffened.

"And you, Sir Murthas, I can't recall—please tell us— where *you* were while the empress's armies fought for their lives. Surely you can relate *your* exploits of the last year and how you fared while other goodly knights died for the cause of Her Eminence's honor?"

Murthas opened his mouth, but Nimbus was quicker. Turning to the woman, he went on, "And, my lady, I want to assure you that you needn't take offense at Sir Hadrian's slight. It is little wonder that he ignored you. For he knows, as we all do, that no honorable lady would *ever* be so bold as to speak first to a strange man in the same manner as a common whore selling her wares on the street."

All three of them stared, speechless, at the tutor.

"If you're still looking for your seat, Sir Hadrian, it's this way," Nimbus said, hauling him along. "Once again, a glorious Wintertide to you all!"

Nimbus directed him to a chair at the end of a table, which so far remained empty.

"Whoa," Hadrian said in awe. "You just called those men cowards and the princess a whore."

"Yes," he said, "but I did so *very* politely." He winked. "Now, please do try to stay out of trouble. Sit here and smile. I have to go." Nimbus slipped back through the crowd, waving to people as he went.

Once more, Hadrian felt adrift amidst a sea of eggshells. He looked back and saw the princess and Murthas pointing in his direction and laughing. Not far away he noted two men watching him. Arms folded, they leaned against a pillar wrapped in red ribbons. The men were conspicuous in that they were the only guests wearing swords. Hadrian recognized the pair, as he had seen them often. They were always standing in the dark, across a room, or just outside a doorway — his own personal shadows.

Hadrian turned away and carefully took his seat. Tugging at his clothes, he tried to remember everything Nimbus had taught him: *sit up straight, do not fidget, always smile, never start a conversation, do not try anything you're unfamiliar with, and avoid eye contact unless cornered into a conversation.* If forced into an introduction, he was supposed to bow rather than shake hands with men. If a lady held out her hand, he should take it and gently kiss its back. Nimbus had advised him to keep several excuses at the ready to escape conversations, and to avoid groups of three or more. The most important thing was to appear relaxed and never draw attention to himself.

Minstrels played lutes somewhere near the front of the room, but he could not see them through the sea of people, who moved in shifting currents. Every so often, insincere laughter burst out. Snide conversations drifted to and fro. The ladies were much better at it than the men. "Oh, my dear, I simply *love* that dress!" A woman's high lilting voice floated from somewhere in the crowd. "I imagine it is insanely comfortable, given that it is so simple. Mine, on the other hand, with all this elaborate embroidery, is nearly impossible to sit in."

"I'm sure you are correct," another lady replied. "But discomfort is such a small sacrifice for a dress that so masterfully masks a lady's physical flaws and imperfections by the sheer complexity of its spacious design."

Trying to follow the feints and parries in the conversations around him gave Hadrian a headache. If he closed his eyes, he could almost hear the clash of steel. He was pleased to see that Princess Beatrice, Prince Rudolf, and Sir Murthas took seats at another table. Across from Hadrian, a man wearing a simple monk's robe took a seat. He looked even more out of place than Hadrian. They nodded silently to each other. Still, the chairs flanking him remained vacant.

At the head table, Ethelred sat beside a massive empty throne. Kings and their queens filled out the rest of the table, and at one end Nimbus was seated next to Lady Amilia. She sat quietly in a stunning blue dress, her head slightly bowed.

The music stopped.

"Your attention, please!" shouted a fat man in a bright yellow robe. He held a brass-tipped staff, which he hammered on the stone floor. The sound penetrated the crowd like cracks of thunder and stifled the drone of conversations. "Please take your seats. The feast is about to begin."

The room filled with the sounds of dragging chairs as the nobility of Avryn settled at their tables. A large man with a gray beard was to the monk's left. To his right sat none other than Sir Breckton, dressed in a pale blue doublet. The resemblance to Wesley was unmistakable. The knight stood and bowed as a large woman with a massive smile sat down on Hadrian's left. The sight of Genevieve Hargrave of Rochelle was a welcome one.

"Forgive me, good sir," she implored as she struggled into her chair. "Clearly they were expecting a dainty princess to sit here rather than a full-grown duchess! No doubt you were hoping for the same." She winked at him.

Hadrian knew a response was expected, and decided to take a safe approach.

"I was hoping not to spill anything on myself. I didn't think beyond that."

"Oh dear, now that *is* a first." She looked across the table at the knight. "I daresay, Sir Breckton, you may have competition this evening."

"How is that, my lady?" he asked.

"This fellow beside me shows all the signs of matching your humble virtue."

"Then I am honored to sit at the same table as he and even more pleased to have you as my view."

"I pity all princesses this evening, for surely I am the luckiest of ladies to be seated with the two of you. What is your name, goodly sir?" she asked Hadrian.

Still seated, Hadrian realized his error. Like Breckton, he should have stood at Genny's approach. Rising awkwardly, he fumbled a bow. "I am...Sir Hadrian," he said, watching for a raised hand. When she lifted it, he felt foolish but placed a light kiss on its back before sitting down. He expected laughter from the others but no one seemed to notice.

"I am Genevieve, the Duchess of Rochelle."

"Pleased to meet you," Hadrian replied.

"Surely you know Sir Breckton?" the duchess asked.

"Not personally."

"He is the general of the Northern Imperial Army and favored champion of this week's tournament."

"Favored by whom, my lady?" Sir Elgar asked, dragging out the seat next to Breckton and sitting with all the elegance of an elephant. "I believe Maribor favors my talents in this year's competition."

"You might like to think that, Sir Elgar, but I suspect your boasting skills are more honed than your riding prowess after so many years of endless practice," the duchess returned, causing the monk to chuckle.

"No disrespect to Her Ladyship," Breckton said in cold seriousness, "but Sir Elgar is correct in that only Maribor will judge the victor of this tournament, and no one yet knows the favor of his choice."

"Do not speak on my behalf," Elgar growled. "I don't need your charity, nor will I be the foundation for your tower of virtue. Spare us your monk's tongue."

"Don't be too quick to shun charity or silence a monk," the robed man across from Hadrian said softly. "Or how else will you know the will of god?"

"Pardon me, good monk. I was not speaking against you but rather rebuking the preaching of this secular would-be priest."

"Wherever the word of Maribor is spoken, I pray thee listen."

A squat, teardrop-shaped man claimed the chair beside the duchess. He kissed her cheek and called her dearest. Hadrian had never met Leopold before, but from all Albert had told him, his identity was obvious. Sir Gilbert took the empty chair next to Elgar.

No one sat to Hadrian's right, and he hoped it would remain that way. With the duchess protecting one flank, if no one took the seat at the other, he had to worry only about a frontal assault. While Hadrian pondered this, another friendly face appeared.

"Good Wintertide, all!" Albert Winslow greeted those at the table with an elegant flourish that made Hadrian envious.

He was certain Albert saw him, but the viscount displayed no indication of recognition.

"Albert!" The duchess beamed. "How wonderful to have you at our table."

"Ah, Lady Genevieve and Duke Leopold. I had no idea I ranked so highly on Her Eminence's list that I should be given the honor of dining with such esteemed personages."

Albert immediately stepped to Genny, bowed, and kissed her hand with effortless grace and style.

"Allow me to introduce Sir Hadrian," the lady said. "He appears to be a wonderful fellow."

"Is he?" Albert mused. "And a knight, you say?"

"That is yet to be determined," Sir Elgar said. "He claims a *Sir* before his name, but I've never heard of him before. Has anyone?"

"Generosity of spirit precludes judging a man ill before cause is given," Sir Breckton said. "As a knight of virtue, I am certain you know this, Sir Elgar."

"Once more, I need no instruction from you. I, for one, would like to know from whence Sir Hadrian hails and how it was he won his spurs."

All eyes turned to Hadrian.

He tried to remember the details drilled into him without looking like he was struggling. "I come from…Barmore. I was knighted by Lord Dermont for my service in the Battle of Ratibor."

"Really?" Sir Gilbert said in a syrupy voice. "I wasn't aware of *that* victory. I was under the impression the battle was lost and Lord Dermont killed. For what were you knighted, and how, pray tell, did His Lordship knight you? Did his spirit fly overhead, dubbing you with an ethereal sword, saying, 'Rise up, good knight. Go forth and lose more battles in the name of the empire, the empress, and the lord god Maribor'?"

Hadrian felt his stomach churn. Albert looked at him with tense eyes, clearly unable to help. Even the duchess remained silent.

"Good evening, gentlemen and lady." From behind him, the voice of Regent Saldur broke the tension, and Hadrian felt the regent's hand on his shoulder.

Accompanying him was Archibald Ballentyne, the Earl of Chadwick, who took the seat to Hadrian's right. Everyone at the table nodded reverently to the regent.

"I was just showing the earl to his seat, but I couldn't help overhearing your discussion concerning Sir Hadrian of Barmore here. You see, it was the empress herself who insisted he attend this festival. I ask him to grant me the guilty pleasure of responding to this honorable inquiry by Sir Gilbert. What do you say, Sir Hadrian?"

"Sure," he replied stiffly.

"Thank you," Saldur said, and after clearing his throat, continued, "Sir Gilbert is correct in that Lord Dermont was lost that day, but reports from his closest aides brought back the tale. Three days of rain made a mounted charge impossible, and the sheer number of the unstoppable Nationalist horde convinced Lord Dermont of the futility of engagement. Overcome with grief, he retreated to his tent in resignation.

"Without Lord Dermont to lead them, the imperial army floundered when the attack came. It was Sir Hadrian—then *Captain* Hadrian of the Fifth Imperial Mounted Guard— who roused the men and set them to ranks. He raised the banner and led them forth. At first, only a handful of soldiers responded. Indeed, only those who served with him answered his call, for they alone knew firsthand his mettle. Ignoring his meager numbers, he trusted in Maribor and called the charge."

Hadrian looked down and fidgeted with an uncooperative toggle on his tunic as the others sat enthralled.

"Although it was suicide, Captain Hadrian rode at the head of the troop into the fen field. His horse threw mud and slop, and a magnificent rainbow burst forth from the spray as he galloped across a stretch of standing water. He drove at the heart of the enemy with no thought of his own safety."

Saldur's voice grew in volume and intensity. His tone and cadence assumed the melodramatic delivery of a church sermon. A few nobles at the other tables turned to listen as he continued.

"His courageous charge unnerved the Nationalist foot soldiers, who fell back in fear. Onward he plunged, splitting their ranks until at last his mount became overwhelmed by the soft earth and fell. Wielding sword and shield, he got to his feet and continued to drive forward. Clashing against steel, he cried out the name of the empress: 'For Modina! Modina! Modina Novronian!'"

Saldur paused and Hadrian looked up to see every eye at the table shifting back and forth between the regent and him.

"Finally, shamed by the bravery of this one lone captain, the rest of the imperial army rallied. They cried to Maribor for forgiveness even as they drew sword and spear and rushed to follow. Before reinforcements could reach him, Hadrian was wounded and driven into the mud. Some of his men bore him from the field and took him to the tent of Lord Dermont. There they told the tale of his bravery and Lord Dermont swore by Maribor to honor Hadrian's sacrifice. He proclaimed his intent to knight the valiant captain.

"'Nay, lord!' cried Captain Hadrian even as he lay wounded and bleeding. 'Knight me not, for I am unworthy. I have failed.' Lord Dermont clutched his blade and was heard to say 'You are more worthy of the noble title of *knight-valiant* than I am of the title of *man*!' And with that, Lord Dermont dubbed him *Sir* Hadrian."

"Oh my!" the duchess gasped.

With everyone staring at him, Hadrian felt hot, awkward, and more naked than when Elgar had interrupted his bath.

"Lord Dermont called for his own horse and thanked Sir Hadrian for the chance to redeem his honor before Maribor. He led his personal retinue into the fight, where he and all but a few of his men perished on the pikes of the Nationalists.

"Sir Hadrian tried to return to the battle despite his wounds, but fell unconscious before reaching the field. After the Nationalists' victory, they left him for dead and only providence spared his life. He awoke covered in mud. Desperate for food and water, he crawled into the forest, where he came upon a small hovel. There he was fed and tended to by a mysterious man. Sir Hadrian rested there for six days, and on the seventh, the man brought forth a horse and told Sir Hadrian to take it, ride to Aquesta, and present himself to the court. After he handed over the reins, thunder cracked and a single white feather fell from a clear blue sky. The man caught the feather before it reached the ground, a broad smile across his face. And with that, the man disappeared.

"Now, gentlemen and ladies." Saldur paused to look out over the other tables whose attention he had drawn. "I tell you truthfully that two days before Sir Hadrian arrived, the empress came to me and said, 'A knight riding a white horse will come to the palace. Admit him and honor him, for he shall be the greatest knight of the New Empire.' Sir Hadrian has been here, recuperating from his wounds, ever since. Today he is fully recovered and sits before you all. Now, if you'll excuse me, I must take my seat, as the feast is about to begin." Saldur bowed and left them.

No one said a word for some time. Everyone stared at Hadrian in wonder, including Albert, whose mouth hung agape.

It was the duchess who finally found words to sum up their collective thoughts. "Well, aren't you just an astonishment topped with surprises!"

∾

Dinner was served in a fashion that Hadrian had never seen before. Fifty servants moving in concert delivered steaming plates of exotic victuals in elaborate presentations. Two peacocks were posed on large platters. One peered up as if surprised, while the other's head curled backward as if it were sleeping. Each was surrounded by an array of succulent carved meat. Ducks, geese, quail, turtledoves, and partridges were displayed in similar fashion, and one pure-white trumpeter swan reared up with its wings outstretched as if about to take flight. Rings of nuts, berries, and herbs surrounded glazed slabs of lean venison, dark boar, and marbled beef. Breads of various shades, from snow white to nearly black, lay in heaping piles. Massive wedges of cheese, cakes of butter, seven different types of fish, oysters steamed in almond milk, meat pies, custard tarts, and pastries drizzled with honey covered every inch of the table. Stewards and their many assistants served endless streams of wine, beer, ale, and mead.

Anxiety welled up as he struggled to remember Nimbus's multiple instructions on table etiquette. The list had been massive, but at that moment he could remember just two things: he was not to use the tablecloth to blow his nose and should not pick his teeth with the knife. Following Saldur's prayer to Maribor, Hadrian's fears vanished when all the guests ripped into the bountiful food with abandon. They tore legs off pigs and heads from birds. Bits of meat and grease sprayed the table as nobles groped and pawed to taste a bite of every dish, lest they miss something that might be the talk of the feast.

Hadrian had lived most of his life on black bread, brown ale, hard cheese, salted fish, and vegetable stews. What lay before him was a new experience. He tried the peacock, which, despite its beauty, was dry and not nearly as good as he had expected. The venison had a wonderful hickory-smoked taste. But the best thing by far was the dish of cinnamon baked apples. All conversation stopped when the eating began. The only sounds in the hall were those of a single lute, a lone singer, and scores of chewing mouths.

> *Long is the day in the summertime,*
> *long is the song which I play,*
> *I will keep your memory in my heart,*
> *till you come to me…*

The music was beautiful and strangely haunting. Its melody filled the great hall with a radiance that blended well with the glow of the fireplace and candles. After the setting of the sun, the windows turned to black mirrors and the mood became more intimate. Consoled with food, drink, and music, Hadrian forgot his circumstance and began to enjoy himself— until the Earl of Chadwick nudged him back to reality.

"Are you entered in the joust?" he asked. From his tone and glassy eyes, Hadrian could tell Archibald Ballentyne had started drinking long before the feast.

"Ah, yes—yes I am, sir—I mean, Your Lordship."

"Then you might be riding against my champion Sir Breckton over there." He waved a limp hand across the table. "He's also competing in the joust."

"Then I don't stand much of a chance."

"No, you don't," the earl said. "But you must do your best. There will be a crowd to please." The earl leaned over in a confidential manner. "Now tell me, was what Saldur told us true?"

"I would never dispute the word of a regent," Hadrian replied.

Archibald guffawed. "I think the phrase you were actually looking for is 'never *trust* the word of a regent.' Did you know they promised me Melengar and then just like that…" The earl attempted to snap his fingers. "…like that…" He attempted again. "…like…" He failed yet a third time. "Well, you know what I mean. They took away what they promised me. So you can see why I'm skeptical. That bit about the empress expecting you, was that true?"

"I have no idea, my lord. How could I know?"

"So you haven't met her? The empress, I mean?"

Hadrian paused, remembering a young girl named Thrace. "No, I haven't actually met *the empress*. Shouldn't she be seated up there?"

The earl scowled. "They leave the throne vacant in her honor. She never dines in public. To be honest, I've lived in this palace for half a year and have only seen her on three occasions: once in the throne room, once when she addressed the public, and once when I… Well, what matters is she never seems to leave her room. I often wonder whether the regents are keeping her prisoner up there. I should have her kidnapped—free the poor girl."

Archibald sat up and said, more to himself than to Hadrian, "That's what I should do, and there's just the man I need to talk to." Plucking a walnut from the centerpiece, he threw it down the table at Albert.

"Viscount Winslow," he shouted with more volume than necessary. "I haven't seen you in quite some time."

"No, indeed, Your Lordship. It has been far too long."

"Are you still in contact with those two… phantoms of the night? You know, the magicians that can make letters disappear and who are equally adept at saving doomed princesses from tower prisons?"

"I'm sorry, Your Lordship, but after what they did to you, I terminated my connection with them."

"Yes...what they did..." the earl slurred while looking into his cup. "What they did was put Braga's head in my lap! While I was sleeping, no less! Did you know that? It was a most disagreeable awakening, I tell you." He trailed off, mumbling to himself.

Hadrian bit his lip.

"I had no idea. You have my sincere apology," Albert said with genuine surprise, which was lost on the earl, who had tilted his head back to take another swallow of wine.

New musicians entered and began playing a formal tune as gentlemen, including Gilbert and Elgar, took the hands of ladies and led them to the dance floor. Hadrian had no idea how to dance. Nimbus had not even tried to instruct him. The Duke and Duchess of Rochelle also left to join in. A clear line of sight opened between Hadrian and Albert.

"So, Sir Hadrian, is it?" the viscount asked, shifting down to take Lady Genevieve's vacated chair. "Is this your first time in the banquet hall?"

"Indeed, it is."

"The palace is large and has an impressive history. I'm sure that during your recent recovery you've not had an opportunity to visit much of it. If you aren't planning to dance, I'd be happy to give you a tour. There are some fine paintings and frescoes on the second floor that are exquisite."

Hadrian glanced at the men still watching him.

"I'm sure they are, Viscount, but I think it might be rude to leave the feast so early. Our hosts might look poorly on me for doing so." He motioned toward the head table, where Saldur and Ethelred sat. "I wouldn't want to incur their disfavor so early in the celebrations."

"I understand completely. Have you found your accommodations at the palace to your liking?"

"Yes, indeed. I have my own room in the knights' wing. Regent Saldur has been most generous, and I have nothing to complain about as far as my quarters are concerned."

"So you have reason to complain otherwise?" Albert inquired.

Carefully choosing his words, Hadrian replied, "Not a complaint, really. I am merely concerned about my performance in the coming tournament. I am going to be competing against many renowned knights, such as Sir Breckton here. It is extremely important that I do well in the joust. Some very distinguished people will be watching the outcome quite closely."

"You should not be so concerned," Breckton mentioned. "If you are true to the knight's code, Maribor will guide you. What others may think has no weight on the field. The truth is the truth, and you know whether you live in accord with it or not. From this you will draw your strength or weakness."

"Thank you for your kind words, but I am not merely riding for myself. A success in this tournament will change the fortunes of those I care about as well...my, ah, retinue."

Albert nodded.

Sir Breckton leaned forward. "You are that concerned about the reputation of your squires and grooms?"

"They are as dear to me as family," Hadrian responded.

"That is most admirable. I can't say I have ever met a knight so concerned with the well-being of those who serve him."

"To be honest, sir, it is mainly for their welfare that I ride. I only hope they do nothing to dishonor me, as some of them are prone to poor judgment—rash and risky behavior— usually on my behalf, of course. Still, in this instance, I prefer they would merely enjoy the holiday."

Albert gave another nod and drained the last of his wine.

Ballentyne took another drink as well. He swallowed, burped loudly, and then slouched with his elbow on the table, resting a palm against his cheek. Hadrian surmised that it would not be long before the earl passed out completely.

The monk and the gray-bearded fellow bid the table good night. The two wandered off while debating the Legend of Kile, the significance of Saldur's story, and the true nature of the man Hadrian had allegedly met in the forest.

"Well, it has been a delight to dine with you all," Albert said, rising. "I am not used to such rich living, and this wine has gone to my head. I fear I will make a fool of myself should I remain, so I will retire."

The two knights bid him farewell, and Hadrian watched as Albert left the hall without looking back.

Having no one else left to converse with, Hadrian turned to Breckton. "Did your father not attend, or is he seated somewhere else?"

Breckton, whose attention was focused toward the front of the hall, took a moment to respond. "My father chose not to come. If not for the request of my lord here"—he gestured at the earl, who did not react—"I would not have attended either. Neither of us is in a mood for celebrations. We only recently learned that my younger brother Wesley died in the empress's service."

Hadrian replied in a somber voice, "I'm sorry for your loss. I'm sure he died with honor."

"Thank you, but death in service is not unexpected. It would be a comfort to know the circumstances. He died far from home, serving aboard the *Emerald Storm*, which was lost at sea." Breckton got to his feet. "Please excuse me. I think I'll also take my leave."

"Of course, good evening to you."

He watched Breckton go. The knight had the same stride as his brother, and Hadrian had to remind himself that the two choices he faced were equally unpleasant. Even without his emotional ties, two lives were more valuable than one. Breckton was a soldier, and as he himself had stated, death in service was not unexpected. Hadrian had no choice, but that fact did little to ease his conscience.

Ballentyne's head slipped off his hand, making a solid thud as it hit the table.

Hadrian sighed. Like knighthood, noble feasts were not as illustrious as he had expected.

## CHAPTER 11

# KNIGHTLY VIRTUE

Albert Winslow walked quickly through Aquesta, holding his heavy cloak tightly around him, its hood raised. He regretted not switching to boots, as his buckled shoes were treacherous on the icy cobblestones. He could have taken a carriage. The palace had a few available for hire, but walking made it easier to determine if he was being followed. Glancing back, Albert found the street empty.

By the time he entered The Bailey Inn, the fire in the common room was burning low. An elderly man slept near the hearth, a cup of brandy nearly spilling in his lap. Albert walked quickly to the stairs and up to his room. He would write out a note, leave it on the table, and then head back to the palace. Formulating the wording in his head, he took out a key and unlocked the door.

*How do I begin to explain what I just saw?*

Instead of entering a cold, dark room, he found a fire burning, lighted candles on the table, and—lying on his bed with boots still on—a dwarf.

"Magnus?"

The door closed abruptly, and Albert spun to see Royce

behind him. "You should remember to lock your door," the thief said.

Albert smirked. "I won't even dignify that with a comment. When did you get back?"

"Not long enough ago to get any rest," Magnus grumbled. "He drove us like dogs to get here."

"Hey, watch the boots," Albert said, slapping them with the back of his hand.

"What's happened with Hadrian?" Royce spoke sharply, his hood still up.

When Albert first met Royce, the viscount had been a drunk living in a farmer's barn outside Colnora. Reduced to selling his clothes piecemeal to buy rum, he was down to little more than his nightshirt and old rags. Wailing about the misfortune of being the noble son of a spendthrift father, he offered Royce and Hadrian his silk nightshirt for five copper tenents. Royce had made him a better offer. Riyria needed a nobleman to work as a liaison to the wealthy and privileged—a respectable face to sell disreputable services. They cleaned him up, paid for new clothes, and provided all the trappings of success that a viscount required. They gave him back his dignity, and Albert was noble once more. From then on the viscount saw Royce as a friend, but at times like this—when Royce's hood was raised, and his voice harsh—even Albert was scared of him.

"Well?" Royce pressed, stepping closer and causing Albert to back up. "Is he in prison? They didn't..."

"What? No!" Albert shook his head. "You're actually not going to believe this. I just came from the Feast of the Nobles, the big opening party for the Wintertide celebration. Everyone was there, kings, bishops, knights, you name it."

"Get to the point, Albert."

"I am. Hadrian was there too."

Albert saw Royce's hands form fists. "What were they doing to him?"

"Oh no, nothing like that—they were feeding him. He was— They made him a knight, Royce—a knight of the empire. You should have seen the outfit he was wearing."

At this, even the dwarf sat up.

"What? Speak sense, you crazy—"

"I swear. It's the truth! Regent Saldur even came over and told the whole table this nutty story about how Hadrian fought for the Imperialists at the Battle of Ratibor and was knighted because of it. Can you believe that?"

"No, I don't. Have you been drinking again?"

"Just a bit of wine. I'm sober. I swear," Albert said.

"But why would they do such a thing? Were you able to get near him? What did he say?"

"He wasn't able to speak freely and hinted that he was being watched, but I think he's competing in the tournament. It sounded like the regents made him some kind of deal."

"The tournament at Highcourt?"

"Yes. He made it pretty clear that we shouldn't interfere or try to help."

"I don't understand."

"That makes two of us."

❦

"I feel ridiculous," Amilia whispered to Nimbus as she pushed her plate away.

One hundred and twenty-three pairs of eyes stared at her. She knew the exact number. She knew which rulers brought wives and which sat with courtesans. She knew who was sensitive to drafts and who was uncomfortable near the heat of the hearth. She knew which princess refused to sit beside which countess. She knew who held power and which ones were just puppets. She knew every quirk and foible, every bias and fear, every name and title—but not a single face.

They were manageable as slips of parchment, but now they were all here—staring. No, not staring. Their expressions were too malicious and filled with contempt for something as benign as staring. In their eyes she could see the exasperation and she knew what they were thinking: *How is it that she— the poor daughter of a carriage maker—sits at the empress's table?* She felt as though one hundred and twenty-three wolves snarled at her with exposed teeth.

"You look beautiful," Nimbus said. His fingers kept tempo with the pavane. The tutor was apparently oblivious to the waves of hatred crashing over them.

She sighed. There was nothing to do now but struggle through the night as best she could. Sitting up straight, Amilia reminded herself to breathe, which was no easy feat in the tight bodice.

Amilia wore the gown the duchess had presented to her that morning. Far from just an ordinary dress, it was a work of art in blue silk. Ribbons woven into elaborate designs resembling swans adorned the front. The fitted bodice pressed her stomach flat and led to a full, billowing skirt that shimmered like rippling water when she moved. A deep neckline left the tops of her breasts exposed. To Lady Genevieve's dismay, Amilia wore a scarf, covering them and the exquisite jeweled necklace the duchess had lent. Perhaps to avoid a similar concealment with the diamond earrings, the duchess had sent three stylists to put Amilia's hair up. They spent the better part of two hours on the coif and were followed by a pair of cosmetic artists, who painted her lips, eyelids, cheeks, and even her fingernails. Amilia never wore makeup of any kind.

She never styled her hair, and she certainly never exposed her breasts. Out of respect for the duchess, she complied, but she felt like a clown—a buffoonish entertainment on display for those one hundred and twenty-three sets of eyes.

*One hundred and twenty-four*, she corrected herself. There had been a last-minute addition.

"Which one is he?" she asked Nimbus.

"Who? Sir Hadrian? I squeezed him in over there. He's the one in purple and gold. Saldur is passing him off as a knight, but I've never met a man so unknightly."

"He's cruel?"

"Not at all. He's considerate and respectful, even to servants. He complains less than a monk, and while I am certain he knows the use of a blade, he seems as violent as a mouse. He drinks only moderately, considers a bowl of porridge a feast, and rises at dawn. He is no knight but rather what a knight *should* be."

"He looks familiar," she said, but could not place him. "How is he coming along?"

"Slowly," Nimbus told her. "I just hope he doesn't attempt to dance. I haven't found time to teach him, and I am certain he hasn't a clue."

"*You* know how to dance?" Amilia asked.

"I am exceedingly talented, milady. Would you like me to teach you as well?"

She rolled her eyes. "I hardly think I will need to know *that*."

"Are you sure? Didn't Sir Breckton seek your favor for the joust?"

"Out of pity."

"Pity? Are you certain? Perhaps you . . . Oh dear, what have we here?" Nimbus stopped as Sir Murthas navigated the tables, walking straight for them. Wearing a ribbed burgundy doublet that was tight in the waist and sported broad, padded shoulders, he looked quite impressive. An elegant gold chain with a ruby hung around his neck. His dark eyes matched his coal-black hair, and his goatee appeared freshly trimmed.

"Lady Amilia, I am Sir Murthas of Alburn." He held out his hand, covered in thick rings.

Confused, she stared at it until the man awkwardly let it fall. Amilia noticed Nimbus cringing beside her. She had done something inappropriate but did not know what.

"I was hoping, dear lady," Sir Murthas said, pushing on, "that you would honor me with a dance."

Amilia was horrified. She sat rigid and stared at him without saying a word.

Nimbus came to her rescue. "I believe Her Ladyship is not interested in dancing at the moment, Sir Murthas. Another time, perhaps?"

Murthas gave the tutor a loathing look, and then his face softened as he returned his attention to Amilia. "May I ask why? If you are not feeling well, perhaps I could escort you to a balcony for some fresh air? If you don't care for the music, I will have them play a different tune. If it is the color of my doublet, I will gladly change."

Amilia remained unable to speak.

Murthas glanced at Nimbus. "Has *he* been speaking ill of me?"

"I have never mentioned you," the tutor replied, but his words had no effect on the knight.

"Perhaps she's put off by that bit of rat hair on your chin, Murthas," Sir Elgar bellowed as he too approached the table. "Or perhaps she is waiting for a real man to ask her to the floor. What do you say, my lady? Will you do me the honor?" Elgar dwarfed Murthas and brushed the smaller knight to one side as he held out his hand.

"I'm—I'm sorry." Amilia found her tongue. "I choose not to dance."

Elgar's expression darkened to a storm, but he said nothing.

"Gentlemen, gentlemen, 'tis I she is waiting for," Sir Gilbert said, striding forward. "Forgive me, my lady, for taking so long to arrive and leaving you in such company."

Amilia shook her head, stood, and hurried away from the table. She neither knew nor cared where she was going. Frightened and embarrassed, she thought only of getting away. Afraid of catching the eye of another knight, she focused on the floor, and it was in this way that she stumbled once more into Sir Breckton.

"Oh my," she gasped, looking up at him. "I...I..."

"We seem to be making a habit of this," Breckton said with a smile.

Amilia was mortified and felt so foolish that tears welled up and spilled down her cheeks.

When Breckton saw this, his smile vanished; he fell to one knee and bowed his head. "Forgive me, dear lady. I am a fool. I spoke without thought."

"No, no, it's all right," she told him, feeling worse than ever. "Please, I am only trying to get to my chambers. I—I've had my fill of feasting."

"As you wish. Please, take my arm and I will see you safely there."

Amilia was beyond resisting and took hold of the knight as they continued down the hall. Away from the noise and the crowd, Amilia felt more like herself. She wiped her cheeks and let go of his arm.

"Thank you, Sir Breckton, but I do not need you to escort me to my room. I have lived in this palace for a long time and know the way quite well. I can assure you there are no dragons or ogres along my path."

"Of course. Forgive me again for my presumption. I only thought because—"

Amilia nodded. "I know. I was just a little overwhelmed. I'm not used to so much attention. Despite the title, I am still a simple girl, and knights...they still frighten me."

Breckton looked wounded and took a step backward. "I would *never* harm you, my lady!"

"Oh, there I go again. I feel like such a fool." Amilia threw up her hands. "I—I don't know how to be noble. *Everything* I *say* is wrong. Everything I *do* or *don't do* is a mistake."

"I am certain it is not you but I who am at fault," Breckton assured her. "I am not accustomed to the courts. I am a soldier—plain and blunt. I will once more ask your forgiveness and leave you alone, as clearly, I am a terror to you."

"No, no, you are not. You are most kind. It's the others I— You are the only one—" She sighed. "Please, I would be honored if you would escort me."

Breckton snapped smartly to attention, bowed, and offered his arm once more. They walked silently to the stairs and up to the fifth floor. Passing by a set of guards, they proceeded to a chamber door. Breckton nodded and smiled at Gerald, who responded with a salute—something Amilia had never seen the guard do before.

"You are well protected," Breckton remarked.

"Not me; this is the empress's chambers. I always check on her before retiring. To be honest, you shouldn't even be on this floor."

"Then I will take my leave."

He started to turn.

"Wait," she said, reaching out to touch his arm. "Here." She pulled off her scarf and handed it to him.

Breckton smiled broadly. "I will wear it at the tournament proudly and represent you with honor."

Taking her hand, he gently kissed the back of it. Then the knight bowed and left. Amilia's gaze followed him until he reached the stairs and disappeared from sight. When she turned back, she found Gerald grinning. She raised an eyebrow and the guard wiped the expression from his face.

Amilia entered the imperial bedchamber. As always, Modina was at the window. Lying on the stone in her thin white nightgown, the empress looked dead. Amilia found her this way most nights. The mirror was still intact and Modina was merely asleep. Still, Amilia could not help thinking that one day... She pushed the thought away.

"Modina?" She spoke softly as she rocked the empress's shoulder. "Come, it's too cold to lie there."

The girl looked up sadly, then nodded. Amilia put her in bed, covered her with a blanket, and gave her a kiss on the forehead before leaving Modina to sleep.

✍

Hadrian was squeezing melted candle wax between his fingers and listening to the rhythmic snores of the earl. Even his *shadows* looked tired, although they were different men since the shift change. He wondered how long he was expected to remain in the hall.

He saw Sir Breckton return to the feast, but rather than resuming his seat, the knight struck up a conversation with Nimbus. He watched them for a moment and then noticed movement at the head table. To Hadrian's dismay, Regent Saldur picked up his wine goblet and walked directly toward him.

"You've done well," the regent said while taking the seat across from Hadrian. "Or at least it appeared so from over there. Sentinel Guy and Lord Marius speak highly of you."

"Lord Marius? You don't mean *Merrick* Marius?"

"Yes, you remember him, don't you? He was at our little meeting. Oh, how foolish. Perhaps we forgot to introduce him. Marius said he was extremely impressed with a recent assignment that you and your partner performed on his behalf. By the sound of things, it was quite difficult. He even told me that he thought only you two could have accomplished such a feat."

Hadrian clenched his teeth.

"I've been thinking...Perhaps when this business with Breckton is over, you might find working for the empire preferable to exile with Gaunt. I am a pragmatist, Hadrian, and I can see the benefit of having someone like you aiding in what we are trying to accomplish. I'm sure you've heard any number of terrible things about me or what I may have done. But you need to realize I'm trying to rid our world of problems that plague all of us, commoner and noble alike. Roads have gone to ruin. You can hardly travel in spring due to mud. Banditry is rampant, which hampers trade and stifles prosperity. Every city is a cesspool of filth and few have adequate fresh water. There are not enough jobs in the north, not enough workers in the south, and not enough food anywhere."

Hadrian glanced across the hall and saw Breckton and Nimbus leaving the feast together. A little while later, Murthas, Elgar, and Gilbert downed their drinks and left in the same direction.

"The world of men has many enemies," Saldur droned on. "When petty kings war with each other, they weaken the nations with their childish feuds. I have long believed these squabbles leave the doors open for invasion and invite destruction. You might not know this, but the Ghazel and Dacca have been raiding from the south. We don't publicize this information, of course, so few know just how severe it has become, but they have even invaded Tur Del Fur."

Hadrian glared. "If you didn't want the Ghazel as neighbors, you probably shouldn't have invited them."

Saldur looked at him curiously for a moment and then said, "I did what was necessary. Now where was I? Oh yes. Not everyone can keep what they have if things are to change. There must be sacrifices. I have tried to be reasonable, but if a leg is infected and cannot be saved, it must be removed for the good of the body. I hope you can see past these small costs and recognize the larger implications. I am not an evil man, Hadrian. It is the world that forces me to be cruel, but no more so than a father forcing his child to swallow an unpleasant medicine. You can see that, can't you?"

Saldur looked at him expectantly.

"Am I allowed to leave?" Hadrian asked. "The feast, I mean."

Saldur sighed and sat back in his chair. "Yes, you can go. You need to get plenty of sleep. The tournament begins in two days."

∽

Pinecones and holly garland, the remnants of wayward revelers, littered the hallways along Hadrian's path to the knights' wing. Rounding a corner, he found Nimbus slumped against the corridor wall. The courtier's tunic was torn, and his nose bleeding. Sir Gilbert stood above him, grinning. Through the doorway of the common room, Hadrian spotted Sir Breckton. Armed with only his dress dagger, the knight defended himself against Murthas and Elgar, each of whom wielded a sword as well as a dagger.

"Look who's joined the party," Gilbert said as Hadrian approached.

"Given this situation," Hadrian asked Nimbus while keeping his eyes on Gilbert, "how much *generosity* am I required to extend to these fellow knights?"

In the common room, Murthas swiped at Breckton, who caught the sword with his little blade and cast the stroke aside.

"Given the situation," Nimbus said quickly, "I think the virtue of generosity is not applicable."

"Indeed!" Breckton shouted. "They have forfeited their right to honorable treatment."

Hadrian smiled. "That makes this a lot easier." Drawing his own dagger, he threw it into Gilbert's thigh. The knight cried out and fell to his knees, looking up in astonishment. Hadrian punched him in the face, and his opponent collapsed. Taking both his and Gilbert's daggers, Hadrian advanced.

Elgar sneered as he turned to face Hadrian, leaving Breckton to Murthas.

"I hope you joust better than you wield a sword," Hadrian said, approaching.

"We haven't even fought yet, you fool," Elgar bellowed.

"That's hardly necessary. You hold your sword like a woman. No, that's not true. I've actually known women who can sword fight. The truth is, you're just terrible."

"What I lack in style, I make up for in strength." Elgar charged Hadrian, raising his blade over his head and leaving his entire chest exposed. Hadrian's training made him instinctively want to aim a single thrust at the man's heart, which would kill Elgar instantly. He fought the urge and lowered his weapon. Saldur and Ethelred would not approve. Besides, Elgar was drunk. Instead, he dodged to one side and left a foot behind to trip the knight. Elgar fell, hitting his head on the stone.

"Is he dead?" Nimbus asked, watching Hadrian roll the big man over on his back.

"No, but I think he might have chipped the slate. Now *that's* a hard head."

Hadrian sat down next to Nimbus and inspected the tutor's wounds.

"Shouldn't you help Sir Breckton?"

Hadrian glanced up as Murthas made another lunge.

"I don't think that's necessary, nor would it be proper to step into another man's fight. However..." Picking up Elgar's sword, Hadrian yelled, "Breckton!" before throwing it across the common room. Breckton caught the weapon and Murthas stepped back, looking less confident.

"Damn you!" Murthas shouted, taking one last swing before fleeing.

Hadrian could not suppress the temptation to stick out his foot once more, tripping Murthas as he ran by. Murthas fell, got back to his feet, and ran off.

"Thank you," Breckton said, offering Hadrian a slight nod.

"It's Murthas who should be thanking me," Hadrian replied.

Breckton smiled. "Indeed."

"I don't understand," Nimbus said. "Murthas lost. Why would he thank you?"

"He's still alive," Hadrian explained.

"Oh," was all Nimbus said.

✧

Hadrian managed to stop Nimbus's bleeding. The tutor's nose did not appear broken. Even so, none of them was interested in returning to the banquet hall. Hadrian and Breckton escorted Nimbus to his room, where the slim man thanked the two knights for their assistance.

"You fight well," Breckton said as he and Hadrian walked the palace corridors back toward the knights' wing.

"Why did they attack you?"

"They were drunk."

"Where I come from, drunks sing badly and sleep with ugly women. They don't attack rival knights and courtly gentlemen."

Breckton was quiet for a moment, then asked, "Where *do* you come from, Sir Hadrian?"

"Saldur explained—"

"Some of the men that fought with Lord Dermont and survived the Battle of Ratibor joined my army in the north. Captain Lowell was one of them. His accounting of that day in no way resembles the tale Regent Saldur described. I would not embarrass the regent or you by mentioning it in public, but now that we are alone..."

Hadrian said nothing.

"What Lowell did tell me was the entire imperial army was caught sleeping on that rainy morning. Most never managed to strap on a sword, much less mount a horse."

Hadrian simply replied, "It was a very confusing day."

"So you say, but perhaps you were never there at all. A knight taking credit for another's valor is most dishonorable."

"I can assure you, I *was* there," Hadrian said sincerely. "And that I rode across the muddy field leading men into battle that morning."

Breckton stopped at the entrance of his own room and studied Hadrian's face. "You must forgive me for my rudeness. You have aided me this evening, and I have responded with accusations. It is unseemly for one knight to accuse another without proper evidence. I will not let it happen again. Good night."

He offered Hadrian a curt nod and left him alone in the corridor.

# Chapter 12

# A Question of Succession

The sun reached its midday peak and Arcadius Vintarus Latimer, the master of lore at Sheridan University, still waited in the grand foyer of the imperial palace. He had been there before, but that was back when it had been called Warric Castle and had been the home of the most powerful king in Avryn. Now it was the seat of the New Empire. The imperial seal etched in the white marble floor was a constant and unavoidable reminder. Arcadius read the inscription that ringed the design, shaking his head in disgust. "They misspelled *honor*," he said aloud, even though he waited alone.

Finally, a steward approached and motioned for him to follow. "The regent Saldur will see you now, sir."

*One step closer*, Arcadius thought as he headed toward the stairs. The steward was nearly to the fourth floor when he realized Arcadius had reached only the second landing.

"My apologies," the lore master called up to him, leaning on the banister and removing his glasses to wipe his brow. "Are you certain the meeting is all the way up there?"

"The regent asked for you to come to his office."

The old professor nodded. "Very well, I'll be right along."

*Another positive development.*

While it was unlikely that Saldur would agree to his proposal, Arcadius judged his odds of success tripled with each flight he climbed. He did not want to speak in a reception hall filled with gossipy courtiers. Not that he held much hope, no matter where the subject was broached. Still, if this meeting went well, he would be free of his guilt and the burden of responsibility. A private meeting with the regent would be perfect. Saldur was an intellectual, and Arcadius could appeal to the regent's respect for education. However, when he reached the office, Saldur was not alone.

"Well, of course we need a southern defense," Ethelred was saying when the steward opened the door. "We have a nation of goblins down there now. You haven't seen them, Sauly. You don't know…er…Yes? What is it?"

"May I present Professor Arcadius Latimer, master of lore at Sheridan University," the steward announced.

"Oh yes, the teacher," Ethelred said.

"He's a bit more than that, Lanis," Saldur corrected.

"Not at all, not at all," Arcadius said with a cheerful smile. "Instructing young minds is the noblest act I perform. I am honored."

The lore master bowed to the four people in the room. In addition to the regents, there were two men he did not recognize. One, however, was dressed in the distinct vestments of a church sentinel.

"You are a long way from Sheridan, Professor." Saldur addressed him from behind a large desk. "Did you come for the holiday?"

"Why no, Your Grace. At my age it takes a bit more than the allure of jingling bells and sweetmeats to rouse one such as I from warm chambers in the depth of winter. I don't know if you noticed, but there's a great deal of snow outside."

Arcadius took a moment to examine his surroundings.

Hundreds of books sat on shelves, locked behind glass cabinets with little keyholes. A pretty carpet, somewhat muddled in its colors and partially hidden by the regent's desk, portrayed what appeared to be a scene of Novron conquering the world while Maribor guided his sword.

"Your office is so... *clean*," the professor remarked.

Saldur raised an eyebrow and then chuckled. "Oh yes, I seem to recall visiting you once. I don't believe I made it through your door."

"I have a unique filing system."

"Lore master, I don't mean to be short, but we are quite busy," Ethelred said. "Exactly what has brought you so far in the cold?"

"Well," he began, smiling at Saldur, "Your Grace, I was hoping to speak to you—in private." He glanced pointedly at the two men he did not recognize. "I have a sensitive matter to discuss concerning the future of the empire."

"This is Sentinel Luis Guy and over there is Lord Merrick Marius. I assume you already know our soon-to-be emperor, Ethelred. If you wish to discuss the empire's future, these are the men you need to speak with."

Arcadius paused deliberately, took off his spectacles, and cleaned them slowly with his sleeve. "Very well, then." The lore master replaced his glasses and crossed the room to one of the soft chairs. "Do you mind? Standing for too long makes my feet hurt."

"By all means," Ethelred said sarcastically. "Make yourself at home."

Arcadius sat down with a sigh, took a deep breath, and began. "I have been thinking about the New Empire you are establishing, and I must say that I approve."

Ethelred snorted. "Well, Sauly, we can sleep better now that the scholars have weighed in."

Arcadius glared at him across the tops of his glasses. "What I mean is that the idea of a central authority is a sound one and will stop the monarchial squabbles, bringing harmony from chaos."

"But?" Saldur invited.

"But what?"

"I just sensed you were going to find fault," Saldur said.

"I am, but please try not to get ahead of me—it ruins the drama. I've spent several days bouncing over frozen ground, preparing for this meeting, and you deserve to experience the full effect."

Arcadius adjusted his sleeves and waited for what he thought was the precise amount of time to draw their full attention. "I'm curious to know if you've put any thought into the line of succession."

"Succession?" Ethelred blurted from where he sat on the edge of Saldur's desk.

"Yes, you know, the concept of producing an heir to inherit the mantle of leadership. Most thrones are lost because of poor planning on this front."

"I'm not even crowned, and you complain because I haven't fathered an heir yet?"

Arcadius sighed. "It is not *your heir* I am concerned about. This empire is founded on a bedrock of faith—faith that the bloodline of Novron is back on the throne. If the bloodline is not maintained, the cohesion that holds the empire together might dissolve."

"What are you saying?" Ethelred asked.

"Only that should something tragic happen to Modina, and no child of *her blood* be available, you would lose your greatest asset. The line of Novron would end, and without this thin strand of legitimacy, the empire could face dissolution. Glenmorgan's Empire lasted only three generations.

How long will this one endure with only a mere mortal at its head?"

"What makes you think anything will happen to the empress?"

Arcadius smiled. "Let's just say I know the ways of the world, and sacrifices are often required to bring about change. I'm here because I fear you might mistakenly think Modina is expendable once Ethelred wears the crown. I want to urge you not to make a terrible, perhaps fatal, error."

Saldur exchanged looks with Ethelred, confirming that the lore master had guessed correctly.

"But there is nothing to fear, gentlemen, for I've come to offer a solution." Arcadius gave them his most disarming smile, which accentuated the laugh lines around his eyes and showed off his round cheeks, which he guessed were still rosy from his trip. "I am proposing that Modina already bore a child."

"What?" Ethelred asked. He stood and his face showed a mixture of emotions. "Are you accusing my fiancée—the empress—of impropriety?"

"I am saying that if she had a child—a child born a few years ago and no longer dependant on the mother—it could make your lives a great deal easier. It would ensure the continued unification of the empire under the bloodline of Novron."

"Speak plainly, man!" Ethelred erupted. "Are you suggesting such a child exists?"

"I am saying such a child *could* exist." He looked at each of their faces before focusing back on Saldur. "Modina is no more the Heir of Novron than I am, but that is not relevant. The only thing that matters is what her subjects believe. If they accept she has a child, then the pretense of the heir can continue and the masses will be satisfied. After ensuring the line of succession, an unfortunate incident involving the empress would not be such a tragedy. Her people would certainly mourn her, but there would still be hope—hope in the form of a child who would one day take the throne."

"You bring up an interesting point, Professor," Ethelred said. "Modina has...been ill as of late, but I'm sure she could hang on long enough to bear a child, couldn't she, Sauly?"

"I don't see why not. Yes. We could arrange that."

The lore master shook his head as if hearing an incorrect response from one of his students. "But what if she were to die in childbirth? It happens far too often and is too great a risk for something as important as this. Do you really wish to gamble all you are trying to accomplish? A child conceived before the empress even knew Ethelred would not reflect poorly on him. There are ways to present the child that would bolster the new emperor's standing. He can profess that his love for Modina is boundless and agree to raise the child as if it were his own. Such sentiments would endear him to the people."

Arcadius waited a minute before continuing. "Take a healthy child and educate it in philosophy, theology, poetry, history, and mathematics. Fill the vessel with training in civics, economics, and culture. Make the child the most learned leader the world has ever known. Picture the possibilities. Imagine the potential of an empire ruled by an intellectual giant rather than the thug with the biggest stick.

"If you want a better empire, you need to create a better ruler. I can provide this. I can bring you a child that I have already begun to educate and will continue to groom. I can raise the child at Sheridan, away from life at court. We don't want a spoiled brat, pampered from birth, swinging little legs on the imperial throne. What we need is a strong, compassionate leader without ties to the nobility."

"One *you* control," Luis Guy accused.

Arcadius chuckled. "It is true that such a child might be fond of me, and while I know that I cut quite a dashing figure for someone my age, I'm a very old man. I will be dead soon. Most likely, I will pass on long before the child reaches coronation age, so you'll not have to worry about my influence.

"I should point out that I don't intend to be the child's only tutor. Nor could I be in order to ensure success. A task of this magnitude would require historians, doctors, engineers, and even tradesmen. You can send as many of your own instructors as you wish. I would hope you, Regent Saldur, would be one of them. I suspect much of the vision of the New Empire comes from you, after all. Once the wedding is over and things are operating smoothly, you could join us at Sheridan. She will require training that you are uniquely qualified to teach."

"She?" Ethelred said.

"Beg pardon?" Arcadius asked, peering over his glasses again.

"You said *she*. Are you speaking of a girl?"

"Well, yes. The child I am suggesting is a young orphan whom I have been taking care of for some time. She is extremely bright and at the age of five has already mastered letters. She is a delightful girl who shows great promise."

"But—a *girl*?" Ethelred sneered. "What good is a girl?"

"I'm afraid my fellow regent is correct," Saldur said. "The moment she married, her husband would rule, and all your education would be wasted. If it was a boy..."

"Well, there is no shortage of orphan boys," Ethelred declared. "Find a handsome one and we can do the same with him."

"My offer is for *this* girl only."

"Why?" Guy asked.

Arcadius detected a tone in the question he did not like.

"Because I sense in her the makings of a magnificent ruler, the kind who could—"

"But she's a *girl*," Ethelred repeated.

"As is Empress Modina."

"Are you saying you would refuse to tutor another child? One of our choosing?" Saldur asked.

"Yes." Arcadius said the word with the stern conviction of an ultimatum. He hoped the value of knowledge that only he could bestow would be enough to win them over, but he could see the answer before it was spoken.

Saldur was respectful at least and politely thanked him for bringing the subject to their attention. They did not invite him to stay for Wintertide, and Arcadius was uncomfortable about the way Luis Guy watched him as he left.

He had failed.

⁊

Royce waited patiently.

He had been in Imperial Square that morning, speaking with vendors who regularly delivered supplies to the palace, when the old battered coach passed by and entered the imperial gates. Recognizing it immediately, Royce wondered what it was doing there.

The palace courtyard had insufficient space for all the visitors' carriages during Wintertide and soon the coach returned and parked along the outer wall. The old buggy, with its paint-chipped wheels, weathered sides, and tattered drapes, looked out of place amidst the line of noble vehicles.

He waited for what must have been hours before he spotted the old man leaving the palace and approaching the carriage.

"What the—" Arcadius began. He was startled by Royce, who sat inside.

The thief placed a finger to his lips.

"What are you doing here?" Arcadius whispered, pulling himself in and closing the door behind him.

"Waiting to ask you that same question," Royce said quietly.

"Where to, Professor?" the driver called as he climbed aboard. The coach bounced with his weight.

"Ah—just circle the city once, will you, Justin?"

"The city, sir?"

"Yes. I'd like to see it before we leave."

"Certainly, sir."

"Well?" Royce pressed as the carriage jerked forward.

"Chancellor Lambert took sick on the day he was to leave for the celebrations here. Because he could not attend, he thought a personal apology was required and asked me—of all people—to deliver his regrets. Now, what about you?"

"We located the heir."

"Did you now?"

"Yeah, and you said finding him would be difficult." Royce drew back his hood and tugged his gloves off one finger at a time. "After Hadrian discovered he was the Guardian of the Heir, he knew exactly what he wanted for a Wintertide present—his very own Heir of Novron."

"And where is this mythical chimera?"

"Right underfoot, as it turns out. We're still pinpointing him, but best guess puts Gaunt in the palace dungeons. He is being held for execution on the 'Tide. We were planning to steal him before that."

"The heir is Degan Gaunt?"

"Ironic, huh? The Nationalist leader trying to overthrow the empire is actually the one man destined to rule it."

"You said *were*...so you're not planning to rescue him anymore?"

"No. Hadrian cut some deal with the regents. They've made him a knight, of all things. If he wins the joust, I think they promised to set Gaunt free. I'm not sure I trust them, though."

The carriage rolled through the streets and up a hill, causing the horse to slow its pace. One of Arcadius's open travel bundles fell to the floor, joining the rest of his clothes, a pile of books, his shoes, and a mound of blankets.

"Have you ever put anything away in your life?" Royce asked.

"Never saw the point. I'd just have to take it back out again. So, Hadrian's in the palace—but what are you doing here? I heard Medford was burned. Shouldn't you be checking on Gwen?"

"Already have. She's fine and staying at the Winds Abbey. That reminds me. You might want to stick around. If all goes well, you can come with us for the wedding."

"Whose?"

"Mine. I finally asked Gwen and she agreed, believe it or not."

"Did she?" Arcadius said, reaching out for one of the blankets to draw over his legs.

"Yeah, and here we both thought she had more sense than that. Can you picture me as a husband and a father?"

"Father? You've discussed children?"

"She wants them and even picked out names."

"Has she now? And how does that sit with you? Whining children and stagnation might be harder for you than all the challenges you've faced before. And this is one you can't walk out on if you decide it's not for you." The old man tilted his head to look over the tops of his glasses, his mouth slightly open. "Are you sure that's what you want?"

"You've been after me to find a good woman for years; now you're second-guessing Gwen? I know I won't find better."

"Oh no, it's not that. I just know your nature. I'm not sure you'll be content with the role of a family man."

"Are you trying to scare me off? I thought you wanted me to settle down. Besides, when you found me, I was a much different person."

"I remember," the wizard said thoughtfully. "You were like a rabid dog, snapping at everything and everyone. Clearly, my genius in matching you up with Hadrian worked wonders. I knew his noble heart would eventually soften yours."

"Yeah, well, travel with a guy long enough and you start picking up his bad habits. You have no idea how many times I almost killed him when we first started. I never bothered, because I expected the jobs would take care of that for me, but somehow he kept surviving."

"Well, I'm glad to see things worked out for you both. Gwen is a fine woman, and you're right—you couldn't do better."

"So you'll wait?"

"I'm afraid not. I was ordered to return immediately."

"But you'll come out to the Winds Abbey afterward, right? If you were not there, it would be like not having my fath—well, an uncle, at least."

Arcadius smiled, but it looked strained. After a moment of silence, the smile disappeared.

"What's wrong?" Royce asked.

"Hmm...oh, nothing."

"No, I've seen that look before. What is it, you old coot?"

"Oh—well, probably nothing," Arcadius said.

"Out with it."

"I was just in with the regents. With them were a sentinel

named Luis Guy and another very quiet fellow. I've never seen him before, but the name was familiar. You used to speak of him often."

"Who?"

"They introduced him as Lord Merrick Marius."

# CHAPTER 13

# THE HOUSE ON HEATH STREET

Mince was freezing.

The dawn's wind ripped through the coarse woven bag around his shoulders as if it were a fishnet. His nose ran. His ears were frozen. His once-numb fingers—now stuffed in his armpits—burned. He managed to escape most of the heavy gusts by standing in the recessed doorway of a millinery shop, but his feet were lost in a deep snowdrift, protected only by double wraps of cloth stuffed with straw. It would be worth it if he learned who lived in the house across the street, and if that name matched the one the hooded stranger had asked about.

Mr. Grim—or was it Mr. Baldwin?—had promised five silver to the boy who found the man he was looking for. Given the flood of strangers in town, it was a tall order to find a single man, but Mince knew his city well. Mr. Grim—it had to be Mr. Grim—explained the fellow would be a smart guy who visited the palace a lot. That right there told Mince to head to the Hill District. Elbright was checking out the inns, and Brand was watching the palace gate, but Mince was sure Heath Street was the place for someone with palace connections.

Mince looked at the house across the street. Only two stories and quite narrow, it was tucked tight between two others. Not as fancy as the big homes but still a fine place. Built entirely of stone, it had several glass windows, the kind you could actually see through. Most of the houses on Heath Street were that way. The only distinguishing marks on this one were the dagger and oak leaf embossment above the door and the noticeable lack of any Wintertide decoration. While the rest of the homes were bedecked in streamers and ropes of garland, the little house was bare. It used to belong to Lord Dermont, who had died in the Battle of Ratibor the past summer. Mince asked the kids who begged on the street if they knew who owned it now. All they could tell him was that the master of the house rode in a fine carriage with an imperial-uniformed driver and had three servants. Both the master and the servants kept to themselves, and all were new to Aquesta.

"This has to be the right house," Mince muttered, his words forming a little cloud. A lot was riding on him that morning. He had to be the one to win the money—for Kine's sake.

Mince had been on his own since he was six. Handouts were easy to come by at that age, but with each year, things got tougher. There was a lot of competition in the city, especially now, with all the refugees. Elbright, Brand, and Kine were the ones who kept him alive. Elbright had a knife, and Brand had killed another kid in a fight over a tunic—it made others think twice before messing with them—but it was Kine, their master pickpocket, who was his best friend.

Kine had taken sick a few weeks earlier. He began throwing up and sweating like it was summer. They each gave him some of their food, but he was not getting better. For the past three days, he had not even been able to leave The Nest. Each time Mince saw him, Kine looked worse: whiter, thinner, blotchier, and shivering—always shivering. Elbright had seen the sickness before and said not to waste any more food on Kine, as he was as good as dead. Mince still shared a bit of his bread, but his friend rarely ate it. He hardly ate anything anymore.

Mince crossed the street to the front of the house, and to escape the bitter wind, he slipped to the right of the porch stairs. His foot sank deeper than expected and his arms windmilled as he fell down a short flight of steps leading to a root cellar. Mince landed on his back, sending up a cloud of powder that blinded him. He reached around and felt a hinge. His frozen hands continued to search and found a large lock holding the door fast.

He stood and dusted himself off. As he did, he noticed a gap under the stairs, a drain of some kind. His fall had uncovered the opening. Hearing the approach of the butcher's wagon, he quickly slithered inside.

"What will you have today, sir?"

"Goose."

"No beef? No pork?"

"Tomorrow starts Blood Week, so I'll wait."

"I have some right tasty pigeons and a couple of quail."

"I'll take the quail. You can keep the pigeons."

Mince had not eaten since the previous morning, and all their talk about food reminded his stomach.

"Very good, Mr. Jenkins. Are you sure you don't require anything else?"

"Yes, I'm sure that will be all."

*Jenkins*, Mince thought, *that is probably the servant's name, not the master of the house.*

Footfalls came down the steps and Mince held his breath as the manservant brushed the snow away from the cellar door with a broom. He opened it to allow the butcher entry.

"It's freezing out here," Jenkins muttered, and trotted out of sight.

"That it is, sir. That it is."

The butcher's boy carried the goose, already plucked and beheaded, down into the cellar and then returned to the wagon for the quails. The door was open. It might have been the cold, the hunger, or the thought of five silver—most likely it was all three—that sent Mince scurrying inside quick as a ferret without bothering to consider his decision. He scrambled behind a pile of sacks that smelled of potatoes and crouched low while trying to catch his breath. The butcher's boy returned with the birds, hung by their feet, and stepped out again. The door slammed, and Mince heard the lock snap shut.

After the brilliant world of sun and snow, Mince was blind. He stayed still and listened. The footsteps of the manservant crossed overhead, but they soon faded and everything was quiet. The boy knew there was no way to escape the cellar undetected, but he chose not to worry about that. The next time there was a delivery, he would just make a run for it. He could get through the door on surprise, and no one could catch him once he was in the open.

When Mince looked around again, he noticed that he could see as his eyes adjusted to the light filtering down through gaps in the boards. The cellar was cool, although balmy when compared to the street, and filled with crates, sacks, and jugs. Sides of bacon hung from the ceiling. A small box lined with straw held more eggs than he could count. Mince cracked one of them over his mouth and swallowed. Finding a tin of milk, he took two big mouthfuls and got mostly cream. Thick and sweet, it left him grinning with delight. Looking at all the containers, Mince felt as if he had fallen into a treasure room. He could live there by hiding in the piles, sleeping in the sacks, and eating himself fat. Hunting through the shelves for more treats, Mince found a jar of molasses and was trying to get the lid off when he heard steps overhead.

Muffled voices were coming closer. "I will be at the palace the rest of the day."

"I'll have the carriage brought at once, my lord."

"I want you and Poe to take this medallion to the silver-smith. Get him started making a duplicate. Don't leave it, and don't let it out of your sight. Stay with him and watch over it. It's *extremely* valuable."

"Yes, my lord."

"And bring it back at the end of the day. I expect you'll need to take it over several times."

"But your dinner, my lord. Surely Mr. Poe can—"

"I'll get my meals at the palace. I'm not trusting Poe with this. He is going along only as protection."

"But, my lord, he's hardly more than a boy—"

"Never mind that, just do as instructed. Where is Dobbs?"

"Cleaning the bedrooms, I believe."

"Take him too. You'll be gone all day, and I don't want him left here alone."

"Yes, my lord."

*My lord, my lord!* Mince was ready to scream in frustration. *Why not just use the bugger's name?*

❧

Mince listened for a long time before deciding the house was empty. He crossed the cellar, climbed the steps, and tried the door to the house. It opened. Careful and quiet as a mouse, he crept out. A board creaked when he put his weight on it. He froze in terror but nothing happened.

He was alone in the kitchen. Food was everywhere: bread,

pickles, eggs, cheese, smoked meats, and honey. Mince sampled each one as he passed. He had eaten bread before, but this was soft and creamy compared to the three-day-old biscuits he was used to. The pickles were spicy, the cheese was a delight, and the meat, despite being tough from curing, was a delicacy he rarely knew. He also found a small barrel of beer that was the best he had ever had. Mince found himself light-headed and stuffed as he left the kitchen with a slice of pie in one hand, a wedge of cheese in the other, and a stringy strip of meat in his pocket.

The inside of the house was more impressive than the exterior. Sculptured plaster, carved wood, finely woven tapestries, and silk curtains lined the walls. A fire burned in the main room. Logs softly crackled, their warmth spreading throughout the lower floor. Crystal glasses sat inside cherry cabinets, fat candles and statuettes rested on tables, and books filled the shelves. Mince had never held a book before. He finished the pie, stuffed the cheese in his other pocket, and then pulled one down. The book was thick and heavier than he had expected. He tried to open it, but it slipped through his greasy fingers and struck the floor with a heavy thud that echoed through the house. He froze, held his breath, and waited for footsteps or a shout.

Silence.

Picking up the book, he felt the raised leather spine and marveled at the gold letters on the cover. He imagined the words revealed some powerful magic—a secret that could make men rich or grant eternal life. Setting the book back on the shelf with a bit of sadness, Mince moved toward the stairs.

He climbed to the second story, where there were several bedrooms. The largest had an adjoining study with a desk and more books. On the desk were parchments, more mysterious words—more secrets. He picked up one of the pages, turned it sideways and then upside down, as if a different orientation might force the letters to reveal their mysteries. He grew frustrated. Dropping the page back on the desk, he started to leave when a light caught his attention.

A strange glow came from within the wardrobe. He stared at it for a long time before venturing to open the door. Vests, tunics, and cloaks filled the cabinet. Pushed to the rear was a robe—a robe that shimmered with its own light. Mesmerized, Mince risked a hesitant touch. The material was unlike anything he had felt before—smoother than a polished stone and softer than a down feather. The moment he touched the fabric, the garment instantly changed from dark, shimmering silver to an alluring purple and glowed the brightest where his fingers contacted it.

Mince glanced nervously around the room. He was still alone. On an impulse, he pulled the robe out. The hem brushed the floor and he immediately draped it over his arm. Letting the robe touch the ground did not seem right. He started to put it on and had one arm in the sleeve when he stopped. The robe felt cold, and it turned a dark blue, almost black. When he pulled his arm out, the beautiful purple glow returned.

Mince reminded himself he was not there to steal.

On principle, he was not against thieving. He stole all the time. He picked pockets, grabbed-and-ran from markets, and even looted drunks. But he had never robbed a house—certainly not a Heath Street house. Thieving from nobles was dangerous, and the authorities were the least of his worries. If the thieves' guild found out, their punishment would be worse than anything the magistrate would come up with. No one would raise a stink over a starving boy taking food, but the robe was a different matter. With all the books and writing in the house, it was obvious the owner was a wizard or warlock of some sort.

It was too risky.

*What would I do with it, anyway?*

While it would put old Brand the Bold's tunic to shame, he could never put it on. The robe was too big for him to wear and Mince would not dare cut it. Even if he managed it, the robe would draw every eye in the city. He reached out to put it back in the wardrobe, deciding he could not risk taking it. Once more the robe went dark. Still holding it, he pulled his arm out, and it glowed again. Puzzled but still determined, Mince hung it back up. The moment he let go, the robe fell to the floor. He tried again and it fell once more.

"All right, go ahead and stay there," he said, and started to turn away.

The robe instantly flared to a brilliant white. All shadows in the room vanished and Mince staggered backward, squinting to see.

"Okay, okay. Stop it. Stop it!" he shouted, and the light dimmed to blue again.

Mince did not move. He stood staring at the robe as it lay on the floor. The light was throbbing—growing bright and dim almost as if it were breathing. He watched it for several minutes, trying to figure it out.

Slowly, he stepped closer and picked it up. "Ya want me to take you?"

The robe glowed the pretty purple color.

"Can I wear you?"

Dark blue.

"So...ya just want me to steal you?"

Purple.

"Don't ya belong here?"

Blue.

"You're being held against yer will?"

The robe flashed purple so brightly that it made him blink.

"You're not—ya know—*cursed*, are you? Ya aren't going to hurt me—are ya?"

Blue.

"Is it okay if I fold ya up and stuff ya inside my tunic?"

Purple.

As big as it was, the garment compressed easily. Mince stuffed it in the top of his shirt, making him look like a busty girl. Because he was already stealing the robe, he also picked up a handful of parchments and stuffed them in as well. He was not going to find out who lived there while the occupants were out, and Mince did not want to stick around for them to discover that the robe was missing. Mr. Grim looked to be the type to know letters, or know someone who did. Maybe he could tell enough from the parchments for Mince to win the silver.

❧

Royce sat on the bleachers in Imperial Square, observing the patterns of the city. Wintertide was less than two weeks away and the city swelled with pilgrims. They filled the plaza, bustled by the street vendors and open shops, and shouted holiday greetings and obscenities in equal measure. Wealthy, blanket-wrapped merchants rode in carriages, pointing at the various sights. Visiting tradesmen carried tools over their shoulders, hoping to pick up work, while established vendors scowled at them. Threadbare farmers and peasants visiting Aquesta to see the holy empress huddled in groups, staring in awe at their surroundings.

*Betrayal in Medford*. Royce read the sign posted in front of a small theater. It indicated nightly performances during the week leading up to Wintertide's Eve. From the barkers on the street, he determined the play was the imperial variation of the popular *The Crown Conspiracy*, which the empire had outlawed. Apparently in this version, the plotting prince and his witch sister decide to murder their father, and only the good archduke stands in the way of their evil plans.

Four patrols of eight men circled the streets. At least one group checked in at each square every hour. They were swift and harsh in their peacekeeping. Dressed in mail and carrying heavy weapons, they brutally beat and dragged away anyone causing a nuisance or being accused of a crime. They did not bother to hear the suspect's side of the story. They did not care who had trespassed on whom, or whether the accusation was truth or fiction. Their goal was order, not justice.

An interesting side effect, which would have been comical if the results had not been so ugly, was that street vendors falsely accused their out-of-town competitors of offenses. Local vendors banded together, forming an alliance to denounce the upstarts. Before long, people learned to gather at the squares just before an imperial patrol was expected to arrive, or follow the men as they patrolled. The spectacle of violence was just one more holiday show.

Two good-sized pigs, attempting to escape their fates of Blood Week, ran through the square, trailed by a parade of children and two mongrel dogs chasing after them. A butcher wearing a bloodstained apron and looking exhausted from running paused to wipe his brow.

Royce spotted the boy deftly dodging his way through the crowd. Pausing briefly to avoid the train chasing the pig, Mince locked eyes with Royce, then casually strolled over to the bleachers. Royce was pleased to see no one watched the boy's progress too closely.

"Looking for me?" Royce asked.

"Yes, sir," Mince replied.

"You found him?"

"Don't know—maybe—never got a name or a look. Got these, though." The boy pulled some parchments from his shirt. "I snatched them from a house on Heath Street. It has a new owner. Can ya read?"

Royce ignored the question as he scanned the parchments. The handwriting was unmistakable. He slipped them into his cloak.

"Where exactly is this house?"

Mince smiled. "I'm right, aren't I? Do I get the coin?"

"Where's the house?"

"Heath Street, south off the top, harbor side, little place right across from Buchan's Hattery. Ya can't miss it. There's a crest of an oak leaf and dagger above the door. Now, what about the money?"

Royce did not respond but focused on the boy's overstuffed tunic, which glowed as if he had a star trapped inside.

Mince saw his look and promptly folded his arms. Tilting his head down, he whispered, "Quit it!"

"Did you take something else from the house?"

Mince shook his head. "It has nothing to do with ya."

"If that's from the same house, you'll want to give it to me."

Mince stuck his lip out defiantly. "It's nothing and it's mine. I'm a thief, see. I took it for myself in case I got the wrong house. I didn't want to risk my neck and get nothing. So it's my bonus. That's how professional thieves work, see? Ya might not like it, but it's how we do things. You and me had a deal and I've done my part. Don't get all high-and-mighty or go on about bad morals, 'cuz I get enough of that from the monks."

The light grew brighter and began flashing on and off.

Royce was disturbed. "What *is* that?"

"Like I said, it's none of yer business," Mince snapped, and pulled away. He looked down once more and whispered, "Stop it, will ya! People can see. I'll get in trouble."

"Listen, I don't have a problem with a little theft," Royce told him. "You can trust me on that. But if you took something of value from *that* house, you'd be wise to give it to me. This might sound like a trick, but I'm only trying to help. You don't understand who you're dealing with. The owner will find you. He's very meticulous."

"What's that mean...*meticulous?*"

"Let's just say he's not a forgiving man. He will kill you, Elbright, and Brand. Not to mention anyone else you have regular contact with, just to be thorough."

"I'm keeping it!" Mince snapped.

Royce rolled his eyes and sighed.

The boy struggled to cover up by doubling over and wrapping his arms around his chest. As he did, the light blinked faster and now alternated different colors. "By Mar, just give me the money, will ya? Before one of the guards sees."

Royce handed him five silver coins and watched as the boy took off. He ran hunched over, emitting a rapidly blinking light that faded and eventually stopped.

❧

Mince entered the loft by climbing to the roof of the warehouse, pulling back a loose board near the eaves, and scrambling through the hole. The Nest, as they dubbed their home, was the result of poor carpentry. A mistake made when the East Sundries Company had built their warehouse against the common wall of the Bingham Carriage House & Blacksmith Shop. A mismeasurement had left a gap, which was sealed shut with side boards. Over the years, the wood had warped.

While trying to break into the warehouse, Elbright had noticed a gap between the boards that revealed the hidden space. He never found a way into the storehouse, but he had discovered the perfect hideout. The little attic was three feet tall and five feet wide and ran the length of the common wall. Thanks to the long hours of the blacksmiths, who usually kept a fire burning, it was also marginally heated.

A collection of treasures gathered from the city's garbage littered The Nest, including moth-eaten garments, burned bits of lumber, fragments of hides tossed out by the tanner, cracked pots, and chipped cups.

Kine lay huddled in a ball against the chimney. Mince had made him a bed of straw and tucked their best blanket around him, but his friend still shivered. The little bit of his face not covered by the blanket was pale white, and his bluish lips quivered miserably.

"How ya doing?" Mince asked.

"C-c-cold," Kine replied weakly.

Mince put a hand to the brick chimney. "Bastards are trying to save coal again."

"Is there any food?" Kine asked.

Mince pulled the wedge of cheese from his pocket. Kine took a bite and immediately started to vomit. Nothing came up, but he retched just the same. He continued to convulse for several minutes, then collapsed, exhausted.

"I'm like Tibith, ain't I?" Kine managed to say.

"No," Mince lied, sitting down beside him. He hoped to keep Kine warm with his body. "You'll be fine the moment the fire is lit. You'll see."

Mince fished the money out of his other pocket to show Kine. "Hey, look, I got coin—five silver! I could buy ya a hot meal, how would that be?"

"Don't," Kine replied. "Don't waste it."

"What do ya mean? When is hot soup ever a waste?"

"I'm like Tibith. Soup won't help."

"I told ya, yer not like that," Mince insisted, slamming the silver in a cup he decided at that moment to use as a bank.

"I can't feel my feet anymore, Mince, and my hands tingle. I ache all over and my head pounds and...and...I pissed myself today. Did you hear me—I pissed myself! I *am* like Tibith. I'm just like he was and I'm gonna die just like him."

"I said ya ain't. Now quit it!"

"My lips are blue, ain't they?"

"Be quiet, Kine, just—"

"By Mar, Mince, *I don't want to die*!" Kine shook even more as he cried.

Mince felt his stomach churn as tears dripped down his cheeks too. Victims never recovered once their lips went blue.

He looked around for something else to wrap his friend in and then remembered the robe.

"There," he muttered, draping the robe over Kine. "After all the trouble you've been, try to be of some use. Keep him warm or I'll toss ya in the smith's fire."

"W-what?" Kine moaned.

"Nothing, go to sleep."

～

Royce heard the key turn. The bolt shifted and the door opened on well-oiled hinges. Four pairs of feet shuffled on the slate of the foyer. He heard the sound of the door closing, the brush of material, and the snap of a cloak. One pair of feet scuffed abruptly as if their owner unexpectedly found himself on the edge of a precipice.

"Mr. Jenkins," Merrick's voice said, "I want you and Dobbs to take the rest of the evening off."

"But, sir, I—"

"This is no time to argue. Please, Mr. Jenkins, just leave. Hopefully I will see you in the morning."

"Hopefully?" This voice was familiar. Royce recognized Poe, the cook's mate on the *Emerald Storm*. It took him a moment, but then Royce understood. "What do you mean you will— Hold on. Is *he* here? How do you know?"

"I want you to go too, Poe."

"Not if he's here. You'll need protection."

"If he wanted me dead, I would already be lying in a bloody puddle. So I think it is fair to surmise that I am safe. You, on the other hand, are a different story. I doubt he knew you would be here. Now that he knows your connection to me, the only thing keeping you alive is that he is more interested in talking to me than slitting your throat, at least for the moment."

"Let him try. I think—"

"Poe, leave the thinking to me. And never tempt him like that. This is not a man to toy with. Trust me, he'd kill you without difficulty. I know. I worked with him. We specialized in assassinations and he's better at it than I am—particularly spur-of-the-moment killings—and right now you're a very tempting spur. Now, get out while you can. Disappear for a while, just to be safe."

"What makes you think he even knows I'm here?" Poe asked.

"He's in the drawing room, listening to us right now. Sitting in the blue chair with its back to the wall, he's waiting for me to join him. I'm sure he has a crystal glass half filled with the Montemorcey wine I bought and left in the pantry for him. He's holding it in his left hand so if, for whatever reason, he has to draw his dagger, he won't need to put the glass down first. He hates to waste Montemorcey. He's swirling it, letting it breathe, and while he's been here for some time, he has yet to taste it. He won't drink until I sit across from him—until I too have a glass."

"He suspects you poisoned it?"

"No, he hasn't tasted the wine because...well, it would just be rude. He'll have a glass of cider waiting for me, as he knows I no longer drink spirits."

"And how do you know all this?"

"Because I know him just as I know you. Right now you're fighting an urge to enter the drawing room to see if I'm right. Don't. You'll never come out again, and I don't want you staining my new carpet. Now leave. I will contact you when I need to."

"Are you sure? Yeah, okay, stupid question."

The door opened, then closed, and footsteps could be heard going down the porch stairs.

There was a pause and then a light flared. Merrick Marius entered the dark room holding a single candle. "I hope you don't mind. I prefer to be able to see you too."

Merrick lit four sconce lights, added some logs to the fire, and stirred the embers to life with a poker. He watched them for a long moment, then placed the tool back on its hook before taking a seat opposite Royce, next to the poured glass of cider.

"To old friends?" Merrick asked, holding up his drink.

"To old friends," Royce agreed, and the two sipped.

Merrick was dressed in a knee-length coat of burgundy velvet, a finely embroidered vest, and a startlingly white ruffled shirt.

"You're doing well for yourself," Royce observed.

"I can't complain. I'm Magistrate of Colnora now. Have you heard?"

"I hadn't. Your father would be proud."

"He said I couldn't do it. Do you remember? He said I was too smart for my own good." Merrick took another sip. "I suppose you're angry about Tur Del Fur."

"You crossed a line."

"I know. I am sorry about that. You were the only one who could do that job. If I could have found someone else..." Merrick crossed his legs and looked over his glass at Royce. "You're not here to kill me, so I'll assume your visit is about Hadrian."

"Is that your doing? This *deal*?"

Merrick shook his head. "Actually, Guy came up with that. They tried to persuade Hadrian to kill Breckton for money and a title. My only contribution was providing the proper incentive."

"They're dangling Gaunt?" Royce asked.

Merrick nodded. "And the Witch of Melengar."

"Arista? When did they get her?"

"A few months ago. She and her bodyguard tried to free Gaunt. He died and she was captured."

Royce took another drink and then set his glass down before asking, "They're going to kill Hadrian, aren't they?"

"Yes. The regents know they can't just let him go. After he kills Breckton, they will arrest him for murder, throw him in prison, and execute him along with Gaunt and Arista on Wintertide."

"Why do they want Breckton dead?"

"They offered him Melengar in order to separate him from Ballentyne. He refused, and now they're afraid the Earl of Chadwick will attempt to use Breckton to overthrow the empire. They're spooked and feel their only chance to eliminate him is by using a Teshlor-trained warrior. Nice skills to have in a partner, by the way—good choice."

Royce sipped his wine and thought awhile. "Can you save him?"

"Hadrian?" Merrick paused and then answered, "Yes."

The word hung there.

"What do you want?" Royce said.

"Interesting that you should ask. As it turns out, I have another job that you would be perfect for."

"What kind?"

"Find-and-recover. I can't give you the details yet, but it's dangerous. Two other groups have already failed. Of course, I wasn't involved in those attempts, and you weren't leading the operation. Agree to take the job and I'll make sure nothing happens to Hadrian."

"I've retired."

"I heard that rumor."

Royce drained his glass and stood. "I'll think about it."

"Don't wait too long, Royce. If you want me to work this, I'll need a couple of days to prepare. Trust me, you'll want my help. A dungeon rescue will fail. The prison is dwarven made."

# Chapter 14

# Tournament Day

The morning dawned to the wails and cries of the doomed. The snow ran red as axe and mallet slaughtered livestock whose feed had run out. Blood Week happened every winter, but exactly what day it began depended on the bounty of the fall harvest. For an orphan in Aquesta, the best part of winter was Blood Week.

Nothing went to waste—feet, snouts, and even bones sold—but with so much to cleave, butchers could not keep track of every cut. The city's poor circled the butcher shops like human vultures, searching for an inattentive cutter. Most butchers hired extra help, but they always underestimated the dangers. There were never enough arms carrying the meat to safety or enough eyes keeping lookout. A few daring raids even managed to carry off whole legs of beef. As the day wore on and workers grew exhausted, some desperate butchers resorted to hiring the very thieves they guarded against.

Mince had left The Nest early, looking for what he could scrounge for breakfast. The sun had barely peeked above the city wall when he managed to snatch a fine bit of beef from Gilim's Slaughterhouse. After a particularly sound stroke from Gilim's cleaver, a piece of shank skipped across the slick table, fell in the snow, and slid downhill. Mince happened to be in the right place at the right time. He snatched it and ran with the bloody fist-sized chunk of meat clutched inside his tunic. Anyone noticing the sprinting boy might conclude he was mortally wounded.

He was anxious to devour his prize, but exposing it would risk losing the meat to a bigger kid. Worse yet, a butcher or guard might spot him. Mince wished Brand and Elbright were with him. They had gone to the slaughterhouses down on Coswall, where most of the butchering would be done. The fights there would be fierce. Grown men would struggle for scraps alongside the orphans. Mince was too small to compete. Even if he managed to grab a hunk, someone would likely take it, beating him senseless. The other two boys could hold their own. Elbright was as tall as most men now, and Brand even larger, but Mince had to satisfy himself with the smaller butcher shops.

Arriving on the street in front of the Bingham Carriage House, Mince stopped. He needed to get inside, but the thought of what he might find there frightened him. In his haste to get an early start, he had forgotten about Kine. For the past few days, his friend's loud wheezing had frequently woken Mince, but he could not remember having heard anything that morning.

Mince had seen too much death. He knew eight boys—friends—who had died from cold, sickness, or starvation. They always went in winter, their bodies stiff and frozen. Each lifeless form had once been a person—laughing, joking, running, crying—then was just a thing, like a torn blanket or a broken lantern. After finding remains, Mince would drag them to the pile—there was always a pile in winter. No matter how short a distance he needed to drag the body, the trip felt like miles. He remembered the good times and moments they had spent together. Then he would look down at the stiff, pale thing.

*Will I be the thing one day? Will someone drag me to the pile?*

He gritted his teeth, entered the alley, climbed to the roof, and pulled back the board. Leaving the brilliant sunlight, Mince crawled blindly into the crevice. The Nest was dark and silent. There was no sound of breathing—wheezing or otherwise. Mince reached forward, imagining Kine's cold, stiff body. The thought caused his hand to shake even as he willed his fingers to spread out, searching. Touching the silken material of the robe, he recoiled as it began to glow.

Kine was not there.

The robe lay on the floor as if Kine had melted during the night. Mince pulled the material toward him. As he did, the glow increased enough to reach every corner of the room. He was alone. Kine was gone. Not even his body remained.

Mince sat for a second, and then a thought surfaced. He dropped the robe in horror and kicked it away. The robe's glow throbbed and grew fainter.

"Ya ate him!" Mince cried. "Ya lied to me. Ya *are* cursed!"

The light went out and Mince backed as far away as possible. He had to get away from the killer robe, but now it was lying between him and the exit.

A silhouette passed in front of the opening, momentarily blocking the sunlight.

"Mince?" Kine's voice said. "Mince, look. I got me lamb chops!"

Kine entered and replaced the board. Mince's eyes adjusted until he could see his friend, holding a pair of bloody bones. His chin was stained red. "I woulda saved you one, but I couldn't find you. By Mar, I was famished!"

"Ya all right, Kine?"

"I'm great. I'm still a little hungry, but other than that, I feel fantastic."

"But last night…" Mince started. "Last night ya—ya—didn't look so good."

Kine nodded. "I had all kinds of queer dreams, that's for sure."

"What kind of dreams?"

"Hmm? Oh, just odd stuff. I was drowning in this dark lake. I couldn't breathe 'cuz water was spilling into my mouth every time I tried to take a breath. I tried to swim, but my arms and legs barely moved—it was a terrible nightmare." Kine noticed the beef shank Mince still held. "Hey! You got some meat too? You wanna cook it up? I'm still hungry."

"Huh? Oh, sure," Mince said as he looked down at the robe while handing the beef to Kine.

"I love Blood Week, don't you?"

⚜

Trumpets blared and drums rolled as the pennants of twenty-seven noble houses snapped in the late-morning breeze. People filed into the stands at Highcourt Fields on the opening day of the Grand Avryn Wintertide Tournament. The contest would last ten days, ending with the Feast of Tides. Across the city, shops closed and work stopped. Only the smoking and salting of meat continued, as Blood Week ran parallel to the tournament, and the slaughter could not halt even for such an august event. Many thought the timing was an omen that signaled the games would produce a higher number of accidents, which only added to the excitement. Every year crowds delighted in seeing blood.

Two years before, the baron Linder of Maranon had died when a splintered lance held by Sir Gilbert pierced the visor of his helm. The same year Sir Dulnar of Rhenydd had his right hand severed in the final round of the sword competition. Nothing, however, compared to the showdown five years ago between Sir Jervis and Francis Stanley, the Earl of Harborn. In the final tilt of the tournament, Sir Jervis—who had already borne a grudge against the earl—passed over the traditional Lance of Peace and picked up the Lance of War. Against council, the earl agreed to the deadly challenge. Jervis's lance pierced Stanley's cuirass as if it were parchment and continued on through his opponent's chest. The knight did not escape the encounter unscathed. Stanley's lance pierced Jervis's helm and entered his eye socket. Both fell dead. Officials judged the earl the victor due to the extra point for a head blow.

Centuries earlier, Highcourt Fields had functioned as the supreme noble court of law in Avryn. Civil disputes inevitably escalated until accused and accuser turned to combat to determine who was right. Soon the only dispute became who was the best warrior. As the realms of Avryn expanded, trips to Highcourt became less convenient. Monthly sessions were eventually reduced to biyearly events where all grievances were settled over a two-week session. These were held on the holy days of Summersrule and Wintertide, in the belief Maribor was more attentive at these times.

Over the years, the celebration grew. Instead of merely proving their honor, the combatants also fought for glory and gold. Knights from across the nation came to face each other for the most prestigious honor in Avryn: Champion of the Highcourt Games.

Adorned in the distinct colors of their owners, richly decorated tents of the noble competitors clustered around the fringe of the field. Squires, grooms, and pages polished armor and brushed their lords' horses. Knights entered in the sword competition limbered up with blades and shields, sparring with their squires. Officials walked the line of the carousel—a series of posts dangling steel rings no larger than a man's fist. They measured the height of each post and the angle of each ring, which men on galloping horses would try to collect with lances. Archers took practice shots. Spearmen sprinted and lunged, testing the sand's traction. On the great jousting field, horses snorted and huffed as unarmored combatants took practice rides across the course.

Amidst all this activity, Hadrian braced himself against a post as Wilbur beat on his chest with a large hammer. Nimbus had arranged for the smith to adjust Hadrian's borrowed armor. Obtaining a suit was simple, but making it fit properly was another matter.

"Here, sir," Renwick said, holding out a pile of cloth to Hadrian.

"What's that for?" Hadrian asked.

Renwick looked at him curiously. "It's your padding, sir."

"Don't hand it to him, lad," Wilbur scolded. "Stuff it in!"

Embarrassment flooded the boy's face as he began wadding up the cloth and shoving it into the wide gap between the steel and Hadrian's tunic.

"Pack it tight!" Wilbur snapped. He took a handful of padding and stuffed it against Hadrian's chest, ramming it in hard.

"That's a bit *too* tight," Hadrian complained.

Wilbur gave him a sidelong glance. "You might not think that when Sir Murthas's lance hits you. I don't want to be accused of bad preparation because this boy failed to pack you properly."

"Sir Hadrian," Renwick began, "I was wondering—I was thinking—would it be all right if I were to enter the squire events?"

"Don't see why not. Are you any good?"

"No, but I would like to try just the same. Sir Malness never allowed it. He didn't want me to embarrass him."

"Are you really that bad?"

"I've never been allowed to train. Sir Malness forbade me from using his horse. He was fond of saying, 'A man upon a horse has a certain way of looking at the world, and a lad such as yourself should not get accustomed to the experience, as it will only produce disappointment.' "

"Sounds like Sir Malness was a real pleasant guy," Hadrian said.

Renwick offered an uncomfortable smile and turned away. "I have watched the events many times—studied them, really—and I have ridden but never used a lance."

"Why don't you get my mount and we'll have a look at you?"

Renwick nodded and ran to fetch the horse. Ethelred had provided a brown charger named Malevolent for Hadrian. Bred for stamina and agility, the horse was dressed in a chanfron to protect the animal from poorly aimed lances. Despite the name, he was a fine horse, strong and aggressive, but not vicious. Malevolent did not bite or kick, and upon meeting Hadrian, the horse affectionately rubbed his head up and down against the fighter's chest.

"Get aboard," Hadrian told the boy, who grinned and scrambled into the high-backed saddle. Hadrian handed him a practice lance and the shield with green and white quadrants, which the regents had supplied.

"Lean forward and keep the lance tucked tight against your side. Squeeze it in with your elbow to steady it. Now ride in a circle so I can watch you."

For all his initial enthusiasm, the boy looked less confident as he struggled to hold the long pole and guide the horse at the same time.

"The stirrups need to be tighter," Sir Breckton said as he rode up.

Breckton sat astride a strong white charger adorned with an elegant caparison of gold and blue stripes. A matching pennant flew from the tip of a lance booted in his stirrup. Dressed in brightly polished armor, he had a plumed helm under one arm and a sheer blue scarf tied around the other.

"I wanted to wish you good fortune this day," he said to Hadrian.

"Thanks."

"You ride against Murthas, do you not? He's good with a lance. Don't underestimate him." Breckton studied Hadrian critically. "Your cuirass is light. That's very brave of you."

Hadrian looked down at himself, confused. He had never worn such heavy armor. His experience with a lance remained confined to actual combat, in which targets were rarely knights. As it was, Hadrian felt uncomfortable and restricted.

Breckton motioned to the metal plate on his own side. "Bolted armor adds an extra layer of protection where one is most likely to be hit. And where is your elbow pocket?"

Hadrian was confused for a moment. "Oh, that plate? I had the smith take it off. It made it impossible to hold the lance tight."

Breckton chuckled. "You do realize that *plate* is meant to brace the butt of the lance, right?"

Hadrian shrugged. "I've never jousted in a tournament before."

"I see." Sir Breckton nodded. "Would you be offended should I offer advice?"

"No, go ahead."

"Keep your head up. Lean forward. Use the stirrups to provide leverage to deliver stronger blows. Absorb the blows you receive with the high back of your saddle to avoid being driven from your horse."

"Again, thank you."

"Not at all, I am pleased to be of service. If you have any questions, I will be most happy to answer them."

"Really?" Hadrian responded mischievously. "In that case, is that a token I see on your arm?"

Breckton glanced down at the bit of cloth. "This is the scarf of Lady Amilia of Tarin Vale. I ride for her this day—for her and her honor." He looked out at the field. "It appears the tournament is about to start. I see Murthas taking his position at the alley, and you are up first. May Maribor guide the arm of the worthy." Breckton nodded respectfully and left.

Renwick returned and dismounted.

"You did well," Hadrian told him, taking the squire's place on the charger. "You just need a bit more practice. Assuming I survive this tilt, we'll work on it some more."

The boy carried Hadrian's helm in one hand and, taking the horse's lead in the other, led the mounted knight to the field. They entered the gate, circled the alley, and came to a stop next to a small wooden stage.

Ahead of Hadrian lay the main arena, which an army of workers had spent weeks preparing by clearing snow and laying sand. The field was surrounded by a sea of spectators divided into sections designated by color. Purple housed the ruler and his immediate family; blue was for the ranked gentry, red for the church officials, yellow for the baronage, green for the artisans, and white for the peasantry, which was the largest and only uncovered section.

Hadrian's father used to bring him to the games, but not for entertainment. Observing combat had been part of his studies. Still, Hadrian had been thrilled to see the fights and cheer the victors along with the rest. His father had no use for the winners and cared to discuss only the losers. Danbury questioned Hadrian after each fight, asking what the defeated knight had done wrong and how he could have won.

Hadrian had hardly listened. He was distracted by the spectacle—the knights in shining armor, the women in colorful gowns, the incredible horses. He knew one knight's saddle was worth more than their home and his father's blacksmith shop combined. How magnificent they had all seemed in comparison to his commoner father. It had never occurred to him that Danbury Blackwater could defeat every knight in every contest.

As a youth, Hadrian had dreamed of fighting at Highcourt a million times. Unlike the Palace of the Four Winds, this field was a church to him. Battles were respectful—not to the death. Swords were blunted, archers used targets, and jousts were performed with the Lance of Peace. A combatant lost points if he killed his opponent, and could be expelled from the tournament even for injuring a competitor's horse. Hadrian had found that strange. Even after his father had explained that the horse was innocent, he had not understood. He did now.

A large man with a loud voice stood on a platform in front of the purple section, shouting to those assembled: "...is the chief knight of Alburn and the son of the Earl of Fentin, and he is renowned for his skill in the games and at court. I give to you—Sir Murthas!"

The crowd erupted in applause, drumming their feet on the hollow planks. Ethelred and Saldur sat to either side of a throne that remained as empty as the one in the banquet hall. At the start of the day, officials had announced that the empress felt too ill that morning to attend.

"From Rhenydd he hails," the man on the box shouted as he gestured toward Hadrian, "only recently knighted amidst the carnage of the bloody Battle of Ratibor. He wandered forest and field to reach these games. For his first tournament ever, I present to you—Sir Hadrian!"

Some clapping trickled down from the stands, but it was only polite applause. The contest was already over in the eyes of the crowd.

Hadrian had never held a Lance of Peace. Lighter than a war lance, which had a metal tip, this one was all wood. The broad flared end floated awkwardly but it was still solid oak and not to be underestimated. He checked his feet in the stirrups and gripped the horse with his legs.

Across the sand-strewn alley, Sir Murthas sat on his gray destrier. His horse was a strong, angry-looking steed cloaked in a damask caparison covered in a series of black and white squares and fringed with matching tassels. Murthas himself held a lozenge shield and wore a matching surcoat and cape of black and white diamonds. He snapped his visor shut just as the trumpeters sounded the fanfare and the flagman raised his banner.

Mesmerized by the spectacle, Hadrian let his gaze roam from the stands to the snapping pennants and finally to the percussionists beating on their great drums. The pounding rolled like thunder such that Hadrian could feel it in his chest, yet the roar of the crowd overwhelmed it. Many leapt to their feet in anticipation. Hundreds waited anxiously, with every eye fixed upon the riders. As a boy in the white stands, Hadrian had held his father's fingers, hearing and feeling that same percussive din. He had wished to be one of those knights waiting at their gates—waiting for glory. The wish had been a fantasy that only a young boy who knew so little of the world could imagine—an impossible dream he had forgotten until that moment.

The drums stopped. The flag fell. Across the alley, Murthas spurred his horse and charged.

Caught by surprise, Hadrian was several seconds behind. He spurred Malevolent and lurched forward. The audience sprang to their feet, gasping in astonishment. Some screamed in fear. Hadrian ignored them, intent on his task.

Feeling the rhythm of the horse's stride, he became one with the motion. Hadrian pushed the balls of his feet down, taking up every ounce of slack and pressing his lower back against the saddle. Slowly, carefully, he lowered the lance, pulling it to his side and keeping its movement in sync with the horse's rapid gait. He calculated the drop rate with the approach of his target.

The wind roared past Hadrian's ears and stung his eyes as the charger built up speed. The horse's hooves pounded the soft track, creating explosions of sand. Murthas raced at him, his black and white cape flying. The horses ran full out, nostrils flaring, muscles rippling, harnesses jangling.

*Crack!*

Hadrian felt his lance jolt, then splinter. Running out of lane, he discarded the broken lance and pulled back on the reins. Hadrian was embarrassed by his slow start and did not want Murthas to get the jump on him again. Intent on getting the next lance first, he wheeled his charger and saw Murthas's horse trotting riderless. Two squires and a groom chased the destrier. Hadrian spotted Murthas lying on his back along the alley. Men ran to the knight's aid as he struggled to sit up. Hadrian looked for Renwick, and as he did, he noticed the crowd. They were alive with excitement. All of them were on their feet, clapping and whistling. A few even cheered his name. Hadrian guessed they had not expected him to survive the first round.

He allowed himself a smile and the crowd cheered even louder.

"Sir!" Renwick shouted over the roar, running to Hadrian's

side. "You didn't put your helm on!" The squire held up the plumed helmet.

"Sorry," Hadrian apologized. "I forgot. I didn't expect them to start the run so quickly."

"Sorry? But—but no one tilts without a helm," Renwick said, an astonished look on his face. "He could have killed you!"

Hadrian glanced over his shoulder at Murthas hobbling off the field with the help of two men and shrugged. "I survived."

"Survived? *Survived?* Murthas didn't even touch you, and you *destroyed* him. That's a whole lot better than just *survived*. Besides, you did it without a *helm*! I've never seen anyone do that. And the way you hit him! You punched him off his horse like he hit a wall. You're amazing!"

"Beginner's luck, I guess. I'm all done here, right?"

Renwick nodded and swallowed several times. "You'll go on to the second round day after tomorrow."

"Good. How about we go see how well you do at the carousel minor and the quintain? Gotta watch that quintain. If you don't hit it clean, the billet will swing around and knock you off."

"I know," Renwick replied, but his expression showed he was still in a state of shock. His eyes kept shifting from Hadrian to Murthas and back to the still-cheering crowd.

⁓

Amilia had never been to the tournament before. She had never seen a joust. Sitting in the stands, Amilia realized she had not even been outside the palace in more than a year. Despite the cold, she was enjoying herself. Perched on a thick velvet cushion, she draped a lush blanket over her lap and held a warm cup of cider between her hands. Everything was so pretty. So many bright colors filled the otherwise bleak winter world. All around her the privileged were grouped according to their stations. Across the field, the poor swarmed, trapped behind fence rails. They blended into a single gray mass that almost faded into the background of muddied snow. Without seats, they stood in the slush, shuffling their feet and stuffing hands into sleeves. Still, they were obviously happy to be there, happy to see the spectacle.

"That's three broken lances for Prince Rudolf!" the duchess squealed, clapping enthusiastically. "A fine example of grand imperial entertainment. Not that his performance compares to Sir Hadrian's. Everyone thought the poor man was doomed. I still can't believe he rode without a helm! And what he did to Sir Murthas... Well, it will certainly be an exciting tournament this year, Amilia. Very exciting indeed."

Lady Genevieve tugged on Amilia's sleeve and pointed. "Oh, see there. They are bringing out the blue and gold flag. Those are Sir Breckton's colors. He's up next. Yes, yes, here he comes, and see—see on his arm. He wears your token. How exciting! The other ladies—they're positively drooling. Oh, don't look now, dear, they're all staring at you. If eyes were daggers and glares lethal..." She trailed off, as if Amilia should know the rest. "They all see your conquest, my darling, and hate you. How wonderful."

"Is it?" Amilia asked, noticing how many of the other ladies were staring at her. She bowed her head and kept her eyes focused on her lap. "I don't want to be hated."

"Nonsense. Knights aren't the only ones who tilt at these tournaments. Everyone comes to this field as a competitor, and there can only be one victor. The only difference is that the knights spar in the daylight, and the ladies compete by candlelight. Clearly, you won your first round, but now we must see if your conquest was a wise one, as your victory remains locked with his prowess. Breckton is riding against Gilbert. This should be a close challenge. Gilbert actually killed a man a few years ago. It was an accident, of course, but it still gives him an edge over his opponents. Although, rumor has it that he hurt his leg two nights back, so we shall see."

"Killed?" Amilia felt her stomach tighten as the trumpet blared and the flag flew.

Hooves shook the ground, and her heart raced as panic flooded her. She shut her eyes before the impact.

*Crack!*

The crowd roared.

Opening her eyes, she saw Gilbert still mounted but reeling. Sir Breckton trotted back to his gate unharmed.

"That's one lance for Breckton," Leo mentioned to no one in particular.

The duke sat on the far side of Genevieve, appearing more animated than Amilia had ever seen him. The duchess ran on for hours, talking about everything and anything, but Leopold almost never spoke. When he did, it was so softly that Amilia thought his words were directed to Maribor alone.

Nimbus sat to Amilia's right, frequently glancing at her. He looked tense and she loved him for it.

"That Gilbert. Look at the way they are propping him up," the duchess prattled on. "He really shouldn't ride again. Oh, but he's taking the lance—how brave of him."

"He needs to get the tip up," Leopold noted.

"Oh yes, Leo. You are right as always. He doesn't have the strength. And look at Breckton waiting patiently. Do you see the way the sun shines off his armor? He doesn't normally clean it. He's a warrior, not a tournament knight, but he went to the metalsmith and ordered it polished so that the wind itself could see its face within the gleam. Now why do you suppose a man who hasn't combed his hair in months does such a thing?"

Amilia felt terrified, embarrassed, and happy beyond what she had believed to be the bounds of emotion.

The trumpet blared, and again the horses charged.

A lance cracked, Gilbert fell, and once again Breckton emerged untouched. The crowd cheered, and to Amilia's surprise, she found herself on her feet along with the rest. She had a smile on her face that she could not wipe away.

Breckton made certain Gilbert was all right, then trotted over to the stands and stopped in front of Amilia's seat in the nobles' box. He tossed aside his broken lance, pulled off his helm, rose in his stirrups, and bowed to her. Without thinking, she walked down the steps toward the railing. As she stepped out from under the canopy into the sun, the cheers grew louder, especially from the commoners' side of the field.

"For you, my lady," Sir Breckton told her.

He made a sound to his horse, which also bowed, and once more the crowd roared. Her heart was light, her mind empty, and her whole life invisible except for that one moment in the sun. Feeling Nimbus's hand on her arm, she turned and saw Saldur scowling from the stands.

"It's not wise to linger in the sun too long, milady," Nimbus warned. "You might get burned."

The expression on Saldur's face dragged Amilia back to reality. She returned to her seat, noticing the venomous glares from the nobles around her.

"My dear," the duchess said in an uncharacteristic whisper, "for someone who doesn't know how to play the game, you are as remarkable as Sir Hadrian today."

Amilia sat quietly through the few remaining tilts, which

she hardly noticed. When the day's competition had ended, they exited the stands. Nimbus led the way and the duchess walked beside her, holding on to Amilia's arm.

"You will be coming with us to the hunt on the Eve's Eve, won't you, Amilia dear?" Lady Genevieve asked as they walked across the field to the waiting carriages. "You simply must. I'll have Lois work all week on a dazzling white gown and matching winter cape so you'll have something new. Where can we find snow-white fur for the hood?" She paused a moment, then waved the thought away. "Oh well, I'll let her work that out. See you then. Ta-ta!" She blew Amilia a kiss as the ducal carriage left.

The boy was just standing there.

He waited on the far side of the street, revealed when the duke and duchess's coach pulled away. A filthy little thing, he stared at Amilia, looking both terrified and determined. In his arms he held a soiled bag. He caught her eye and with a stern resolve slipped through the fence.

"Mi-milady Ami—" was all he got out before a soldier grabbed him roughly and shoved him flat. The boy cowered in the snow, looking desperate. "Lady, please, I—"

The guard kicked him hard in the stomach and the boy crumpled around his foot. His eyes squeezed shut in pain as another soldier kicked him in the back.

"Stop it!" Amilia shouted. "Leave him alone!"

The guards paused, confused.

On the ground, the boy struggled to breathe.

"Help him up!" She took a step toward the child, but Nimbus caught her by the arm.

"Perhaps not here, milady." His eyes indicated the crowd around the line of carriages. Many were straining to see what the commotion was about. "You've already annoyed Regent Saldur once today."

She paused, then glanced at the boy. "Put him in my carriage," she instructed the guards.

They lifted the lad and shoved him forward. He dropped his bundle and pulled free in time to grab it before scurrying into the coach. Amilia glanced at Nimbus, who shrugged. The two followed the youth inside.

A look of horror on his face, the boy cowered on the seat across from Amilia and Nimbus.

The courtier eyed the lad critically. "I'd have to say he's ten, no more than twelve. An orphan, certainly, and nearly feral by the look of him. What do you suppose he has in the bag? A dead rat?"

"Oh, stop it, Nimbus," Amilia rebuked. "Of course it's not. It's probably just his lunch."

"Exactly," the tutor agreed.

Amilia glared. "Hush, you're frightening him."

"Me? He's the one who came at us with the moldy bag of mystery."

"Are you all right?" Amilia asked the boy softly.

He managed a nod, but just barely. His eyes kept darting around the interior of the carriage but always came back to Amilia, as if he were mesmerized.

"I'm sorry about the guards. That was awful, the way they treated you. Nimbus, do you have some coppers? Anything we could give him?"

The courtier looked helpless. "I'm sorry, my lady. I'm not in the habit of carrying coin."

Disappointed, Amilia sighed and then tried to put on a happy face. "What was it you wanted to say to me?" she asked.

The boy wetted his lips. "I—I have something to give to the empress." He looked down at the bag.

"What is it?" Amilia tried not to cringe at the possibilities.

"I heard...well...they said she couldn't be at the tournament today because she was sick and all. That's when I knew I had to get this to her." He patted the bag.

"Get what to her? What's in the bag?"

"Something that can heal her."

"Oh dear. It *is* a dead rat, isn't it?" Nimbus shivered in disgust.

The boy pulled the bag open and drew out a folded shimmering robe unlike anything Amilia had ever seen before. "It saved the life of my best friend—healed him overnight, it did. It's...it's magical, it is!"

"A religious relic?" Nimbus ventured.

Amilia smiled at the boy. "What's your name?"

"They call me Mince, milady. I can't say what my real name is, but Mince works well enough, it does."

"Well, Mince, this is a generous gift. This looks very expensive. Don't you think *you* should keep it? It's certainly better than what you're wearing."

Mince shook his head. "I think it wants me to give it to the empress—to help her."

"*It* wants?" she asked.

"It's kind of hard to explain."

"Such things usually are," the courtier said.

"So can you give this to her?"

"Perhaps you should let *him* give it to her," Nimbus suggested to Amilia.

"Are you serious?" she replied.

"You wanted to atone for the misdeeds of the guards, didn't you? For the likes of him, meeting the empress will more than make up for a few bruises. Besides, he's just a boy. No one will care."

Amilia thought a moment, staring at the wide-eyed child.

"What do you think, Mince? Would you like to give it to the empress yourself?"

The boy looked as if he might faint.

❧

Modina had found a mouse in her chamber three months earlier. When she had lit the lamp, it had frozen in panic in the middle of the room. Picking it up, she felt its little chest heave as it panted for breath. Clearly terrified, it looked back at her with its dark, tiny eyes. Modina thought it might die of fright. Even after she set it down, it still did not move. Only after the light had been out for several minutes did she hear it scurry away. The mouse had never returned—until now.

He was not that mouse, but the boy looked just the same. He lacked the fur, tail, and whiskers, but the eyes were unmistakable. He stood fearfully still, the only movement the result of his heaving chest and trembling body.

"Did you say his name was *Mouse*?"

"Mince, I think he said," Amilia corrected. "It is *Mince*, isn't it?"

The boy said nothing, clutching the bag to his chest.

"I found him at the tournament. He wants to give you a gift. Go on, Mince."

Instead of speaking, Mince abruptly thrust the bag out with both hands.

"He wanted to give this to you because Saldur announced that you were too sick to attend the tournament. He says it has healing powers."

Modina took the bag, opened it, and drew forth the robe. Despite having been stuffed in the old, dirty sack, the garment shimmered—not a single wrinkle or stain on it.

"It's beautiful," she said sincerely as she held it up, watching it play with the light. "It reminds me of someone I once knew. I will cherish it."

When the boy heard the words, tears formed in his eyes and streaked his dirty cheeks. Falling to his knees, he placed his face on the floor before her.

Puzzled, Modina glanced at Amilia, but the imperial secretary only offered a shrug. The empress stared at the boy for a moment and then said to Amilia, "He looks starved."

"Do you want me to take him to the kitchen?"

"No, leave him here. Go have some food sent up."

After Amilia left the room, Modina laid the robe on a chair and then sat on the edge of the bed, watching the boy. He had not moved, and remained kneeling with his head still touching the floor. After a few minutes, he looked up but said nothing.

Modina spoke gently. "I'm very good at playing the silent game too. We can sit here for days not saying a word if you want."

The boy's lips trembled. He opened his mouth as if to speak and then stopped.

"Go ahead. It's okay."

Once he started, the words came out in a flood, as if he felt the need to say everything with a single breath. "I just want ya to get better, that's all. Honest. I brought ya the robe because it saved Kine, see. It healed him overnight, I tell ya. He was dying, and he woulda been dead by morning, for sure. But the robe made him better. Then today, when they said you was too sick to see the tournament, I knew I had to bring ya the robe to make ya better. Ya see?"

"I'm sorry, Mince, but I'm afraid a robe can't heal what's wrong with me."

The boy frowned. "But...it healed Kine and his lips were blue."

Modina walked over and sat down on the floor in front of him.

"I know you mean well, and it's a wonderful gift, but some things can never be fixed."

"But—"

"No buts. You need to stop worrying about me. Do you understand?"

"Why?"

"You just have to. Will you do that for me?"

The boy looked up and locked eyes with her. "I would do anything for you."

The sincerity and conviction in his voice staggered her.

"I love you," he added.

Those three words shook her, and even though she was sitting on the floor, the empress put a hand down to steady herself.

"No," she said. "You can't. You just met—"

"Yes, I do."

Modina shook her head. "No, you don't!" she snapped. "No one does!"

The boy flinched as if struck. He looked back down at the floor and, nevertheless, added in a whisper, "But I do. Everyone does."

The empress stared at him.

"What do you mean—'everyone'?"

"Everyone," the boy said, puzzled. He gestured toward the window.

"You mean the people in the city?"

"Well, sure, them, but not just here. Everywhere. Everyone loves you," the boy repeated. "Folks been coming to the city from all over. I hear them talking. They all come to see ya. All of them saying how the world's gonna be better 'cuz you're here. How they would die for you."

Stunned, Modina stood up slowly.

She turned and walked to the window, where she gazed into the distance—above the roofs to the hills and snow-covered mountains beyond.

"Did I say something wrong?" Mince asked.

She turned back. "No. Not at all. It's just that..." Modina paused. She moved to the mirror and ran her fingertips along the glass. "There are still ten days to Wintertide, right?"

"Yes. Why?"

"Well, because you gave me a gift, I'd like to give you something in return, and it looks like I still have time."

She crossed to the door and opened it. Gerald stood waiting outside, as always. "Gerald," she said, "could you please do me a favor?"

# Chapter 15

# The Hunt

"Merry Eve's Eve, Sir Hadrian," a girl said brightly when he poked his head outside his room. She was just one of the giggling chambermaids who had been extending smiles and curtsies to him since the day of the first joust. After his second tilt, pages bowed and guards nodded in his direction. His third win, although as clean as the others, had been the worst, as it brought the attention of every knight and noble in the palace. After each joust, he had his choice of sitting in his dormitory or going to the great hall. Preferring to be alone, Hadrian usually chose his room.

That morning, like most days, Hadrian found himself wandering the palace hallways. He had seen Albert from a distance on a few occasions, but neither attempted to speak with the other, and there had been no sign of Royce. Crossing through the grand foyer, he paused. The staircase spiraled upward, adorned in fanciful candles and painted wood ornaments. Somewhere four flights up, the girl he had known as Thrace was probably still asleep in her bed. He put his foot on the first step.

"Sir Hadrian?" a man he did not recognize asked. "Great joust yesterday. You really gave Louden a hit he'll not soon forget. I heard the crack even in the high stands. They say Louden will need a new breastplate, and you gave him two broken ribs to boot! What a hit. What a hit, I say. You know, I lost a bundle betting against you the first three jousts, but since then I've won everything back. I'm sticking with you for the final. You've made a believer out of me. Say, where you headed?"

Hadrian quickly drew back his foot. "Nowhere. Just stretching my legs a bit."

"Well, just wanted to tell you to keep up the good work and let you know I'll be rooting for you."

The man exited the palace through the grand entrance, leaving Hadrian at the bottom of the stairs.

*What am I going to do, walk into her chambers unannounced? It's been over a year since I spoke with her. Will she hate me for not trying to see her earlier? Will she remember me at all?*

He looked up the staircase once more.

*It's possible she's all right, isn't it? Just because no one ever sees her doesn't necessarily mean anything, does it?*

Modina was the empress. They could not be treating her too badly. When she lived in Dahlgren, she had been happy, and that had been a squalid little village where people were killed nightly by a giant monster.

*How much worse can living in a palace be?*

He took one last look around and spotted the two shadows leaning casually near the archway to the throne room. With a sigh, Hadrian turned toward the service wing, leaving the stairway behind.

The sun was not fully up, but the kitchen was already bustling. Huge pots billowed clouds of steam so thick that the walls cried tears. Butchers hammered on cutting blocks, shouting orders. Boys ran with buckets, shouting back. Girls scrubbed cutlery, pans, and bowls. The smells were strong and varied. Some, such as that of baked bread, were wonderful, but others were sulfurous and vile. Unlike in the rest of the palace, no holiday decoration adorned the walls or tables. Here, behind the scenes, the signs of Wintertide were reduced to cooling trays of candied apples and snowflake-shaped cookies.

Hadrian stepped into the scullery, fascinated by the activity. As soon as he entered, heads turned, work slowed, and then everything came to a stop. The room grew so quiet that the only sounds came from the bubbling pots, the crackling fires, and water dripping from a wet ladle. All the staff stared at him, as if he had two heads or three arms.

Hadrian took a seat on one of the stools surrounding an open table. The modest area appeared to be the place where the kitchen staff ate their own meals. He tried to look casual and relaxed, but it was impossible with all the attention.

"What's all this now?" boomed a voice belonging to a large, beefy cook with a thick beard and eyes wreathed in cheerful wrinkles. Spotting Hadrian, those eyes narrowed abruptly. He revealed—if only for a moment—that he had another side, the same way a playful dog might suddenly growl at an intruder.

"Can I help you, sir?" he asked, approaching Hadrian with a meat cleaver in one hand.

"I don't mean any harm. I was just hoping to find some food."

The cook looked him over closely. "Are you a knight, sir?"

Hadrian nodded.

"Up early, I see. I'll have whatever you want brought to the great hall."

"Actually, I'd rather eat here. Is that okay?"

"I'm sorry?" the cook said, confused. "If you don't mind me asking, why would a fine nobleman like yourself want to eat in a hot, dirty kitchen surrounded by the clang of pots and the gibbering of maids?"

"I just feel more comfortable here," Hadrian said. "I think a man ought to be at ease when eating. Of course, if it's a problem..." He stood.

"You're Sir Hadrian, aren't you? I haven't found the time to see the jousts, but as you can see, most of my staff has. You're quite the celebrity. I've heard all kinds of stories about you and your recent change in fortune. Are any of them true?"

"Well, I can't say about the stories, but my name is Hadrian."

"Nice to meet you. Name's Ibis Thinly. Have a seat, sir. I'll fix you right up."

He hurried away, scolding his crew to return to work. Many continued to glance over at Hadrian, stealing looks when they felt the head cook could not see. In a short while, Ibis returned with a plate of chicken, fried eggs, and biscuits and a mug of dark beer. The chicken was so hot that it hurt Hadrian's fingers, and the biscuits steamed when he pulled them open.

"I appreciate this," Hadrian told Ibis, taking a bite of biscuit.

Ibis gave him a surprised look and then chuckled. "By Mar! Thanking a cook for food! Them stories *are* true, aren't they?"

Hadrian shrugged. "I guess I have a hard time remembering that I'm noble. When I was a commoner, I always knew what noble meant, but now, not so much."

The cook smiled. "Lady Amilia has the same problem. I gotta say it's nice to see decent folk getting ahead in this world. The news is you've ruled the field at Highcourt. Beat every knight who rode against you. I even heard you opened the tournament by tilting against Sir Murthas without a helm!"

Hadrian nodded with a mouthful of chicken, which he shifted from side to side, trying to avoid a burnt tongue.

"When a man does that," Ibis went on, "and comes from the salt like the rest of us, he wins favor among the lower classes. Yes, indeed. Those of us with dirty faces and sweaty backs get quite a thrill from one such as you, sir."

Hadrian did not know how to respond and contented himself with swallowing his chicken. He had ridden to the sound of roaring crowds every time he had competed, but Hadrian was not there for applause. His task was dark, secret, and not worthy of praise. He had unsaddled five knights and, by the rules of the contest, owned their mounts. Hadrian had declined that privilege. He had no need for the horses, but it was more than just that—he did not deserve them. All he wanted was the lives of Arista and Gaunt. In his mind, the whole affair was tainted. Taking anything else from his victories—even the pleasure of success—would be wrong. Nevertheless, the crowds cheered each time he refused his right to a mount, believing him humble and chivalrous instead of what he was—a murderer in waiting.

"It's just you and Breckton now, isn't it?" Ibis asked.

Hadrian nodded gloomily. "We tilt tomorrow. There's some sort of hunt today."

"Oh yes, the hawking. I'll be roasting plenty of game birds for tonight's feast. Say, aren't you going?"

"Just here for the joust," Hadrian managed to say even though his mouth was full again.

Ibis bent his head to get a better look. "For a new knight on the verge of winning the Wintertide Highcourt Tournament, you don't seem very happy. It's not the food, I hope."

Hadrian shook his head. "Food's great. Kinda hoping you'll let me eat my midday meal here too."

"You're welcome anytime. Ha! Listen to me sounding like an innkeeper or castle lord. I'm just a cook." He hooked a thumb over his shoulder. "Sure, these mongrels quiver at my voice, but you're a knight. You can go wherever you please. Still...if my food has placed you in a charitable mood, I would ask one favor."

"What's that?"

"Lady Amilia holds a special place in my heart. She's like a daughter to me. A sweet, sweet lass, and it seems she's recently taken a liking to Sir Breckton. He's good, mind you, a fine lancer, but from what I've heard, you're likely to beat him. Now, I'm not saying anything against you—someone of my station would be a fool to even insinuate such a thing—but..."

"But?"

"Well, some knights try to inflict as much damage as they can, taking aim at a visor and such. If something were to happen to Breckton...Well, I just don't want Amilia to get hurt. She's never had much, you see. Comes from a poor family and has worked hard all her life. Even now, that bas—I mean, Regent Saldur—keeps her slaving night and day. But even so, she's been happy lately, and I'd like to see that continue."

Hadrian kept his eyes on his plate, concentrating on mopping up yolk with a crust of bread.

"So anyway, if at all possible, it'd be real nice if you went a bit easy on Breckton. So he doesn't get hurt, I mean. I know a'course that you can't always help it. Dear Maribor, I know that. But I can tell by talking with you that you're a decent fellow. Ha! I don't even know why I brought it up. You'll do the right thing. I can tell. Here, let me get you some more beer."

Ibis Thinly walked away, taking Hadrian's mug and appetite with him.

≈

In many ways Amilia felt like a child Saldur had brought into the world that day in the kitchen when he had elevated her to the rank of lady. Now she was little more than a toddler, still trying to master simple tasks and often making mistakes. No one said anything. No one pointed and laughed, but there were knowing looks and partially hidden smiles. She felt out of her element when trying to navigate the numerous traps and hazards of courtly life without a map.

When addressed as *my lady* by a finely dressed noble, Amilia felt uncomfortable. Seeing a guard snap to attention at her passing was strange. Especially since those same soldiers had grinned lewdly at her little more than a year earlier. Amilia was certain the guards still leered and the nobles still laughed, but now they did so behind polite eyes. She believed the only means of banishing the silent snickers was to fit in. If Amilia did not stumble as she walked, spill a glass of wine, speak too loudly, wear the wrong color, laugh when she should remain quiet, or remain quiet when she should laugh, then they might forget she used to scrub their dishes. Any time Amilia interacted with the nobility was an ordeal, but when she did so in an unfamiliar setting, she became ill. For this reason, Amilia avoided eating anything the morning of the hawking.

The whole court embarked on the daylong event. Knights, nobles, ladies, and servants all rode out together to the forest and field for the great hunt. Dogs trotted in their wake. Amilia had never sat on a horse before. She had never ridden a pony, a mule, or even an ox, but that day she found herself precariously balanced atop a massive white charger. She wore the beautiful white gown and matching cape Lady Genevieve had provided her, which, by no accident, perfectly matched her horse's coat. Her right leg was hooked between two horns of the saddle and her left foot rested on a planchette. Sitting this way made staying on the animal's back a demanding enterprise. Each jerk and turn set her heart pounding and her hands grasping for the charger's braided mane. On several occasions, she nearly toppled backward. Amilia imagined that if she were to fall, she would wind up hanging by her trapped leg, skirt over her head, while the horse pranced proudly about. The thought terrified her so much that she barely breathed and sat rigid with her eyes fixed on the ground below. For the two-hour ride into the wilderness, Amilia did not speak a word. She dared to look up only when the huntsman called for the party's attention.

They emerged from the shade of a forest into the light of a field. Tall brown rushes jutted from beneath the snow's cover. The flicker of morning sunlight was reflected by moving water where a river cut the landscape. Lacking any wind, the world was oddly quiet. The huntsman directed them to line up by spreading out along the edge of the forest and facing the marsh.

Amilia was pleased to arrive at what she hoped was their destination and proud of how she had managed to direct her horse without delay or mishap. Finally at a standstill, she allowed herself a breath of relief only to see the falconer approaching.

"What bird will you be using today, my lady?" he asked, looking up at her from within his red coif. His hands were encased in thick gloves.

She swallowed. "Ah...what would you suggest?"

The falconer appeared surprised, and Amilia felt as if she had done something wrong.

"Well, my lady, there are many birds but no set regulation. Tradition usually reserves the gyrfalcon for a king, a falcon for a prince or duke, the peregrine for an earl, a bastard hawk for a baron, a saker for a knight, a goshawk for a noble, tercel for a poor man, sparrow hawk for a priest, kestrel for a servant, and a merlin for a lady, but in practice it is more a matter of—"

"She will be using Murderess," the Duchess of Rochelle announced, trotting up beside them.

"Of course, Your Ladyship." The falconer bowed his head and made a quick motion with his hand. A servant raced up with a huge hooded bird held on his fist. "Your gauntlet, milady," the falconer said, holding out a rough elk-hide glove.

"You'll want to put that on your left hand, darling," the duchess said with a reassuring smile and mischievous glint in her eyes.

Amilia felt her heart flutter as she took the glove and pulled it on.

"Hold your hand up, dear. Out away from your face," Lady Genevieve instructed.

The falconer took the raptor from the servant and carried her over. The hawk was magnificent and blinded by a leather hood with a short decorative plume. While being transferred to Amilia, Murderess spread her massive wings and flapped twice as her powerful talons took hold of the glove. The hawk was lighter than she had expected, and Amilia had no trouble holding her up. Still, Amilia's fear of falling was replaced by her fear of the bird. She watched in terror as the falconer wrapped the jess around her wrist, tethering her to the hawk.

"Beautiful bird," Amilia heard a voice say.

"Yes, it is," she replied. Looking over to see Sir Breckton taking station on her left, Amilia thought she might faint.

"It's the Duchess of Rochelle's. She—" Amilia turned. The duchess had moved off, abandoning her. Panic made her stomach lurch. As friendly as Lady Genevieve was, Amilia was starting to suspect the woman enjoyed tormenting her.

Amilia tried to calm herself as she sat face to face with the one man in the entire world she wanted to impress. With one hand holding the bird and the other locked on to the horse's reins, she realized the cold was causing her nose to run. She could not imagine the day getting any worse. Then, as if the gods had heard her thoughts, they answered using the huntsman's voice.

"Everyone! Ride forward!"

*Oh dear Maribor!*

Her horse tripped on the rough, frost-heaved ground, throwing her off balance. The sudden jolt also startled Murderess, who threw out her great wings to save herself by flying. Tethered to Amilia's wrist, the hawk pulled on her arm. She might have stayed in the saddle—if not for the bird's insistence on dragging her backward.

Amilia cried out as she fell over the rump of the horse, her nightmare becoming reality. Yet before she cleared the saddle, she stopped. Sir Breckton had caught her around the waist. Though he wore no armor, his arm felt like a band of steel—solid and unmovable. Gently, he drew her upright. The bird flapped twice more, then settled down and gripped Amilia's glove again.

Breckton did not say a word. He held Amilia steady until she reseated herself on the saddle and placed her foot on the planchette. Horrified and flushed with humiliation, she refused to look at him.

*Why did that have to happen in front of him!*

She did not want to see his face and find the same condescending smirk she had seen on so many others. On the verge of tears, she wanted desperately to be back at the palace, back in the kitchen, back to cleaning pots. At that moment she preferred the thought of facing Edith Mon—or even her vengeful ghost—to that of enduring the humiliation of facing Sir Breckton. Feeling tears gathering, she clenched her jaw and breathed deeply in an effort to hold them back.

"Does it have a name?"

Sir Breckton's words were so unexpected that Amilia replayed them twice before understanding the question.

"Murderess," she replied, thanking Maribor that her voice did not crack.

"That seems...appropriate." There was a pause before he continued. "Beautiful day, isn't it?"

"Yes." She tasked her brain to think of something to add, but it came back with nothing.

*Why is he talking like that? Why is he asking about the weather?*

The knight sighed heavily.

Looking up at him, she found he was not smirking but appeared pained. His eyes accidentally met hers while she studied his face, and he instantly looked away. His fingers drummed a marching cadence on his saddle horn.

"Cold, though," he said, and quickly added, "Could be warmer, don't you think?"

"Yes," she said again, realizing she must sound like an idiot with all her one-word answers. She wanted to say more. She wanted to be witty and clever, but her brain was as frozen as the ground.

Amilia caught him glancing at her again. This time he shook his head and sighed once more.

"What?" she asked fearfully.

"I don't know how you do it," he said.

The genuine admiration in his eyes only baffled her further.

"You ride a warhorse sidesaddle over rough ground with a huge hawk perched on your arm and are still managing to make me feel like a squire in a fencing match. My lady, you are a marvel beyond reckoning. I am in awe."

Amilia stared at him until she realized she was staring at him. In her mind, she ordered her eyes to look away, but they refused. She had no words to reply, which hardly mattered, as Amilia had no air in her body with which to speak. Breathing seemed unimportant at that moment. Forcing herself to take a breath, Amilia discovered she was smiling. A second later, she knew Sir Breckton noticed as well, as he abruptly stopped drumming and sat straighter.

"Milady," said the falconer's servant, "it's time to release your bird."

Amilia looked at the raptor, wondering just how she was going to do that.

"May I help?" Sir Breckton asked. Reaching over, he removed Murderess's hood and unwound her tether.

With a motion of his own arm, the servant indicated that she should thrust her hand up. Amilia did so, and Murderess spread her great wings, pushed down, and took to the sky. The raptor climbed higher and higher yet remained circling directly overhead. As she watched the goshawk, Amilia noticed Breckton looking at her.

"Don't you have a bird?" she asked.

"No. I did not expect to be hawking. Truth be told, I haven't hunted in years. I'd forgotten the joy of it — until now."

"So you know how?"

"Oh yes. Of course. I used to hunt the fields of Chadwick as a lad. My father, my brother Wesley, and I would spend whole weeks chasing fowl from their nests and rodents from their burrows."

"Would you think ill of me if I told you this was my first time?"

Breckton's face turned serious, which frightened her until he said, "My lady, be assured that should I live so long as to see the day that the sun does not rise, the rivers do not flow, and the winds do not blow, I would *never* think ill of you."

She tried to hide another smile. Once more, she failed, and once more, Sir Breckton noticed.

"Perhaps you can help me, as I am befuddled by all of this," Amilia said, gesturing at their surroundings.

"It is a simple thing. The birds are *waiting on*—that is to say, hovering overhead and waiting for the attack. Much the way soldiers stand in line preparing for battle. The enemies are a crafty bunch. They lay hiding before us in the field between the river and ourselves. With the line made by the horses, the huntsman has ensured that the prey will not come this way, which, of course, they would try to do—to reach the safety of the trees—were we not here."

"But how will we find these hidden enemies?"

"They need to be drawn out, or in this case *flushed* out. See there? The huntsman has gathered the dogs."

Amilia looked ahead as a crowd of eager dogs moved forward, led by a dozen boys from the palace. After they were turned loose, the hounds disappeared into the undergrowth. Only their raised tails appeared, here and there, above the bent rushes as they dashed into the snowy field without a bark or a yelp.

With a blue flag, the huntsman signaled to the falconer, who in turn waved to the riders. He indicated they should move slowly toward the river. With her bird gone, Amilia found it easier to control her horse and advanced along with the rest. Everyone was silent as they crept forward. Amilia felt excited, although she had no idea what was about to happen.

The falconer raised a hand and the riders stopped their horses. Looking up, Amilia saw the birds had matched their movement across the field. The falconer waved a red flag and the huntsman blew a whistle, which sent the dogs bursting forth. Immediately, the field exploded with birds. Loud thumping sounds erupted as quail broke from cover, racing skyward. In their efforts to evade the monstrous dogs, they never saw the death awaiting them in the sky. Hawks swooped down out of the sun, slamming into their targets and bearing them to the ground. One bore its prey all the way to the river, where both hawk and quail hit the water.

"That was Murderess!" Amilia shouted, horrified. Her mind filled with the realization that she had killed Lady Genevieve's prized bird. Without thinking, she kicked her horse, which leapt forward. She galloped across the field and, as she neared the river, spotted a dog swimming out into the icy water. Another quickly followed in its wake. Two birds flapped desperately on the surface, kicking up a white spray.

Just before Amilia charged headlong into the river, Breckton caught her horse by the bit and pulled them both to a halt.

"Wait!"

"But the bird!" was all Amilia could say. Her eyes locked on the splashing.

"It's all right," he assured her. "Watch."

The first dog reached Murderess and, without hesitation, took the hawk in its jaws. Holding the raptor up, the hound circled and swam back. At the same time, the second dog raced out to collect the downed prey. The quail struggled, but Amilia was amazed that the hawk did not fight when the dog set its teeth.

"You see," Breckton said, "dogs and birds are trained to trust and protect one another. Just like soldiers."

The hound climbed out of the water still holding the hawk. Both Amilia and Breckton dismounted as the dog brought the bird to them. Gently, the animal opened its jaws and Murderess hopped onto Amilia's fist once more. She stretched out her wings and snapped them, spraying water.

"She's all right!" Amilia said, amazed.

A boy ran up to her, holding out a dead bird by a string tied around its feet. "Your quail, milady."

✧

When Hadrian returned later that day, Ibis Thinly was waiting with more than just a plate. The entire table was laden with a variety of meats, cheeses, and breads. The scullery had been cleaned such that extra sacks were removed, shelves dusted, and the floor mopped. The table was set with fresh candles, and a larger, cushioned chair replaced the little stool. He guessed not all of this was strictly Ibis's doing. Apparently, word of his visit had spread. Twice as many servants populated the kitchen as had that morning—most standing idle.

Ibis did not speak to Hadrian this time. The cook was feverishly busy dealing with the flood of game brought in by nobles returning from the hunt. Already maids were plucking away at quail, pheasant, and duck from a long line of beheaded birds that was strung around the room like a garland. With so much to process, even Ibis himself skinned rabbits and squirrels. Despite his obvious urgency, the cook immediately stopped working when Amilia arrived.

"Ibis! Look! I got two!" she shouted, holding the birds above her head. She entered the kitchen dressed in a lovely white gown and matching fur cape.

"Bring them here, lass. Let me see these treasures."

Hadrian had seen Lady Amilia from a distance at each of the feasts, but this was the first time he had seen her up close since he had posed as a courier. She was prettier than he remembered. Her clothes were certainly better. Whether it was the spring in her step or the flush in her cheeks brought on by the cold, she appeared more alive.

"These are clearly the pick of the lot," Ibis said after inspecting her trophies.

"They're scrawny and small, but they're *mine*!" She followed the declaration with a carefree, happy laugh.

"Can I infer from your mood that you did not hunt alone?"

Amilia said nothing and merely smiled. Clasping her hands behind her back, she sashayed about the kitchen, swinging her skirt.

"Come now, girl. Don't toy with me."

She laughed again, spun around, and announced, "He was at my side almost the whole day. A *perfect* gentleman, I might add, and I think..." She hesitated.

"Think what? Out with it, lass."

"I think he may fancy me."

"Bah! Of course he fancies you. But what did the man say? Did he speak plainly? Did he spout verse? Did he kiss you right there on the field?"

"*Kiss me?* He's *far* too proper for such vulgarity, but he was *very* nervous...silly, even. And he couldn't seem to take his eyes off me!"

"Silly? Sir Breckton? Ah, lass, you've got him hooked. You have. A fine catch, I must say, a fine catch indeed."

Amilia could not contain herself and laughed again, this time throwing back her head in elation and twirling her gown. Doing so, she caught sight of Hadrian and halted.

"Sorry, I'm just having a late lunch," he said. "I'll be gone in a minute."

"Oh no. You don't have to leave. It's just that I didn't see you. Other than the staff, I'm the only one who ever comes down here—or so I thought."

"It's more comfortable than the hall," Hadrian said. "I

spend my days tilting with the knights. I don't feel like competing with them at meals too."

She walked over, looking puzzled. "You don't talk like a knight."

"That's Sir Hadrian," Ibis informed Amilia.

"Oh!" she exclaimed. "You helped Sir Breckton and my poor Nimbus when they were attacked. That was very kind. You're also the one who rode in the tournament without a helm. You've—you've unseated every opponent on the first pass and haven't had a single lance broken on your shield. You're...very good, aren't you?"

"And he's riding against Sir Breckton tomorrow for the championship," Ibis reminded her.

"That's right!" She gasped, raising a hand to her lips. "Have you *ever* been unseated?"

Hadrian shrugged self-consciously. "Not since I've been a knight."

"Oh, I wasn't—I didn't mean to—I just wondered if it hurt terribly. I guess it can't feel good. Even with all that armor and padding, being driven from a galloping horse by a pole must not be pleasant." Her eyes grew troubled. "But all the other knights are fine, aren't they? I saw Sir Murthas and Sir Elgar on the hawking just today. They were trotting and laughing, so I'm certain everything will be all right no matter who wins.

"I know tomorrow is the final tilt and winning the tournament is a great honor. I understand firsthand the desire to prove yourself to those who look down on you. But I ask you to consider that Sir Breckton is a good man—a very good man. He would never hurt you if he could help it. I hope you feel the same." She struggled to smile at Hadrian.

He put down the bread he was eating as a sickening

sensation churned his stomach. Hadrian had to stop eating in
the kitchen.

~

The acrobats rapidly assembled their human pyramid. Vaulting one at a time into the air, they somersaulted before each
landed feetfirst on the shoulders of the one below. One after
another they flew, continuing to build the formation until the
final man reached up and touched the ceiling of the great hall.
Despite the danger involved in the exciting performance,
Amilia was not watching. She had seen the act before at the
audition and rehearsals. Her eyes were on the audience. As
Wintertide neared, the entertainment at each feast became
grander and more extravagant.

Amilia held her breath until the hall erupted in applause.
*They liked it!*

Looking for Viscount Winslow, she spotted him clapping,
his hands above his head. The two exchanged wide grins.

"I thought I would die from stress toward the end," Nimbus whispered from the seat next to Amilia. The bruises on
the tutor's face were mostly gone and the annoying whistling
sound had finally left his nose.

"Yes, that was indeed excellent," said King Roswort of
Dunmore.

At each feast, Nimbus always sat to Amilia's left and the
queen and king sat to her right.

King Roswort was huge. He made the Duke and Duchess
of Rochelle appear petite. His squat, portly build was
mimicked—in miniature—in his face, which sagged under its
own weight. Amilia imagined that even if he were thin, King
Roswort would still sag like an old riding horse. His wife,
Freda, while no reed herself, was thin by comparison. She was

dry and brittle both in looks and manner. The couple were fortunately quiet most of the time, at least until their third glasses of wine. Amilia lost count that evening but assumed number three had arrived and perhaps already gone.

"Are the acrobats friends of yours?" the king asked, leaning around his wife to speak to Amilia.

"Mine? No, I merely hired them," she said.

"Friends of friends, then?"

She shook her head.

"But you know them?" the king pressed further.

"I met them for the first time at the auditions."

"Rossie," Freda said. "She's clearly trying to distance herself from them now that the doors of nobility are open to her. You can't blame her for that. Anyone would abandon the wretches. Leave them in the street. That's where they belong."

"But I—" Amilia began before the king cut her off.

"But, my queen, many are rising in rank. Some street merchants are as wealthy as nobles now."

"Terrible state of affairs," Freda snarled through thin, red-painted lips. "A title isn't what it used to be."

"I agree, my queen. Why, some knights have no lineage at all to speak of. They are no better than peasants with swords. All anyone needs these days is money to buy armor and a horse, and there you have it—presto—a noble. Commoners are even learning to read. Can you read, Lady Amilia?"

"Actually, I can."

"See!" The king threw his hands up. "Of course, you are in the nobility now, but I assume you learned letters before that? It's a travesty. I don't know what the world is coming to."

"At least the situation with the elves has improved," his wife put in. "You have to give Ethelred credit for reducing their numbers. Our efforts to deal with them in Dunmore have met with little success."

"Deal with them?" Amilia asked, but the monarchs continued under their own momentum.

"If they had any intelligence, they would leave on their own. How much plainer can it be that they are not welcome?" the king said. "The guilds prohibit them from membership in any business, they can't obtain citizenship in any city, and the church declared them unclean enemies of Novron ages ago. Even the peasants are free to take measures against them. Still, they don't take the hint. They keep breeding and filling up slums. Hundreds die each year in church-sanctioned Cleansing Days, but they persist. Why not move on? Why not go elsewhere?"

As the king ran out of breath, the queen took over. "They are like rats, festering in every crack. Living among their kind is a curse. It's what brought down the first empire, you know. Even keeping them as slaves was a mistake. And mark my words, if we don't get rid of them all, so that not a single elf walks a civilized street or country lane, this empire will fall to the same ruin."

"True, true, the old emperors were too soft. They thought that they could *fix* them—"

"Fix them!" Freda erupted. "What a ridiculous notion. You can't fix a plague. You can only run from it or wipe it out."

"I know, darling, I agree with you wholeheartedly. We have a second chance now, and Ethelred is off to a good start."

Realizing that the king and queen ran through a conversation as familiar and comfortable to them as a pair of well-worn shoes, Amilia nodded politely without really listening. She had seen elves only once in her life. When she had still been living in Tarin Vale, three of them had come to the village—a family, if they had such notions of kinship. Apparently content to dress in rags, they were dirty and carried small, stained bundles, which Amilia guessed were all they had. They were so thin they looked sick, and walked with their heads bowed and shoulders slumped.

Children had called the elves names and villagers had thrown stones and shouted for them to leave. A rock struck the female's head and she cried out. Amilia did not throw any rocks, but she watched as the family was bruised and bloodied before they fled from town. At the time, she did not understand how they could be a threat. The monk who had been teaching her letters explained elves were responsible for the downfall of the empire. They had seemed helpless, and Amilia could not help feeling sorry for them.

Roswort concluded his tirade by accusing the elves of being responsible for the drought two years before, and Amilia caught Nimbus rolling his eyes.

"You don't share their opinions?" she whispered.

"It's not my place to counter the words of a king, milady," the courtier responded politely.

"True, but I sometimes wonder just what goes on under that wig of yours. Something tells me there's more than courtly etiquette rattling around."

Off to Amilia's right, Roswort and Freda had moved on. "Dwarves aren't much better, but at least they have skills," the king was saying. "Fine stonemasons and jewelers, I'll give them that, but niggardly as an autumn squirrel facing an early snow, the entire lot of them. They can't be trusted. Any one of them would slit your throat to steal two copper tenents. They stick to their own kind and whisper their outlawed language. Living with dwarves is like trying to domesticate a wild animal, can't ever truly be done."

The conversation died down as another performance started. This time a pair of conjurers pulled apples and oddments from their sleeves, then juggled the items. When the act was over, and all the knives and goblets safely caught, Nimbus asked, "Doesn't the empress hail from your kingdom, Your Majesty?"

"Oh yes." Roswort perked up and nearly spilled his drink. "Lived right there in Dahlgren. What a terrible mess that was. Afterward, the deacon ran about babbling his tall tales—and no one believed him. I certainly didn't. Who would have thought that the Heir of Novron would come from that tiny dust speck?"

"How is it that we never see her?" the queen asked Amilia. "She *will* be at the wedding, won't she?"

"Of course, Your Majesty. The empress is saving her strength for just that. She's still quite weak."

"I see," the queen replied coolly. "Surely she is well enough by now to admit guests. Several of the ladies feel it has been most unseemly the way she has been ignoring us. I would very much like a personal audience with her before the ceremony."

"I am afraid that's really not up to me. I only follow her directions."

"How can you follow her directions on something I have just now suggested? Are you a mind reader?"

"Who would have expected Sir Hadrian to be in the finals of the tournament?" Nimbus said loudly. "I certainly didn't think a novice would be challenging for the title tomorrow. And against Sir Breckton! You must admit Lady Amilia certainly backed the right arm-and-shield there. Who are you favoring, Your Majesty?"

Roswort pursed his lips. "I find both of them disagreeable. The whole tournament has been too tame for my taste. I prefer the theatrics of Elgar and Gilbert. They know how to play to a crowd. This year's finalists are as solemn as monks, and neither has done anything other than unseat their opponents. That's bad form, if you ask me. Knights are trained for war.

They should instinctually seek to kill rather than merely bust a pole on a reinforced plate. I think they should be required to use war tips. Do that, and you'll see something worth watching!"

When the last performance finished, the lord chamberlain rapped his brass-tipped staff on the flagstones and Ethelred stood. Conversations trailed off as the banquet hall fell silent.

"My friends," Lanis Ethelred began in his most powerful voice, "I address you as such to assure you that even though you will soon be my loyal subjects, I will always think of you, first and foremost, as my friends. We have weathered a long hard struggle together. Centuries of darkness, hardship, barbarianism, and threats from Nationalists have plagued us. But in just two days' time, the sun will dawn on a new age. This Wintertide we celebrate the rebirth of civilization—the start of a new era. As our lord Maribor has seen fit to bestow onto me the crown of supreme power, I will pledge to be faithful to his design and lead mankind armed with the firm hand of righteousness. I will return to traditional values in order to make the New Empire a beacon to light the world and blind our enemies."

The hall applauded.

"I hope you all enjoyed your game birds, courtesy of the hawking. Tomorrow the finalists of the joust will tilt for the honor of best knight. I hope you will all enjoy the contest between two such capable men. Sir Breckton, Sir Hadrian— where are you?—please stand, both of you." The two knights hesitantly rose to their feet, and the audience applauded. "A toast to the elite of the New Empire!"

Ethelred, along with everyone else in the hall, drank in their honor. The regent sat back down, and Amilia motioned to the musicians to take their places.

As on the previous nights, couples took to the open floor to dance. Amilia spotted Sir Breckton, dressed in a silver tunic, striding her way. When he reached the head table, he bowed before her.

"Excuse me, my lady. Might I enjoy the pleasure of your company for the dance?"

Amilia's heart beat quickly at his invitation, and she could not think clearly. Before remembering that she could not dance, she stood, walked around the table, and offered her hand.

Taking it, the knight gently led her to where pairs of dancers formed into lines. Accompanying him in such an intimate setting felt like a dream. When the first notes of music hit the air, that dream turned to a nightmare. Amilia had no idea what to do. She had watched the dances the past several evenings but not to learn their steps. All she could recall was that the dance started in rows and ended in rows, and at some point in the middle, the dancers touched hands and traded places several times in rapid succession. All other details were a mystery. For a moment, Amilia considered returning to the security of her chair, but to do so now would embarrass her and humiliate Breckton. Light-headed, she hovered on the verge of fainting but managed a curtsy in response to Breckton's bow.

Nothing could save her from the pending disaster. In her mind played a scene, in which she staggered, tripped, and fell. The other nobles would laugh and sneer while tears ran down her cheeks. She imagined them saying, *What possessed you to think you could be one of us?* Not even Breckton's calm gaze was able to reassure Amilia.

She shifted her weight from left to right, knowing some action would be required in a half bar of music. If only she knew which foot to use, she might manage the first step.

Suddenly the music stopped and the entire assemblage halted.

A hush fell as conversations died, replaced by scattered gasps. Everyone stood and all eyes were transfixed as into the great hall strode Her Most Serene and Royal Grand Imperial Eminence, Empress Modina Novronian.

Two fifth-floor guards flanked her as they crossed the hall. The empress was dressed in the formal gown she had worn for the speech on the balcony, the luxurious mantle trailing behind her. Modina's hair was pulled under a mesh cowl, upon which rested the imperial crown. She walked with stunning grace and dignity—chin high, shoulders squared, back straight. As she passed through the silent crowd, she appeared ethereal, like a mythical creature slipping through trees in a forest.

Amilia blinked several times, unsure what she was actually seeing and remained as transfixed as the others. The effect of Modina's appearance was astounding and was reflected by every face in the room. No one moved and few appeared to breathe.

Reaching the front of the room, Modina walked down the length of the main table to the imperial throne left vacant each of the previous nights. The empress paused briefly in front of her seat, raised a delicate hand, and simply said, "Continue."

There was a long pause, and then the musicians began to play once more. Saldur and Ethelred both glared at Amilia, who promptly excused herself from the dance. Her leaving the floor was quite understandable now, though she was sure it no longer mattered. Amilia doubted anyone, except perhaps Sir Breckton, noticed or cared.

She returned to the main table and stood behind Modina.

"Your Eminence, are you certain you are strong enough to be here? Wouldn't you like me to escort you back to your room?" she asked softly.

Modina did not look at Amilia. The empress's eyes scanned the room, taking in the revelry. "Thank you, my dear. You are so kind to inquire, but I am fine." Amilia exchanged glances with Ethelred and Saldur, both of whom looked tense and helpless.

"I think you should not be risking yourself so," Saldur told Modina. "You need to save your strength for your wedding."

"I am certain you are quite correct, Your Grace—as you always are—and I will not stay long. Still, my people deserve to see their empress. Maribor forbid that they come to suspect I don't exist at all. I am certain many couldn't distinguish me from a milkmaid. It would be a sad thing indeed if I arrived at my wedding and no one could tell the bride from the bridesmaids."

Saldur's look of bewilderment was replaced with a glare of anger.

Amilia remained behind the empress's chair, unsure what to do next. Modina tapped her fingers and nodded in rhythm with the music while watching the dance. By contrast, Saldur and Ethelred were as rigid as statues.

At the end of the song, Modina applauded and got to her feet. The moment she rose, all the guests stopped once more, fixing their eyes on her.

"Sir Breckton and Sir Hadrian, please approach," the empress commanded.

Saldur shot another concerned glance at Amilia, who could do nothing but clutch the back of Modina's chair.

The two knights came forward and stood side by side before the empress. Hadrian followed Breckton's lead, bending to one knee and bowing his head.

"Tomorrow you will compete for the glory of the empire, and Maribor will decide your fate. You are clearly both beloved by this court, but I see Sir Breckton wears the token of my secretary, Lady Amilia. This grants him an unfair advantage, but I will not ask him to refuse such a gift. Nor would I ask Lady Amilia to seek its return, as a favor once given is a sacred endorsement of faith. Instead, I will mirror her gesture by granting Sir Hadrian my token. I proclaim my faith in his skill, character, and sacred honor. I know his heart is righteous, and his intentions virtuous." Modina drew out a piece of pure white cloth that Amilia recognized as part of her nightgown, and held it out.

Hadrian took the cloth.

Modina continued, "May you both find honor in the eyes of Maribor and compete *as true and heroic knights*."

The empress clapped her hands and the hall followed her lead, erupting in cheers and shouts. In the midst of the thunder, Modina turned to Amilia and said, "You may escort me back to my room now."

The two walked down the length of the table. As they passed the Queen of Dunmore, Freda looked stricken. "Lady Amilia, what I said earlier—I—I didn't mean anything by that, I just—"

"I'm sure you meant no disrespect. Please sit, Your Majesty. You look pale," Amilia said to the queen, and led Modina out of the room. Saldur watched them go, and Amilia was thankful he did not follow. She knew there would be an interrogation, but she had no idea how to explain Modina's behavior. The empress had never done anything like this before.

Neither woman said anything as they walked arm in arm to the fifth floor. The door to Modina's bedchamber stood unguarded. "Where is Gerald?" Amilia asked.

"Who?" the empress replied with a blank look.

Amilia scowled. "You know very well who. Gerald. Why isn't he guarding your door? Did you send him on an errand to get him out of the way?"

"Yes, I did," the empress replied casually.

Amilia frowned. They entered the bedroom and she closed

the door behind them. "Modina, what were you thinking? Why did you do that?"

"Does it matter?" the empress replied, settling onto her bed with a soft bounce.

"It matters to the regents."

"It's only two days until Ethelred comes to my bedroom and takes me to the cathedral for our marriage. I did no damage. If anything, I reassured the nobles that I exist and am not just a myth created by the regents. They should thank me."

"That still doesn't explain why."

"I have only a few hours left and felt like getting out. Can you begrudge me this?"

The anger melted from Amilia and she shook her head. "No."

Ever since the mirror had appeared in Modina's room, the two had avoided discussing the empress's plans for Wintertide. Amilia considered having it removed, but knew that would not matter. Modina would just find another way. The secretary's only other alternative was to tell Saldur, but the regent would imprison the empress. The ordeal had nearly destroyed Modina once, and Amilia could not be responsible for inflicting that on her again—even to save the empress's life. There seemed to be no solution. Especially considering that if their places were reversed, Amilia would probably do the same thing. She had tried to delude herself into believing that Modina would change her mind, but the empress's words and the reminder of Wintertide's approach brought her back to reality.

Amilia helped Modina out of her gown, tucked the empress into the big bed, and hugged her tightly while trying to hide her tears.

Modina patted Amilia's head. "It will be all right. I am ready now."

❧

Hadrian trudged back to the knights' wing, carrying the white strip of cloth as if it weighed a hundred pounds. Seeing Thrace had removed one burden, but her words had replaced it with an even heavier load. He passed by the common room, where a handful of knights still lingered. They handed around a bottle, taking swigs from it.

"Hadrian!" Elgar shouted. The large man stepped into the hall, blocking his path. Elgar's face was rosy, and his nose red, but his eyes were clear and focused. "Missed you at the hawking today. Come on in and join us."

"Leave me alone, Elgar, I'm in no mood tonight."

"All the more reason to come have a drink with us." The big warrior grinned cheerfully, slapping Hadrian on the back.

"I'm going to sleep." Hadrian turned away.

Elgar gripped him by the arm. "Listen, my chest still hurts from when you drove me off my saddle."

"I'm sorry about that but—"

"Sorry?" Elgar looked at him, clearly confused. "Best clobbering I've taken in years. That's how I know you can take Breckton. I've wagered money on it. I thought you were a joke when you first showed up, but after that flying lesson... Well, if you're a joke, it's not a terribly funny one."

"You're apologizing?"

Elgar laughed. "Not in your lifetime! Summersrule is only six months away, and I'll have another chance to repay in kind. But just between you and me, I'm looking forward to seeing Sir Shiny eat some dirt. Sure you won't have a drink? Send you off to bed right proper?"

Hadrian shook his head.

"All right, go get your beauty rest. I'll keep the boys as

quiet as I can, even if I have to bash a few skulls. Good luck tomorrow, eh?"

Elgar returned to the common room, where at least two of the knights were trying to sing "The Old Duke's Daughter" and doing a terrible job of it. Hadrian continued to his room, opened the door, and froze.

"Good evening, Hadrian," Merrick Marius greeted him. He was dressed in an expensive crimson silk garnache. Around his neck was a golden chain of office. Merrick sat nonchalantly at the chamber's little table, upon which sat the chessboard from the common room. All the pieces were in their proper starting places except for a single white pawn, which was two spaces forward. "I have taken the liberty of making the first move."

The room was too small for anyone to hide in—they were alone. "What do you want?" Hadrian asked.

"I thought that was obvious. I want you to join me. It's your turn."

"I'm not interested in playing games."

"I think it is a bit presumptuous to consider this a mere game." Merrick's voice was paradoxically chilling and friendly, a mannerism Hadrian had witnessed many times before—in Royce.

Merrick's demeanor distressed him. Hadrian had learned to read a man by his tone, his body language, and the look in his eye, but Merrick was impossible to peg. He appeared completely relaxed, yet he should not be. Although larger and heavier than Royce, Merrick was not a big man. He did not look like a fighter, nor did he appear to be wearing any weapons. If Merrick was half as smart as Royce had suggested, he knew Hadrian could kill him. Given how he had manipulated them on the *Emerald Storm*, which had resulted in the death of Wesley Belstrad and the destruction of Tur Del Fur, Merrick should further know it was a real possibility, yet the man showed no sign of concern. It unnerved Hadrian and made him think he was missing something.

Hadrian took the seat across from Merrick and, after glancing at the board for only a moment, slid a pawn forward.

Merrick smiled with the eagerness of a small boy starting his favorite pastime. He moved another pawn, putting it in jeopardy, and Hadrian took it.

"Ah, so you accept the Queen's Gambit," Merrick said.

"Huh?"

"My opening moves. They are referred to as the Queen's Gambit. How you respond indicates acceptance or not. Your move has signaled the former."

"I just took a pawn," Hadrian said.

"You did both. Are you aware chess is known as the King's Game due to its ability to teach war strategy?"

Almost without thought, Merrick brought another pawn forward.

Hadrian did not reply as he looked at the board. His father had taught him the game when he was a boy to strengthen Hadrian's understanding of tactics and planning. Danbury Blackwater had made a board and set of pieces from metal scraps. His father had been the best chess player in the village. It had taken years for Hadrian finally to checkmate him.

"Of course, the game has broader implications," Merrick went on. "I've heard bishops base whole sermons on chess. They draw parallels indicating how the pieces represent the hierarchy of the classes, and the rules of movement depict an individual's duty as ordained by God."

Merrick's third pawn was in jeopardy, and Hadrian took it as well. Merrick moved his bishop, again without pause. The man's playing style disturbed Hadrian, as he expected more contemplation after Hadrian had taken two of his pieces.

"So you see, what you deem a simple, frivolous game is actually a mirror to the world around us and how we move in it. For example, did you know that pawns were not always allowed to move two squares at the start? That advent was the result of progress and a slipping of monarchial power. Furthermore, upon reaching the opposite side of the board, pawns used to only be promoted to the rank of councilor, which is the second-weakest piece, after the pawn itself."

"Speaking of pawns…We didn't appreciate you using us at Tur Del Fur," Hadrian said.

Merrick raised a hand. "Royce has already scolded me on that score."

"Royce—he spoke to you?"

Merrick chuckled. "Surprised I'm still alive? Royce and I have a…an understanding. To him I am like that bishop on the board. I'm right there—an easy target—and yet the cost is too high."

"I don't understand."

"You wouldn't."

"You tricked us into helping you slaughter hundreds of innocent people. Royce has killed for far less."

Merrick looked amused. "True, Royce usually requires a reason *not* to kill. But don't deceive yourself. He's not like you. The deaths of innocents, no matter how many, are meaningless to him. He just doesn't like being used. No, I would venture to say that only one murder has ever caused him to suffer remorse, and that is why I'm still alive. Royce feels the scales are not balanced between us. He feels he still owes me."

Merrick gestured toward himself. "Were you waiting on me? I believe it's your move."

Hadrian decided to be more daring and pulled out his queen to threaten Merrick's king. Merrick moved instantly, sliding his king out of harm's way, almost before Hadrian removed his hand.

"Now where was I?" Merrick continued. "Oh yes, the evolution of chess, which changes just as the world does. Centuries ago there was no such thing as castling, and a stalemate was considered a win for the player causing it. Most telling, I think, is the changing role of the queen in the game."

Hadrian brought forward a pawn to threaten the bishop, and Merrick promptly took it. Hadrian moved his knight out and Merrick did the same.

"Originally there was no queen at all, as all the pieces were male. Instead, a piece called the king's chief minister held that position. It wasn't until much later that the female queen replaced this piece. Back then she was restricted to moving only one square diagonally, which made her quite weak. It wasn't until later that she obtained the ability to move the entire length of the board in any direction, thus becoming the most powerful piece in the game—and the most coveted target to trap or kill."

Hadrian started to move his bishop but stopped when he realized that Merrick's knight was threatening his queen.

"That was an interesting speech the empress delivered at the feast, don't you think?" Merrick asked. "Why do you think she did that?"

"No idea," Hadrian replied, studying the board.

Merrick smiled at him. "I see why Royce likes you. You're not big on conversation. You two are quite the odd pairing, aren't you? Royce and I are far more similar. We each maintain a common pragmatic view of the world and those in it, but you are more an idealist and dreamer. You look like an ale drinker to me, and Royce prefers his Montemorcey."

Another quick succession of moves made Hadrian slow down his play and left him studying the board.

"Did you know I introduced him to that particular wine? That was years ago, when I brought him a case for his birthday. Well, that's not precisely correct. Royce has no idea about the actual date of his birth. Still, it could have been, so we celebrated like it was. I liberated the wine from a Vandon caravan loaded with merchandise, and we spent three whole days drinking and debauching a tiny agrarian village. That town had a surprisingly large proportion of attractive maids. I had never seen Royce drunk before that. He's usually so serious— all dark and brooding—or at least he was back then. For those three days he relaxed and we had arguably the best time of our lives."

Hadrian focused on the board.

"We were quite the team back in our day. I'd plan the jobs and he'd execute them. We had quite a contest going. I tried to see if I could invent a challenge too difficult, but he always surprised me. His skills are legendary. Of course, back then the shackles of morality didn't weigh him down. That's your doing, I suppose. You tamed the demon, or at least think you have."

Hadrian found Merrick's conversation irritating and realized that was the point. He moved his queen to safety. Merrick innocently, almost absentmindedly, slid a pawn forward.

"It's still there, though—the demon within—hiding; you can't change the nature of someone like Royce. In Calis they try to tame lions, did you know that? They take them as cubs and raise them in palaces as pets for princes. They think them safe until one day the family dogs are gone. 'Perhaps the dogs warranted it,' the love-struck prince says. 'Perhaps the hounds attacked the cat or antagonized it,' he says as he strokes his loyal beast. The next day they find the carcass of the prince in a tree. No, my friend, you can't tame a wild animal. Eventually it will return to its true nature."

Hadrian made a series of moves that succeeded in taking the white bishop. He could not determine if Merrick was just toying with him or was not nearly as good at the game as Hadrian had expected.

"Does he ever speak of me?" asked Merrick.

"You sound like an abandoned mistress."

Merrick sat straighter and adjusted the front of his tunic. "You've had a chance to see Breckton joust. Is there any doubt about whether you can defeat him?"

"No."

"That's good. But now comes the important question... will you?"

"I made an agreement, didn't I? You were there."

Merrick leaned forward. "I know you—or at least your type. You're having second thoughts. You don't think it's right to kill an innocent man. You've met Breckton. He's impressive. The kind of man you want to be. You're hating yourself right now, and you hate me because you think I helped arrange it. Only I didn't. I have no part in this—well, beyond suggesting they offer you the princess. Whether you want to thank me or kill me for that, I'd just like to point out that at the time you were threatening to kill everyone in the room."

"So if this is none of your business, then why are you here?"

"I need Royce to do another job for me—an important one—and he'll be far less inclined if you die, which you will if you don't kill Breckton. If, however, you keep your promise, everything should work out nicely. So I've come to affirm what you already know, and what Royce would tell you if he were here. You *must* kill Breckton. Keep in mind you will be trading the life of the most capable enemy of Melengar for its princess and the leader of the Nationalists. Together, they could revitalize the resistance. And let's not forget your legacy. This is your one chance to correct the sin of your father and bring peace to his spirit. If nothing else, don't you think you owe Danbury that much?"

"How do you know about that?"

Merrick merely smiled.

"You're a smug bastard, aren't you?" Hadrian glared at him. "But you don't know everything."

Hadrian reached out to move, but Merrick raised a hand and stopped him.

"You're about to take my rook with your bishop. After that, you will take the other with your queen. How can you not? The poor castle is completely undefended. You'll be feeling quite pleased with yourself at that point. You'll be thinking that I don't play this game anywhere near as well as you expected. What you won't realize is that while you have gained materially, you've systematically given up control of the board. You'll have more troops but discover too late that you can't effectively mount an attack. I will sacrifice my queen. You will have no choice but to kill her. By that time, I will be perfectly positioned to reach your king. In the end, you will have taken a bishop, two rooks, and my queen, but none of this will matter. I will checkmate you on the twenty-second turn by moving my remaining bishop to king's seven." Merrick stood and moved toward the door. "You've already lost, but you lack the foresight to see it. That's your problem. I, on the other hand, do not suffer from that particular malady. I am telling you for your own good, for Royce's sake, for Arista, Gaunt, and even for your father—you must kill Sir Breckton. Good night, Hadrian."

## Chapter 16

# Trials by Combat

The sky was overcast, the day a dull gray, and the wind blew a chilled blast across the stands. And yet the crowd at Highcourt was larger and louder than ever. The entire imperial court, and most of the town, had turned out to see the spectacle. Every inch of the bleachers was jammed, and a sea of bodies pushed against the fence. On the staging field only the blue and gold tent of Sir Breckton and the green and white tent of Sir Hadrian remained.

Hadrian arrived early that morning alongside Renwick, who went right to work feeding and brushing Malevolent. Hadrian did not want to be in the palace and risk an encounter with Breckton, Amilia, or Merrick. All he wanted was to be left alone and for this day to be over.

"Hadrian!" a strangely familiar voice called. Along the fence line, he spotted a man amidst the crowd waving at him while a pike-armed guard held him back. "It's me, Russell Bothwick from Dahlgren!"

Leaving Renwick to finish dressing Malevolent, Hadrian walked over to the fence to get a better look. As he did, his shadows from the palace moved closer.

Hadrian shook Russell's hand. His wife, Lena, and his son

Tad stood next to Hadrian's old host. Behind them was Dillon McDern, the town smith, who had once helped Hadrian build bonfires to fend off a monster.

"Let them through," Hadrian told the guard.

"Look at you!" Dillon exclaimed as they passed under the rail to join Hadrian at his tent. "Too bad Theron's not here. He'd be braggin' about how he had taken fencing lessons from the next Wintertide champion."

"I'm not champion yet," Hadrian replied solemnly.

"That's not what Russell here's been saying." Dillon clapped his friend on the back. "He's done his own fair share of bragging at every tavern in town about how the next champion once spent a week living in his home."

"Four people bought me drinks for that," Russell said with a laugh.

"It's very nice to see you again," Lena said, taking Hadrian's hand gently and patting it. "We all wondered what became of you and your friend."

"I'm fine and so is Royce, but what happened to all of you?"

"Vince led us all to Alburn," Dillon explained. "We manage to scratch a living out of the rocky dirt. It's not like it was in Dahlgren. My sons have been taken for the imperial army, and we have to hand over most of what we grow. Still, I guess it could be worse."

"We saved all our coppers to come up here for the holidays," Russell said. "But we had no idea we'd find *you* riding in the tournament. Now that really is something! Rumor is they knighted you on the field of battle. Very impressive."

"Not as much as you might think," Hadrian replied.

"How's Thrace?" Lena asked, still holding his hand.

He hesitated, not sure what to say. "I don't know. I don't get to see her much. But she came to the banquet last night and she looked well enough."

"We just about died when we heard Deacon Tomas was calling for her to be crowned empress."

"Thought the old boy had gone mad, really," Dillon put in. "But then they went and did it! Can you imagine that? Our little Thrace—I mean, Modina—empress! We had no idea she and Theron were descended from Novron. That's probably where the old man got all his stubbornness and she her courage."

"I wonder if she's in love with Regent Ethelred," speculated Verna, Dillon's daughter. "I bet he's handsome. It must be wonderful to be the empress and live in that palace with servants and knights kissing your hand."

"You'd think she woulda remembered some of us *little folk* who cared for her like a daughter," Russell said bitterly.

"Rus!" Lena scolded him. Her eyes drifted to the high walls of the palace visible over Highcourt's tents. "The poor girl has gone through so much. Look up there. Do you think she's happy with all these problems she has to deal with? Wars and such. Do you think she has time to think about old neighbors, much less track us down? Of course not, the poor dear!"

"Excuse me, Sir Hadrian, but it's time," Renwick announced, leading Malevolent.

With the help of a stool, Hadrian mounted the horse, which was decorated in full colors.

"These are friends of mine," Hadrian told the squire. "Take care of them for me."

"Yes, sir."

"'Yes, *sir*'! Did you hear that?" Dillon slapped his thigh. "Wow, to be knighted and in the final bout of the Wintertide tournament. You must be the happiest man in the world right now."

Hadrian looked at their faces and tried to smile before trotting toward the gate.

The crowd exploded with applause as the two knights rode onto the field. The clouds overhead were heavier than before and appeared to have drained the color from the banners and flags. He felt cold, inside and out, as he took his position at the gate.

Across from him, Breckton waited in the same fashion. His horse's caparison waved in the bitter wind. The squires arrived and took their positions on the podium, beside the lances. The herald, a serious-looking man in a heavy coat, stepped up to the platform. The crowd grew silent when trumpeters blew the fanfare for the procession to begin.

Ethelred and Saldur rode at the head of the line, followed by King Armand and Queen Adeline of Alburn, King Roswort and Queen Freda of Dunmore, King Fredrick and Queen Josephine of Galeannon, King Rupert of Rhenydd—recently crowned and not yet married—and King Vincent and Queen Regina of Maranon. After the monarchs came the princes and princesses, the lord chancellor and lord chamberlain, Lady Amilia and Nimbus, and the archbishop of each kingdom. Lastly, the knights arrived and took their respective seats.

The trumpeters blew once more and the herald addressed the crowd in loud, reverent tones.

"On this hallowed ground, this field of tourney where trials are decided, prowess and virtue revealed, and truth discovered, we assemble to witness this contest of skill and bravery. On this day, Maribor will decide which of these two men shall win the title of Wintertide champion!"

Cheers burst forth from the crowd and the herald paused, waiting for them to quiet.

"To my left, I give you the commander of the victorious Northern Imperial Army, hero of the Battle of Van Banks, son of Lord Belstrad of Chadwick, and favored of our lady Amilia of Tarin Vale—Sir Breckton of Chadwick!"

Again, the crowd cheered. Hadrian caught sight of Amilia in the stands, clapping madly with the rest.

"To my right, I present the newest member to the ranks of knightly order, hero of the Battle of Ratibor, and favored of Her Most Serene and Royal Grand Imperial Eminence, Empress Modina Novronian—Sir Hadrian!"

The crowd roared with such intensity that Hadrian could feel their shouts vibrating his chest plate. Looking at the sea of commoners, he could almost imagine a small boy standing next to his father, waiting in excited anticipation.

"For the title of champion, for the honor of the empire, and for the glory of Maribor these two battle. May Maribor grant the better man victory!"

The herald stepped down to the blasts of trumpets, which were barely noticeable above the cry of the crowd.

"Good luck, sir." A stranger dressed in gray stood at Hadrian's station, holding out his helm.

Hadrian looked around but could not see Renwick any-where. He took the helm and placed it on his head.

"Now, *the lance*, sir," the man said.

The moment Hadrian lifted it, he could tell the difference. The weapon looked the same, but the tip was heavy. Holding it actually felt better to him, more familiar. There was no doubt he could kill Breckton with it. His opponent was a good lancer, but Hadrian was better.

Hadrian glanced once more at the stands. Amilia stood with her hands pressed to her face. He tried to think of Arista and Gaunt. Then his eyes found the empty space between Ethelred and Saldur—the throne of the empress—Modina's empty seat.

*I proclaim my faith in his skill, character, and sacred honor. I know his heart is righteous, and his intentions virtu-ous. May you both find honor in the eyes of Maribor and compete as true and heroic knights.*

The flags rose and he took a deep breath, lowering his visor. The trumpets sounded, the flags dropped, and Hadrian spurred his horse. Breckton responded at the same instant and the two raced toward each other.

Hadrian crossed only a quarter of the field before pulling back on the reins. Malevolent slowed to a stop. The lance remained in its boot, pointing skyward.

Breckton rode toward him. A bolt of gold and blue thundering across the frozen ground.

*Excellent form.*

The thought came to Hadrian as if he were a spectator, safe in the stands, like that boy so long ago holding his father's hand along the white rail, feeling the pounding of the hooves. He closed his eyes and braced for the impact. "I'm sorry, Da. I'm sorry, Arista," he muttered within the shell of his helm. With luck, Breckton's blow might kill him.

The hoofbeats drummed closer.

Nothing happened. Hadrian felt only the breeze of the passing horse.

*Did he miss? Is that possible?*

Hadrian opened his eyes and turned to see Breckton riding down the alley.

The crowd died down, shuffling as a low murmur drifted on the air. Hadrian removed his helm just as Breckton pulled his horse to a stop. The other knight also removed his helm and trotted back to meet Hadrian at the rail.

"Why didn't you tilt?" Breckton asked.

"You're a good man. You don't deserve to die by treachery." Hadrian let the tip of his lance fall to the ground. Upon impact, the broad ceramic head shattered to reveal the war point.

"Nor do you," Breckton said. He slammed his own pole and revealed that it too had a metal tip. "I felt its weight when

I charged. It would seem we are both the intended victims of deceit."

The sergeant of the guard led a contingent of twenty soldiers onto the field and said, "The two of you are ordered to dismount! By the authority of the regents, I place you under arrest."

"Arrest?" Breckton asked, looking confused. "On what charge?"

"Treason."

"Treason?" Breckton's face revealed shock at the accusation.

"Sir, dismount now or we will use force. Try to run and you *will* be cut down."

On the far side of the field, a contingent of seret entered in formation, and mounted troops blocked the exits.

"Run? Why would I run?" Breckton sounded bewildered. "I demand to hear the details of this charge against me."

No answer was provided. Outnumbered and out-armed, Breckton and Hadrian dismounted. Seret surrounded them and rushed the two knights off the field. As they did, Hadrian spotted Luis Guy in the stands near Ethelred and Saldur.

The crowd erupted. They booed and shouted. Fists shook and Highcourt Fields was pelted with whatever they could find to throw. More than once Hadrian heard the question "What's going on?"

The seret shoved them out of the arena through a narrow corridor of soldiers that created a path leading them out of the crowd's sight and into a covered wagon, which hauled them away.

"I don't understand," Breckton said, sitting among the company of five seret. "Someone conspires to kill us and we are accused of treason? It doesn't make sense."

Hadrian glanced at the hard faces of the seret and then down at the wagon floor. "The regents were trying to kill you…and I was supposed to do it. You were right. I'm not a knight. Lord Dermont never dubbed me. I wasn't even a soldier in the imperial army. I led the Nationalists *against* Dermont."

"Nationalists? But Regent Saldur vouched for you. They confirmed your tale. They—"

"Like I said, they wanted you dead and hired me to do it."

"But why?"

"You refused their offer to serve Ethelred. As commander of the Northern Imperial Army, that makes you a threat. So they offered me a deal."

"What *kind* of deal?" Breckton asked, his voice cold.

"I was to kill you in exchange for the lives of Princess Arista and Degan Gaunt."

"The Princess of Melengar and the leader of the Nationalists?" Breckton fell into thought once more. "Are you in her service? His?"

"Neither. I never met Gaunt, but the princess is a friend." Hadrian paused. "I agreed in order to save their lives. Because if I failed to kill you, they will die tomorrow."

The two traveled in silence for some time, rocking back and forth as the wooden wheels of the wagon rolled along the snow-patched cobblestone. Breckton finally turned to Hadrian and asked, "Why didn't you do it? Why didn't you tilt?"

Hadrian shook his head and sighed. "It wasn't right."

∽

"There are over a hundred rioters just in Imperial Square," Nimbus reported. "And more arriving every minute. Ethelred has pulled the guards back and closed the palace gates."

"I heard some guards were killed. Is that true?" Amilia asked from her desk.

"Only one, I think. But several others were badly beaten. The rioters are calling for the empress."

"I've heard them. They've been chanting for the last hour."

"Since the tournament, they don't trust Ethelred or Saldur. The crowd wants an explanation and they'll accept it only from the empress."

"Saldur will be coming here, won't he? He'll want me to have Modina say something. He'll order me to have the empress make a statement about Breckton and Hadrian plotting to take the throne."

Nimbus sighed and nodded. "I would suspect so."

"I won't do it," Amilia said defiantly. She rose and slapped her desk. "Sir Breckton isn't a traitor and neither is Sir Hadrian. I won't be a party to their execution!"

"If you don't, it's likely you will share their fate," Nimbus warned. "After tomorrow, Ethelred will be the emperor. He will officially rule and there will be precious little need for Modina's nursemaid."

"I love him, Nimbus." This was the first time she had said the words—the first time she had admitted it, even to herself. "I can't help them kill him. I don't care what they do to me."

Nimbus gave her a sad smile and sat down in the chair near her desk. This was the first time that Amilia could remember him sitting in her presence without first asking permission. "I suppose they will have even less need for a tutor. Hadrian obviously did *something* wrong and I will likely be blamed."

Someone walked by outside the office and both shot nervous glances at the closed door.

"It's like the whole world is ending." Tears ran down Amilia's cheeks. "This morning I was so happy. I think I woke up happier than I'd ever been."

They paused anxiously as they heard several more people running past the door.

"Do you think I should check on Modina?" Amilia asked.

"It might be wise." Nimbus nodded. "The empress always sits by that window. She's bound to hear the protests. She'll be wondering what's going on."

"I should talk to her. After the way she acted at the feast, who knows what she's thinking?" Amilia stood.

Just as the two moved toward the door, it burst open and Saldur stormed in. The regent was red-faced, his jaw clenched. He slammed the door behind him.

"Here!" Saldur shoved a parchment in Amilia's face. A few lines of uneven text were scrawled across it. "Make Modina learn this and have her reciting it on the balcony in one hour— *exactly* as written!"

Wheeling to leave, he opened the door.

"No," Amilia said softly.

Saldur froze. Slowly, he closed the door and turned around. He glared at her. "What did you say?"

"I won't ask Modina to lie about Sir Breckton. That's what this is, isn't it?" She looked at the parchment and read aloud, "'My loyal subjects…'" She skipped down. "'…found evidence…Sir Breckton and Sir Hadrian…guilty of treason against the empire…committed the vilest crime both to man and god and must pay for their evil.'" Amilia looked up. "I won't ask her to read this."

"How dare you." Saldur rose to his full height and glowered down at her.

"How dare *you*?" she retorted defiantly. "Sir Breckton is a great man. He is loyal, considerate, kind, honora—"

Saldur struck Amilia hard across the face, sending her to the floor. Nimbus started to move to her but stopped short. Saldur ignored him.

"You were a scullery girl! Or have you forgotten? I *made* you! Have you enjoyed pretending to be a lady? Did you like

wearing fine dresses and riding off to the hunt, where knights
fawned all over you? I'm sure you did, but don't let your feelings for Breckton go to your head. This is no game and you
should know better. I understand you're upset. I understand
you like the man. But none of this matters. I am building an
*empire* here! The fate of future generations is in our hands.
You can't toss that aside because you have a crush on someone
you think looks dashing in a suit of armor. You want a knight?
I'll arrange for you to have any knight in the kingdom. I promise. I can even arrange a marriage with a crown prince, if that
is what you wish. How's that? Is that *grand* enough for you,
Amilia? Would you like to be a queen? Done. What matters
right now is that we keep the empire from crumbling. I've
given you power because I admire your cunning. But *this* is
not negotiable. Not this time.

"There might only be a few hundred rioters out there now,"
Saldur said, pointing to her window, "but word will spread
and in a day or two we could be facing a civil war! Do you
want that? Do you want to force me to send the army out to
slaughter hundreds of citizens? Do you want to see the city set
on fire? I will not have it. Do you hear me?"

Saldur grew angrier and more animated as his tirade continued. "I like you, Amilia. You've served me well. You're
smarter than any ten nobles, and I honestly plan to see you
rewarded handsomely for your service. I'm serious about making you a queen. I will need loyal, intelligent monarchs governing the imperial provinces. You've proved I can count on
you and that you can think for yourself. I value such qualities.
I admire your spirit, but not *this* time. You will obey me,
Amilia, or by Maribor's name, I'll have you executed with the
rest!"

Amilia shook. Her lower lip trembled even as she clenched
her jaw. Still clutching the paper, she balled her hands into

tight fists and breathed deeply as she tried to control herself. "Then you'd better order another stake for the bonfire," she said, tearing the parchment in two.

He glared at her for a moment longer and then threw open the door and two seret entered. "Take her!"

# CHAPTER 17

# THE FINAL DARKNESS

J asper was back.

Arista lay on her side, face flat against the stone. She heard the rat skittering somewhere in the dark. The sound sent chills through her.

Everything hurt from lying on the floor. Worst of all, her feet and hands were numb nearly all the time now. Occasionally, Arista woke to the feel of her leg moving—the only indication that Jasper was eating her foot. Horrified, she would try to kick only to find her effort barely shifted her leg. She was too weak.

No food had arrived for a very long time, and Arista wondered how many days ago they had stopped feeding her. She was so feeble that even breathing took concentrated effort. The coming flames were now a welcome thought. That fate would be better than this slow death, being eaten alive by a rat she called by name.

Terrible ideas assailed her exhausted, unguarded mind.

*How long will it take for a single rat to eat me? How long will I stay conscious? Will he remain content to gnaw off my foot, or once he realizes I can no longer resist, will he go for softer meat? Will I be alive when he eats my eyes?*

Shocked to realize there were worse things than burning alive, Arista hoped Saldur had not forgotten her. She found herself straining, listening for the sounds of the guards and praying to Maribor that they would arrive soon. If she had the strength, Arista would gladly light the pyre herself.

She heard pattering, scratching on the floor, tiny nails clicking. Her heart fluttered at the sounds. Jasper was moving toward her head. She waited.

*Patter, patter, patter*—he came closer.

She tried to raise a hand, but it did not respond. She tried to raise her head, but it was too heavy.

*Patter, patter, patter*—closer still.

Arista could hear Jasper sniffing, smelling. He had never come this close to her face before. She waited—helpless. Nothing happened for several minutes. Starting to fall asleep, she stopped herself from drifting off. She did not want to be unconscious with Jasper so close. There was nothing she could do to keep him from feeding, but being awake was somehow better than not knowing.

When a minute had passed with no further noise, Arista thought the rat might have moved away. The sound of sharp teeth clicking told her Jasper was right next to her ear. He sniffed again and she felt him touch her hair. As the rat tugged, Arista began to cry, but she had no tears to weep.

*Rumble.*

Arista had not heard the sound in quite some time. The stone-on-stone grinding told her the door to the prison was opening.

There were sounds of gruff voices and several sets of footsteps.

*Tink-tink!*

Guards, but others were with them, others with softer shoes—boots perhaps? One walked; the other staggered.

"Put 'em in numbers four and five," a guard ordered.

More steps. A cell door opened. There was a scuffle and then the door slammed. More steps and the sound of a burden dragged across the stone. They came closer and closer but stopped just short of her door.

Another cell opened. The burden dropped—a painful grunt. *Tink-tink.*

The guards went back out and sealed them in. It was only a deposit. There would be no food, no water, no help, not even the salvation of an execution.

Arista continued to lie there. The noise had not scared Jasper away. She could hear him breathing near her head. In a moment or two, the rat would resume his meal. She began to sob again.

"Arista?"

She heard the voice but quickly concluded she had only imagined it. For the briefest moment she thought it was—

"Arista, it's Hadrian. Are you there?"

She blinked and rocked her head side to side on the stone floor.

*What is this? A trick? A demon of my own making? Has my mind consumed itself at last?*

"Arista, can you hear me?"

The voice sounded so real.

"Ha—Hadrian?" she whispered in a voice so faint she feared he would not hear.

"Yes!"

"What are you doing here?" Her words came out as little more than puffs of air.

"I came to save you. Only I'm not doing very well."

There was the sound of tearing cloth.

Nothing made sense. Like all dreams, this one was both silly and wonderful.

"I messed up. I failed. I'm sorry."

"Don't be…" she said to the dream, her voice cracking. "It means a lot…that you…that anyone tried."

"Don't cry," he said.

"How long until…my execution?"

There was a long pause.

"Please…" she begged. "I don't think I can stand this much longer. I want to die."

"*Don't say that!*" The dungeon boomed with his voice. The sudden outburst sent Jasper skittering away. "Don't you *ever* say that."

There was another long pause. The prison grew silent once more, but Jasper did not return.

*The tower was swaying. She looked under the bed, but still she couldn't find the brush. How was that possible? They were all there except the first one. It was the most important. She had to have it.*

*Standing up, she accidently caught sight of her reflection in the swan mirror. She was thin, very thin. Her eyes had sunk into their sockets like marbles in pie dough. Her cheeks were hollow, and her lips stretched tight over bone, revealing rotted teeth. Her hair was brittle and falling out, leaving large bald areas on her pale white skull. Her mother stood behind her with a sad face, shaking her head.*

*"Mother, I can't find the brush!" she cried.*

*"It won't matter soon," her mother replied gently. "It's almost over."*

*"But the tower is falling. Everything is breaking and I have to find it. It was just here. I know it was. Esrahaddon told me I needed to get it. He said it was under the bed, but it's not here. I've looked everywhere and time is running out. Oh, Mother, I'm not going to find it in time, am I? It's too late. It's too late!"*

Arista woke. She opened her eyes, but there was no light to indicate a difference. She still lay on the stone. There was no tower. There were no brushes, and her mother was long dead. It was all just a dream.

"Hadrian...I'm so scared," she said to the darkness. There was no answer. He had been part of the dream too. Her heart sank in the silence.

"Arista, it will be all right." She heard his voice again.

"You're a dream."

"No. I'm here."

His voice sounded strained.

"What's wrong?" she asked.

"Nothing."

"Something's wrong."

"Just tired. I was up late and—" He grunted painfully.

"Wrap the wounds tight," another man said. Arista did not recognize him. This voice was strong, deep, and commanding. "Use your foot as leverage."

"Wounds?" she asked.

"It's nothing. The guards just got a bit playful," Hadrian told her.

"Are you bleeding badly?" the other voice asked.

"I'm getting it under control...I think...Hard to tell in the dark. I'm...feeling a bit dizzy."

The dungeon's entrance opened again and once more there was the sound of feet.

"Put her in eight," a guard said.

The door to Arista's cell opened and the light of the guard's torch blinded her. She could barely make out Lady Amilia's face.

"Eight's taken," the guard shouted down the corridor.

"Oh yeah, number eight gets emptied tomorrow. Don't worry about it, for one night they can share."

The guard shoved the secretary inside and slammed the door, casting them into darkness.

"Oh dear Novron!" Amilia cried.

Arista could feel her kneeling beside her, stroking her hair. "Dear Maribor, Ella! What have they done to you?"

"Amilia?" the deep voice called out.

"Sir Breckton! Yes, it's me!"

"But—why?" the knight asked.

"They wanted me to make Modina denounce you. I refused."

"Then the empress knew nothing? This is not her will?"

"Of course not. Modina would never agree to such a thing. It was all Saldur's and Ethelred's doing. Oh, poor Ella, you're so thin and hurt. I'm so sorry."

Arista felt fingers brushing her cheek gently and realized she had not heard Hadrian in a long time. "Hadrian?"

She waited. There was no response.

"Hadrian?" she called again, fearful this time.

"Ella—er—Arista, calm down," Amilia said.

Arista felt her stomach tighten as she realized just how important it was to hear his voice, to know he was still alive. She was terrified he would not speak again. "Had—"

"I'm...here," he said. His voice was weak and labored.

"Are you all right?" Arista asked.

"Mostly, but drifting in and out."

"Has the bleeding stopped?" Breckton asked.

"Yeah...I think."

◅

As the night wore on, Modina could still hear them—voices shouting in anger and crying out in rage. There must be hundreds, perhaps thousands, by then. Merchants, farmers, sailors, butchers, and road menders all shouted with one voice.

They beat on the gate. She could hear the pounding. Earlier, Modina had seen smoke rising just outside the walls. In the darkness she could see the flicker of torches and bonfires.

*What is burning? An effigy of the regents? The gate itself? Maybe it is just cook fires to feed all of them while they camp.*

Modina sat at the window and listened to the wails the cold wind brought her.

The door to her bedroom burst open. She knew who was there before turning around.

"Get up, you little idiot! You're going to make a speech to calm the people."

Regent Saldur crossed the dim chamber with Nimbus in tow. He held out a parchment toward Nimbus.

"Take this and have her read it."

Nimbus slowly approached the regent and bowed. "Your Grace, I—"

"We don't have time for foolishness!" Saldur exploded. "Just make her read it."

The regent paced with intensity while Nimbus hurriedly lit a candle.

"Why is there no guard at this door?" Saldur asked. "Do you have any idea what could happen if someone else had waltzed up here? Have soldiers stationed as soon as we leave or I'll find someone *else* to replace Amilia."

"Yes, Your Grace."

Nimbus brought over the candle and said, "His Grace respectfully requests that—"

"Damn you." Saldur took the parchment from Nimbus. He brought it over and held it so close to Modina's face that she could not have read it even if she had known how. "*Read it!*"

Modina did not respond.

"You spoke well enough for Amilia. You always speak for *her*. You even opened your mouth when I threatened her for letting you play with that damn dog. Well, how's this, my little empress? You get out there and read this—clearly and accurately—or I will have your sweet little Amilia executed tomorrow along with the rest. Don't think I won't. I've already sent her to the dungeon."

Modina remained as unmoving as a statue.

Saldur struck her across the face. She rocked back but made no sound. Not a hand rose in defense. She did not flinch or blink. A tear of blood dripped from her lip.

"You insane little bitch!" He hit her again.

Once more, she showed no notice, no fear, no pain.

"I'm not certain she can even hear you, Your Grace," Nimbus offered. "Her Eminence has been known to go into a kind of trance when overwhelmed."

Saldur stared at the girl and sighed. "Very well, then. If the crowd doesn't disperse by morning, we'll send out the army to cut us a path to the cathedral. But the wedding *will* go on as scheduled and then we can finally be rid of her."

Saldur turned and left.

Nimbus paused to set the candle on Modina's table. "I'm so very sorry," he whispered before following the regent from the room.

The door closed.

Cool air on her face soothed the heat left by Saldur's hand.

"You can come out now," Modina said.

Mince crawled out from under the bed. He was pale in the light of the single flame.

"I'm sorry you had to hide, but I didn't want you to get into trouble. I knew he would be coming."

"It's okay. Are you cold? Do you want the robe?" he asked.

"Yes, that would be nice."

Mince crawled back under the bed and pulled out the shimmering cloth. He shook it a few times before gently draping it over her shoulders.

"Why do you sit next to this window? It's awfully chilly and the stone is hard."

"You can sit on the bed if you like," she said.

"I know, but why do *you* sit here?"

"It's what I do. It's what I've done for so very long now."

There was a pause.

"He hit you," Mince said.

"Yes."

"Why did you let him?"

"It doesn't matter. Nothing matters anymore. Soon it will all be over. Tomorrow is Wintertide."

They sat in silence for several minutes. She kept her eyes on the city, reflected by the flickering fires beyond her window. Behind her, Mince shifted and fidgeted occasionally, but he did not speak.

Eventually Modina said, "I want you to do something for me."

"You know I will."

"I want you to go back to the city again. This time I want you to stay there. You need to be careful and find somewhere safe until the rioting is over. But—and this is the important thing—I don't want you to come back here again. Will you promise me that?"

"Yes, if that is what you want," Mince told her.

"I don't want you to see what I must do. Or be hurt afterward because of it. I want you to remember me the way I've been over these last few days with you."

She got up, crossed to the boy, and kissed him on the forehead. "Remember what I said, and keep your promise to me."

Mince nodded.

Modina waited until he left the room and his footsteps faded down the hall. She blew out the candle, took the water pitcher from the dresser, and shattered the mirror.

◆

From under the tarpaulin draped over a potato cart, Royce peered around the courtyard. He took special care to study the darkened corners and the gap behind the woodpile. A yellow glow rose from beyond the front gate as if the city was ablaze. Shouts were still coming from the far side, growing louder and demanding the release of Hadrian and Breckton. The unseen mob called for the empress to show herself. It was a perfect diversion but also put every guard in the palace on alert.

"Are we going in or not?" Magnus grumbled, half buried in tubers. Royce answered by slipping out. The dwarf followed, and as they made their way to the well, Royce was impressed by how quietly Magnus moved. Royce kept a constant check on the guards facing the gate. No one was paying attention to the courtyard.

"You want to crank me down, or do you want to go first?" Magnus whispered.

"There's no power in existence that could cause me to let you do the lowering."

Magnus muttered something about a lack of trust and sat on the bucket, holding the rope tight between his legs. Royce waited for the dwarf to get settled, then lowered him until Magnus signaled him to stop. When the weight left the bucket, Royce lowered the pail to the bottom, braced the windlass, and climbed down the rope.

Albert had gained the dwarf access to the inner ward as a member of the wedding event crew. It had taken Magnus just five minutes to determine the dungeon's location. A few stomps told him where to find empty spaces below. A nighttime lowering into the well by Royce had revealed the rest. Magnus deduced that the well, peppered with small air ducts, ran along the outer wall of the prison, granting the dwarf access to the face of the ancient stone. For eleven nights, Magnus had worked, cutting an entry. Merrick had been right—the prison was dwarven made—but he had never expected Royce to bring his own dwarf, especially one with experience in burrowing through stone.

As Royce descended, he spotted a faint glow from an opening in the side of the shaft. The hole itself was really more like a tunnel, due to the thickness of the ancient stone. He removed the bundle he carried, containing a sword and lantern, and passed it through the hole to the dwarf. Even with all Magnus's skill, the stone must have been difficult to dig through, as the passage was narrow. While sufficient for a dwarf, it was a tight squeeze for Royce, and he hoped Hadrian would fit.

Emerging from the tunnel, Royce found himself peering around a small cell, where a dead body was lying on the floor. Dressed in a priest's habit and curled into a tight ball, the dead man gave off a terrible stench. The room was tiny, barely large enough to accommodate the corpse. Magnus stood awkwardly against the wall, holding a crystal that glowed with a faint green radiance.

Royce pointed at the rock. "Where'd you get the stone?"

"Beats the heck out of flint and steel, eh?" Magnus grinned and winked. "I dug it up. I'm a dwarf, remember?"

"Really trying to forget that," Royce said. He crossed to the door, picked the lock, and peered down the hallway outside. The walls had the same kind of markings he had seen in Gutaria Prison—small spidery patterns. He examined the seam where the walls met the floor.

"What are you waiting for? Let's get on with it," Magnus said.

"You in a hurry?" Royce whispered.

"It's cold. Besides, I can think of a lot better places to be than here. Heck, the stench is reason enough. I'd like to be done with this."

"I'm heading in. You wait here and watch for anyone coming behind us—and be careful."

"Royce?" Magnus asked. "I did good, right? With the stonework, I mean."

"Sure. You did fine."

"After this is over…you think you could let me study Alverstone for a while? You know, as kind of a reward—to show your appreciation and all."

"You'll be paid in gold, just like Albert. You've got to get over this obsession of yours."

Royce entered the hallway. The darkness was nearly absolute, the only illumination coming from Magnus's green stone.

He made a quick sweep of the corridors—no guards. Most of the cells were empty but he could hear faint movement and breathing from behind four doors. The only other sound was the *drip, drip, drip* of the well echoing off the stone walls. After he was sure it was safe, Royce lit the lantern but kept the flame low. He picked the lock on one of the cells and found a man lying motionless on the floor. His blond hair was a little longer than Royce remembered, but Royce was certain this was the man he had seen in the tower of Avempartha—Degan Gaunt. He was dangerously thin but still breathing. Royce shook him, but he did not wake. Royce left the door open and moved on.

He unlocked the next cell, and a man sitting on the floor looked up. The resemblance was unmistakable and Royce recognized him immediately.

"Who's there?" Breckton Belstrad asked, holding up a hand to block the glare of the lantern.

"No time to chat. Just wait here for a minute. We'll be leaving soon."

Royce moved to the next cell. Inside, two women slept. One he did not know, and the other he almost did not recognize. Princess Arista was ghastly thin, dressed in a rag, and covered with what looked to be bite marks. He left them and moved to the last cell.

"Fourth time's the charm," he whispered under his breath as he opened the final door.

Hadrian sat leaning against the wall. He was shirtless. His tunic had been torn into strips and tied around his leg, arm, and midsection. His shirt was fashioned into a pad pressed tight to his side. Each piece of material was soaked dark, but Royce's partner was still breathing.

"Wake up, buddy," Royce whispered, nudging him. Hadrian was damp with sweat.

"About time you got here. I was starting to think you ran off and left me."

"I considered it, but the thought of Magnus as my best man kinda forced the issue. Nice haircut, by the way. It looks good on you—very knightly."

Hadrian started a laugh that turned to grunts of pain.

"They skewered you good, didn't they?" Royce asked, adjusting the cloth strips. He pulled the midsection one tighter.

Hadrian winced. "The prison guards don't like me much. They lost money betting against me five jousts in a row."

"Oh, well, that's understandable. I would have stuck you too."

"You got Arista, right? And Gaunt? Is he alive?"

"Yeah, she's sleeping next door. As for Gaunt, he's in pretty bad shape. I'll have to drag him out. Can you walk?"

"I don't know."

Royce gripped Hadrian around the waist and slowly helped him up. Together they struggled down the corridor to the end cell with the well breach. Royce pushed on the door but it did not budge. He put more effort into it but nothing happened.

"Magnus, open the door," Royce whispered.

There was no answer.

"Magnus, come on. Hadrian is hurt and I'm gonna need your help. Open up."

Silence.

# CHAPTER 18

# WINTERTIDE

In the darkness of the prison, Amilia lay cradled in Breckton's arms, pondering the incomprehensible—how it was possible to drown simultaneously in bliss and fear.

"Look," Sir Breckton whispered.

Amilia raised her head and saw a weak light leaking around the last cell's door. In the pale glow, the figures in the prison appeared ghostly faint, devoid of all color. Princess Arista, Sir Hadrian, and Degan Gaunt lay in the corridor, on a communal bed built from straw gathered from all the cells. The three looked like corpses awaiting graves. Sir Hadrian's torso was wrapped in makeshift bandages stained frighteningly red. The princess was so thin that she no longer looked like herself, but Degan Gaunt was the worst of all. He appeared to be little more than skin stretched over bone. If not for his shallow breathing, he could have been a cadaver, several days dead.

During the night, a man had broken into the prison in an attempt to free them. He had opened the doors to the cells, but the plan to escape had failed. Now the man prowled around the prison.

"It's morning," Sir Breckton said. "It's Wintertide."

Realizing the light indicated a new day, Amilia began to cry. Breckton did not ask why. He simply pulled her close. From time to time the knight patted her arm and stroked her hair in a manner she could hardly have thought possible less than a day before.

"You'll be all right," he reassured her with surprising conviction. "As soon as the empress discovers the treachery of the regents, I am certain nothing will stop her from saving you."

Amilia pressed her quivering lips tightly together. She gripped the knight's arm and squeezed it.

"Modina is also a prisoner," Arista stated.

Amilia had thought the princess was sleeping. Looking over, she saw Arista's eyes were open and her head was tilted just enough to see them.

"They use her as a puppet. Saldur and Ethelred run everything."

"So she's a complete fabrication? It was *all* just a ruse? Even that story about slaying Rufus's Bane?" Breckton asked her.

"That was real," Arista replied. "I was there."

"You were there?" Amilia asked.

Arista started to speak, then coughed. She took a moment, then drew in a wavering breath. "Yes. She was different then—strong, unwavering. Just a girl, but one determined to save her father and daunted by nothing. I watched her pick up a bit of broken glass to use as a weapon against an invincible monster the size of a house."

"There now, my lady," Breckton said. "If the empress can do that, I am certain—"

"She can't save us!" Amilia sobbed. "She's dead!"

Breckton looked at her, stunned.

She pointed at the light under the door. "It's Wintertide. Modina killed herself at sunrise." She wiped her face. "The empress died in her room, in front of her window, watching the sun rise."

"But...why?" he asked.

"She didn't want to marry Ethelred. She didn't want to live. She didn't have a reason to go on. She...she..." Overcome with emotion, Amilia rose and moved down the corridor. Breckton followed.

✥

Hadrian woke to the sound of Arista coughing. He struggled to sit up, surprised at his weakness and wincing at the pain. He inched close enough to lift the princess's head and rest it on his thigh.

"How are you?" he asked.

"Scared. How about you?"

"I'm great. Care to dance?"

"Maybe later," Arista said. Her body was bruised and covered with ugly red marks. "This sounds terrible," she said, "but I'm glad you're here."

"This sounds stupid," he replied, "but I'm glad I am."

"That is stupid."

"Yeah, well, I've had a run of stupidity as of late."

"I think we all have."

Hadrian shook his head. "Not like mine. I actually trusted Saldur. I made a deal with him—and Luis Guy, of all people. You and Royce wouldn't have made that mistake. Royce would have used the time between jousts to break you out. And you—you would've probably figured some way to take over the whole empire. No, you two are the smart ones."

"You think I'm smart?" she asked softly.

"You? Of course. How many women could have taken a

city in armed conflict with no military training? Or saved their brother and kingdom from a plot to overthrow the monarchy? And how many would have tried to single-handedly break into the imperial palace?"

"You could have stopped before that last one. If you didn't notice, that was a colossal failure."

"Well, two out of three isn't so bad." He grinned.

"I wonder what is happening up there," Arista said after a time. "It's probably midday. They should have come and taken us to the stakes by now."

"Well, maybe Ethelred had a change of heart," Hadrian said.

"Or maybe they've decided to just leave us down here to starve."

Hadrian said nothing and Arista stared at him for a long time.

"What is it?" he asked.

"I want to ask you to do me a favor."

"What is it?"

"It's not an easy favor to ask," she said.

He narrowed his eyes. "Name it."

She still hesitated and then took a deep breath. Looking away at first, she said, "Will you kill me?"

Hadrian felt the air go out of him.

"What?"

She looked back at him but said nothing.

"Don't talk like that."

"You could strangle me." Reaching out, she took his hand and placed it to her neck. "Just squeeze. I'm certain it won't take long. I don't think it will hurt much. Please, I'm so weak already, and Royce didn't bring any food or water. I—I want it to be over. I just want this nightmare to end..." She started to cry.

Hadrian stared at her, feeling the warmth of her neck against his hand. His lips trembled.

"There's this rat, and he's going to..." She hesitated. "Please, Hadrian. Oh, please. Please?"

"No one is going to be eaten alive." Hadrian looked again at the marks on her skin. "Royce is working on a way out. This is what he does, remember? This is what we always do. We're miracle workers, right? Isn't that what Alric calls us? You just need to hang on."

Hadrian took his hand from her throat and pulled her close with his good arm. He felt dead inside, and only the stab wounds reminded him he was otherwise. He stroked Arista's hair while her body jerked with the sobs. Gradually, she calmed down and drifted back to sleep. Hadrian faded in and out as well.

"You awake?" Royce asked, sitting down next to Hadrian.

"Am now. What's up?"

"How you feeling?"

"I've had better days. What have you come up with? And it better be good, because I already told Arista how brilliant you are."

"How's she doing?" Royce asked.

Hadrian looked at the princess, who remained asleep, her head still resting against him.

"She asked me to kill her."

"I'll take that as *not well*."

"So? What have you found out?" Hadrian asked.

"It's not good. I've been over every inch of this dungeon three times now. The walls are solid and thick. There are no cracks or worn areas. Even with Magnus doing the digging with his special chisels, it took over a week to dig in. No telling how long it would take to tunnel out. I found some stairs leading up to what I assume is the entrance, but there's no lock. Heck, there isn't even a door. The stairway just ends at the stone ceiling. I still don't know what to make of that."

"It's a gemlock. Like Gutaria. A seret in the north tower has a sword with an emerald in the hilt."

"That would explain it. The door I came through won't budge. It's not locked, so it must be jammed somehow. It's probably our best chance at getting out. It's made of wood, so feasibly we could try to burn it down. It's pretty thick, though, so I'm not sure I can get it to catch even by using the straw and oil from the lantern. And the smoke—if it doesn't kill us first—could signal our escape and guards would be waiting at the top."

"Arista and Gaunt can't climb out through a well," Hadrian pointed out.

"Yeah, but that's just one of the problems. I'm positive the rope isn't there anymore. I'm not sure if they grabbed Magnus or if he's responsible. Either way, anyone bothering to spike the door would take the rope too."

"So where does that leave us?"

Royce shrugged. "The best I can come up with is to wait for dark and then try to burn down the door. Maybe no one will see the smoke. Maybe we won't suffocate before we can break it down. Maybe I can slip out unnoticed. Maybe I can kill the guards. Maybe I can rig a way to pull you out of the well."

"That's a lot of maybes."

"No kidding. But you asked." Royce sighed. "You got anything?"

"What about Arista?" Hadrian looked down at her sleeping face again, which he held cradled with his good arm. "She's weak but maybe—"

Royce shook his head. "There are runes all over the walls. Just like the ones in the prison Esrahaddon was in. If she could do anything, I'm pretty sure she would have by now."

"Albert?"

"If he has half a brain, he'll lie low. At this point he can't do anything but draw attention to himself."

"What about the deal Merrick offered?"

"How do you know about that?" Royce asked, surprised.

"He told me."

"You two talked?"

"We played chess."

Royce shrugged. "There's no deal. He'd already told me what I wanted to know."

They sat side by side in silence awhile. Finally Hadrian said, "I doubt this is any consolation, but I do appreciate you coming. I know you wouldn't be here if it weren't for me."

"Don't you ever get tired of saying that?"

"Yeah, but I'm pretty sure this will be the last time. At least I finally got to Gaunt. Some bodyguard I turned out to be. He's nearly dead."

Royce glanced over. "So that's the Heir of Novron, eh? I sort of expected more, you know? Scars, maybe, or an eye patch—something interesting, distinctive."

"Yeah, a peg leg, maybe."

"Exactly."

They sat together in the dim light. Royce was conserving the lantern oil. Eventually Breckton and Amilia returned and sat beside Arista. Lady Amilia's eyes were red and puffy. She placed her head on Breckton's shoulder, and he nodded a greeting to Hadrian and Royce.

"Royce, this is Sir Breckton," Hadrian said, introducing them.

"Yeah, I recognized him when I opened the door. For a moment, I thought it was Wesley looking back at me."

"Wesley? You've met my brother?"

Hadrian said, "We both have. I'm sorry I couldn't say

anything at the feast. Royce and I served with him on the *Emerald Storm*. Your brother had taken command after the captain was killed. I've followed many officers over the years, but I can truthfully say I never served under a more worthy and honorable man. If it wasn't for Wesley's bravery in battle, Royce and I both would have died in Calis. He made a sacrificial charge so others would live."

Royce nodded in agreement.

"You never cease to amaze me, Sir Hadrian. If that is indeed true, then I thank you. Between the two of us, Wesley was always the better man. I only hope I shall meet my end half as well as he did."

꿎

Saldur fumed as he started up the stairs to the fifth floor. It was past midday and they should have left for the cathedral hours earlier. The Patriarch himself was waiting to perform the ceremony.

As far back as Saldur could recall, which was a good many years, the Patriarch had never left his chambers in Ervanon. Those wishing to see him, to seek his council or blessing, had to travel to the Crown Tower. Even then, he accepted audiences only on rare occasions. The Patriarch had a reputation for refusing great nobles and even kings. Even the highest-ranking members of the church never saw him. Saldur had been bishop of Medford for nearly ten years without ever meeting the man. As far as the regent knew, even Galien, the former Archbishop of Ghent, who lived with the Patriarch in the Crown Tower, had never had a face-to-face meeting. That the sentinels made frequent visits to the tower was common knowledge, but Saldur doubted if any actually stood in the presence of the Patriarch.

That the Patriarch had left the Crown Tower for this auspicious occasion was a personal triumph for Saldur. He genuinely looked forward to meeting the great leader of the Nyphron Church—his spiritual father. The wedding was supposed to be a wondrous and moving event, a lavish production complete with a full orchestra and the release of hundreds of white doves. This day was the accumulation of years of careful planning, dating back to that fateful night in Dahlgren when the plan to elevate Lord Rufus to emperor had failed.

At that time, Deacon Tomas had been raving like a lunatic. He claimed to have witnessed the miracle of a young girl named Thrace killing the Gilarabrywn. Seeing as how Saldur himself had proclaimed that only the *true* Heir of Novron could slay that beast, the deacon's claim was perceived as a problem. Sentinel Luis Guy planned to erase the incident by killing both the deacon and the girl, but Saldur saw other possibilities.

The Patriarch had wanted to name Saldur as the next Archbishop of Ghent, to take the place of Galien, who had died in the Gilarabrywn's attack. The position was the highest in the church hierarchy, just below the Patriarch himself. The offer was tempting, but Saldur knew the time had arrived for him to take the reins of shaping a New Empire. He abandoned his holy vestments and donned the mantle of politics—something no officer of the church had done since the days of Patriarch Venlin.

Saldur weathered the condemnation of kings and bishops in his battle against ignorance and tradition. He pressured, cajoled, and murdered to reach his goal of a strong, unified empire that could change the world for the better. With his guidance, the glory of the Old Empire would rise once more. To the feeble minds of Ethelred and his ilk, that just meant one man on one throne. To Saldur it meant *civilization*. All that once was would be again. Wintertide marked the culmination of all his efforts and years of struggle. This was the last uphill battle and it was proving to be a challenge.

Saldur had expected the peasants to tire themselves out overnight, but their fury seemed to have increased. He was irked that the city, which had been quiet and orderly for years, chose this moment to rampage. In the past, people had been taxed penniless and starved to provide banquets for kings. Despite all this, they had never revolted. That they did so now was strange, but moreover, it was embarrassing.

Even Merrick had been surprised by the reprisal, which had appeared to come out of nowhere and everywhere at once. Saldur had expected some disappointment at the outcome of the joust and anticipated a few troublemakers. He knew there was a chance that one of the knights would live and supporters of the fallen champion might lash out. What he had not counted on was both competitors surviving. With no obvious crime, their arrests appeared unwarranted. Still, the response was curiously impassioned.

At first he thought it would be an easy matter to contend with, and ordered a dozen heavily armed soldiers to silence the agitators. The men returned bloodied and thinned in ranks. What they had met was not a handful of dissidents but a citywide uprising. The whole matter was frustrating, but of no actual concern. He had sent for the Southern Army, and it was on its way to restore order. That would take a day or so. In the meantime, Saldur proceeded with the wedding.

The ceremony had been delayed a few hours, as Saldur had needed the morning to arrange armed escorts for the carriage's trip to the cathedral. That had gone well and now he just needed to transport the bride and groom. He was anxious to get the final procession under way, but Ethelred had not returned with Modina. If he had not known better, Saldur might have thought Lanis was exercising his husbandly rights a bit early. Whatever the delay, he was tired of waiting.

Saldur reached the empress's bedroom and found two guards posted outside the door. At least Nimbus was following orders. Without a word to either guard, Saldur threw the door open, entered, and halted just past the threshold. The regent stood, shocked, as he took in the grisly scene.

The first thing he saw was the blood. A large pool spread across the white marble floor of the chamber. The second was the broken mirror. Its shards were scattered like brilliant islands in a red sea.

"What have you done!" he exclaimed before he could catch himself.

Modina casually turned away from the window to face him, the hem of her white nightgown soaked red to the knee. She looked at the regent without qualm or concern.

"He dared to place a hand on the empress's person," she said simply. "This cannot be allowed."

Ethelred's body lay like a twisted doll, an eight-inch shard of glass still protruding from his neck.

"But—"

Modina cocked her head slightly to one side like a bird and looked curiously at Saldur.

She held another long, sharp shard. Despite its being wrapped in material, her grip was so tight blood dripped down her wrist.

"I wonder how a feeble old man such as yourself would fare against a healthy, young farm girl armed with a jagged piece of glass."

"Guards!" he shouted.

The two soldiers entered the room but showed little reaction at the scene before them.

"Restrain her," Saldur commanded.

Neither of them moved toward the empress. They simply stood inside the doorway, unheeding.

"I said restrain her!"

"There's no need to shout," Modina said. Her voice was soft, serene. Modina moved toward Saldur, walking through the puddle. Her feet left macabre tracks of blood.

Panic welled in Saldur's chest. He looked at the guards, then back at the empress, who approached with the knifelike glass in her hand.

"What are you doing?" he demanded of the soldiers. "Can't you see she's crazy? She *killed* Regent Ethelred!"

"Your forgiveness, Your Grace," one guard said, "but she *is* the empress. The descendant of Novron. The child of god."

"She's *insane!*"

"No," Modina said, cold and confident. "I'm not."

Saldur's fear mingled with a burning rage. "You might have these guards fooled, but you won't succeed. Men loyal to me— the whole Southern Imperial Army—are already on their way."

"I know," she told him in her disturbingly dispassionate voice. "I know everything." She nodded at the guard and added, "As is fitting for the daughter of Novron.

"I know, for example, that you killed Edith Mon for aiding Arista, which incidentally she didn't—I did. The princess lived for weeks in this very room. I know you arranged to have Gaunt captured and imprisoned. I know you hired Merrick Marius to kill Esrahaddon. I know you made a deal with him that handed the port city of Tur Del Fur over to the Ba Ran Ghazel. I know how you bargained with a dwarf named Magnus to betray Royce Melborn in exchange for a dagger. I know you convinced Hadrian to kill Sir Breckton in the tournament. I know you slipped Breckton a war tip. Only neither knight killed the other. I like to think I had a hand in that.

"You thought you had anticipated everything, but you hadn't expected a riot. You didn't know about the rumors circulating through the throngs of the city to expect treachery at the joust as proof of your treason. Yesterday's crowd wasn't watching for entertainment—but for confirmation of that rumor.

"I also know that you were planning to kill me." She glanced down at Ethelred's body. "That was actually his idea. He doesn't care for women. You, on the other hand, just wanted to lock me up again in that hole. That hole that nearly drove me mad."

"How do you know all this?" Saldur felt real fear. This girl, this child, this peasant's daughter *had* slain the Gilarabrywn. She had butchered Ethelred, and now she knew— She knew everything. It was as if...as if she really were...

She smiled.

"Voices came to me. They told me everything." She paused, seeing the shock on his face. "No, the words were not Novron's. The truth is worse than that. Your mistake was appointing Amilia, who loved and cared for me. She freed me from my cell and brought me to this room. After so many months in the dark and cold, I was starved for sunlight. I spent hours sitting beside the window." She turned and looked at the opening in the wall behind her. "I had nothing to live for and had decided to kill myself. The opening was too small, but when I tried to fit through it, I heard the voices. Your office window is right below mine. It's easier to hear you in the summer, but even with your window closed, I can still make out the words.

"When I first came here, I was only a stupid farm girl, and I didn't care what was being said. After my family died, I didn't care about anything. As time went on, I listened and learned. Still there was nothing to care about—no one to live for. Then one day a little mouse whispered a secret in my ear that changed everything. I learned I have a new family, a family that loves me, and no monster will ever take them from me again."

"You won't get away with this! You're just a—a—"

"The word you are searching for is *empress*."

༂

That morning Archibald woke feeling miserable, and his spirits only fell as the day progressed. He did not bother going to the cathedral. He could not bear to see Ethelred taking *her* hand. Instead, he wandered the palace, listening to the sounds of the peasants shouting outside. There was the blast of an army trumpet coming from somewhere in the city. The Southern Army must be arriving.

*A pity*, he thought.

Even though he would fare poorly at the hands of the mob, should the rioters breach the gate or walls, he still reveled in the knowledge that the regents would suffer more.

He entered the great hall, which was empty except for the servants readying it for the wedding feast. They scurried about like ants, feverishly carrying plates, wiping chairs, and placing candles. A few of the ants bowed and offered the obligatory *my lord* as he passed. Archibald ignored them.

Reaching another corridor, he found himself walking toward the main stair. Archibald was halfway up the first flight before he realized where he was headed. The empress would not be there, but he was drawn to her room just the same. Modina would be at the altar by now, her room empty. A vacant space never to be filled again now that she was...He refused to think about it.

Out of the corner of his eye, he caught the movement of figures. Turning, he spotted Merrick Marius standing at the end of the corridor, speaking to someone Archibald did not recognize—an old man wrapped in a cloak. When they spotted him, the pair abruptly slipped around a corner. Archibald wondered whom Merrick was speaking with, as he was always up to no good. Just then, a commotion overhead interrupted his thoughts. Hearing a man cry out, he ran for the stairs.

When he reached the fourth floor, he found a guard lying dead. Blood dripped down the marble steps in tiny rivers. Archibald drew his sword and continued to climb. On the fifth floor he discovered two more slain guards.

In the corridor ahead, Luis Guy was fighting another palace guard. Archibald had almost reached them when the sentinel delivered a quick thrust and the guard fell as dead as the others.

"Thank Maribor you've arrived!" Saldur's voice echoed from Modina's room as Guy entered the chamber. The regent sounded shaken. "We have to kill her. She's been faking all this time and eavesdropping. She knows everything!"

"But the wedding?" Guy protested.

"*Forget the wedding!* Ethelred is dead. Kill her and we'll tell everyone she is still sick. I will rule until we can find a replacement for Ethelred. We will announce that the new emperor married her in a private ceremony."

"No one will believe that."

"We don't have a choice. Now kill her!"

Archibald peered in. Guy stood, sword in hand, with Saldur. Beyond them, near the window, was Modina in her red-stained nightdress. Presumably the blood belonged to Ethelred, who lay dead on the floor. Sunlight glinted off a shard of glass gripped tightly in the empress's hands.

"How do I know you're not going to just saddle *me* with both their murders?"

"Do *you* see another way out of this? If we let her live, we are all dead men. Look around you. Look at the guards you just killed. Everyone believes she really *is* the empress. You *have* to kill her!"

Guy nodded and advanced on her.

Modina took a step back, still holding the shard out.

"Good afternoon, gentlemen," the Earl of Chadwick announced as he entered. "I hope this isn't a private party. You see, I was growing bored. Waiting for this wedding is very dull."

"Get out of here, Archie," Saldur snapped. "We don't have *time* for you. *Get out!*"

"Yes, I can see you're very busy, aren't you? You have to hurry up and kill the empress, but before you do…perhaps I can be of assistance. I would like to propose an alternative."

"Such as?" Saldur asked.

"I've wanted to marry Modina for some time—and still do. Now that the old bugger's dead"—he looked down at Ethelred's body and offered a wry smile—"why not choose me? I'll marry her and things can go on as planned, only with me on the throne instead of Ethelred. Nothing has to change. You could say I dueled him for the right of her hand. I won and she swooned for me."

"We can't let her leave the room. She'll talk," Saldur said.

Archibald considered this as he strolled around Saldur. He eyed the empress, who stood defiantly even though Guy's sword was only a few feet away.

"Consider this. I'll hold the point of a dagger hidden by my cloak at her ribs during the ceremony. She either does as we want or dies on the altar. If I kill her in front of all the crowned heads, neither of you will be held responsible. You can claim innocence of the whole affair. Her death will fall on me—that crazy lunatic *Archie* Ballentyne."

Saldur thought for a moment, then shook his head. "No,

we can't risk letting her out of this room. If she gets to people, she can take control. Too many are devoted to her. It has to end here. We'll pick up the pieces afterward. Kill her, Guy."

"Wait!" Archibald said quickly. "If she's going to die—let me do it. I know it sounds strange, but if I can't have her, I will take some satisfaction from denying her to anyone else."

"You are a twisted little git, aren't you, Ballentyne?" Guy said with a disgusted look.

Archibald moved closer. For each step he took forward, Modina took a step back, until she had no more room to retreat.

Archibald raised his sword, and while keeping his eyes focused on Modina, he plunged the blade toward Luis Guy. The sentinel did not see the attack coming, but Archibald's ruse prevented an accurate strike. His thrust landed poorly. Instead of piercing Guy's heart, the blade glanced off a rib and merely sliced through his side. Archibald quickly withdrew his blade, turned, and tried to strike again. Guy was faster.

The earl felt Guy's blade enter his chest. The last thing Archibald Ballentyne saw before he died was Modina Novronian running past Saldur, slicing his arm as he unsuccessfully tried to stop her.

⋟

Royce's head turned abruptly.

"What—" Hadrian began, but stopped when Royce held up a hand.

Getting to his feet in one fluid motion, Royce paused mid-stride on a single foot, listening. He waited a moment and then moved swiftly to the cell door, which admitted the light. He lay down and placed his ear to the crack at the bottom.

"What is it?" Hadrian asked.

"Fighting," he replied at last.

"Fighting? Who?" Hadrian asked.

"I can't hear the color of their uniforms." Royce smirked. "Soldiers, though. I hear swords on armor."

They all looked at the door. Soon Hadrian heard it too. Very faint at first, like the rustle of leaves in autumn, but then he picked out the sounds of steel on steel and the unmistakable cries of men in pain. Within the prison, new sounds rose—the main entrance opened, shouts rang out, and footsteps echoed down the hall.

Royce picked up the sword he had brought and held it out toward Hadrian.

He shook his head. "Give it to Breckton. I doubt I can even hold it."

Royce nodded, handed the weapon to the knight, and raced down the hall with Alverstone drawn.

Breckton left Amilia's side and moved to stand in front of them all. Hadrian knew whoever was coming would have to kill the knight to get by.

Hard heels and soles echoed off the stone. A man cried out in terror.

"By Mar!" Hadrian heard Royce say. "What are *you* doing here?"

"Where is she?" responded a young man's voice. Hadrian recognized him but could not understand how he could possibly be there.

Torchlight filled the hall, growing brighter as footsteps hurried near. The group appeared first as dark silhouettes, the prisoners wincing at the brilliance. Hadrian raised an arm to shield his eyes.

"Alric? Mauvin?" Hadrian asked, stunned, then quickly added, "Breckton, *stop*! Don't fight!"

The King of Melengar and his best friend were leading a

party of men into the dungeon. Renwick, Ibis Thinly, and several others Hadrian did not know crowded the stone corridor. When Alric Essendon saw the prisoners, he wavered and a sickened expression crossed his face.

"You two—go back." Alric barked orders to his retinue. "Fetch stretchers." He raced to his sister's side. "Arista! Good Maribor, what have they done to you?" Over his shoulder he shouted, "Bring water! Bring bandages and more light!"

"You're not looking too good, my friend," Mauvin Pickering said, kneeling beside Hadrian. Mauvin was dressed in shimmering mail, his blood-spattered tabard bearing the crest of the Essendon falcon.

"They have indeed treated you poorly, sir," Renwick agreed, looking distraught. He was also dressed in bloodstained mail, and his face and hair were thick with sweat.

"I don't understand," Royce said. "Last we heard, Drondil Fields was under siege and about to fall."

"It was," Mauvin replied. "Then the damndest thing happened. The flag of truce went up from the vanguard of the Northern Imperial Army. A rider advanced and asked permission to speak at the gates. He explained that new orders had arrived along with a personal message to King Alric. If that wasn't strange enough, the personal guard of Empress Modina had delivered them."

He nodded toward a palace guard who was providing water to Amilia. "His name is Gerald. Anyway, the message said that Regents Ethelred and Saldur were traitors, and they were keeping the empress a prisoner in her own palace. It also said the war against Melengar was their personal quest for power, and that their commander, Sir Breckton, was either dead by treachery or falsely imprisoned and awaiting execution."

Hadrian started to speak, but Mauvin stopped him. "Wait... wait... it gets better. The orders commanded the acting leader of the Northern Army to cease all aggression against Melengar, extend the empress's sincerest apologies to King Alric, and return to Aquesta with all haste. The messenger went on to explain that Arista was scheduled for execution on Wintertide, and Empress Modina requested Alric to send whatever assistance he could spare."

"What did Alric say?" Hadrian asked Mauvin, as the king was consumed with aiding his sister.

"Are you kidding? He figured it was a ploy. Some trick to get us to come out. We all thought so. Then Alric yells down, more as a joke than anything, 'To prove you are telling the truth, lay down your weapons!' We laughed real hard until the commander, a guy named Sir Tibin—who's a decent enough fellow once you get to know him—did just that. We all stood on the parapet watching in disbelief as the Imperialists made this huge pile of spears, swords, and shields.

"That convinced Alric. He told them that not only would he send help, but he would personally lead the detachment. We rode day and night and expected to have a rough time breaching the city walls, but when we arrived, the gates were open. The people were rioting in the empress's name and shouting for Ethelred's and Saldur's heads. We stormed the palace and found only token resistance—just some foot soldiers and a few seret."

"Your sword has blood on it," Hadrian noted, pointing to Mauvin's blade.

"Yeah, funny that. I was determined never to draw it again, but when the fighting started, it just kind of came out by itself."

"What about Modina?" Amilia asked. "Is she...is she..."

Gerald's face was grave.

"What?" Amilia begged.

"There was an unfortunate incident in her bedroom this morning," the guard said.

Tears rose in Amilia's eyes. "Did she..."

"She killed Regent Ethelred."

"She what?"

"She stabbed him with a piece of broken glass from her mirror. She escaped an attempt on her life and ran to the courtyard. She rallied the soldiers who were loyal to her. When we arrived, she was ordering her men about like a seasoned general. Her troops managed to open the palace gates for us. Along with the Melengarians and the Northern Army, we suppressed the remaining seret and the palace guards loyal to the regents."

"Where is she now?" Amilia asked.

"She's on her throne, accepting vows of allegiance from the monarchs, nobles, and knights—everyone that had come for the wedding."

Men with stretchers appeared in the hall. Amilia turned to Sir Breckton. With tears in her eyes, she let out an awkward laugh and said, "You were right. She did save us."

## CHAPTER 19

# NEW BEGINNINGS

Modina stood alone on the little hill just beyond the city. This was the first time she had been outside the palace gates in more than a year. Four men with pickaxes had worked the better part of three days, cutting through the frozen ground to make a hole deep enough for the grave. What had taken days to dig was filled in just minutes, leaving a dark mound on a field of white.

Her reunion with the world was bittersweet, because her first act was to bury a friend. The gravediggers tried to explain it was customary to wait until spring, but Modina insisted. She had to see him put to rest.

Seventeen soldiers waited at the base of the hill. Some trotted a perimeter on horseback, while others kept a watchful eye on her or the surrounding area. As she stood quietly in that bleak landscape, her robe shimmered and flapped in the wind like gossamer.

"You did this to me," she accused the dirt mound before her.

Modina had not seen him since Dahlgren. She knew *of* him the way she knew about everything.

Saldur enjoyed the sound of his own voice, which made him an excellent tutor. The regent even talked to himself when no one else was around. When he did not know something, he always summoned experts to the sanctity of his office, the one place he felt safe from prying ears. Most of the names and places had been meaningless at first, but with repetition, everything became clear. Modina learned of Androus Billet from Rhenydd, who had murdered King Urith, Queen Amiter, and their children. Androus succeeded where Percy Braga had failed when trying to seize control of Melengar. She learned how Monsignor Merton, though loyal to the church, was becoming a liability because he was a true believer. She heard that the regents could not decide if King Roswort of Dunmore's biggest asset was his cowardice or his greed. She learned the names of Cornelius and Cosmos DeLur, men the regents saw as genuine threats unless properly controlled. Their influence on trade was crucial to maintaining imperial stability.

In the beginning Modina heard without listening as the words just flowed past. Over time, their constant presence filtered through the fog, settling like silt upon her mind. The day *his* name floated by was the first time she actually paid attention to what was being said.

The regents were toasting him for their success. Initially, Modina thought he was in Saldur's study, sharing a glass of spirits with them, but eventually it became apparent they were mocking him. His efforts were instrumental to their rise, but he would not share in the rewards. They spoke of him as a mad lunatic who had served his purpose. Instead of executing him, he had been locked in the secret prison—that oubliette for refuse they wanted to forget.

He died alone in the darkness. The doctors said it was due to starvation, but Modina knew better. She was intimately familiar with the demons that visited prisoners trapped in that darkness: regret, hopelessness, and most of all, fear. She knew how the fiends worked—entering in silence, filling a void, and growing until the soul was pushed out, until nothing remained. Like an old tree, the trunk could continue to stand while the core rotted away, but when all strength was gone, the first breeze would snap the spirit.

She knelt down and felt the gritty texture of a cold clump of dirt in her hand. Her father had loved the soil. He would break it up with his huge leathery fingers and smell it. He even tasted it. Field and farm had been his whole world, but they would not be hers.

"I know you meant well," she said. "I know you believed. You thought you were standing up for me, protecting me, saving me. In some ways, you succeeded. You might have saved my life, but you did not save *me*. What fate might we have had if you hadn't championed my cause? If you hadn't become a martyr? If we stayed in Dahlgren, you could have found us a new home. The Bothwicks would have raised me as their own daughter. I would have carried wounds, but perhaps I would have known happiness again. Eventually. I could have been the wife of a farmer. I would have spun wool, pulled weeds, cooked turnips, raised children. I would have been strong for my family. I would have fought against wolves and thieves. Neighbors would say, *She got that strength from the hardships of her youth.* I could have lived a small, quiet life. But you changed all that. I'm not an innocent maid anymore. You hardened and hammered me into a new thing. I know too much. I've seen too much. And now I've killed."

Modina paused and glanced up at the sky. There were only a few clouds on the field of blue, the kind of clear blue seen only on a crisp winter day.

"Perhaps the two paths really aren't so different. Ethelred was just a wolf who walked like a man, and the empire is my family now."

Placing a hand on the grave, she softly said, "I forgive you." Then Modina stood and walked away, leaving behind the mound with the marker bearing the name Deacon Tomas.

～

The candles had burned down to nubs and still they were not through the list. Amilia's eyes drooped and she fought the urge to lay her head down on the desk. She sat wrapped in a blanket with part of it made into a hood.

"Should we stop here and come back to it tomorrow?" she asked hopefully.

The empress shook her head. She was wearing the robe Mince had given her. Amilia had not seen her wear anything else since Modina had taken control of the empire. Other than on the night of the hawking feast, the empress had never donned the crown or mantle of her office. "I want to get through this last set tonight. I can't afford to have these positions left vacant. Isn't that right, Nimbus?"

"It would be best to settle on the remaining prefects, at least. If I may speak plainly, Your Eminence, you relieved over one-third of all office holders. If new ones are not appointed soon, the resulting void might give warlords an opportunity to exert authority and fracture the empire."

"How many do we still have to go?" Modina asked.

Nimbus shuffled through parchments. "Ah, there are still forty-two vacant positions."

"Too many. We have to finish this."

"If only you hadn't removed *so* many," Amilia said in a tired voice.

Since taking power, Modina had worked tirelessly and demanded the same of her aides. The change in her was amazing. The once quiet, shy waif, who had sat before a window each day, had transformed into an empress, commanding and strong. She organized meetings of state, judged the accused, appointed new officials, and even demanded that Nimbus teach her letters and history.

Amilia admired her but regretted Modina's dedication. With so much required of her, Amilia had only a few moments each day to spend with Sir Breckton. The secretary found herself strangely nostalgic for the hours they had spent imprisoned together.

Each day the empress, Nimbus, and Amilia met in Saldur's old office. Modina insisted on working there because it contained numerous charts, maps, and scrolls. These imperial records were meticulously organized and provided details on all aspects of the kingdom. Not being able to read, Modina had to rely on Nimbus and Amilia to sift through the documents and find answers to her questions. Nimbus was a greater help than Amilia, but still Modina insisted on her presence.

"I just wish I could remove some of the nobles as well," Modina said. "There are several kings and dukes that are as bad as Saldur. Saldur got King Armand of Alburn his throne through the assassination of King Reinhold, and I hate that he is rewarded for such treachery. Are you certain I can't remove him?"

Nimbus cringed. "*Technically* you can. As empress and the descendant of Novron, you are semidivine and your authority is absolute to all those who call Maribor god. However, such notions are fine in *theory*, but you must function based on *reality*. A ruler's power comes from the support and loyalty of her nobles. Offend enough of them and not only will they not obey you, they will almost certainly raise armies against you. Unless you are prepared to govern by the strength of Maribor's will alone, I suggest we keep the ruling nobles, if not happy, at least content."

Nimbus shifted in his seat. "A number of Ethelred and Saldur supporters are most likely preparing for a coup. Given the current situation, however, I am certain they are puzzled how best to proceed. For over a year the regents actively promoted you as empress and a goddess—supreme and infallible. Now that you actually wield power, it will take some creative manipulation to convince others to act against you. Finding allies won't be easy, but they have some advantages. For instance, you are inexperienced and they expect you to make mistakes, which they will hope to exploit. The key is to avoid making any."

Modina thought for a moment and then asked, "So although I am all powerful, I have to obey the nobles?"

"No, you merely have to keep them from wanting to get rid of you. You can do this in two ways. Keep them placated by providing things they want, such as wealth, power, and prestige. Or make the idea of opposing you more distasteful than bowing to you. Personally, I suggest doing both. Feed their egos and coffers, but build your base around loyal leaders. Men like Alric of Melengar would be a good start. He's proven himself to be trustworthy, and you've already won his gratitude by saving his kingdom. Bolster his position by providing income through preferential trade agreements. Grow that seed of an alienated monarchy into an economic, political, and military ally. With powerful supporters, the nobles will not be so quick to attack you."

"But Melengar isn't even in the empire."

"All the better. Those inside the empire will compete for power amongst themselves. Everyone on the ladder wants to be on a higher rung. Because Alric isn't part of that ladder, no one will feel slighted when he receives preferential status. If you were to act similarly with a noble within the empire, you will generate resentment of that favoritism. You can proclaim aid to Melengar as *prudent foreign affairs*. By endorsing Alric, you'll be building a supporter who won't be easily assailable. And one who will be more grateful than those who consider it their due."

"But won't this be expensive? Where will I get the funds? The people are already suffering under a heavy tax," the empress said.

"I would suggest meeting with the DeLurs. They generally operate outside *official* channels, but offering them legitimacy can provide mutual benefit. Given recent events with the Ba Ran Ghazel in Delgos, Cornelius DeLur in particular should be most receptive to a proposal of imperial protection."

"I've been thinking about Cornelius DeLur quite a bit lately. Do you think I should appoint him as trade secretary?"

Nimbus smiled, started to speak, paused, and then eventually said, "I think that might be a little too much like placing a drunk in charge of a tavern, but you're thinking along the proper lines. Perhaps a better choice might be to appoint Cornelius DeLur Prefect of Colnora. Until recently, Colnora was a merchant-run city, so recognizing this officially would go a long way toward good relations with merchants in general and the DeLurs in particular. Best of all, it won't cost you anything."

"I like the idea of Cornelius as prefect," Modina said, and turned to Amilia. "Please summon him for an audience. We can present the idea and see what he says." The empress returned her attention to Nimbus. "Is there anything else I need to be looking into at present?"

"I suggest creating sanctioned imperial representatives, trained here in Aquesta, to travel and relay instructions. They can be your eyes and ears to check up on local administrators. You might consider drawing these representatives from the monasteries. Monks are usually educated, used to living in poverty, and will be especially devoted because of your Nov-ronian lineage. Religious fervor can often be more powerful than wealth, which will keep your agents bribe-resistant. Oh, one other thing, be certain to avoid appointing anyone to a province who is from that area, and be sure to rotate them often. This will prevent them from becoming too familiar with those they administer."

"As if I didn't have enough to do." Modina sighed. "The best approach is to divide and conquer. Do you have a short list for the remainder of the prefects, Nimbus?"

"Yes." He reached into his piles and pulled out a stack of parchments. "I've compiled what I think are the best candidates. Shall we go through them?"

"No, I trust your judgment."

Nimbus looked disappointed.

"To save time, call in your top choices and interview them yourself. If you're satisfied, I want you to go ahead and appoint them. What's next?"

"What about Saldur?" Nimbus asked.

Modina sighed once more and slouched in her chair.

"Many of the others can be tried for treason, but he's different," Nimbus explained. "He wasn't just the regent. He was also once a very powerful officer in the Nyphron Church. An execution would be...well...*awkward*. Saldur is too dangerous to let go and too dangerous to execute. I suppose we could keep him imprisoned indefinitely."

"No!" Modina suddenly said. "I can't do that. You're right in that his situation is unique, but we must settle the matter one way or another. Even though he's in the tower and not the dungeon, I won't let anyone stay locked up forever. Even with adequate food, water, and light, the knowledge that you'll never be free has a way of destroying you from the inside. I'll not do that to anyone, not even *him*."

"Well, the Patriarch hasn't left for Ervanon yet. He's taken up residence in the cathedral. If we could convince him to denounce Saldur, that would make it possible to execute the ex-regent without fear of reprisal. Shall I set up a meeting?"

Modina nodded.

"Is that it?" Amilia asked. "Can we go to bed?"

"Yes, I think that will do for now," Modina told them. "Thank you both for all of your assistance. I couldn't hope to do any of this without you."

"You're most welcome, Your Eminence," Nimbus replied.

"You know, Nimbus, you don't have to be so formal. We are alone, after all. You can call me Modina."

"Don't bother," Amilia said. "You can't stop him. Trust me. I've tried. I've badgered him for nearly a year, yet he still calls me milady."

"My respect for you both prevents me from doing otherwise."

"Honestly, Nimbus," Modina told him, "you should be chancellor permanently. You are already doing the job behind the scenes. I don't know why you won't officially take the position."

"I am happy to serve now, in your time of need, but who is to say what the future might bring?"

Modina frowned.

"Oh, one more thing," Nimbus said. "There have been some strange rumors from the north. The information is sketchy, but there appears to be some kind of trouble."

"Like what?"

"I don't know exactly. All I've heard is that the roads from Dunmore are choked with refugees fleeing south."

"You might want to send someone to find out what's happening," Modina told him.

"I already did. I asked Supreme General Breckton to investigate, and he has sent three separate patrols. Quite some time ago, in fact."

"And?" the empress inquired.

"None of them have returned," Nimbus replied.

"What do you make of it?"

Nimbus shrugged. "Perhaps they are delayed by bad weather or flooding. Although, to be honest, the most likely answer would point toward pestilence. If the patrols visited a plague-ridden city, they would remain rather than risk bringing the disease back with them. Even so, illnesses have a way of traveling on their own. It might be best to brace for an epidemic."

Modina sighed. "Will it never end?"

"Wishing you were back at your window now, aren't you?" Amilia asked.

᪥

Hadrian had found himself in the infirmary along with Arista Essendon and Degan Gaunt. For the first three days, he did little more than sleep and was only marginally aware that his wounds had been stitched and wrapped. Whenever he woke, Royce was beside the bed, enveloped in a cloak with the hood covering his face. With his feet propped up on a chair, the thief appeared to be sleeping, but Hadrian knew better.

As Hadrian regained enough strength to focus, Royce entertained him with current events. The good news was that Modina seemed to have matters concerning the empire well in hand. The bad news was that Merrick Marius and Luis Guy had managed to escape and had not been seen since Wintertide.

By the seventh day, Hadrian felt strong enough to try walking, and he had been moved out of the infirmary and into a bedroom on the third floor. Each day he walked down the corridor, holding on to Royce, Albert, or Renwick. The squire and viscount were frequent visitors, but Hadrian did not have the opportunity to thank the Duke and Duchess of Rochelle for their help before they returned home. Like the other nobles gathered for the wedding, they swore fealty to Modina before departing. Albert continued to stay in Genny and Leo's suite, as the viscount was in no hurry to trade the luxurious palatial accommodations for his austere cell at the monastery. From time to time, Mauvin and Alric stopped by, usually on their way to visit Arista. Even Nimbus peeked in once or twice, but Royce and Renwick, who took turns as his steadfast sentries, tended to Hadrian day and night.

The princess rested two doors down. Though still thin and weak, Arista was recovering faster than Hadrian, judging by the pace of her strides past his door. At first Alric or Mauvin escorted her, but recently she had started passing by unaided. Hadrian was disappointed that she never came to his room, and he, in turn, never visited hers.

Degan Gaunt had been at death's door when first pulled from the dungeon, and few had expected him to survive. At Hadrian's insistence, Royce checked in on him and relayed updates on his condition. Even when given thin chicken broth, Gaunt had choked and vomited. One night the doctors had called in a priest of Nyphron, but somehow Gaunt pulled through. The latest reports indicated Degan was now eating solid foods and starting to regain weight.

"Ready for another walk?" Royce asked, handing Hadrian a cloak.

Recently woken, Hadrian was still rubbing his eyes. "Wow, you're in a hurry. Mind if I relieve myself first? Is somebody getting a bit anxious to get back to Gwen?"

"Yes, and you're milking all the attention. Now get up."

Royce helped Hadrian to his feet. Feeling the tug on his stitches, Hadrian grimaced as he slowly stood.

"How's the head today?" Royce asked.

"Much better. Not dizzy at all. I think I can walk on my own."

"Maybe so, but lean on me anyway. I don't want you falling down the stairs and ripping your side open. If you do, I'll be stuck here playing nursemaid another week."

"Your compassion is overwhelming," Hadrian said, wincing as he slipped a tunic over his head.

"Let's just start by getting you down to the courtyard. If you're still feeling okay after that, then you can try going on your own."

"Oh, may I?" Hadrian replied.

Using Royce as a crutch, Hadrian limped out to the hallway. He let his friend lead him toward the main landing. He expected pain but felt only a modest twinge.

"You know, I meant what I said in the dungeon. I appreciate you coming for me," Hadrian said.

Royce laughed. "You do realize that I really didn't *do* anything? Everything would have turned out exactly the same if I had stayed at Windermere with Gwen. She keeps insisting I'm needed to save you, but you seem pretty self-sufficient these days. Well, not right now, but you know what I mean."

They reached the courtyard and Royce helped Hadrian down the stairs. A warm spell had moved in and the weather was unusually pleasant. Hadrian heard the sound of dripping water everywhere as the snow melted.

"Early spring?" Hadrian asked.

"Only temporary, I'm sure," Royce replied. "Nothing this nice stays long. Okay, now that you're on level ground, try walking to the gate. I'll wait here."

Even after two weeks, the courtyard still bore signs of combat. Dark smears and sooty smudges on the walls, a broken cart, a missing door, and several shattered windows all told the story of what had happened while he had been in the prison.

Hadrian spotted another patient out for her daily exercise. Arista wore a simple blue dress and had gained enough weight to start looking like herself again. She swung her arms and took deep breaths of fresh air while circling the ward. Her hair was down and blowing in the breeze.

"Hadrian!" Arista cried out after seeing him.

He tried to straighten up and winced.

"Here, let me help you." She rushed forward.

"No, no, I'm trying to go solo today. Royce is releasing some of his tyrannical control." He hooked a thumb toward his friend, waiting at the palace doors. "I'm surprised Alric lets you wander around alone."

She laughed and pointed at two well-armed guards whose eyes never wavered from her as they stood a short distance away. "He has turned into a mother hen. It's kind of embarrassing, but I'm not going to complain. Did you know he cried the night they carried us out? Alric has always been more like our mother than I am. How can I be mad at someone for caring?"

They walked together to a bench. It was clear of snow; the warm sun had dried it clean. The two of them sat down and Hadrian was grateful for the rest.

"Alric did well," he said. "I'm sure it was difficult for him to leave Medford and go to Drondil Fields. Royce tells me he took quite a few of the citizenry with him."

She nodded. "Yes, and doing so made the siege difficult. Hundreds of people were jammed into the corridors, halls, and all around the courtyard. Food was scarce after only a month because there were so many mouths to feed. Alric's advisors told him he had to deny food to the sick to save others, but he refused to listen. Some of the weak actually died. Count Pickering said Alric needed to surrender in order to save those he could. I heard from Mauvin that Alric was planning to do just that. He was just waiting until after Wintertide. I'm proud of my brother. He knew they would kill him, but he was willing to sacrifice himself for his people."

"How are things now at Drondil Fields?"

"Oh, fine. Supplies are flowing again and Count Pickering is administrating from there. I'm not sure if you know, but Medford was destroyed. Drondil Fields will need to function as the capital until Alric can rebuild. That's funny, as it served just such a purpose in the beginning."

Hadrian nodded and the pair continued to sit while quietly looking around the courtyard. Arista unexpectedly took his hand and squeezed. Glancing down, he saw her looking at him with a warm smile.

"I want to thank you for trying to rescue me," Arista said. "You have no idea how much it meant. When I was in the..." She paused and looked away, staring at some distant, unseen point. A shadow crossed her face and lingered long enough to make her lip quiver. When she spoke again, her voice was softer and less confident. "I felt very alone. More so than I imagined a person could be."

Arista chuckled softly. "I was so naive. When I was first captured, I believed I could face death bravely—like Alric was going to." Arista paused again, studying the fallow garden and wetting her lips. "I'm ashamed to say that I'd completely given up by the end. I didn't care about anything. I just wanted the fear to stop. I was terrified, so terrified that...And then... then I heard your voice." She gave another sad little smile. "I couldn't believe what I heard at first. You sounded like a birdsong in the dead of winter...so warm, so friendly, so very out of place. I was falling into an abyss, and at the very last moment, you reached out and caught me. Just your voice. Just your words. I don't think I can ever express how much they meant."

He nodded and squeezed her hand back. "I'm pleased to have been of service, my lady." Hadrian gave a reverent little bow of his head.

They sat quietly again for some time. When the silence was nearly uncomfortable, Hadrian asked, "What are you going to do now? Go with Alric to Drondil Fields?"

"Actually, that's something I need to talk to you about—but not today. We both have healing yet to do. It will wait until we are stronger. Did you know Esrahaddon is dead?"

"Yeah, we found that out."

"He came to me the night he was killed and told me something. Something involving Degan Gaunt..." Her voice faded as she glanced toward the main gate, a look of curiosity crossing her face. "Who is that?" She pointed.

Hadrian followed her gaze and saw a lone figure entering on horseback. The rider was thin, small, and wearing a monk's frock. The man rode slumped over the horse's neck. Once inside the palace's gate, he fell face-first into the slush. Royce was the farthest away, but he was still able to reach the man first. Several servants were right behind him. Hadrian and Arista approached, and by the time they arrived, Royce had already rolled the man over and pulled back his hood.

"Myron?" Hadrian said in disbelief. He stared down at the familiar face of their friend from the Winds Abbey. The monk was unconscious, but there was no sign of a wound.

"Myron?" Arista asked, puzzled. "Myron Lanaklin of Windermere? I thought he never left the abbey."

Hadrian shook his head. "He doesn't."

✧

The little monk lay on a cot in the infirmary. Two chambermaids and the palace physician busied themselves tending to
him. They brought water and cleaned the mud from his face,
arms, and legs, looking for wounds. Myron woke with a startled expression, looked around in a panic, and collapsed again.
A miserable moan escaped his lips, followed by, "Royce?"

"What's wrong with him?" Hadrian asked.

"Just exhausted, as far as I can tell," the doctor replied.
"He needs food and drink." Just as he said this, a maid entered
with a steaming bowl.

"I'm so sorry," Myron said, opening his eyes again and
focusing on Royce. "I'm so sorry. I'm sure it was my fault. I
should have done *something*...I don't know what to say."

"Slow down," Royce snapped. "Start at the beginning and
tell me everything."

"*Everything?*" Hadrian asked. "Remember who you're
talking to."

"It was four days ago and me and Miss DeLancy were out
talking with Renian. I was telling him about a book I had just
finished. It was early and no one was in the garden but us.
Everything was so quiet. I didn't hear anything. Maybe if I
had heard..."

"Get to the point, Myron." Royce's irritation increased.

"He just appeared out of nowhere. I was talking with
Renian when I heard her gasp. When I turned, he was behind
her with a knife to her throat. I was so scared. I didn't want
to do anything that might get Miss DeLancy hurt."

"What did he look like? *Who* put a knife to her throat?"
Royce asked intently.

"I don't know. He didn't say his name. He looked a little

like you, only larger. Pale skin, like new vellum—and dark eyes—very dark. He told me, 'Listen carefully. I've been told you can remember exactly what you hear or read. I hope that is true for *her* sake. You will travel to the palace in Aquesta, find Royce Melborn, and deliver him a message. Any delay or mistake may cost her life, so pay attention.'"

"What's the message?" Royce asked.

"It was very strange, but this is what he told me: 'Black queen takes king. White rooks retreat. Black queen captures bishop. White rook to bishop's four, threatening. Check. White's pawn takes queen and bishop. Jade's tomb, full face.'"

Royce looked devastated. He stepped back and actually stumbled. Breathing hard, he sat on a vacant bed.

"What is it?" Hadrian asked anxiously. "Royce?"

His friend did not answer. He did not look at him or at anyone. He merely stared. Hadrian had seen the look before. Royce was calculating, and from his intense expression, Hadrian could tell he was doing so in earnest.

"Royce, talk to me. What did that mean? I know it's a code but for what?"

Royce got up. "Gwen's in danger. I have to go."

"Let me get my swords."

"No," he said bluntly. "I want you to stay out of this."

"Stay out of it? Stay out of what? Royce, since when do—"

Royce's face turned to a mask of calm. "Look at you— you're hobbling around. I can handle this. You get some rest. It's not that bad."

"Don't do that. Don't try to manage me. Something terrible is happening. It's Merrick, isn't it? He likes chess. What did that message mean? I was the one who got you to help me find Gaunt, and if there is a price to be paid, I want to help. What's Merrick up to?"

Royce's face changed again. The calm faded, and what lay

behind it was an emotion Hadrian had never seen on his partner's face before—terror. When he spoke, his voice quavered. "I have to go, and I *need* you to stay out of it."

Hadrian noticed Royce's hands were shaking. When Royce saw them too, he pulled them under his cloak.

"Don't follow me. Get well and take your own path. We won't be seeing each other again. Goodbye."

Royce bolted from the room.

"Wait!" Hadrian called. He struggled to stand and follow, but it was useless. Royce was already gone.

## CHAPTER 20

# THE QUEEN'S GAMBIT ACCEPTED

It was late as Arista walked the balcony of her room. The storm from the night before had left the handrails mounded with snow, and icicles dangled from the eaves. In the light of the nearly full moon everything was so pretty, like a fairy tale. Pulling her cloak tight, Arista lifted the hood such that she looked out through a fur-lined tunnel. Still the cold reached her. She considered going back inside, but she needed to be out. She needed to see the sky.

Arista could not sleep. She felt uneasy—restless.

Despite her exhaustion, sleeping was nearly impossible. The nightmares were not a surprise, given what she had gone through. She often woke in the dark, covered in sweat, certain she was still in the dungeon—certain that the sounds of snow blowing against the window were the scratches of a rat named Jasper. Afterward, lying awake brought thoughts of Hadrian. The hours of darkness trapped in that hole had stripped her bare and forced her to face the truth. In Arista's most desperate moment, her thoughts had turned to him. The mere sound of his voice had saved her, and the thoughts of her own death were extinguished when she feared he was hurt.

She was in love with Hadrian.

The revelation was bitter, as it was clear he did not feel the same. In those last hours, the only words that passed his lips were ones of common comfort, the same encouragement anyone would give. He might care about her, but he did not love her. In one way, she found that a blessing, as every man who ever had loved her had died. She could not bear to see Hadrian die as well. She concluded they would remain friends. Close friends, she hoped, but she would not endanger that friendship by admitting anything more. She wondered if somewhere Hilfred was watching her and laughing at the irony or crying in sympathy.

Still, it was not thoughts of Jasper or Hadrian that kept Arista walking the balcony that night. Another ghost stalked her troubled mind, whispering memories. Something was happening. She had felt it building ever since they had pulled her from the prison. At first she assumed it was the lingering effect of starvation, a form of light-headedness affecting her senses. Now she realized it was more than that.

*...at Wintertide the* Uli Vermar *ends. They will come— without the horn everyone dies. Only you know now—only you can save...*

The words of Esrahaddon echoed in her head, but she could not understand what they meant.

*What is the* Uli Vermar? *And who is coming?*

Something had clearly happened. Somehow the world had changed on Wintertide. She could feel it. She could taste it. The air sizzled with the sensation. While she had known how to tap the natural power of the world, Arista was shocked to discover that the world could talk back, speaking to her in a language she did not fully understand. It came in subtle impressions, vague feelings she might have previously dismissed as imagination. All the signals spoke of a great shift. She, like all living things in tune with the natural world, was aware of the change just as if it were the coming dawn. Something about *this* Wintertide had been different. Something rare, something old, something great had transpired. She looked to the northeast. It was there, hurtling toward them.

*They are coming.*

A voice startled her. "Anna said you were out here."

Arista spun to see Modina standing behind her. She wore a simple kirtle dress. Her arms folded across her chest, fending off the cold. She looked more like the girl Arista had first met in Dahlgren than an empress.

"Sorry, didn't mean to scare you," Modina said.

Arista gathered herself and curtsied as best she could. "Not at all, Your Eminence."

Modina sighed. "Please don't. I have enough people kissing the floor. I refuse to take it from you. And I'm sorry for taking so long to visit."

"You are the empress—the *real* empress. I'm sure your time is limited. And because I am still the Ambassador of Melengar, I really should greet and address you properly."

Modina frowned. "Perhaps, but can't we skip the formalities when in private?"

"If that is your wish."

"I wanted to let you know that we are officially allies now. I signed a preferred trade agreement and defense pact this morning with Alric."

"That's wonderful." Arista smiled. "Although you're putting me out of a job by going over my head like that."

"Can we go inside? It's freezing out here." Modina led the way back into Arista's room.

In the dim light, Arista noticed something lying folded neatly on the bed.

"I was so worried about you," Modina whispered as she unexpectedly hugged the princess, squeezing her tight. "And just so you know, I did visit you—nearly every night. You've just been asleep."

"You saved my life, my brother, and my kingdom," Arista replied, returning the embrace. "Do you really think I can feel slighted by you?"

Modina let go. "I'm sorry it took so long. I'm sorry that you had to stay in that...that...place. I didn't save Deacon Tomas, and I didn't save Hilfred. Perhaps if I had acted sooner..."

"Don't," Arista said, seeing the empress's eyes watering. "You have nothing to apologize for."

Modina wiped the tears and nodded. "I wanted to give you something...something special." She walked to the bed and held up a familiar robe, which unfolded in shimmering cascades.

"Do you recognize it?"

Arista nodded.

"I can't imagine there are two such robes in all the world. I think he would want you to have it, and so do I."

∽

Modina had just left Arista's room and was passing Degan's half-open door when he called out, "Hang on there!"

She pushed the door open and stood on the threshold, looking at him.

Tall and still very thin, he sat propped against a bank of pillows in bed. "My chamber pot needs emptying, and the room is starting to stink. Wanna get in here and take care of it?"

"I'm not the chambermaid," Modina replied.

"Oh? Are you a nurse? 'Cause I'm still not feeling well. I could use some more food. Some beef would be nice—steak, perhaps?"

"I'm not a nurse or scullery maid either."

Degan looked irritated. "What good are you, then? Listen, I just got out of the dungeon, and they literally starved me. I deserve some sympathy. I need more food."

"If you want, I can walk you down to the kitchen and we can find something there."

"You're joking, right? Didn't you just hear what I said? I'm sick. I'm weak. I'm not about to go rummaging around like a rodent."

"You won't regain your strength by sitting in bed."

"I thought you said you weren't the nurse. Listen, if you won't bring it to me, find someone who will. Don't you realize who I am?"

"You're Degan Gaunt."

"Yes, but do you know *who* I am?"

She looked at him, puzzled. "I'm sorry...I don't kn—"

"Can you keep a secret?" he asked, leaning forward and speaking in a conspiratorial tone.

Modina nodded.

"As it turns out, I'm the Heir of Novron." Modina feigned surprise and Gaunt grinned in reply. "I know—I was shocked too. I only recently learned myself."

"But I thought Empress Modina was the heir."

"From what I heard, that's just what the old regents wanted everyone to believe."

"So do you plan to overthrow the empress?"

"Don't need to," he said with a wink. "I heard she's young and beautiful, so I figure I'll just marry her. I also hear she's popular too, so I can benefit from the goodwill she already has. See how smart that is?"

"What if she won't marry you?"

"Hah! Why wouldn't she? I'm the Heir of Novron. You can't do no better than that."

Modina noticed Gaunt looking her over more intently. His tongue licked his upper lip, sliding back and forth. "Say, you're kinda pretty, you know that?" He glanced past her, into the hallway. "What do ya say you shut the door and slip on over here?" He patted the covers.

"I thought you were sick and feeble."

"I said I was weak, not feeble, and I'm not *that* weak. If you won't get me something to eat, the least you can do is help warm my bed."

"I don't think that is the least I can do. Yes, I can definitely think of less."

He furrowed his brow at her. "You know, I'm gonna be the emperor just as soon as I get well enough. You might want to be nicer to me. We can keep this thing going, even after the wedding. I expect I'll have several *ladies-in-waiting*, if you know what I mean. I'll be taking good care of them too. This is your chance to get in early and be the first."

"And what exactly does that mean?"

"Oh, you know. I take care of you. Give you a room here at the palace. See that you get some fine dresses. That kind of stuff."

"I already have those things."

"Sure, but you might not after I take over. This way you can make sure that your future is protected. So, what do you say?"

"Remarkably, I think I will pass."

"Suit yourself." Gaunt waved her away. "But hey, if you do see a maid, tell her to get her ass in here and get rid of this pot, okay?"

When Modina reached the stair, she met a gate soldier climbing up.

"Your Eminence." He approached, bowed, and waited.

"Yes?" she asked.

"A man at the palace gates is requesting an audience."

"What? Now?"

"Yes, Your Eminence. I told him it wasn't possible."

"It's getting kind of late. Ask him to see the palace clerk in the morning."

"I already told him that, but he says he and his family must leave at first light. They came for Wintertide, and he wanted to make one last attempt to see you before departing. He said you would know him."

"Did he give you his name?"

"Yes, Russell Bothwick of Dahlgren."

Modina lit up. "Where is he now?"

"I had him wait at the gate."

When she had lived in Dahlgren, the Bothwicks had been as close as family. They had taken her in after the death of her mother, and the excitement of seeing her old friends overtook Modina. She trotted down the stairs to the main entry, causing the guards to rush to open the huge double doors for her. Modina hurried into the snowy courtyard and regretted not having brought a cloak the moment she stepped outside. The night was dark, and as she crossed the courtyard toward the front gate, she realized she could have used a lantern as well. Seeing Russell and Lena was too good to be true. She would give them the finest suite in the palace and stay up all night reminiscing about old times... better times.

As she passed the stable, a voice close by said, "Thrace?"

She spun around and was surprised to find Royce there. "What are you doing out here? Come with me to the gate. The Bothwicks are here."

"I want you to know I am very sorry about this," Royce told her.

"About what?"

He had a sad expression in his eyes as one hand clamped

over her mouth. She struggled for a moment, but it was over quickly. The last thing she heard was his voice whispering in her ear, "*I'm sorry.*"

᧞

The palace bell rang before dawn. Hadrian and the other residents of the third floor stepped into the hallway. Arista wore Esrahaddon's glimmering robe, and Degan Gaunt yawned while clutching a blanket around his shoulders.

Amilia and Breckton led a troop of guards into the corridor.

"Have any of you seen the empress?"

"Not since last night," Arista said.

"What's going on?" Gaunt grumbled irritably. This was the first time Hadrian had seen him since the dungeon.

"The empress is missing," Breckton announced. He motioned to the soldiers, who opened doors and swept into the rooms.

"So what's all the fuss? Check the quarters of the best-looking servant," Gaunt said. "She probably just fell asleep afterward."

"Bishop Saldur is also missing," Breckton said. "And the guard at the tower and two gate sentries are dead."

The soldiers finished searching the rooms and returned to the hallway.

"How could Saldur have gotten out?" Arista asked. "And why would he take Modina?"

Hadrian glanced at her and then at the floor. "It wasn't Saldur."

"But who could have—" Arista started.

Hadrian interrupted her. "Royce took her. He has taken them both. 'White's pawn takes queen and bishop.' It's the Queen's Gambit and Royce has accepted."

## Chapter 21

# Langdon Bridge

Directly overhead the full moon peered through a break in the clouds, making the Bernum River glisten like a dark, oily snake as it wound through the heart of Colnora. Numerous warehouses perched on the high banks, sleeping like behemoths on the cold winter night. Far from the residential neighborhoods, the mercantile district was desolate at this hour. Frost-covered lampposts fashioned in the shapes of swans dotted the length of the Langdon Bridge, illuminating icicles hanging from every ledge and ornament. Snow started to fall once more, and fluffy flakes caught in the lamplight twirled and drifted on air currents rising from the river gorge. The sound of the Bernum roared up from the depths as if the river were some monstrous, insatiable beast.

Royce stood in the shadows on the north side of the bridge. Despite the cold, he was drenched in sweat. Behind him, Saldur and Modina stood silently with their wrists tied behind their backs. Royce did not use gags—they were not required. He had given his prisoners several reasons to remain silent.

Extracting Saldur from the prison tower had been easy enough. The ex-regent offered no resistance and obeyed every whispered command promptly and quietly. Royce had been disappointed, as he was eager for any excuse to correct that particular captive's behavior. Modina was another matter. He honestly regretted taking her. He simply had no choice. Royce had squeezed her neck with the least amount of pressure and for the shortest interval necessary to drop her painlessly into unconsciousness. He was certain she woke with a terrible headache but suffered no other harm.

Royce studied the warehouses on the far side of the bridge. One had a four-leaf clover painted on its side. That was the place where he had mistakenly killed Merrick's lover. It had happened back when all three of them had been assassins in the Black Diamond thieves guild. *Jade's tomb.* He worried about the message Merrick was sending with his choice of location.

After glancing up again and checking the location of the moon, Royce lit a lantern and stepped into the street. Two nerve-wracking moments later, another light appeared in reply from the far end of the bridge. Merrick was there. And Gwen was with him.

*She's alive!*

Royce's heart leapt. Relief mixed with anxiety. She was so close, yet not close enough. No one else was visible—the Black Diamond were conspicuously absent. Royce had expected members of the thieves' guild to descend the instant he entered the city. Either Merrick had arranged for safe passage, or they had decided they did not want any part of *this* transaction.

"Show them." Merrick's voice carried on the cool, crisp air.

Royce motioned and Modina and Saldur stepped from the shadows next to him.

"I'll double your reward for this, Marius," Saldur shouted. "You'll be Marquis of Melengar. I'll—" He cried out in pain as Royce dragged Alverstone along his shoulder blade. The gleaming knife sliced through the regent's robes and into his skin.

"Did we forget our agreement?" Royce snapped.

Royce looked at Modina, who stood quiet and still. The empress displayed no fear, anger, or malice. She did not struggle. She merely waited.

"Send them across," Merrick ordered.

"Don't run, Saldur," Royce said. "You need to match Gwen's pace. I'm good at throwing a dagger, and you won't be out of my range until you reach the bridge's midpoint. If you pass it before she does, it will be the last step you ever take."

The captives stepped forward at the same time as Gwen. She wore a heavy wool cloak and boots that were not her own. Tears streamed down her cheeks. With her arms tied behind her back, she could not push away her tangled hair or free her mouth from the gag. They walked toward each other at an agonizingly slow pace.

For Royce, nothing on the face of the world stirred except for the three hostages on the bridge. The prisoners passed at the bridge's center, exchanging only brief glances. The wind blew harder, throwing the snow and Gwen's hair askew. Royce's heart thundered in his chest as she broke into a run. He no longer cared about the others. Saldur could rule all of Elan, so long as he could have Gwen. They would go to Avempartha—leave that very night. The wagon was already filled with supplies and hitched to a strong team. He would take her beyond everyone's reach. Royce would finally have a place to call home and have a life worth living. Every night he would sleep with Gwen in his arms, knowing he would never need to leave her again. Together they would walk through open fields without Royce having to look over his shoulder. They would have children, and he would delight in watching them grow. Royce would be content to grow old with Gwen at his side.

He was sprinting to her. He did not recall telling his feet to move, yet they raced toward her. As the distance between them closed, Royce threw out his arms to embrace Gwen. Suddenly her eyes widened with shock, then shut tight with anguish. She stiffened and arched her back as the crossbow bolt exited the front of her body. Royce felt a spray of blood.

She fell.

"*Gwen!*" he screamed.

He slid to his knees and turned her over so they could see each other. Dark blood pooled around her, staining the snow. He cradled Gwen in his arms, pulled her to him, and brushed the hair from her face. Royce's hands shook as he cut her restraints. He pulled away the gag, which was soaked in blood.

She coughed. "Roy-Roy-ce." She struggled to speak. "Roy-ce...my love..."

"Shh," he told her. "It will be all right. I'll find a doctor. I'll take care of you. We're going to get married right away. No more waiting. I swear it!"

"No." She shook her head in his hands. "I don't...need a doctor."

Royce wiped the blood from her mouth and supported her head as her eyes fought for focus.

Her hand twitched as she tried to lift it toward his face. "Don't cry," she said.

Royce had not been aware that he was until that moment. Tears ran down his cheeks and fell to her face, mixing with the thin line of blood that trickled from the side of her mouth.

*This cannot be happening*, his mind screamed. *We are going away together. The wagon is ready!*

He shook and shuddered as if he might break in two.

"Don't leave me, Gwen. I love you. Please don't leave me."

"It's okay, R-Royce...Don't you see?"

"No, no—it's not. It's not okay! It's—" His voice broke. He swallowed. "How can this be okay? How can you leaving me alone be all right?"

She jerked in his arms. Her eyes closed and she coughed once more. When her eyes opened again, her chest heaved for breath. A thick gurgling sound came from her throat.

"It's the fork in your lifeline," she managed to say, her voice weaker now—only a coarse whisper. "You reached it…The death of the one you love most. Only I was wrong…I was wrong. It wasn't Hadrian…It was me…It was me all along."

"Yes," he cried, kissing her forehead.

"And what did I tell you about that? What did I say? Do you remember?"

"You said…You said that you could die a happy woman if only that were true."

She looked up at him tenderly, but her eyes lost focus and began to wander. "I can't see you, Royce. It's dark. I can't see in the dark like you can. I'm scared."

He clenched her hand. "I'm here, Gwen. I'm right beside you."

"Royce, listen to me. You have to hang on," she said, her voice suddenly urgent. "Don't let go. Don't you dare let go. Do you hear me? Are you listening to me, Royce Melborn? You have to hang on, Royce. Please…give me your hand. Give me your hand!"

He squeezed her hand tighter. "I'm here, Gwen. I have you. I'm not letting go. I'll never let go."

"Promise me. You must promise. Please, Royce."

"I promise," he told her.

"I love you, Royce. Don't forget…Don't let go…"

"I love you."

"Don't…let…"

Her body hitched again. She struggled to breathe, stiffened

in his arms, and then slowly...gradually...fell limp. Her head tilted backward. Clutching her tightly to his chest, he kissed her face. Gwen was gone and Royce was alone.

◆

Amilia, Breckton, Hadrian, and Arista led thirty horsemen to the gates of Colnora. The cavalry detachment was selected from the Northern Imperial Army and included Breckton's best soldiers. Most of them had been at the siege of Drondil Fields only weeks before. These were not the sons of counts and dukes. They did not wear elaborately decorated armor of full plate. They were grim, battle-hardened men who honed their skills on bloody fields.

In the wake of Modina's abduction, Amilia found herself in the surreal position of imperial steward. The former scullery maid now ruled the empire. She tried not to think about it. Unlike Modina, she was not descended from Novron and held no pedigree to protect her station. And she had no idea how long she had before her power, her station, and perhaps her very life ended.

She had no idea what to do, but to her great relief, Sir Breckton mobilized his men and vowed to find the empress. When Sir Hadrian and Arista volunteered to join them, Amilia decided to ride as well. She could not sit in the palace. She did not know how to administrate, so she left Nimbus in charge until her return. If she could not find Modina, there might be no point in returning at all. They had to find her.

"Open the gate!" Sir Breckton shouted toward the watch-tower that sat atop the wall in Colnora.

"City gate opens at dawn," someone replied from above.

"I am Sir Breckton, commander of the imperial hosts, on a

mission of grave importance to Her Eminence. I demand that you open at once!"

"And I am the gatekeeper with strict orders to keep this gate sealed between dusk and dawn. Come back at first light."

"What are we going to do?" Amilia asked as panic threatened to consume her. The absurdity of the situation was overwhelming. The empress's life was at stake, and they were at the mercy of a foolish man and a wooden gate.

Breckton dismounted. "We can lash tree branches together to make ladders and go over the walls. Or we can build a ram—"

"We don't have time for that," Hadrian interrupted. "The full moon's high. Royce is doing the exchange at the Langdon Bridge. We have to get inside and down to that bridge—now!"

"This is all your fault!" Amilia burst out, and shook with fury. "You and your *friend*. First you attempt to kill Sir Breckton, and now *he's* taken Modina."

Breckton reached up and took her hand. "Although he had the power to do so, Sir Hadrian did not kill me. He is not responsible for the actions of his associate. He is trying to help."

Amilia wiped tears from her eyes and nodded. She did not know what to do. She was no general. She was just a stupid peasant girl whom the nobility would soon execute. Everything was so hopeless. The only one who did not seem upset was Arista.

The princess was humming.

Already off her horse, she stood with her eyes closed and her hands outstretched. Her fingers moved delicately through the air and a low vibration echoed from deep in her throat. The sound was not a tune or a song of any kind. There was no discernible melody, and as Arista's voice grew louder, the air seemed to grow thick and heavy. Then there was another hum. An echo resonated from the gate. The wooden beams moved like a man quivering in the cold. They cracked and buckled. The great hinges rattled, and bits of stone fractured where they met the walls. Arista stopped humming. The gate ceased its trembling. Then, in one burst of voice, she uttered an unrecognizable word, and the gate exploded in flying bits of splintered wood and scattered snow.

෯

Modina tested the ropes on her wrists, but the movement only caused them to bite deeper. Merrick Marius and two men she did not know had dragged her off the bridge and into a nearby warehouse. Saldur was allowed to walk freely. The building was cavernous, abandoned, and in need of repair. Broken windows let in snow, which drifted across the bare floorboards. Torn sacks and broken glass littered the floor.

"Excellent, my boy. Excellent." Saldur addressed Merrick Marius as another man cut his hands free. "I will honor my offer to reward you handsomely. You will—"

"Shut up!" Merrick ordered harshly. "Get them both upstairs."

One of the men threw Modina over his shoulder like a sack of flour and carried her up the steps.

"I don't understand," Saldur said, even as the other stranger steered him upstairs too.

"This isn't over," Merrick replied. "DeLancy is dead. You have no idea what that means. The scales are balanced. The demon is unleashed."

He said more, but his voice faded as Modina was carried up several flights. The man carrying her dropped her in an empty room on the third floor. He pulled a wad of twine from his pocket and bound her ankles tight. When he was done, he moved to the broken window and peered out.

Moonlight fell across his face. He was a short, husky brute with a rough beard and flat nose. He wore a dark cowl over a coarse woolen garnache, but Modina's eyes were focused on the leather girdle from which two long daggers hung. He crouched on one knee, looking at the street below.

"Be very quiet, miss," he murmured, "or I'll have to slit your throat."

✑

With trembling hands, Royce laid Gwen's lifeless body near the side of the bridge. He closed her eyes and kissed her lips one last time. Folding her arms gently across her chest, he covered her as best he could with the rough, oversized cloak as if putting her to bed. He could not bring himself to cover her face and stared at it for a long while, noting the smile she wore even in death.

Turning from her, he got up and, without conscious thought, found himself crossing the bridge.

"Stop right there, Royce!" Merrick shouted when he had reached the far side.

From the sound and angle of his voice, Royce knew Merrick was on the second floor of the warehouse.

"All of the lower doors and windows are sealed. I have a man with a dagger to the empress's throat."

Royce ignored him. He deftly climbed up the closest lamppost, shattered the lantern, and snuffed out the flame. He repeated this twice more, darkening the area.

"I mean it, Royce," Merrick shouted again. The tinge of panic in his voice betrayed that his old partner could no longer see him. "Don't make the mistake of killing another innocent woman tonight."

Royce tore the bottom of his cloak and soaked the scrap in the lamppost reservoir. Then he walked to the warehouse.

"You can't get to me without killing her!" Merrick shouted again. "Get back where I can see you."

Royce began coating the base of the walls with oil.

"Damn it, Royce. I didn't do it. I didn't kill her. It wasn't me."

Royce struck a light, catching the oiled cloth on fire, and pushed it under the door. The wood was old and dry, and the flames hungrily took hold. The brisk winter wind did its part, spreading flames to the clapboard sides.

"What are you doing?" asked Saldur's voice, rising in terror. "Marius, do something. Threaten to cut Modina's throat if he doesn't—"

"I did, you idiot! He doesn't care about the empress. He's going to kill us all!" Marius shouted.

The flames spread quickly. Royce went back for more oil to lure the fire across the timbers. The exterior of the storehouse blazed, and sheets of flame raced upward. Royce stepped back and watched the building burn. He felt the heat on his face as the flaming building lit up the street.

Shouts came from inside, fighting to be heard over the crackling of the fire. Royce waited, watching the cloverleaf insignia burn away.

It was not long before the first man jumped from a second-story window. He managed to land well enough, but Royce was on him in an instant. Alverstone flickered in the firelight. The man screamed, but Royce was in no hurry and took his time. He cut the tendons of the man's legs, making it impossible for him to run. Then, sitting on his chest, he severed the man's fingers. It had been a long time since Royce had used Alverstone to dismember someone. He marveled at how well the white dagger cut through the toughest cartilage and even through bone. Royce left the first man to bleed when he noticed another one jump. This one came from a third-story window. He landed awkwardly, and Royce heard a bone break.

"No!" the man cried, struggling to crawl away as Royce's dark form flew toward him. The man scraped desperately at the snow. Once more, Royce was slow and methodical. The man howled with each cut. When he stopped moving, Royce removed his heart. He stood up, drenched in blood, his right arm soaked to the elbow, and threw the organ through the window the man had leapt from.

"You're next, Saldur," he taunted. "I can't wait to see if you actually have one or not."

There was no response.

Out of the corner of his eye, Royce saw a dark figure moving from the back of the building. Merrick was barely noticeable as he slipped through the dancing shadows. Royce guessed he was planning to hide on the lip under the Langdon Bridge, which the Black Diamond used to ambush targets. Royce left Saldur to burn. The fire completely engulfed the second floor. It would be just a matter of time. The only way out was for the regent to jump, and a man his age would fare poorly in a three-story drop to frozen ground.

Royce chased after Merrick, who abandoned stealth to make an open run for it. Royce caught up quickly, and Merrick gave up near the middle of the bridge. He turned, his dagger drawn, his face covered in sweat and soot.

"I didn't kill her," he shouted.

Royce did not respond. He rapidly closed the remaining distance and attacked. The white dagger lashed out like a snake. Merrick dodged. He avoided the first swipe but Royce caught him on the return stroke, slicing across his chest.

"Listen to me," Merrick said, still trying to back away.

"Why would I kill her? You *know* me! Don't you think I knew she was my protection? Have you *ever* seen me do anything as stupid as that? Just ask yourself—why would I do such a thing? What would I gain? Think, Royce, think. What reason would I have to kill her?"

"The same reason that I'm going to kill you—revenge."

Royce lunged. Merrick tried to move, but he was too slow. He would have died instantly if Royce had aimed for his heart or throat. Instead, Alverstone caught Merrick in the right shoulder.

It plunged deep and Merrick dropped his weapon.

"*It doesn't make sense!*" Merrick screamed at him. "This has nothing to do with Jade. If I wanted revenge, I could have killed you years ago. I only wanted Saldur and the empress. I was never going to hurt her. We've made our peace with each other, Royce. I was serious about that offer to work together again. We are not enemies. Don't make the same mistake I did. You were set up when Jade died, but I couldn't see that—I didn't want to. Now someone is doing the same thing to me. I've been set up, don't you see? Just like you were. Use your brain! If I had a bow, would I have let you burn the warehouse? It wasn't me. It was someone else!"

Royce made a show of looking around. "Funny, I don't see anyone else here."

He pounced again. Merrick retreated and his heel hit the short curb of the bridge.

"You're running out of room."

"Damn it, Royce, you have to believe me. I would never kill Gwen. I swear to you—I didn't do it!"

"I believe you," Royce said. "I just don't care."

With one final thrust, he stabbed Alverstone into Merrick's chest.

Merrick toppled backward. He reached out for the only

thing he could grab, and together he and Royce fell over the edge.

๛

When the gate had burst open, Hadrian did not wait for the others. Instead, he spurred his horse and raced toward the river. Malevolent slipped on the snow and nearly fell as he rounded the corner to Langdon Bridge. On the far side, the warehouse burned like a giant pyre. The streetlamps on that side of the bridge were dark. On his side, the iron swans, dusted with snow, flickered with an eerie orange light. The tall lampposts cast wavering shadows—thin, dark, dancing spears that fluttered and jabbed.

Hadrian saw her lying near the side of the bridge.

"Oh dear Maribor, no!" He ran to Gwen's side. Flakes of snow gathered on her closed eyes and clung to her dark lashes. He put his head to her chest. There was no heartbeat—she was dead.

"*It doesn't make sense!*" Hadrian heard someone cry out. Looking down the bridge, he saw them at the very apex of the span. Royce had Merrick backed up along the edge. Merrick was hurt, unarmed, and screaming. Jumping to his feet, Hadrian sprinted forward, his boots slipping on the slick snow. From only a few strides away, Hadrian saw Royce stab Merrick and watched as both of them tumbled over the side.

He slid, caught himself against the lip, and looked over. His heart pounded in his chest. Far below, the churning water of the Bernum River revealed itself as a dark line broken by moonlit explosions where water crashed against rocks. He saw something dark still falling. A moment later, it hit the surface with a brief flash of white.

❧

Arista flexed her fingers and climbed back on her horse. Breckton remounted as well and rode forward to speak with the shouting gate guards. Hadrian had already disappeared into the twisting streets.

No one mentioned anything about the exploding gate.

Without Hadrian to guide them, Sir Breckton led the detachment through Colnora. They crossed the Bernum using the Warpole Bridge and were midway across when they saw the warehouse ablaze near a bridge farther down the river, signaling their destination. Rather than backtrack, Breckton continued across the Warpole and arrived at the Langdon Bridge on the warehouse side, causing them to pass in front of the monstrous blaze.

The building was an inferno. The burning hulk mesmerized Arista. Huge spirals of flames reached to the sky. All four stories were on fire. The north wall blistered and snapped. The east wall curled and partially collapsed, releasing a burst of sparks and a rain of burning debris that hissed when it struck snow. White smoke billowed out from shattered windows and a nearby oak tree blazed, its naked limbs turned into a giant torch.

Arista heard a woman cry out.

"That's Modina!" Amilia shrieked, pulling back so hard on her horse's reins that the beast shook its head and backed up a step. *"She's inside!"*

Sir Breckton and several of his men dismounted and rushed to the doorway. They broke down the bolted door, but the heat forced them back. Breckton pulled his cloak over his head and started to enter.

"Stop!" Arista shouted as she slid from her horse.

The knight hesitated.

"You'll die before you reach her. I'll go."

"But—" Breckton said, then stopped. Rubbing his jaw, he looked at the fire and then back at Arista. "Can you save her?"

Arista shook her head. "I don't know. I've never done this before, but I stand a better chance than you do. Just keep everyone else back."

She pulled the sleeves of Esrahaddon's robe over her hands and the hood up around her head and face as she approached the crumbling warehouse. Realizing she could sense the fire's movements was exhilarating. The blaze moved and acted like a living thing. It withered, snapped, and fed on the old wood like a ravenous beast. It was hungry, starved for nourishment, a never-ending want, boundless greed. Approaching the blaze, she sensed it noticing her, and the fire regarded Arista with desire.

*No,* she told it. *Eat the wood. Ignore me.*

The fire hissed.

*Leave me alone or I will snuff you out.*

Arista knew she could conjure a rainstorm, or even a whirlwind, but rain would take too long, and wind would collapse the fragile building. Perhaps there was a way to eliminate the fire altogether, but she was not certain how to go about it and Modina could not wait for her to figure it out.

The fire snapped. She felt its elemental eye turn away and Arista entered the blackened doorway. She walked into an inferno of smoke and fire. Everything around her was burning. Hot currents of air whipped and gusted, blasting through the building's interior. She moved through a raging river of smoky air that parted around her.

After finding the scorched wooden stairs, she carefully began to climb. Beneath her feet the planks fractured, splintered, and popped. With the protection of Esrahaddon's robe, she felt warmth but nothing more. Breathing through the material, Arista found fresh, cool air.

"Thanks, Esra," she muttered, pushing forward into the thick, surging smoke.

She heard a muffled cry from above and climbed. On the third floor, she found Modina. The empress was in the center of a small room, hands and feet bound. The fire was busy enjoying the older, drier timber of the main brace on the far side of the room and ignored the greener floorboards where Modina lay. Running along the rafters, it ate into the supporting beams with wolfish delight.

"Not much time," the princess said, glancing up. "Can you walk?"

"Yes," Modina answered.

Arista cursed herself for not wearing a dagger as her fingers struggled to untie the empress's hands. Once loose, they worked to free her feet.

Modina coughed and gagged. Arista removed the robe. Instantly the intense heat slammed into her. She wrapped the garment over their shoulders like a blanket and held one of the sleeves to her mouth.

"Breathe through the robe," she told Modina over the roaring blaze.

The two women moved down the stairs together. Arista kept her focus on the fire's intentions and warned it away when it came too close. A timber cracked overhead and crashed with the sound of thunder. The building shuddered with the blow. A step snapped under Arista, and Modina pulled her forward in time to save the princess from a two-story fall.

"We can thank the dungeon for you not weighing much," Modina said through the sleeve pressed against her mouth.

They reached the ground floor and raced out together. The moment Modina emerged, Amilia threw her arms around her.

"There's someone else up there," Sir Breckton announced. "In that upper window near the end."

"Help!" Saldur cried. "Someone help me!"

A few looked to Arista, but she made no move to reenter the building.

"*Help me!*" he screamed.

Arista stepped back to get a better view. The old man was in tears. His face was transfigured with horror.

"Arista!" he pleaded, spotting her. "In the name of Novron...help me, child."

"It's a shame," she shouted back, her voice rising above the roar of the fire, "that *Hilfred* isn't here to save you."

There was another loud *crack* and Saldur's eyes filled with panic. He grabbed the windowsill and clung to it as the floor gave way beneath him. With a final scream, his fingers slipped and Maurice Saldur, former bishop of the Nyphron Church, co-regent and architect of the New Empire, vanished from view into the flames.

✎

Hadrian was bent over the bridge's edge, looking over the side. His eyes fixated on the spot far below where the body had hit the river. A gust of wind revealed a familiar cloak that flapped out from below the skirt of the bridge.

His heart beat faster as he spotted four fingers clinging to a hidden lip that ran beneath the span. He hurriedly wrapped his feet around a lamppost and lowered himself farther. Royce was there, just out of reach. His left hand held the underside of the Langdon, his feet dangling free.

"Royce!" Hadrian called.

His partner did not look up.

"Royce—damn you, look at me!"

Royce continued to stare down into the foaming waters as the wind whipped his black cape like the broken wings of a bird.

"Royce, I can't reach you," Hadrian shouted, extending his arm toward his friend. "You have to help me. You need to reach with your other hand so I can pull you up."

There was a pause.

"Merrick is dead," Royce said softly.

"I know."

"Gwen is dead."

Hadrian paused. "Yes."

"I—I burned Modina alive."

"Royce, goddamn it! That doesn't matter. Please, look at me."

Slowly, Royce tilted his head up. His hood fell away and tears streaked his cheeks. He refused to meet Hadrian's eyes.

"*Don't do it!*" Hadrian yelled.

"I—I don't have anything left," Royce muttered, his words almost stolen by the wind. "I don't—"

"Royce, listen to me. You have to hang on. Don't let go. Don't you dare let go. Do you hear me? Are you listening to me, Royce Melborn? You have to hang on, Royce. Please... give me your hand. Give me your hand!"

Royce's head snapped up. He focused on Hadrian and there was a curious look in his eyes. "What—what did you say?"

"I said I can't reach you. I need your help."

Hadrian extended his arm farther.

Royce sheathed Alverstone and swung his body. The momentum thrust his right hand upward. Hadrian grabbed it and lifted.

# BOOK VI

# PERCEPLIQUIS

## Chapter 1

## The Child

Miranda had been certain that the end of the world would begin like this — without warning, but with fire. Behind them, the sky glowed red as flames and plumes of sparks rose into the night sky. The university at Sheridan was burning.

Holding Mercy's little hand, Miranda was terrified she might lose the girl in the dark. They had been running for hours, dashing blindly through the pine forest, pushing their way past unseen branches. Beneath the laden boughs, the snow was deep. Miranda fought through drifts higher than her knees, breaking a path for the little girl and the old professor.

Struggling somewhere behind, Arcadius called out, "Go on, go on, don't wait for me."

Hauling the heavy pack and dragging the little girl, Miranda was moving as fast as she could. Every time she heard a sound or thought a shadow moved, Miranda fought back a scream. Panic hovered just below the surface, threatening to break free. Death was on their heels and her feet were anchors.

Miranda felt sorry for the child and worried that hauling her forward was hurting her arm. Once, Miranda had pulled too hard and dragged Mercy across the surface of the snow. The girl had cried when her face skimmed the powder, but her whimpering was short-lived. Mercy had stopped asking questions, stopped complaining about being tired. She had given up talking altogether and trudged behind Miranda as best she could. She was a brave girl.

They reached the road and Miranda knelt down to inspect the child. Her nose ran. Snowflakes clung to her eyelashes. Her cheeks were red, and her black hair lay matted with sweat to her forehead. Miranda took a moment to brush several loose strands behind her ears while Mr. Rings kept a close eye on her. As if he were a fur stole, the raccoon curled around the girl's neck. Mercy had insisted on freeing the animals from their cages before leaving. Once released, the raccoon had run up Mercy's arm and held tight. Apparently, Mr. Rings also sensed something bad was coming.

"How are you doing?" Miranda asked, pulling the girl's hood up and tightening the broach holding her cloak.

"My feet are cold," she said. The child's voice was little more than a whisper as she stared down at the snow.

"So are mine," Miranda replied in the brightest tone she could muster.

"Ah, well, that was fun, wasn't it?" the old professor said while climbing the slope to join them. He puffed large clouds and shifted the satchel over his shoulder, his beard and eyebrows thick with snow and ice.

"And how are *you* doing?" Miranda asked.

"Oh, I'm fine, fine. An old man needs a bit of exercise now and again, but we need to keep moving."

"Where are we going?" Mercy asked.

"Aquesta," Arcadius replied. "You know what Aquesta is, don't you, dear? That's where the empress rules from a big palace. You'd like to meet her, wouldn't you?"

"Will she be able to stop them?"

Miranda noticed the little girl's gaze had shifted over the old man's shoulder to the burning university. Miranda looked as well, watching the brilliant glow rising above the treetops. They were many miles away now, and yet the light still filled the horizon. Dark shadows flew above the fire's light. They swooped and circled over the burning university, and from their mouths spewed torrents of flame.

"We can hope, my dear. We can hope," Arcadius said. "Now let's keep moving. I know you're tired. I know you're cold. So am I, but we have to go as fast as we can. We have to get farther away."

Mercy nodded or shivered. It was difficult to discern which. Miranda dusted the snow from the child's back and legs in an attempt to keep her from getting wetter than she already was. This drew a cautious glare from Mr. Rings.

"Do you think the other animals got away?" Mercy asked.

"I'm certain they did," Arcadius assured her. "They are smart, aren't they? Maybe not as smart as Mr. Rings here— after all, he managed to get a ride."

Mercy nodded again and added in a hopeful voice, "I'm sure Teacup got away. She can fly."

Miranda checked the girl's pack and then her own to ensure they were still closed and cinched tight. She looked down the dark road before them.

"This will take us through Colnora and right into Aquesta," the old wizard explained.

"How long will it take to get there?" Mercy asked.

"Several days—a week, perhaps. Longer if the weather stays bad."

Miranda saw the disappointment in Mercy's eyes. "Don't worry, once we are farther away, we will stop, rest, and eat. I'll make something hot and then we'll sleep for a bit. But for now, we have to keep going. Now that we are on the road, it will be easier."

Miranda took the little girl's hand and they set off again. She was pleased to discover that what she had told the child turned out to be true. Trenches left by wagons made for easy going, even more so due to the downhill slope. They kept a brisk pace, and soon the forest rose to blot out the fiery glow behind them. The world became dark and quiet, with only the sound of the cold wind to keep them company.

Miranda glanced at the old professor as he trudged along, holding his cloak tight to his neck. The skin of his face was red and blotchy, and he labored to breathe. "Are you sure you are all right?"

Arcadius did not respond at first. He drew near, forced a smile, and whispered softly in Miranda's ear, "I fear you may need to finish this journey without me."

"What?" Miranda said too loudly, and glanced down at the little girl. Mercy did not look up. "We'll stop soon. We'll rest and take our time tomorrow. We've gone a good distance today. Here, let me take your satchel." She reached out.

"No. I'll hang on to it. It's very fragile, as you know — and dangerous. If anyone dies carrying it, I want it to be me. As for resting, I don't think it will make a difference. I'm not strong enough for this sort of travel. We both know that."

"You can't give up."

"I'm not. I'm handing off the charge to you. You'll manage."

"But I don't know what to do. You've never told me the plan."

Arcadius chuckled. "That's because it changes frequently. I had hoped the regents would have accepted Mercy as Modina's heir, but they refused."

"So now what?"

"Modina is on the throne now, so we have a second chance.

The best you can do is get to Aquesta and seek an audience with her."

"But I don't know how—"

"You'll figure it out. Introduce Mercy to the empress. That will be a start in the right direction. Soon you will be the only one who knows the truth. I hate placing this burden on you, but I have no choice."

Miranda shook her head. "No, it was my mother who placed the burden on me. Not you."

"A deathbed confession is a weighty thing." The old man nodded. "But doing so allowed her to die in peace."

"Do you think so? Or is her spirit still lingering? Sometimes I feel as if she is watching—haunting me. I'm paying the price for her weakness, her cowardice."

"Your mother was young, poor, and ignorant. She witnessed the death of dozens of men, the butchery of a mother and child, and narrowly escaped. She lived in constant fear that someday, someone would discover there were twins and she rescued one of them."

"But," Miranda said bitterly, "what she did was wrong and unconscionable. And the worst part is she couldn't let the sin die with her. She had to tell me. Make it my responsibility to correct her mistakes. She should—"

Mercy came to an abrupt halt, tugging on Miranda's arm.

"Honey, we need to..." She stopped upon seeing the girl's face. The faint light of an early dawn revealed fear as Mercy stared ahead to where the road dipped toward a large stone bridge.

"There's a light up ahead," Arcadius said.

"Is it...?" Miranda asked.

The old teacher shook his head. "It's a campfire—several, it looks like. More refugees, I suspect. We can join with them and the going will be easier. If I'm not mistaken, they are camped on the far bank of the Galewyr. I had no idea we'd come so far. No wonder I'm puffing."

"There now," Miranda said to the girl as they once more started forward. "See? Our troubles are already over. Maybe they will even have a wagon that an old man can ride in."

Arcadius gave her a smirk but allowed himself a smile. "Things may be looking up at that."

"We'll be—"

The girl squeezed Miranda's hand and stopped once more. Up the road, figures on horseback trotted toward them. The animals snorted white fog as their hooves drove through the iced tracks. The riders sat enveloped in dark cloaks. With hoods drawn up and scarves wrapped, it was difficult to determine much, but one thing was certain—they were just men. Miranda counted three. They came from the south but not from the direction of the campfires. These were not refugees.

"Who do you think?" Miranda asked. "Highwaymen?"

The professor shook his head.

"What do we do?"

"Hopefully nothing. With luck they are just good men coming to our aid. If not..." He patted his satchel grimly. "Get to those campfires and ask for shelter and protection. Then see to it that Mercy reaches Aquesta. Avoid the regents and try to tell the empress Mercy's story. Tell her the truth."

"But what if—"

The horses approached and slowed.

"What do we have here?" one rider asked.

Miranda could not tell who spoke, but guessed it was the foremost. He studied them while they stood still, listening to the deep throaty pant of the horses.

"Isn't this convenient?" he said, and dismounted. "Of all the people in the world—I was just coming to see you, old man."

The leader was tall and held his side gingerly, moving stiffly. His piercing eyes glared out from under his hood, his nose and mouth shrouded by a crimson scarf.

"Out for an early stroll in a snowstorm?" he asked, closing the distance between them.

"Hardly," Arcadius replied. "We're in flight."

"I'm sure you are. Clearly if I had waited even a day, I would have missed you, and you might have slipped away. Coming to the palace was a foolish mistake. You exposed too much. And for what? You should have known better. But age must bring with it a degree of desperation." He looked at Mercy. "Is this the girl?"

"Guy," Arcadius said, "Sheridan is burning. The elves have crossed the Nidwalden. The elves have attacked!"

*Guy!* Miranda knew him, or at least his reputation. Arcadius had taught her the names of all the church sentinels. From the professor's viewpoint, Luis Guy was the most dangerous. All sentinels were obsessed, all chosen for their rabid orthodoxy, but Guy had a legacy. His mother's maiden name was Evone. She had been a pious girl who had married Lord Jarred Seret, a direct descendant of the original Lord Darius Seret, who had been charged by Patriarch Venlin to find the heir of the Old Empire. In the realm of heir hunters, Luis Guy was a fanatic among fanatics.

"Don't play me for a fool. This is the girl-child you spoke to Saldur and Ethelred about, isn't it? The one you wanted to groom as the next empress. Why would you do that, old man? Why pick *this* girl? Is this another ruse? Or were you actually trying to slip her past us? To atone for your mistake." Guy crouched down to get a better look at Mercy's face. "Come here, child."

"No!" Miranda snapped, pulling Mercy close.

Guy stood up slowly. "Let go of the child," he ordered.

"No."

"Sentinel Guy!" Arcadius shouted. "She's just a peasant girl. An orphan I took in."

"Is she?" He drew his sword.

"Be reasonable. You have no idea what you're doing."

"Oh, I think I do. Everyone was so focused on Esrahaddon that you went by unnoticed. Who could have imagined that you would point the way to the heir not just once, but twice?"

"The heir? The Heir of Novron? Are you insane? Is that why you think I spoke to the regents?"

"Isn't it?"

"No." He shook his head, an amused smile on his face. "I came because I suspected they hadn't thought about the question of succession, and I wanted to help educate the next imperial leader."

"But you insisted on this girl—only *this* girl. Why would you do that unless she really is the heir?"

"That makes no sense. How could I know who the heir is? Or even if an heir still lives?"

"How indeed. That was the missing piece. You are actually the only one who could know. Tell me, Arcadius Latimer, what did your father do for a living?"

"He was a weaver, but I fail to see—"

"Yes, so how did the poor son of a weaver from a small village become the master of lore at Sheridan University? I doubt your father even knew how to read, and yet his son is one of the most renowned scholars in the world? How does that happen?"

"Really, Guy, I would not think I would need to explain the merits of ambition and hard work to someone such as you."

Guy sneered back. "You disappeared for ten years, and when you came back, you knew a lot more than when you left."

"You're just making things up."

Guy smirked. "The church doesn't let just anyone teach at their university. Did you think they didn't keep records?"

"Of course not. I just didn't think you'd see them." The old man smiled.

"I'm a sentinel, you idiot! I have access to every archive in the church."

"Yes, but I didn't think my scholastic examination would be of any interest. I was a rebel in my youth—handsome too. Did the records indicate that?"

"It said you found the tomb of Yolric. Who was Yolric?"

"And here I thought you knew everything."

"I didn't have time to linger in libraries. I was in a hurry to catch you."

"But why? Why are you after me? Why is your sword out?"

"Because the Heir of Novron must die."

"She's not the heir. Why do you think she is? How could I even know who the heir was?"

"Because that is one of the secrets you brought back. You discovered how to locate the heir."

"Bah! Really, Guy, you have quite an imagination."

"There were other records. The church called you in for questioning. They thought you might have gone to Percepliquis like that Edmund Hall fellow. And then, only days after that meeting, there was a fight in the city of Ratibor. A pregnant mother and her husband were killed. Identified as Linitha and Naron Brown, they and their child were executed by Seret Knights. After centuries of looking, I find it interesting that my predecessor managed to locate the Heir of Novron just days after the church interrogated you." Guy glared at the professor. "Did you make a deal with the church? Did you trade information in exchange for freedom? I'm sure they told you they wanted to find the heir so they could make him king again. When you discovered what they really did, I imagine you felt used—the guilt must be awful."

Guy paused for Arcadius to respond but the professor said nothing.

"After that everyone thought the bloodline had ended, didn't they? Even the Patriarch had no idea another heir still lived. Then Esrahaddon escapes and he goes straight to Degan Gaunt. Only Degan isn't the heir. I was fooled for a long time too, but imagine my shock when he failed the blood test that he previously passed. No doubt the result of the same potion Esrahaddon used on King Amrath and Arista that made Braga suspect the Essendons. I suppose, looking back on it, we should have guessed a wizard of the Old Empire wasn't a fool and would never lead us to the real heir.

"But there was another, wasn't there? And you performed whatever trick you did the first time to find her." Guy peered at Mercy. "What is she? A bastard child? A niece?" He advanced toward Miranda. "Hand her over."

"No!" the old professor shouted.

One of the soldiers grabbed Miranda, and the other pulled the girl from her.

"But let's be certain, shall we? I will not make the same mistake twice." With a deft sweep of his wrist, Guy slashed Mercy across her hand. She screamed and Mr. Rings hissed.

"That's uncalled for!" Arcadius said.

"Watch them," Guy ordered his men while he moved to his horse.

"Hush now, be a brave girl for me," Miranda told Mercy.

Guy carefully laid his sword on the ground, then withdrew a small leather case from his saddlebag. From it, he pulled forth a set of three vials. He uncorked the first, tilted it slightly, and tapped on it with his finger until a bit of powder sprinkled onto the bloodstained end of his sword.

"I want to leave now," Mercy whimpered as the guard held her fast. "Please can we go?"

"Interesting," Guy muttered to himself, then applied the contents of the next vial. This one held a liquid that hissed and fizzled when it landed on the blade.

"Guy!" Arcadius shouted at him as he stepped forward.

"*Very* interesting," Guy continued. He uncorked the last vial.

"Guy, don't!" the old man yelled.

He poured a single drop on the tip of the sword.

*Pop!*

The sound was like a wine bottle cork coming free and the flash was as brilliant as lightning.

The sentinel stood up, staring at the end of his sword, and began to laugh. It was a strange and eerie sound, like the song of a madman. "At last. At long last, I have found the Heir of Novron. The quest of my ancestors will be achieved through me."

"Miranda," Arcadius whispered, "you can do nothing more by yourself." The old man's eyes glanced toward the refugee camp.

As the morning light rose, Miranda could see several columns of smoke. Possible help was tantalizingly close. Only a few hundred yards at most.

"I've devoted my life to correcting my mistake. But now it is up to you to do what must be done," Arcadius said.

Luis Guy took the girl and hoisted her onto his horse. "We'll take her to the Patriarch."

"What about these two, sir?" one of the hooded men asked.

"Take the old man. Kill the woman."

Miranda's heart skipped as the soldier reached for his sword.

"Wait!" Arcadius said. "What about the horn?" The old

professor was backing away, clutching his satchel. "The Patriarch will want the horn too, won't he?"

Guy's eyes flashed at the bag Arcadius held.

"You have it?" the sentinel asked.

Arcadius shot a desperate look toward Miranda, then turned and fled back down the road.

"Watch the child," Guy ordered one of his men. Turning to the other, he waved, and together they chased after Arcadius, who ran faster than Miranda would have ever imagined possible.

She watched him—her closest friend—racing back the way they had come, his cloak flying behind him. She might have thought the sight comical except she knew what Arcadius actually had in his satchel. She knew why he was running away, what that meant, and what he wanted her to do.

Miranda reached for the dagger under her cloak. She had never killed anyone before, but what choice did she have? The man standing between her and Mercy was a soldier, and likely a Seret Knight. He turned his back on her to get a better grip on Guy's horse, focusing his attention on Mercy and the hissing raccoon that snapped at him.

Miranda had only seconds before Guy and the other man caught up to Arcadius. Knowing what would happen made her want to cry. They had come so far together, sacrificed so much, and just when it seemed like they were finally close to their goal...to be stopped like this...to be murdered on a roadside... *Tragic* was too weak a word to frame the injustice. There would be time for tears later. The professor was counting on her and she would not let him down. That one look had told her everything. This was the final gamble. If they could get Mercy to Modina, everything might be made right again.

She drew the dagger and rushed forward. With all her strength, Miranda stabbed the soldier in the back. He was not wearing mail or leather and the sharp blade bit deep, passing through clothes, skin, and muscle.

He spun and swatted her away. The back of his fist connected with her cheek and left her reeling from the blow. She fell to the snow, still holding the dagger, the handle slick with blood.

On the horse, Mercy held tight to the saddle and screamed. The raccoon chattered, its fur up.

Miranda got back to her feet as the soldier drew his sword. He was badly hurt. Blood soaked his pant leg and he staggered toward her. She tried to get away, reaching for Mercy and the horse, but the seret was faster. His sword pierced her side somewhere near her waist. She felt it go in. The pain burned, but then she suddenly felt cold. Her knees buckled. She managed to hold fast to the saddle as the horse, frightened by the violence and Mercy's screaming, moved away, dragging her with it.

Behind them, the soldier fell to his knees, blood bubbling from his lips.

Miranda tried to pull herself up, but her legs were useless. They hung limp and she felt the strength draining from her arms. "Take the reins, Mercy, and hang on tight."

Down the road, Guy and the other man had caught up to Arcadius. Guy, who had stopped at the sound of the girl's screams, lagged behind, but the other soldier tackled the old professor to the snow.

"Mercy," Miranda said, "you need to ride. Ride over there—ride to the campfires. Beg for help. Go."

With her last bit of strength, she struck the horse's flank. The animal bolted forward. The saddle ripped from Miranda's hands and she fell once more into the snow. Lying on her back, she listened to the sound of the horse as it raced away.

"Get on your—" she heard Guy shout, but it was too late. Arcadius had opened the satchel.

Even from hundreds of feet away Miranda felt the earth shake from the explosion. An instant later, a gust of wind threw stinging snow against her face as a cloud billowed into the morning sky. Arcadius, and the man who wrestled with him, died instantly. Guy was blown off his feet. The remaining horses scattered.

As the snowy cloud settled, Miranda stared up at the brightening sky, at the rising dawn. She was not cold anymore. The pain in her side was going away, growing numb along with her legs and hands. She felt a breeze cross her cheek and noticed her legs and waist were wet, her dress soaked through. She could taste iron on her tongue. Breathing became difficult— as if she were drowning.

Guy was still alive. She heard him cursing the old man and calling to the horses as if they were disobedient dogs. The crunch of snow, the rub of leather, then the sound of hooves galloping away.

She was alone in the silence of the cold winter's dawn.

It was quiet. Peaceful.

"Dear Maribor, hear me," she prayed aloud to the brightening sky. "Oh Father of Novron, creator of men." She took her last breath and with it said, "Take care of your only daughter."

∽

Alenda Lanaklin crept out of her tent into the brisk morning air. She wore her thickest wool dress and two layers of fur, but still she shivered. The sun was just rising—a cold milky haze in the soup of a heavy winter sky. The clouds had lingered for more than a week and she wondered if she would ever see the sun's bright face again.

Alenda stood on the packed snow, looking around at the

dozens of tents pitched among the pine forest's eaves. Campfires burned in blackened snow pits, creating gray tails of smoke that wagged with the wind. Among them wandered figures, hooded and bundled such that it should have been difficult to identify male from female. Yet there was no such dilemma—they were all women. The camp was filled with them as well as children and the elderly. People walked with bowed heads, picking their way carefully through the trampled snow.

Everything appeared so different in the light, so quiet, so still. The previous night had been a terror of fire, screams, and a flight along the Westfield road. They had paused only briefly to take a head count before pushing on. Alenda had been so exhausted that she barely recalled the camp being set.

"Good morning, my lady," Emily greeted her from beneath a blanket, which was wrapped over her cloak. Her words lacked their normal cheerfulness. Alenda's maid had always been bright and playful in the morning. Now she stood with somber diligence, her reddened hands quivering, her jaw shaking with the chill.

"Is it, Emmy?" Alenda cast another look around. "How can you tell?"

"Let's find you some breakfast. Something warm will make you feel better."

"My father and brothers are dead," Alenda replied. "The world is ending. How can breakfast possibly help?"

"I don't know, my lady, but we must try. It's what your father wanted—for you to survive, I mean. It's why he stayed behind, isn't it?"

A loud boom, like a crack of thunder, echoed from the north. Every head turned to look out across the snowy fields. Every face terrified that the end had arrived at last.

Reaching the center of the camp, Alenda found Belinda Pickering; her daughter, Lenare; old Julian, Melengar's lord high chamberlain; and Lord Valin, the party's sole protector. The elderly knight had led them through the chaos the night before. Among them, they composed the last vestiges of the royal court, at least those still in Melengar. King Alric was in Aquesta lending a hand in the brief civil war and saving his sister, Arista, from execution. It was to him they now fled.

"We have no idea, but it is foolish to stay any longer," Lord Valin was saying.

"Yes, I agree," Belinda replied.

Lord Valin turned to a young boy. "Send word to rouse everyone. We will break camp immediately."

"Emmy," Alenda said, turning to her maid. "Run back and pack our things."

"Of course, my lady." Emily curtsied and headed toward their tent.

"What was that sound?" Alenda asked Lenare, who only shrugged, her face frightened.

Lenare Pickering was lovely, as always. Despite the horrors, the flight, and the primitive condition of the camp, she was radiant. Even disheveled in a hastily grabbed cloak, with her blonde hair spilling out of her hood, she remained stunning, just as a sleeping baby is always precious. She had gotten this blessing from her mother. Just as the Pickering men were renowned for their swordsmanship, so too were the Pickering women celebrated for their beauty. Lenare's mother, Belinda, was famous for it.

All that was over now. What had been constants only the day before were now lost beyond a gulf too wide to clearly see across, although at times it appeared that Lenare tried. Alenda often had seen her staring north at the horizon with a look somewhere between desperation and remorse, searching for ghosts.

In her arms, Lenare still held her father's legendary sword.

The count had handed it to her, begging that she deliver it safely to her brother Mauvin. Then he had kissed each member of his family before returning to the line where Alenda's own father and brothers waited with the rest of the army. Since then, Lenare had never set the burden down. She had wrapped it in a dark wool blanket and bound it with a silk ribbon. Throughout the harrowing escape, she had hugged the long bundle to her breast, at times using it to wipe away tears.

"If we push hard today, we might make Colnora by sunset," Lord Valin told them. "Assuming the weather improves." The old knight glared up at the sky as if it alone were their adversary.

"Lord Julian," Belinda said. "The relics...the scepter and seal—"

"They are all safe, my lady," the ancient chamberlain replied. "Loaded in the wagons. The kingdom is intact, save for the land itself." The old man looked back in the direction of the strange sound, toward the banks of the Galewyr River and the bridge they had crossed the night before.

"Will they help us in Colnora?" Belinda asked. "We haven't much food."

"If news has reached them of King Alric's part in freeing the empress, they should be willing," Lord Valin said. "Even if it has not, Colnora is a merchant city, and merchants thrive on profit, not chivalry."

"I have some jewelry," Belinda informed him. "If needs be, you can sell what I have for..." The countess paused as she noticed Julian still staring back at the bridge.

Others soon lifted their gazes, and finally Alenda looked up to see the approach of a rider.

"Is it...?" Lenare began.

"It's a child," Belinda said.

Alenda quickly realized she was right. A little girl raced at them, clutching to the back of the sweat-soaked horse. Her hood had blown back, revealing long dark hair and rosy cheeks. She was about six years old, and just as she clutched the horse, a raccoon held fast to her. They were an odd pair to be alone on the road, but Alenda reminded herself that "normal" no longer existed. If she should see a bear in a feather cap riding a chicken, that too might be normal now.

The horse entered the camp and Lord Valin grabbed the bit, forcing the animal and rider to a stop.

"Are you all right, honey?" Belinda asked.

"There's blood on the saddle," Lord Valin noted.

"Are you hurt?" the countess asked the child. "Where are your parents?"

The girl shivered and blinked but said nothing. Her little fists still clutched the horse's reins.

"She's cold as ice," Belinda said, touching the child's cheek. "Help me get her down."

"What's your name?" Alenda asked.

The girl remained mute. Deprived of her horse, she turned to hugging the raccoon.

"Another rider," Lord Valin announced.

Alenda looked up to see a man crossing the bridge and wheeling toward them.

The rider charged into the camp and threw back his hood, revealing long black hair, pale skin, and intense eyes. He bore a narrow mustache and a short beard trimmed to a fine point. He glared at them until he spotted the girl.

"There!" he said, pointing. "Give her to me at once."

The child cried out in fear, shaking her head.

"No!" Belinda shouted, and pressed the girl into Alenda's hands.

"My lady," Lord Valin said. "If the child is his—"

"This child does not belong to him," the countess declared, her tone hateful.

"I am a Sentinel of Nyphron," the man shouted so all could hear. "This child is claimed for the church. You will hand her over now. Any who oppose me will die."

"I know very well who you are, Luis Guy," Belinda said, seething. "I will not provide you with any more children to murder."

The sentinel peered at her. "Countess Pickering?" He studied the camp with renewed interest. "Where is your husband? Where is your fugitive son?"

"I am no fugitive," Denek said as he came forward. Belinda's youngest had recently turned thirteen and was growing tall and lanky. He was well on his way to imitating his older brothers.

"He means Mauvin," Belinda explained. "This is the man who murdered Fanen."

"Again I ask you," Guy pressed. "Where is your husband?"

"He is dead and Mauvin is well beyond your reach."

The sentinel looked out over the crowd and then down at Lord Valin. "And he has left you poor protection. Now, hand over the child."

"I will not," Belinda said.

Guy dismounted and stepped forward to face Lord Valin. "Hand over the child or I will be forced to take her."

The old knight looked to Belinda, whose face remained hateful. "My lady does not wish it, and I shall defend her decision." The old man drew his sword. "You will leave now."

Alenda jumped at the sound of steel as Guy drew his own sword and lunged. In less than an instant, Lord Valin was clutching his bleeding side, his sword arm wavering. With a shake of his head, the sentinel slapped the old man's blade away and stabbed him through the neck.

Guy advanced toward the girl with a terrifying fire in his eyes. Before he could cross the distance, Belinda stepped between them.

"I do not make a habit of killing women," Guy told her. "But nothing will keep me from this prize."

"What do you want her for?"

"As you said, to kill her. I will take the child to the Patriarch and then she must die, by my hands."

"Never."

"You cannot stop me. Look around. You have only women and children. You have no one to fight for you. Give me the child!"

"Mother?" Lenare said softly. "He is right. There is no one else. Please."

"Mother, let me," Denek pleaded.

"No. You are still too young. Your sister is right. There is no one else." The countess nodded toward her daughter.

"I am pleased to see someone who—" Guy stopped as Lenare stepped forward. She slipped off her cloak and untied the bundle, revealing the sword of her father, which she drew forth and held before her. The blade caught the hazy winter light, pulling it in and casting it back in a sharp brilliance.

Puzzled, Guy looked at her for a moment. "What is this?"

"You killed my brother," Lenare said.

Guy looked to Belinda. "You're not serious."

"Just this once, Lenare," Belinda told her daughter.

"You would have your daughter die for this child? If I must kill all your children, I will."

Alenda watched, terrified, as everyone backed away, leaving a circle around Sentinel Guy and Lenare. A ripping wind shuddered the canvas of the tents and threw Lenare's golden hair back. Standing alone in the snow, dressed in her white traveling clothes and holding the rapier, she appeared as a mythical creature, a fairy queen or goddess—beautiful in her elegance.

With a scowl, Luis Guy lunged, and with surprising speed and grace, Lenare slapped the attack away. Her father's sword sang with the contact.

"You've handled a blade before," Guy said, surprised.

"I am a Pickering."

He swung at her. She blocked. He swiped. She parried. Then Lenare slashed and cut Guy across the cheek.

"*Lenare*," her mother said with a stern tone. "Don't play games."

Guy paused, holding a hand to his bleeding face.

"He killed Fanen, Mother," Lenare said coldly. "He should be made to suffer. He should be made an example."

"No," Belinda said. "It's not our way. Your father wouldn't approve. You know that. Just finish it."

"What is this?" Guy demanded, but there was a hesitation in his voice. "You're a woman."

"I told you—I am a Pickering and you killed my brother."

Guy began to raise his sword.

Lenare stepped and lunged. The thin rapier pierced the man's heart and was withdrawn before he finished his stroke.

Luis Guy fell dead, facedown in the blood-soaked snow.

## Chapter 2

# Nightmares

Arista woke up screaming. Her body trembled; her stomach suffered from a sinking sensation—the remaining residue of a dream she could not remember. She sat up, her left hand crawling to her chest, where she felt the thundering of her heart. It was pounding so hard, so fast, beating against her ribs as if needing to escape. She tried to remember. She could only recall brief snippets, tiny bits that appeared to be disjointed and unrelated. The one constant was Esrahaddon, his voice so distant and weak she could never hear what he said.

Her thin linen nightgown clung to her skin, soaked with sweat. Her bedsheets, stripped from the mattress, spilled to the floor. The quilt, embroidered with designs of spring flowers, lay waded up nearly on the other side of the room. Esrahaddon's robe, however, rested neatly next to her, giving off a faint blue radiance. The garment appeared as if a maid had prepared it for her morning dressing. Arista's hand was touching it.

*How is it on the bed?* Arista looked at the wardrobe. The door she remembered closing hung open, and a chill ran through her. She was alone.

A soft knock at the door startled her.

"Arista?" Alric's voice came from the other side.

She threw the robe around her shoulders and immediately felt warmer, safer. "Come in," she called.

Her brother opened the door and peered in, holding a candle a bit above his head. Dressed in a burgundy robe, he had a thick baldric buckled around his waist, the Sword of Essendon hanging at his side. The weapon was huge, and as he entered, Alric used one hand to tilt it up to keep the tip from dragging on the floor. The sight reminded her of the night their father was murdered—the night Alric became king.

"I heard you cry out. Are you all right?" he asked, his eyes searching the room and settling on the glowing robe.

"I'm fine—just a nightmare."

"Another one?" He sighed. "You know, it might help if you didn't sleep in that *thing*." He gestured toward the robe. "Sleeping in a dead man's clothes...it's creepy—sort of sick, really. Don't forget he was a wizard. That thing could be— well, I'll just say it—it *is* enchanted. I'm sure it is responsible. Do you want to talk about your dream?"

"I don't remember much. Like all the others, I just...I don't know. It's hard to describe. There's this sense of urgency that's overwhelming. I feel this need to find something—that if I don't, I'll die. I always wake up terrified, like I am walking off a cliff and don't see it."

"Can I get you something?" he asked. "Water? Tea? Soup?"

"Soup? Where will you get soup in the middle of the night?"

He shrugged. "I just thought I'd ask. You don't have to beat me up for it. I hear you scream, I jump out of bed and rush to your door, I offer to play servant for you, and this is the thanks I get?"

"I'm sorry." She frowned playfully but meant what she

said. Having him there did chase the shadows away and took her mind off the wardrobe. She patted her bed. "Sit down."

Alric hesitated, then set the candle on her nightstand and took a seat beside her. "What happened to the sheets and quilt? Looks like you were wrestling."

"Maybe I was. I can't remember."

"You look terrible," he said.

"Thanks."

He sighed.

"I'm sorry. I'm sorry. But you're still my little brother and this new protective side of yours is hard to get used to. Remember when I fell off Tamarisk and broke my ankle? It hurt so bad that I couldn't see straight. When I asked you to get help, you just stood there laughing and pointing."

"I was twelve."

"You were a brat."

He frowned at her.

"But you're not anymore." She took his hand and cupped it in both of hers. "Thank you for checking on me. You even wore your sword."

Alric looked down. "I didn't know what beast or scoundrel might be attacking the princess. I had to come prepared to do battle."

"Can you even draw that thing?"

He frowned at her again. "Oh, quit it, will you? They say I fought masterfully in the Battle of Medford."

"Masterfully?"

He struggled to stop himself from smiling. "Yes, some might even say heroically. In fact, I believe some did say heroically."

"You've watched that silly play too many times."

"It's good theater, and I like to support the arts."

"*The arts*." She rolled her eyes. "You just like it because it makes all the girls swoon and you love all the attention."

"Well…" He shrugged guiltily.

"Don't deny it! I've seen you with a crowd of them circling like vultures and you grinning and strutting around like the prize bull at the fair. Do you make a list? Does Julian send them to your chambers by hair color, height, or merely in alphabetical order?"

"It's not like that."

"You know, you do have to get married, and the sooner, the better. You have a lineage to protect. Kings who don't produce heirs cause civil wars."

"You sound like Father. Maribor forbid I should have any enjoyment in my life. I have to be king—don't make me have to be a husband and father too. You might as well just lock me up and get it over with. Besides, there's plenty of time. I'm still young. You make it sound like I am teetering on the edge of my grave. And what about you? You're pushing old-maid status now. Shouldn't we be searching for suitable nobles? Do you remember when you thought I arranged a marriage for you with Prince Rudolf, and—Arista? Are you all right?"

She turned away, wiping the moisture from her eyes. "I'm fine."

"I'm sorry." She felt his hand on her shoulder.

"It's okay," she replied, and coughed to clear her throat.

"You know I would never—"

"I know. It's all right, really." She sniffled and wiped her nose. They sat in silence for a few minutes; then Arista said, "I would have married Hilfred, you know. I don't care what you or the council would have said."

A look of surprise came over him. "Since when have you ever cared…Hilfred, huh?" He smirked and shook his head.

She glared back.

"It's not what you think," he said.

"What is it, then?" she asked with an accusing tone, thinking that the boy who had laughed at her falling from her horse had reappeared.

"No slight to Hilfred. I liked him. He was a good man and loved you very much."

"But he wasn't noble," she interrupted. "Well, listen—"

"Wait." Her brother held up a hand. "Let me finish. I don't care if he was noble or not. Truth is he was nobler than just about anyone I can think of, except maybe that Breckton fellow. How Hilfred managed to stand by you every day, while not saying anything—that was real chivalry. He wasn't a knight, but he's the only one I ever saw who acted like one. No, it's not because he wasn't noble-born, and it's not because he wasn't a great guy. I would have loved to have him as a brother."

"What, then?" she asked, this time confused.

Alric looked at her, and in his eyes was the same expression she had seen when he had found her in the dark of the imperial prison.

"You didn't love him," he said simply.

The words shocked her. She did not say anything. She could not say anything.

"I don't think there was anyone in Essendon Castle who didn't know how Hilfred felt. Why didn't you?" he asked.

She could not help it. She started crying.

"Arista, I'm sorry. I just…"

She shook her head, trying to get enough air into her lungs to speak. "No—you're right—you're right." She could not keep her lips from quivering. "But I would have married him just the same. I would have made him happy."

Alric reached out and pulled her close. She buried her head into the thick folds of his robe and squeezed. They did not say anything for a long while and then Arista sat up and wiped her face.

She took a breath. "So when did you get so romantic, anyway? Since when does love have anything to do with marriage? You don't love any of the girls you spend your time with."

"And that's why I'm not married."

"Really?"

"Surprised? I guess I just remember Mom and Dad, you know?"

Arista narrowed her eyes at him. "He married Mother because she was Ethelred's niece and he needed the leverage with Warric to combat the trade war with Chadwick and Glouston."

"Maybe at the start, but they grew to love each other. Father used to tell me that wherever he was, if Mom was there, it was home. I always remembered that. I've never found anyone who made me feel that way. Have you?"

She hesitated. For a moment she considered telling him the truth, then just shook her head.

They sat again in silence; then finally Alric rose. "Are you sure I can't get you anything?"

"No, but thank you. It means a lot to know that you care."

He started to leave, and as he reached the door, she said, "Alric?"

"Hmm?"

"Remember when you and Mauvin were planning on going to Percepliquis?"

"Oh yeah, believe me, I think about that a lot these days. What I wouldn't give to be able to—"

"Do you know where it is?"

"Percepliquis? No. No one does. Mauvin and I were just hoping we'd be the ones to stumble on it. Typical kid stuff, like slaying a dragon or winning the Wintertide games. It sure would have been fun to look, though. Instead, I guess I have to go home and look for a bride. She'll make me wear shoes at dinner—I know she will."

Alric left, closing the door softly behind him and leaving her in the blue glow of the robe. She lay back down with her eyes open, studying the stone and mortar above her bed. She saw where the artisan had scraped his trowel, leaving an impression frozen in time. The light of the robe shifted with her breaths, creating the illusion of movement and giving her the sensation of being underwater, as if the ceiling were the lighted surface of a winter pond. It felt like she was drowning, trapped beneath a thick slab of solid blue ice.

She closed her eyes. It did not help.

*Soup*, she thought—warm, tasty, comforting soup. Perhaps it was not such a bad idea after all. Maybe someone would be in the kitchen. She had no idea what time it was. It was dark, but it was also winter. Still, it had to be early, since there had been no scuttling of castle servants past her door. It did not matter. She would not fall back to sleep now, so she might as well get up. If no one was awake, she might manage on her own.

The idea of doing something for herself, of being useful, got her going. She was actually excited as her feet hit the cold stone and she looked around for her slippers. The robe glowed brighter, as if sensing her need. When she entered the dark hall, it remained bright until she descended the stairs. As she entered into torchlight, the robe dimmed until it only reflected the firelight.

She was disappointed to find several people already at work in the kitchen. Cora, the stocky dairymaid with the bushy eyebrows and rosy cheeks, was at work churning butter near the door, pumping the plunger in a steady rhythm, trading one hand for another. The young boy Nipper, with his shoulders powdered in snow, stomped his feet as he entered from the dark courtyard, carrying an armload of wood, pausing to shake his head like a dog. He threw a spray that garnered a curse from Cora. Leif and Ibis stoked the stoves, grumbling to each other about damp tinder. Lila stood on a ladder like a circus performer, pulling down the teetering bowls stacked on the top shelf. Edith Mon had always insisted on having them dusted at the start of each month. While the ogre herself was gone, her tyranny lived on.

Arista had looked forward to rustling around in the darkened scullery, searching for a meal like a mouse. Now her adventure was ruined and she considered returning upstairs to avoid an awkward encounter. Arista knew all the scullery servants from her days posing as Ella the chambermaid. She might be a princess, but she was also a liar, a spy, and, of course, a witch.

*Do they hate me? Fear me?*

There was a time when the thought of servants had not bothered her, a time when she had hardly noticed them at all. Standing at the bottom of the steps, watching them scurry around the chilly kitchen, she could not determine if she had gained wisdom or lost innocence.

Arista pivoted, hoping to escape unnoticed back up the stairs to the sheltered sanctuary of her chamber, when she spotted the monk. He sat on the floor near the washbasins, where the stone was wet from a leaky plug. His back rested against the lye barrel. He was small, thin, and dressed in the traditional russet frock of the order of the Monks of Maribor. Delighted by rubbing the shaggy sides of Red, the big elkhound who sat before him, he had a great smile on his face. The dog was a fixture in the kitchen, where he routinely cleared scraps. The dog's eyes were closed, his long tongue hung dripping, and his body rocked as the monk scratched him.

Arista had not seen much of Myron since the day he had

arrived at the castle. So much had happened since then that she forgot he was still there.

Walking forward, she adjusted her robe, straightening it and fixing the collar. Heads looked up. Cora was the first to see her. The pace of her plunging slowed. Her eyes tracked Arista's movements with interest. Nipper, having dropped his load, stood up and was in the process of brushing the snow off when he stopped in mid-stroke.

"Ella—ah, forgive me, Your Highness." Ibis Thinly was the first to speak.

"Actually, I'd prefer Arista," she replied. "I couldn't sleep. I was hoping to maybe get a little soup?"

Ibis grinned knowingly. "It can get cold up in them towers, can't it? As it happens, I saved a pot of last night's venison stew, froze it out in the snow. If that's all right, I'll have Nipper fetch it. I can heat it up in two shakes. It'll warm you nicely, and how about some hot cider and cinnamon to go with it? Still got some that ain't quite turned yet. It will have a bit of a bite, but it's still good."

"Yes, thank you. That would be wonderful."

"I'll have someone run it up to your chambers. You're on the third floor, right?"

"Ah, no. Actually, I was thinking of eating down here—if that's okay?"

Ibis chuckled. "Of course it is. Folks been doing that a good deal these days, and I'm sure you can eat anywhere that pleases you, 'cepting maybe the empress's bedroom—course rumor has it you did that already." He chuckled.

"It's just that"—she looked at the others, all of whom were watching and listening—"I thought I might not be welcome after…after lying to all of you."

The cook made a dismissive *pfft* sound. "You forget, we worked for Saldur and Ethelred. All they ever did was lie and they sure never scrubbed floors or emptied no chamber pots along with us. You take a seat at the table, Your Highness. I'll get you that stew. Nipper, fetch the pot and get me the jug of cider too!"

She took a seat as instructed and whether they agreed with Ibis's sentiments or not, none of them said a word. They returned to work and only occasionally glanced at her. Lila even ventured a tiny smile and a modest wave before returning to her struggle with the bowls.

"You're Myron Lanaklin, aren't you?" Arista asked, turning on her stool to face the monk and the dog.

He looked up, surprised. "Yes, yes, I am."

"Pleased to meet you. I'm Arista. I believe you know my brother, Alric?"

"Of course! How is he?"

"He's fine. Haven't you seen him? He's just upstairs."

The monk shook his head.

No longer being scratched, Red opened his eyes and looked at Myron with a decidedly disappointed expression.

"Isn't he wonderful?" Myron declared. "I've never seen a dog this big. I didn't know what he was at first. I thought he might be a shaggy breed of deer that they housed in the kitchen, much like we used to keep pigs and chickens at the abbey. I was so happy to discover he was not a future meal. His name is Red. He's an elkhound. Although, I think his days of hunting wolves and boar are over. Did you know that in times of war, they can take knights down off horses? They kill their prey by biting the neck and crushing the spine, but really he's not vicious at all. I come down here every day to see him."

"Do you always get up this early?"

"Oh, this isn't early. At the abbey this would be lazy."

"You must go to sleep early, then."

"Actually, I don't sleep much," he said as he resumed petting the dog.

"Me neither," she admitted. "Bad dreams."

Myron looked surprised. Again, he stopped stroking Red, who nosed his hand in protest. She thought he was about to say something, but then he returned his attention to the dog.

"Myron, I'm wondering if you can help me?" she asked.

"Of course. What are the nightmares about?"

"Oh no. I wasn't speaking of that. It's just that my brother mentioned you read quite a bit."

He shrugged. "I found a little library on the third floor, but there are only about twenty books there. I'm on my third time through."

"You've read all the books in the library three times?"

"Almost. I always have trouble with Hartenford's *Genealogy of Warric Monarchs*. It's almost all names and I have to sound most of them out. What do you need to know?"

"I was actually thinking about information you might have read about while at the Winds Abbey. Have you ever heard of the city of Percepliquis?"

He nodded. "It's the capital city of the original empire of Novron."

"Yes," she said eagerly. "Do you know where it is?"

He thought a moment and smiled to himself. "In every text, they always refer to everything else by way of it. Hashton was twenty-five leagues southeast of Percepliquis. Fairington, a hundred leagues due north. No one ever mentioned where Percepliquis was, I presume because everyone already knew."

"If I got you a map, would it be possible to find it based on the references to other places?"

"Maybe. I'm pretty sure that's how Edmund Hall found it. Although, all you really need is his journal. I've always wanted to read that one."

"I thought reading his journal is considered heresy. Isn't that why they locked Hall and his journal in the top of the Crown Tower?"

"Yes."

"And yet you would still read it? Alric never mentioned what a rebel you are."

Myron looked puzzled, then smiled. "It is heresy for a member of the Nyphron Church to read it."

"Oh, that's right. You're a Monk of Maribor."

"And blessedly, we have no such restrictions on our reading material."

"It makes you wonder, doesn't it?" Arista said. "All the things that might be hidden at the top of the Crown Tower."

"Makes you wish you could get inside, doesn't it?"

"Yes—yes, it does."

◆

They arrived late that evening, the whole castle buzzing with the news. Trumpets blared, servants rushed, and before she could get dressed, two servants, as well as Alric and Mauvin, had stopped by to tell Arista of the caravan that had just arrived from the north bearing the falcon crest and the banners of gold and green.

She hoisted the hem of the robe and raced down the steps with the rest. A crowd formed on the front steps. Servants, artisans, bureaucrats, and nobles mingled and pushed to see the sight. Guards formed an aisle allowing her to pass to the front, where she stood next to Mauvin and Alric. To her left, she spotted Nimbus draping Amilia's shoulders with his cloak, leaving the skinny man looking like a twig in the wind. She did not see the empress.

Wind-whipped torches and a milky moon illuminated the

courtyard as the caravan entered. There were no soldiers, just elderly men who walked behind carriages. Toward the rear of the procession came wagons bearing a shivering cargo. Women and children, crammed tightly together, huddled for warmth beneath communal blankets. The first carriage reached the bottom of the steps and Belinda and Lenare Pickering stepped out, followed by Alenda Lanaklin. The three women looked up at the crowd before them hesitantly.

Mauvin ran forward to embrace his mother.

"What are you all doing here?" he exclaimed excitedly. "Where's Father, or didn't he—" Arista saw Mauvin stiffen and pull back.

There was no joy at this meeting. The women's faces were sorrowful. They were pale, drawn, and gray, and only their eyes and noses held color—red and sore from crying and the bitter wind. Belinda held her son, wringing his clothes with her fists.

"Your father is dead," she cried, and buried her face in his chest.

Moving slower than the rest, Julian Tempest, the elderly lord chamberlain of Melengar, climbed carefully down out of the carriage. When Arista saw him, her stomach tightened. She could think of very few things that might cause Julian to leave Melengar, and none of them good.

"The elves have crossed the Nidwalden River," Julian announced to the crowd. His voice fought against the wind that viciously fluttered the flags and banners. He walked gingerly, placing his feet upon the frozen ground as if it might be pulled out from beneath him. The old man's stately robes snapped about him like living things, his cap threatening to fly off. "They've invaded and taken all of Dunmore and Ghent." He paused, looked at King Alric, took a breath, and said, "And Melengar."

"The north has fallen? To elves?" Alric sounded incredu-
lous. "But how?"

"These are not the *mir*, Your Majesty. They are not the
half-breeds we are familiar with. Those that attacked are
pure-blooded elves of the Erivan Empire. Terrible, fierce, and
merciless, they came out of the east and crushed all in their
path." The wind gained a grip on the old man's cap, throwing
it across the yard and revealing his balding head, wreathed in
thin white hair. His hands flew up in a futile effort and
remained at face level, quivering and forgotten. "Woe to the
House of Essendon, the kingdom is lost!"

Alric's gaze lifted to the caravan. He stood staring at the
long line of wagons, studying its length, the number of faces
crawling from them, and Arista knew what he was thinking.

*Is this all?*

Julian and the ladies were ushered inside. Arista watched
them enter but remained on the steps. She recognized a face or
two. One had been a barmaid at The Rose and Thorn.
Another, a seamstress at the castle. Arista had often seen her
daughter playing near the moat with a doll her mother had
made from scraps. She did not have the doll now and Arista
wondered, *What became of it? What became of everything?*

"There's not that many," Amilia was saying to Sebastian.
He was a ranking castle guard, but she could not recall his
specific position. "Find room for them in the gallery for now."

He snapped a salute.

"And have someone run and tell Ibis to get some food prepared; they look hungry."

Amilia turned back toward the castle doors when she made
eye contact with Arista. She bit her lip in a sad expression.
"I'm sorry," she managed to say, and then walked away.

Arista remained on the steps as the stable hands broke

down the harnesses and the wagons emptied. A line of refugees filed past her, heading inside.

"Melissa!" Arista called.

"Your Highness." Melissa curtsied.

"Oh, forget that." She ran down the remaining steps and gave the girl a hug. "I'm so happy you are all right."

"Are you the empress?" a little girl asked, holding on to Melissa's hand.

Arista had been away from Melengar for some time—only a few months short of a year—but this child could not have been Melissa's. The girl had to be six or seven. She stood on the step beside Arista's maid, bouncing on anxious feet and clutching a bundle to her chest with her free hand.

"This is Mercy," Melissa said, introducing her. "We found her on the way here." She lowered her voice and whispered, "She's an orphan."

There was something familiar about the little girl. Arista was certain she had seen her before. "No, I'm sorry. I'm not the empress. My name is Arista."

"Can I see the empress?"

"I'm afraid not. The empress is very busy."

The child's eager expression collapsed to one of disappointment, and her head drooped to look at her feet. "Arcadius said I would meet the empress when we got to Aquesta."

Arista studied her face a moment. "Arcadius? Oh yes, I remember you. We met last summer, wasn't it?" Arista looked around the few remaining refugees but did not see her old teacher among them. Just then, she noticed the bundle move. "What have you got in there?"

Before the girl could answer, the head of a raccoon poked out. "His name is Mr. Rings."

Arista bent down, and as she did, the robe brightened slightly—a soft pink glow. The girl's eyes widened excitedly.

"Magic!" she exclaimed. She reached out, then paused and looked up.

"You can touch it," Arista told her.

"It's slippery," she said, rubbing the material between her fingers. "Arcadius could do magic too."

"Where is Arcadius?" The little girl did not answer as she shivered in the cold. "Oh, I'm sorry, you both must be freezing. Let's get inside."

They stepped from the pale blue winter into the dark fire-lit hall. The howl of the wind silenced at the closing of the doors, which boomed, echoing in the vaulted chamber. The little girl looked up in awe at the flight of steps, the stone columns and arches. A number of refugees, wrapped in blankets, shivered as they waited for directions.

"Your Highness," Melissa whispered. "We found Mercy alone on a horse."

"Alone? But where is..." She hesitated, seeing Melissa's downcast eyes.

"Mercy hasn't said much, but... well, I'm sorry."

The light of her robe dimmed and the color turned blue. "He's dead?" *First Esrahaddon, now Arcadius.*

"The elves burned Ghent," Melissa said. "Sheridan and Ervanon are gone."

"Gone?"

"Burned."

"But the tower of Glenmorgan, the Crown Tower..."

Melissa shook her head. "We joined with some people fleeing south. Several saw it fall. One said it looked like a child's toy being toppled. Everything is gone." Melissa's eyes glistened. "They're... unstoppable."

Arista expected tears, but all she felt was a numbness—too much loss all at once. She gently touched Mercy's cheek.

"Can I let Mr. Rings play in here?" Mercy asked.

"What? Oh, I suppose, as long as you keep a sharp eye on him," Arista said. "There's an elkhound that might gobble him up if he goes too far."

She set the raccoon down. It sniffed the floor and cautiously skittered to the wall near the steps, where it began a systematic smelling along all the baseboards. Mercy followed and took a seat on the lowest step.

"I can't believe Arcadius is dead."

*…at Wintertide the* Uli Vermar *ends. They will come— without the horn everyone dies.* The words of Esrahaddon echoed in Arista's head. Words of warning mingled with words she still did not fully understand.

Mercy yawned and rested her chin on her hands as Mr. Rings inched along the length of the step, exploring the world.

"She's tired," Arista said. "I think they are handing out soup in the great hall. Would you like some soup, Mercy?"

The girl looked up, smiled, and nodded. "Mr. Rings is hungry too, aren't you, Mr. Rings?"

❧

*The city was more beautiful than anything Arista had ever seen. White buildings, taller than the highest tree, taller than any building she had ever seen, rose up like slender fingers reaching for the sky. Sweeping pennants of greens and blues trailed from their pinnacles snapping in the breeze and shimmering like crystal. A road, broad enough for four carriages, straight as a maypole, and paved with smooth stone, led into the city. Upon it moved a multitude of wagons, carts, wains, coaches, and buggies. No wall or gate hindered the flow of traffic. No guardhouse gave them pause. The city lacked towers, barbican, and moat. It stood naked and beautiful— fearless and proud with only a pair of sculptured lions to intimidate visitors. The breadth of the city was hard to accept, hard for her to believe. It dominated three full hills and filled the vast valley where a gentle river flowed. It was a lovely place—and it was so familiar.*

Arista, you must remember.

*She felt the urgency, a tightness in her stomach, a chill across her back. Arista had to think; she needed to solve the puzzle. So little time remained, but such a sight as this would be impossible to forget. She could not have seen it before.*

You were here.

*She was not. Such a place as this could not even exist. This was a dream, an illusion.*

You must trust me. You were here. Look closely.

*Arista was shaking her head. It was ridiculous…and yet…something about the river, the way it curved near the base of the northern hill. Yes, the hill. The hill did look familiar. And the road—not so wide. It had been overgrown and hidden. She remembered finding it in the dark; she remembered wondering how it had come to be there.*

Yes, you were here. On the hill, look at the Aguanon.

*Arista did not understand.*

The northern hill, look at the temple on the crest.

*She spotted it. Yes, it was familiar, but it did not look the same in her memory. It was broken, fallen, mostly buried, but it was the same. Arista had been there and it frightened her to remember. Something bad had happened to her here. She had nearly died on this hill before the broken stones, amidst the splintered remains of shattered columns and breaching slabs. But she had not died. She did something on that hill, something awful, something that made her rip the dewy grass with her fists and beg Maribor for forgiveness.*

*At last, Arista understood where she was, what she was seeing.*

This is it. This was my home. Go there, dig down, find the tomb, bring forth the horn. Do it, Arista! You must! There is no time left! Everyone will die! Everyone will die! EVERYONE WILL—

Arista woke up screaming.

# CHAPTER 3

# PRISONS

"Get out of the way!" Hadrian shouted, his voice booming through the corridor. He stood just a few feet from the guard glaring at him, breathing on him. The two guards who watched from the end of the hall ran forward. He heard their chain mail jingling, their empty scabbards slapping their thighs. Both stopped short of sword's length.

"It's the Teshlor," one warned in a whisper.

The soldier who blocked the door stood his ground. Hadrian sensed the tension, the fear, the lack of confidence, but he also felt the courage and loyalty that refused to let him waver. He usually respected such qualities in a man, but not this time. This man was merely in his way.

Behind him, a latch lifted and a door creaked. "What's going on?" a befuddled woman's voice asked.

Hadrian glanced. It was Amilia. She shuffled forward, wiping her eyes and fumbling with the tie of her robe.

"I need to speak to the empress," he growled. "Tell them to stand down."

"It's the middle of the night!" she exclaimed in a whisper. "You can't see her. If you want, I'll try to arrange an appointment in the morning, but I must tell you, Her Eminence is very busy. The news—"

Hadrian's hands rose and he took hold of his sword grips. The three soldiers tensed and all but the door guard took a step back. The man before him let his own hand settle slowly on his weapon but he did not pull it.

*This guard is a cool one*, Hadrian thought, and took another half step closer, until their noses nearly touched. "Get out of my way."

"Hadrian? What are you doing?" This time it was Arista's voice echoing down the hallway.

"I'm seeking an audience with the empress," he said through gritted teeth. He broke his stare to turn and see the princess trotting up the fifth-floor corridor. As always these days, she was dressed in Esrahaddon's robe, which was a dull blue and, at the moment, only reflected the fire of the torches hanging in the wall sconces.

"They have him locked up. They won't even let me see him," Hadrian told her.

"Royce?"

"He didn't want to kidnap the empress, but he would have done anything to get Gwen back. They should give him a medal for killing Saldur and Merrick." Hadrian sighed. "Gwen died in his arms and he wasn't thinking straight. He never meant to harm Modina. I found out he's being held in the north tower. I don't think Modina even knows. So I'm going to tell her. Don't try and stop me."

"I'm not," she said. "I have to see her as well."

"What for?"

The princess looked uncomfortable. "I had a bad dream."

"*What?*"

"No one is seeing the empress tonight!" Amilia declared.

Six more guards arrived, trotting toward them. "I'll turn out the whole castle regiment if I have to!"

Hadrian glanced at the imperial secretary. "Do you think they'll stop me?"

"The door has a bolt on the inside," the door guard said. "Even if you got past us, there's half a foot of solid oak in your way."

"That won't be a problem," Arista assured them. "But I should warn you, I can't be responsible for wounds from flying splinters." Her robe began to glow. It gave off a hazy gray light that slowly brightened, bleaching their faces and weakening the torch-fed shadows. Hadrian noticed a faint breeze in the corridor. A warm wind was rising, swirling around Arista like a tiny cyclone, fluttering the hem of her robe and the ends of her hair.

Amilia stared, horrified.

"Open the door, Amilia, or I'll remove it."

Amilia looked as if she might scream.

"Let them in, Gerald." The voice emanated from the other side of the door.

"Your Eminence?"

"Yes, Gerald. It isn't locked. Let them in."

The door guard lifted the latch and gave a push. The door swung inward, revealing the darkness of the imperial bedroom. Amilia said nothing. She was breathing faster than normal, her fists clenched at her sides. Hadrian entered first, with Arista behind, both followed by Amilia and Gerald.

It was cold in the bedroom. The fireplace was dark and the only light came in through the open window in the far wall. To either side, sheer white curtains billowed inward, dancing in the faint moonlight like a pair of ghosts. Dressed in only her nightgown, Empress Modina rested on the floor, looking out at the stars. She sat on her knees, hands in her lap, her shoulders drawn up against the cold. Bare toes poked out from within the pool of white linen that gathered around her. Blonde hair fell down her back in tangles. She appeared much like the girl Hadrian had seen under the Tradesmen's Arch in Colnora so long ago.

"They arrested Royce," Hadrian told her. "They've locked him in a cell in the tower."

"I know."

"You know?" he said incredulously. "How long have—"

"I ordered it."

Hadrian stared at her, stunned. "Thrace—I mean, Modina," he said softly. "You don't understand. He never meant to harm you. He only did what he had to. He was trying to save the person he loved most in the world. How could you do this to him?"

At last she turned. "Have you ever lost the one person in the world that meant everything to you? Did you watch them die, knowing it was your fault?"

Hadrian said nothing.

"When my father was killed," she continued, looking back out the window, "I remember I found it almost too painful to breathe. I had not just lost my father; it was as if the whole world had died, but somehow I was left behind—alone. I just wanted it to end. I was tired. I wanted the pain to stop. If I had the chance—if they hadn't taken me away, if they hadn't locked me up, I would have thrown myself into the falls." She turned and looked at Hadrian once more. "Believe me. He is well cared for—at least, as much as he will allow. Ibis makes him good meals that he doesn't eat. Can you think of a better place for Royce right now?"

Hadrian's shoulders slumped; his arms fell loose at his sides. "Can I at least see him?"

Modina thought a moment. "Yes, but only you. In his present state, he is a danger to anyone else. Still, I'm not sure he will hear you. You can visit him in the morning." She leaned over so she could see Amilia. "Can you see to it that he has access?"

"Yes, Your Eminence."

"Good," the empress said, then looked at Arista. "Now what is it that you have that can't wait until morning?"

The Princess of Melengar stood shifting her feet, folding and refolding her hands before her, the robe a tranquil dark blue. She looked at the empress, then at Hadrian, Amilia, and even Gerald, who stood stiffly just inside the door. When her eyes once more returned to Modina, she said, "I think I know how to stop the elves."

❧

Hadrian had just descended to the third floor, where several people were returning to their rooms now that all the shouting had died down. He caught a glimpse of Degan Gaunt. The ex-leader of the Nationalists stood in his nightshirt, peering up the steps, both curious and irritated. This was the first time Hadrian had seen the man since the two of them had been released from the dungeon. His neck and nose were narrow, and his lips were so thin they were almost nonexistent. There were creases across his brow and lines about his eyes that spoke of a hard life. Hadrian could tell by the way he carried his weight, and the motions of his body, that he felt awkward, lost in his own skin. He had a faraway look in his eyes, two days' growth of beard, and a plume of hair that hung out of place. If he had to guess, Hadrian might have pegged him as a poor poet. He seemed nothing like the descendant of emperors.

"What's going on up there?" Gaunt asked a passing servant.

"Someone looking to see the empress, sir. It's over now."

Gaunt appeared dubious.

This was not how Hadrian had planned on meeting Gaunt. Hadrian had waited, giving them both time to fully heal. After that, he hesitated out of nerves. He wanted their meeting to go well, to be perfect. This was not perfect, but now that they stood face to face he could hardly walk away.

"Hello, Mr. Gaunt, I am Hadrian Blackwater," he said, introducing himself with a bow.

Degan Gaunt greeted him with his nose crinkled up as if he smelled something bad. He critically observed Hadrian, then frowned. "I thought you'd be taller."

"I'm sorry," Hadrian apologized.

"You're supposed to be my servant, right?" Gaunt asked. He began walking around Hadrian, orbiting him in slow, lazy circles, carrying a frown around with him.

"Actually, I'm your bodyguard."

"How much am I expected to pay for this privilege?"

"I'm not asking for money."

"No? What is it, then? You want me to make you a duke or something? Is that why you're here? Boy, people come out of the woodwork when you've got money and power, I guess. I mean, I don't even know you and here you come begging for privileges before I'm even crowned emperor."

"It's not like that. You're the Heir of Novron; I am the defender of the heir, just like my father before me. It's a... tradition."

"Uh-huh." Gaunt stood slouching, sucking on his teeth for a moment before jamming his pinky finger into his mouth to struggle with something caught between them. After a few minutes, he gave up.

"Okay, here's what I don't get. I'm the heir. That makes me head of the empire, and head of the church. I'm even part god, if I get that right—great-great-grandson of Maribor or some kind of which or whether. So if I'm gonna be emperor and have a whole castle of guards and an army to protect me, what do I need you for?"

Hadrian didn't say anything. He didn't know what he could say. Gaunt was right. His role as bodyguard was only important so long as the heir was in hiding.

"Well, guarding you is sort of a family tradition that I would hate to break," he finally told Gaunt. The words sounded silly even to him.

"You any good with a sword?"

"Pretty good."

Gaunt scratched his stubbly chin. "Well, since you aren't charging anything, I guess I'd be stupid not to take you on. Okay, you can be my servant."

"Bodyguard."

"Whatever." Gaunt waved at him as if shooing away a pesky fly. "I'm going back to bed. You can wait outside my door and do your guard thing if you like."

Gaunt returned to his room and Hadrian waited outside, feeling decidedly foolish. That had not gone as well as he had hoped. He failed to impress Gaunt, and he had to admit, Gaunt did nothing to impress him. He did not know what exactly he had expected. Maybe he thought Gaunt would be the embodiment of the noble poor. A man of staggering integrity, a beacon of enlightenment, who had grown out of the earth's salt and struggled to the pinnacle. Sure, his standards were high, but after all, Degan was supposed to be part god. Instead, just being near him made Hadrian want to go bathe.

He leaned against the wall outside the door, looking up and down the quiet hallway.

*This is ridiculous. What am I doing?*

The answer was obvious—nothing. But there was nothing to do. He had missed his opportunity and was now useless. From somewhere inside, he heard Gaunt begin to snore.

☙

The next morning Hadrian found Royce sitting on the floor of the cell, his back resting against the wall, one knee up, cocked like a tent pole. His right arm rested on it, his hand hanging limp. He wore only his black tunic and pants. His belt and boots were missing, his feet bare, the soles blackened with dirt. He hung his head back, tilted upward resting against the wall and revealing a week's worth of dark stubble that covered his chin, cheeks, and neck. Lengths of straw littered his hair and clothing, but on his lap lay a neatly folded, meticulously clean scarf.

He did not look up when Hadrian entered the cell. He was not sleeping—no one could get this close to Royce without his waking, but more obviously, his eyes were open. He stared at the ceiling, not seeing it.

"Hey, buddy," Hadrian said, entering the cell.

The guard closed the door behind him. He heard the lock slide in place. "Call me when you want out," he told Hadrian.

The cell had a small window near the ceiling, which cast a square of light where the wall and floor met. Through its shaft, he could see straw dust lingering in the air. A cup of water, a glass of wine, and a plate of potato and carrot stew sat beside the door. All untouched, the stew having dried into a solid brick.

"Am I interrupting breakfast?"

"That was dinner," Royce said.

"That bad, huh?" Hadrian sat across from him on the bed. It had a thick mattress, a half dozen warm blankets, three soft pillows, and fine linen sheets. It had not been slept in. "Not too bad in here," he said, making a show of looking around. "We've been in much worse, but you know, this was pretty much the last place I was thinking you'd be. I sort of thought the idea was for you to disappear and give me time to explain why you kidnapped the empress. What happened?"

"I turned myself in."

Hadrian smirked. "Obviously."

"Why are you here?" Royce replied, his eyes dull and empty.

"Well, now that I know you're here, I thought you could use some company. You know, someone to talk to, someone who can smuggle you fig pudding and the occasional drumstick. I could bring up a deck of cards. You know how much you love beating me at... Well, you just like beating me."

Royce made an expression that was almost like a smile. He reached out with his left hand and grabbed up a handful of straw. He crushed it in his fist letting the bits fall through his fingers and watching them in the shaft of light. When the last of it fell, he opened his hand palm-up, stared at it, turning it over and back as if he had never really seen it before.

"I want to thank you, Hadrian," he said, still looking at his hand, his voice soft, lingering, disconnected.

"Awfully formal, aren't you? It's just a card game," Hadrian said, and smiled.

Royce lowered his hand, laying it on the floor like a forgotten toy. His attention turned vaguely toward the ceiling again. "I hated you when we first met, did you know that? I thought Arcadius was crazy making me take you along on that heist."

"So why did you?"

"Honestly? I expected you'd be killed; then I could go to the nutty wizard, laugh, and say, *See? What did I tell you? The clumsy fool died*. Only you didn't. You made it all the way to the top of the Crown Tower, no complaining, no whining."

"Did you respect me then?"

"No. I figured you suffered from beginner's luck. I expected you'd die on the return trip that next night when he made us put it back."

"Only, again I lived."

"Kinda made me mad, actually. I'm not usually wrong, you know, about people? And man, you could fight. I thought Arcadius was feeding me a load of crap the way he went on about you. 'The best warrior alive,' he said. 'In a fair fight Hadrian can best anyone,' he said. That was the telling part— a fair fight. He knew not all your battles would be fair. He wanted me to educate you in the world of backstabbing, deceit, and treachery. I guess he figured I knew something about that."

"And I was supposed to teach honor, decency, and kindness to a man raised by wolves."

Royce rolled his head to the side and looked at him. "He told you about me?"

"Not everything, just some of the ugly parts."

"Manzant?"

"Just that you were there, that it almost killed you, and that he got you out."

Royce nodded. His face drooped, his eyes stared again, his hand absently scooped up another handful of straw to crush.

Hadrian's eyes drifted around the cell. Centuries of captives had left a dark smoothness to all the stones a bit higher than halfway up, like a flood line. On the far wall, a year's worth of old hatch marks scratched a pattern that looked like a series of bound bales of wheat. Up in the window, a bird had built a nest, tucked on the outside corner of the sill. It was empty, frosted in snow. Occasionally, he heard a cart, a horse, or the sound of people in the courtyard below them, but mostly it was quiet, a heavy, dull-gray silence.

"Hadrian," Royce began. He'd stopped playing with the straw, his hands flat, his stare focused on the wall, his voice weak and hesitant. "You and Arcadius...you're the only family I've ever known. The only two people in this whole world—" He swallowed and bit his lower lip, pausing.

Hadrian waited.

Finally he went on. "I want you to know—It's important that..." He turned away from Hadrian, facing the wall. "I wanted to say thank you for being there for me, for being here. For being the closest thing to a brother I'll ever know. I just— I just want you to know that."

Hadrian did not say anything. He waited for Royce to turn back, to look at him. It took several minutes, but the silence drew the look. When he did, Hadrian glared at him. "Why? Why do you want me to know that?"

"What do you mean?"

"Tell me—no, don't look at the wall; look at me. Why is it so important that I know this?"

"It just is, okay?" Royce said.

"No, it's not *okay*. Don't give me this crap, Royce. We've been together for twelve years. We've faced death dozens of times. Why is it you're telling me this now?"

"I'm upset. I'm distraught. What do you want from me?"

Hadrian continued to stare but slowly began to nod. "You've been waiting, haven't you? Just sitting here, leaning against that wall, waiting—waiting for me to show up."

"In case you forgot, they arrested me. I'm in a locked cell. There's not much else I can do."

Hadrian snorted.

"What?"

Hadrian stood. He needed to move. There wasn't much

space but he still paced back and forth between the wall and the door. Three steps each way. "So when are you going to do it? As soon as I leave? Tonight? How about a nice morning suicide? Huh, Royce? You could be poetic and time it with the rising of the sun, or just the drama of midnight, how would that be?"

Royce scowled.

"How are you gonna do it? Your wrists? Throat? Gonna challenge the guard to fight when he brings dinner? Call him names? Or are you gonna make an even bigger splash? Head for Modina's room and threaten the empress's life again. You'll find some young idiot, a big one, someone with an ego. You'll draw a blade, something little, something not too scary. He'll draw his sword. You'll pretend to attack, but he won't know you're faking."

"Don't be this way."

"*This way?*" Hadrian stopped and whirled on him. He had to take a breath to calm down. "How do you expect me to be? You think I should be—what? Happy, maybe? Did you think I'd just be okay with this? I thought you were stronger. If anyone could survive—"

"That's just it—I don't want to! I've always survived. Life is like a bully that gets laughs by seeing how much humiliation you'll put up with. It threatens to kill you if you don't eat mud. It takes everything you care about—not because it wants what you have, or needs it. It does it just to see if you'll take it. I let it push me around ever since I was a kid. I did everything it demanded just to survive. But as I've gotten older, I realize there are limits. You showed me that. There's only so far I can go, only so much I can put up with. I'm not going to take it anymore. I won't eat mud just to survive."

"So it's my fault?" Hadrian slumped down on the mattress once more. He sat there running his hand through his hair for a moment, then said, "Just so you know, you're not the only one who misses her. I loved her too."

Royce looked up.

"Not like that. You know what I mean. The worst part is…" His voice cracked. "It really is my fault, and that's what I will be left with. Did you think of that? You were right and I was wrong. You said not to take the job from DeWitt, but I talked you into it. 'Let's leave Dahlgren; this isn't our fight,' you said, but I got you to stay. 'You can't win against Merrick,' you said, so you went to protect me. You told me Degan Gaunt would be an ass, and you were right about that too. You didn't do what you knew was right because of me. I pulled you along while trying to redeem myself to the memory of a dead father. Gwen is gone because of me. I destroyed what little good there was in your life trying to accomplish something that in the end means nothing.

"I'm not the hero who saves the kingdom and wins the girl. Life isn't like that." Hadrian laughed bitterly. "You finally taught me that one, pal. Yep. Life isn't a fairy tale. Heroes don't ride white horses, and the good don't always win. I just—I guess I just *wanted* it to be that way. I didn't think there was any harm in believing it. I never knew it would be you and Gwen that would pay."

"It's not your fault," Royce told him.

"You tell me that a few million more times and I might actually start believing it. Only that's not going to happen, now is it? You're not going to be around to remind me, are you? You're going to give up. You're going to walk out on me and that will be my fault too. Damn it, Royce! You *have* a choice. I know it doesn't seem like it, and I know I'm a fool that believes in a fantasy world where good things can happen to good people, but I do know this. You can either head into darkness and despair or into virtue and light. It's up to you."

Royce jerked his head up and looked at Hadrian, a shocked expression on his face. Shock turned quickly to suspicion.

"What?" Hadrian asked, concerned.

"How are you doing that?" Royce demanded, and for the first time since Hadrian had entered the cell, he saw the old Royce—cold, dark, and angry.

"How am I doing what?"

"That's the second time you've quoted Gwen, once on the bridge and now—this. She said that same thing to me once, those exact words."

"Huh?"

"She read my palm and told me there was a fork—a point of decision. I had to choose to head into darkness and despair or into virtue and light. She told me this would be precipitated by a traumatic event—the death of the one I loved the most."

"Gwen?"

He nodded. "But you weren't there. You couldn't have heard her say that. We were alone in her office at the House. It was *a year* ago. I only remember because it was the night Arista came to The Rose and Thorn, and you were getting drunk and ranting about being a parasite. So how did you know?"

Hadrian shrugged. "I didn't, but…" He felt a chill run up his spine. "What if *she* did? What if I'm not quoting her—what if she was quoting me?"

"*What?*"

"Gwen was a seer," Hadrian said. "What if she saw your future, bits and pieces like Fan Irlanu did in that Tenkin village?" Now he was staring at the wall, his eyes wandering aimlessly as he thought. "She could have seen us on the bridge, and here in this cell. She knew what I would say, and she also knew you wouldn't listen to me. She must have known you wouldn't listen to me at the bridge either. That's why she said those things." He was speaking quickly now, seeing it all before him. "She knew you would ignore me, but you can't ignore her. Royce, Gwen doesn't want you to die. She agrees with me. I may have been wrong in the past, but not this time. This time I'm right, and I know I'm right because Gwen saw the future and she's backing me up." He sat against the wall, folding his hands behind his head in victory. "You can't kill yourself," he said jubilantly, as if he had just won some unspoken bet. "You can't do it without betraying her wishes!"

Royce looked confused. "But if she knew, why didn't she stop it? Why did she let me go with you? Why didn't she tell me?"

"It's obvious, isn't it? She wanted us to go, and either she couldn't avoid her death, or—"

"Or what? She wanted to die?" he said sarcastically.

"No, I was going to say, she knew she *had* to die."

"Why?"

"I don't know—something else she saw, maybe, something that hasn't happened yet. Something so important it was worth dying on the bridge for, but whatever it is, it doesn't include you killing yourself. She made that pretty clear, I think."

Royce threw his head back against the stone wall hard enough to make an audible thud and clenched his eyes shut. "Damn it."

◈

Mauvin Pickering stood on the fourth-floor balcony, looking out at the palace courtyard. It was snowing again, thick wet flakes. They fell on the muddy earth, slowly filling in where carts had left deep ruts. One after another, the flakes hit the ground and melted, but somehow, they managed to overcome.

The puddles receded; the dirt disappeared; the world turned white and pure once more.

Beyond the wall he could see the roofs of the city. Aquesta stretched out below him, hundreds of snow-covered thatched peaks clustered together, huddling against the winter storm. The buildings ran to the sea and up the hill north. His gaze rose to the gap he knew was Imperial Square, and farther out to Bingham Square, where he could see the top of the Tradesmen's Tower marking the artisan district. He continued to look up, his gaze reaching out beyond the open patches of farm fields to the forested hills—a hazy gray line in the distance, and the suggestion of higher hills beyond—masked by the snowy curtain. He imagined he could see Glouston, and beyond it, across the river, Melengar, the kingdom of the falcon-crested kings, the land of his birth, his home. Drondil Fields would be blanketed in snow, the orchard frosted, the moat frozen. Vern would be out breaking the ice on the well, dropping his heavy hammer tied to the end of a rope. He would be fearful the knot would come loose like it had five years earlier, leaving his favorite tool at the bottom of the well. It was still there, Mauvin thought, still lying in the water, waiting for Vern to claim it, but now he never would.

"You'll catch your death out there," his mother said.

He turned to see her standing in the doorway in her dark blue gown—the closest thing she had to black. Around her shoulders was the burgundy shawl Fanen had given her for Wintertide three years before—the year he died. It became a permanent part of her attire that she wore year-round, explaining how it kept the chill away in the winter and the sun off her shoulders in the summer. That morning he noticed she was also wearing the necklace. The awkward thick chain weighed down by the huge pendant was hard to miss. It was supposed to look like the sun. A big emerald pressed into the gold setting, and lines of rubies forming the rays of light. It was an ugly, gaudy thing. He had seen it only a few times before in the bottom of her jewelry box. It had been a gift from his father.

Even after bearing four children, Belinda Pickering still turned heads. Too many for his father's comfort, if the stories were true. Rumors had circulated for decades of the numerous duels fought over her honor. Legend asserted there were as many as twenty, all sparked by some man looking at her too long. They all ended the same, with the death of the offender via Count Pickering's *magic* sword. That was the legend, but Mauvin knew of only two actual incidents.

The first had occurred before he was born. His father had told him the story on his thirteenth birthday, the day he had mastered the first tier of the Tek'chin. His father explained that he and Mauvin's mother had been traveling home alone and were waylaid by highwaymen. There had been four bandits and his father was willing to give up their horses, his purse, and even Belinda's jewelry to escape without incident. But his father had seen the way the thieves looked at Belinda. As they whispered back and forth, he saw the hunger in their eyes. His father killed two, wounded one, and sent the last one running. They had given his father a scar nearly a foot long.

The second had happened when Mauvin was just ten. They had come to Aquesta for Wintertide and the Earl of Tremore became angry when Count Pickering refused to enter the sword competition. The earl knew that even if he had won the tournament, he would still be considered second best, so he challenged Pickering to a duel. Mauvin's father refused. The Earl of Tremore had grabbed Belinda and kissed her before the entire court. She slapped him and pulled away. When he made a grab for her, he tore free the neckline of her gown, exposing her. She fell to the floor, crying, struggling to cover herself. Mauvin remembered with perfect clarity his father drawing his sword and telling him to help his mother back to their room. He did not kill the Earl of Tremore, but the man lost a hand in the battle.

Still, it was easy to see how the stories spread. Even he could see how lovely his mother was. Only now, for the first time, did he notice the gray in her hair and the lines on her face. She had always stood so straight and tall, but now she leaned forward, bowed as if by an invisible weight.

"I haven't seen you much," she said. "Where have you been?"

"Nowhere."

He waited for her to press, to demand more information. He expected it—but she just nodded. His mother had been acting this way since arriving and it unnerved him.

"Chancellor Nimbus was by earlier. He wanted to let you know that the empress is calling a meeting this evening and you are requested to attend."

"I know. Alric already told me."

"Did he say what it was to be about?"

"It'll be about the invasion, I'm sure. She will want to mount a full-scale retaliation. Alric expects she will use this crisis to demand Melengar join the empire."

"What will Alric do?"

"What can he do? Alric isn't a king without a kingdom. I should warn you that I intend to join him. I will gather what men Alric still has, form a troop, and volunteer to fight."

Once more the quiet, submissive nod.

"Why do you do that? Why must you give in to me without even a protest? If I had said I was going off to war a month ago, I would have never heard the end of it."

"A month ago you were my son; today you are Count Pickering."

He watched her clutch the shawl with a white-knuckled fist, her mouth set, her other hand holding the doorframe.

"Maybe he survived," Mauvin said. "He's gotten through tough situations before. There's a chance he could have fought his way out. With his sword no one could ever beat him—not even Braga."

Her lips trembled; her eyes grew glassy. "Come," she said, and disappeared back into the castle. He followed as she led the way to her chambers. There were three beds in the room. With all the refugees, space was tight in the palace these days. The chamberlain did his best to accommodate them according to rank, but there was only so much he could do. Mauvin bunked with Alric and now his brother Denek as well. Mauvin knew his mother shared her room with his sister, Lenare, and the lady Alenda Lanaklin of Glouston, neither of whom was there at that moment.

The room was a fraction of the size of her bedchamber back home. The beds themselves were small single bunks. The plain headboards were dressed with quilts adorned with patterns of roses. Leaded glass windows let the light in, but sheer white curtains turned the brilliance into a muted fog, which felt heavy and oppressive. The room had the air of a funeral. On the dresser he spotted the familiar statuette of Novron that used to be in their chapel. The demigod sat upon his throne, one hand upraised in a gesture of authority. Beside it was a single salifan candle, still burning. On the floor before it lay her bed pillow, two dents side by side where she had knelt.

His mother walked to the wardrobe and withdrew a long blanket-wrapped bundle. She turned and held it out. There was a formality in her movement, a solemnness in her eyes. He looked at the bundle—long and thin, tied with a green silk ribbon, the kind she and Lenare used to bind their hair. The blanket it held was like a shroud over a dead body. Mauvin did not want to touch it.

"No," he said without meaning to, and took a step backward.

"Take it," she told him.

The door opened abruptly.

"I don't want to go alone," Alenda Lanaklin said as she and his sister, Lenare, entered. The two women were also dressed in dark conservative gowns. Lenare carried a plate of food, and Alenda a cup. "It's awkward. I don't even know him. Oh—" They both stopped.

Mauvin hastily took the bundle from his mother. He did not look at it and quickly moved toward the door.

"I'm sorry," Alenda said. She was staring at him, her face troubled.

"Excuse me, ladies," Mauvin muttered, and walked past them. He kept his eyes focused on the floor as he went.

"Mauvin?" Alenda called down the hallway.

He heard her steps behind him and stopped, but he did not turn.

He felt her touch his hand. "I'm sorry."

"You said that."

"That was for interrupting."

He felt her press against him, and she kissed his cheek.

"Thank you." He watched as she worked hard to force a smile even as a tear slipped down her cheek.

"Your mother hasn't eaten. She hardly even leaves the room. Lenare and I went to get her something."

"That's very kind."

"Are *you* all right?"

"I should be asking you that. I lost a father, but you lost a father and two brothers as well."

She nodded and sniffled. "I've been trying not to think

about it. There's so much—too much. Everyone has lost someone. You can't have a conversation anymore without people crying their eyes out." She half laughed, half cried. "See?"

He reached up and wiped her tears. Her cheeks were amazingly soft; the wetness made them shine.

"What were you and Lenare talking about?" he asked.

"Oh, that?" she said, sounding embarrassed. "It will sound foolish."

"Perhaps foolishness is needed right now." He made a face and winked at her.

She smiled, this time more easily.

"Com'on," he said, taking her hand and pulling her with him down the hall. "Tell me this terrible secret."

"It's not a secret. I just wanted Lenare to come with me when I meet my brother."

"Myron?"

She nodded. "I'm a little nervous about it—frightened, actually. How do I explain why I never bothered to see him?"

"Why didn't you?"

She shrugged self-consciously. "I should have. I just— He was a stranger. If only my father had taken me, but he didn't. He seemed like he wanted to forget Myron existed. I think he was ashamed of him and some of that rubbed off on me, I guess."

"And now?"

"Now I'm scared."

"Scared of what?"

"Of him."

"You're scared of *Myron*?" He started to chuckle, but he stopped abruptly when he saw the seriousness in her eyes.

"I knew you'd think me foolish!"

"It's just that we're talking about Myron and—"

"He's the marquis now!" she exclaimed. "He's the head of my house. By law, I have to do as he says, go where he orders, marry whom he chooses. What if he hates me? What if he decides to punish me for the hardships he has had to endure? I've lived in a castle with servants who dressed, fed, and bathed me. I've attended feasts and tournaments, galas and picnics. I've worn silk, lace, finely embroidered gowns, and jewelry. While he—" She stopped. "Since the age of four, Myron has been sequestered at the Winds Abbey. He has been forced to work with his hands in the dirt, worn coarse wool, and never gone anywhere or seen anyone—not even his family. Now they are all dead, except for me. Of course he hates me. Why wouldn't he? He'll curse me and I'll be the target of all his pain and frustration. He'll deny me, just as we denied him. He'll send me away, strip me of my title, and leave me penniless. And…and…I can't even blame him."

She looked up at Mauvin's face, confused. "What? What?"

## CHAPTER 4

# FALL THE WALL

"How is Royce?" Arista asked Hadrian as they took seats next to each other near the end of the table. There were no place cards, and Hadrian had no clue where they might want him to sit. He looked to the princess for guidance, but all she offered was a shrug.

"Not great, but who is these days?" He glanced at Alric, who was taking a seat across from Arista, then at Mauvin, who sat next to his king. "I was sorry to hear about your father," he offered.

Mauvin replied with an almost imperceptible nod. Arista stood, reached across the table, and took Mauvin's hand. She did not say a word but merely looked into his eyes, offering a weak smile.

"See, that's the difference," Mauvin said. "I suffer a loss and people console me. Royce suffers a loss and whole towns evacuate." He offered a sad smile. "I'm fine, really. My father led a good life, married the most beautiful woman in the realm, raised four children, outlived one, and died in battle defending his home. I should hope to do half as well."

"It's hard to imagine that anyone could break through Royce's shell," King Alric said.

Only a few years had passed since Hadrian had first met Alric. He, Royce, and later Myron spent three days roaming the hills of Melengar with the prince just after King Amrath's death. It seemed like only yesterday, but Alric appeared decades older. His eyes showed a maturity and his boyish face was gone—hidden behind a full beard. He looked more like his father now, brooding and withered. The small white scar on his forehead was still there—a ghostly reminder of that day he nearly died, when his face was pushed into the dirt.

"She was a remarkable woman," Hadrian explained.

"I wish I had met her," Arista said, sitting back down.

"You would have liked Gwen, and I know she thought highly of you. She was"—Hadrian paused—"unique."

They gathered in the great hall, the largest chamber in the palace. Four stone hearths filled the room with warmth and a ruddy-orange glow. Above each massive fireplace, arrays of steel shields and glimmering swords were displayed as a sign of power. Thirty-two banners displaying the emblems of all the noble houses of Avryn hung from the ceiling in two rows along the length of the room. Five had been added since the last time Hadrian had sat there. The banners of the House of Lanaklin of Glouston, the House of Hestle of Bernum, the House of Exeter, the House of Pickering of Galilin, and the gold crowned falcon on a red field of the House of Essendon of Melengar— all restored to their rightful places.

The table where they waited was the only one in the room. Placed in the center of the hall, it was longer than the bar at The Rose and Thorn, and nine chairs lined each side, along with one at the end. This was the same room where Hadrian spent his first feast masquerading as a noble. He felt as out of place now as he had then as the room filled with the other invited guests—each noble.

He knew most of the faces that entered. Armand, King of

Alburn, claimed a seat near the head of the table, his son, Prince Rudolf, at his right hand. Not to be outdone, Fredrick, King of Galeannon, sat across from him. King Vincent of Maranon chose to sit two chairs down from Fredrick, making Hadrian wonder if there was an issue between the two bordering kingdoms. Not everyone was a royal. Sir Elgar, Sir Murthas, and Sir Gilbert, as well as Sir Breckton, who wore the gold sash of his new office as imperial high marshal, entered together.

Stewards began pouring wine while seven seats remained open, including the one at the head of the table, where no one dared sit. Hadrian took a sip from the goblet before him and grimaced.

"That's right," Arista mentioned. "You aren't a wine drinker, are you?"

Hadrian set the goblet back down and continued to sneer at it. "It's probably very good," he said. "It just tastes like spoiled grape juice to me, but you have to remember I was raised on Armigil's beer."

Hadrian's old tutor, the awkwardly thin imperial chancellor, Nimbus, entered along with Amilia, the imperial secretary, and they took their seats to the immediate left and right of the table's head. Degan Gaunt wandered in, looking lost. He was dressed in an expensive doublet and breeches with buckle shoes, none of which suited him. Looking at the heir, Hadrian could not help comparing him to the Duchess of Rochelle's pet poodle, which she dressed in tailored vests. Gaunt circled the table three times before choosing a lonely seat in the vacant space two up from Mauvin and one down from Sir Elgar, both of whom he eyed suspiciously.

Two more men entered. The first he did not know, a heavy-set elderly man with a bald head and sagging cheeks. He was dressed in a long, handsomely brocaded coat with large silver buttons, accompanied by a ruffled silk shirt. Following him was a younger but fatter duplicate of the first. Hadrian recognized him as Cosmos DeLur, the wealthiest man in Avryn and infamous head of the Black Diamond thieves guild. He guessed the other man must be his father, Cornelius DeLur, formerly the unofficial leader of the Republic of Delgos.

Two chairs left.

Several conversations occurred simultaneously. Hadrian tried to make sense of them. Tilted heads, knowing smiles, sidelong glances, murmurs, whispers. He could catch only a handful of words here and there. Most often, what he caught were discussions about the empress. Many of those at the table had seen her only that one night before the final Wintertide joust, when she made her brief, but dramatic, appearance, and once more when they swore fealty after the uprising. This would be the first opportunity for them to have an audience with her.

Trumpets blared.

All conversations halted, each head turned, and everyone stood as the empress entered the hall. Her Eminence Modina Novronian passed through the arched doorway, looking every inch the daughter of a god. She wore a black gown gorgeously hand embroidered with a rainbow of colored thread and adorned with diamonds, rubies, and sapphires. Around her neck, a starched ruff rose in the shape of a Calian lily. She wore long sleeves with wrist ruffs that scalloped her hands. On her ears dangled sparkling earrings, and on her breast lay a necklace of pearl. As she walked, a long black velvet mantle embroidered with the imperial crest trailed behind her. The days of begging a clerk for dress material were long gone.

The woman Hadrian saw before him had the face of Thrace Wood, but she was not the little girl he had once pulled from the gutter on Capital Street in Colnora. She walked tall, her shoulders back, her gaze elevated. She did not look at anyone, nor turn her head prematurely, her sight fixed by the direction she faced. She took her time, walking elegantly, in an arc that allowed her train to straighten before she reached the head of the table.

Hadrian smiled to himself as he remembered how a madam had once suggested that, to save her from starvation, she should join the roster at the Bawdy Bottom Brothel. He had responded with the prophetic words "Something tells me she's not a prostitute."

A steward removed the mantle from her shoulders and placed the chair behind her, but the empress did not sit. Hadrian noted a slight stiffening of her posture as she surveyed her guests. He followed her line of sight, noting the last empty chair.

She addressed Nimbus. "Did you notify the Patriarch of my summons?"

"I did, Your Eminence."

She sighed, then looked upon her subjects.

"Lords and ladies, forgive me. I will forgo customary traditions. My chancellor tells me there are many formalities I am expected to follow; however, such things take time and time is a luxury we can't afford."

It was eerie, Hadrian thought, seeing her addressing heads of state, as calmly as if she were holding a tea party for children.

"As most of you already know, Avryn has been invaded. We believe the attack began more than a month ago, but we were uncertain until very recently. The information comes from the refugees fleeing south and twelve teams of scouts I had sent north, many of whom never returned. Sir Breckton, if you will please explain the situation as it now stands..."

Sir Breckton rose and stood before the assembly, wearing a

long black cape over his dress tunic. All eyes turned to him, not just because he was about to speak, but because Sir Breckton was one of those men who commanded attention. There was something in the way he held himself. He managed to appear taller, straighter, and stouter than other men. Breckton made a formal bow to the empress, then faced the table.

"While none of the scouts managed to pierce the advance troops to report on the main body of the elven army, what we have learned is unsettling enough. We now believe that at midnight on Wintertide, elements of the Erivan Empire crossed the Nidwalden River with a force estimated at over a hundred thousand. They conquered the kingdom of Dunmore in less than a week and Glamrendor is gone. King Roswort, Queen Freda, and their entire court—lost, presumably on their return trip from the Wintertide celebration."

Heads turned left and right and Hadrian heard the words *hundred thousand* and *less than a week* repeated between them. Breckton paused for only a moment before speaking again.

"The elven host continued west, entering unopposed into Ghent. Estimates suggest they conquered it in eight days. Whether Ghent put up a fight, we don't know. It has been confirmed, however, that the university at Sheridan was burned and Ervanon destroyed."

The men at the table shifted with more anxiety but less was said.

"They entered Melengar next," he told them, and a few heads turned toward Alric. "Drondil Fields made a last stand, heroically providing time for as many as possible to escape south. The fortress managed to hold out for one day."

"A day?" King Vincent exclaimed. He looked at Alric, who nodded solemnly. "How can this be?"

"King Fredrick." The empress addressed the monarch seated to her left. "Please repeat what you told us."

King Fredrick stood up, brushing the folds from his clothes. He was a squat, balding man with a round belly that pressed the limits of the front of his tunic.

"Not long after the Wintertide holiday—perhaps a few days at most—travelers brought news of trouble in Calis. They told stories of Ghazel hitting the coast in droves. They called it The Flood. Hundreds of thousands of the mongrels stormed the cliffs at Gur Em Dal."

"Are you saying the elves are in league with the Ghazel?" Cornelius DeLur asked.

The king shook his head. "No, they weren't warriors. Well, some may have been, but the impression I got was that they too were refugees. They were fleeing and running where they could. The Calian warlords slaughtered many on the eastern coast, but the deluge was so great they could not entirely stem the wave. Within a week, bands of Ghazel were on the border of Galeannon and slipping into the Vilan Hills. We lost all communication with Calis—no more travelers have come out."

Fredrick took his seat.

"As of this very afternoon," Sir Breckton said, "we received word that a ship by the name of the *Silver Fin* was five days out of its port in Kilnar when it saw Wesbaden burning. Beyond it, the captain said he saw another column of smoke rising in the distance, which he guessed to be Dagastan."

"Why would the elves launch an attack on both the Ghazel and us? Why open two fronts?" Sir Elgar asked.

"It's likely they don't consider either the Ghazel or ourselves to be a serious threat," Breckton told them. "Sources report the elven host is accompanied by scores of dragons who burn everything in their path. Other reports speak of equally disturbing capabilities, such as the ability to control the weather and call down lightning. There are stories of huge monsters that shake the earth, burrowing beasts, lights that blind, and a mist that...devours people."

"Are these fairy stories you would have us believe, Breckton?" Murthas asked. "Giants, monsters, mists, and elves? Who were these scouts? Old wives?"

This brought chuckles from both Elgar and Gilbert and a smile from Rudolf.

"They were good men, Sir Murthas, and it does not befit you to speak ill of the courageous dead."

"I grieve for the lives of the men who died," King Armand said. "But seriously, Breckton, a mist that kills people? You make them out to be the sum of all nightmares, as if every tale of boogeyman, ghost, or wraith spills out of the wood across the Nidwalden. These are only elves, after all. You make them sound like invincible gods that—"

> *They came with hardly a warning,*
> *thousands both beautiful and terrible;*
> *They came on brilliant white horses*
> *wearing shining gold and shimmering blue;*
> *They came with dragons and whirlwinds,*
> *and giants made of stone and earth;*
> *They came and nothing could stop them.*
> *They are coming still.*

The voice issued from the doorway and all heads turned as into the great hall entered an old man. It was hard to say what caught Hadrian's eyes first, as so much was startling. The man's hair, which did not begin until well behind his balding forehead, was long enough to reach the back of his knees and was beyond gray, beyond white, appearing almost purple, like the edges of a rotting potato. His mouth lacked lips, his eyes were without brows, and his cheeks were shriveled. He wore a cascade of glittering purple, gold, and red—robes displayed with relish—flaunting it with dramatic sweeps of his arms as he walked using a tall staff. Brilliant blue eyes shifted restlessly around the room, never pausing for too long on any one person. His jaw, held taut in an openmouthed grin, showed a surprising full complement of teeth, his expression a silent laugh.

Behind him entered two equally shocking guards. They wore shimmering gold breastplates over top shirts of vertical red, purple, and yellow stripes with long cuffs and billowing sleeves. Matching pants plumed out, gathering just below the knee into long striped stockings. Across their chests, stretching from their shoulders, hung silver braids and tassels of honor. They wore gold helms with messenger wings that hid their faces. Each held unusual weapons, long halberds with ornately curved blades at both ends, which they held tight to their sides with one arm straight down and the other high across their chests.

The guards halted in perfect unison, snapping their heels in one audible *clack*. The old man continued forward, approaching Modina. He stopped before her, slamming the metal tip of his staff down on the stone floor.

"Forgive me, Your Eminence," the old man announced in a loud voice, and followed with an elaborate bow, which allowed him the opportunity to further display the grandeur of his robes. "My apologies cannot begin to elevate the depth of my sadness at having failed to arrive at the appointed time, but alas, I was irrevocably detained. I do hope you can forgive a feeble old man."

Modina stared at him, her expression blank. She said nothing.

The old man waited, shifting his weight, tilting his head from side to side.

Modina glanced at Nimbus.

"Patriarch Nilnev," the chancellor addressed the old man. "If you will please take your seat."

The Patriarch looked at Nimbus, then back to Modina. With a curious expression, he nodded, walked to the empty chair, clacking his staff with each step, and sat down.

"Patriarch Nilnev," Breckton said. "Can you explain your interruption of King Armand's comments?"

"I was quoting an ancient text: '*And lo the sylvan gods prey on Man. They that death does not visit and time does not mar. Firstborn fairy kings, undisputed lords, mankind cowers before thee.*'" He recited the words with reverence and paused before continuing, "The ancient writings speak clearly of the power of the elves. So much time has passed, so much dust covers the years, that man has forgotten the world as it was before the coming of our lord Novron. Before his sacred birth, the elves ruled all the land. Every fair place, every sunlit hill and green valley, lay under their dominion. They were firstborn, greatest of the inhabitants of Elan. We forgot because the miracle of Novron made such amnesia possible. Before his coming, the elves *were* invincible."

"Forgive me, Your Holiness." Sir Elgar spoke up, his voice like the growl of a bear. "But that's a load of bull. Elves are as weak as women and dumber than cattle."

"Have you crossed the Nidwalden, Sir Elgar? Have you seen a true member of the Erivan Empire? Or are you speaking of the *mir*?"

"What's a *mir*?"

"A *mir*—or *kaz* in Calian—is one of those wretched, vile creatures that so often used to defile the streets of cities throughout Apeladorn. Those emaciated, loathsome perversions with pointed ears and slanted eyes who carry a muddied mix of human and elven blood are abominations. *Mirs* are remnants of a conquered people that have less in common with elves than you do with a goldfish. Elf and human cannot coexist. They are mortal enemies by divine providence. The mixing of their blood in a single body has produced a contemptible walking insult to both Maribor and Ferrol, and the gods' wrath has fallen upon them. You should not presume to look at a *mir* and guess at the nature of an elf."

"Okay, I get the point. Still, I've never come across any creature that draws breath who is immune from the sharpened tip of a sword," Elgar said.

This produced pounding of fists on the table and grunts of agreement from the other knights—all except Breckton.

"The ancient text tells us that prior to the coming of Novron, no elf was ever killed by a man. Moreover, due to their long life, no human ever saw an elven corpse. This gave rise to the belief that they were immortal gods. '*Soft of foot, loud as thunder, terrible as lightning, greater than the stars, they come, they come, they come to conquer.*'"

"So if they were so great, how did Novron stop them?" Elgar challenged.

"He was the son of a god," the Patriarch replied simply. "And"—he paused briefly, his grin widening to display even more teeth—"he had help in the form of the Rhelacan."

"The divine sword?" Sir Breckton asked skeptically.

The Patriarch shook his head. "It was created by the gods, but the Rhelacan is not a sword; it is the Trumpet of Ferrol, the Call of Nations, the *Syord duah Gylindora* that Novron used to defeat the Erivan Nation. Many make the same mistake. In the Old Speech the word *syord* means *horn*, but that bit of information was lost when some sloppy translator thought it meant *sword*. The name Rhelacan is merely Old Speech for *relic* or *artifact*. So the *Syord duah Gylindora*, or Horn of Gylindora, became the *sword that is a great relic*, or the Rhelacan—the weapon that Novron used against the elves."

"How can this...*horn*...defeat an army?" Sir Breckton asked.

"It was made by the hand of their god, Ferrol, and holds dominion over them. It gave Novron the power to defeat the elves."

"And where might this marvelous trumpet be?" Cornelius DeLur spoke up. "I only ask because in our present circumstances, such a delightful treasure could prove to be quite useful."

"Herein lies the great question. The Rhelacan has been lost for centuries. No one knows what became of the Horn of Gylindora. The best accounts place it in the ancient capital of Percepliquis, just before the city vanished."

"Vanished?" Cornelius asked, leaning forward as far as his immense girth would allow.

"Yes," the Patriarch said. "All accounts from that time report that the city was there one day and gone the next. Percepliquis was consumed, lost, it is said, in a single day." The Patriarch closed his eyes and spoke in a musical tone:

> *Novron's home, seat of power*
> *White roads, walls, roofs, and towers*
> *Upon three hills, fair and tall*
> *Gone forever, fall the wall.*
>
> *Birthplace of our wondrous queen*
> *Mounted flags of blue and green*
> *Exquisite mansions, wondrous halls*
> *Goodbye forever, fall the wall.*
>
> *City of Percepliquis*
> *Ever sought, forever missed*

*Pick and shovel, dig and haul*
*Search forever, fall the wall.*

*Gala halted, city's doom*
*Spring warmth chilled with dust and gloom*
*Darkness sealed, blankets all*
*Death upon them, fall the wall.*

*Ancient stones upon the Lee*
*Dusts of memories gone we see*
*Once the center, once the all*
*Lost forever, fall the wall.*

"I know that," Hadrian blurted out, and regretted it the moment he did, as all eyes looked his way. "It's just that I remember hearing that as a kid. Not the whole thing, just the last part. We used to sing it when we played a game called Fall-the-Wall. We didn't know what it meant. We didn't think it meant anything. Although some of the kids thought it had something to do with the ruins of Amberton Lee."

"It does!" Arista broke in. "Amberton Lee is all that remains of the ancient capital of Percepliquis."

Hadrian heard the reactions of disbelief around the table.

"How do *you* know this?" Sir Murthas asked inquisitorially. "Scholars and adventurers have searched for centuries and a wit—" He caught himself. "A *princess* just happens to know where it is? What proof do you have?"

"I had—" Arista began when the empress cut her off.

"Princess Arista has provided to me irrefutable proof that what she says is indeed true." Modina glared at the knight.

Sir Murthas looked as if he might protest, but he closed his mouth in defeat.

"I believe the city is buried," Arista went on. "I think Edmund Hall found a way in. If only we had his journal...but the Crown Tower is gone, along with everything in it."

"Wait a minute," Hadrian said. "Was it a beat-up brown leather notebook? About this big?" He gestured with his hands.

"Yes," the Patriarch said.

Arista looked back and forth between them. "How do you know that?"

"I know it because I have lived in the Crown Tower," the Patriarch said.

"And you?" Arista looked at Hadrian, who hesitated.

"Ha-ha! Of course, of course. I knew it!" Cosmos DeLur chuckled and clapped his hands together in single applause while smiling at Hadrian. "Such a wonderfully delightful rumor as that had to be true. That is an exquisite accomplishment."

"You stole it?" Arista asked.

"Yes, he did," the Patriarch declared.

"Actually," Hadrian said, "Royce and I did, but we put it back the next night."

"Riyria's reputation is well founded," Cosmos said.

"I did not wish to lose such an important treasure again, so since then, I've kept it with me at all times." The Patriarch pulled out a small ruddy-brown leather book and lay it on the table. "This is the journal of Edmund Hall, the daily account of his descent into the ancient city of Percepliquis and what lies within."

Everyone stared at the book for a moment in silence.

"The princess is correct," the Patriarch continued. "The city lies beneath Amberton Lee and Hall did find a means in. He also found a great deal more than that. The journal speaks of a terrible shaft of darkness, an underground sea that must be crossed, insidiously complex tunnels and tight crevices, bloodthirsty tribes of Ba Ran Ghazel, and a monster so terrible Hall could not fully describe it."

"You're saying the ancient capital is only three miles from Hintindar?" Hadrian asked.

"Yes," Modina said, "and I plan on sending in a party to retrieve this horn."

"Having read Hall's journal," the Patriarch said, "I believe you will need several skilled warriors, someone with historical knowledge of the city, someone with spelunking skills, and someone with sailing experience. I have already sent three teams on this very mission. Perhaps I—"

"I know," the empress said. "They all failed. Princess Arista will organize my team."

"If we could borrow Hall's journal," Arista said, "that would be of great assistance. I promise you'll have it returned before the party sets out."

The Patriarch's smile seemed to waver, but he nodded. "Of course. It is the least I can do."

Modina gestured toward Arista. "Your Highness, if you will…"

The princess stood up and faced the table. Before she could talk, however, Sir Elgar got to his feet. "Hold on," he said. "Are you saying we aren't even going to try and fight them? We're just going to sit here and wait for some fairy-tale horn that might not even exist anymore? I say we form ranks, march north, and hit them before they hit us!"

"Your courage is commendable," Sir Breckton said, "but in this instance foolish. We have no idea where our enemy is, the size or strength of their force, or their path of movement. Without even the faintest hint about our enemy we would be as a blind man fumbling around for a bear in the forest. And all attempts to discover anything about our foe have met with failure. I have sent dozens of scouts and few have returned."

"It seems wrong to just wait."

"We won't just be waiting," the empress said. "You can be assured that Sir Breckton has drawn up excellent plans for the defense of Aquesta, which I expect each of you to support. We have already begun overstocking the city with supplies and reinforcing the walls. We should not deceive ourselves: this war—this storm—is coming and we must be prepared for it. I assure you, we will stand, we will fight, and we will pray. As I find myself faced with annihilation, I am not above throwing support to even the thinnest promise. If there is a chance that finding this horn can save my people—my family—we must try. I will do whatever it takes to protect us. I would even make a deal with Uberlin himself if that is what is needed."

When she was done, no one said a word until she once more gestured toward Arista.

The princess took a breath. "I have already discussed this with the empress. The team will be small, no more than twelve, I think. Two people must go. For the rest, I will ask for volunteers, starting from a list we have already prepared. I will speak with those on the list individually, in order to allow for the privacy of each person's decision."

"And who are these two?" Murthas asked. "The ones that must go. Can we know their names?"

"Yes," Arista said. "They are Degan Gaunt and myself."

Several people spoke at once. Sir Elgar and the other knights laughed, and Alric started to protest, but by far the loudest voice in the room came from Degan Gaunt.

"Are you insane?" he shouted, jumping to his feet. "I'm not going anywhere! Why do I have to go? This is just another plot of the aristocracy to silence me. Can't you see what this really is? This elven threat is a hoax, an excuse to oppress the common man once more!"

"Sit down, Mr. Gaunt," Modina said. "We'll discuss this in private as soon as the meeting is over."

Gaunt dubiously sat down and slumped in his chair.

The empress rose and the room went silent. "This concludes this meeting. Sir Breckton will begin by convening a war council here in one hour to specify in detail the reorganization of troops and the requisition of supplies and arms necessary to develop a proper defense for the city. Those not asked to join the Percepliquis party should meet back here at that time. In the future, Chancellor Nimbus and Secretary Amilia will be on hand in their offices to answer any additional questions. May Maribor protect us all."

⌘

The room filled with the sounds of scraping chairs and low conversations. Hadrian rose to his feet but stopped when he felt Arista's hand on his arm.

"We stay here," she told him.

He glanced up the length of the table as the kings and knights began filing out of the room. The empress made no indication of leaving, nor did Amilia or Nimbus. He even caught the spindling chancellor subtly patting the table with his hand, as further indication that Hadrian should sit back down. Alric and Mauvin stood but did not advance toward the exit.

The Patriarch, flanked by his bodyguards, exited the hall. He looked back, nodding and smiling, his staff clicking on the stone. He was the last one out of the hall, and with a nod from Nimbus, guards closed the doors. A dull but—Hadrian felt—ominous thud echoed with their closing.

"I'm going," Alric told his sister.

"But—" she started.

"No buts," he said firmly. "You went to meet with Gaunt against my wishes. You tried to free him from these dungeons instead of coming home. You even managed to be on hand when Modina slew the Gilarabrywn. I'm tired of being the one sitting home worrying. I may no longer have a kingdom, but I am still the king! If you go, I go."

"Me too," Mauvin put in. "As Count of Galilin, it falls to me to keep both of you safe. My father would have insisted."

"I was just going to say, before you interrupted," Arista began, "that you're both already on the list. I'll just check you both off as agreeing."

"Good." Alric smiled triumphantly, folding his arms across his chest, then grinned at Mauvin. "Looks like we'll make it to Percepliquis after all."

"And you can take me off your bloody list!" Degan Gaunt shouted. He was on his feet. "I'm not going!"

"Please sit down, Degan," Arista told him. "I need to explain."

Degan remained furious, his eyes wide, his hands tugging at his doublet and his tight collar. "You!" He pointed at Hadrian. "Are you just going to sit there? Aren't you supposed to protect me?"

"From what?" he asked. "They only want to talk."

"From the brutish manhandling of the common man by the rich aristocracy!"

"That's actually what we need to speak about," Modina explained. "You are the true Heir of Novron, not I. That is why Ethelred and Saldur locked you up."

"Then why haven't I been acknowledged? I've seen precious little benefit from that wondrous title. I should be the emperor—I should be on the throne. Why hasn't my pedigree been announced? Why do you feel it is necessary to speak about my lineage in private? If I really am this heir, I should be sitting for my coronation right now, not going on some suicide mission. How stupid do you think I am? If I really were this descendant of a god, I would be too valuable to risk. Oh no, you want me out of the way so you can rule! I am an inconvenience that you have found a convenient way to dispose of!"

"Your lineage hasn't been announced for your own safety. If—"

Gaunt cut Modina off. "My own safety? You people are the only ones that threaten me!"

"Will you let her finish?" Amilia told him.

Modina patted her hand and then continued. "The heir has the ability to unite the four nations of Apeladorn under one banner, but I have already accomplished that, or rather the late regents, Saldur and Ethelred, have. Through their diligent, misguided efforts, the world already believes the heir sits on the imperial throne. At this moment, we are in a war with an adversary we have little chance of defeating. This is no time to shake the people's belief. They must remain strong and confident that the heir already rules. We must remain united in the face of our enemy. If we revealed the truth now, that confidence would be shaken and our strength destroyed. If we manage to survive, if we live to see the snow melt and the flowers bloom again, then you and I can talk about who sits on the throne."

Degan stood with less conviction now. He leaned on the table, pulling on his collar. "I still don't see why I need to go on this loony trip into a buried city."

"The ability to unite the kingdoms was thought to be the sum of the heir's value, but we now believe it is trivial compared to your true importance."

"And that is?"

"Your ability to both find and use the Horn of Gylindora."

"But I don't know anything about this—this horn thingy. What is it I'm supposed to do, exactly?"

"I don't know."

"What will happen if I use it?"

"I don't know."

"Then I don't know that I am going. You said that if everything works out, we'll talk about who sits on the imperial throne, but I say we have that discussion now. I will go on this quest of yours, but in return I demand the throne. I want it in writing, signed with your hand, that I will be Emperor of Apeladorn upon my return, regardless of success. And I want two copies, one which I will take with me in case the other is *somehow* lost."

"That's outrageous!" Alric declared.

"Perhaps, but I won't go otherwise."

"Oh, you'll go," Mauvin assured him with a smirk.

"Sure, you can tie me up and drag me, but I'll hang limp—a dead weight that will slow you down. And at some point you'll need me to do something, which I assure you I will not. So if you want my cooperation, you will give me the throne."

Modina stared at him. "All right," she said. "If that is your price, I will pay it."

"You're not serious!" Alric exclaimed. "You can't agree to put this—this—"

"Careful," Gaunt said. "You are speaking of your next emperor, and I remember slights against me."

"What will happen to Modina?" Amilia asked.

Gaunt pursed his lips, considering. "She was a farmer once, wasn't she? She can go back to that."

"Empress," Alric began, "think about what you are doing."

"I am." She turned to Nimbus. "Take Gaunt. Have the scribe write up whatever he wants. I will sign it."

Gaunt smiled broadly and followed the chancellor out of

the hall. A silence followed. Alric started to speak several times but stopped himself and finally slumped in his seat.

Arista looked at Hadrian and took his hand. "I want you to go."

Hadrian glanced at the door. "Being his bodyguard, I don't suppose I have a choice."

She smiled, then added, "I also want Royce to come."

Hadrian ran a hand through his hair. "That might be a bit of a problem." He looked toward Modina.

"I have no objection," she said.

"We need the best team I can put together," Arista added.

"That's right," Alric said. "If ever there was a need for my miracle team, this is it. Tell him I'll make it worth his time. I still have *some* fortune left."

Hadrian shook his head. "This time it won't be about money."

"But you will talk to him?" Arista asked.

"I'll try."

"Hey," Alric said to Arista, "why is it that *you* feel compelled to go? I never remember you having any interest in Percepliquis before."

"To be honest, I would rather not go, but it's my responsibility now."

"Responsibility?"

"Perhaps *penance* is a better word. You could say I am haunted." Her brother did not appear to understand, but she did not elaborate. "We still need a historian. If only Arcadius had...but now..."

"I know someone," Hadrian said, picking up Hall's journal. "A friend with an appetite for books and an uncanny memory."

Arista noded. "What about someone with sailing experience?"

"Royce and I spent a month on the *Emerald Storm*. We know a little about ships. It's a shame I don't know where Wyatt Deminthal is, though. He was the helmsman on the *Storm* and a fantastic seaman."

"I'm familiar with Mr. Deminthal," Modina said, drawing a curious look from Hadrian. "I'll see if I can convince him to sign on."

"That just leaves the dwarf," Arista said.

"The what?" Hadrian stared at her.

"Magnus."

"You've found him?" Alric asked.

"Modina did."

"That's wonderful!" Alric exclaimed. "Can we execute him before our departure?"

"He's going with you," Modina told him.

"He killed my father!" Alric shouted. "He stabbed him in the back while he was at prayer!"

"While I can see your point, Your Majesty," Hadrian said to Alric, "there is a more pressing issue. He nearly killed Royce twice. If he sees Magnus, the dwarf is dead."

"Then perhaps you should be the one to hang on to this." Modina produced the white dagger and slid it down the table, where it came to rest, spinning slightly before Hadrian. "I know all about Magnus's crimes. His obsession with Royce's dagger caused him to make poor decisions, including the one that got him arrested when he tried to steal it from the store-house. You are going underground, perhaps deep underground. There will be no maps or road signs and I can't afford for you to get lost."

"Alric, Modina and I agree on this," Arista said. "Remember he was my father as well. We are setting out on a journey that may decide the fate of our race! The elves don't want to push us from our lands and lock us in slums. They plan to eradicate us. They won't ever let us have a second chance to hurt them. If we don't succeed, it's over—all of it. No more Melengar, no more Warric, no more Avryn. We will cease to exist. If I must tolerate—even forgive—a murderer as payment for the safety of everyone and everything I've ever known…Why, I'd marry the little cretin if that was the modest price Maribor put on *this* prize."

There was a silence after the princess stopped speaking.

"All right," Alric said grudgingly. "I guess I can put up with him."

Hadrian reached out and picked up Alverstone. "I will definitely need to hold on to this."

"Wow," Mauvin said, looking at Arista. "You'd marry him? That's really sick."

"Supplies are being prepared," Modina explained. "Food kits designed by Ibis Thinly will be packed along with lanterns, ropes, harnesses, axes, cloth, pitch, blankets, and everything else we can think of that you might need."

"Then we will leave as soon as the supplies are ready," Arista declared.

"So it's settled." Modina stood and all the others followed suit. "May Maribor guide your steps."

# CHAPTER 5

# THE MARQUIS OF GLOUSTON

Myron sat curled up on his bunk, bundled deep in several layers of blankets. He had his hood up and a candle in his hand, which hovered over a giant book spread across his knees. He shared Hadrian's room in the knights' dormitories. The room lacked a window and fireplace, leaving it dark as well as cold. Only a plain green drape covering one wall interrupted the drab space. Myron did not mind; he liked the room.

He took his meals in the kitchen. Breakfast was early and supper late, working on abbey time. He visited Red, the elkhound, daily and said his prayers alone. In many ways, it reminded him of the abbey. He had expected he would be homesick by now, but the feeling never came. This surprised him at first, but *home*, he realized, was not so much a place as an idea that, like everything else, grew and blossomed along with the person. Being away gave him a new insight that the abbey was no longer his home—he carried his home with him now, and his family was not just a handful of monks.

He forced his eyes to focus on the book before him. Lord Amberlin of Gaston Loo had just discovered that he was descended from the Earl of Gast, who had defeated the invading Lumbertons at the Battle of Primiton Tor. He had no idea who Lord Amberlin was nor who the Lumbertons might be, but it was fascinating just the same. Everything he read still fascinated him.

A knock at the door caused him nearly to spill the candle. He put the book away and, opening up, was greeted by a familiar page.

"My lord."

Myron smiled. The boy always called him that, and Myron found each instance funny. "The lady Alenda requests an audience with you in the small east parlor. She is there now. Will you see her or shall I respond with a message?"

Myron stood puzzled for a moment. "Lady who?"

"The lady Alenda of Glouston."

"Oh," he said. "Ah, I'll go, but...ah, could you show me the way? I don't know where the east parlor is."

"Certainly, my lord."

The page turned and began walking, leaving Myron to quickly close the door and trot after him. "What is Lady Alenda like?" Myron asked.

The page glanced at him, surprised. "She's your sister, my lord. At least, that is what she said."

"Yes, she is, but...Do you know what she wants?"

"No, my lord. The lady Alenda did not say."

"Did she sound angry?"

"No, my lord."

They reached the small parlor, with its hearty fire's warm glow. The room was filled with many soft upholstered chairs and couches, lending the chamber a friendly feel. Rich tapestries depicting a hunt, a battle, and a spring festival covered the walls.

Two women jumped to their feet the moment he entered. The foremost was dressed in a beautiful black gown of brocade with a high collar and tight bodice composed of many buttons, lace, and trimming. The second wore a much simpler, but nonetheless rich, black gown of kersey.

Having spent almost his entire life in a monastery on top of a remote hill, Myron had met few people, and even fewer women—and none like these two. They were both as beautiful as a pair of deer.

They promptly curtsied and Myron was not sure what that meant.

*Am I supposed to curtsy as well?*

Before he could decide, one of them spoke. "My lord," the nearest woman said while still bent down. "I am your sister, Alenda, and with me is my maid Emily."

"Hello," he said awkwardly. "I'm Myron."

He held out his hand. Alenda, still in full curtsy, looked up, confused. She spotted his outstretched arm and gave an odd glance to the other woman before taking it. She kissed the back of his hand.

Myron hauled his hand back, shocked. A long uncomfortable silence followed.

"I really wish I had some cookies to offer you," he said at length.

Again, silence.

"We always had cookies at the abbey for guests."

"I want to ask your forgiveness, Your Lordship," Alenda burst out in a quavering voice, "for failing to meet you before this. I know it was wrong of me and that you have every reason to be angry. I have come now to beg you to be merciful."

Myron looked at the woman before him, baffled. He blinked several times.

"You are begging mercy—from *me*?"

Alenda looked at him, horrified. "Oh please, my lord, have pity. I didn't even know you lived until I was fourteen, and then I heard about you only in passing during a dinner conversation. It really wasn't until I was nineteen that I fully realized I had another brother and that Father had sentenced you to that awful place. I know I am not blameless. I realize my misdeeds and fully admit to you my foul nature. When I heard you lived, I should have come at once and embraced you, but I did not. Still, you must understand I am not accustomed to traveling abroad and visiting strange men, even if they are my long-lost brother. If only our father had brought me to you— but he refused and sadly I did not press."

Myron stood frozen in place.

Looking at him, Alenda wailed, "Sentence me as you must, but please do not torture me any longer. My heart cannot stand it."

Myron's mouth opened, but nothing came out. He stepped back, stunned.

Alenda stood wavering on her feet. In the silence between them, she looked at the frayed, coarse woolen frock he wore and her eyes filled with tears. She stepped toward him, her hands shaking. She reached out, touching his garment, letting it play between her fingers, and whispered with a closing throat, "I am sorry for how Father treated you. I am sorry for how I treated you. I am sorry for all that you have been forced to endure by our selfishness, but please don't turn me out into the cold. I'll do whatever you ask, but please have pity." Alenda fell to her knees before him weeping into her hands.

Myron fell to his own knees and, reaching out, put his arms around his sister and hugged her. "Please stop crying. I don't know what I did to hurt you, but I'm very sorry." He looked up at Emily and mouthed, "Help me."

The maid just stared at him in shock.

Alenda looked up, dabbing the tears from her eyes with a lace handkerchief. "You aren't going to strip me of my title? Drive me off our land and force me to fend for myself?"

"Oh dear Maribor, no!" Myron exclaimed. "I could never do that! But—"

"You won't?"

"Of course not! But—"

"Will you—could you also grant me my dowry of the Rilan Valley?" she said, and then very quickly added, "I only ask because no decent man would ever marry a woman without an adequate dowry. Without this I would continue to be a burden to you and the estate. Of course, the Rilan is very good land and I understand that you may not want to part with it, but Father promised it to me. Still I would be happy with anything you are willing to grant."

"But I can't give you anything. I'm only a monk of the Winds Abbey." He pulled the cloth of his frock out from his chest. "This is all I own. This is all I've ever owned. And technically I think this belongs to the abbey."

"But—" Alenda looked at him, stunned. "Don't you know?"

Myron waited, blinking again.

"Our father and brothers are all gone, fallen in the battle against the elves. They died at Drondil Fields—"

"I'm so sorry to hear that," Myron said. He patted her hand. "I mourn for your loss. You must feel awful."

"They were your family as well."

"Yes, of course, but I was not as close to them as you were. Actually, I only met Father, and just once. But that does not diminish my sympathy for you. I am so sorry for you. Is there anything I can do?"

A questioning furrow across her brow, Alenda exchanged looks with Emily.

"I'm not sure you understand. With their passing, our family's fortune and title passes to you. They left you your inheritance. You are the Marquis of Glouston. You own thousands of acres of land, a castle, villages—barons and knights are all yours to command. You control the lives of hundreds of men and women who live or die at your decree."

Myron shivered and grimaced. "No, no. I'm sorry, you must be mistaken. I want none of that. I don't suppose I could trouble you to take care of those things?"

"So I can have the Rilan Valley?"

"Oh no—well, I mean, yes—I mean, everything. I don't want it. You can have it all—well, are there any books?"

"A few, I think," Alenda said, dazed.

"Then can I have those?" he asked. "You can have them back if you want after I read them, but if you don't, I'd like to make them part of the library at Windermere. Would that be all right?"

"Are you saying you want me to assume ownership of all of Glouston? Everything—except the books?"

Myron nodded and glanced at Emily. "If that is too much trouble, perhaps your friend could help. Maybe she could have some of those castles and knights—you know, many hands make light work."

Alenda nodded with her mouth still open.

Myron smiled. "Was there anything else?"

Alenda shook her head slowly.

"Okay, well, it was very nice meeting you." He reached out and shook Alenda's hand. "Both of you." He shook Emily's as well. Neither said a word.

He exited through the door and leaned with his back against the wall, feeling as if he had just escaped death itself.

"There you are," Hadrian called to him as he approached up the corridor, clutching a small notebook. "The page told me you were here."

"The strangest thing just happened," Myron told him, pointing back at the parlor door.

"Save it." He held out the book. "You need to read this tonight. The whole thing. Can you do that?"

"Just the one?"

Hadrian smiled. "I knew I could count on you."

"What is it?"

"Edmund Hall's journal."

"Oh my!"

"Exactly. And tomorrow you can tell me all about it on the road. It will help to pass the time."

"Road—tomorrow?" Myron asked. "Am I going back to the abbey?"

"Better—you're going to be a hero."

## CHAPTER 6

# VOLUNTEERS

As far as prison cells went, Wyatt Deminthal had seen far worse. Despite the stone, it was surprisingly warm and remarkably similar to the solitary cell he had been occupying for the past several weeks. The small bed he sat on was nicer than most of the rooms he had rented and much better than the ship hammocks he was used to. A small window, high up, allowed light to splash the far wall. Wyatt had to admit it was a fine room. He might have even found it comfortable if not for the locked door and the dwarf staring at him.

The dwarf had already been in the cell when they had brought Wyatt in, and the guards had not bothered with introductions. He had a brown braided beard and a broad flat nose, and he was dressed in a blue leather vest, with large black boots. Despite having been roommates for several hours, neither had said a word. The dwarf grumbled occasionally, shuffled his boots as he shifted position, but said nothing. Instead, he had a nasty habit of staring. Little round eyes peered out from beneath bushy eaves—eyebrows that matched his beard in color if not in neatness. Wyatt had known few dwarves, but they always sported carefully groomed beards.

"So you're a sailor," the dwarf muttered.

Wyatt, who had been passing the time by playing with the feather in his hat, raised his head and nodded. "And you're a dwarf."

"What was your first clue?" The little fellow smirked. "What'd you do?"

Wyatt did not see any point in avoiding the question. Lies were told to protect one's future, and Wyatt had no illusions of his. "I'm responsible for destroying Tur Del Fur."

The dwarf sat up, interested. "Really? What part?"

"The whole city—well, technically all of Delgos, if you think about it. I mean, without the protection of Drumindor, the port is lost and the rest is helpless."

"You destroyed an entire country?"

"Pretty much." Wyatt nodded miserably, then sighed.

The dwarf continued to stare at him, now in fascination.

"How about you?" Wyatt asked. "What did you do?"

"I tried to steal a dagger."

Now it was Wyatt's turn to stare. "Really?"

"Sure, but you have to remember—I'm a dwarf. You'll probably get a slap on the wrist. After all, you only destroyed a country. I'll likely be ripped apart by wild dogs."

The door to the chamber opened, and while Wyatt had never actually seen her before, there was no mistaking Empress Modina Novronian. She entered flanked by guards and a spindly man in a foppish wig.

"Both of you are guilty of crimes," she said. "Punishable by execution."

Wyatt was surprised at the sound of her voice. He had expected an icier tone, a shrill superiority common to high nobility. She sounded—oddly enough—like a young girl.

"Wyatt Deminthal," the spindly man in the wig said formally. "For wanton acts that precipitated and enabled the invasion of Delgos and the destruction of Tur Del Fur by the

Ba Ran Ghazel, you are hereby found guilty of high treason against mankind and this empire. Punishment will be execution by beheading, to be carried out immediately."

The empress then turned to the dwarf and once more the thin man spoke. "Magnus the dwarf, for the murder of King Amrath, you are hereby found guilty and sentenced to death by beheading, also to be carried out at once."

"Seems you left something out," Wyatt said to the dwarf, who only grumbled in response.

"Both of your lives are over," Modina said. Then: "When I leave this room, the headsman will escort you to the block in the courtyard, where your punishment will be administered. Is there anything you would like to say before I leave?"

"My daughter…" Wyatt began, "she's innocent. So is Elden—the big guy with her. I beg you, please don't punish them."

"They are safe and free to go. But where do you think they will go once you're dead? You've been caring for them both for many years, haven't you? While Elden may make a fine babysitter, he's not much of a provider, is he?"

"Why are you saying this?" It mystified Wyatt that such a young girl could be so cruel.

"Because I would like to make you an offer, Mr. Deminthal. I would like to make both of you an offer. Given your positions, I think it is a very good one. I want the two of you to do a task for me. It will involve a difficult journey that I suspect will be very dangerous. If you agree, then upon your return, I shall absolve you both of your crimes."

"And if I don't come back? What happens to Elden and Allie?"

"Elden will go with you. I need experienced sailors and strength. I think he'll be useful."

"What about Allie? I won't have her going to some prison or orphanage. Can she come as well?"

"No, as I mentioned, the trip will be dangerous, so she will remain with me. I will be her guardian while you are away."

"What if I don't come back? What if neither Elden or I..."

"If that happens, I promise that I will personally adopt her."

"You will?"

"Yes, Mr. Deminthal. If you succeed, you will be forgiven of all crimes you have committed. If you fail, I will make your daughter my daughter. Of course, you can refuse my offer, in which case I have to ask if you would prefer a blindfold or not. It's your choice."

"And me?" Magnus asked.

"I offer you the same thing. Do as I ask, and you'll live. I'll consider your service as fulfillment of your sentence. In your case, however, there is one additional stipulation. Mr. Deminthal has proved that his ties to his daughter are strong enough to hold him to his commitments. You, on the other hand, have no such attachments and have a talent for disappearing. I can't afford to let you out of this cell without some insurance. I know a sorceress who can find anyone, anywhere, using only a strand of hair, and your beard is ever so long."

Magnus's eyes widened in alarm.

"It's your choice, master dwarf, your beard or your neck."

"Do we at least get to know where we are going, and what we will be doing?" Wyatt asked.

"Does it matter?"

Wyatt thought a moment, then shook his head.

"You'll be accompanying a team to the ancient city of Percepliquis to find a very important relic that might just save mankind. If you succeed at that, I think you deserve to be forgiven for any crime.

"There is just one more thing. You'll be accompanied by Royce Melborn and Hadrian Blackwater. As for you, Wyatt, they know nothing of your involvement with Merrick. I suggest you keep it that way. Merrick is dead, and nothing good can come from revealing your involvement in Tur Del Fur."

Wyatt nodded toward the dwarf. "I already told him."

"That's all right. I doubt Master Magnus will be speaking to them much. Magnus has had, shall we say, his own misunderstandings with Riyria, not to mention the children of King Amrath, who will also be along for the trip. I suspect he'll be on his best behavior, won't you, Magnus?"

The dwarf's face showed concern but he nodded.

"So, gentlemen, the choice is yours. Risk your lives for me and have a chance to become heroes of the empire, or refuse and die now as criminals."

"That's not much of a choice," the dwarf growled.

"No—no, it isn't. But it is all you have."

⸙

Hadrian slowly climbed the steps. It felt like there were more of them this time. Aside from speaking to Myron, Hadrian had spent all night, and a good part of the next day, walking the corridors and courtyard, trying to formulate an argument— a reason that would convince Royce to go.

The guard heard him coming and was on his feet, key in hand. He looked bored. "You've come to take him?" he asked without interest. "I was told you'd be by—expected you earlier."

Hadrian only nodded in reply.

"So much fuss about this little guy? From hearing the talk around the palace, you'd think he was Uberlin himself," the guard continued as he placed the key in the lock. "He's been quieter than a mouse. A few nights ago, I heard him crying— muffled sobs, you know? Not exactly the demon I was warned about."

Royce had not moved. Nothing in the cell had changed since Hadrian's last visit.

"You wanna give me a minute?" Hadrian asked the guard, who stood behind him.

"Huh? Oh—sure. Take your time."

Hadrian stood silently at the open door. Royce did not move. He continued to sit with his head bowed.

Hadrian sighed. After all his searching, his thinking, his wandering, his solution seemed feeble at best. He had held dozens of mental debates in which he had played both sides of the arguments, but when he sat across from Royce, he had only one thing he could say. "I need your help."

Royce looked up as if his head weighed a hundred pounds, his eyes red, his face ashen. He waited.

"One last job," Hadrian told him, then added, "I promise."

"Is it dangerous?"

"Very."

"Is there a good chance I'll get killed?"

"Odds are definitely in favor of that."

Royce nodded, looked down at the scarf in his lap, and replied, "Okay."

## CHAPTER 7

# THE LAUGHING GNOME

Arista lugged her pack out into the cold. Three stewards and one soldier, an older man with a dark beard who held the door open, offered to carry it for her. She shook her head and smiled. The pack was light. Gone were the days of bringing six silk dresses, hoopskirts, corsets, girdles, and a headdress—just in case. She planned to sleep in the clothes she traveled in and learn to do without almost everything else. All she really needed was the robe. The wind blew snow in her face, freezing her nose. Her feet felt the cold, but the rest of her was immune, protected by the shimmering garment.

As she crossed the courtyard, the only light came from within the stable, and the loudest noise from her boots as they crushed the snow.

"Your Highness!" A boy chased after her, gingerly holding a steaming cup in both hands. "Ibis Thinly sent this to you." He shivered, dressed only in light wool.

She took the cup. "Tell him thank you."

The boy made a feeble bow and turned so fast to run back that his foot slipped and he fell to one knee.

The cup contained tea, and it felt wonderfully hot in her chilled fingers. The steam warmed her face as she sipped. Ibis had prepared a wonderful meal for everyone, laying it out across two tables. Arista had only glanced at the plates. It was too early to eat. She rarely ate breakfast. Her stomach needed time to wake up before going to work. That morning the thought of food was abhorrent. Her stomach was knotted and riding high. She knew she would pay later for skipping the meal. Somewhere along the road she would regret not having eaten something.

The stable smelled of wet straw and horse manure. Both doors stood open, leaving a path for the wind, which jingled the harnesses. Gusts harassed the lanterns and ripped through gaps in the walls, producing a loud fluttering howl as if a massive flock of sparrows were taking flight every few seconds.

"I'll take that, Your Highness," a groom offered. He was a short, stocky older man with a bristling beard and a knit hat that slumped to one side. He had two bridles draped around his neck and a bale hook hanging from his belt. He grabbed her pack and walked to the wagon. "You'll be riding back here," he told her. "I've made a right comfortable spot for you. I got a soft pillow from a chambermaid and three thick blankets. You'll ride in style, you will."

"Thank you, but I'll be needing a horse and a sidesaddle."

The groom looked at her with a blank stare, his mouth open, his lips thick and cracked. "But—Your Highness, where you're going—it's quite a ways from here, ain't it? Right awful weather too. You won't want to be atop no horse."

She smiled at him, then turned and walked up the aisle between the stalls. The aisle was brick, the stalls were dirt, and everything lay covered in bits of straw. The rear ends of a dozen horses faced her, swishing tails and shifting weight from one hoof to the other. Cobwebs gathered in corners, catching hay and forming snarled nests even in the rafters. The walls all bore a stain a full foot from the bottom—the high manure mark, she guessed. She stopped without thinking before a stall. This was where she had spent a night with Hilfred, where he had held her, where he had stroked her hair—kissed her. A pleasant-looking gray mare was there now. The horse turned her head and Arista saw a white nose and dark eyes. "What do you call this one?"

The groom slapped the horse's rump fondly. "This here girl is called Princess."

Arista smiled. "Saddle her for me."

Arista led Princess out into the courtyard. The groom followed close behind with the wagon. The team of horses puffed great clouds into the morning air. A crowd of people came out to the steps of the palace wrapped in dark cloaks, heads draped in hoods. They spoke in soft voices and whispers, clustering in small groups; some cried. The gathering reminded Arista of a funeral.

She knew many of the faces, even if she did not know all the names.

Alenda Lanaklin stood beside Denek, Lenare, and Belinda Pickering as they said goodbye to Mauvin and Alric. Mauvin threw his head back, laughing at something. It sounded wrong—too loud, too much effort. With her left hand, Belinda dabbed at her eyes with a cloth; her right hand gripped Mauvin's sleeve with white fingers. Alenda looked over the crowd, managing to catch Myron's attention. She waved to him. The monk paused in his efforts to pet the noses of the team of brown geldings harnessed to the wagon. He smiled and hesitantly waved back.

Not far away, two men Arista did not know spoke with the empress. One wore a plumed cavalier hat, a red and black doublet, high leather boots, and a heavy sailor's wrap. The other man towered over everyone present. His head reminded Arista of a barrel, wide and flat on top and bottom, with

vertical creases like wooden slats. He was mostly bald and
missing one ear and sporting several ugly scars, one that split
his lower lip. A thick, untailored cape draped him like a tent.
Arista speculated he had merely cut a hole in a thick blanket
and pulled his head through. At his side was a huge, crude
axe, hanging naked from a rough bit of raw leather.

"Do what the empress tells you," Arista heard the sailor
say. "She'll take care of you until I come back."

A few feet away, Hadrian stood speaking with a man, a
refugee from Melengar. He was a viscount, but she did not
know his name. An attractive young woman rushed up, went
up on her toes, and kissed Hadrian. The viscount called her
Emerald.

*What kind of name is that?*

Hadrian hugged her, pulling Emerald off the ground. She
giggled. Her left leg bent at the knee. She was very cute—
smaller than Arista, thinner, younger. The princess wondered
if he had dozens of women like this all over Avryn, or if this
Emerald was special. Watching them together, seeing his arms
around her, watching them kiss, she felt an emptiness, as if
there were a hole inside her. She felt an ache, a pain like a
weight pressing on her chest, and told herself to look away.
After another minute, she actually did.

Twelve riding horses and two hitched to the wagon, fourteen animals in all, stood waiting in the snow. On four of the
horses sat five young boys—squires, Hadrian called them—
who he had recruited to act as servants and watch after the
animals. All Arista knew about them were their names: Renwick, Elbright, Brand, Kine, and Mince. The last boy was so
small that he rode double with Kine. They waited sitting
straight and trying to look serious and grown up.

The buckboard, filled with their provisions and covered
with a heavy canvas tarp, had its wheels removed and was fit-

ted with snow runners. Huddled on the forward bench, glancing only occasionally at the crowd and adjusting his hood with a disgusted, angry expression, was the dwarf. Beneath his heavy brows, beneath his large nose and frowning mouth, his long braided beard had recently been cut short. The dwarf's fingers absently played with it the way a tongue might play with the space left by a missing tooth. He grumbled and sneered, but she could not find any sympathy for him. It was the first time she had seen Magnus since the day he had slammed the door in her face—less than a week after his hand had murdered her father.

Royce Melborn stood alone in the snow. He waited silently across the courtyard near the gate, his dark cloak fluttering lightly with the breeze—a small shadow near the wall. No one appeared to notice him except Hadrian, who kept a watchful eye, and Magnus, who repeatedly glanced over nervously. Royce never looked at any of them. His head faced the gate, the city, and the road beyond.

Amilia exited the palace, wrapped in heavy wool. She pushed through the crowd and crossed the yard to Arista. Trapped under her arm was a parchment, wrinkled and creased. In her hands was what looked to be a short whip.

"This is for you," she said, holding out what Arista now recognized as the severed half of the dwarf's beard, still neatly braided. "Being aware of Magnus's tendency to disappear, Modina took the precaution of snipping some hair for you."

She nodded. "Give her my thanks. Do you know where Gaunt is?"

"He's coming."

The castle doors opened once more and Degan Gaunt stepped out. He was clad in a belted fur-lined houppelande and a chaperon hat with a full bourrelet wrapped around his head and a long cornette that streamed nearly to the ground.

The elaborate houppelande was worn complete with huge bell sleeves and a long train, which dragged across the ground, softly grading the snow behind him.

"The future emperor has arrived," Amilia whispered, and then added, "He thought his clothes needed to reflect his future status and he didn't want to be cold."

"Can he ride in that?"

Before the secretary could answer, a page ran out before Gaunt carrying two large silk pillows and a blanket. He proceeded to lay them out on the wagon's bench. The dwarf forgot his beard as he looked at the pillows beside him with another sneer.

"I'm not riding beside a dwarf. Get that runt off of there," Gaunt said. "Hadrian will drive the wagon." When no one made a move, he added, "Do you hear me?"

Arista pulled herself onto Princess's back, swung her leg over the sidesaddle horn, and trotted rapidly to Gaunt. She reined the animal only a few feet short of Gaunt, causing him to step back. She glared down at him. "Magnus rides on the wagon because he's too short for the horses, and he is perfectly capable of driving it, true?"

The dwarf nodded.

"Good."

"But I do not wish to travel with him."

"Then you may ride on a horse."

Gaunt sighed. "I've been told this will be a long journey and I do not wish to spend it on the back of a horse."

"Then you can sit beside Magnus. Either way—it doesn't matter."

"I just told you I don't want to sit beside a dwarf." Gaunt glared at Magnus with a grimace. "And I don't appreciate your tone."

"And I don't appreciate your obstinacy. You can ride beside

Magnus, ride on a horse, or walk, for all I care. But regardless, we are leaving." She raised her head and her voice. "Mount up!"

At her command, they all found their rides and climbed aboard. Looking livid, Gaunt stood staring at the princess.

Arista pulled on the reins and turned her mare to face Modina, who was holding Allie's hand. This left Gaunt facing the rear of her mare.

"I swear I will do all I can to find the horn and return with it as soon as possible."

"I know," Modina replied. "May Maribor guide your path."

✎

Alric and Mauvin rode at the head of the party, although the king did not know where they were going. He had studied many maps but only set foot out of Melengar on three occasions. Alric had never traveled that far south and he had never heard of Amberton Lee before the meeting. He trusted someone would tell him when to turn—Arista, most likely.

They traveled the Old Southern Road, which Alric knew from maps ran all the way to Tur Del Fur, at the southern tip of Delgos. As they passed through the Adendal Durat, the road was little more than a cleft in the ridge that sliced through the rocky mountains as it dropped down from the plateau of Warric to the plain of Rhenydd. Snow drifted in the pass such that on occasion, they needed to dismount and pull the horses through, but the road remained passable. Months of sun followed by bitter nights had left a crust on the surface that crunched under the horses' hooves and left icicles, hanging thick like frozen waterfalls, across the face of the rocky cliffs. The height of winter was over, days grew longer, and while the world lay buried, it was not as deep as it once had been.

No one talked much during the course of the morning. Gaunt and Magnus were particularly quiet, neither saying a word nor looking at each other. Degan sat bundled, his long train wrapping his body and head so only his nose remained exposed. Magnus appeared oblivious to the cold as he drove the wagon with bare ruddy hands. His breath iced his mustache and what remained of his beard, leaving him with a frozen grimace of irritated misery. Alric felt better seeing his discomfort.

Royce and Hadrian rode at the rear of the party, and Alric never noticed either speak. Royce rode absently, his hood up, his head down, bobbing as if he were asleep. The five boys were with them. They whispered among themselves occasionally, as servants were prone to do. The sailor they called Wyatt rode beside his giant friend. Alric had never seen a man that size before. They had provided him a draft horse and still his feet hung nearly to the ground, the stirrups left dangling. Wyatt had whispered a few words to the giant at the start, but Elden never spoke.

The only conversation, the only break from the droning crunch of snow and panting breath of the animals, was that of Myron and Arista. A quarter hour did not pass without the monk pointing out some curiosity to her. Alric had forgotten Myron's fascination with everything—no matter how trivial. Myron found the twenty-foot icicles hanging from the cliffside nothing short of a miracle. He also pointed out designs he found in the rock formations—one he swore looked like the face of a bearded man. Arista smiled politely and even offered a laugh on occasion. It was a girl's laugh, high and light, natural and unburdened. Alric would feel self-conscious to laugh so openly. His sister did not seem to care what those around her thought.

Alric hated how she had taken charge when setting out. As

much as he had enjoyed the look on Gaunt's face when she had barked at him in the courtyard, he disliked the bold way his sister acted. If only she had given him the time to act. He was the king, after all. The empress might have given Arista authority to *organize* the expedition, but that did not extend to leading it. She had never satisfactorily explained why she was along, anyway. He had assumed she would ride quietly in the wagon and leave commanding the venture to him but he should have known better. Given her theatrics in the courtyard, it was surprising that she still rode sidesaddle and had not taken to wearing breeches. They escaped the tight pass before noon as morning clouds finally gave up their tight grip on the world. Ahead the land dropped away, leaving a magnificent view to the south. Alric spotted Ratibor in the distant valley. The whole city appeared no larger than his thumb and from that distance it looked beautiful, a clustered glen in a sea of forest and field.

"There," Hadrian announced from the rear, pointing toward a shining river to the east. "You can see Amberton Lee—sort of. Down near the Bernum River, where it bends. See there, how the land rises up into three hills."

"Yes, that's it," Arista agreed. "I remember." She looked up at the sky. "We won't make it today."

"We could spend the night in Ratibor," Hadrian offered. "It's only a few miles. We could reach it by nightfall."

"Well, I don't—" Arista began.

"We will head to Ratibor," Alric declared quickly, causing Arista to look at him in surprise.

"I was just going to say," she went on, "if we veer east now, we'll be that much closer in the morning."

"But there is no road," Alric told her. "We can't be wandering through the snowy fields."

"Why not?"

"Who knows how deep that snow is and what lies beneath?"

"Royce can find us a route through; he's good at that," Hadrian said.

"That's what I was thinking," Arista agreed.

"No, Ratibor is a much better choice," Alric said loudly. "We'll get a good night's rest, then push on at first light and be there by noon."

"But, Alric—"

"You heard my decision!" He kicked his horse and trotted down the road, feeling their eyes on his back.

Hooves trotted up behind him. He expected it to be his sister and dreaded the argument, but he would not back down. Alric turned hotly only to see Mauvin with his hair flying. The rest of the group followed twenty feet behind them, but they were moving in his direction. He let his horse slow to a walk.

"What was that all about?" Mauvin asked, moving alongside, where the two horses naturally fell into the same pace.

"Oh, nothing." He sighed. "Just trying to remind her who's king. She forgets, you know."

"So many years, so few changes," Mauvin said softly, brushing the hair out of his eyes.

"What's that supposed to mean?"

Mauvin only smiled. "Personally, I prefer your idea. Who wants to sleep in the snow if you can have a bed? Besides, I'd like to see Ratibor. It was on our list, remember?"

Alric nodded. "We were also supposed to go to Tur Del Fur."

"Yeah, but let's save that for another time, since it's under new management and all," Mauvin mentioned. "I still can't believe we are on our way to Percepliquis. That was always the big prize—the dream."

"Still hoping to find the Teshlor Codes?"

Mauvin chuckled. "That's right. I was going to discover the secret techniques of the Teshlor Knights. You remember that, do you? I was supposed to be the first one in a thousand years to possess that knowledge. I would have guarded it jealously and been the greatest warrior alive." Mauvin glanced behind them. "Not much chance of that now. Even if I did find them, I could never match Hadrian. He grew up with it and was taught by a master. That was a stupid dream, anyway. A boy's fantasy. The kind of thing a kid thinks before actually seeing blood on a blade. When you are young, you think you can do anything, you know? And then..." He sighed and turned away. Alric noticed his hand go up to his face briefly before settling on the pommel of his sword, only it was not Mauvin's sword.

"I didn't notice before," Alric told him, nodding toward Mauvin's side.

"This is the first time I've worn it." He pulled his hand away self-consciously. "I've wanted it for so long. I used to see my father wield it—so beautiful, so elegant. I dreamed of it sometimes. All I ever wanted to do was hold it, swing it, and hear it sing in the air for me."

Alric nodded.

"What about you?" Mauvin asked. "Are you still interested in finding Novron's crown?"

The king huffed and might have laughed if the statement had not seemed so ironic. "I already have a crown."

"Yeah," Mauvin said sadly.

Alric spoke in a voice just loud enough for Mauvin to hear. "Sometimes the price of dreams is achieving them."

&

They were just closing the city gate for the night when the party arrived in Ratibor. Arista did not recognize the guard. He was a burly, balding man in a rough stitched rawhide coat who waved at them impatiently to get inside.

"Where is a good place to find lodgings for the night, my good man?" Alric asked, circling his mount on the guard as he went about locking down the city.

"Aquesta. Ha!" The man laughed.

"I meant here."

"I knows what ya meant," he said gruffly. "The Gnome has open rooms, I think."

"The Gnome?"

"It's a tavern," Arista explained. "The Laughing Gnome — King's Street and Lore."

The guard eyed her curiously.

"Thank you," she said, quickly kicking her horse. "This way."

The heavy scent of manure and urine that Arista had remembered as the prominent smell of Ratibor was replaced by the thick smell of wood smoke. Other than that, the city had changed little from the last time she had been there. Streets ran in awkward lines, forcing adjoining buildings to conform to the resulting spaces often with strange results, such as shops in the shapes of wedges of cheese. The wooden planks that used to bridge the rivers of muck lay buried beneath a thick layer of snow. The winter had stolen the leaves from the trees and the wind ripped along empty streets. Nothing but the snow moved. Arista had expected winter would brighten the place and bury the filth, but instead she found it bleak and barren.

She rode in the lead now. Behind her, she could hear Alric grumbling. He spoke too low for her to catch the words, but his tone was clear. He was unhappy with her — again. Any other time, she might have fallen back, apologized for whatever it was she had done wrong, and tried to make him feel better. But she was cold, hungry, and tired. She wanted to get to the tavern. His feelings could hurt at least until they were settled.

As they approached Central Square, she tried to keep her eyes down and focus on the snow where Princess walked, but she could not resist. When they were in the exact middle of the square, her eyes ignored her will and looked up. The post was still there, but the ropes were gone. Dark and slender, nearly blending into the background, it was a physical reminder of what might have been.

*There is blood under the snow*, she thought.

Her breath shortened and her lip began to quiver. Then she noticed someone riding beside her. Arista was not aware if she had heard his approach, or merely sensed his presence, but suddenly Hadrian was an arm's length away. He did not look at her or speak. He merely rode quietly alongside. This was the first time he had left Royce's side since they had started out, and she wondered what had brought him forward. Arista wanted to believe he joined her because he knew how she felt. It was silly, but it made her feel better to think it.

The signboard above the door at the public house was crowned in snow and yet remained as gruesome as ever. The obscenely large open mouth, hairy pointed ears, and squinting eyes of the namesake gnome glared down at them.

Arista halted, slid off her mount, and stepped onto the boardwalk. "Perhaps the rest of you should wait here while Hadrian and I make arrangements."

Alric coughed and she caught him glaring at her.

"Hadrian and I know this city. It will just be faster if we go," she told him. "*You* were the one that wanted to come here."

He frowned and she sighed. Waving for Hadrian to follow, she passed under the sign of The Laughing Gnome. A flickering yellow light and warm air that smelled of grease and smoke greeted them. A shaggy spotted dog scampered over, trying to lick their hands. Hadrian caught him just as he jumped up toward her. He let the dog's forepaws rest on his thighs as he scrubbed behind its ears, causing the animal to hang its tongue.

The common room was empty except for two people huddled near the hearth—so different from the first time she had been there. She stared off at a spot near the center where a fiery-haired young man had once held the room spellbound.

*This was the place. It was here I saw Emery for the very first time.*

She had never thought about it before, but this revelation made the room sacred to her. She felt a hand on her shoulder. Hadrian gave her a gentle squeeze.

She spotted Ayers behind the bar, wiping out mugs. He was wearing the same apron, which appeared to have the same stains. The innkeeper had not shaved in a day or two, and his hair was mussed, and his face moist.

"What can I do ya for?" he asked as they approached, the dog trailing behind, pawing at Hadrian for more attention.

"We'd like rooms." Arista counted on her fingers. "There are fifteen in our party, so maybe four rooms? Do your rooms sleep four?"

"They can, but I usually charge by the pair."

"Oh, okay, so then seven rooms if you have them, I guess— the boys can all sleep in one room. Do you have vacancy?"

"Oh, I've got 'em. No one here but the mice. All the folk heading down from Wintertide passed through weeks ago. No one travels this time a' year. No need to…" He trailed off as he looked intently at Arista. His narrow eyes began widening. "Why, ain't you—I mean, yer her—ain't you? Where have you been?"

Embarrassed, she glanced at Hadrian. She had been hoping to avoid this. "We'd just like the rooms."

"By Mar! It is you!" he said, loud enough to catch the

attention of the two near the fire. "Everyone said you was dead."

"Almost. But really, we have people waiting in the cold. Can we get rooms? And we have horses too that—"

"Jimmy! Jimmy! Get your arse in here, boy!"

A freckle-faced kid, as thin as a Black Diamond member, rushed out of the kitchen, bursting through the doors with a startled look on his face.

"Horses outside need stabling. Get on it."

The boy nodded, and as he stepped by Ayers, the proprietor whispered something in his ear. The lad looked at Arista and his mouth opened as if it had just gained weight. A moment later he was running.

"You understand we're tired," Arista told the innkeeper. "It has been a long day of riding and we need to leave early in the morning. We are just looking for a quiet night."

"Oh, absolutely! But you'll be wantin' supper, right?"

Arista glanced at Hadrian, who nodded. "Yes, of course."

"Wonderful. I'll get something special for you."

"That's not necessary. We don't want to cause any—"

"Nonsense," Ayers told her. "Rusty!" he shouted over her head toward the two at the hearth, who were now on their feet, hesitantly inching closer. "Run and tell Engles I want his cut of pork."

"Pork?" the man replied. "You can't serve her no smoked pork! Benjamin Braddock got a prize lamb he's kept alive all winter, feeds it like a baby, he does."

"Yeah, real sweet animal," the other man said.

"Okay, okay, tell him to get it to Engles and have it butchered."

"How much you willing ta pay?"

"Just tell him who it's for, and if he wants to come ask *her* for money, let him."

"Oh please, this isn't necessary," Arista said.

"He's been saving that lamb for a special occasion," Rusty told her, and smiled. "I can't see how he can expect a better one."

The door opened and the rest of the party entered, dusting snow off their heads and shoulders and stomping their feet. Once inside, Gaunt let go his train and threw back his hood, shivering. He walked directly toward the fire with his hands outstretched and brought to Arista's mind the image of a giant peacock.

Rusty nudged his buddy. "That's Degan Gaunt."

"By Mar," Ayers said, shaking his head. "If'n you get a drop, it's a flood. And look at him all dressed up like a king. He's one of your group?"

Arista nodded.

"Blimey," Rusty said, staring now at Hadrian. "I seen this fella afore too—just a few weeks ago. He's the tourney champion. He unhorsed everyone 'cept Breckton, and he only missed 'cuz he didn't want ta kill him." He looked at Hadrian with admiration. "You woulda dropped him if'n you'd had the chance. I know it."

"Who else you got with you?" Ayers asked, looking overwhelmed. "The Heir of Novron?"

Arista and Hadrian exchanged glances.

"Our rooms—where are they?" Alric asked, joining them as he shook the wet out of his hood.

"I—ah—let me show you." Ayers grabbed a box of keys and led the way up the stairs.

As she climbed, Arista looked down at the empty space below and remembered how they had spent forty-five silver to sleep there. "How much for the rooms?"

Ayers paused, turned, and chuckled.

When they reached the top of the stairs, he threw his arms out. "Here you are."

"Which rooms?"

Ayers grinned. "Take the whole floor."

"How much?" Alric asked.

Ayers laughed. "I'm not charging you—I can't charge you. I'd be strung up. You get settled in and I'll call you when dinner is ready."

Alric grinned. "See? I told you it was worth coming. They are very friendly here."

"For her," Ayers said, nodding in Arista's direction, "nothing in this city has a price."

Alric frowned.

"That is very kind," she told him. "But given our situation, I think five rooms will still be best."

"What? Why?" Alric said.

"I don't think we want to leave Magnus or Gaunt unsupervised, do you?"

Hadrian, Royce, Myron, and Gaunt took one room. Wyatt, Elden, Magnus, and Mauvin took the second, and the boys took the third. Alric insisted on his own room, which left Arista alone as well.

"Relax as long as you like," Ayers told them. "Feel free to come down and enjoy the hearth. I'll roll out my best keg and uncork my finest bottles. If you choose to sleep, I'll send Jimmy to knock on your doors as soon as the meal is ready. And I just want to say, it's a great honor to have you here." He said the last part while staring at Arista.

She heard Alric sigh.

⌁

Wyatt lay on one of the beds, stretching out his sore muscles. Elden sat across from him on the other bed, his huge head in his hands, his elbows on his knees. The bed bent under the pressure. Wyatt could see the ropes drooping down below the frame. Elden caught Wyatt's look and stared back with sad, innocent eyes. Like Allie, Elden trusted him. He gave the big man a reassuring smile.

"Stop! Don't touch that!" Mauvin shouted, and every head in the room turned. The count was hanging his cloak on a string with the other wet clothes. He glared at Magnus, who had a hand outreached toward the pommel of Pickering's sword, which was sheathed and hanging by a belt slung over the bedpost.

Magnus raised a bushy eyebrow and frowned. "What is it with you humans? And you call us misers! Do you think I'll stuff it under my shirt and walk off with it? It's as tall as I am!"

"I don't care. Leave it be."

"It's a fine weapon," the dwarf said, his hand retreating, but his eyes drinking it in. "Where did you get it?"

"It was my father's." Mauvin advanced to the end of the bed and grabbed his sword.

"Where did he get it?"

"It's a family heirloom, passed down for generations." Mauvin held the sword in his hand gingerly, as if it were an injured sparrow needing reassuring after its narrow escape from the dwarf. Wyatt had not noticed the weapon before, but now that his attention was drawn, he saw that it was an uncommonly attractive sword. It was elegant in its simplicity; the lines were perfect and the metal of the hilt shone bright. Almost imperceptible were fine decorative lines.

"I meant, how did yer family come to have it? It is a rare man who owns such a blade as this."

"I suppose one of my ancestors made it, or paid for it to be made."

The dwarf made a disgusting noise in his throat. "This was

not made by some corner blacksmith with a brat pumping a bellows. That there, lad, was forged in natural fires in the dark of a new moon. Your kind didn't touch it for centuries."

"My kind? Are you saying this is dwarven?"

Again the noise of reproach. "Bah! Not by my kin—that blade is elvish and a fine one at that, or I've never worn a beard."

Mauvin looked at him skeptically.

"Does she sing when she travels the air? Catch the light around her and trap it in her blade? Never grow dull even if used as a shovel or an axe? Cut through steel? Cut through other blades?"

Mauvin's face answered the dwarf. The count slowly drew it out. The blade shimmered in the lamplight like glass.

"Oh yes, she's an elven blade, boy, drawn from stone and metal, formed in the heat of the world, and tempered in pure water by the First Ones, the Children of Ferrol. No finer blade have I laid my eyes on save one."

Mauvin slipped it back and frowned. "Just don't touch it, okay?"

Wyatt heard the dwarf grumble something about having his beard cut off; then Magnus moved to the bed on the other side of the room, where he was too far for Wyatt to hear. Mauvin still held the blade, rubbing his fingers over the pommel; his eyes had a faraway look.

They were strangers to Wyatt. Mauvin, he knew, was a count of Melengar and close friend of King Alric. He had also heard that he was a good sword fighter. His younger brother had been killed in a sword fight some years back. His father had died recently—killed by the elves. He seemed a decent sort. A bit moody, perhaps, but all right. Still, he was noble and Wyatt had never had many dealings with them, so he decided to be cautious and quiet.

He kept a closer eye on the dwarf and wondered about the "misunderstandings" the empress had spoken of.

*How do I keep getting myself into these situations?*

Poor Elden. Wyatt had no idea what he made of all this.

"How you feeling?" Wyatt asked.

Elden shrugged.

"Want to go down for the meal, or have me bring you back a plate?"

Again a shrug.

"Does he talk?" Mauvin asked.

"When he wants to," Wyatt replied.

"You're the sailors, right?"

Wyatt nodded.

"I'm Mauvin Pickering," he said, putting out his hand.

Wyatt took it. "Wyatt Deminthal, and this is Elden."

The count looked Elden over. "What does he do on a ship?"

"Whatever he wants, I should think," Magnus muttered. This brought a reluctant smile to everyone's lips, including those of the dwarf, who clearly had not meant it as a joke but gave in just the same.

"Where are you from—Magnus, is it?" Wyatt asked. "Is there a land of dwarves?"

The dwarf's smile faded. "Not anymore." He clearly meant that to be the end of it, but Wyatt continued to stare and now Mauvin and Elden were doing likewise. "From up north—the mountains of Trent."

"Is it nice there?"

"It's a ghetto—dirty, cramped, and hopeless, like every place they let dwarves live. Satisfied?"

Wyatt regretted saying anything. An awkward silence followed until the tension was broken by a pounding at the door and a cheerful shout: "Meal is ready!"

❦

The knock came to their door announcing supper and Hadrian and Myron were first on their feet. Royce, who sat on a stiff wooden chair in the corner by the window, did not stir. His back was to them as he stared out at the dark. Perhaps his elven eyes could see more than the blackness of the glassy pane, perhaps he was watching people moving below, or the windows of the shops across the street, but Hadrian doubted he was even aware of the window itself.

Royce had not said a word since they had left Aquesta. When he bothered, he communicated in nods. Royce was always quiet, but this was unusual even for him. More disturbing than his silence were his eyes. Royce always watched the road, the eaves of the forest, the horizon, always looking, scanning for trouble, but not that day. The thief rode for over nine hours without once looking up. Hadrian could not tell if he stared at the saddle or the ground. Royce might have been asleep except that his hands continually played with the ends of the reins, twisting them with such force that Hadrian could hear the leather cry.

"Hadrian, fetch me a plate of whatever they are handing out down there," Degan told him as he lay on his bed, staring up at the ceiling.

Upon first entering the room, Gaunt had immediately claimed the bed nearest the fireplace. He had cast off his houppelande and chaperon, throwing them on the floor. Then he had flung himself on the mattress, where he sprawled, moaning about his aches.

"And make sure it's lean," Gaunt went on. "I don't want a bunch of fat. I want the good stuff. And I'll take dark bread if they have it, the darker the better. And a glass of wine— no, make that a bottle, and be sure it's good stuff, not—"

"Maybe you should come down and pick out what you want. That way there won't be any mistakes."

"Just bring it up. I'm comfortable—can't you see I'm comfortable here? I don't want to mingle with all the local baboons. An emperor needs his privacy. And for Novron's sake, pick up my clothes! You need to hang those up so they can dry properly." He looked quizzical. "Hmm...I suppose that should be *for my ancestor's sake*, now wouldn't it? Perhaps even for *my* sake." He smiled at the thought.

Hadrian rolled his eyes. "Let me rephrase. Get your own food or go hungry."

Gaunt glowered and slapped his mattress so that even Royce looked over. "What bloody good is it having a personal servant if you never do anything for me?"

"I'm not your servant; I'm your...bodyguard," he said with reluctance, the word tasting stale. "How about you, Royce? Can I bring you something?"

Royce didn't bother even to shake his head. Hadrian sighed and headed for the door.

When he descended the stairs, Hadrian found The Laughing Gnome filled to the walls. People packed the common room. Considering their numbers, the crowd was keeping remarkably quiet. Rather than being filled with a roar of conversation and laughter, the room barely buzzed with a low hum of whispers. All heads turned expectantly when he and Myron emerged from the steps. That was followed quickly by signs of disappointment.

"Right this way, gentlemen," Ayers called, pushing forward. "Clear a path! Clear a path!"

Hadrian caught a few muttered *false knight* and *joust champion* comments as Ayers escorted them from the bottom of the stairs around to a large table set up in a private room.

"I'm keeping them out so you can eat in peace," Ayers told

them. "But I can't kick them out of the inn altogether. I have to live in this town, and I'd never hear the end of it."

Wyatt, Mauvin, Magnus, and Alric already sat at the table with empty plates before them. Jimmy, dressed now in a stained apron, rushed about filling cups. He held a pitcher in each hand and danced around the table like a carnival juggler. The room was a small space adjacent to the kitchen. Fieldstone made up half of the wall, along with the corner fireplace. Thick milled timbers and plaster formed the upper portion. The room's three windows remained shuttered and latched.

"Are they all here to see *us*?" Myron asked. He paused at the doorway, looking back at the crowd, mirroring their expressions of awe.

Hadrian had just taken a seat when a cheer exploded beyond the closed door in the common room. Alric drained his glass and held it up to Jimmy, shaking it.

"Are you all right? Where have you been?" voices, muffled by the wooden door, called out in the common room. "Were you kidnapped? Will you resume your office? We missed you. Will you drive out the empire again?"

"Forgive me, dear people, but I have traveled long today," Arista said from the other room. "I am very tired and cannot hope to answer all your questions. Just know this: the tyrants that once controlled the empire are gone. The empress now— and for the first time—rules, and she is good and wise."

"You met her?"

"I have. I lived with her for a time and have just come from Aquesta. Evil men held her prisoner in her own palace and ruled in her name. But…she rose up against her captors. She saved my life. She saved the world from a false imperium. Now she is in the process of building the true successor to the Empire of Novron. Show her the trust you have given me, and

I promise you will not be disappointed. Now, if you will allow me, I am very hungry."

Cheering. Applause.

The door opened and Arista stepped inside, then closed it behind her and leaned on it as if she were barricading it with her body. "Where'd they all come from?"

"Word spread," Ayers replied, looking self-conscious. "I need to get back to the bar. I can't leave the mob too long without refreshment."

As Ayers exited, Hadrian spotted Mince standing with the other boys just outside the doorway. Hadrian waved them in. All five entered the dining room in single file and stood just inside—afraid to move farther.

"They came to our room and told us there was food down here, sir," Renwick said to Hadrian. "But we don't know where to go."

"Take a seat at the table," Hadrian replied.

All the boys reacted with the same shocked expression, a mixture of fear and wonder.

"Oh, we aren't going to have the servants eat with us," Alric said, causing the boys to halt.

"There are enough chairs," Arista pointed out.

"But honestly, stableboys? Look at them. They're not just servants; they're children. There must be somewhere else they can eat."

"Actually, if I may . . ." Hadrian spoke loudly, stood up, and grabbed a hold of Mince, who was attempting to worm his way out of the room. "These young men here," Hadrian said, pointing to Elbright, Kine, and Brand, "assisted in rousing the people of Aquesta to open the gates for you and your army. And Renwick"—Hadrian pointed at the oldest—"was a tremendous help to me as my squire during the time I pretended to be a knight."

"Still am, sir. I don't care what they say."

Hadrian smiled at him. "He also fought in the palace court-yard and was one of the first into the dungeon, if you recall. And this young man here," he said, holding the squirming boy with both hands, "is Mince. This *child*, as you call him, has been singled out by the empress herself as being instrumental in the overthrow of Ethelred and Saldur. Without them, it is very likely that your sister, Royce, I, and even the empress would all be dead. Oh, and of course, so would you and Mauvin. Not bad for a stableboy. So for all that they have done, don't you think they deserve a place at our table?"

"Yes, yes, of course, of course," Alric said quickly, looking a bit ashamed.

"Sit down," Hadrian told them, and they each took a seat, smiles across their faces.

A rotund woman with short, ratty hair and saddlebag cheeks backed into the room from the kitchen, carrying a deep tray of spit-roasted lamb. She wore a gray wool dress and yet another grease-stained apron.

She approached the table and stopped abruptly, looking at the diners with a disappointed—even irritated—expression. "Missing three," she said, her high voice reminding Hadrian of a squeaking door.

"I'll bring a plate up for Royce. He's…he's not feeling well," Hadrian explained.

Arista glanced at him. "Is it okay to leave him alone?"

Hadrian nodded. "I think so. Besides, if he wanted to do something, who's going to stop him?"

"Elden will also be staying in his room," Wyatt mentioned. "He has a thing about crowds."

The cook nodded. Her large breasts, outlined by the apron, hung over the edge of the pan, threatening to nudge the steaming lamb. No one else spoke. Finally she asked, "And where's that scoundrel Degan Gaunt? I can't imagine him turning down a free meal."

"Scoundrel?" Hadrian said, surprised. "I thought he was a hero here in Ratibor."

"Hero?"

He nodded. "Yeah, you know. Local boy who went off to seek his fortune, became a pirate, and returned to lead the liberation movement."

The cook laughed, though it was more like a cackle that juggled its way out of her round throat. She put down the tray and began cutting the meat.

Everyone at the table exchanged glances.

Wyatt shrugged. "I don't know his background, but Gaunt was no pirate. That I do know."

Again, the cook cackled and this time put a hand to her lips, which turned the laughter inward and caused her shoulders and chest to bounce.

"Are you going to let us in on the joke?" Alric asked.

"Oh, well, it's not my place to be spreading rumors, now is it?" she said, and followed the statement by making a show of biting her lower lip. Her hands slowed in their work and then stopped. She looked up and a huge grin pushed the saddlebags apart.

"Okay, so it's this way," she said, lowering her voice. "I grew up only a few doors down from Gaunt—right there on Degan Street. Did you know that his mother named him Degan because it was the only word she knew how to spell, having seen the street sign for so many years?"

Now that her mouth was going, so were her hands, and she sliced portions and delivered them to their plates, heedless of the little trails of grease she left. "Anywho, his mother and mine were close and I used to be best friends with his sister, Miranda. She was a joy, but Degan—well, even as a boy he was a demon.

We stayed clear of him when we could. He was a pitiful little wretch. He got caught stealing dozens of times, and not because of need. I mean, I don't agree with theft, but pinching a loaf of bread from Briklin's Bakery when the old man has his back turned to surprise your mother with on Wintertide is one thing. I ain't saying it is right, but I overlook something like that.

"Well, as for Degan, he goes in for stuff like smashing the window on the curio shop so he can have a porcelain rabbit he had his eye on. Thing is, everyone knows he's a no-good. You can see it in the way shopkeepers watch him or shoo him out the door. They can spot the likes of him a mile away."

Just then, Ayers barged in. "Jimmy, get to the cellar and roll out another keg. They've already drained the one we pulled up earlier." The boy put down his pitchers and ran toward the kitchen. Ayers stared at the cook. "You're not bothering these folks, are you, Bella? Is she bothering any of you?"

"Not at all," Arista replied, and all the heads at the table nodded in agreement.

"Well, keep it that way. She has a way of yammering, she does."

Bella blinked her eyes innocently.

Jimmy appeared, rolling a barrel from the kitchen.

"How many we got left?" the innkeeper asked.

"Four."

Ayers frowned. "I shoulda ordered more, but who knew…" He pointed at the diners and shrugged. Ayers took control of the barrel and returned to the tavern. Bella waited a moment, staring at the door. Then a grin filled her face and she went on.

"Now, just ta give you an idea about how bad things got for ole Degan, he even received a visit from the BD telling him to cut it out. Course he don't and yet somehow managed to avoid punishment. Miranda and I used to talk about how that boy was charmed. But after his mother's death, he got into

some *real* trouble. Now, I wasn't there to see it, but rumor is —
and it sure seemed like the kinda thing that idiot would do —
he got drunk and raped Clara, the candle maker's daughter.
Well, her old man had connections. Not only was he a favorite
merchant to the royal chamberlain, but his nephew was in
the BD."

"BD?" Myron asked. "I don't understand."

"BD — Black Diamond," Mauvin told him.

Myron still looked confused.

"Not a lot of literature on them," Hadrian said. "The Black
Diamond is a very powerful thieves' guild. They control all
the illegal activity in a city, just like a potters' guild controls
the pottery market."

The monk nodded. The cook was standing still again,
holding a lamb chop between two greasy, stubby fingers, waiting, as if her body could not move unless her mouth was.

"I'm sorry, please continue," Myron said. "This is a wonderful story."

"Well now," she went on, dumping the chop onto Myron's
plate so roughly and off center that it nearly flipped over. "I
remember there were patrols combing the streets for him.
They was angry too, shouting that they was gonna hang him,
only they never found ole Degan. Turns out that a press-gang
near the docks caught him that very night. They didn't know
who he was. They just needed hands for a ship and hauled him
off to sea. Like I said, the man is charmed.

"Okay, so this next part I know from reliable folk. Some
years later, the ship he was on was attacked by pirates. They
done killed the whole crew but somehow ole Degan survived.
Who knows how he done it? He probably convinced them
pirates he knew where a treasure was buried er sumptin. Anywho, he gets away. Some folks say a storm wrecked the pirate
ship, and again he's the lone survivor. That seems a mite bit

lucky for anyone, but for Degan it doesn't seem so strange. So he ends up in Delgos and gets into trouble again. He's back to his old tricks, this time stealing from the merchant families at the border villages. He's going to be executed for sure this time, but then he spins his greatest tale.

"He says he was only taking the money to finance his dream of freeing the common man from the boot of the aristocracy. Can you believe it? Degan Gaunt, a man of the people? Well, that kinda talk plays real well down that way. Those folks on the peninsula hate the monarchies. They swallow it and, what do you know, not only do they let him go—they give him money for his cause! Well, this just tickles Degan, as you could imagine, and he decides to keep the thing going. He travels all over, giving speeches and getting donations. I heard him once when he was preaching his spiel in Colnora. He was actually pretty good at it—all shouts for liberty and freedom, banging his fist on a podium and working up a sweat. Then a'course he passes the hat. But then—" She stopped talking as she struggled to free a troublesome lamb chop from the rest.

"But then?" Alric asked.

"Oh, sorry," she said. "Somehow he goes from being this traveling sideshow to actually running an army—and a successful one at that! That's just strange. It's one thing to be—"

The crowd outside the door began clapping, and a moment later the door to the dining room opened and Degan stepped inside. He had a disapproving sneer on his face.

"You started serving without me?"

No one answered and the cook puckered her lips, continuing to dish out the meal in silence. Degan took a seat and waited impatiently for his plate. Everyone stared at him until he glared back, irritated. "What?"

"This is very good." Wyatt spoke up, pointing to the lamb on his plate.

"Thank you," the cook replied.

"If it is, it will be the first time this place has served anything eatable," Gaunt muttered. "Hurry up, woman!"

The cook, who stood behind him, made a *see what I mean?* face and dropped a chop on his plate.

"What time will you folks be getting up?" the cook asked. "You'll be wanting breakfast, won't you?"

"We'll be leaving early," Arista said. She caught a look from her brother. "Isn't that right, Alric?" she added.

"Yes, yes, ah—dawn, I should think," he said. "Breakfast should be before that. Something hot, I hope."

"Seeing the business you're bringing him, old Ayers would pay to poach venison if you wanted it. Course he ain't gonna be too pleased you're leaving tomorrow. I'm sure he's hoping you'll be here a week at least."

"We're in a hurry," Arista explained.

Bella looked as if she might say more when the common room door opened again. "Bella, quit bugging them. I don't pay you to chatter. I have orders for food. I need five stews and a plowman's meal."

"All right, all right!" she bellowed back. She turned to the diners and, with an awkward curtsy, rushed off to the kitchen.

&

The room was dark except for the moonlight that entered through the window and the glow of hot coals in the fireplace. Outside, the wind blew snow against the building. Royce could hear the muffled sounds of voices rising through the floorboards as everyone ate dinner. The shift of furniture, the clink of glasses—he had heard it all before.

Royce's eyes focused on the street corner outside. He could see the start of the alley between Ingersol's Leather Shop and a silversmith. It was right there—on that very corner, that exact spot.

"That's where I came from." Royce spoke to the empty room, his words condensing on the window's glass, making a tiny fog.

He remembered nights like this—cold, windy nights when it was hard to get to sleep. Most nights he had slept in a barrel packed with straw, but when it was really cold—the kind of cold that killed—he had climbed into barns and squeezed between sheep and cattle. Doing so was dangerous. Farmers listened to their animals, and if they found intruders, they assumed they were stealing.

Royce had been only eight, maybe ten years old. He had been freezing, his feet and hands numb, his cheeks burning. It was late and he had crawled into the stable on Legends Avenue. The rear stall was blocked off into a makeshift manger for four sheep. They lay curled up as one big wooly bed, their sides rising and falling like breathing pillows. Royce carefully crawled into the middle, feeling their body heat and the soft wool. They bleated at his intrusion, but given the size of the stall, they suffered his presence. In just a few minutes he fell asleep.

He woke to a farmer with a pitchfork. The farmer jabbed and nearly got Royce in the stomach. Royce rolled, taking the tongs in his shoulder. He screamed and scattered the sheep, which bounced off the walls. In the confusion, Royce escaped into the snow. The hour was late. It was still dark, and blood ran down his arm. He had not yet discovered the sewers and had no place to go. He returned to the barrel on the corner and climbed in, pulling as much straw over him as he could.

Royce remembered hearing "Ladies of Engenall" played on a fiddle from inside the Gnome. He listened to them all night: people singing, laughing, clinking glasses—all warm, safe, and happy while outside he shivered and cried. His shoulder screamed in pain. The rags he wore hardened as the blood froze. Then it started to snow. He felt the flakes on his face and thought he would die that night. He was so certain that he prayed, and that was the first and last time he had ever asked the gods for help. The memory was so vivid he could almost smell the straw. He recalled lying there shivering, his eyes shut tight as he had whispered aloud to Novron, asking to be saved. He pleaded, reminding the god that he was only a child—a boy—only he knew that was a lie. He was not a boy—boys were human.

Royce was not human—not entirely. He was a *mir*, a half-breed, a mongrel.

He knew Novron would not help him. Novron and his father, Maribor, were the gods of men. Why would they listen to the words of an elf, a hated cur whose own parents had thrown him away as trash? Still, he begged for his life anyway. Because he did not look like an elf, the young Royce reasoned that maybe Novron would not notice.

Right down there, on that corner, Royce had begged to live.

He traced a circle on the window with his finger.

He always remembered it as the worst night of his life—he had been alone, terrified, dying. And he had been so happy the next morning when he was still alive. Starved, shaking from the cold, stiff from sleeping in a ball, shoulder throbbing, but as happy as a person could be.

*Here I am, warm and comfortable in The Laughing Gnome, and I'd give anything to be in that barrel again.*

A board creaked and Myron entered quietly. He hesitated at the door, then slowly crossed the room toward Royce and sat down on the bed near him.

"I used to sit for hours too," the monk said, his voice soft, just a tad above a whisper. "I used to remember things... times and places, both good and bad. I would see something that reminded me of my past and wish I could go back. I wished I could be the way I used to be, even if that meant pain. Only I could never find my way around the wall. Do you know what I mean by *the wall*?"

Royce refused to answer. Myron did not seem to mind.

"After the burning of the abbey, I never felt whole again. Half of me was missing—gone—more than half. What was left was lost, like I didn't know where I was or how to get back."

Royce stared. He was breathing faster without knowing why.

"I tried to find a way to go on. I could see familiar traces of the path that was my life, but there was always the wall behind me. Do you know what I mean? First you try and climb, pretending it never happened, but it's too tall. Then you try to go around, thinking you can fix it, but it is too far. Then, in frustration, you beat on it with your hands, but it does nothing, so you tire and sit down and just stare at it. You stare because you can't bring yourself to walk away. Walking away means that you're giving up, abandoning them.

"There is no way back. There is only forward. It's impossible to imagine there's any reason to move ahead, but that isn't the real reason you give up. The real fear—the terror that keeps you rooted—is that you might be wrong."

Royce reeled. It was as if Myron were rifling through his heart, opening sealed closets and exploring locked drawers. Royce gave Myron a withering look. If he were a dog, Royce would be growling, yet Myron seemed not to notice.

The little monk went on.

"Instead of passion, you have regret. In place of effort, you are mired in memory. You sink in nothingness and your heart drowns in despair. At times—usually at night—it's a physical pain, both sharp and dull. The anguish is unbearable."

Royce reached out and grabbed Myron by the wrist. He wanted him to stop—needed him to stop.

"You feel you have no choices. Your love for those who have gone makes you hold tight to their memory and the pain of their loss. You feel to do anything else would be disloyal to them," Myron went on, placing his free hand on top of Royce's and patting it gently.

"While the idea of leaving is at first impossible to contemplate, the question you need to ask is, how would they feel knowing that you are torturing yourself because of them? Is this what they would want? Is that what you would want them to do if the situation was reversed? If you love them, you need to let go of your pain and live your life. To do otherwise is a selfish cruelty."

Hadrian opened the door and nearly dropped the plate of lamb. He stepped in hesitantly. "Everything all right here?" he asked.

"Get him away from me, before I kill him," Royce growled between gritted teeth, his voice unsteady, his eyes hard.

"You can't kill Myron, Royce," Hadrian said, rapidly pulling the monk away as if he had found a child playing with a wild bear. "It would be like killing a puppy."

Royce did not want to kill Myron. He honestly did not know what he wanted, except for him to stop. Everything the monk had said hurt, because it was all true. The monk's words were not close. They were not worrisomely accurate. What he said was dead-on, as if he were reading Royce's mind and speaking his innermost thoughts aloud—holding his terrors to the light and exposing them.

"Are you all right, Royce?" Hadrian asked, still holding Myron close. His tone was cautious, nervous.

"He'll be fine," Myron replied for him.

≈

The five boys and Myron had left the dinner table, followed shortly by Hadrian and Wyatt, who took plates up to Royce and Elden respectively. Alric, who had eaten his fill, loosened his belt but made no move to leave. He sat back, smiling, as Ayers brought out another bottle of wine and set it on the table before them. For the first time since they had started this trip, Alric was feeling good. This was more like it. He could see the same expression in Mauvin's eyes. This was the dream of their youth: riding hard, exploring, seeing strange new sights, and in the evening settling in at a local inn for a fine meal and a night of drinking, laughing, and singing. At last, the carefree days of his boyhood—once stolen—now returned. This was an adventure at last. This was a man's aspiration, a chance to live life to the fullest.

"My finest stock," Ayers told them with pride.

"That's awfully kind of you," Arista said. "But we need to be getting up early tomorrow."

"It's not polite to insult a host like that, Arista," Alric said, feeling her hands trying to strangle his dream.

"I didn't—Alric, you can't stay up all night drinking and expect to get an early start in the morning."

He frowned at her. This was why she had never been included in his and Mauvin's plans. "The man wants to honor us, all right? If you're tired, go to bed and leave us be."

Arista huffed loudly and threw her napkin on the table before walking out.

"Your sister isn't pleased with you," Gaunt observed.

"Are you just discovering that now?" Alric replied.

"Shall I open it?" Ayers asked.

"I don't know," Alric muttered.

"It would be best to do as she tells you," Gaunt said.

"What's that?"

"I only meant her being in charge and all. You don't want to become the nail sticking out. I can see why you're afraid of her and I sympathize, believe me. You saw the way she treated me when we left—but what can we do? She holds all the power."

"She's not in charge," Alric growled. "I am." He looked at Ayers. "Open that bottle, my good man, and pour liberally."

Gaunt smiled. "I guess I misjudged you, Your Majesty. I've actually been doing too much of that. Take Magnus here, for example."

Alric preferred not to. The idea that he had just finished a meal with—and was about to drink at the same table with—his father's killer sickened him.

"I was offended that I had to ride with a dwarf, but it turns out he's not a bad companion. True, he's not exactly a big talker, but he's interesting just the same. Did you know he's held here by the hairs of his beard—literally? He's another member of our exclusive club who your sister controls and forces to do her bidding."

"My sister doesn't control me," Alric snapped.

"And you had best watch your tongue, my friend," Mauvin advised Gaunt. "You are treading on dangerous ground."

"My apologies. Perhaps I am mistaken. Please forgive me. It's just that I've never seen a woman lead a mission like this before. It's shocking to me, but then again, you come from the north, and I come from the south, where women are expected to stay behind while their men go off to fight. Allow me to toast her." He raised his glass. "To the princess Arista, our lovely leader."

"I told you, she's not in charge. I am," Alric said with more force.

Gaunt smiled and raised his other hand defensively. "I meant no offense." He raised his glass again. "To you, then, to King Alric, the true leader of this mission."

"Hear! Hear!" Alric joined him and drank.

# CHAPTER 8

# AMBERTON LEE

*P*eople were singing in the streets. They danced and it did
not seem to matter with whom. Streamers flew through
the air and explosions of light illuminated the sky like magic.
Bands played and every face reflected their joy. The doors to
all the shops were open, their wares free to the people on the
street—free bread, free cakes, free meats, free drinks. People
took whatever they liked and the owners smiled and waved.

"Good Founding!" they shouted to each other. "Good
Founding to you! May Novron bless his home and people!"

She felt disturbed at this, although she did not know why.
Something was wrong. She looked at the faces. They did not
know.

Know what? *she wondered. She had to hurry. Time was
running out.* Running out? What is going to happen?

She had to move, but not too quickly. It was important not
to give them cause for suspicion. She must get to the rendezvous. She squeezed the necklaces in her hand. Working the
spell had taken all night. There was not even time to say goodbye to Elinya and that broke her heart.

As she hurried along, she knew she would never see Elinya
again. Turning onto the Grand Mar, she saw the imperial

guards waiting in the eaves. Each group was led by a Teshlor knight. The three swords the knights carried marked them as surely as their imperial armor did. Heroes of the realm, the protectors of the emperor—assassins all.

She had to find Nevrik and Jerish.

Pausing at the Column of Destone, she turned. The palace was straight ahead, not more than another half mile. She could see the great golden dome. Emperor Nareion and his family were there. Her heart pounded, and her breath came in short gasps. She could go. She could face them. She could fight. They would not expect that and she could get the first incantation. She would blow the whole miserable palace apart and let the glass and stone rip through the bleeding bastards. But she knew it would not be enough. This would not stop them, but she would kill a few and hurt many others. Not Venlin, though, and not Yolric. They would kill her— maybe not Yolric, but Venlin certainly. Venlin would not hesitate. She would be dead, the imperial family would follow, and Nevrik and Jerish would be lost.

No, she needed to sacrifice the father for the son. It was the emperor's wish, his order. The line must endure at all costs. The line must survive.

She turned and ran down Ebonydale, weaving her fingers, masking her movement. She had to get the necklaces to them. Then they could hide. The empire would be safe—at least one small piece. Once the amulets were safely around their necks and they were on their way, she would turn back. And Maribor help the traitors then, for she was done hiding. They would see the power of a Cenzar unleashed, unrestrained by edict. She would destroy the entire city if she needed to. Lay it all to waste. Bury it deep beneath the earth and let them spend eternity picking through the rubble.

For now, though, she had to hurry. It was time to go.

*Time to go.*

*Time to—*

Arista woke up.

It was dark, but as always, the robe was glowing faintly, revealing the small, sparse room. She felt as if she had fallen from one world to another. She was in a hurry to do something, but that was only a dream. Out the window, she could just make out the first hints of morning light. Slowly she remembered she was in The Laughing Gnome in Ratibor. She kicked off the blankets and reached out with her toes, looking for her boots. The fire was out and the room was cold. Touching the floorboards was like standing on ice.

In just a few moments, she was moving up the corridor, knocking on doors, hearing people groan from behind them. Downstairs, the crowd from the night before was gone; the common room looked like a storm had passed through. Bella was up and Arista smelled leftover lamb and onions. The rest staggered down groggily, wavering as they wiped their eyes. Mauvin's hair was worse than ever, as several locks stood up on one side. Magnus could not stop yawning, and Alric kept dragging his hands over his face as if trying to remove a veil. Only Myron appeared alert, as if he had been up for some time.

While they ate, Ayers ordered Jimmy into the cold to saddle the animals. Hadrian and Mauvin took pity on the boy, and along with the other boys, they all went out to help him. By the time the sun breached the horizon, they were ready to leave.

"Arista?" Alric stopped her as she headed for the door. They were alone in the common room, standing beside the bar, where a dozen mugs reeked of stale beer. "I would appreciate it if you were a little less quick to give orders in my presence. I am king, after all."

"What did I... Are you mad that I woke everyone up?"

"Well, yes—to be honest—I am. That and everything else you've done. You are constantly undermining my authority. You make me...well, you make me look weak and I want you to stop."

"All I did was get people out of bed so we could get an early start. If you were up pounding on doors, I wouldn't have to. I told you that staying up late wasn't a good idea, but you didn't listen. Or would you rather we had waited until noon?"

"Of course not, and I'm glad you got everyone up, but..."

"But what?"

"It's just that you are always doing that, always taking command."

"Seems to me I wanted to ride on to Amberton Lee yesterday, but you ordered us here. Did I argue?"

"You started to. If I hadn't ridden off, we'd still be debating it."

Arista rolled her eyes. "What do you want me to do, Alric, not talk anymore? You want me to crawl in with the rest of the supplies in the sled and pretend I'm not here?"

"That's just it. You—you insert yourself into everything. You shouldn't be here at all. This is no place for a woman."

"You may be king, but this is *my* mission. Modina didn't assign this task to me. I went to her to explain where I was going. This was my idea—my responsibility. I would have gone even if no one else did, even if Modina forbade me. And let me remind you that unless we succeed, you won't be king of anything."

Alric's face was red, his cheeks full, his eyes angry.

"Lovers' quarrel?" Mauvin asked, walking in with a smile. When neither replied, he dropped the expression. "Okay— never mind. I just forgot my gloves—but, ah...the horses are ready." He picked the gloves up off a table and quickly slipped back out.

"Listen," Arista said in a quieter tone. "I'm sorry, okay? I'll try to be more of a *lady* if you want, and I'll let you lead." She gestured outside. "They would probably prefer taking orders from a man, anyway."

There was a long pause and she said, "Still hate me?"

Alric wore a nasty look on his face, but the storm had passed. "Let's go. People are waiting."

He walked past her and Arista sighed and followed him.

⋘

By midmorning, they found the ancient road. Royce seemed better and rode with Hadrian at the head of the column, guiding them along narrow trails, paths, and even frozen rivers. Alric took his position right behind them. Arista stayed back. She rode with Myron once more, this time just behind the wagon. They left the farmlands and entered an unclaimed wilderness of fields and thickets. Not long after reaching the woods, they came upon a broad avenue. It did not look the same as when Arista had ridden on it with Etcher. The snow hid the paving stones and weeds. Arista stopped Princess broadside in the avenue and looked up and down its length. "Straight as a maypole," she muttered.

The monk looked at her.

"This is it," she told him. "The road to Percepliquis. Under this snow are stones laid thousands of years ago by order of Novron."

Myron looked down. "It's nice," he replied politely.

They followed the tracks left by the sled ahead of them. There was silence as they rode through the trees. Here the snow was a soft powder and muffled everything, the sound of the horses and sled smothered to a whisper.

Once more, they traveled without much comment. Not

long after they had started up the road, Magnus brought up the subject of lunch, and she was pleased to hear Alric say they would eat when they reached the Lee. The sun had passed overhead and shadows were forming on the other side of the trees when they began climbing a steep hill. As they cleared the gray fingers of the forest, Arista saw the snow-crowned summit ahead. On it were broken shapes of cut stone, ruins of a great city poking up through the surface. Ancient walls buried now in earth and snow caught the pale light of a late-winter afternoon.

*It is a grave*, she thought, and wondered how she could have missed this before. A sense of sadness and loss radiated from the mounds now that she understood what she was seeing. Pillars lay half buried in the hillside, mammoth headstones of a giant's graveyard; broken steps of marble and walls of stone lay crumbled. Only one tree stood upon the hill—it appeared dead but, like the rest of the ruins, still stood long after its time. The strange shapes rose from the earth, casting blue shadows. The scene was beautiful—beautiful but sad, in the way a lake can still be beautiful even when frozen.

Royce raised a hand for them to stop when they reached the base of the open hillside. He dismounted and went ahead on foot. They all waited, listening to the jangle of the bridles as the horses shook their heads, unhappy with the interruption.

When he returned, he spoke briefly with Hadrian and Alric. Arista's brother glanced back at her as if he might say something or call her up to ask advice. He looked away and the party moved on once more. Arista fought the urge to trot ahead and inquire about what was happening. It was frustrating to sit in the dark, sentenced to the corner like a naughty child, but it was important for Alric to hold the reins. She squeezed her hands into fists. She loved her brother, but she did not trust him to make the right decisions.

*Hadrian is up there with him*, she thought. *He won't let him do anything stupid.* Thank Maribor she had Hadrian with her. He was the only one in the party she felt she could rely on, the only one she could lean on without fear of breaking or offending. Just looking at the back of him as he bounced on his horse was comforting.

They climbed to the summit and dismounted.

"We'll have lunch," Alric announced. "Myron, come up here, will you?"

Royce, Alric, and Myron spoke together for several minutes while Arista sat on some stone, absently eating strips of smoked beef and exhausting her jaws in the attempt. Ibis had sent full meals, but she was in no mood. The chewing gave her something to do besides walking over there.

She turned away to see Elden staring at her. He looked away bashfully, pretending to search in his pack for something.

"Don't mind him, my lady," Wyatt said. "Or should I address you as Your Highness?"

"You can call me Arista," she said, and watched his eyes widen.

"Seriously?"

She nodded. "Of course."

He shrugged. "Okay, then, *Arista*." He spoke the word gingerly. "Elden here, he doesn't get out much, and when he has, it's been on board ships where there aren't any women. I suspect you're the first lady he's seen up close in—well, as long as I've known him. And I'm sure you're the only noblewoman he's ever seen."

She touched her matted hair and the robe that hung on her like a smock. "Not a very good example, I'm afraid. I'm not exactly Lady Lenare Pickering, am I? I'm not even the best-looking princess here. My horse takes that title. Her name is Princess." She smiled.

Wyatt looked at her, puzzled. "You sure don't speak like a noblewoman. I mean, you do—but you don't."

"That's very coherent, Mr. Deminthal."

"There, you see? Those are the words of a princess—putting me in my place with eloquence and grace."

"As well she should," Hadrian said, appearing beside her. "Do I need to keep an eye on you?" he asked Wyatt.

"I thought you were *his* bodyguard." He pointed at Gaunt, who remained on the wagon with the dwarf, their lunches resting on the bench between them.

"You'd think that, wouldn't you?"

"What did Royce find?" Arista asked.

"Tracks, but they're old."

"What kind of tracks?"

"Ghazel—probably a scouting party. Looks like King Fredrick was right about *the flood*. But we are still a ways from Vilan Hills. I'm surprised they are scouting out this far."

She nodded thoughtfully. "And Alric has Myron and Royce trying to find the entrance?"

"Yep, they're looking for a river. Hall's book tells of a river flowing into a hole."

"What about the tracks?"

"What about them?"

"Have you followed them?"

"They're too old to be a threat. Royce guesses they were made more than a week ago."

"Maybe they aren't from Vilan Hills. The Patriarch said Ghazel were in Percepliquis. Follow the tracks...They might lead to the entrance. And get Magnus off the wagon. Isn't he supposed to be an expert at finding underground passages?"

Hadrian stared at her stupidly. "You're absolutely right." He started to return to the others.

"Hadrian?" She stopped him.

"Yeah?"

"Don't tell Alric I said anything. Say it was your idea."

He looked confused for a second, then said, "Oh—right." He nodded with sympathy. Hadrian started to climb the hill, then waved at Wyatt. "Com'on, sailor, you can help look too."

"But I'm still—"

Hadrian gave him a smirk.

"Okay, okay. Excuse me, my lady—ah—Arista."

The two climbed to the top of the hill and disappeared over the rise. Elden came over and sat beside her. He reached into his pocket and withdrew a small bit of wood, holding it out in his huge palm. It was a figurine, deftly carved in the shape of a woman. She took it and, upon closer inspection, realized it was her. The detail was perfect, right down to her messy hair and Esrahaddon's robe.

"For you," she heard him whisper.

"It's beautiful, thank you."

Elden nodded; then, standing up slowly, he moved off to sit by himself.

Arista held the statuette in her fingers, wondering when he had found time to make it. She tried to determine whether he had whittled in the saddle or carved it the night before while the rest of them were eating dinner.

Myron left the top of the hill and Arista waved him over.

"So what does Mr. Hall have to say about how he got in?"

Myron smiled comically. "Not a lot that is of much help. Although, he did have some nice diagrams that showed the ruins, so we are in the right place. As for getting in, all he said was that he went into a hole. From his accounts, it was really deep. He started climbing down and fell. A nasty fall by the sound of it too. His handwriting afterwards was shaky and he only bothered to write short sentences: *Fell in a hole. No way out. The pile! They eat everything! Cyclone of darkness. River running. Stars. Millions. Crawling, crawling, crawling. They eat everything."*

Arista sneered. "Doesn't sound all that pleasant, does it?"

"It gets worse," he said. "Down near the underground sea, just before he reached the city, he encountered the Ba Ran Ghazel, but that wasn't the worst of it. He actually made it to the great library when—"

A whistle sounded.

"Found it!" Alric shouted.

⚬

The hole was not on the summit of the hill.

Hadrian had watched as Magnus and Royce had located the passage, each coming at it from a different direction. Royce traced Ghazel tracks and Magnus followed what he called the sound of an underground hollow. They came together down the back side of the slope, where the angle grew steep and dangerous. A patch of trees and thick thorny brambles wreathed what appeared to be a minor depression. The only clue that something more lurked there was the faint echo of falling water.

"Looks slippery," Mauvin said as they all gathered on the icy ridge above. "Who's going first?"

Before anyone could answer, Royce appeared carrying a heavy coil of rope, wearing his climbing harness and slipping on his hand-claws—brass wraps with sharpened hooks that jutted out of his palms. Hadrian helped him get situated; then Royce lay on his stomach and inched along, leaving a trough in the soft snow as he eased off the ridge.

As he started down the slope, Royce began to slide. He tried to get a grip, but his hands and claws found only snow. He picked up speed like a sled and Hadrian worked at taking up the slack in the rope. Then Royce crashed through the thickets and disappeared from view. Mauvin joined Hadrian on the rope, which was now as taut as a bowstring.

"Get the end," Hadrian ordered. "Tie it to that tree."

Magnus moved to grab the line.

"No, not you!" Hadrian shouted, and the dwarf scowled. Hadrian looked to the next-closest person. "Wyatt, could you tie the end off?"

The sailor grabbed the end of the rope and dragged it around the base of the little birch.

"How ya doing, Royce?" Hadrian called.

"Dangling," Royce replied. "Pretty slick up there. Give me some slack."

They stood in a circle, each keeping a safe distance, all of them standing on their toes, trying to see down. Overhead, the winter clouds made it hard to tell the time. There was no sun, just a vague gray light that filled the sky, leaving everything murky and drained of color. Hadrian guessed they had only four hours of light left.

Mauvin and Hadrian let out the rope until it hung from the tree, although Hadrian continued to hold on to it just the same. He could not see Royce and stared instead at the thin rope. It too was mostly lost, buried in the snow, leaving only a telltale mark.

"Can you reach the bottom?"

"How much rope do we have?" Royce's voice returned like an echo from the bottom of a well.

Hadrian looked at Arista.

"Ten coils of fifty feet each," she replied. "All told, there should be five hundred feet's worth," she shouted, tilting her head up a bit as if throwing her voice into the hole.

"Not half good enough," Royce replied.

"That's a deep hole," Hadrian said.

The rope shifted and twisted at the edge.

"What're you doing, buddy?"

"Trying something."

"Something stupid?"

"Maybe." He sounded winded.

The rope stopped moving and went slack.

"Royce?" Hadrian called.

No answer.

"Royce?"

"Relax," came his reply. "This might work. I'm on a ledge, big enough for all of us, I think. Icy, but doable. We can tie on here too. Looks like we'll have to work our way a leg at a time. Might as well start sending down the gear."

They brought up the wagon and began lowering supplies, each package disappearing through the opening in the brush.

"I'll go first," Alric announced when the wagon was empty.

Hadrian and Mauvin tied the safety rope around his waist and legs. Once tethered, the king took hold of the guide rope and, sitting down on the snow, scooted forward. Mauvin and Hadrian were careful this time to let out the rope slowly, and soon Alric reached the thickets and peered through.

"Oh dear Maribor!" Alric exclaimed. "You have me, right?" he shouted back at them.

"You're not going anywhere until you want to," Mauvin replied.

"Oh lord," he repeated several times.

Royce was offering suggestions, but too faintly for Hadrian to hear exactly what they were.

"Okay, okay, here I go," Alric said. He turned himself over and, lying flat on his stomach, started backing into the hole, clutching tightly to the guide rope. "Slowly now," he warned as Mauvin and Hadrian let out the tether, and inch by inch he slipped over the edge and out of view.

"Oh sweet Maribor!" they heard him exclaim.

"You okay?" Hadrian called.

"Are you crazy? Of course I'm not! This is insane."

"Lower him," Royce shouted.

They let out the line until Hadrian felt a tug that he guessed was Royce pulling Alric to the ledge. The rope went slack, Royce shouted the all clear, and they reeled up the empty harness. Feeling it best to send him early so they still had enough people to man the rope, they sent Elden next. He went over the side quietly, although his eyes told a story similar to Alric's.

"Degan, you're next," Hadrian informed him.

"You are joking," Gaunt replied. "You don't expect me to go down there?"

"Kinda why you're here."

"That's insane. What if the rope breaks? What if we can't reach the bottom? What if we can't get back up? I'm not doing this. It's—it's ridiculous!"

Hadrian just stared at him, holding the harness.

"I won't."

"You have to," Arista told him. "I don't know why, but I know the Heir of Novron must accompany us for this trip to be successful. Without you there's no need for any of us to go."

"Then fine, none of us go!"

"If we don't, the elves will kill everyone."

He looked at her and then at the others with a desperate, pleading face. "How do you know this? I mean, how do you know I have to come?"

"Esrahaddon told me."

"That loon?"

"He was a wizard."

"He's dead. If he was so all-knowing, how come he's dead? Huh?"

"Waiting down here," Alric shouted up.

"You have to go," Arista told him.

"And if I refuse?"

"You won't be emperor."

"What good is being emperor if I'm dead?"

No one spoke; they all just looked at him.

Degan slumped his shoulders and grimaced. "How do you put this damn thing on?"

"Put your feet through the loops and buckle it around your waist," Hadrian explained.

After Gaunt and Arista were down, Wyatt took over Hadrian's position on the rope, freeing him to speak with Renwick. "You have supplies to last a week, perhaps more if you conserve," he told him and the other boys as they gathered around. "Take care of the horses and stay off the hilltop. Make camp in that hollow. For your own safety, I'd avoid a fire in the daylight. The smoke will be visible at a distance. It would be best not to attract any uninvited guests."

"We can handle ourselves," Brand declared.

"I'm sure you can, but still it would be best not to wander, and try to keep unnoticed."

"I want to go with you," Renwick said.

"Me too," Mince added.

Hadrian smiled. "You're all very brave."

"Not me," Elbright said. "A man would have to be a royal fool to go into something like that."

"So you're the sensible one," Hadrian told him. "Still, we need all of you to do your job here. Keep the camp, and take care of the horses for us. If we aren't back in a week, I suspect we won't be coming back and it will probably be too late if we do. If you see fire in the north or west, that will likely mean the elves have overrun Aquesta or Ratibor. Your best bet would be to go south. Perhaps try to catch a ship to the Westerlins. Although I have no idea what you'll find there."

"You'll be back," Renwick said confidently.

Hadrian gave the boy a hug, then turned to look at the monk, who was, as usual, with the horses. "Com'on, Myron, it's nearly your turn."

Myron nodded, petting his animal one last time, whispering to it. Hadrian put an arm around him as they walked toward the ridge, where Wyatt and Mauvin were in the process of lowering Magnus.

"What did you say to Royce last night?" Hadrian asked the monk.

"I just spoke with him briefly about loss and coping with it."

"Something you read?"

"Sadly, no."

Hadrian waited for more, but the monk was silent. "Well, whatever it was, it worked. He's—I don't know—alive again. Not singing songs and dancing, of course. If he did that, I suppose I'd worry. But you know, kinda normal, in a Royce sort of way."

"He's not," Myron replied. "And he'll never be the way he was again. There's always a scar."

"Well, I'm just saying the difference is like summer and winter. You should be thanked, even if Royce will never say it. There aren't many who would face him like that. It's like pulling a thorn from a lion's paw. I love Royce, but he *is* dangerous. The life he's lived denied him a proper understanding of right and wrong. He wasn't kidding when he said he might have killed you."

"I know."

"Really?"

Myron nodded. "Of course."

"You didn't even seem worried. What happened to my little naive shut-in who walked in awe of the world? Where did all the wisdom come from?"

Myron looked at him, puzzled. "I'm a monk."

❧

Hadrian was the last to enter the hole, lowering himself hand over hand, sliding on his stomach to the edge, where at last he looked over and saw what Alric and the rest already had. An abyss opened below him. From the rim of the bowl, the opening looked small, but it was an illusion. The aperture was huge, an almost perfect circle of irregular rock, like the burrow of some enormous rabbit, and it went straight down. As in the pass, long icicles decorated the upper walls, stretching down from stony cliffs, and snow dusted the crevices.

He could not see the bottom. The setting sun cast an oblique light across the opening and against the far wall, leaving the depths lost to darkness. Far below, so far he would not have ventured an arrow shot, swallows flew, their tiny bodies appearing as insects, highlighted by the sunlight and brilliant against the black maw as they swirled and circled.

A bit light-headed, Hadrian stared down into the space below his feet. His stomach lightened and it took conscious effort to breathe. He got a firm hold of the rope, slipped over the side, and dangled in midair. The sensation was disturbing. Only the thin line separated him from eternity.

"You're doing great," Arista called to him as if she were an old pro now, her voice hollow as it echoed across the mouth of the shaft. He felt Royce pulling him in toward the side. Looking down, he saw all of them crouched on a narrow ledge that was glassy with ice, their gear stacked at one end.

He touched down, feeling hands on his waist pulling him to the safety of the wall.

"That was fun," he joked, only then realizing how fast his heart was racing.

"Yeah, we should do this all the time," Mauvin said, and followed it with a nervous laugh.

"Want us to leave the rope or untie it?" Renwick called down.

"Have him leave it," Royce said. "That lip will be a problem otherwise. From this point on, I'll come last and bring the rope with me. Wyatt, you have the most climbing experience. Why don't you find the next ledge?"

Hadrian could see tension on the sailor's face as they tied on the harness.

The interior of the hole was a wall of stone with many handholds. Hadrian guessed that even he could climb it with little fear if not for the ice and the knowledge that he was hundreds of feet from the ground.

Wyatt found a landing point, a new ledge some ways down, and they began the moving process again. The next ledge was narrower and shorter. There was not enough room for everyone, and Wyatt was forced to move on before all of them were down. Royce brought up the rear, untying the rope, coiling it around his body, and climbing down untethered, using just his claws.

The next two levels Hadrian did not consider ledges at all. They were merely a series of hand- and footholds where only three could pause. As they were forced to cling to the rock without ropes, their gear was left to dangle.

The next ledge was the widest yet, being the width of a country lane, and upon reaching it, several of them collapsed, lying down on their backs, their chests heaving, sweat dripping. Hadrian joined them, yawning to relieve the growing pressure in his ears. When he opened his eyes, he saw a circle of white light above them that was no larger than his thumb held at arm's length. A seemingly solid shaft of light, like a pale gray pillar, beamed down into the hole. Through its luminescent column, the swallows swooped at eye level, rising and falling, dancing through the shaft. The far wall was still so distant it appeared hazy in the ethereal light.

"It's like being bloody spiders," Alric remarked.

"I'm not sure even being ruler of the world is worth all this," Degan moaned.

"I can see how Edmund Hall fell now, but he must have gotten down a long way to have survived," Arista said. "Could you imagine doing this alone?"

"He wasn't alone," Myron said. "He had two friends and several servants."

"What happened to them? Were they locked up as well?"

"No," Myron replied.

"They didn't survive, did they?"

"I'm afraid not."

Hadrian sat up. His clothes were wet. Around him droplets fell, cascading down the walls. Looking across the shaft, he could see a clear division between a bright level of ice and snow and a much darker level of damp stone. "It's warmer," he said.

"We need to keep going," Royce told them. "The light is fading. Anyone want to do this holding a torch?"

"Try and find thicker ledges," Alric told Wyatt.

"I find what I find."

The lower they went, the darker it became, regardless of the daylight, which, to Hadrian's dismay, was fading quickly. They dropped down four more ledges. Their efficiency grew with repetition, but their progress was being hampered by the failing light. The walls were black, while overhead the opening had changed from a brilliant gray to a sickly yellow, with one side dipping into a rosy purple as the sun began to set.

Arista was on the rope, climbing down, when he heard her scream. Hadrian's heart skipped. He was holding the rope—had it wrapped around his waist—when he felt her weight jerk him.

"Arista!" he shouted.

"I'm all right," she called up.

"Did you slip?" Alric yelled from farther below.

"I—I put my hand on a bat," she said.

"Everyone quiet," Royce ordered.

Hadrian could hear it too, a faint squeaking, but on a massive droning scale. That was followed by a hum, a vibration that bounced within the shaft until it grew to a thunder. The air moved with a mysterious wind, swirling and gusting.

"What's going on?" Arista called out, her voice hard to hear behind the growing roar.

"Hang on!" Hadrian shouted back.

They felt a rushing movement, like an eruption that issued from below, as the world filled with the fluttering of endless wings and high-pitched squeals. Hadrian braced himself, holding tight to the rope, as Arista screamed once more and the shaft filled with a cloud of bats that swirled with the force of a cyclone.

With his head down, Hadrian clutched the rope, wrapping it tight around his forearm. Mauvin and Royce grabbed hold of him. Arista was not going anywhere.

In less than a minute the hurricane of bats passed by.

"Lower me down!" Arista called. "Before something else happens."

He felt her touch down, and as he reeled up the harness, Hadrian looked up. The small patch of mauve sky was filled with a dark swirling line. A cloud of bats snaked like the tail of a serpent, twisting, looping, circling. Like a magic plume of smoke, they were mesmerizing to watch. Hadrian guessed there had to be millions.

Looking back down, he noticed there was a light below, a bright light that filled the shaft, revealing the glistening walls.

"What's going on down there?" he called.

"I'm tired of not being able to see," Arista yelled back.

"She's got her robe glowing," Alric said uncomfortably.

When Hadrian got down, he saw the princess perched on an outcropping of rock. Her legs dangled over the edge, scissoring in the air, her robe glowing white. Whenever she moved, the shadows shifted. Everyone stole repeated glances, as if it might be impolite to stare. Gaunt had no such reservation as he gaped, openly horrified.

On they went, following the same order, all of them doing their job with a rhythm. They traveled in silence except for the necessary calls of "down" and "clear." It took five more descents before he heard Wyatt call up, "Stop! I'm at the bottom!"

"You're still on the rope," Hadrian shouted back, confused. "You haven't touched down yet? You need more slack?"

"*No!* No slack! I would prefer not to touch down."

"River?" Arista asked.

"Nope, but it's moving."

"What is?"

"Can't really tell. It's too dark down here. Give me a minute to find a place to land."

In time, they all descended to an island of rock that jutted up from the floor of the cavern. Even with Arista beside him, it was too dark for Hadrian to see clearly what lay around them. All he knew was that they stood on an island within a sea of dark movement. He smelled a foul odor and heard a soft chattering coming from the floor. The smell was very much like an old chicken coop. "What is it, Royce?"

"I really think you need to see this for yourself," Royce replied. "Arista, can you turn that thing up?"

Before he finished his sentence, Esrahaddon's robe increased in brilliance, a phosphorous light illuminating the entire base of the shaft. What they saw left them speechless. They were not actually at the bottom. They stood on the tip of an up-thrusted rock, tall enough to breach the surface of a monolithic pile of bat droppings. The cone-shaped mound of guano stood easily three hundred feet high. Every inch of it moved, as across its surface scurried hundreds of thousands of cockroaches.

"By Mar!" Mauvin exclaimed.

"That's disgusting," Alric said.

There was more there than cockroaches. Hadrian spotted something white and spidery darting across the surface—a crab, and there was not just one, but hundreds all scuttling along. There was a faint squeal lower down and he saw a rat. The rodent was scrambling to escape the pile as a horde of beetles swarmed it. The rat toppled and was pulled onto its back, where it floundered, struggling in the soft guano. It squealed again. Its feet, tail, and head quivered and thrashed above the surface as an endless mob of beetles pulled it down, until only the trembling, hairless tail was visible, and then it too vanished.

" 'Crawling, crawling, crawling. They eat everything,' " Myron quoted.

"Anyone want to try walking across that?" Royce asked.

Wyatt replied with an uncomfortable laugh, then said, "No, seriously, how do we get down?"

"What if we jump and run real fast?" Mauvin offered.

This idea garnered several grimaces.

"What if it's not solid? Can you imagine it being so soft that you went under, like water?" Magnus muttered.

"You're thinking something," Hadrian said to Royce. "You saw this from above. You wouldn't have come down if you didn't have some kind of plan."

He shook his head. "Not me, but I was hoping she would." He gestured at Arista.

All eyes turned to the princess and she returned the looks with an expression of surprise and self-doubt.

"You need to provide us with a path or something," Royce told her. "Some means of getting down the slope of this pile. There's an opening over there, a crack in the wall—see it?" He pointed. "It will be tight, but I think we can get through. Of course, we'll have to crawl, possibly even dig our way out. So really, anything you can do to distract the meat-eating beetles would be nice."

She nodded and sighed. "I really don't have a lot of experience at this."

"You do what you can," Hadrian told her.

"The only other alternative is Mauvin's idea—we run for it and hope to get out before we're completely eaten."

Arista made a face and nodded again. "Everyone should stand behind me. I don't know exactly what will happen."

"What's she gonna do?" Gaunt asked. "What's going on?"

"Just do as she says," Royce told him.

The princess took a position on the edge of the rock and faced the mound. The rest gathered behind her, shifting their feet so as not to fall. Arista stood with her arms at her sides, rotating her palms out toward the mound, and slowly, softly, she began to hum. Then the light of her robe went out.

Darkness swallowed them.

Their only reference point was the tiny circle of starlit sky that lingered overhead, and in the absence of sight, the chattering sounds of a million roaches echoed. They all stood close to each other, huddled against the black, when tiny lights began appearing. Pinpricks flashed and died in the air before them. While the sparks lived, they swirled and drifted, riding currents of spinning air. More appeared, until Hadrian felt he was seeing the top of a giant campfire. There was no flame, only the swarm of sparks that rose high into the air, carried up as if the shaft were an enormous chimney.

In addition to the sparks, there was heat. It felt as if Hadrian stood before his father's forge. He could feel it baking his clothes and flushing his skin. With the heat came a new smell; far worse than the musty ammonia scent, this was thick and overpowering—the gagging stench of burning hair. As they watched, the pile before them began to radiate light, a faint red glow, like embers in a neglected fireplace. Then spontaneously flames caught, flaring here and there, throwing tall demonic shadows dancing on the walls.

"All right! All right!" Alric shouted. "That's enough! That's enough! You're burning my face off!"

The flames subsided, the red glow faded, and the soaring sparks died. Arista's robe once more glowed, but fainter and with a bluish tint. Her shoulders slumped and her legs wavered. Hadrian grabbed hold of her by the elbow and waist.

"Are you all right?"

"Did it work? Is anyone hurt?" she asked, turning to look.

"A little seared, perhaps," he said.

Royce ventured a foot out onto the pile. There was an audible crunch, as if he were stepping on eggshells. The surface of the mound looked dark and glassy. Nothing moved anymore.

Royce took two steps, then returned promptly to the island. "Still a tad warm. We might want to wait a bit."

"How did you do that?" Degan asked, astonished, while at the same time shifting away from her as far as the tiny perch allowed.

"She's a witch," Magnus said.

"She's not a witch!" In the otherwise silent cave, the volume of his own voice embarrassed Hadrian. It echoed twice. He noticed Alric looking at him, surprised, and he felt suddenly crowded. He stepped off and started walking.

He felt the surface of the pile crackle beneath his weight, the heat under his boots as if he were striding across sunbaked sand. He shuffled down the side of the pile, kicking the roasted remains of crabs aside. Light bobbed behind him and he knew at least Arista followed. They reached the crack. It was larger than it had seemed at a distance, and he was able to pass through without so much as ducking.

# CHAPTER 9

# WAR NEWS

The two girls sprinted along the parapet, their dark winter cloaks waving in their wake. Mercy jerked to a halt and Allie nearly ran her down. They bumped and both giggled into the cold wind. The sky was as gray as the castle walls they stood on, their cheeks a brilliant red from the cold, but they were oblivious to such things.

Mercy got to her hands and knees, and crawling between the merlons, she peered down. Huge blocks of unevenly colored stone formed a twenty-foot-high wall, the squares seeming to diminish in size the farther away they were. At the bottom lay a street, where dozens of people walked, rode, or pushed carts. The sight made Mercy's stomach rise, and her hands felt so weak that squeezing anything caused a tickling sensation. Still, it was wonderful to see the world from so high, to see the roofs of houses and the patterns formed by streets. With the snow, almost everything was white, but there were splashes of color: the side of a red barn on a distant hill, the three-story building painted sky blue, the bronze patches of road where snow retreated before the heat of traffic. Mercy had never seen a city before, much less one from this height. Being on the battlements of the palace made her feel as if she were the empress of the world, or at least a flying bird—both of equal delight in her mind.

"He's not down there!" Allie shouted, her voice buffeted by the wind so that her words came to Mercy as if from miles away. "He doesn't have wings!"

Mercy crawled back out of the blocks of stone and, bracing her back against the battlement, paused to catch her breath.

Allie was standing before her—grinning madly, her hood off, dark hair flying in the wind. Mercy hardly noticed Allie's ears, or the odd way her eyes narrowed, anymore. Mercy had been fascinated by her that first day, when they had met in the dining hall. She had wandered away from the Pickerings' table to get a closer look at the strange elven girl. Allie had been just as interested in Mr. Rings, and from then on the two were inseparable. Allie was her best friend—even better than Mr. Rings, for although Mercy confided all her secrets to each, Allie could understand.

Allie sympathized when Mercy told her how Arcadius had refused to let her roam the forests near the university. She had suffered equally from similar hardships, such as when her father refused to let her roam their home city of Colnora. Both girls spent long nights by candlelight sharing horror stories of their adventure-impoverished childhoods, rendered such by overprotective guardians who refused to see the necessity of finding tadpoles or obtaining the twisted metal the tinsmith threw away.

They tried on each other's clothes. Allie's wardrobe consisted of boyish outfits, mostly tunics and trousers, all faded and worn, with holes in the knees and elbows, but Mercy found them marvelous. They were much easier to wear than dresses when climbing trees. Allie had very few clothes compared to the many dresses, gowns, and cloaks Mercy used to have at the university, but of course, now Mercy had only the one outfit Miranda had dressed her in the day they had fled Sheridan. In the end, all they managed to do was trade cloaks. Mercy's was thicker and warmer, but she liked how Allie's old tattered wrap made her look dashing, like some wild hero.

Allie let Mercy play with the spare sextant her father had given her, showing her how to determine their position by the stars. In return, Mercy let Allie play with Mr. Rings, but began regretting the decision now that he climbed on Allie's shoulder more often than her own. Late at night she would scold the raccoon for his disloyalty, but he only chattered back. She was not at all certain he understood the gravity of the problem.

"There!" Allie shouted, pointing farther up the parapet, where Mercy spotted the raccoon's tiny face peering at them from around the corner. The two bolted after him. The face vanished, a ringed tail flashed and was gone.

The two slid on the snow as they rounded the corner. They were at the front of the palace now, above the great gates. On the outside was a large square, where vendors sold merchandise from carts and barkers shouted about the best leather, the slowest-burning candles, and the bargain price of honey. On the inside lay the castle courtyard and, beyond it, the tall imposing keep, rising as a portly tower with numerous windows.

The raccoon was nowhere to be seen.

"More tracks!" Mercy cried dramatically. "The fool leaves a trail!"

Off they ran once more, following the tiny hand-shaped imprints in the snow.

"He went down the tower stairs, lasses," the turret guard informed them as they raced by. Mercy only glanced at him. He was huge, as all the guards were, wearing his silver helm and layers of dark wool, and holding a spear. He smiled at her and she smiled back.

"There!" Allie shouted, pointing across the courtyard at a dark shadow darting under a delivery cart.

They scrambled down the steps, bounded to the bottom, and raced across the ward. They caught up to him when he neared the old garden. The two split up like hunters driving their quarry. Allie blocked Mr. Rings's path, forcing him toward Mercy, who was closing in. At the last minute, Mr. Rings fled toward the woodpile outside the kitchen. He easily scaled the stacked logs and scampered through a window, left open a crack to vent smoke.

"Crafty villain!" Allie cursed.

"You can't escape!" Mercy shouted.

Mercy and Allie entered the yard door to the kitchen and raced through the scullery, startling the servants, one of whom dropped a large pan, which rang like a gong. Shouts and curses echoed behind them as they sped up the stairs, past the linen storeroom, and into the great hall, where Mercy finally made a spectacular diving grab and caught Mr. Rings by the back foot. His tiny claws skittered over the polished floor, but to no avail. She got a better grip and pulled him to her.

"Gotcha!" she proclaimed, lying on her back, hugging the raccoon and panting for breath. "It's the gallows for you!"

"A-hem."

Mercy heard the sound and instantly knew she was in trouble. She rolled over and, looking up, saw a woman glaring down, her arms folded and a stern look across her face. She wore a brilliant black gown decorated with precious stones that twinkled like stars. At the nearby table, another woman and eight men with grim faces stared at them.

"I don't recall inviting you to this meeting," the woman told Mercy. "Or you," she said to Allie, who had tumbled in behind Mercy. She then focused on Mr. Rings. "And I know I didn't invite you."

"Forgive us, Your Eminence," the two door guards said in near unison as they rushed forward, the foremost taking a rough hold of Allie. The second guard grabbed for Mercy, who scrambled to her feet, frightened.

The lady raised a delicate hand, bending it slightly at the wrist, and instantly the guard halted.

"You are forgiven," she told him. "Let her go."

The guard holding Allie obeyed and the little girl took a step away, looking at him warily.

"You're the empress?" Mercy asked.

"Yes," she replied. "My name is Modina."

"I'm Mercy."

"I know. Allie has told me all about you. And this is Mr. Rings, correct?" the empress asked, reaching out a hand and stroking the raccoon's head. Mr. Rings tilted his snout down in a shy gesture as he was awkwardly held to Mercy's chest, his belly exposed. "Is he the one causing all the trouble?"

"It's not his fault," Mercy blurted out. "We were just playing a game. Mr. Rings was the despicable thief who stole the crown jewels and me and Allie were on the hunt tracking him down to face the axman's justice. Mr. Rings just happens to be a really good thief."

"I see, but alas, we are in the middle of a very important meeting that does not include thieves, axmen, or little girls." She focused on Mr. Rings, as if she were speaking only to him. "And raccoons, no matter how cute, are not allowed. If you two would be so kind as to take him back to the kitchen and ask Mr. Thinly to make him a plate of something, perhaps that will keep him out of mischief. See if he can also find some sweetmeats for the two of you—toffee, perhaps? And while he is being so kind, you might return the favor by asking if there are any chores you can do for him."

Mercy was nodding even before she finished.

"Away with you, then," she said, and the two sprinted back the way they had come, exchanging wide-eyed looks of relief.

⌖

Modina watched them race out, then turned back to the council. She did not resume her seat but preferred to walk, taking slow steps, circling the long table where her ministers and knights waited. The only sounds in the room were the crackle of the fire and the click of her shoes. She walked more for effect than from need. As empress, she had discovered the power and necessity of appearances.

The dress was an outward expression of this. Stiff, tight, restraining, noisy, and generally uncomfortable, it was nonetheless impressive. She noticed the expressions of awe in the eyes of all who beheld her. Awe begot respect; respect begot confidence; confidence begot courage, and she needed her people to be brave. She needed them to cast aside their doubts even in the face of a terrible growing shadow. She needed them to believe in the wisdom of a young woman even when faced with annihilation.

The men at the table were not fools. They would not be there if she thought them so. They were practical, clear-thinking, war-hardened leaders. Such romantic notions as the infallibility of a daughter of Novron did not impress them. The count of spears and a calculated plan were more to their liking. Still, even such efforts she knew to be futile. Warriors on a battlefield and the belief in a demigod empress would stand equal chance of saving them now. They had but one hope and—as a goddess, or as a thoughtful ruler—she needed their blind acceptance to raise the payment needed to buy time. So she walked with her head bowed, her fingers tapping her lower lip in apparent contemplation, giving the impression that she calculated the number of swords and shields, their positions at the choke points, the river dams set to be broken, the bridges set to be destroyed, the units of cavalry, the state of preparedness of the reserve battalions. More than anything she did not wish to appear to these old men as a flighty girl who held no understanding of the weight she bore.

She paused, looking at the fire, leaving her back to the table. "You are certain, then?" she asked.

"Yes, Your Eminence," Sir Breckton replied. "A beacon is burning."

"But only one?"

"We know that the elves are capable of swiftness and stealth. It's why we had so many signal patrols."

"Still, only one?"

"It's no accident."

"No, of course not," she said, pivoting on a heel so that her mantle swept gracefully around. "And I do not doubt it now, but it shows something of their ability. Out of twenty-four, only one man had enough time to lay a torch to a pile of oiled wood." She sighed. "They have crossed the Galewyr, then. Trent has fallen. Very well, send orders to clear the country-side, evacuate the towns and villages, and break the dams and bridges. Seal us off from the rest of the world—except for the southern pass. That we leave open for the princess. Thank you, gentlemen."

The meeting was over and the council stood. Breckton turned to Modina. "I will leave immediately to personally take charge of destroying the bridges in Colnora."

She nodded and noticed Amilia wince at his words. "Sir Breckton, I hope you do not take offense, but I would like to have my secretary accompany you so that she can report to me. I don't want to take you away from your duties just to keep me informed."

Both of them looked shocked. "But, Your Eminence, I will be riding north—there is risk—"

"I will leave it to her, then. Amilia? Will you go?"

She nodded. "As my empress wishes," she said solemnly, as if this were a terrible hardship that she would endure only for the sake of the empire. Amilia, however, was not a very good actress.

"As you will be passing by Tarin Vale, see that you check on Amilia's family, and ensure they are sent here to the palace." This time Amilia lit up with genuine surprise.

"As you wish," Sir Breckton said with a bow.

Amilia said nothing but reached out and squeezed Modina's hand as she passed her.

"One more thing," Modina said. "See to it that the man— the one that lit the fire—see that he receives a commendation of some kind. He should be rewarded."

"I will indeed, Your Eminence."

Servants entered the hall carrying plates but pulled up short with guilty looks.

"No, no, come in." She waved them forward. "Chancellor, you and I will continue in my office to allow these people to set up for the evening meal."

Outside the great hall, the corridors and public rooms buzzed with dozens of people walking, working, or just gathering to talk. She liked it this way; the castle felt alive. For so long she had lived within a cold hollow shell—a ghost within a mausoleum. But now, packed tightly with guests, all fighting for access to washbasins and seats at tables, and arguing over snoring and blanket stealing, it felt like a home. At times, she could almost imagine they were all relatives arriving as guests for a grand party or, perhaps, given the lingering mood, a funeral. She had never met most of those she saw, but they were family now. They were all family now.

Guards escorted them through the corridor and up the central stairs. Since the Royce Incident, as Breckton called it, he insisted she have bodyguards at all times. They ordered people in gruff tones to step back. "Empress!" they would call out, and crowds would gasp, look around nervously, dividing and bowing. She liked to smile and wave as she passed, but on the stairs she had to hold the hem of her dress. The dress, for all its expense, was no end of problems and she looked forward to the end of the day, when she could retire to her room and slip into her linen nightgown.

She half considered going there now. Nimbus would not mind. He had seen her in it hundreds of times, and while he was a shining example of protocol himself, he was silent to the foibles she made. As Modina climbed the stairs, it occurred to her she would have no more reservation about changing her clothes in front of him than she would about doing so in front of Red or Amilia, as if he were a doctor or priest.

They entered what had once been Saldur's office. She had had most of the church paraphernalia and personal items removed. The chambermaids might even have scrubbed it— as the room did smell better.

The sun was setting outside the window, the last of the light quickly fading.

"How long has it been?" she asked Nimbus as he closed the office door.

"Only two days, Your Eminence," Nimbus replied.

"It seems so much longer. They must have reached Amberton Lee by now, right?"

"Yes, I should think so."

"I should have sent riders with them to report back. I don't like this waiting. Waiting to hear from them, waiting to hear the trumpet blare of invasion." She looked out at the dying light. "When they seal the northern pass and destroy the bridges in Colnora, the only way in or out of this city will be by sea or the southern gate. Do you think I should put more ships out to guard against a water invasion? We are vulnerable to that."

"It's possible, yet unlikely. I've never heard of elves being ones for sea going. I don't believe they brought ships with them across Dunmore. Breckton destroyed the Melengar fleet and—"

"What about Trent? They might have gone there for the ships."

The slender man nodded his powdered-wig-covered head. "Except that there was no need at that time. There will be no need until your men close the roads. Usually one doesn't go to great lengths unless one has to, and so far—"

"They have had an easy time of killing us. Will it be any harder for them here?"

"I think so," Nimbus said. "Unlike the others, we have had time to prepare."

"But will it be enough?"

"Against any human army we would be impregnable, but..."

Modina sat on the edge of her desk, her gown puffing out as she did. "The reports said swarms of Gilarabrywn. You've never seen one, Nimbus, but I have. They're giant, brutal, terrifying flying monsters. Just one of them destroyed my home—burned it to ash. They are unstoppable."

"And yet you stopped it."

"I killed one—the man said swarms! They will burn the city from the sky."

"The shelters are almost complete. The buildings will be lost, but the populace will be safe. They will not be able to take the city by Gilarabrywn. You have seen to that."

"What about food?"

"We've been lucky there. It was a good year. We have more

in store than is usual for late winter. Fishermen are working around the clock harvesting, salting, and smoking. All meats and grain are rationed and underground. Even here at the castle the bulk of the stores are already in the old dungeon."

"It should slow them down, shouldn't it?"

"I think so," he said.

She looked back out the window at the snow-covered roofs. "What if Arista and the others had trouble? What if they were attacked by thieves? They might have died even before reaching the city."

"Thieves?" Nimbus asked, stifling a laugh. "I daresay I should pity any band of *thieves* that had the misfortune of assaulting that party. I am certain they have entered Amberton Lee safely."

She turned to face him. His tone was so confident, so certain that it set her at ease. "Yes, I suppose you're right. We just have to hope they are successful. What obstacles they will face beneath the Lee will certainly be more formidable than a band of thieves."

# Chapter 10

# Beneath the Lee

Arista had no idea what time it was or how long they had walked since reaching the bottom of the shaft. Her feet, sore and heavy, slipped and stumbled over rocks. She yawned incessantly and her stomach growled, but there was no stopping—not yet.

They followed a series of narrow crevices so small and tight it often required crawling and, in the case of Elden, a sucked-in stomach and the occasional tug-of-war. It was frighteningly claustrophobic at times. She moved sideways through narrow slits where her nose passed within inches of the opposite side. During this period, Arista's robe was the only source of light. At times, she noticed it dim or flicker briefly, which gave her concern. She would stiffen and instantly the light grew steady, often brighter, but as the night dragged on, the light drifted steadily from white to darker shades of blue.

The passage widened and constricted, but Royce usually found a way to move ahead. On a few occasions, he was wrong and they needed to backtrack and find another way. At such times, Arista heard Magnus mumble. Royce must have heard him too, but the thief never spoke or looked in his direction. The dwarf, who moved through the tunnels like a fish in water, did not elaborate on his grumblings. He remained generally quiet and traveled in the rear or middle of the group, yet occasionally when Royce entered a crevice, Magnus might cough with a disapproving tone. Royce ignored him and invariably returned with a scowl. After a few missteps, Royce started turning away from an appealing path the moment Magnus made a sound, as if a new thought had just occurred to him. Silently worked out and agreed upon, the system functioned well enough for both of them.

The rest of the party followed mindlessly, focused only on their own feet. After the first hour, Alric, who had begun the march giving the occasional obvious direction or asking questions, then nodding his head as if approving some sort of action, gave up the pretense altogether. Soon he dragged himself along like the rest, blindly following wherever Magnus and Royce led.

"Mmm," Arista heard Magnus intoning somewhere ahead, as if he had just tasted something wonderful.

The princess was fumbling forward, ducking and twisting to get by as they struggled through another long narrow fissure. The blue light of her robe made the rock appear to glow.

"Wonderful," the dwarf muttered.

"What is?"

"You'll see."

They inched onward through the crevice, which became tighter. She felt forward with her feet, kicking away loose stones to find footing.

"Whoa." She heard Royce's voice from somewhere up ahead, speaking the word slowly with uncharacteristic awe. She attempted to look forward, but Mauvin and Alric, standing ahead of her in the narrow pass, blocked her view.

Alric soon exclaimed, "By Mar! How is that possible?"

"What's happening?" Degan said behind her.

"No clue—not there yet," she replied. "Mauvin's big head is blocking me."

"Hey!" he retorted. "It's not my fault. It gets really narrow in—Oh my god!"

Arista pushed forward.

Mauvin was right—the path did grow very tight—and she had to bend, squeeze, and step through. Her shoulders brushed the stone, her hair caught on jagged rocks, and her foot was almost stuck as she shifted her weight. She held her breath and pulled her body through the narrowest gap.

Once on the far side, the first thing she noticed was that she was standing in a large cavern, which, after the hours of crawling like a worm, was wonderful. The action of some forgotten river had cut the walls out in scoops and brushed them to a smooth wavy finish. Elongated pools of water that littered the floor shone as mirrors divided from each other by smooth ridges of rock.

The second thing she noticed was the *stars*.

"Oh my," she found herself saying as she looked up. The roof of the cavern appeared just like the night sky. Thousands of tiny points of light glowed bright. Captured in the enclosed space, they illuminated the entire chamber. "Stars."

"Glowworms," Magnus corrected as he walked out ahead of her. "They leech on to the ceiling stone."

"They're beautiful," she said.

"Drome didn't put all his grandeur on the outside of Elan. Your castles, your towers, they are sad little toys. Here are the real treasures we hoard. They call us misers on the surface— they have no idea. They scrape for gold, silver, and diamonds, never finding the real gems beneath their feet. Welcome to the house of Drome; you stand on his porch."

"There's a flat table of rock up there," Royce told them, pointing ahead at a massive plate of stone that lay at a slight angle. "We'll camp, get some food, and sleep."

"Yes, yes, that sounds wonderful," Alric agreed, bobbing his head eagerly.

They walked around the pools filled with the reflected starlight. Myron and Elden, both with their eyes locked on the distant ceiling, missed their footing several times, soaking their feet—neither seemed to care. They climbed to the surface of the table rock, which was as large as the floor of the palace's great hall. It was a vague triangle, and the long point rose at the center of the cavern like the prow of a ship breaching a wave.

With no wood and no need for tents, making camp consisted entirely of dropping their packs and sitting down. Arista had the lightest pack, carrying only her own supplies of food, bedding, and water, but still, her shoulders ached and did so even more noticeably once she set her burden down. She planted herself on the prow, her legs dangling over the edge, and leaned back on her hands, rolling her head. She felt the aches in her neck and looked up at the false night sky. Elden was the first to join her; he settled in and mimicked her actions exactly. He smiled bashfully when he caught her looking. The big man's forehead and his left cheek had ugly scrapes and his tunic was torn across the chest and along his right shoulder. It was a wonder he had made it through at all.

From her pack she pulled one of the meals, in a neatly sewn bag. She tore it open and found salted fish, a preserved egg with a green look to it, a bit of hard bread, walnuts, and a pickle. Just as she had once devoured the pork stew Hadrian and Royce had given her the first night she had traveled with them, she consumed this meal, and when finished, she searched the bag for any remaining crumbs. Sadly, she found only two more walnuts at the bottom. She considered opening another bag, but reason fought against the idea. Partially sated, her hunger lost its edge and gave up.

Most of the group found seats along the edge of the shelf and lined up like birds on a fence, their legs dangling at various rates of swing. Royce was the last to settle. As in the past, he spent some time exploring ahead and checking behind. Degan and Magnus sat together some distance from the rest, speaking together softly.

"Blessed Maribor, am I starved!" Mauvin declared as he tore open a bag of his own. His expression showed his disappointment, but he was not discouraged. After he tasted the contents, a smile returned. "That Ibis is a genius. This fish is wonderful!"

"I—have—the pork," Alric managed to get out around the food in his mouth. "Good."

"I feel as if I am back on a ship," Wyatt mentioned, but did not pause to explain why as he tore his bread with his teeth.

Myron negotiated a trade with Elden over walnuts—a discussion held without words. The little monk looked exhausted but managed to smile warmly at the giant as they debated with hand gestures and nods. Elden grinned back, delighted by the game.

After eating, Arista looked around for a place to sleep. It was not like bedding down in a forest, where you looked for a flat area clear of roots and stones. Here everything was rock. One place was as good as another, and all appeared to offer little in the way of comfort. With her pack in hand, she wandered toward the center of the shelf, thinking that at the very least she did not want to roll off. She spotted Hadrian far down at the low end of the rock. He was lying on his back, his knees up, his head on his blanket, which he had rolled into a pillow.

"Something wrong?" she asked, approaching cautiously.

He turned on his side and looked up. "Hmm? No."

"No?" She got down on her knees beside him. "Why are you all the way over here?"

He shrugged. "Just looking for some privacy."

"Oh, then I'm probably bothering you." She got up.

"No—you're not." He stopped her. "I mean..." He sighed. "Never mind."

He sounded upset, frustrated, maybe even angry. She stood hovering over him, unsure of what to do. She hoped he would say something, or at least smile at her. Instead, he refused to look her way. His eyes focused on the darkness across the cavern. The miserable, bitter sound of the words *never mind* echoed in her head.

"I'm going to sleep," she said at last.

"That's a good idea," he replied, still not bothering to look at her.

She walked slowly back to the center of the table, glancing at him over her shoulder. He continued to lie staring at nothing. It bothered her. If it were Royce, she would not give it a second thought, but this was not like him. She spread out her blankets and lay down, feeling suddenly awful, as if she had lost something valuable. She just was not sure what.

Her robe was dark. She had not noticed until that moment and could not recall when it had faded. They were all tired, even the robe. She looked up at the glowworms. They did look like stars. There must be hundreds of thousands.

∞

*The boy was pale, ghostly, his eyes sallow. His mouth hung slightly agape as if perpetually on the verge of asking a ques-*

tion, only he could no longer form words. She guessed it took all his mental capacity to keep from screaming. Jerish stood next to him. The fighter towered over the lad with a look that reminded her of a cornered mother bear. They were both dressed in common clothes, his armor and emblems left at the palace. He appeared to be a poor merchant or tradesman, perhaps, except for the long sword slung to his back, the pommel rising over his left shoulder as if keeping watch.

"Grinder," the boy said as she entered the station.

"Nary," she greeted him, and it took effort not to bow. He looked so much like his father—the same lines, the same clarity in his eyes, the cut of his mouth—the lineage of the emperor so obvious.

"Were you followed?" Jerish asked.

She smirked.

"A Cenzar cannot be followed?"

"No," she said bluntly. "Everyone still thinks I am loyal to the cause. Now we have to be quick. Here." She held out the necklaces. "This one is for you, Nary, and this is Jerish's. Put them on and never take them off. Do you understand me? Never take them off. They will hide you from magical eyes, protect you from enchantments, allow me to find you when the time is safe, and even provide you with a bit of luck."

"You intend to fight them?"

"I will do what I can." She looked at the boy. Her efforts had to be for him now, for his safety and his return.

"You cannot save Nareion," Jerish told her bluntly. She looked at the boy and saw his lips tremble.

"I will save what is dearer to him, his son and his empire. It may take time—a long time, perhaps—but I swear I will see the empire restored even if it costs me my life." She watched as they slipped the necklaces on. "Be sure to hide him well. Take him into the country, assume the life of a commoner. Do nothing to draw attention, and await my call."

"Will these really protect us from your associates?"

"I will have no associates after today."

"Even old Yolric?"

She hesitated. "Yolric is very powerful, but wise."

"If he is so wise, why is he with them? Is it not wisdom to preserve the empire and show loyalty to the emperor?"

"I am not certain Yolric is with them. He has always remained an island. Even the emperors do not influence him. Yolric does as he wishes. I cannot say what he will do. I hope he will join with me, but should he side with Venlin..." She shook her head sadly. "We must hope."

Jerish nodded. "I trust you to watch our backs. I never thought I would ever say that—not to a Cenzar...not to you."

"And I entrust you with the future of the empire and ultimately the fate of mankind—I certainly did not expect to be saying that to you."

Jerish tore off his glove and held out his hand. "Goodbye, Brother."

She took his hand in hers. This was the last time she would ever shake anyone's hand.

How do I know that?

"Goodbye, Nary," she told the boy. At the sound of her voice, Nevrik rushed forward and threw his arms about her. She hugged him back.

"I'm scared," he said.

"You must be brave. Remember, you are the son of Nareion, the emperor of Apeladorn, the descendant of Novron, the savior of our race. Know that the time will come when the blood descendant of Novron must protect us again—your descendant, Nary. It may take many years for me to defeat

*the evil that has risen today, so you must not wait. If you find
a girl who makes your heart smile, make her your wife.
Remember, Persephone was a mere farmer's daughter and she
mothered a line of emperors. You must find a girl like that
and have a family. Give your child your necklace and stay
safe. Do what Jerish says. After this day, there will be no warrior greater than he. I will see to that as well." She noticed a
dark look come over Jerish. "It is necessary," she told him,
surprised at the ice in her own voice.*

*Jerish nodded miserably.*

*"What exactly do you intend to do?"*

*"Just make certain you are not in the city when I do it."*

*Tink! Tink! Tink!*

Arista woke up cold and confused. The sense of urgency,
the fear and concern, lingered. Her back hurt. The hard, damp
stone tortured her strained muscles, leaving her feeling crippled.
She rolled to her side with a miserable groan.

*Tink! Tink! Tink!* The sound of stone striking stone echoed.

She looked up but saw nothing. It was all black now. The
worms were gone or no longer giving off light.

*Tink!*

There was a spark of white light and in that brief flash she
spotted Magnus, hunched over a pile of rocks, only a few feet
from her.

*Tink!*

"*Ba, durim hiben!*" he growled. She heard him shift
position.

"How long have I been asleep?" she asked.

"Six hours," the dwarf replied.

*Tink!* Another flash, another incomprehensible grumble.

"What is it you are doing?"

"Frustrating and embarrassing myself."

"What?"

"It's just been so long, although that's really no excuse. I can hardly call myself a Brundenlin if—"

*Tink!* Another flash—this time it did not go out. The spark appeared to linger, amazingly bright. Instantly Magnus bent down and she could hear him blowing. The spark grew brighter with each puff. Soon she could clearly see the face of the dwarf—the ridges of his cheeks, the tip of his nose, the beard trimmed short, all highlighted by the flickering glow. His dark eyes glistened, eagerly watching the flame he breathed life into.

"We have no wood," she said, puzzled, as she sat up.

"Don't need wood."

She watched him pile fist-sized stones on top of the little flame. He blew again and the fire grew. The stone was burning.

"Magic?"

"Skill," he replied. "Do you think they only have fire on the outside? Drome taught the dwarves first. In the deep, the blood of Elan bubbles up. There are rivers of burning stone, red and yellow, flowing thick and hot. We taught the secret of fire to the elves, much to our regret."

"How old are you?" she asked. It was common knowledge that elves lived longer—much longer—than humans, but she had no idea about dwarves.

Magnus looked at her through squinting eyes and pursed his lips as if he had tasted something bitter. "That's not a polite question, so I will be just as rude and ignore it. Since you feel you still need me, I trust you won't burn me to a cinder for it."

Arista rocked back. "I would never do such a thing. Perhaps you've forgotten I am not the one who randomly commits murder."

"No? My mistake. Apparently you're only content with enslavement." He tugged at his cropped beard.

"Would you have come if the empress had merely asked?"

"No. What care is it of mine if the elves erase you? It would restore the world. Humans have always been a blight, like the Ba Ran Ghazel, only with the Ghazel you know where you stand. They don't pretend to accept you when they want something, then shove you out in the cold when they're done with you. No, the Ghazels' hatred is up front and honest, not like the lies of the humans."

"I'd listen to him, Princess. He is an expert on betrayals."

The voice, low and threatening, came out of the darkness and Magnus jumped up, scrambling toward her, as if for protection. A moment later Royce appeared at the edge of the fire's light.

"I just wanted the dagger," Magnus replied, a hint of desperation in his voice, which rose an octave higher than normal.

"I understand, and I promise that the moment this business is done, I will make a present of it to you," Royce told him with a hungry look in his eyes that gave even Arista's heart pause. "Be sure to keep me informed of his usefulness, won't you, Your Highness?"

"He's actually being very helpful—so far," she replied.

"Too bad," Royce said. "Still, I have every confidence that will change. Won't it, Magnus?" He glared at the dwarf for several minutes as if expecting an answer; then the thief looked at her. "Better get everyone up. It's time we got moving."

Royce turned and disappeared silently into the cave's gloom. When she looked back at the dwarf, Magnus was staring at her with a surprised, almost shocked, expression, as if something about her suddenly mystified him. He turned away and grumbled something she did not catch before returning to his pile of burning rocks.

Magnus's campfire made the process of getting up and having breakfast almost cheerful and lent a sense of normality to their queer surroundings. The bright yellow flicker reminded Arista of her days traveling with Royce and Hadrian, and of her trip to Aquesta. It was shocking to think of those days as better times. Her life since the death of her father had been one long cascading fall that had left her tripping over ever greater troubles.

She could hardly imagine a more desperate state than the one she faced now. There wasn't much that could top the extinction of mankind. She was certain, however, that it would never come to that. Even should the elves prevail, even if they sought to eradicate humans, she suspected there would be pockets that survived. It would be like trying to kill all the mice in the world. A few would always survive. She looked around the cave as she sat tying up her hair for the day's journey. Hundreds, perhaps thousands, could live down there alone. Like her father, she was not an overly religious person, and yet she could not believe that Maribor would let his people vanish from the face of Elan. He had saved them before. He had sent Novron to snatch them from the brink, and she suspected he would do so again.

Myron ate breakfast with Elden much as he had dinner. The two communicated in silence while Wyatt rolled up blankets. She had no idea what to make of Wyatt. He and Elden kept mostly to themselves, rarely speaking, and usually only to each other. They did not seem a bad sort, not like Gaunt. Degan bothered her like a splinter in her skin. How he could be the descendant of Novron was bewildering, and not for the first time she wondered if perhaps Esrahaddon had gotten it wrong.

They lit lanterns from the dying flames of the campfire,

and after packing up, Royce roamed about the cavern, disappearing from view occasionally. Only the glow of his lantern showed his position.

"Wrong way," she heard Magnus mutter, his arms folded, his foot tapping the stone. "Better…better…now up… up—yes!"

From across the cavern they could see Royce swinging his light and they marched forward. They climbed a sheer cliff to a crack in the rock and sliced through to another chamber. Then they climbed down into another long passage into yet another cavity. Each looked the same as the ones before, smooth walls and wet, pool-scattered floors.

"I thought caverns were supposed to have long cone-shaped stones hanging down from the ceiling," Alric mentioned as they entered yet another chamber.

"Not old enough," Magnus said.

"What's that?" the king asked.

"These caves, they're not old enough for dripstones to form. It takes tens of thousands of years. These…" He looked around, pursing his pudgy lips. "These tunnels are young. I doubt they have existed for more than a few thousand years and most of that time this was underwater from a powerful river. That's what carved the walls and rounded the rocks. You also need limestone and this isn't that kind of cave. Actually…" He paused, then stopped to pick up a rock. As he weighed it in his hand, a puzzled look came over his face.

"What is it?" Mauvin asked.

"The rocks here are from the surface." He shrugged. "Perhaps the river carried them." He continued to stare, licking his teeth, for several seconds before dropping it and moving on.

They entered another narrow space but not nearly so tight as before. This was an irregular passage about the size of a typical second-story castle corridor. Low ceilings caused them to duck and rough ridges made them step around, but the way was considerably easier and more comfortable than those previously encountered. The passage was in a constant descent, growing more pronounced with each step. They followed the glow of Royce's lantern and kept track of the back of their procession by the bob of Hadrian's. As on the previous day, Arista walked in the middle, her robe glowing softly.

They heard a rush, as if someone far away was beating a drum. The sound echoed, making it hard to determine what direction it was coming from. They all paused, looking around nervously. Arista felt a slight breeze forming and realized what was coming. At the same instant, she knew that outside, the sun had just risen.

"Here they come," Hadrian called out.

Arista crouched down, pulling the hood of her robe up over her head as through the corridor swept the same multitude of bats that had frightened her in the shaft the evening before. The world around her filled with squeaks and flutters; then the wind passed and the sound moved away. She stood up and peeked out and saw the others lowering their arms as well. A few slow strays continued to fly by when one not far from Myron was snatched from the air. The monk staggered backward with a gasp and fell in front of Elden, who picked the monk up as if he were a doll.

"Snake," Wyatt announced. "A big black one."

"There's dozens of them," Royce explained.

"Where?" Alric asked.

"Mostly behind you on the walls."

"What?" the king said, aghast. "Why didn't you say something?"

"Knowing would only make traveling slower."

"Are they poisonous?" Mauvin asked.

They could all see the silhouetted shoulders of Royce's shadow on the far wall shrug.

"I demand you inform me of such things in future!" Alric declared.

"Do you want to know about the giant millipedes, then too?"

"Are you joking?"

"Royce doesn't make jokes," Arista told him as she looked around, anxiously hugging herself. Immediately her robe brightened and she spotted two snakes on the walls, but they were a safe distance away.

"He must be joking," Alric muttered quietly. "I don't see any."

"You aren't looking up," the thief said.

Arista did not want to. Some instinct, a tiny voice, warned her to fight the impulse, but in the end she just could not help herself. On the low ceiling, illuminated brightly by the robe, slithered a mass of wormlike bugs with an uncountable number of hairlike feet. Each was nearly five inches in length and close to the width of a man's finger. There were so many that they swarmed over each other until it was hard to tell if the ceiling was rock at all. Arista felt a chill run down her back. She clenched her teeth, forced her eyes to the floor, and focused on walking forward as quickly as possible.

She promptly passed Alric and Mauvin, both moving quicker than normal. She reached Royce, who stood outside the corridor on a boulder at the entrance to a larger passage.

"I guess I was wrong. Looks like I should have told you earlier," Royce said, watching them race forward.

"Are there...?" she asked, pointing upward without looking.

Royce glanced up and shook his head.

"Good," she replied. "And please, if Alric wants to know these things, fine, but don't tell me. I could have gone the rest of my life not knowing they were there." She shivered.

Everyone scurried out of the corridor except Myron, who lingered, staring up at the ceiling and smiling in fascination. "There are millions."

They entered another chamber, a smaller cavern of dramatic boulders that thrust up and out. Arista thought they appeared how the timbers of a house might look if a giant stepped on it. As soon as they entered, they faced a mystery on the far wall, where three darkened passages awaited, one large, one small, and one narrow. The party waited as Royce disappeared briefly into each one. When he returned, he did not look pleased.

"Dwarf!" he snapped. "Which one?"

Magnus stepped forward and poked his head into each. He placed his hands on the stone, groping over the surface as if he were a blind man. He pressed his ear to the rock, sniffed the air in each opening, and stepped back with a perplexed look. "They all go deep, but in separate directions."

Royce continued to stare at him.

"The stone doesn't know where we want to go, so it can't tell me."

"We can't afford to pick the wrong path," Arista said.

"I say we choose the largest," Alric stated confidently. "Wouldn't that be the most sensible?"

"Why is that sensible?" Arista asked.

"Well—because it is the biggest, so it ought to go the farthest and, you know—get us there."

"The largest might not remain that way," Magnus replied. "Cracks in rock aren't like rivers. They don't taper evenly."

Alric looked irritated. "Okay, what about you?" he asked Arista. "Can you do anything to—well—you know—find which is the right one?"

"Like what?"

"Do I need to spell it out? Like…" He waved his hands in the air in a mysterious fashion that she thought made him look silly. "Magic."

"I knew what you meant, but what exactly do you expect me to do? Summon Novron's ghost to point us in the right direction?"

"Can you do that?" the king asked, sounding both impressed and apprehensive.

"No!"

Alric frowned and slapped his thighs with his hands as if to indicate how horribly she had let him down. It irritated her how everyone seemed so disgusted by her talent and yet was even more upset when they found her ability lacking.

"Myron?" Hadrian said softly to the monk, who stood silently, staring at the passages.

"*Three openings. What to do?*" Myron said eerily.

"Myron, yes!" Alric smiled. "Tell us, which way did Hall go?"

"That's what I am reciting to you," he replied, trying to hide a little smile. " 'Three openings. What to do? I sat for an hour before I gave up trying to reason it out and just picked. I chose the closest.' "

Myron stopped, and when he failed to say more, Alric spoke. "The closest? What does that mean? Closest to what?"

"Is that all Hall wrote?" Arista asked. "What came next?"

Everyone crowded around the little man as he cleared his throat.

" 'Down, down, down, always down, never up. Slept in the corridor again. Miserable night. Food running low. Big-eyed fish looking better all the time. This is hopeless. I will die in here. I miss Sadie. I miss Ebot and Dram. I should never have come. This was a mistake. I have placed myself in my own grave. Feet are always wet. Want to sleep, but don't want to lie in water.

" 'A pounding. Pounding up ahead. A way out maybe!

" 'Pounding stopped. I don't think it was from the outside. I think someone else is down here—something else. I hear them—not human.

" 'Ba Ran Ghazel. Sea goblins. A whole patrol. Nearly found me. Lost my shoe.

" 'Bread moldy, salted ham nearly gone. At least there is water. Tastes bad, brackish. Slept poorly again. Bad dreams.

" 'I found it.' "

"The shoe?" Wyatt asked.

"No," Myron replied, smiling, "the city."

"Interesting," Gaunt said. "But that doesn't help us with the passages, does it? By the sound of things he traveled for days and never listed any landmark. It's pointless."

"We could split up," Alric said, considering. "Two groups of three and one of four. One group is bound to reach Percepliquis."

Arista shook her head. "That only works if we can divide up Mr. Gaunt in three parts. He is the one who has to reach the city."

"So you keep reminding me," Gaunt said. "But you refuse to tell me exactly what you expect me to do. I am not a man of many talents. There is nothing I can do that someone else in this party can't. I hope to Maribor you don't expect me to slay one of those Gilly-bran things. I'm not much of a fighter."

"I suppose you have to—I don't know—blow the horn."

"Couldn't I have done that after you returned with it?"

Arista sighed. "There's something else. I don't know what. I just know you have to be here."

"And yet we have no idea where *here* is," he said indignantly.

Arista sighed and sat down on a rock, staring at the entrances. As she did, Alric stared at her.

"What?" she asked.

Alric smiled and glanced back at the passages. "I was wrong. Hall went in the narrow passage on the right."

He sounded so certain that everyone looked at him.

"Care to tell us how you know that?" Arista asked.

He grinned, obviously very pleased with himself. "Sure, but first you have to tell me why you sat there," he said to her.

"I don't know. I was tired of standing and this might take a while."

"Exactly," Alric said. "What did you say, Myron? It took an hour for Hall to decide which passage?"

"Close. 'I sat for an hour before I gave up trying to reason it out and just picked,' " the monk corrected.

"He sat for an hour trying to decide," Alric replied. "He sat right where you are."

"How do you know?" Gaunt asked. "How do you know it was on *that* rock and not someplace else?"

"Ask Arista," the king replied. "Why did you sit there and not someplace else?"

She shrugged and looked around. "I didn't really think about it. I just sat. I guess because it looked like the most comfortable place."

"Of course it is. Look around. That rock is perfect for sitting. All the others are sharp on the top or at steep angles or too big or small. That is the perfect sitting rock for looking at those passages! And that's the same reason Hall chose that spot, and the closest passage is the narrow one. Hall went in there. I'm positive."

Arista looked at Royce, who looked at Hadrian, who shrugged. "I think he might be right."

"Sounds good to me," Royce said.

Arista nodded. "I think so too."

Everyone seemed pleased except for Gaunt, who frowned but said nothing.

Alric adjusted his pack and, taking the lantern from Royce, promptly led the way.

"That lad might amount to something yet," Mauvin said, chuckling, as he followed his king.

# CHAPTER 11

# THE PATRIARCH

Monsignor Merton shuffled along the dark snowy road, his black hood up, his freezing fingers gripping the neck of his frock. He shuffled for fear of falling on the ice he could not feel. The tip of his nose and the tops of his cheeks had gone from feeling cold to burning unpleasantly.

*Maybe I have frostbite*, he thought. *What a sight I will be without a nose*. The thought did not bother him much; he could get along fine without one.

The hour was late. The shop windows were all black, dull sightless eyes reflecting his image. He had passed fewer than a dozen people since leaving the palace and all of them were soldiers. He felt sorry for the men who guarded the streets. The shopkeepers complained when they collected taxes, the vagrants wailed when they drove them off, and the criminals cursed them. They were half-shaven, blunt-nosed, loud, and always seen as bullies, but no one saw them on nights like this. The shopkeepers were all asleep in their beds, the vagrants and thieves tucked in their holes, but the soldiers of the empress remained. They felt the cold, suffered the wind, and endured exhaustion, but they bore their burdens quietly. As he shuffled on, Merton said a quiet prayer to Novron to give them strength and make their night rounds easier. He felt foolish doing so. *Surely Novron knows the plight of his own. He does not need me reminding him. What an utter annoyance I must be, what a bother. It's little wonder that I should lose my nose. Perhaps both feet should be taken as well.*

"Without feet, Lord, how will I serve?" He spoke softly. His voice came out in clouds that drifted by as he walked. "For I am not fit for much else these days beyond carrying messages."

He stopped. He listened. There was no answer.

Then he nodded. "I see, I see. Stop being a fool and walk faster and I will keep my feet. Very wise, my lord."

On he trudged, and reaching the top of the hill, he turned off Majestic Avenue and entered Church Square. At the center of the dark void glowed the clerestory lights of the great cathedral, the Imperial Basilica of Aquesta. Now that Ervanon was no more—crushed and defiled by the elven horde—this was the seat of power of the Nyphron Church. Here emperors would be crowned, married, and laid to rest. Here Wintertide services would be performed. Here the Patriarch and his bishops would administer to the children of Maribor. While it had nowhere close to the majesty of the Basilica of Ervanon, it had something Ervanon had never had—the Heir of Novron, their earthly god returned. And not a moment too soon, was how Merton saw it, but gods had a flair for dramatic timing. He considered himself blessed to be granted life in such a wondrous time. He would be a living witness to the fulfillment of the promise and the return of Novron's Empire, and in some small way he might even be allowed to contribute.

He climbed the steps to the massive doors and tugged on the ring. Locked. It always mystified Merton why the house of Novron should be sealed. He beat against the oak with his frozen fist.

The wind howled; the cold ripped mercilessly through his thin wool. He looked up, disappointed not to see stars overhead. He liked the stars, especially how they looked on cold nights, as if he could reach up and pluck one. As a boy, he had imagined that he might scoop them up and slip them into his pocket. He never imagined doing anything with the stars; he would just run his fingertips through them like grains of sand.

The door remained closed.

He hammered again. His hand made a feeble fleshy sound against the heavy wood.

"Is it your will that I freeze to death here on your steps?" he asked Novron. "I certainly should not think it would look good to have the body of your servant found here. People might get the wrong idea."

He heard a latch slide.

"Thank you, my lord, forgive my impatience. I am but a man."

"Monsignor Merton!" Bishop DeLunden exclaimed as he held up a lantern and peered out. "What are you doing out so late on a night like this?"

"God's will."

"Of course, but certainly our lord could wait until morning. That's why he makes new ones every day." DeLunden was more the curator of the church than its bishop these days, now that the Patriarch had taken up residence. He was like the captain of a ship that ferried an admiral.

Bishop DeLunden had unusually dark skin even for a Calian, which made his wreath of short white hair stand out against his balding head, the top of which looked like a dark olive set in cream. The bishop had a habit of wandering the halls at night like a ghost. Exactly what he did on his walks about the cathedral Merton had no idea, but tonight he was more than thankful for his nocturnal habits. "And it wasn't

Novron who sent you out on such a night; it was Patriarch Nilnev." He pulled the great door closed and slid the bolt. "Back from the palace again, are you?"

"These are troubled times and he needs to keep informed. Besides, if not for my wanderings, who would praise the beauty of our lord's nights?"

"Those farther south, I imagine," DeLunden retorted gruffly. "Put your hands on the lantern. Warm them lest they fall off."

"Such compassion," Merton said. "And for the likes of an Ervanonite like me."

"Not all Ervanonites are bad."

"There's only four of us."

"Yes, and of the four I can say that you are a good, devout, and gentle man."

"And the others?"

"I don't speak of them at all. I still find it altogether strange that only he and his guards managed to escape the desolation of Ervanon while all others perished."

"I am here."

"Novron loves you. Our lord pointed you out on the day of your birth and told his father to watch over you."

"You are too kind, and surely Novron loves everyone, and the leader of his church most of all."

"But the Patriarch is not—not anymore." The bishop peered from the vestibule toward the interior. "I don't like how he treats you."

Since the Patriarch had arrived, Bishop DeLunden had been very vocal about how the Patriarch treated everyone and, more importantly, *his* cathedral. It was a matter of jealousy, but Merton would never say anything. If Novron wished the bishop to learn this lesson, he would find a worthier vessel than him to explain.

"I also don't like how he holds court in the holy chancel, as if he were Novron himself. The altar deserves more respect. Only the empress should occupy that space, only the blood of Novron, but he sits there as if *he* is the emperor."

"Is he there now?"

"Of course he is—him and his guards. Why does he need guards, anyway? I don't have guards and I meet dozens of people every day. He meets no one but is never separated from them—and what strange men. They speak only to him, and always in whispers. Why is that? He unnerves me. I am glad I never met the man when I was a deacon, or I should never have devoted my life to Novron."

"And that would have been a terrible loss to us all," Merton assured him. "Now if you do not mind, I must speak with the Patriarch."

"Patriarch! That's another thing. The man has a name—he was born with a name, just like the rest of us—but no one ever uses it. We refer to our lords as Novron and Maribor, but Nilnev of Ervanon must be referred to as *the Patriarch*, out of respect for his office as head of the church, but as I said, he's not the head anymore. Novron's child has returned to us, but still he sits there. Still he rules. I don't like it—I don't like it one bit, and I don't think the empress approves either. If she doesn't, we can be assured our lord Novron isn't too pleased."

"Would you like me to speak to him about your concerns?"

DeLunden scowled. "Oh, he knows. Believe me, he knows."

Merton left the bishop in the narthex and entered the nave. He stopped briefly, looking down the long cavernous room with its magnificent arched ceiling, shaped like a great ship's keel—the word *nave*, Merton had learned, was derived from the ancient term *navis*, meaning *ship*. Towering rows of ribbed pillars, like bunches of reeds bound together, rose hundreds of feet, spilling out at the tops, which spread to form the vaulted ceiling. To either side, lower aisles flanked the nave, encased in the arcades—the series of repeating archways and columns. Above them, the clerestory, or second story, was pierced by tall quatrefoil windows, which normally flooded the floor with light. Tonight they remained black and oily as they reflected the fire of the candles. The same was true of the great rose window at the far end of the cathedral, which appeared as one giant eye. Merton often thought of it as the eye of god watching them, but just as the clerestory lights were dark, so too the great eye remained shut.

Reaching the altar, Merton found alabaster statues of Maribor and Novron. Novron, depicted as a strong handsome man in the prime of his youth, was kneeling, sword in hand. The god Maribor, sculpted as a powerful, larger-than-life figure with a long beard and flowing robes, loomed over Novron, placing a crown on the young man's head. The statues were the same in every church and chapel; only the materials differed, depending on the means of the parishioners.

"Come forward, Monsignor," he heard the Patriarch say. His voice carried in echoes from the altar. The cathedral was so large that from where he stood, those in the chancel appeared tiny, dwarfed by distance and made small by the height of the ceiling and the breadth of the walls.

Merton walked the long pathway, listening to the sounds of his shoes against the stone floor.

Just as DeLunden had described, the Patriarch sat at the altar on a chair, his gold and purple robes draped to the floor. Rumors circulated it was the same chair he had used in Ervanon, which he had ordered brought with him at great effort. Merton had never interviewed with His Holiness while in Ervanon, so he could not say if that rumor was true. Few could—His Holiness had rarely seen anyone in his days sequestered in the Crown Tower.

He might have been sleeping, the way the old did, regardless of where they happened to be. To either side of him stood the guards, matching their charge perfectly in color and fashion. DeLunden was right, at least about the guards: they were a peculiar pair. They stood like statues, without expressions, and for a moment he considered how their eyes reminded him of the windows.

Upon reaching the Patriarch, Merton knelt and kissed his ring, then stood once more. The Patriarch nodded. The guards did not move—not even to blink.

"You have news," Nilnev prompted.

"I do, Your Holiness. I have just come from a meeting with Her Eminence and her staff."

"So tell me, what is the empress doing to protect us?"

"She has done a great deal. Supplies have been stored to last the city an estimated two years with proper rationing, which she has already instituted. In addition, the grounds of Highcourt Fields will be opened to farmers come spring. This and other areas of the city will produce grain and vegetables from stored seed. Already manure is being delivered as fertilizer. Fish are being netted around the clock and salt houses are preserving the cod in bulk. A saltworks has been built near the docks to provide pans for raking. These measures could very well provide the city and its people with food for years— indefinitely, perhaps, should the fishing fleet be free to farm the sea.

"All stores are being kept underground in bunkers being dug by the populace in the event of attacks from the sky similar to what was seen at Dahlgren. In most instances, this is merely an expansion or adaptation of an existing dungeon. A series of tunnels have already been built that allow access to freshwater. The wastes from latrines are being channeled through newly built sewers. Given the frozen ground, progress is slow, but it is believed that adequate space is already available to save the population—although it will be most uncomfortable. Plans to continue the expansion underground could take two or three more months. The empress actually feels that having it uncompleted is beneficial, as it gives the people something to do."

"So she plans to become a city of moles, hiding in the dirt?"

"Well, yes and no, Your Holiness. She has also strengthened the defenses of the city. A series of catapults are in various states of construction around the outer walls, and soldiers are being drilled by officers appointed by Marshal Breckton. He has devised a number of redundant procedures for every contingency, allowing a means of giving commands in the form of horns, drums, and flags to be flown from the high towers. Archers have stockpiled thousands of arrows and any able-bodied citizen not already employed is working to gather wood for more. Even children are scouring the forest floors. Oil and tar vats are prepared and in ample supply at all gates.

"Signal fires were placed to burn the moment the elves were spotted. One was lit and the empress has ordered all of the roads leading to the city to be destroyed, save the southern gate. All bridges and dams are to be broken in order to prevent—"

"Destroyed?" the Patriarch interrupted. "When did she give this order?"

"Just last night."

"Last night?" The Patriarch looked concerned. "Is there anything else?"

"The empress asked me to inquire what precautions you will be taking."

"That is none of her business," he replied.

Merton was shocked. "Begging your pardon, Your Holiness, but she is the empress as well as the head of the church.

How is it not her business to know what efforts you have taken to secure her flock?"

The Patriarch glared at him for a moment, then softened his expression. "You are a good and devout member of the church, Merton of Ghent, and as our lord has seen fit to make you my liaison to the empress, I think perhaps it is time you were made aware of certain truths."

"Your Holiness?"

"Empress Modina is not the head of this church," the Patriarch declared simply.

"But she's the Heir of Novron—"

"That's exactly the problem—she is not." The Patriarch licked his nonexistent lips and continued. "Bishop Saldur and Archbishop Galien overstepped their mandate while in Dahlgren. They took it upon themselves to declare the girl the anointed heir. It was a well-intentioned mistake. They were too impatient to wait for Novron to show the way, so they sought to artificially create a new empire. They picked this girl at random, using the unexpected incidents on the Nidwalden to serve as proof. What happened there, however, was proof of nothing. It's a fabrication that a Gilarabrywn can only be slain by the blood of Novron. They used the ignorance of the masses to build this false empire."

"Why didn't you stop it?"

"What could I do? Did you think I *chose* to live my life in seclusion?"

Merton looked at the Patriarch for a moment, confused; then the revelation dawned on him. "You were a prisoner?"

"Why else would I be locked away at the top of the Crown Tower all these years, never seeing anyone?"

"These guards?"

"The only two souls I know to be truly loyal to me. They tried to free me once. They spoke out and Galien had their tongues sliced off. Only now, with Saldur and the others dead, and Ervanon destroyed, am I able to speak freely."

"I can hardly believe it," the monsignor said. "The archbishop, and Saldur as well? But they both seemed so kindly."

"You have no idea of their ruthlessness. Now, as a result of their actions, a false god sits on the throne of our lord and our fate is in peril."

"But you can do something about it now, can't you?"

"What can I do? You've heard the mutterings of even old Bishop DeLunden. Imagine what the world would think if I tried to tell the truth. I would be labeled a jealous old man, clinging to lost power. No one would believe me. The empress would see me murdered, just as she eliminated Ethelred and Saldur when they stood in her way. No, I cannot act openly—not yet."

"What do you intend to do, then?"

"There is a greater issue at stake. We do not face just the extinction of the empire, but of mankind. Modina and her actions will doom all of us."

"Her preparations to defend the city certainly appear to—"

"Her efforts are useless, but that is not of which I speak."

"You're referring to the mission to Percepliquis?"

"Yes! It's by this that she imperils all."

"But you were at the meeting. Why didn't you say anything?"

"Because that mission *is* necessary. It's imperative that the horn be found. The danger lies in *who* finds it. That horn is a weapon of incredible power. What Modina does not know—what even Saldur and Ethelred did not know—is that they have been fooled into searching for it. The enemy needs to lay hands on it as much as we do. Whoever wields it controls all. It's *he* who they obey. They have always been his pawn. For centuries, he has planned this, his hand guiding every move, hidden in the shadows, manipulating forces unseen. They think he is gone, that he is dead, but he is not. He is clever and crafty, his magic is beyond imagining, and he seeks revenge. A millennium of preparation comes down to this moment and it is he who desires the horn and with it will make all of mankind bow to him. Even the elves will pay for crimes committed a thousand years ago. They will hand the horn to him, for they do not see the danger traveling with them.

"Right now, in the depths of this world, ten individuals are delving into the past and discovering what never should be known, and with that knowledge the world will be undone, unless…"

Merton waited, and when the Patriarch said nothing more, he asked, "Unless what?"

The old man, with his barren brows and bluish hair, looked back as if pulled from a terrible nightmare. "I did what I could. I managed to strike a deal with a member of the empress's team. At the right moment, my agent will betray them."

"Who?"

"I will not say. You are a good servant of Novron, but I cannot take a chance of revealing his identity even to you — not with so much at stake."

"Can you at least tell me who this evil one is? Who can span the course of a thousand years to bring this about?"

"Think hard, Monsignor, and you will know, but for now pray — pray to Novron that my agent will succeed in his charge."

"I will, Your Holiness. I will."

"Good, and pack your bags lightly."

"Am I going somewhere?"

"We both are."

## Chapter 12

# Thieves End

R oyce heard whispering.

He estimated it was an hour before dawn. Although he wasn't certain, it would surprise him if he was very far off. Royce had experience keeping track of time underground. He had developed a surprisingly accurate method during his incarceration in Manzant. During those days, tracking minutes had focused his mind, keeping it off other, more painful thoughts. This was the first time in many years he had allowed himself to remember those days. He had carefully locked them away, packaged them into a back corner of his mind with a dark blanket laid over top, just in case he accidentally looked that way. Only now did he welcome the memories. The pain they caused worked much the same way as keeping track of time had in Manzant, much the same as biting a finger, or squeezing his fist until the fingernails dug half-moons into his palm. They distracted him from thoughts of loss far more fresh—far more crippling.

More than a decade had passed since the First Officer of the Black Diamond had betrayed him, since he had tragically killed Jade and as a result was sent to Manzant Prison by his best friend. Manzant was a dwarven-constructed prison and salt mine. He could still remember the dark rock with streaks of white and fossils of shellfish. The walls were shored up with timber. Dwarves never used wood. Men added that years later as they carved deeper, hauling the chunks of rock salt out to the elevator in baskets. It was easy to tell the man-made sections from the dwarven by the height of the ceiling. Those being punished worked in the dwarven tunnels, and Royce often found himself there.

He recalled the constant clink of pick on stone and the heat of the fires boiling the brine out of underwater lakes. Huge pans, bubbling and hissing, filled the stale air with steam. If he closed his eyes, he could see the line of bucket men and the walkers chained by their necks to the huge wheel powering the pump. He could also see men driven to exhaustion until they collapsed into the furnace pit.

Water was plentiful, so it was available to those who worked, but Ambrose Moor, the owner of the prison mine, did not waste his profits on food. They were lucky to receive a single small meal a day, usually the spoiled remnants of what a crew of indentured sailors refused to eat. This was just one of many deals Ambrose arranged to minimize operation costs. Royce would fall asleep to dreams of killing Ambrose and the thoughts lingered throughout the day. In the two and a half years he spent in Manzant, he killed Ambrose five hundred and thirty-seven times—no two alike. He killed many people in Manzant and not all of them were imaginary. He never thought of them as people. They were all animals, monsters. Whatever humanity a man had possessed going in was leached out by the salt, pain, and despair. They all fought for rotten food, a place to sleep, a cup of water. He learned how to sleep light and how to appear like he was sleeping when he was not.

Never seeing daylight, never breathing fresh air, and being worked to exhaustion each day, and beaten for mere recreation, had killed many and driven others insane. For Royce, Manzant was only part of his prison, the latest incarnation. The real walls he had been building up brick by brick for years. Escaping Manzant was impossible, but it was ultimately easier than escaping the prison of his own making.

Nim had started him on the path, and later Arcadius and Hadrian had guided his way, but it was Gwen who had finally unlocked the cell door. She shoved it open and stood just outside calling, assuring him it was safe. He could smell the fresh air and see the brilliance of the sun. He was almost through, almost out—almost.

The whispering came from near the pool.

He thought everyone was asleep. They had traveled a long distance that day over hard terrain. No one had called for him to stop, but he had seen them stumbling—all except the dwarf. The little rat never seemed to tire but continued to scurry, and more than once, Royce had spotted a little smile behind the mustache and remains of his beard.

He had almost killed Magnus that first night they had spent at The Laughing Gnome. The thought had danced teasingly on his mind. That was before Myron came back from dinner and got all chatty. Royce would not admit it to anyone, but the dwarf was useful, and on surprisingly good behavior—which showed even more good sense. More than that, he discovered he no longer had the desire. Like everything else, the dwarf's crime had been made trivial by Gwen's death. Both love and hate were banished from him. He was a desert, dry of all passion. Mostly he was tired. He had one last job to do and he would do it, not for the empire, not even for Hadrian—this was for Gwen.

He got to his feet silently, out of curiosity more than concern. The whispering was definitely coming from the party— not some intruder. He spotted the princess lying on her side, wrapped in twisted blankets. She was jerking and thrashing again, that creepy robe glowing different colors, fading out and lighting up. He had no idea if the robe was causing her to dream so violently or if her dreams sparked the robe's response. He did not see how it was any of his business and moved on.

At first, he thought it might be Magnus and Gaunt whispering. He frequently spied them traveling together and talking when the rest were too far to hear. Drawing closer, he discovered the source—it was Elden. He could see the huge reclined form up on one elbow under the blanket. His conspirator was on the far side and blocked from view. Wyatt lay a short distance away. He too was awake and watching.

"What's going on?" Royce whispered to the sailor. "Who's Elden talking to?"

"The monk."

"Myron?"

Wyatt nodded.

"Is it normal for him to talk to strangers like that?"

Wyatt looked at him. "He's talked more to that little monk in the last three days than he has to me in the last decade. They were doing this last night too, and I swear I heard Elden crying. I once watched while a ship's surgeon put a red-hot poker to a wound on his thigh. Elden didn't make a sound, but last night that little monk had him weeping so bad his eyes were red the next morning."

Royce said nothing.

"Funny thing, though, he was smiling. All day long, I saw Elden grinning from ear to ear. That's just not like him."

"Best get back to sleep," Royce told him. "I'll be waking everyone in another hour."

❧

Royce stopped again.

Hadrian could see him over the heads of the others from

his position at the rear. This time, Royce knelt down, placed the lantern on the ground beside him, and scraped the dirt. Alric approached and stood slightly to one side.

The party spent most of that day, like the one before, traveling in a single column in the narrow corridor. Overhead, water dripped, soaking their heads and shoulders; likewise, their feet felt pickled from wading through ankle-deep pools.

"What is it this time?" he heard Degan mutter with disdain. "He's stopping every twenty feet now. This is the problem with monarchies and the whole feudal system, for that matter. Alric is in charge by no other virtue than his birth, and the man is clearly incompetent. He lost his own kingdom twice over in a single year, and now he is in charge of us? We should have a leader who is elected on merit, not lineage. Someone who is the most talented, the most gifted, but no—we have Alric. And the king in all his minuscule wisdom has chosen Royce to guide us. If I were in charge, I would put Magnus out front. He's obviously far more gifted. He's constantly correcting Royce's mistakes. We would be making twice the time we are now. I've observed that people respect you."

Hadrian noticed Gaunt was looking at him. Up until that moment, he had not known who Gaunt was speaking to.

"No one says it, no one bows or anything, but you are highly regarded, I can tell—more than Alric, that's for certain. If you were to support me, I think we could persuade the others to accept my command of this group. I know Magnus would."

"Why you?" Hadrian asked.

"Huh?"

"Why should you be in charge?"

"Oh—well, for one thing I am the descendant of Novron and will be emperor. And second, I am smarter than that oaf Alric, by far."

"I thought you said you wanted a system based on merit, not lineage."

"I did, but like I said, I am far better suited to the task than he is. Besides, why else am I here if not to lead?"

"Alric has led men into battle, and when I say *led*, I mean it. He personally charged the gates of Medford under a hail of arrows ahead of everyone, even his bodyguards."

"Exactly, the man is a fool."

"All right, it might not have been the smartest choice, but it did show courage and an unwillingness to sit back in safety while sending others into peril. That right there gives him credit in my book. But okay, I see your point. He might not be the smartest leader. So if you want someone with brains and merit, then Princess Arista is your clear choice."

Degan chuckled, apparently taking his comments as a joke. When he saw Hadrian's scowl, he stopped. "You're not serious? She's a woman—an irritating, manipulative, bossy woman. She shouldn't even be on this trip. She's got Alric wrapped around her finger and it will get us all killed. Did you know she tried to free me from that dungeon all by herself? She failed miserably, got herself captured and her bodyguard killed. That's what she does, you know. She gets people killed. She's a menace. And on top of that she's also a wit—"

Degan struck the wall with the back of his head, bounced off, and fell to his knees. Hadrian felt the pain in his knuckles and only then realized he had hit him.

Gaunt glared up, his eyes watering, his hands cupping his face. "Crazy fool! Are you mad?"

"What's going on?" Arista called back down the line.

"This idiot just punched me in the face! My nose is bleeding!"

"*Hadrian* did?" the princess said, stunned.

"It was…an accident," Hadrian replied, knowing it sounded

feeble, but not knowing how else to describe his actions. He had not meant to hit Gaunt; it had just happened.

"You *accidentally* punched him?" Wyatt asked, suppressing a chuckle. "I'm not sure you have a full understanding of the whole bodyguard thing."

"Hadrian!" Royce called.

"What?" he shouted back, irritated that even Royce was going to join in this embarrassing moment.

"Come up here. I need you to look at something."

Degan was still on his knees in a pool of water. "Um— sorry 'bout that."

"Get away from me!"

Hadrian moved up the line as Wyatt, Elden, and Myron pressed themselves against the walls to let him pass, each one looking at him curiously.

"What did he do?" Arista whispered as he reached her.

"Nothing, really."

Her eyebrows rose. "You punched him for no reason?"

"Well, no, but—it's complicated. I'm not even sure I understand it. It was sort of like a reflex, I guess."

"A...reflex?" she said.

"I told him I was sorry."

"Anytime today would be nice," Royce said.

Arista stepped aside, looking at him suspiciously as he passed.

"What was all that about?" Alric asked as he approached.

"I, ah—I punched Gaunt in the face."

"Good for you," Alric told him.

"About time someone did," Mauvin said. "I'm just sorry you beat me to it."

"What do you make of this?" Royce asked, still on his knees and pointing to something on the ground beside his lantern.

Hadrian bent down. It was a leather string with a series of stone beads, feathers, and what looked like chicken bones threaded through it.

"It's a Trajan ankle bracelet," he told them. "Worn for luck by warriors of the Ankor tribe of the Ghazel."

"The ends aren't torn," Royce said. "But look how they are bent and twisted. I think it just came untied. And it is partially buried under the dirt, so I am thinking it's been here awhile. Regardless, we are in their neighborhood, so we'd better start moving a bit more cautiously. See if you can keep the chatter down to a minimum."

Hadrian looked at the bracelet and caught Royce by the arm as he was about to move forward again.

"Here," he said, keeping his body positioned to block the view of the rest of the party. He placed Alverstone into Royce's hand.

"I was wondering where that went."

"Time to re-claw the cat, I think," Hadrian said. "Just be a good boy, okay?"

"Look who's talking."

The party moved forward again. Hadrian did not return to the rear. He thought it was more likely they would encounter Ghazel from the front, and he also did not relish the idea of returning to Gaunt.

The corridor widened until they could walk three abreast. Then abruptly the passageway ended. It stopped in a small room where the far side narrowed to no more than a crack. In the center was nothing more than a sizable pile of rocks.

Gaunt shook his head in disgust. "I told you he was incompetent," he said, pointing at Alric. "He was so sure this was the right passage, and here we are days later standing at a dead end."

"You said *I* was incompetent?" the king asked, then looked to Hadrian. "No wonder you hit him. Thanks."

"What about us?" Gaunt asked. "How many days of food do we have? How much time have we wasted? We've been down here—what? Three days now? And it took us two days from Aquesta. That's five days. Add five days to get back and even if we were to leave right now, we will have been gone ten days! How long do you think we have until the elves reach Aquesta? Two weeks? We'll blow most of that time just retracing our steps."

"I did not hear you suggesting a different choice," Arista said. "Alric picked as best he could and I don't think anyone here could have chosen any better."

"How surprising—*his sister* is defending him."

Mauvin stepped toward Gaunt and drew his blade. The sword picked up the light from the lanterns on its mirrored surface and flashed as Mauvin raised the point to Gaunt's neck. "I warned you before. Do not speak of my king without respect in my presence."

"Mauvin, stop!" Arista ordered.

"I'm not going to kill him," he assured her. "I'll just carve my initials in his face."

"Alric." She turned to her brother. "Tell him to stop."

"I'm not certain I should."

"See! This is the oppression I spoke of!" Gaunt shouted. "The evils of a hereditary authority."

"Somebody shut him up," Royce snapped.

"Mauvin," Hadrian said.

"What?" Mauvin looked at him, confused. "You punched him!"

"Yeah, well—that was then."

"Lower your blade, Mauvin," Alric said, relenting. "My honor can wait until we are through with this."

Mauvin sheathed his weapon and Gaunt pushed himself

away from the wall, breathing heavily. "Threatening me doesn't change the situation. We are still at a dead end and it is—"

"It's not a dead end," Magnus stated. He stomped his boot twice, got to his knees, and placed his ear to the ground. Then he looked up and glared at the pile of rocks. He got back to his feet and began throwing the rocks aside. Beneath were several pieces of wooden planking and, below them, a hole.

"That was hidden on purpose," Wyatt said.

"This doesn't mean we are in the right passage," Gaunt argued. "I don't remember the monk ever saying anything about going in a hole. There's no way to tell this is the right way."

"It is," Myron replied.

Gaunt turned on the little monk. "Oh, so you're keeping information from us, is that it? Or are you merely incompetent and just forgot to tell us about this part of the journal?"

"No," he said meekly. "There's nothing in the journal about this."

"Then surely you are more pious than I thought, for Maribor himself must be giving you information he keeps from the rest of us."

"Maybe," Myron replied. "All I know is that's Edmund Hall's mark." He pointed. "See there, carved into the stone."

Royce was first to it and, holding his light above the floor, revealed the etched inscription:

$$\boxed{F\!H}$$

"E.H.," Gaunt read. "How do we know that stands for Edmund Hall?"

"You think there's a parade of people coming through here with those initials, do you?" Royce asked.

"That's the exact way he wrote his initials in the journal," Myron explained.

"What about these, Myron?" Royce asked as he pushed more rocks away to reveal more etchings. These were much brighter—fresher than the *EH*.

Myron glanced at them for only a moment before saying, "I don't know anything about those."

Hadrian stepped up, blew the dirt away. Then he turned to Arista and Alric. "Didn't the Patriarch say he sent other teams?"

"Yes, he did," Alric agreed. "Three of them, I think."

"According to the empress, they all failed," Arista added.

Hadrian glanced at Royce. "I think we know about the third group he sent, but they didn't come this way. Still, I'm guessing these are the initials of either the first or the second team." He looked at Royce again. "If you were going to hand-pick a group to come down here, and you could choose any-one, who would you pick to lead such a group?"

"Breckton, maybe," Royce replied. "Or possibly Gravin Dent of Delgos."

"Well, we know they didn't pick Breckton, and look at the first initials, GD. Now when was the last time anyone saw Gravin? He wasn't at the Wintertide games this year."

"Not last year either," Alric said.

"He was at Dahlgren," Mauvin said.

"Yes, he was!" Arista confirmed. "I remember Fanen point-ing him out and saying what a great adventurer he was and how he worked mainly for the Church of Nyphron. He called him something…a—a—"

"Quester?" Mauvin asked.

"Yes, that's it!"

"Now let's think about that," Hadrian said. "They would need a scholar, a historian. Dent was at Dahlgren. Wasn't there someone else too? That funny guy with the catapult, what was his name?"

"Tobis Rentinual?" Mauvin asked. "He was a real nut."

"Yeah, but do you remember him saying something about how he named the catapult after Novron's wife, because of all the research he did into ancient imperial history?"

"Yes. He said something about having to learn a language or something, didn't he? He was all boastful about it, remember?"

"That's right." Hadrian was nodding. "Look at that second set of initials, TR."

"Tobis Rentinual," Mauvin said. "It even looks like how he would draw his letters."

"What about the others?" Alric asked.

Hadrian shrugged. "I'm really only guessing at the first two. I have no idea about the others."

"I do," Magnus said. "Well, one of them, at least. HM, that's Herclor Math."

"Who?" Hadrian asked, and looked around, but everyone shrugged.

"Of course none of you would know him. He's a mason—a *dwarf* mason—and a good one. I would recognize his inscription anywhere. The Maths are an old family. A Math even worked on the design team of Drumindor. His clan goes back a long way."

"Why did they initial the stone?" Wyatt asked.

"Maybe to let anyone who might follow know they got this far," Magnus replied.

"Why didn't they mark the bloody three-choice passage?" Mauvin asked.

"Maybe they planned to," Arista said. "Maybe—like us—they didn't know if they picked the right one, but planned to mark it on the way out, only—only they never came out."

"Maybe we should carve our initials too," Mauvin suggested. "So others will know we were here."

"No," Arista said. "If we don't come back out, there will be no others to follow us."

Each of them looked toward the hole with apprehension.

"At any rate," Royce said, "this looks like the place. Who's carrying the rope?"

They tied three lengths of rope together, and with Hadrian on the line, Royce climbed in. They fed out two-thirds of it before Hadrian felt the line stop and Royce's weight come off.

He waited.

They all waited. Some sat down on whatever flat spots they could find. Elden remained standing. He had an unpleasant look on his face as he eyed the hole. Despite Arista's comments, the dwarf busied himself carving each of their initials into the stone.

"You want to call down to him?" Alric asked. "He's been in there a while."

"It's better to be patient," he replied. "Royce will either call up or yank on the line when he wants us to come down."

"What if he fell?" Mauvin asked.

"He didn't. On the other hand, what is more likely is that there's a patrol of Ghazel and he's waiting for them to pass. If you get nervous and start yelling down, you'll get him killed, or angry. Either way it's not a good idea."

Mauvin and Alric both nodded gravely. Hadrian had learned his lesson the hard way on that first trip the two made to Ervanon. Learning to trust Royce when it was dark, you were alone, and the world was so quiet you could hear your own breathing was not something you did overnight.

Hadrian remembered the wind whipping them as they climbed the Crown Tower. *That* was a *big* tower. He must have climbed a hundred of them with Royce since, but aside from Drumindor, that was the tallest—and the first. He had marveled at how the little thief could scale the sheer wall like a fly with nothing but those hand-claws. He gave Hadrian a pair and sat smirking as he tried to use them.

"Hopeless," was all he said, taking the claws back. "Can you at least climb a rope?"

Hadrian had just returned from his days in the arenas of Calis, where he had been respected and cheered by roaring crowds as the Tiger of Mandalin. He was less than pleased with this little twig of a man treating him as if he were the village idiot. So infuriated had he been by Royce's smug tone that Hadrian had wanted to beat him unconscious, only Arcadius had warned him to be patient. "He's like the pup of a renowned hunting dog who's been beaten badly by every master he's had," the old wizard had told him. "He's a gem worthy of a little work, but he'll test you—he'll test you a lot. Royce doesn't make friends easily and he doesn't make it easy to be his friend. Don't get angry. That's what he's looking for. That's what he expects. He'll try to drive you away, but you'll fool him. Listen to him. Trust him. That's what he won't expect. It won't be easy. You'll have to be very patient. But if you do, you'll make a friend for life, the kind that will walk unarmed into the jaws of a dragon if you ask him to."

Hadrian felt a light tug on the rope.

"Everything okay, pal?" he called down softly.

"Found it," Royce replied. "Come on down."

It was like a mine shaft, tight and deep. Hadrian had descended only a short distance when his eyes detected a faint light below. The pale blue-green light appeared to leak into the base of the shaft, which, he could now estimate, was no more than a hundred feet deep. As he reached the bottom, he felt a strong breeze and heard a sound. A very out-of-place sound—the crash of waves.

He stood in an enormous cavern so vast he could not see the far wall. At his feet were shells and black sand, and before him lay a great body of water with waves that rolled in white and frothy. Along the beach, he spotted clumps of seaweed and algae that glowed bright green and the ocean gave off an emerald light, which the ceiling reflected in such a way as to make it seem like they were not underground at all. He felt like he was standing on the beach at night under a cloudy, albeit green, sky. His nose filled with the pungent scent of salt, fish, and seaweed. To the right lay nothing but endless water, but straight out, just visible at the horizon, were structures—the outlines of buildings, pillars, towers, and walls.

Across the sea lay the city of Percepliquis.

Royce stood on the shore, staring across the water, and glanced over his shoulder when Hadrian touched down. "Not something you see every day, is it?"

"Wow," he replied.

It did not take long before all of them stood on the black sand, gazing out at the sea and the city beyond. Myron looked as if he were in shock. Hadrian realized the monk had never seen an ocean, much less one that glowed bright green.

"Edmund Hall mentioned an underground sea," Myron said at length. "But Mr. Hall is not terribly good at descriptions. This—*this* is truly amazing. I've never thought of myself as big in any sense, but standing here, I feel as small as a pebble."

"Anyone lose an ocean? 'Cause I think we just found it," Mauvin announced.

"It's beautiful," Arista said.

"Whoa," Wyatt muttered.

"How are we going to get across it?" Gaunt asked.

They all looked to Myron. "Oh, right—sorry. Edmund Hall made a raft from stuff he found washed up on the beach.

He said there was a lot of it. He lashed planking with a rope he had with him and formed a rudder out of one side of an old crate. His sail was a patchwork of sewn bags, his mast a tall log of driftwood."

"How long did it take him?" Gaunt asked.

"Three weeks."

"By Mar!" he exclaimed.

Alric scowled at him. "There's ten of us and we have an expert sailor and better gear. Let's get looking for our raw material."

They all spread out like a group of beachcombers looking for shells and starfish on a lovely summer's day.

There was a good deal of debris on the shore. Old bottles and broken crates, poles and nets, all amazingly well preserved after having been down there for a thousand years. Hadrian picked up a jug with writing on one side. He carefully turned it over, realizing he was holding an artifact that by its mere age was profoundly valuable. He did not expect to be able to read it. Everything from the ancient time of Percepliquis would be in Old Speech. He looked at the markings and was stunned to find he could understand them: BRIG'S RUM DISTILLERY. DAGASTAN, CALIS.

He blinked.

"Where's Myron?" It was not so much the question as the voice that pulled Hadrian's attention away from the jug.

Elden had spoken. The big man stood like a wave break on the sand, his head twisting around, searching. "I don't see him."

Hadrian glanced up and down the beach. Elden was right—the monk was gone.

"I'll find him," Royce said, annoyed, and trotted off.

"Elden?" Wyatt called. "Can you give me a hand here?" he said, trying to pull up a large weathered plank mostly buried in the sand. "We can use this as the keel, I think."

Alric and Mauvin were dragging over what looked like the side of a wooden crate. "There's another side to this back there among those rocks," the king informed Wyatt.

"That's great, but right now can the two of you help us dig this beam out?"

Gaunt wandered the beach halfheartedly, kicking over rocks, as if he might find a mast hiding under one. Magnus noticeably avoided the water, sticking to the high beach area and glancing over his shoulder at the waves as if they were barking dogs he needed to constantly assure himself were chained.

Arista came running down to where the four dug the beam out of the sand. "I found a huge piece of canvas!" she said, and did a little dance.

Hadrian noticed her feet were bare. She held her shoes in her hands, swinging them by the heels, her robe swaying. As he looked at her just then, she could have been any number of girls he had known from taverns or small towns—not a princess at all.

"Don't you like my celebratory dance?" she asked him.

"Is that what that is?"

She rolled her eyes. "Com'on and help me get the canvas. It will make the perfect sail."

She ran back down the beach and Hadrian followed. She stopped and, bending down, pulled on the corner of a buried piece of canvas. "We'll have to dig it out, but I bet it is big. I think—" She stopped when she spotted Royce and Myron walking toward them.

"There you are," Hadrian said in a reprimanding tone. "You had Elden worried, young man."

"I saw a crab," Myron said, embarrassed. "They have these huge claws and run sideways—they scurry very fast—like big spiders. I chased him down the beach, but he disappeared into a hole before I could get a good look. Have you ever seen a crab?"

"Yes, Myron. I've seen crabs before."

"Oh, so you know how fascinating they are! I was literally carried away—well, not literally. I mean, I wasn't actually *carried* by the crab; *lured* is more accurate."

"Royce, look at the canvas I found!" Arista said, repeating her little dance for him.

"Very nice," the thief replied.

"You don't seem suitably impressed. It's going to be our sail," she told him proudly. "Maybe we should have a contest for the person who finds the best part of the raft." She followed this with a greedy grin.

"We could do that." Royce nodded. "But I don't think you'll win."

"No? Did you find something better?"

"Myron did."

"Better than the crab?" Hadrian asked.

"You could say that." Royce motioned for them to follow.

They walked around an arm of the cliff wall that jutted into the sea, causing them all to wade up to their ankles for a short bit. On the far side, resting on the sand about a half mile down the beach, was a small single-mast boat that listed off the keel. Its pair of black sails dangled from the yards, feebly flapping in the sea breeze.

"By Mar!" Hadrian and Arista said together.

꒰ꜱ

A loose board on the boat's deck creaked under Hadrian's weight and Royce glared at him. Twelve years they had worked together, and still Royce did not seem capable of understanding that Hadrian could not float. The problem was that Royce apparently could. He made it look so easy. Hadrian walked like the caricature of a thief—on his toes, his arms out for balance, wavering up and down as if he were on a tightrope. Royce walked as casually as if he were sauntering down a city street. They communicated as they always did on the job, with facial expressions and hand gestures. Royce had learned sign language as part of his guild training but had never bothered teaching Hadrian more than a few signals. Royce was always able to communicate what he needed by pointing, counting with his fingers, or making simple obvious signs like scissoring his fingers across his level palm, imitating legs walking on a floor. He expressed most of his silent dialogue the way he was now: through rolled eyes, glares, and the pitiable shaking of his head. Given how irritated he so often looked, it was a mystery why he put up with Hadrian. After the first trip to the Crown Tower, both were convinced Arcadius was insane in paring them. Royce hated him and the feeling was mutual. Just as Royce recently confirmed, the only reason they had gone back together was out of spite—their shared dislike compelled them. Royce wanted to see Hadrian give up, or die, and Hadrian refused to give him the satisfaction of either. Of course, what ended up happening was something neither of them expected—they were caught.

Royce held a hand out palm up, and Hadrian stopped moving, freezing in place as if he were playing a kid's game. He could see Royce tilting his head like a dog trying to listen. He shook his head and motioned for him to follow again.

The two had left the rest of the party on the beach, safely back near where Arista had found the canvas, as they scouted the ship. It looked abandoned, but Royce refused to take chances. What they found on deck only further suggested it was deserted. The wood was rough and weathering badly, paint was peeling, and crabs scurried about as if they had lived there for some time. The bow plaque indicated the name: *Harbinger*. Still, one last mystery needed investigation. The little ship was tiny compared to the *Emerald Storm*, just large enough to support a below-deck cabin, and they needed to see what was inside.

The door lay closed and Royce inched up on it as if it were a viper ready to strike. When he reached the cabin, he glanced back at Hadrian, who drew his swords. Royce carefully twisted the latch. The corroded metal stuck and he struggled to free it. Then the door fell inward with a creek and banged against the inner wall. Hadrian rushed forward just in case. He fully expected the cabin to be empty, but to his surprise, the faint light falling through the doorway revealed a man.

He lay on a small bed within the small cabin. He was dead, his face rotted, the eyes and lips gone and most of the flesh eaten, perhaps by the crabs. Hadrian guessed the man had died not too long ago, less than a year certainly, perhaps only six months. He wore sailors' clothes and around his neck was a white kerchief.

Hadrian whispered, "My god, is that…"

Royce nodded. "It's Bernie."

Hadrian remembered Bernie as the wiry topman from the *Emerald Storm*. He along with Staul—whom Royce had killed—Dr. Levy, and the historian Antun Bulard had worked for Sentinel Thranic. They were the third and final team the Patriarch had sent in to obtain the horn. The last Hadrian had seen of them was in the dungeons beneath the Palace of the Four Winds.

"This looks like blood on the bed and floor," Royce said.

"I'll take your word for it—I just see a shadow—but what's that around his belly?"

"Linen—bloodstained. Looks like he died from a stab

wound to the stomach, but it was slow." Royce climbed out of the cabin and looked around the ship, bending down to study the decking and the lines.

"What are you looking for?"

"Blood," he replied. "There's blood all over the place, spots on the deck, handprints on the ropes, and on the wheel. I think he set sail wounded."

"He could have been attacked on board."

"Maybe, but I doubt it. He looks to have initially survived whatever fight gave him the wound, that means the other guy must have been hurt worse, only there's no other body."

"Might have dumped it in the sea."

"Mighta, but there would still be signs of a fight and blood—a lot of blood—somewhere. All I see are dribbles and drips. No, I think he was wounded, got the boat rigged, and set sail..." Royce ran to the wheel, then the stern. "Yep, rudder is tied. He set the ship, tied the rudder; then, feeling weak, he lay down below, where he slowly bled to death."

"So who knifed him?"

Royce shrugged. "Ghazel?"

Hadrian shook his head. "It's been—what? Three, four months? You saw that bracelet back there. The Ghazel have passed by here. They've seen this ship but haven't touched it. If they killed him, they would have taken it. No, Thranic had a deal with the Ghazel, remember? He said something about a guide and safe passage."

"So Merrick or the Patriarch managed to cut a deal with the Ghazel, letting them come in here?"

"Seems to be the case."

Hadrian waved to the others and dropped a rope ladder over the side.

"All safe and sound, I trust?" Alric asked, coming aboard.

"Safe," Hadrian said. "As for sound, I defer to our resident expert in the ways of seafaring."

Wyatt stood in the middle of the ship and slammed his feet down on the wood of the deck. He then grabbed a rope and climbed up to the masthead, inspecting the lines and the canvas. Lastly, he went below. When he returned, he said, "A little worn and neglected, but she's a fine ship as far as Tenkin doggers go."

"Tenkin?" Mauvin asked.

Wyatt nodded. "And that's Bernie in the cabin, right?"

"Pretty sure," Hadrian replied.

"Then that means this isn't just some underground salt lake."

"What do you mean?"

"This boat sailed here from the Palace of the Four Winds. This must open out to the Goblin Sea—some cove the Ba Ran Ghazel discovered that goes underground and is navigable all the way under Alburn to here."

"That's how the Ghazel have been getting in and managing to send scouting parties around Amberton Lee," Hadrian said.

"As nice as all that is," Alric began, "how are we going to get this ship into the water?"

"We aren't," Wyatt told him. "It will do that all by itself, in about six hours."

"Huh?"

"This ship is just going to jump in the water in six hours?" Mauvin asked incredulously.

"He's talking about the tide," Arista said.

"It's low tide right now, or near it. I'm guessing at high tide the watermark will be up to the cliff's edge. There won't even be a beach here. Of course, the ship may still be touching bottom. We'll set sail and hope the wind can pull us. If not, we'll have to kedge off."

"Kedge off?" Mauvin asked, and glanced at Arista, who this time shrugged.

"You take the ship's anchor, put it on a launch, paddle it out, drop it in the water, and then with the capstan you crank and pull the ship toward the anchor. It's not a fun drill. Sometimes the anchor doesn't catch, and sometimes it catches too well. Either way, turning the capstan is never pleasant. All I can say is thank Maribor we have Elden.

"Of course, a ship this size doesn't have a launch, so we'll need to make something to float the anchor out with. Since we have six hours to kill, we might as well do that. I'll need Royce, Hadrian, and Elden to help me set the ship in order, so could His Majesty grab a few of the remaining people and make a raft?"

"Consider it done, Captain," Alric told him.

"We should also dispose of old Bernie, I'm afraid," Wyatt said. "While it is tempting to just dump him in the sea, we probably should bury him."

"Don't look at me," Gaunt said. "I didn't even know the man."

"I'll do it," Myron told them. "Can someone help me get him to the beach?"

"Good, then we're all squared away," Wyatt said. "We'll set sail in six hours—hopefully."

## Chapter 13

# The Voyage of the Harbinger

The tide had come in and Arista noticed most of the shore was gone. Waves slammed against the cliff edge, hammering the wall. Seawater sluiced in and out of the shaft they had come down, making a vague sucking sound with each roll out. The ship sat upright, the deck flat, and the whole thing rocked with each new set of waves, which lifted the stern.

Myron stood on the deck of the *Harbinger*, casting his eyes upward at the sails as Royce flew about on ropes, tying off the braces. Soaked to the bone, the monk created a puddle where he stood. His frock stuck to his skin, a bit of glowing seaweed was on his shoulder, and he had black sand in his hair and on his cheeks.

"All done, then?" Hadrian asked, tying the end of one of the lines Royce had dropped to him.

Myron nodded. "Well, mostly, but I thought..." He looked up once more. "I thought Royce might be willing to say a few words, since he knew him best."

"Royce is a bit busy," Hadrian replied.

Myron's shoulders slumped.

"How about if I come? I knew him too."

"Can I come?" Arista asked. She had been on deck coiling ropes and generally clearing the clutter. No one had asked her to. No one had asked her to do anything. Women were unexpected on board a ship and she did not think Wyatt knew what to do with her. She had tried helping Alric with building the raft for the anchor, but that had gone badly. Her brother noticeably winced each time she suggested something to Mauvin, Degan, or Magnus. After only an hour, she excused herself, saying she was not feeling well, and returned to the ship. She hoped Wyatt would have some use for her, but he only smiled and nodded politely as he passed.

"Of course," Myron said eagerly, a smile brightening his face.

Arista jumped to her feet, feeling oddly relieved. Somehow she had expected Myron would exclude her as well. She regretted volunteering, as getting off the ship required wading in chest-deep water. It was very cold and took her breath away. Her robe billowed around her as she struggled to find traction in the ground below.

A strong wave struck her from behind and she started to fall face forward. Hadrian caught her by the elbow and held her up.

"Thank you. I thought I was going for a swim there," she told him.

"Bad form on the wave's part, sneaking up and attacking you from the back like that."

"Not very chivalrous, was it?"

"Not at all—I'd complain."

Myron moved ahead of them, splashing his way to a high point where the water was only a few inches deep. "He's under here—at least, he used to be." Myron looked about, concerned.

"I'm sure he still is," Hadrian said.

"We'd best get started before he slips away," Arista said as a wave's retreat sucked her feet into the sand. "You start us off, Myron."

"Dear Maribor, our eternal father, we are gathered here to say farewell to our brother Bernie. That's his name, right?" Myron whispered.

Hadrian nodded.

"We ask that you remember him and see that he crosses the river to the land of the dawn." He looked to Hadrian, motioning with his hand for him to speak.

"Ah…" Hadrian thought a moment. "Bernie wasn't a good man, exactly. He was a thief, and a grave robber, and he tried to knife Royce once—"

Seeing Myron's expression, Arista nudged Hadrian.

"But, um…he didn't actually ever try to kill any of us. He was just doing his job, I guess. I suppose he was pretty good at it." Hadrian stopped there, looking awkward.

"Would *you* like to say something?" Myron asked Arista.

"I didn't know him."

"At this point I don't think he'd mind," Myron said.

"Okay. I suppose." She thought a second, then said, "Although none of us knew him well, I am certain Mr. Bernie had virtues as well as shortcomings, like any of us. He likely helped people, or showed courage in the face of adversity when others might not. He must have had some good in him; otherwise Maribor would not have sent one of his most compassionate and thoughtful servants here to ensure he had a proper passing."

"Wow, that was much better than mine," Hadrian whispered.

"Shh," Arista said.

"And so, Lord," Myron concluded with a bowed head, "we say farewell to Bernie. May the light of a new dawn rise upon his soul." Then in a light voice Myron sang:

*Unto Maribor, I beseech thee*
*Into the hands of god, I send thee*
*Grant him peace, I beg thee*
*Give him rest, I ask thee*
*May the god of men watch over your journey.*

"Is that it?" Hadrian asked.

"That's it," Myron replied. "Thank you both for coming and standing in the cold water."

"Let's get back. My feet are going numb," Arista said, hopping through the surf.

"Your Highness?" Myron asked, chasing her. "I can't help but ask. Who is the servant of Maribor you were speaking of?"

She looked at him, surprised. "You, of course."

"Oh."

When they got back, Alric and the rest were tying up their makeshift raft to the side of the *Harbinger.* Arista was impressed. The raft was eight feet square, lashed tight and caulked with pitch.

On board, Wyatt and Elden were pushing everything that could be moved from the bow to the stern. The back of the ship began to rock in earnest, making it hard to stand.

Once everyone was on board, Wyatt looked up as if to the heavens and shouted, "Loose the tops'l!"

She gasped as Royce pulled a line, then without hesitation ran across the yard to the far side and pulled another. The topsail fell open and Royce dropped to the masthead and, running along the top of the mainsail yard, tied off the sheets.

"Loose the mains'l!" Wyatt shouted, and Royce released the big sail. "Hands to the sheets!"

Hadrian and Elden, on opposite sides of the ship, pulled ropes connected to the lower corners of the sail, stretching it out taut.

"Hands to the braces! Back all sails!"

Elden and Hadrian grabbed hold of ropes attached to the ends of the yards and pulled, twisting them around so that they caught the wind on an angle, pushing the ship backward toward the sea. They looked to Wyatt, who waved them over until they had the right angle; then they tied off the braces.

"Everyone to the stern!" Wyatt called, and each of them moved to the back of the ship. The wind and the waves rocked them, and at times it seemed they were lifting, but the ship failed to move.

"The keel's dug in," Wyatt said, then sighed. "We'll need to kedge off. Elden and Hadrian, hoist the anchor to the raft and lash it tight. Alric—forgive me, Your Majesty, but I need to use you like a deckhand and will be dispensing with formalities. I hope you understand. Please take Mauvin and launch the raft as soon as the anchor is on it. Now this is what you must remember: paddle out *directly* behind the ship. Any angle will reduce our traction. We want to pull the ship in perfect line with the keel. When you are out so far that the chain is fully extended, drop the anchor, then return to the ship as fast as you can."

Alric nodded, and with Mauvin following, they climbed over the side of the ship. Using the pulleys attached to the main yard, Hadrian and Elden hoisted the anchor out over the raft, which bobbed and bucked in the surf. Alric and Mauvin straddled it, tying the anchor fast to the deck; both were sprayed and soaked by crashing waves. Hadrian handed paddles down, and with one on each side, the two worked to push the weighted craft out over the swells.

The chain played out through Wyatt's own hands as he stood at the stern, carefully watching their progress. Alric and Mauvin appeared like two rats on a barrel lid when the chain went taut. Arista saw the flash of Mauvin's blade, and the anchor went into the water, nearly flipping the raft.

"Hands to the capstan!" Wyatt called. "That's everyone—except, of course, you, Your Highness."

Arista sighed but was just as happy to stand at the stern rail and watch Alric and Mauvin, who were paddling back. They were moving much faster now that they had the swells pushing them.

In the center of the ship, poles were passed through the holes in the big wheel and everyone put their weight into pushing the capstan around. Arista could hear the rapid *clank*, *clank*, *clank* of the pawls as they took up the slack. Then the sound grew slower, the time between the clanks longer.

Everyone aside from her, including Wyatt, heaved on the capstan. Each pole had two people on it except for Elden's. The giant commanded his own pole and his face was turning red from the strain. Arista heard a fearful creaking as the anchor and the ship fought each other.

"Show us the waves, Arista!" Wyatt called to her. "Put your arms up and drop them just before a wave is about to hit the ship!"

She nodded and looked out to sea. Alric and Mauvin were already coming alongside. She looked at the swells. They were in a lull, but she could see three humps in the distance rolling toward them like the slithering backs of serpents.

"It will be a minute," she shouted back.

"Everyone rest," Wyatt told them. "When you see her drop her arms, really put your back into it."

Mauvin and Alric scrambled over the side, soaked and exhausted. They flung themselves down on the deck.

"No time to rest!" Wyatt shouted at them. "Find a spot on the poles."

The swells were nearing and Arista raised her arms. "Get ready!"

They all braced themselves and took deep breaths.

The first swell rushed in and Arista dropped her arms, but she did so too late.

They heaved. There was a grinding sensation; then it stopped and the men fell, exhausted, hanging from the poles.

"I timed it wrong," Arista shouted. "I was too late. Here comes another." She raised her arms and they all braced again, with Mauvin and Alric finding places at the poles.

Arista watched the swell rushing at her. This time she lowered her arms while the wave was still a few feet away. By the time the men heaved, the rear of the ship was rising. There were a noticeable lurch and more grinding. This time she heard the sound of wood scraping and felt movement.

"One more!" she shouted, raising her arms and then dropping them almost as soon as they were up.

Once more the men pushed, the chain tightened, and the boat rose. This time a gust of wind managed to catch the topsail and the ship lurched dramatically. The bottom scraped and broke out of the sludge. They rocked smooth and free, drifting backward.

A cheer rose and everyone was grinning. Wyatt ran back to the stern beside Arista and grabbed hold of the wheel. "That was lucky," he said, sweat dripping from his forehead. "Great job, by the way."

"Thanks."

"Keep cranking! Let's see if we can save the anchor."

The men pushed the capstan around easily now. They quickly covered the distance Alric and Mauvin had paddled and passed it. Arista watched the cable swing down beneath them. There was a sudden lurch that staggered her; then she heard the rapid clanking of the pawls as the anchor came in.

"Man the braces!" Wyatt shouted. "Stand by to come about!"

Wyatt looked out at the swells and gave the wheel a hard

spin. The ship turned. "Swing round the yards—starboard tack!"

Everyone else cleared out of the way as Hadrian, Elden, and Royce went to work twisting the yards and tying off. The ship turned its nose out to sea and the wind filled the sails, pushing it over to one side. "Tacks and sheets, catch that wind!"

Arista grabbed hold of the rail, frightened at the sudden speed the ship acquired and the disturbing tilt of the deck. Concerned that they were about to capsize, she watched apprehensively as the mast leaned and the ship rode on its side.

"There she goes!" Wyatt exclaimed with a great smile on his lips. "Fly, *Harbinger*, fly!" As if the ship heard him, the bow broke through a crest, dove forward, and hurdled the surface until it splashed down with a burst of spray. "Atta girl!"

❧

Arista carried the hot cup with difficulty. She held it with both hands, but the deck refused to stay in one place for long and caused her to stagger. She approached Myron, who sat shivering with his back against the base of the mast.

"Here," she said, kneeling down and holding out the steaming cup.

"For me?" he asked, and she nodded. He took the cup and sniffed. "It's tea?" he said as if the drink were some kind of miracle. "It's hot tea."

"You seemed like you could use something warm to drink."

Myron looked at her with an expression of such gratefulness she thought for a moment that he might cry. "I—I don't know what to say."

"It's just tea, Myron. It wasn't much work."

"You had to get the stove going, and that must have been difficult. I wouldn't know how to do that on board a ship."

"I—ah, I didn't use the stove."

"But you had to boil the water…Oh," he said, lowering his voice.

"Yeah, I used a little trick." She wiggled her fingers.

He looked back down at the cup.

"If you don't want it, that's okay. I just thought—"

He lifted the cup and took a noisy sip. "It's wonderful. Created by magic and made for me by a royal princess. This is the best tea I've ever had. Thank you."

She laughed a bit and sat down before the lurching of the ship knocked her over. "Lately, I sometimes forget I am a princess. I haven't thought of myself that way for a really long time."

"Still, it is astoundingly thoughtful."

"It's what I can do," she said. "I feel useless lately. The least I can do is cook. Problem is, I really don't know how. But I can boil water like nobody's business. I'd like to make a cup for Royce. Hadrian says he gets seasick and I always thought tea soothed the stomach, but he's up in the rigging. Still, at the rate we're traveling I don't think it will be much longer before we land."

Myron tilted the cup to his lips and sipped. "It tastes wonderful. You did an excellent job."

She smirked at him. "You'd say that even if it was awful. I get the impression I could serve you dishwater and you'd act perfectly happy."

He nodded. "That is true, only I wouldn't be acting."

She opened her mouth to protest, then stopped. "You really mean that, don't you?"

He nodded and took another sip.

"It doesn't take much to please you, does it, Myron?"

"Antun Bulard once wrote 'When you expect nothing from the world—not the light of the sun, the wet of water, nor the air to breathe—everything is a wonder and every moment a gift.'"

"And you expect nothing from the world?"

He looked at her, puzzled. "I'm a monk."

She smiled and nodded. "You need to teach me to be a monk. I expect too much. I want too much…things I can't have."

"Desire can be painful, but so can regret."

"*That* is the one thing I have too much of."

"Sail!" Royce shouted from somewhere above them.

"Where?" Wyatt called from the wheel.

"Off the starboard bow, you'll be able to see it in another minute."

Arista and Myron got to their feet and moved to the rail. The dark prow of the *Harbinger* cut a white slice through the luminous green waves. Ahead, the city was much closer. Arista could see some detail in the buildings—windows, doorways, stairs, and domes.

"Which side is the starboard side?" she asked.

"The right side," Myron told her. "*Starboard* is derived from what they used to call the rudder—the sterobord—which was always on the right side of a ship, because most people are right handed. As a result, when docking, the one steering a ship always pulled up placing the opposite side of the ship next to the pier so it didn't interfere with his paddling, or the rudder. And of course that side, the left side, was the *port* side. Or so Hill McDavin explained in *Chronicles of Maritime Commerce and Trade Practices of the Kilnar Union*."

"Hadrian said you could do stuff like that—but until you see it, it's hard to believe. It's amazing that you can remember so many things."

"Everyone has talents. It's like magic, I guess."

"Yes," she said, nodding slowly. "I suppose it is."

"Look," Myron told her, pointing.

She spotted dark sails coming out of the dim light. They were far larger than their own—big sweeping triangles of black canvas with a white mark emblazoned on them. The design was a symbol of slashes that looked vaguely like a skull.

"Everyone get down!" Wyatt shouted. "Royce, tell me if they change course toward us!"

Arista and Myron lay down on the deck but continued to peer out at the approaching vessel. The hull came into view as if out of a green fog. It too was black and glistened with the ocean's spray, looking like smoked glass. With the underside reflecting the unholy glow of the sea, the ship appeared ominous. It looked as if it were something not of their world at all.

A light flashed from the top of the masts.

"They are signaling us," Royce called down.

"Damn," Wyatt said. "That's going to be a problem."

"She's changing course toward us."

"Hands to the braces!" Wyatt shouted as he spun the wheel and the *Harbinger* turned away from the oncoming ship. "They're onto us now."

Arista heard a faint shout across the water and she could see movement; small dark figures loped across the deck. As she saw them, a chill ran through her. Like anyone, she had heard tales of the Ba Ran Ghazel—the sea goblins. They were the stuff of legends. Nora, Arista's nursemaid, had told her fairy stories at bedtime. Most often the tales were about greedy dwarves that kidnapped spoiled princesses, who were always saved by a dashing prince in the end. But sometimes, she spoke about the Ghazel. No prince ever saved a princess from them, no matter how dashing. The Ghazel were vile creatures of the dark, inhuman monsters, the children of a malevolent god. Nora's tales of the Ghazel always included villages burned, warriors killed, and children taken—not to be ransomed but to be feasted on. The Ghazel always ate their victims.

When Arista was sitting in her bed, wrapped in blankets, surrounded by pillows, and safe in the warmth and light of a crackling fireplace, Nora's tales were fun. She always imagined dwarves as nasty little men and fairies as tiny winged girls, but the Ghazel she could never conjure entirely—even in the vast imaginings of her childish mind. They were always as they appeared now: distant threatening shadows exhibiting fast jerky movements that no human could make. Nora had always begun her stories the same way: "Not all of this story is true, but enough is…" Looking out at the ship, and the dark figures on the deck, Arista wondered if Nora had realized just how true they were.

The *Harbinger* pivoted under Wyatt's deft hand, sheering away to the left. Arista and Myron lost sight of the Ghazel ship. They ran back to the stern, where Wyatt stood holding the wheel with one hand while looking back over his shoulder. The Ghazel ship had matched their tack and was coming up on their stern.

"Everyone to the lee side!"

"Oh, now which side is that?" Arista asked Myron.

"Opposite of windward, ah—right now it is the starboard side."

"What in Maribor's name is wrong with *left* and *right*?"

As soon as they reached the starboard rail, she knew why Wyatt had ordered them there. As he cranked the wheel, the wind pressed the *Harbinger's* sails and bent the ship over on its beam, forcing it dangerously close to capsizing. The starboard side rose higher and higher.

Arista wrapped her arms around the rail to keep from sliding and Myron did the same. Farther up the deck, Magnus looked terrified as he clutched the side, his feet skidding and slipping on the wet boards. If the ship had flown before, it was doing something unheard of now. They no longer dipped and rose, but like a bar of soap running across a washboard, they hammered the crests as they went. The ship felt like a stone being skipped across a lake.

"Ha-ha!" Wyatt jeered, the wind ripping the words from his mouth so that she barely heard him. "Match that with your overweight trow!"

She watched Wyatt, with his feet in place against the stock, his arms holding the wheel, hugging it to his chest like a lover, his hair blowing, the spray bathing him. He wore a grin and she was not certain whether she should be happy or concerned. The rest of them hung on in desperation as the race sent them across the luminous sea.

Arista noticed the pain in her arm lessening, the ship righting itself, their speed dropping. She glanced at Wyatt and saw a look of concern.

"They're stealing our wind," he grumbled.

"How are they doing that?" Alric asked.

"They are putting us in their wind shadow, moving their ship in line with ours, blocking it—depriving us. Hands to the braces! Starboard tack!"

The ship was nearly flat now, allowing Hadrian and Elden to run. They cast off ropes and pulled the yard around again, the big sail flapping as Wyatt turned the ship to catch the wind from the other side. Overhead, Royce moved among the top lines, working the upper sail.

"Haul those sheets in!" They caught the wind once more and the ship set off again. "All hands to port!"

Arista was ahead of him, already running across the deck to renew her grip on the rail. She knew what was coming this time and got her feet planted securely before the side of the ship rose. Beyond the stern, she could see the following ship already turning to mimic their action, the great black sails with the skull-like symbols flapping loose as they came around. They were much closer now. She could clearly see the creatures crawling across the deck, climbing ropes. Dozens of them had gathered near the bow. It frightened her to see them move. They skidded along on all fours like spiders—a shipload of huge black tarantulas—so tightly packed they climbed over each other just to move about.

The *Harbinger* skipped the waves again, racing directly at the city, but it was no use. The following ship, with its larger bank of sails, was still eating up the distance between them and moved to cut their wind again.

"Elden, Hadrian!" Wyatt called. "I will be going about, but when I do, I will then change my mind and go back to my previous tack, do you understand? The moment you get my signal, run the jib up to port."

Hadrian looked at Elden, who was nodding. "Show him, Elden. This has to go perfectly or we're dead in the water. Also, get Alric and Mauvin on the lines. More hands will make this easier. The moment we are back on tack and under way, drop the jib. Let's see how good their crew is. They have the advantage of more canvas, so let's turn that against them. With all that sail, it will take them longer to recover, and if they don't pull back in time, they will stall."

"Your Highness," he said, addressing Arista, "I will need to be facing forward to time this just right, so you need to be my eyes astern. I need you to watch the Ghazel ship and tell me the moment you see them starting to come around, got that?"

"Yes," she replied, nodding in case her feeble voice was lost in the wind.

"Then get forward and hang on."

She nodded again and began crawling to the front of the ship, moving hand over hand along the rail.

"Stand by to come about!" Wyatt shouted.

He waited. She watched as the Ghazel ship once more glided over, aligning itself, eclipsing their wind. Wyatt flexed his fingers on the wheel and took a deep breath. He even closed his eyes for a moment, perhaps saying a silent prayer; then he stiffened his back and turned the wheel hard over.

The ship sheered back to port. "Tacks and sheets!"

Elden and Hadrian went to work once more, and Mauvin and Alric followed their directions, pulling the yards round. Arista focused her gaze on the Ghazel ship behind them. She could feel the *Harbinger* shifting, sensed it slowing underneath her as it started to lose the wind.

"They're turning!" she shouted as she saw the Ghazel coming about. The tiny spiders scattered across their deck in sudden fury. They were not just trying to match their turn; they were trying to beat them to it.

Wyatt did nothing.

"They're turning," she yelled again.

"I heard you," he said. "We need to wait for them to be fully committed."

Arista gripped the rail with nervous hands, feeling the ship moving slower and slower.

"Avast!" he finally shouted. "Back all braces! Raise the jib!"

The ship still had some wind, still some forward motion to it, and when Wyatt turned the wheel, it responded. The jib out front had the angle and caught what was left of the wind, turning the bow. A wave caught them dead on and broke, washing the deck, but the ship held true. The sails caught the wind and filled. Elden hauled down the jib as once more the *Harbinger* flew.

Behind them, the Ghazel realized their mistake but were

too late. They tried to mimic the turn and she watched as their sails went slack.

Wyatt looked behind them. "They're lost, stalled in the eye of the wind," he declared, grinning, his chest heaving with excitement. "It will take them several minutes to catch it again. By then we will—"

"Sail!" Royce shouted. "Starboard bow!"

Wyatt's grin melted as his head turned. Ahead of them appeared a ship that looked nearly identical to the one behind. It flashed a light and behind them the other Ghazel ship replied.

Wyatt looked fore and aft and she could see the story written clearly in lines of fear on his face. Through great skill, and a bit of luck, they had barely managed to avoid one ship. They would not fare well against two.

"Sail! Port bow!" Royce shouted, and she could see Wyatt visibly slump against the wheel as if struck from behind.

Wyatt lay off the wheel and let the ship slow and level off. There was no need to hasten their approach. Everyone on board looked to him.

"What now?" Alric asked, coming aft.

Wyatt did not reply. He just turned his head, looking back and forth at the ships. His forehead glistened. He bit his lip, and Arista noticed his left hand starting to shake.

"We're out of options, aren't we?" Alric asked.

"This ship doesn't even have nets to impede boarders," Wyatt replied.

"How will they attack?" Hadrian asked. "Will they board?"

"Eventually, yes, but first they will clear the deck with arrows."

"Fire?"

"No," Wyatt replied. "They have us. We're boxed in, overwhelmed. They will want the ship."

"Do we have to surrender?" Alric asked.

"Ghazel don't take prisoners," Hadrian told him. "They don't even have a word in their language for *surrender*."

"What do we do, then?" the king asked.

"We don't really have a lot of options, Your Majesty," Wyatt told him. "Those ships hold sixty, maybe as many as a hundred Ghazel each, and we don't even have a means of shooting back. Their archers will drive us into the cabin; then they will grapple on and come aboard uncontested. At that point they could lock us in and sail us to their port."

"Which they will do," Hadrian added. "Then they will drag us into a ring and…and, well, you get the idea. No sense in spoiling the surprise."

"I hate ships!" Magnus growled. "Infernal things. There's nowhere to go. Nowhere to hide."

"We're going to…die?" Gaunt asked, stunned. "I—I can't die. I'm going to be emperor."

"Yeah, well, we all had plans, didn't we?" Hadrian said.

"I didn't," Royce said, climbing down from the rigging. Arista noted a modest smile on his lips. "I don't think I'll be joining you in the cabin. I don't mind a game of arrow dodging."

"Actually only Arista and Myron should go in the cabin," Hadrian said. "The rest of us will remain on deck. We'll need shields—anything of wood about an inch thick will do, or metal even thinner. Trilons don't have much penetration power. We can also use the mast as cover."

Arista looked out at the approaching ships, coming at angles to intercept them. The Ba Ran Ghazel were coming and there would be no rescue by a dashing prince—*the Ghazel always ate their victims.*

"Not this time," she told herself, and letting go of the rail, she walked forward. She stepped around Wyatt at the wheel and passed through the group of men in the waist.

"Arista?" Hadrian called. "You should get in the cabin."

She looked out at the water.

"Mr. Deminthal," she shouted, "take hold of that wheel. Everyone else...hang on to something."

Taking a breath, Arista calmed herself and reached out into the dark—into the energy that lay around them, above and below. She could feel the depths of the ocean, the weight of the water, the floor of the sea, the fish, the seaweed, the glowing algae. She felt the breeze and grabbed it tight.

The wind, which had been a constant presence since they had climbed out of the shaft to the beach, abruptly died. The sails drooped; the incessant quiver and clank of pulleys and ropes halted. Not a breath remained and the world became silent. Even the waves perished. The ships stopped as the sea became as tranquil as a bathtub. The silence was deafening.

Then across the water the hush was broken by Ghazel voices. She could hear them, like the barks and howls of dogs. She felt them too. She felt everything and held it all in her grip.

She raised her hand, holding her fingertips lightly.

*Fire?* she thought. She had played that note before. She knew just how to do it. But as enticing as the thought of three flaming pyres against the water was, the light would alert the shore.

*Wind?* She could sense that chord. It was powerful. She could shatter the ships. *No.* Too unwieldy, like trying to pick up a coin with mittens.

*Water? Yes!* It was everywhere. She twisted three fingers in the air and the world responded with movement.

The sea swirled.

Currents formed, churning, building, rotating, and spinning. The three Ghazel ships began to rotate, revolving as if they were toy boats in a tub she had flicked with a finger.

Whirlpools formed.

Beneath the goblin ships, circles appeared—large swirling funnels of spinning water. Faster and faster they moved, the centers giving way, dropping lower as the speed of the rotation increased. They widened, spreading out, and grew in strength. Even the *Harbinger* began to rock noticeably as the maelstroms reached out to pull on the strength of the whole sea.

The barks of the Ghazel became cries and screams as the ships continued to spin. A *crack* issued across the water as a mast snapped. Then another, and another, poles the size of tree trunks popped like twigs. The Ghazel shrieked and wailed, their voices blurring into one note, which Arista also held.

The sheer enormity of the power she worked was incredible. It was so easy and all at her command. Everything— every droplet, every breath, every heartbeat—it was all hers. She felt them, touched them, played with them. It was irresistible, like scratching a terrible itch. She let the power run. It was so big, so potent. She did not just control the power; she *was* the power, and it was her. She whirled, she frothed, and she wanted to run, to spin and grow. Like a ball sent off a hill, she felt the building momentum. It excited her and she loved the motion—the *freedom*! She felt herself letting go, giving herself to it, spreading out and becoming a part of the symphony she played—so grand—so beautiful. All she wanted was to blend with the whole, to become—

*Stop it!*

The idea was a discord. An off note. A broken thread.

*Stop it! Pull back!*

A distant voice called to her, struggling to be heard over the crescendo of the music she played.

*Regain control!*

She didn't want to listen; she didn't like the sound. It clashed with the melody.

*You're killing them!*
Of course I'm killing them. That is the whole point.
*The Ghazel are gone. That is not who you are killing! Stop!*
No. I can't.
*You can!*
I won't. I don't want to. It's too wonderful to stop, too in-credible. I have to keep going. I love it so —

⌁

Arista woke with a wrenching headache. It was so painful her eyes hurt just from opening. She was in the cabin, lying on the bed where they had found Bernie. A lantern hanging from a hook on the ceiling swayed back and forth, casting shadows that sloshed from one wall to the next.

She turned her head and pain swelled behind her eyes. "Ow," she whispered.

Arista raised a hand and found a bandage wrapped around her head. There was stiffness at the back of her head where the bandage pulled at her hair. Drawing her hand away, she found blood on her fingertips.

"Are you all right?" Myron asked. He sat beside her on a little stool and took her hand in his.

"What happened?" she asked. "My head is killing me."

"Excuse me a moment," the monk said, and opened the door to the deck. "She's awake," he called.

Immediately, Hadrian and Alric entered, ducking inside and dodging the lantern. "Are you all right?"

"Why does everyone keep asking me that? And yes, I'm fine...mostly. But my head hurts." She sat up slowly.

Hadrian looked pained. "I'm sorry about that."

She narrowed her eyes at him, which made her head hurt even more. "You hit me?"

He nodded.

"Why?"

"He had to," Alric put in, his expression grave. "You—you lost control, or something."

"What do you mean?"

Arista saw him glance toward the doorway. "What is it? What happened?"

She stood up, weaving a bit, her head still not right, and she felt tired to the point of being groggy. Hadrian extended a hand and steadied her. She ducked her head, careful to avoid banging it against the doorframe, and stepped out onto the deck.

"Oh dear Maribor!" she gasped.

The *Harbinger* was in shambles. The mast was gone; all that remained was a splintered stump. The beams of the deck were warped. One board was cracked to the point of splintering, and on the starboard side near the bow there was a gaping hole that revealed the hull below. The topsail was gone, along with the topsail yard, but the mainsail lay across the bow, torn and tattered. The railing on the port side was missing as well, sheared away.

"*I* did this?" she asked, shocked. "Oh my—is anyone…" She looked around, searching for faces—Gaunt, Magnus, Mauvin, Alric, Hadrian… "Where's Royce, Wyatt, and Elden?"

"They're okay. They're working on the ship. Everyone's okay," Alric told her. "Thanks to Hadrian. We tried talking to you, shaking you. Wyatt even poured water over your head. You just stood there mumbling and fiddling with your fingers while the ship came apart."

Mauvin was smiling at her and nodding. On his forehead a deep cut stood out, and his cheek was red and blotchy.

"Did I do that?"

"Actually a flying pulley did that. I was just too stupid to duck." He was still smiling at her, but there was something behind it—something terrible—something she had never seen on Mauvin's face before: fear—fear of her.

She sat down where she was, feeling the strength melt out of her legs. "I'm so sorry," she whispered.

"It's all right," her brother told her, again with apprehension in his voice. They made a circle around her, but no one came near.

"I'm sorry," she repeated. Her eyes filled with tears and she let them run down her cheeks. "I just wanted..." Her voice gave up on her and she began to weep.

"There's nothing to be sorry for," Hadrian said. He came forward and knelt beside her. "You saved us. The Ghazel are gone."

"Yeah," Mauvin said. "Scariest thing I've ever seen. It was like—like what they said Esrahaddon could do, only *he* never did. It was—"

"It was what we needed," Hadrian broke in over him. "If she hadn't, we'd all be dead now, and trust me, it would have been a very unpleasant death. Thank you, Your Highness."

She looked up at Hadrian. He appeared blurry through her watering eyes. He was smiling. She wiped her face and peered at him again carefully. She studied his eyes.

"What?" he asked.

"Nothing," she said.

His hand reached out and brushed her cheeks dry. "What?" he asked again.

"I—I don't want—" She hesitated and took a breath. "I just don't want people to be afraid of me."

"That arrow's already flown," Degan Gaunt said.

"Shut it, Gaunt," Alric snapped.

"Look at me," Hadrian told her, and putting his hand under her chin, he gently lifted it. He took her hands in his. "Do I look frightened?"

"No," she said. "But…maybe you should be."

"You're tired."

"I am—I'm really very tired."

"We're going to be drifting here for a bit, so why don't you lie down and get some rest? I'm sure things will look better when you wake up."

She nodded and her head felt like a boulder rocking on her shoulders.

"Com'on," he said, pulling her to her feet. She wavered and he slipped an arm around her waist and escorted her back into the cabin, where Myron had the bed ready.

"Myron will watch over you," Hadrian assured Arista as he tucked the blankets tightly around her. "Get some sleep."

"Thank you."

He brushed her wet hair from her eyes. "It's the least I can do for my hero," he said.

✧

*She walked swiftly up the Grand Mar, the broad avenue beautifully lined with flowering trees. The rose-colored petals flew and swirled, carpeting the ground, scenting the air, and creating a blizzard in spring.*

*It was festival day, and blue and green flags were everywhere. They flew over houses and waved in the hands of passersby. People clogged the streets. Wandering minstrels filled the air with music and song. Drums announced another parade, this one a procession of elephants followed by chariots, prancing horses, dancing women, and proud soldiers. Stall keepers called to the crowd, handing out cakes, nuts, confections, and fermented drinks called Trembles, made from the sweet blossoms of the trees. Young girls rushed from door to door, delivering small bouquets of flowers in the imperial colors.*

Noblemen on their chariots wore their bright-colored tunics; gold bracelets flashed in the afternoon sun. Older women stood on balconies, waving colored scarves and shouting words impossible to hear. Boys who dodged and slipped through the crowd carried baskets and sold trinkets. You could get three copper pins for three piths, or five for a keng. There was always a contest to collect the largest variety of pins before the day was out.

It was a beautiful day.

She hurried past the rivers of people into Imperial Square. To her right stood the stone rotunda of the Cenzarium and to the left the more brutish columned facade of the blocked Hall of Teshlor. Before her, at the terminus of the boulevard, rose the great golden-domed imperial palace—the seat of the emperor of the world. She walked past the Ulurium Fountain, across the Memorial Green, to the very steps of the palace— not a single guard was on duty. No one noticed. Everyone was too busy celebrating. That was part of the plan that Venlin had laid well.

She entered the marbled hall, so cool, so elegant, and scented with incense that made her think of tropical trees and mountaintops. The palace was a marvel, large, beautiful, and so sturdy it was hard to imagine what she knew was happening.

She reached the long gallery, the arcade of storied columns, each topped with three lions looking down from their noble perch at all who passed that way.

Yolric was waiting for her.

The old man leaned heavily on his staff. His long white beard was a matted mess. "So you have come," he greeted her. "But I knew you would. I knew someone would. I could have guessed it would be you."

"This is wrong. You of all people should see that!"

Yolric shook his head. "Wrong, right—these words have no meanings except in the minds of men. They are but illusions. There is only what is and what isn't, what has been and what will be."

"I am here to define that value for you."

"I know you are. I could have predicted it. My suspicions, it would seem, have weight. This is the second time now. It has taken a long time to find, but there is a pattern to the world. Wobble it and it corrects, which should be impossible; chaos should beget chaos. Order should be only one possibility and drowned by all the other permutations. But if it corrects again, if order prevails, then there can be only one answer. There is another force at work—an invisible hand—and I think I know what that force is."

"I don't have time to discuss this theory of yours again."

"Nor do I have need of you. As I said, I have finally worked it out. You see, the legends are true."

She was irritated with him; he barred her path but did not attack. He merely babbled on about unimportant theories. This was no time for metaphysical debates about the nature of existence, chaos versus order, or the values of good and evil. She needed to get by him, but Yolric was the one person she could not hope to defeat. She could not take the chance of instigating a battle if it could be avoided. "Do you side with Venlin or not?"

"Side with the Bishop? No."

She felt a massive sense of relief.

"Will you help me? Together we could stop him. Together we can save the emperor. Save the empire."

"I wouldn't need your help to do that."

"So you will let it happen?"

"Of course."

"Why?"

"I need the wobble. One does not a pattern make. I need to see if it will correct again and, perhaps, how. I must find the fingerprint, the tracks that I can trace to the source. The legends are true—I know that now, but I still want to see his face."

"I don't know what you are talking about!"

"I know you don't. You couldn't."

"Are you going to try and stop me or not?"

"The wobble, my boy. I never touch it once I have it going. You go, do what you must. I am only here now to watch. To see if I can catch a glimpse at the face behind the invisible hand."

She was confused, baffled by Yolric's unconcerned attitude, but it did not matter; what did was that he would not interfere. Her greatest obstacle was gone. Now it was just between her and Venlin.

"Goodbye, then, old master, for I fear I shall never see you again."

"No, you won't. I would wish you luck, but I do not believe it exists. Still, I suspect you have better than mere luck on your side—you have the invisible hand."

# CHAPTER 14

# THE COLD

The ceiling of the grand imperial throne room was a dome painted to mimic the sky on a gentle summer's day, and Modina still thought it beautiful. Dressed once more in her formal gown, she sat on the gaudy bird-of-prey throne with the wings, spread into a vast half circle, forming the back of the chair. The throne was mounted on a dais that had twelve steps to climb. She could not help remembering the days they had forced her to practice before it.

"Do you remember the board you ordered sewn into my dress?" she asked Nimbus, who looked suddenly uncomfortable.

"It worked," he replied.

"Who's next?"

Nimbus studied the parchment in his hands. "Bernard Green, a candlemaker from Alburn."

"Send him in, and get another log on the fire. It's freezing in here."

Unlike the great hall, the throne room was rarely used, or at least that had been the case until now. When the empress had been a mythical creature, the room had been sealed. Now that she existed in the flesh, the room was opened once more, but it always felt cold, as if it would take time to recover the warmth after those years of neglect.

Nimbus waved to the clerk, and a moment later, a short, soft-looking man entered. His eyes were small, his nose narrow and sharp. Modina immediately thought of a squirrel and recalled how she used to remember the court of Ethelred by similar associations before she learned their names.

"Your Grand Imperial Eminence," he said with a shaky voice, and bowed so low his forehead touched the floor.

They all waited. He did not move.

"Ah—please stand up," she told him. The man popped up like a child's toy, but he refused to look at her. They all did that. She found it irritating but understood it was a tradition and it would be even more unnerving for them to try to change. "Speak."

"Ah—Grand Imperial Eminence—I, ah—that is—ah—I am from Alburn, and I—am a candlemaker."

"Yes, I know that, but what is your problem?"

"Well, Your Grand Imperial Eminence, since the edict, I have moved my family here, but—you see—I have little means and no skills other than making candles, but the merchant guild refuses to grant me a license of business. I am told that I cannot have one as I am not a citizen."

"Of course," Nimbus said. "Citizenship is a prerequisite for applying to a guild and only guild members are allowed to conduct a trade within the city."

"How does one obtain citizenship?" Modina asked.

"Usually by inheritance, although it can be granted to individuals or families as recognition for some extraordinary service. Regardless, one must be a member of a guild to gain citizenship."

"But if you need to be a guild member to apply for citizenship and you need to be a citizen to be a guild member, doesn't that make it extraordinarily difficult to become a citizen?"

"I believe that is the point, Your Eminence. Cities guard against invasions from outside tradesmen that might disrupt the order of established merchants and reduce the profitability of existing businesses."

"How many citizens are there?"

"At present, I believe about ten to fifteen percent of the city's population are citizens."

"That's ridiculous."

"Yes, Your Eminence. It's also a drain on the treasury, because only citizens are required to pay taxes. Also, only citizens have the right of a trial in a court, or are required to serve to protect the city walls in the event of attack."

Modina stared at him.

"Shall I summon the city's merchant council and organize a meeting in order to review the guild policy, say, tomorrow?" Nimbus asked.

"Please do." She looked back down at Bernard Green. "Rest assured I will address this matter immediately, and thank you for bringing it to my attention."

"Bless you, Your Grand Imperial Eminence, bless you." He bowed once more with his head to the floor.

Modina waved her hand and the master-at-arms escorted him out. "I don't so much mind the bowing—that's actually nice. It's the scraping I can't stand."

"You are not just the empress," Nimbus told her. "You are a demigod. You must expect a little scraping."

"Who's next?"

"A fellow by the name of Tope Entwistle, a scout from the north," he replied.

"A scout? A scout follows the candlemaker?"

"He just has a status report—nothing urgent," Nimbus

told her. "And the candlemaker had been waiting for three days."

A stocky man entered wearing a heavy wool tunic with a little copper pin in the shape of a torch on his breast. He also sported wool pants wrapped in leather strips. His face was blotchy, his skin a ruddy leather. The tip of his nose was more than red; it was a disturbing shade of purple. His knuckles and the tips of his fingers were a similar color. He walked with an unusual gait, a hobbled limp, as if his feet were sore.

"Your Imperial Eminence." The man bowed and sniffled. "Sir Marshal Breckton sends word. He reports that there has been no confirmed movement by the elves since the initial crossing. In addition, he sends word that all bridges and roads have been closed. As for the lack of movement on the part of the elven force, it is his estimated opinion that the elves may have gone into winter quarters. He has also sent several quartermaster lists and a detailed report, which I have here in this satchel."

"You can give those to the clerk," Nimbus told him.

He slipped the satchel off and sneezed as he held out the bag.

"And how are things in Colnora?"

"Excuse me, Your Highness." He stuck a finger in his ear and wiggled it. "I've been fighting a cold for a month and my head is so clogged I can barely hear."

"I asked, how are things in Colnora?" she said louder.

"They are fine in Colnora. It's the road between that gets a tad chilly. Course I can't complain. I've been up on the line in the wilderness and there it is colder than anything. Not even a proper fire allowed, on account of not wanting to give away our positions to the elves."

"Is there anything you need?"

"Me? Oh, I don't need much. I already had me a good hot

meal and a sit near a hearth. That's all I need. Course a soft, warm place to sleep awhile before I head back would certainly be appreciated."

Modina looked at Nimbus.

"I will inform the chamberlain," he told her.

"Thank you, Your Eminence," the scout said, and bowed again before leaving.

"I never really thought about how it must be out there for them, waiting," Modina said.

"Next is Abner Gallsworth, the city administrator," Nimbus said, and a tall, thin man entered. He was the best dressed of the lot that morning, wearing long heavy robes of green and gold draped nearly to the floor. On his head was a tall hat with flaps that drooped down the sides of his head like a hound's ears. His face was long and narrow, qualities made more noticeable by the sagging of age.

"Your Imperial Eminence." He bowed, but more shallowly than anyone else so far, and there was no scraping to be seen. "While I am pleased to report that all the provisioning you have commanded has been achieved, and that the city is functioning at high efficiency, I nevertheless regret to tell you that there is a problem. We are becoming overcrowded. Refugees are still arriving from the surrounding towns and villages—even more so since the news of troops sealing the roads and passes has leaked into the countryside.

"We now have several hundred people living on the streets, and with the winter's cold, I have daily reports coming across my desk of frozen corpses in need of disposal. At present we are carting the bodies outside the walls and piling them in a fallow field to await a spring burial. This solution, however, has attracted wild animals. Packs of wolves have been reported and those still outside the city walls are complaining. I would like to request permission to dispose of the bodies at sea. To do this, I will require access to a barge. As all ships are presently under imperial edict, my request has been repeatedly denied. Hence I am here, appealing to you."

"I see," Modina said. "And what provisions have you made to prevent the future deaths of more refugees?"

"Provisions?" he asked.

"Yes, what have you done to stop the peasants from freezing to death?"

"Why…nothing. The peasants are dying because they have no shelter. They have no shelter because they cannot afford any or none can be found. I can neither create money nor construct housing. Therefore, I do not understand your question."

"You cannot commandeer ships to dispose of bodies either and yet you stand before me requesting that."

"True, but a barge is an achievable goal. Preventing future peasants from dying is not. The city has been overcrowded for weeks and yet just this morning another large group has arrived from Alburn. There are perhaps fifty families. If a viable solution is what you desire, I suggest preventing any more displaced people from entering the city. Seal it off and be done with it. Let those that come here looking for charity learn that they must provide for themselves. Allowing them entry will only cause a higher rate of mortality."

"I suspect you are right," Modina told him. "I also suspect you would feel quite differently if it was you and your family standing on the other side of our locked gate. I am the empress of all the people. It is my responsibility to keep them safe, not the other way around."

"Then please tell me what you would like me to do, for I can see no solution to this problem. There is simply no place for all these people."

Modina looked around her, at the painted dome and the great stone hearth burning the new log she had ordered.

"Chancellor?" she said.

"Yes, Your Eminence?" Nimbus replied.

"How many people could we fit in this hall?"

He raised his eyebrows in surprise, then pursed his lips. "Perhaps a hundred if they do not mind squeezing together."

"I think if faced with freezing to death, they will not mind."

"You will open the throne room to the public?" Gallsworth asked, stunned. "How will you conduct the business of the empire?"

"This *is* the business of the empire, and no, I am not going to open the throne room to the public." She looked at Nimbus. "I am opening the entire palace. I want the gates opened at once. Line the halls, corridors, even the chapel. I want every square inch used. There will not be a single man, woman, or child left in the cold as long as there is any room to spare. Is that understood?"

"Absolutely, Your Eminence."

"Furthermore," she said, turning to Gallsworth, "I want a study done of the city to locate any other sources of shelter that could be utilized. I don't care how hallowed or privileged. This is an emergency and all space is to be used."

"You're serious?" he said, amazed.

"I will not have my people dying on my doorstep!" she declared in a raised voice that left no room for question.

Guards looked up, concerned by her unusual outburst. Servants appeared nervous and several noticeably cringed. The city administrator did not. He remained straight, his eyes focused on her own. He said nothing for a moment; then his lips began to move about as if he were sucking on something, and finally he began to nod.

"Very well," he said. "I will begin to look into the matter, but I can tell you right now where there is a large unused space. The Imperial Basilica of Aquesta has the capacity to house perhaps a thousand and at present is home to no more than eight individuals."

"If you knew this, why did you not say something before?"

"I would never presume to fill the house of god with poor, filthy peasants."

"Then what in Maribor's name is it for?"

"The Patriarch will not be pleased."

"Damn the Patriarch!" Modina barked. "Nimbus—"

"At once, Your Eminence."

❧

"Why are the two of you not asleep?" Modina asked, entering her bedroom to find Mercy and Allie wide-awake.

Modina insisted that Allie stay in her room as part of her initiative to free up as much space as possible. When Allie asked for Mercy to join them, Modina could not refuse. Now both girls were in their nightgowns, wrapped in blankets, facing the darkened, frost-covered window. At her question, the girls looked at her and then quickly wiped their cheeks.

"Too cold," Mercy replied unconvincingly, and sniffled.

"It's freezing," Allie agreed. "We couldn't even play outside today."

"Even Mr. Rings won't set foot out there." Mercy glanced to where the raccoon was curled up near the fire.

"It is very cold, isn't it?" Modina said, looking out the window at the starry sky. The night was always clear when the temperature was frigid.

"It freezes the water in your eyes!"

"It makes my ears hurt."

Modina put her hand to the frosted glass—the same window she had spent so many hours kneeling before. It was like ice to her touch. "Yes, the cold is troublesome, but it might just be the miracle we need."

"We need it to be cold?" Allie questioned.

"Well, if Mr. Rings won't go outside, I don't suspect anyone else will want to be out there either."

"You mean the elves?" Mercy asked.

"Yes," she replied. She didn't see the point in lying.

"Why do they want to kill us? Allie is an elf, but she doesn't want to kill us, do you?"

Allie shook her head.

"I don't know why," Modina said. "I'm not certain anyone knows. The reason is likely very old, too old for anyone to remember."

"Will they—will they kill us when it gets warmer?" Allie asked.

"I'm not going to let them. Your father isn't going to let them either. Is that why you were crying? You miss him, don't you?"

The girl nodded.

"And you?" Modina looked at Mercy.

"I miss Arcadius and Miranda. She used to put me to bed at night, and he would tell me stories when I couldn't sleep."

"Well, I think I can help with that. I know a story—a story that a dear friend once told me when I was feeling very bad. So bad, in fact, that I couldn't even eat. How about we get more wood for the fire, curl up in my big bed, and I will tell it to you?"

She watched the two padding about in their bare feet, collecting armloads of split logs.

The empress smiled.

Everyone commented on how gracious she was for taking them in and sharing her personal chambers. Although, there were some who thought that it was a political ploy—that her generosity was extended to make it impossible for any duke to suggest such indignities were beneath him. This was not the reason, only a convenient secondary benefit. Modina did it because she had promised Wyatt she would look after Allie, and she meant to fulfill that oath. As there was no separating the two girls, Modina inherited twins. Having done so, she realized that even if Wyatt returned that night, and the winter melted to summer and all the problems with her kingdom were swept away by some miracle, she would still want the children to live with her. Carefree laughter was something Modina had not heard in a great while. She had stared out her window at a free blue sky to avoid the gray world of grim-faced men. Now a bit of that sky bounced within her chambers. They reminded her of Maria and Jessie Caswell, childhood friends who had died too soon.

She tucked the girls in and lay beside Allie, stroking her hair.

"This is called *Kile and the White Feather*. The father of the gods, Erebus, had three sons: Ferrol, Drome, and Maribor. They were the gods of elves, dwarves, and men. He also had a daughter, Muriel, who was the loveliest being ever created. She held dominion over all the plants and animals. Well, one night Erebus became drunk and... well, he hurt his own daughter. In anger, her brothers attacked their father and tried to kill him, but of course, gods can't die.

"Filled with guilt and grief, Erebus returned to Muriel and begged her forgiveness. She was moved by her father's remorse but still could not bear to look at him. He begged, pleading for her to name a punishment. He would do anything to win her forgiveness. Muriel needed time to let the fear and pain pass, so she told him, 'Go to Elan to live. Not as a god, but as a man to learn humility.' To repent for his misdeeds, she charged him with doing good works. Erebus did as she requested and took the name of Kile. It is said that to this day, he walks the world of men, working miracles. For each act that pleases her, Muriel bestows upon him a white feather from her magnificent robe, which he keeps in a pouch forever by his side. Muriel decreed that when the day came when all the feathers were bestowed, she would call her father home and forgive him. It is said when all the gods are reunited, all will be made right and the world will transform into a paradise."

"Empress?" Mercy said.

"Yes?"

"When you die, do you meet others who have died?"

"I don't know. Who is it you want to meet?"

"I miss my mother."

"Oh, that's different," she told her. "I am quite certain daughters and mothers are *always* reunited."

"Really?"

"Of course."

"She was very pretty, my mother. She used to say I was pretty too."

"And you are."

"She told me I would grow up to be a fairy princess one day, but I don't think I will now. I don't think I will grow up at all."

"Don't talk like that. If your mother said you would be a fairy princess, you trust her—mothers know these things." She hugged the girl and kissed her cheek. Mercy felt so small, so delicate. "Now it is late and time for you to go to sleep."

A bright moon was rising.

Modina thought of the fifty-eight men outside, pitched on a snowy hillside, ordered by her to remain in the cold. Some would lose fingers, others toes, noses, or ears, and some might be dying right then, like her father almost had the night of the blizzard. They might be huddled in a shallow frozen hole they had chipped out of the snow, trying in vain to keep warm with only a thin wool blanket and a few layers of clothes separating them from the bitter winds. They would shiver uncontrollably, their teeth chattering, their muscles tight as they pulled into balls, snow and ice forming on their beards and eyelashes. The unlucky ones would fall into a deep warm sleep, never to wake up.

She thought of the men, imagined their pain and fear, and felt guilt. They were dying on her command, but she needed them to be there. As much as she wished it could be better for them, as much as she wished she could pray for warmer weather, she looked out at the sparkling stars and whispered, "Please, Maribor, I know I am not your daughter. I am but a poor peasant girl who shouldn't even be here, but please, please make it stay cold."

She fell asleep and woke a few hours later. The room was dark, the new logs having burned low, and everything outside the covers felt chilled.

It was Mercy who had woken her. She was kicking and twisting in the covers, her eyes still closed. She wrestled, her arms twitching, her eyes darting fretfully under her lids. From her mouth came fearful utterances like the cries of terror from one gagged.

"What's wrong with her?" Allie asked with a sleepy face and matted hair.

"Bad dream, I suspect." Modina took hold of Mercy's shoulder and gave it a gentle squeeze. "Mercy?" she said. "Mercy, wake up."

The little girl kicked once more, then lay still. Her eyes fluttered open and then shifted left and right nervously.

"It's okay. It was just a bad dream." Mercy clutched at Modina, shaking. "It's all right, everything is okay now."

"No," the little girl replied with a hitching voice. "It's not.

I saw them. I saw the elves coming into the city. Nothing stopped them."

Modina patted her head. "It was just a dream, a nightmare brought on because of what we were saying just before you fell asleep. I told you I won't let them hurt us."

"But you couldn't stop them—no one could. The walls fell down and flying monsters burned the houses. I heard the men screaming in the fog. There was lightning, the ground broke, and the walls fell. They poured in riding white horses all dressed in gold and blue."

"Gold and blue?" Modina asked.

She nodded.

Modina's heart felt as if it skipped a beat. "Did you see the elves when you escaped the university?"

"No, just the flying monsters. They were really scary."

"How did you know they dressed in gold and blue?"

"I saw them in my dream."

"What else did you see? Which way did they come?"

"I don't know."

"You said they were on horses. Did they arrive here on horses or did they come by boat?"

"I don't know. I just saw them on horses coming into the city."

"Do you know which gate?"

She shook her head, looking more frightened as Modina quizzed her. The empress tried to calm down, tried to smile, but she could not. Instead, she stood up. The floor was cold, but she barely noticed. She paced, thinking.

*It's not possible for a child to see the future in a dream—is it? But that's what the Patriarch said when he was quoting at the meeting. "They came on brilliant white horses, wearing shining gold and shimmering blue." Still, that ancient account might not apply to these elves.*

"Can you remember where you were when you saw them enter the gate?"

Mercy thought a moment. "We were on the wall out front of the courtyard, where Allie and I play with Mr. Rings."

"Was it day or night?"

"Morning."

"Could you see the sun?"

She shook her head and Modina sighed. If only she—

"It was cloudy," Mercy told her.

"Could you tell which side the sea was on while looking at the gate?"

"Ah—this side, I think," she said, taking her right hand out of the covers and shaking it for her.

"Are you sure?"

The girl nodded.

"You were looking at the *southern* gate," Modina said.

"You two get back to sleep," she told the girls, and left them staring as she rushed out of the bedroom, pulling on a robe. The guard outside spun around, startled.

"Wake up the chancellor and tell him I want to see that scout Entwistle right now. I will meet them in the chancellor's office. Go."

She closed the door and ran down the steps to the fourth floor without bothering to get dressed.

"You there!" She caught a guard yawning. He snapped to attention. "Get a light on in the chancellor's office."

By the time Nimbus and the scout arrived, she had the map of the kingdom of Warric off the shelf and spread out over the desk.

"What's going on?" the chancellor asked.

"You are from the south, aren't you, Nimbus?"

"I am from Vernes, Your Eminence."

"That's down here at the mouth of the Bernum?"

"Yes."

"Do you know of any place south of Colnora to cross the Bernum River?"

"No, Your Eminence."

She looked back at the map for a moment and the two men waited patiently. "So the elves can't get at us from the west unless they have seaworthy ships, and they can't approach us from the north because of the mountains?"

She looked up, this time at the scout.

"Yes, Your Eminence, we started an avalanche on the Glouston road and it won't be clear until late spring. The bridges in Colnora were destroyed as well."

"And they can't come at us from the east or the south because of the Bernum. What about the Rilan Valley? Can't they get through there?"

"No, the snow is too deep in the fields. An elf might be able to walk over it with proper shoes, but he won't be able to bring horses or wagons. And even if they did, they would still have to cross the Farendel Durat, and those passes are closed."

She looked again at the map, studying the little lines on it.

"If the elven army was to attack us from our southern gate, how best would they get here?"

"They can't," the scout said. "The only bridges across the Bernum River gorge were in Colnora and they have been destroyed."

"What if they went *around* Colnora? What if they crossed the Bernum south of there?"

"The river south of Colnora is wide and deep. There's no ford or bridge except those in Colnora, which aren't there anymore."

Modina drummed her fingers on the desk, staring at the map.

"What is it, Your Eminence?" Nimbus asked.

"I don't know," she said. "But we're missing something.

It's not the cold slowing down their advance. Maybe they want us to think it is, but I'm certain they're circling around us. I think they will attack from the southeast."

"But that's not possible," the scout said.

"These are elves. Do we really know what is possible for them? If they were able to get across, what would that do?"

"That would depend on where they crossed. It could wind up dividing us from Breckton's forces in the east, or they could walk in unopposed from the south."

"Your Eminence, I know every inch of the Bernum. I used to float goods down it from Colnora to Vernes with my brother as boys. We worked it year-round. There is no place to cross. It is as wide and deep as a lake and has a deadly current. Even in summer, without a boat, a man can't get across. In winter it would be suicide."

The decision was too important to base on the nightmare of a child even though her heart told her she was right. Her eyes fell on the little copper pin in the shape of a torch on Tope Entwistle's chest. "Tell me," she said. "What is that you are wearing on your breast?"

He glanced down and smiled self-consciously. "Sir Breckton awarded that to me for successfully lighting the fire signaling the elves' move across the Galewyr."

"So you actually saw the elven army?"

"Yes, Your Eminence."

"Tell me, then, what color are the uniforms of the elves?"

He looked surprised at the question and then replied, "Blue and gold."

"Thank you, you can leave. Go back to sleep. Get some rest."

The scout nodded, bowed, and left the office.

"What are you thinking, Your Eminence?" the chancellor asked.

"I want word sent to Colnora to recall Breckton and his troops," she said. "We aren't going to survive, Nimbus. Even after everything we've done. They are going to break through our defenses, throw down our walls, and burst into this palace."

Nimbus said nothing. He remained straight and calm.

"You knew that already, didn't you?"

"I harbor few illusions, Your Eminence."

"I won't let my family be slaughtered—not again."

"There is still hope," he told her. "You have seen to that. All we can do is wait."

"And pray."

"If you feel that will help."

"You don't believe in the gods, Nimbus?"

He smiled wryly. "Oh, I most certainly believe in them, Your Eminence. I just don't think they believe in me."

# CHAPTER 15

# PERCEPLIQUIS

The *Harbinger* limped to shore without much dignity. Wyatt managed to create a small sail from what remained, and hoisted it to a pole he lashed to the stump of the old mast. They no longer flew across the waves; they barely drifted, but it was enough to make the far shore. Farther down the shore Royce spotted what looked to be a dock, which they avoided, and instead they anchored in at a sheltered cove. Here the beach was only a small spit of land surrounded by large blocks of broken stone, each one half the height of a man. They lay tumbled and scattered like the toys of some giant toddler after a tantrum. The stones glistened from the sea spray, and those closest to the water wore glowing beards of what looked like long stringy moss.

"What bothers me is the lack of gulls," Wyatt said, tying off the bowline to a rock that rose out of the sand like a colossal finger. "Only a godforsaken beach is without seagulls."

"Really?" Hadrian asked. "The gulls? I would have figured the glowing green water would have you more concerned."

"There's that too."

Magnus was one of the first off the boat. He hit the sand and ran up the slope to the stone blocks, touching them with his hands as if to assure himself they were real. Royce was off next. His face had started to take on a green all its own. His elven heritage made him subject to seasickness and Hadrian recalled the days of misery his friend had spent aboard the *Emerald Storm*. Royce climbed to the top of a large sturdy rock and lay down. Alric and Mauvin arrived on the beach wide-eyed, looking up at the ruined stone with awe. Arista was the last off, accompanied by Myron, who held her hand. She had slept for more than two hours and still had deep shadows beneath her eyes. After reaching the beach, she turned around to view the *Harbinger* and a look of remorse crossed her brow.

"She's not in much shape for a return trip," Wyatt stated, looking at the princess. "I was thinking that maybe Elden and I ought to stay here and work on her while the rest of you fetch that horn. I could rig a few pulleys in these rocks, and with Elden's help, I might be able to set a new mast if we manage to find something we can use for one. At the very least, I could run a jib line and reinforce the pole we have. I also think the rudder needs some work and I need to stop the leaks that opened up or she'll sink on the way back. I have the pitch for that; I just need to make a fire and get the hull out of the water, which the tide should help with."

"And if the Ghazel spot you?" Arista asked.

"Well, I will do my best to avoid that, but if they come around, I suppose we'll hide among the rocks. I'm hoping that after today, we won't be seeing any more of them for a while. Perhaps we have at least a few days before another ship arrives.

"Thing is, I'm on this trip for my sailing skills, right? I can't handle a sword as well as a Pickering or Hadrian, and I wasn't brought along for that, anyway. Neither was Elden. Besides, you can leave the excess gear here, and travel lighter."

Arista nodded. She did not look strong enough to argue.

"I really didn't mean to hit you so hard," Hadrian told her as Arista sat down on the sand.

"What?" she asked sluggishly. "Oh no, it's not my head. It's just that I feel exhausted, even after sleeping. I feel like I've walked for miles and been up for weeks. You know better than I do—do you get that from being whacked in the head?"

"No, not really," he replied. "It just usually throbs awhile and aches after that."

"I feel sort of like you do when coming down with a cold—weak, tired. My mind just wanders and I can't stay focused. It doesn't help that anytime I sleep, I have dreams."

"What kind of dreams?"

"You'll think I'm crazy," she said, embarrassed.

"I thought that from the first time we met."

She smirked at him. "In my dreams I'm not me—I actually think I'm Esrahaddon, only it's years ago, before this city was destroyed, before the emperor was killed, before he was locked up."

"That's what you get from wearing that robe."

She looked down. "It's a really nice robe—very warm, and have you ever seen one that lights up for you?"

"It's a little creepy."

"Maybe."

They sat in silence for a minute. Elden and Wyatt walked around the ship, looking at the hull. They were wasting no time assessing the damage. Alric and Mauvin climbed up in the rocks, exploring like children. Myron sat only a few feet away and appeared to be watching them.

Hadrian stared at the waves as they rolled ashore, splashing just beyond their feet. They would head off soon, but for now, it was good to sit on solid ground. He would nudge Royce in a bit, but he wanted to give him a few minutes. He expected dangers would be greater from that point on, and preferred Royce to be in top form.

"I should thank you," Arista said with downcast eyes and a quiet voice, as if it were a confession.

He looked at her curiously. "For what?"

"For the crack on the head," she replied, raising a hand to rub the spot. She took the bandage off. "Alric was right. I'd lost control." Her hair fell across her face—an auburn curtain hiding everything but the tip of her nose. "It's hard to explain the feeling of it—the power—it's as if I can do anything. Can you imagine knowing you can do *anything*? It's exciting, alluring—it draws you in and you want it like a hunger. You feel yourself becoming part of something bigger, joining with it, working with it. You sense every drop of water, every blade of grass, and you become them—everything—the air and the stars. You want to see how far you can go, where the edges are, only some part of you knows—there are no edges.

"I never did anything that big before. I spread out too far. I joined with it too much. I was losing myself, I think. It was just so amazing, feeling the world respond to me like it was a part of me, or I was a part of it. I don't know—I wasn't thinking anymore. I was just feeling and I don't know what might have happened if you hadn't..."

"Whacked you?"

"Yeah."

"I'm just glad you aren't mad," he said, and meant it. "Most people I hit wake up with a slightly different attitude."

"I suppose they do." She pulled the curtain of hair back and tilted her head up at him. She had a self-conscious smile on her face. "I'd also like to thank you for something else."

He looked at her once more—confused and a little worried.

"I want to thank you for not being afraid of me."

Her hair was tangled, her face drawn and weary. She had drooping eyes and thin pale pink lips. There was a pinch of sand on the tip of her nose. Creases marked her forehead, thin lines of worry.

*Is there anyone quite like her?*

He fought an urge to brush the sand from her nose.

"Who says I'm not afraid of you?" he asked her.

He saw her turning that comment over in her mind and felt it was best to end the conversation before he said something stupid. He got up, dusted the sand off himself, and went looking for his pack. He had just reached the ship, where Wyatt was coiling a length of rope, when the two scouts returned.

"There's a passage up that way," Mauvin announced, grinning.

They came to the side of the ship, where they found their packs and, pulling out their water sacks, threw their heads back and guzzled to quench their thirst.

"It's amazing," Alric said, wiping the water from his beard. "There are these huge statues of lions—their paws are taller than I am! This really is Percepliquis. I want to go in. We should get going."

"Wyatt and Elden are planning to stay here," Hadrian told him.

"Why?" he asked, concerned and perhaps a bit annoyed.

"They plan to fix the ship while we're gone and have it ready for us by the time we get back."

"Oh, okay, that makes sense—good sense. That's great. Now let's get our stuff and get going. I've waited all my life to see this." Alric and Mauvin trotted back aboard the *Harbinger* to find the rest of their gear.

"Kings," Hadrian said to Wyatt with a shrug.

"Be careful," Wyatt told him. "And keep an eye on Gaunt."

"Gaunt?"

"You're too trusting," Wyatt said. He nodded to where Gaunt sat near the dwarf on a large stone slab. "He spends a lot of time with Magnus and he was unusually friendly with me and Elden, like he was buddying up with the drafted members of the party, trying to form a group of dissenters. Remember what I told you on the *Emerald Storm*? There's always one member of any crew who's looking for a mutiny."

"And he's our only hope," Hadrian replied with a lilt of irony in his voice. "You'd better be careful too. As you know, the Ghazel are no joke. Keep an eye out. Don't sleep on the ship. Don't light any fires."

"Trust me, I remember the arena at the Palace of the Four Winds. I have no desire to cross swords with them a second time."

"That's good, because this isn't an arena and there are no rules. Out here they'll swarm over you like an army of ants."

"Good luck."

"Same to you and make sure this ship is ready to sail when we get back. I've been on enough jobs with Royce to know that while the going in may be slow, the coming out is usually a race."

The ruins of the city began at the water's edge, although this was not entirely evident until they left the sand and moved inland, where they had a wider perspective. The large stone blocks were part of the broken foundation of white marble columns that had once stood a hundred feet tall. They knew this by discovering three remaining columns still upright, yet how they had managed to remain this way was bewildering, as the blocks had shifted precariously.

They found the passage Alric and Mauvin had discovered, which began at the feet of two huge lions carved from stone. Each was easily two hundred feet tall, although one was missing its head, which had fallen away. The remaining lion showed a fierce face with teeth bared and a full and flowing mane.

"The Imperial Lions," Myron muttered as they passed under their shadow and Royce paused to light his lantern.

"I've seen these before," Arista whispered, her head back, looking up at the sculptures. "In my dreams."

"What do you know of this place, Myron?" Royce asked, lifting his light and peering forward into a vast labyrinth of crumbled stone and silhouetted ruins.

"Which author would you like to hear from? Antun Bulard did a wonderful study of the ancient texts as well as—"

"Summarize, please."

"Right, okay, well, legend has it that this was once a small agrarian village, the home of a farmer's daughter named Persephone. They lived in fear of the elves, who had reportedly burned nearby villages and slaughtered the inhabitants right down to every man, woman, and child. Persephone's village was next but a man called Novron appeared in the village. He fell in love with Persephone and vowed to save her. He begged her to leave the village but she refused, so he decided to stay and swore to protect her.

"He took charge and rallied the men. When the attack came, he defeated the forces of the elves, saving the village. He revealed himself to be Novron, the son of Maribor, sent to protect his children from the greed of the Children of Ferrol.

"Many battles later, Novron defeated the elves at the Battle of Avempartha and a time of peace with the elves began. Novron wished to build a capital for his great empire and a home for his wife. Although he ruled vast tracks of land, Persephone refused to live anywhere other than her village. So it was here that Novron built his capital, naming it Percepliquis—*the city of Persephone.*

"Over the years it became the largest and most sophisticated city in the world. It is chronicled as being five miles across and the seat of a famous university and library. Scholars came from across the empire to study. The Grand Imperial Palace was built here and it was a place of temples, gardens, and parks. Records report that the city had clean water fountains open to the public and baths where citizens lounged in heated pools.

"Percepliquis was also the home of the imperial bureaucracy, a vast system of offices that administered the empire, controlling its economy and social and political institutions. There were agents responsible for rooting out potential dissidents, suspected criminals, and corrupt officials. And of course, it was home to the Teshlor Guild and the Cenzar Council—the imperial knights and the college of wizards that advised and protected the emperor.

"Through his bureaucracy the emperor controlled everything, from the forests to mines, farms, granaries, shipyards, and cloth mills. Corruption was held in check by appointing more than one head of each department and by rotating them out frequently. They never appointed local men who might have ties to those they administered to. Even prostitution was regulated by the empire.

"Percepliquis was a place of great wealth. The center of the empire's trade that spanned all of Apeladorn and reached even into the exotic Westerlins and north into Estrendor, it bustled with richly dressed merchants and the roads were legendary. They were huge, wide thoroughfares of well-laid stone, perfectly straight, that ran for miles in all directions. Trees were planted on either side of them to provide shade, and they were well maintained and marked with milestones. Wells and shelters were placed at regular intervals for the comfort of travelers.

"There was no famine, no crime, no disease or plague. No

droughts were ever recorded, nor floods, nor even harsh frosts. Food was always plentiful, and no one was poor."

"I can see why the Imperialists want to recapture that ideal," Alric observed.

"Which just goes to show how foolish people can be," Gaunt said. "No famine, no drought, no disease, no poor? There's about as much chance of that happening as—"

"As you becoming emperor?" Royce asked.

Gaunt scowled.

"So what should we be looking for?" Royce asked.

Myron shook his head. "I don't know," he replied, and glanced at Arista.

"The tomb of Novron," the princess told them.

"Oh." Myron brightened. "That would be under the palace in the center of the city."

"Any way to identify it?"

"It's a huge white building with a solid-gold dome," Arista answered for him, gaining several surprised looks. She shrugged. "I'm guessing."

Myron nodded. "Good guess."

They moved on as before, with Royce in the lead, fleet of foot as always, investigating shadows and crevices, his light bobbing. Alric and Mauvin followed at a distance in a manner that reminded Hadrian of a fox hunt. Arista and Myron walked together, both staring up at their surroundings with great interest. Gaunt and Magnus followed them, occasionally speaking in whispers. Hadrian brought up the rear once more, glancing over his shoulder repeatedly. He already missed Wyatt and Elden.

They followed a passage that wove between collapsed rockfalls until they reached a street of neatly paved stones, each cut in a hexagon and fitted with stunning precision.

Here, at last, the mounds of rubble gave way, allowing them to view the shattered remains of the once-magnificent city that rose around them.

Great buildings of rose or white stone, tarnished by age and curtained in debris, had lost none of their beauty. What immediately captured Hadrian's attention was how tall they were. Pillars and arches soared hundreds of feet in the air, supporting marvelously decorated entablatures and pediments. Great domes of burnished bronze and stone-crowned buildings with diameters in excess of a hundred feet were far larger than anything he had ever seen before. Colonnades supporting a row of arches ran for hundreds of yards as mere decoration, standing out before load-bearing walls. Statues of unknown men were exquisitely sculpted such that they might move at any minute. They adorned silent fountains, pedestals, and building facades.

The grandeur of the city was stunning, as was its rattled state. Each building, each pillar, each stone appeared to have dropped from some great height. Blocks of stone lay askew and shifted out of place. Some teetered beyond imagination, loose, twisted, and misaligned so that it looked as if the weight of a sparrow would topple a structure of a thousand tons. The devastation was not even or predictable. Some buildings missed whole walls. Most no longer had roofs, while others revealed the shift of only a few stones. Despite the disarray, other aspects of the city were astonishingly preserved. A seller's market stood untouched; brooms remained standing, stacked on display. A pot stall exhibited several perfect clay urns, their brilliant ceramic glazes of red and yellow dimmed only by a coat of fine dust. On the left side of the street, in front of a disheveled four-story residence, lay three skeletons, their clothes still on them but rotted nearly to dust.

"What happened to this place?" Gaunt asked.

"No one knows exactly," Myron replied, "although there have been many theories. Theodor Brindle asserted that it was the wrath of Maribor for the murder of his blood. Deco Amos the Stout found evidence that it was destroyed by the Cenzar, in particular the wizard Esrahaddon. Professor Edmund Hall, whose trail we are on, believed it was a natural catastrophe. After crossing the salty sea and seeing the state of the city, he concluded in his journal that the ancient city sat upon a cavern of salt, which was dissolved with a sudden influx of water, thus causing the city above to collapse. There are several other more dubious explanations, such as demons, and even one rumor concerning the bitterness of dwarves and how they pulled it down out of spite."

"Bah!" Magnus scoffed. "Humans always blame dwarves. A baby goes missing and it was a dwarf that stole it. A princess runs off with a second son of a king and it was a dwarf who lured her to a deep prison. And when they find her with the prince—lo, she was rescued!"

"A king is stabbed in the back in his own chapel, and a princess's tower is turned into a death trap," Royce called back to them. "Friends are betrayed and trapped in a prison— yes, I can see your surprise. Where do they get such ideas?"

"Damn his elven ears," Magnus said.

"What?" Gaunt asked, shocked. "Royce is an elf?"

"No, he's not," Alric said. He looked back over his shoulder. "Is he?"

"Why don't you ask him?" Arista replied.

"Royce?"

The bobbing light halted. "I don't see how this is the time or place for discussing my lineage."

"Gaunt brought it up. I was just asking. You don't look elven."

"That's because I am a *mir*. I'm only part elven, and since I never met my parents, I can't tell you any more than that."

"You're part elven?" Myron said. "How wonderful for you. I don't think I've ever met an elf. Although I have met you, so perhaps I have met others and don't know it. Still, it is quite exciting, isn't it?"

"Is this going to be an issue?" Royce asked the king. "Are you planning on questioning my allegiance?"

"No, no, I wasn't," Alric said. "You've always been a loyal servant—"

Hadrian started walking forward, wondering if he had returned Royce's dagger too soon.

"Servant? Loyal?" Royce asked, his voice growing lower and softer.

*Never a good sign*, Hadrian thought. "Royce, we need to keep moving, right?"

"Absolutely," he said, staring directly at Alric.

"What did I say?" the king asked after Royce resumed his advance. "I was merely—"

"Stop," Hadrian told him. "Forgive me, Your Majesty, but just stop. He can still hear you and you'll only make matters worse."

Alric appeared as if he would speak again, but then scowled and moved on. Arista offered her brother a sympathetic look as she passed him.

They continued in silence, following the light. On occasion Royce whispered for them to wait, and they sat in silence, tense and worried. Hadrian kept his hands on the pommels of his swords, watching and listening. Then Royce would return and off they would go once more.

They moved to a much wider boulevard. The buildings became more elaborate, taller, often with facades of chiseled columns. Pillars lined the avenue, tall monoliths covered in detailed engravings, epigraphs and images of men, women, and animal figures. One very large building was totally shattered, forcing them to climb over a mountain of rubble. The going was treacherous, with slabs of broken rock the size of houses that were loose enough to shift with their weight. Driven to inch along ledges and crawl through dark holes, they all welcomed a rest on the far side.

They sat on what had once been a great flight of marble steps, which now went nowhere and looked down the city's main road. Each building was tall and made from finely carved stone, usually a white marble or rose-colored granite. Fountains appeared intermittently along the wide thoroughfare, and as he stared, Hadrian could imagine a time when children ran in the streets, splashing in the pools and swinging from the spear arm a statue held out. He could almost see the colorful awnings, the markets, the crowds. Music and the smells of exotic food would fill the air, much like in Dagastan, only here the streets were clean, the air cool. What a wonderful place it must have been, what a wonderful time to have lived.

"A library," Myron whispered as they sat, his eyes fixed on a tall circular building with a small dome and a colonnade surrounding it.

"How do you know?" Arista asked.

"It says so," he replied. "On top there: IMPERIAL REPOSITORY OF TOMES AND KNOWLEDGE, roughly translated, at least. I don't suppose I could…" He trailed off, his eyes hopeful.

"If you go in there, we might never get you out," Hadrian said.

"We need to camp and we still don't know anything about the horn," Arista said. "If Myron could find something…"

"I'll take a look," Royce said. "Hadrian, come with me. Everyone else wait here."

Just as if he were on a job, Royce circled the library twice, making a careful study of the entrances and exits before moving to the two great bronze doors, each decorated in ornate sculptured relief depicting a bisected scene of a man handing a scroll and a laurel to a younger man amidst the aftermath of a great battle. Hadrian noticed a river and a familiar-looking tower at the edge of a waterfall in the upper right. The doors were marred badly, dented and bent, bearing marks from a large blunt hammer.

Hadrian slowly, quietly drew one sword. Royce set down and hooded the lantern, then pulled the doors open and slipped inside. One of the many rules Hadrian had learned from the start was never to follow Royce into a room.

That was how it all had gone so bad in Ervanon.

Royce had slipped into the Crown Tower as delicately as a moth through a window. Yet unlike on the previous night, the room was not empty. A priest sat in the small outer chamber. It did not matter, as he had not seen or heard Royce, but then Hadrian blundered in. The man screamed. They ran—Royce one way, Hadrian the other. It was a coin flip that Hadrian won. The guards came around the tower on Royce's side. While they were busy chasing and wrestling Royce down, Hadrian made it back to the rope. He was safe. All he had to do was climb back down, retrieve his horse from the thickets, and ride away. That was exactly what Royce expected him to do, what Royce would have done in his place, but back then Royce did not know him.

Hadrian heard the three taps from inside the library and, grabbing the lantern, crept inside. It was black and he was met with a terrible confluence of smells. The dominant odor was a thick burnt-wood scent, but a more pungent rotted-meat stink managed to cut through. From the darkness, he heard Royce say, "We're clear, light it up."

Hadrian lifted the lantern's hood to reveal a scorched hall. Burned black and filled with piles of ash, the room was still beautiful beyond anything else Hadrian had ever seen. Four stories tall, the walls circling him were marvelously crafted tiers of marble arcades. Towering pillars ringed the coffered dome and supported the great arches joining the arcades to each other. Around the rim, a colonnade of white marble was interspersed with lifelike bronze statues of twelve men, each of which had to be at least twenty feet tall. From the floor they appeared life-sized. Great chandeliers of gold hung around the perimeter. The black cracked remains of tables formed a circular pattern of desks with a great office in the center. A fresco painting of wonderful scenes of various landscapes formed the lower part of the dome, while the greater portion, made of glass, now lay in shards scattered across the beautiful mosaic floor.

In the center of the room, near the office bench, was its only inhabitant. Surrounded by a few singed books, papers, quills, three lanterns, and an oilcan lay what remained of an old man. He was on his back, his head resting on a knapsack, his legs wrapped in a blanket. Like Bernie, this man was dead, and as he had Bernie, Hadrian recognized him.

"Antun Bulard," he said, and knelt beside the body of the elderly man he had befriended in Calis. He was not as ravaged by death as Bernie—no sea crabs here. Bulard, who had always been pale in life, was now a bluish gray, his complexion waxy. His white hair was brittle and spectacles still rested on the end of his nose.

"Bernie was right," Hadrian told Bulard. "You didn't survive the trip, but then again, neither did he."

Hadrian used the old man's blanket to wrap him up and together they carried his body out and set it off to the side under a pile of rocks. The smell lingered, but it was not nearly as pungent.

When the others arrived, they stared with disappointment, Myron most of all. Exhaustion won out and they threw their packs down while Royce relocked the door.

Myron looked up, his eyes scanning the tiers and countless aisles where books must have once lay, but now they housed only piles of ash, and Hadrian noticed the monk's hands tremble.

"We'll rest here for a few hours," Royce said.

"Here?" Gaunt asked. "The smell is awful, charcoal and something else…What is that disgusting—" Gaunt asked.

"We found a body," Hadrian told them. "Another member of the last team the Patriarch sent in, from the same group as Bernie, from the *Harbinger*…and a friend. We took his remains out."

"Was he burned?" Myron asked fearfully.

"No." Hadrian placed a hand on his shoulder. "I don't think anyone was here when it caught fire."

"But it was burned recently," the monk said. "It wouldn't still smell like this after a thousand years."

"Perhaps our resident sorceress can do something about the stench?" Gaunt asked.

This brought stern looks from Hadrian, Alric, and Mauvin.

"What?" Degan asked. "Are we to continue to tiptoe around it? She is a magician, a mage, a wizardess, a sorceress, a witch—pick whatever term you prefer. Beat me senseless if you like, but after our little boat ride, there is no debating the reality of that fact."

Alric strode toward Gaunt with a threatening look and a hand on his sword.

"No." Arista stopped him. "He's right. There's no sense hiding it or pretending. I suppose I am a— Did you say *wizardess*? That one's not too bad." As she said this, her robe glowed once more and a mystical white light filled the chamber with a wonderful brilliance, as if the moon had risen in their midst. "That's fine—best that it is out in the open, best that we can all say it. Royce is an elf, Hadrian a Teshlor, Mauvin a count and a Tek'chin swordsman, Alric a king, Myron a monk with an indelible mind, Magnus a dwarven trap smith, Degan the Heir of Novron, and I—I am a wizardess. But if you call me a witch again, I promise you'll finish this journey as a frog in my pocket. Are we clear?"

Gaunt nodded.

"Good. Now, I am exhausted, so you will have to live with the smell."

With that, Arista threw herself down, wrapped up in her blankets, and closed her eyes. As she did, the robe dimmed and faded until at last it was dark. The rest of them followed her lead. Some swallowed a handful of food or a mouthful of water before collapsing but no one spoke. Hadrian tore open another packaged meal, surprised at how few he had left. They had better find the horn soon or they might all end up like Bulard.

*What happened to him?*

It was the question he drifted to sleep on.

᪥

Hadrian felt a nudge and opened his eyes to Mauvin's face and wild hair hanging over him.

"Royce told me to wake you. It's your watch."

Hadrian sat up groggily. "How long and who do I wake?"

"You're last."

"Last? But I just fell asleep."

"You've been snoring for hours. Give me the chance to get a little sleep."

Hadrian wiped his eyes, wondering how he could best estimate the length of an hour, and shivered. He always felt chilled when he woke up, before his blood got running properly. The cool subterranean air did nothing to help. He wrapped his blanket around his shoulders and stood up.

The party all lay together like blanket-shrouded corpses, bundles of dark lumps on the floor. Each had swept the broken glass back and it clustered in a ring marking the border of their camp. The lantern was still burning, and off to one side, near where he had found Bulard's body, huddled in a ball and wrapped in his hooded frock and blanket, sat Myron.

"Tell me you did not stay up reading," he whispered, sitting down next to him among the piles of papers and books, which Myron had neatly stacked.

"Oh no," he replied. "I was beside Mauvin when Alric woke him for his watch. I just couldn't get back to sleep, not in here. These papers," he said, picking up a handful. "They were written by Antun Bulard, a famous historian. I found them scattered. He was here. I think he is the one who died."

"He used to say he couldn't remember anything unless he wrote it down."

"Antun Bulard?" Myron looked astonished. "You've met him!"

"I traveled briefly with him in Calis. A nice old man and a lot like you in many ways."

"He wrote the *The History of Apeladorn*, an incredible work. It was the book I was scribing the night you found me at the Winds Abbey." Myron lifted the parchments, holding them up to Hadrian. "His legs were broken. They left him here with some food and water and the lantern for light. His notes are sloppy, lines running over one another. I think he wrote them in the dark to save oil for reading, but I can read most of it. He was with three others, a Dr. Levy, Bernie—who we laid to rest—and Sentinel Thranic, who I gather was their leader. Antun wasn't very pleased with him. There was also a man named Staul, but he died before they set sail."

"Yes, we knew them too. What happened?"

"Apparently, they acquired the *Harbinger* from a warlord of some sort called Er An Dabon. He also arranged for a Ghazel guide to take them into the city. All went well, if not a bit tense, until they arrived at this library. Here they found evidence that this had been the last stand for a previous team and he mentioned the names Sir Gravin Dent, Rentinual, Math, and Bowls."

"So it *was* them."

"They apparently barricaded themselves inside, but the doors were forced open. Bulard's group found their gear, bloodstains, and lots of Ghazel arrows—but no bodies."

"No, they wouldn't."

"Antun suggested they leave him to sit and read while they went on to explore for the horn."

"So the library—"

"It was fine—*perfect*, to use the words of Antun Bulard—filled with thousands and thousands of books. Bulard wrote, 'There is perhaps a hundred tomes on birds—just birds—and above those, another hundred on the imperial seafaring mercantile industries. I followed an aisle back to a swirling brass stair that corkscrewed up to yet another floor, like an attic, and it was filled to the ceiling with records of the city—births, deaths, land titles, and transfers—amazing!' "

"What happened?"

"Thranic burned it," Myron said. "They had to hold Antun down. After that, he refused to go any farther. Thranic broke both his legs to prevent him from escaping the city and left him here, just in case they had a question he needed to answer.

"Antun salvaged these from the ash." He pointed to the small stack of five books. "He lived for nearly three months. In the end, with the oil gone, he was trying to feel the words on the page with his fingertips."

"Nothing about what happened to the others?"

"No, but he appeared to realize something of tremendous importance. He began writing about it in earnest, but it must have been after the oil ran out and I suspect starvation was taking its toll. His quill work was abysmal. He wrote something about a betrayal, a murder, and something he referred to as the Great Lie, but the only thing he wrote clearly was the phrase *Mawyndulë of the Miralyith*, which was underlined twice. The rest is indecipherable, although it goes on for ten more pages and there are many exclamation points. Only the last line is fully readable. It says, 'Such a fool was I, such fools are we all.' "

"Any idea what this Maw-drool-eh of the Mirrorleaf *is*?"

"Maw-in-due-lay and Meer-ah-leeth," he corrected. "The Miralyith is, or was, one of the seven tribes of elves."

"Seven tribes?"

"Yes, actually Bulard wrote of them in his first book years ago. There were seven tribes of elves named from the ancestors that founded them. The Asendwayr, known as the hunters; the Gwydry, the farmers; the Eilywin, the builders; the Miralyith, the mages; the Instarya, the warriors; the Nilyndd, the crafters; and the Umalyn, the priests of Ferrol. Everyone knows that Ferrol created the elves first and for thousands of years only they and the creations of Muriel existed on the face of Elan. Bulard discovered that there was friction from the beginning. Elves once fought elves, clan against clan. A feud existed between the Instarya and the Miralyith to where—"

Arista quivered in her sleep and let out a muffled cry.

"She's been like that all night," Myron told him.

Hadrian nodded. "She told me she's been suffering from

nightmares, but I think they are more than dreams." Hadrian watched her. As he did, he felt Myron's hand on his. Looking up, he saw the monk offer him a sad smile.

Hadrian drew his hand away. "I think I'd better start waking people."

Myron nodded as if he understood more than Hadrian had meant to say.

# CHAPTER 16

# THE WHITE RIVER

Mince was convinced that the vast majority of his ten long years—soon to be eleven—had been spent with frozen feet. Even the empress's gifts of thick wool cloaks, hats, mittens, boots, and scarves were incapable of withstanding the biting winds. His fingers kept going numb, and he had to make fists to keep the blood flowing.

*This must be the coldest winter the world has ever seen. If the water in my eyes freezes, will I be unable to blink?*

Mince stood with a bucket in hand and stomped on the river with his frozen feet—solid as stone. He heard no cracking, nor the gurgle of liquid lapping beneath the surface. There would be no water again, which meant another miserable day warming cups of snow under their tunics. Hadrian had ordered them not to build a fire and Renwick was adamant about obeying. The task was unpleasant, but they could make do. Mince was not sure how much longer the horses could go without.

Lack of water was not the horses' only problem. Even though the boys had tethered them in a tight pack, and built a windbreak from pine boughs and thickets, the animals were still suffering from the cold. Ice formed on their backs, icicles hung from their noses, and that morning Mince had seen two of them lying down. One was producing a small puff of white mist at frighteningly long intervals. The other did not appear to breathe at all. The ones lying down were the horses on the outside of the pack—the ones exposed to the most wind.

The Big Freeze, as Kine had named it, had occurred three days earlier and come upon them overnight. The previous day they had run around in warm sunshine, playing tag without scarves or hats; then the sky had turned gray and a frigid air blew in. That morning Elbright had returned from fetching the water reporting that only a narrow stream ran down the center of the river. The day after, the river was gone completely— replaced by a smooth expanse of white. That afternoon when the snow started to fall, the flakes were no larger than grains of sand.

The five boys had been living in a snow cave beneath the eaves of a holly tree, and when the freeze came, they dug their shelter deeper and built a windbreak by covering the opening with lashed pine boughs.

Time passed slowly after the Big Freeze. With the temperature so bitter, they no longer went out except to relieve themselves. The only fun they had had was when Brand discovered the *trick*. He got up miserable, shivering, and cursing, and in a fit of frustration, he spit. It was so cold that the liquid cracked in the air. They spent the next few hours trying to see who could get the loudest snap. Kine was the best, but he had always been the best spitter. As fun as cracking spit was, it pushed away the boredom only temporarily and they tired of the game. As the cold wind blew, and the temperature continued to drop, Mince could not help wondering how long they would have to stay.

He should have headed back to the Hovel, what they began calling their snow cave, but instead scanned the length of the broad white trail that ran north and south like a shining crystal road. Mince was trying to see if some portion was clear. Perhaps there was a place where the current prevented the ice from forming. He looked for a change in color, but there was nothing but a never-ending expanse of white. Still, something caught his eye. Far to the north he saw movement.

A long gray line crossed the river. There were people, tall and slender, wearing identical cloaks. He stared, amazed at the sight, and wondered if perhaps they were ghosts, for in the stillness of the winter's morning he heard no sound of their passing. Mince stood staring but it was not until he saw a glint of armor that it occurred to him what he was actually seeing. The revelation froze him as instantly as if he were spit turning solid in the morning air.

*Elves!*

As he watched the spectral cavalcade, they marched three abreast in the muted light, passing like phantoms on the ridge. They rode on steeds that even at a distance Mince could tell surpassed any breed raised by men. With broad chests, tall ears, proud arched necks, and hooves that pranced rather than walked, these animals were ethereal. Their bridles and equestrian gowns were adorned in gold and silk, as if the animals were statelier than the noblest human king. Upon them, each rider wore a golden helm and carried a spear with a streaming silver banner licking the air.

The sound of music reached his ears—a wild, capricious but beautiful euphony that haunted his spirit and caused him to unwillingly take a step forward. Joining the sound was the wonderful lilt of voices. They were light and airy and reminded Mince of flutes and harps speaking to one another. They sang in a language Mince could not understand, but he did not need to. The melody and plaintive beauty of the sound carried him with it. He felt warm and content and took another step forward. Before long, the music faded, as did the sight of them as they finished crossing the river and disappeared into the foothills.

"Mince!" He heard Elbright and felt hands shaking him. "He's over here! The little idiot fell asleep on the ice. Wake up, you fool!"

"What's he doing way up here? I found the bucket a half mile back." Kine's voice was more distant and out of breath.

"It's almost dark. We need to get him back. I'll carry him. You run ahead and tell Renwick to get a fire started."

"You know what he'll say."

"I don't care! If we don't get him warm, he'll die."

There were the sounds of feet on snow, sounds of urgency and fear, but Mince did not care. He was warm and safe and still remembered the music lingering in his head, calling to him.

≺⸙

When Kine returned to camp, only Brand was there—Brand the Bold, as he liked to call himself. It was a bold boast for a kid of thirteen, but no one questioned it. Brand had survived a knife fight, and that was more than any of them could claim.

"We need to get a fire started," Kine said, returning to the Hovel. "We found Mince and he's near dead with cold."

"I'll get kindling," Brand replied, and ran out into the snow.

Kine got the tinderbox from the supplies they had not touched and cleared a space near the front of the shelter. Brand was back in minutes with a sheet of birch bark, a handful of brown grass, tiny dry twigs, and even a bit of rabbit fur. He dropped the treasures off and set back out. As he did, Kine spotted Elbright carrying Mince on his back. The boy's head rolled with each step. It reminded him of how deer looked when hunters brought them in.

Elbright said, "Make a bed, put down lots of needle branches—pile them up—we want to keep him off the snow."

Kine nodded and ran out of the shelter past the horses— two more were lying down. He entered a grove of spruce trees, where he tore the branches from the trunks, getting his mittens sticky from the sap. He made four trips, and when he finished, Mince had a thick bed to lie on.

Elbright had a small, delicate flame alive on the birch sheet. His mittens were on the snow beside him. His bare fingers were red, and he frequently breathed on them or slapped his thigh as he squatted in the snow. "Fingers go numb in seconds."

"What are you doing?" Renwick said, coming up the slope from the south.

When Mince had not returned after going for water, they all went searching in different directions. Renwick took the southern riverbank and returned only now that the sky was darkening and the temperature plummeted.

Although he was also an orphan, Renwick was not one of their gang. He lived at the palace, where his father used to be a servant. While really no more than a page, the boy had served as squire to Sir Hadrian during Wintertide. All the boys were impressed by Hadrian's spectacular success during the games and this admiration spilled over to Renwick. The boy was also older—perhaps a year or two Elbright's senior. Unlike those of the rest, Renwick's clothes fit him properly and even matched in color.

"We have to get a fire going," Elbright told him even as he fed the tongues of flame little sticks. "We found Mince on the ice. He's freezing to death."

"We can't build a fire. Hadrian—"

"Do you want him to die?"

Renwick looked at the growing fire and the tendrils of white smoke snaking from it, then at Mince lying on the spruce bed. Kine could see the debate going on inside him.

"He's my best friend," Kine told him. "Please."

Renwick nodded. "It's getting dark. The smoke won't be visible, but we need to contain the light as much as we can. Let's bank the snow walls higher. Damn, it *is* cold."

Brand returned with more wood, larger branches and even a few broken logs. His cheeks and nose were red and ice crystals formed around his nose and mouth.

"You need to keep him awake," Elbright told him as he tended the fire as if it were a living thing. "If he stays asleep, he'll die."

Kine shook Mince and even slapped him across the face, but the boy did not seem to notice. Meanwhile, Renwick and Brand boosted the windbreak wall, which not only contained the light, but also reflected the heat. Elbright coaxed the fire, cooing to it like it was a child he had brought into the world. "Com'on, baby, eat that branch. Eat it, that's right, there you go. Tastes good, doesn't it? Eat all of it. It will make you strong."

Elbright's baby became a full-grown fire and soon the frigid cold fell back. It was the first time in days any of them had known real warmth. Kine's feet and fingers began to ache and his cheeks and the tip of his nose burned as he thawed out.

Beyond the mouth of their snow cave, darkness fell, made deeper by the bright light of the fire. Renwick grabbed a pot from the supplies, filled it with snow, and set it near the fire to melt. Elbright refused to let him put it on his fire. They sat in silence, listening to the friendly sound of the flames.

Soon the shelter was warm enough that Elbright took off his hat and even his cloak. The rest of them followed his lead, with Kine laying his over Mince.

"Can we eat now?" Brand asked.

Renwick had established a firm rule that they ration their food and they all ate together to make certain no one had more than his share. Like the cups of water, they kept their meals inside their shirts, up against their skin, since it was the only way to keep the food from freezing solid.

"I suppose," Renwick said passively, but looked just as hungry as any of them.

Brand pulled out his stick of salt pork and set it near the fire. "I'm having a hot meal tonight."

The rest of them mimicked him, and before long, the smell of hot meat filled the cave. They all waited to see how long Brand could hold out. It was not long and soon everyone was ripping into the pork and making exaggerated smacks of ecstasy.

In the midst of their revelry, Mince sat up.

"Supper?"

"You're alive!" Kine exclaimed.

"You're not eating my share, are you?"

"We should!" Elbright yelled at him. "You little idiot. Why did you decide to take a nap on the ice?"

"I fell asleep?" Mince asked, surprised.

"You don't remember?" Kine asked. "We found you curled up on the river, snoring."

"You should thank Maribor for your life," Elbright added. "And what were you doing so far north?"

"I was watching the elves."

"Elves?" Renwick asked. "What elves?"

"I saw the elven army crossing the river, a whole line of them."

"There were no elves," Elbright declared. "You dreamed it."

"No, I saw them on horseback, and they played this beautiful music. I started listening and—"

"And what?"

"I don't know."

"Well, you fell asleep is what," Elbright told him. "And if I hadn't heard you snoring, you'd be dead by now."

"He would, wouldn't he?" Renwick muttered, looking out at the dark. "The elves—you said they were all on horseback? None on foot? How about wagons?"

"No, no wagons, just elves on horses, beautiful horses."

"What is it?" Elbright asked.

"He didn't see the elven army."

"I know that," Elbright replied with a chuckle. "It was a dream."

"No—no, it wasn't," Renwick corrected. "He saw elves, but it wasn't the army. It was only the vanguard—the advance patrol. I heard the knights talking—the elven army travels at night, but hardly anyone has ever seen them and no one knows why, but I think I do—I do now."

They all looked at Mince.

"He'd be dead," Elbright said, nodding. "But that means the army is—It's night!"

They all looked at the fire, which had melted down a half foot into the snow so that it burned in its own little well. Elbright was the one who kicked it out. It made a dying hiss as the snow swallowed the flames. They all worked to bury the embers until it was a small mound of dirty brown with sticks and grass sticking out.

No one said a word as they felt around in the faint light for their cloaks and mittens. Silence hung in the air. Since it was winter, they did not expect the sounds of birds or frogs, but now not even the wind breathed. The constant rustle of naked branches was absent, as were the random cracks and snaps.

They poked their heads out of the cave, lifting them attentively above the blind and around the bundle of pine boughs. They could not see anything.

"They're out there," Renwick whispered. "They are crossing the frozen river and sneaking up on Aquesta from the south. We have to warn them."

"You want us to go out *there*?" Elbright asked incredulously. "Where *they* are?"

"We have to try."

"I thought we had to stay here and watch the horses."

"We do, but we also have to warn the city. I'll go. The rest of you stay here. Elbright, you'll be in charge. You can explain to Hadrian why I left." As he spoke, he moved to the gear and began picking supplies. "Keep the fire out. Stay inside and…" He paused a moment, then said, "Cover your ears if you hear any music."

No one said a word as he slipped out. They all watched as he inched nervously to the horses. He picked the one closest to the middle of the bunch and saddled it. When he was gone, all that remained was the deep silence of a cold winter's night.

# CHAPTER 17

# THE GRAND MAR

The party had stopped again. Since they'd left the library, their progress through the ancient city had been tedious, as Royce was pausing frequently. Sometimes he forced them to wait for what felt like hours as he scouted ahead—the rest of them sitting among the rubble. This time, he had left them in the middle of what appeared to be an alley with tall buildings towering on either side. Arista sighed and leaned against one wall. Someone ahead of her had stepped on a piece of fabric, the boot print revealing the faded colors of blue and green. She bent down and picked a small flag from under a thick coating of dust and dirt. This one was a handheld version, the sort people waved at celebrations. Looking up, she spotted a window, and hanging from that was an old and faded banner that read FESTIVIOUS FOUNDEREIONUS!

"What does that say?" she asked Myron, but she was certain she already knew.

" 'Happy Founder's Day,' " the monk replied.

Next to where she found the flag, she noticed a small object. Reaching out, she found a copper pin in the shape of the letter *P*. Now more than ever she wished she could remember the dream from the night before, but the more she tried to recall, the more it slipped away.

Royce returned, waving them forward, and then he led them in a circle back to the boulevard. Here they began to see skeletons. They were in groups of twos and threes, lying crumpled to the ground as if they had died right where they stood. The only way to tell how many there were was by the number of skulls in the piles. As they progressed, the bone count increased. Skeletons lined either side of the road with skull counts of ten deep.

They entered a small square, a portion of which was flooded where the ground was cracked and sank away at a dramatic angle. The same green light that illuminated the sea lit the square and revealed a raised platform on which was a great statue of a man. He stood twenty feet tall, with a strong, youthful physique. A sword was in his right hand and a staff in the other. Arista had seen similar statues several times throughout the city and in each case the head was missing, broken at the neck and shattered.

Royce stopped again.

"Any idea if we are getting close to the palace?" he asked, looking at Myron.

"I only know that it is near the center," the monk replied.

"The palace is at the end of the Grand Mar," Arista told them. "That's what they used to call the boulevard we're on now. So it is just up ahead."

"The Grand Mar?" Myron said, more to himself than to her, and then nodded. "The Marchway."

"What are you babbling about?" Alric asked.

"There was said to be a great avenue in Percepliquis called the Grand Imperial Marchway, so called as it was often the site of parades. Ancient descriptions declared it to have been wide enough for twelve soldiers to walk abreast and that it was made up of two lanes divided by a row of trees. Imperial troops would march down the right side to the palace, where the emperor would review them from his balcony, and then they would return down the other side."

"They were fruit trees," Arista said. "The trees that grew in the center of the Grand Mar—fruit trees that blossomed in spring. They used to make a fermented drink from the blossoms called...Trembles."

"How do you know that?" Myron asked.

She looked at him and pretended to be surprised. "I'm a wizardess."

They paused to have a short meal on the steps of an impressive building off the main boulevard. Stone lions, similar to those that guarded the entrance to the city, sat on either side. A fountain stood in the street at the center of an intersection. The water no longer sprayed and the pool was filled with a black liquid.

"What books have you got there?" Alric asked, seeing Myron sift through his pack and pull out one of the five that Bulard had saved.

"This one is called *The Forgotten Race* by Dubrion Ash. It deals mostly with the history of the dwarves."

"What's that now?" Magnus asked, leaning over to look closer at the pages.

"According to this, mankind is actually native to Calis—isn't that interesting? And dwarves started in what we know as Delgos. The elves of course are from Erivan, but they quickly occupied Avryn."

"What about the Ghazel?" Hadrian asked.

"Funny you should ask," he said, flipping back several pages. "I was just reading about that too. You see, men appeared in Calis during the *Urintanyth un Dorin* and would have—"

"Huh?" Mauvin asked.

"It means *the Great Struggle with the Children of Drome*. You see, the dwarves warred with the elves for centuries, nearly six hundred years, in fact, until the fall of Drumindor in 1705—that's pre-imperial reckoning, of course—about two thousand years before Novron built this city. The dwarves went underground after that. As it turns out, the early human tribes would have failed—perished—if not for the contact they had with the exiled dwarves who traded with them."

"Aha!" the dwarf said. "And how do they treat us for our kindness now? Ghettos, refusals of citizenship, bans on dwarven guilds, special taxes, persecution—it's a sad reward."

"Quiet!" Royce suddenly told everyone, and stood up. He looked left and then right. "Get ready to move," he said, and leaving the lantern, he climbed down the steps, heading back the way they had come.

"You heard him," Hadrian said.

"But we just sat down," Alric complained.

"If Royce says get ready to move, and he has that look on his face, you do what he says if you want to live."

They gathered their belongings back into their bags. Arista took one more mouthful of salt pork and a swallow of water before stashing the rest in her pack. She was just pulling the straps over her shoulders when Royce reappeared.

"We're being tracked," he told them in a whisper.

"How many?" Hadrian asked.

"Five."

"A hunting party." Hadrian drew his swords. "Everyone get moving. Royce and I will catch up."

"But they're just five," Arista protested. "Can't we avoid them?"

"It's not the five I am worried about," Hadrian told her. "Now go. Just keep moving up the avenue."

He and Royce moved back down the road at a trot. She watched them go as a sinking feeling pulled at her stomach. Alric led them forward at a run, past the fountain and on up the Grand Mar.

This part of the city was familiar to her. This road, these buildings — she had seen them before. Gone were the brilliant white alabaster walls and brightly painted doors. Now they were dingy and brown, cracked, fractured, chipped, and like everything else, covered in a layer of dirt. As in the rest of the city, the columned halls stood on misaligned stones.

Alric led them around a massive fallen statue whose head had severed at its neck and lay on its side, its features bashed and broken. They then leapt a fallen column, and as soon as she cleared it, Arista stopped. She knew this pillar; it was the Column of Destone. She turned left and saw the narrow road Ebonydale. That was the way Esrahaddon had gone to meet Jerish and Nevrik. She looked forward down the Mar. She should be able to see the dome, but it was not there. Ahead was only rubble.

"Arista!" She heard Alric calling to her and she ran once more.

⁓

Royce and Hadrian paused near the headless statue, where the algae in the water cast an eerie green radiance to the underside of all things. Royce motioned with two spread fingers that a pair were coming up one side of the street and two on the other. While the two pairs were mere shadows to Hadrian, the fifth was quite visible as he loped up the center of the boulevard like an ape hunched over and traveling on three limbs. His massive claws clicked intentionally on the stone as signals to the others. Every few feet he would pause, raise his head, and sniff the air with his hooked, ring-pierced nose. He wore a headdress made from the blackened fin of a tiger shark, a mark of his station—a token he would have obtained alone in the sea with no more than his claws. He was the chief warrior of the hunting party—the largest and meanest—and the others looked to him for direction. They all carried the traditional sachel blades—curved scimitars, narrow at the hilt and wider at the tip, where a half-moon scoop formed a double-edged point. Like all Ghazel, he also carried a small trilon bow with a quiver slung over one shoulder.

Royce drew out Alverstone and nodded to Hadrian as he slipped into the darkness. Hadrian gave him a minute; then, taking a breath, he also moved forward. He closed the distance, keeping the statue between him and the Ghazel. To his surprise, he was able to reach the platform before the warrior noticed him and let out the expected howl. Immediately arrows whistled and glinted off the stone.

The warrior rushed him, his sachel slicing the air. Fighting a Ghazel was always different from fighting men, but the moment the two swords connected, Hadrian no longer needed to think. His body moved on its own, a step, a lunge. The fin-endowed warrior responded exactly as Hadrian wanted. Hadrian caught the warrior's next stroke with his short sword and saw the momentary shock in the Ghazel's eyes when his bastard sword came around, removing his arm at the elbow. A short spin and Hadrian took the warrior's head, fin and all.

A high-pitched shriek announced the charge of two more Ghazel. Hadrian always appreciated how they announced their attacks. He was able to step out from his shelter now—the rain of arrows having ended.

The two bared their pointed teeth and black gums, cackling.

Hadrian shoved the length of his short sword into the stomach of the closest. Dark blood bubbled up from the wound. Without looking to see the reaction of the remaining Ghazel, he swung his other blade behind him and felt it sink into flesh.

Hadrian heard fast-moving footsteps and looked up. Across the open square Royce ran at him, carrying a Ghazel bow and quiver of arrows. The thief was making no attempt at stealth, his cloak flying behind him.

"What's up? Did you get the others?"

"Yep," he said. As he ran by, he tossed the bow and quiver to Hadrian and added, "You might need these."

Hadrian chased after him as he ran back up the Grand Mar. "What's the hurry?"

"They weren't alone."

Hadrian glanced back over his shoulder but saw nothing. "How many?"

"A lot."

"How many are a lot?"

"Too many to stand around and count."

⚜

The party reached the end of the boulevard, which looked nothing like what Arista remembered from her dream. The Ulurium Fountain—with its four horses bursting out of the frothing waters—was gone, crushed by giant stones. To the right, the rotunda of the Cenzarium still stood, but it was a faded, broken version of its former self, the dome gone, the walls blackened. To the left, the columned facade of the Hall of Teshlor remained intact. While it had weathered the years better, the building was just as grime-covered as the rest. Most importantly, the great golden dome of the magnificent palace— in fact, the whole palace—was missing. Before her, only a

hopeless mountain of rubble remained. All around the param-
eter, every inch of space was carpeted with bones of the dead.

Reaching the end of the road, Alric spun around and held
the lantern high. "Arista! Which way?"

She shook her head and shrugged. "The palace—it should
be just ahead of us. I think—I think it's destroyed."

"That's just great!" Gaunt bellowed. "Now what do we do?"

"Shut up!" Mauvin barked at him.

"Is this as far as Hall got?" Alric asked Myron.

"No," the monk replied. "He wrote that he entered the
palace."

"How?"

"He found a crevice."

"Crevice? Where?"

"He wrote 'Fearful of the drums in the darkness, and
afraid to sleep in the open, I sought refuge in a pile of rocks. I
found a crevice just large enough for me to slip through.
Expecting nothing more than a mere pocket to sleep in, I was
elated to discover a buried corridor. On my way out I was
careful to mark it so that I might find it should I return this
way again.'"

They began searching, crawling among the boulders and
broken stones. The collapse of the building covered the entire
breadth of the broad boulevard with a mass of fallen stones
containing hundreds of crevices, each of which might hide an
entrance. They had only begun looking when Royce and
Hadrian returned, their weapons still drawn and slick with
dark blood.

"That's not good," she heard Hadrian say the moment he
saw the pile.

"There's a crevice somewhere that leads inside," Arista
said.

"There's a horde of Ghazel right behind us," Royce told her.

"Everyone inside that building on the left," Hadrian shouted.

They ran across the square, struggling over the piles of bones and rocks that blanketed the walk and steps to the Hall of Teshlor. Yelps and cries erupted behind them. Looking back, Arista spotted goblins skidding across the stone, scratching their claws like dogs on a hunt. Their eyes flashed in the darkness with a light from within, a sickly yellow glow rising behind an oval pupil. Muscles rippled along hunched backs and down arms as thick as a man's thigh. Mouths filled with rows and rows of needle-like teeth spilled out the sides as if there was not enough room in their mouths to contain them.

"Don't watch, run!" Hadrian shouted, grabbing hold of her arm and pulling her across the loose mounds of bones.

Alric and Mauvin sped up the steps, heaving themselves simultaneously against the great doors.

Hadrian threw Arista to the ground, where she fell, scraping her knee and bruising her cheek.

"Wha—" Her protest was silenced as a hail of arrows peppered around them, sparking off the stones. He hauled her to her feet once more and shoved her forward.

"Go!" Hadrian ordered.

She ran as fast as she could, charging up the steps. Myron and Magnus, who had just slipped inside the big double doors, waved at her to hurry. She glanced behind her. Gaunt was just reaching the base of the steps.

Arrows flew again.

Arista heard the hiss and Hadrian pulled her behind the pillars, but Gaunt had no such protection. An arrow caught him in the leg and he fell, sliding to a stop.

He rolled over to his back and cried out as the first goblin reached him.

"Degan!" Arista screamed.

A white dagger slit the Ghazel's throat, and the princess

spotted Royce straddling the fallen Gaunt. Three more Ghazel rushed forward. Two fell dead almost instantly as Hadrian joined Royce, taking one with each of his swords. Distracted, the third turned toward the new threat just as Royce stepped behind him and the goblin fell.

"Get up, you fool!" Royce shouted at Gaunt, grabbing him by his cloak and pulling him to his feet. "Now run!"

"Arrow in my leg!" was all Gaunt managed to say through gritted teeth.

"Look out!" Arista shouted as nearly a dozen more Ghazel charged.

Hadrian's swords flashed as he threw himself into the fight. Royce vanished only to reappear and vanish again, his white dagger flashing like a sparkling star in the night.

"Back into your holes, you beasts!" Alric shouted as he suddenly ran out with a lantern in one hand and his sword in the other. Mauvin chased after his king as Alric leapt into the fray fearlessly, cleaving into the nearest goblin. Her brother took an arm off his opponent and then ran him through. Arista's heart stopped as Alric failed to see the blade of another Ghazel swinging from the side at his head. Mauvin saw it. A lightning-quick flash of his sword blocked the attack, sliced through the blade, and killed the goblin in one stroke.

Gaunt was up and hobbling forward.

Arista hiked up her robe and ran back down the stairs to him. "Put your arm around me!" she shouted, moving to his wounded side.

Gaunt put his weight on her. From behind them more goblins entered the square. Twenty — perhaps as many as thirty — ran forward shrieking and yelping, their claws clicking the stone, and a drone came from them like the sound of a swarm of locusts.

"Time to go!" Hadrian declared. Reaching Alric, he pulled

the lantern from the king's hand and smashed it on the stone before the attacking Ghazel. A burst of flame rose along with more cries and squeals.

"I've got him!" Hadrian told her. "Run!"

They all bolted for the doors that Magnus and Myron held open. As soon as they entered, the monk and the dwarf pulled them shut. Royce slid the latch.

"Get that stone bench in front of the door!" Royce shouted.

"What bench?" Mauvin asked. "It's pitch-black in here!"

Arista barely thought about it and her robe glowed with a cold blue light that revealed the entrance hall. Musty and stale, it was much like the library, covered in cobwebs and dust. The white-and-black-checkered floor was cracked and uneven. A chandelier that had hung from the ceiling rested in the center of the floor. Braziers lay toppled, stone molding was scattered, and plaster chips littered the ground. Great tapestries still clung to either wall. Faded and dirty, they were otherwise unmarred, as were long curtains that draped the walls. Stairs led up from either side of the front doors and past two tall, narrow windows that looked out onto the square. It was then that Arista realized how much like a small castle-fortress the Teshlor Guild was.

*Boom! Boom!* The goblins hammered against the door, shaking the dust off the walls.

Having laid Gaunt down near the center of the room, Hadrian pulled the goblin bow from his shoulder and ran up the steps. He made use of the arrow slits to fire on the goblins outside. She heard a cry for every twang of the tiny bow and soon the hammering stopped.

"They've moved off," Hadrian said, leaning heavily against the wall. "Out of bow range, at least, but now that they know they have guests, they won't leave us alone."

Royce looked around, scanning the stairs, the ceiling, and the walls. "Question is...is there another way in here? And perhaps more importantly, another way out?" He pulled the remaining lanterns from Myron's pack and began lighting them.

Arista moved to Gaunt's side. The short, foul-looking arrow had penetrated through his calf with both ends sticking out. "I can see why you were having such trouble running," she told him as she pulled her dagger and started to cut his trouser leg.

"At least someone gives me credit," he growled.

"You're lucky, Mr. Gaunt," Hadrian said, coming down the stairs and approaching them. He grabbed the first lit lantern and knelt down beside him. "If the tip was still inside your leg, this next process would hurt a lot more."

"Next process?"

Hadrian bent down, and before Arista or Gaunt knew what was happening, he snapped off the arrow's tip. Gaunt howled in pain.

"Get some bandages ready," he told Arista. Myron was already there holding two rolls out to her. "Now this will hurt some."

"*This* will?" Gaunt asked incredulously. "What you did befo—"

Hadrian pulled the shaft from his leg. Gaunt screamed.

Blood flowed from the wounds on either side of the leg and Hadrian quickly began wrapping and pulling the cloth.

"Put your hands on the other side and squeeze tight—real tight," he told Arista. Blood soaked through the white linen, turning it red.

"Squeeze harder!" he told her as he unrolled a second length of cloth.

As she did, Gaunt cried out again, throwing his head back. His eyes went wide for a moment and then squeezed shut.

"I'm sorry," she told him.

Gaunt groaned through gritted teeth.

Blood seeped through her fingers. It was warm—and slicker than she had expected, almost oily. This was not the first time she had found her hands covered in blood. In the square of Ratibor, with Emery in her arms, there was much more, but she did not notice it then.

"Okay, let go," Hadrian told her, and he redressed the wound. Once again he had her squeeze as soon as he was finished. More blood soaked the bandages, but it was spotty this time and did not consume the whole linen.

Hadrian wrapped another length and tied it off. "There," he said, wiping his hands. "Now you just have to hope there was nothing nasty on that shaft."

Royce handed him a lantern. "We should look for other entrances."

"Mauvin, Alric? Keep watch out the windows, shout if they return."

"I need water," Gaunt said, his face dripping with sweat. Arista slipped a pack under his head and grabbed his water pouch. It appeared more of it dribbled down his chin than went in his mouth.

"Rest," she said, and brushed the hair from his brow.

He gave her a suspicious look.

"Don't worry, I'm not going to enchant you," she said.

❧

When she entered, her robe illuminated the grand hall with a cold azure light. A great stone table stood in the center with dozens of tall chairs surrounding it. A few had fallen to their sides, as had a half dozen metal goblets that rested on the table. The chamber was four stories tall, with great windows lining the high gallery and skylights in the ceiling. She imagined that they had once filled this room with a wonderful radiance of sunlight. Painted on the upper walls and parts of the ceiling were astounding scenes of battle. Knights rode on horseback with streamers flying from long poles, vast valleys were filled with thousands of soldiers, and castle gates, defended by archers, were assailed by machines of war. In one scene, three men battled on a hilltop against three Gilarabrywn. Those same men were seen in other images, and in one, they were pictured in a hall with a throne where one sat with a crown and to either side stood the other two. Below the paintings, a varied array of weapons lined the room: swords, spears, shields, bows, lances, and maces. The one thing they all had in common: even after a thousand years, they still gleamed.

Words were engraved in a band encircling the room and could also be found on recessed plaques, yet Arista's training in the Old Speech was verbal, not written. Unable to decipher the meanings, she did spot the words *Techylor* and *Cenzlyor*.

A majestic stair gave access to the gallery above and she climbed it. At the top were a series of doors. Some rooms lay open and she spied small chambers, living quarters with beds, shelves, and closets. Lantern light spilled from one.

She found Hadrian standing near the bed, staring up at the opposite wall as if entranced. He was looking at a suit of armor, a shield, and a set of weapons. The armor was not at all like the traditional heavy breastplates, pauldrons, vambraces, and tassets of typical knight attire. This was one piece and appeared as a long formal coat, but made from leaves of gold-colored metal. It hung from a display with a great plumed helm like the head of an eagle resting on top.

"Planning on moving in?" she asked. "I got a little worried when you didn't come back."

"Sorry," he said, embarrassed. "I didn't hear any shouts. Is everything all right?"

"Gaunt is sleeping, Myron reading, Magnus is arguing with Alric, Royce still hasn't returned, and Mauvin wandered off. And what are you doing?"

She sat down on the bed, which promptly collapsed under her weight, issuing a cloud of dust.

"You all right?" he asked, helping her up.

"Yes," she said, coughing and waving her hand before her face. "I guess the wood rotted over the years."

"This is it," he said.

"What?" She brushed the dust from her robe.

"This is Jerish's room, Jerish Grelad, the Teshlor Knight who went with the emperor's son into hiding."

"How do you know?"

"The shield," he said, and pointed across the room at the heater shield hanging on the wall. On it was an emblem of twisted and knotted vines around a star supported by a crescent moon. Hadrian reached back and drew forth the long spadone sword. He held it up so that she could see the small engraving at the center of the pommel that matched the one on the shield. Then he stood up and crossed the room. As he did, she noticed for the first time that the suit of armor had no sword, but there was a sheath of gold and silver. Hadrian fitted the tip into the opening and let the great sword slide home. "You've been parted a long time."

"Doesn't quite match anymore," Arista said, noticing how the sword was marred to a dull finish.

"It has seen a thousand years of use," Hadrian said, defending it. He looked back at the armor. "The sword was the only thing he took. I suppose he couldn't expect to hide very well dressed in shiny gold armor." His fingers played over the gleaming surface of the metal.

"Looks like it would fit," she said.

He smirked. "What would I do with it?"

She shrugged. "Still, it seems like you should have it. Goes with the sword, anyway."

"It does, doesn't it?"

He lifted the coat. "So light," he said, stunned.

Arista looked back down at the bed and, as she did, noticed a small object—a figurine carved from a bit of smoky quartz. She picked it up and rubbed it clean. It was a statuette of three people, a boy flanked by two men, one in leaf armor and the other in a robe. The likeness of Esrahaddon was remarkable, except that this figure had hands. Whoever the artist was had a rare gift.

"Interested in what he looked like?" she said, and held out the figurine.

"He was young," Hadrian replied, taking the statuette and turning it over in his hands. "A good face, though." Then his eyes shifted and he smiled and she knew he was looking at Esrahaddon. "So this must be Nevrik, the heir. Doesn't look like Gaunt, does it?"

"How many generations are there in a thousand years?" she asked. "Funny that he left this. It's so beautiful you would have thought he'd taken it with him, or at least..." She paused and glanced around the room. Except for the expected silt of a thousand years, the room was neat and ordered, the bed made, drawers and cabinets closed, a pair of boots standing side by side at the foot of the bed.

"Did you...straighten up in here at all?" she asked.

He looked at her curiously and appeared as if he might laugh. "No," he told her.

"It's just that it's so tidy."

"What, because he was a knight you think— Okay, so there is Elgar, but he's more of an exception. No one is as messy as he is, but—"

"That's not what I meant. It's just that after Jerish left— after he took Nevrik and ran—I would have thought they would have searched this room, tore it apart looking for clues, but nothing looks out of place. And this figurine—don't you think they would have taken it? Why didn't they ransack the room? It's been a thousand years. You'd think they would have gotten around to it by now, unless…maybe they never got the chance."

"What do you—"

The blare of a horn blowing from somewhere outside the guildhall reached them, followed by the distant beat of drums.

❧

"What's happening?" Hadrian asked, returning with Arista to the front of the hall, where Alric was once again at the windows. He carried the armor in a bundle and the shield over his back.

Alric shrugged. "I don't know. I can't see a thing out there. Did you find an exit?"

"No, everything is sealed by rubble. So on the one hand, we're safe, but on the other, trapped."

"I think more are arriving out there," Alric mentioned.

"Get your head back from the window before you catch an arrow," Royce told him, returning from a side hall Arista had not taken.

She knelt down beside Gaunt and looked over his wound. The bleeding had finally stopped, but his face was still moist despite the chill in the air.

"Anything?" Hadrian asked.

Royce shook his head; then he looked around, concerned. "Where's Myron and Mauvin?"

"This is the Teshlor Guild," Alric said. "Mauvin has wanted to explore this since he was ten."

"And Myron?"

Alric glanced at Gaunt, who looked up painfully, blinking. Then all of them turned to Magnus.

"Don't look at me like that. I don't know where he went. He wandered off."

"I'll look for him," Royce said.

"Wait." Alric stopped him. "How are we going to get out of here?"

"Don't know," Royce replied.

Alric slumped against the front wall with a miserable look on his face. "He's not serious, is he?"

"You're the king," Gaunt said. "You tell us. You wanted to be in charge. What does your family heritage and blue-blood breeding say now? What insight has it provided you that we commoners can't see?"

"Shut it, Gaunt," Mauvin ordered, trotting down the stairs.

"There you are," Royce said.

"I'm just saying that he's the king," Gaunt went on. "He's in charge. So far all that he's managed is to get me bleeding to death and all of us trapped. This is a perfect chance for him to shine and prove his worth. All the other teams that came in here didn't have a noble king to lead them. Surely he will not leave us to the same fate as they. Isn't that right, Your Majesty?"

"I said, shut it," Mauvin repeated in a lower, more threatening voice. "Have you forgotten he just risked his life to help save yours?"

Alric looked at each of them as they sat around the entrance hall in the flickering light of four lanterns, each casting four separate shadows of everything.

"I don't know," he said. He peeked back out the window. "You heard the horn and the drums. There could be dozens of goblins out there by now."

"I doubt that," Hadrian replied, and Alric looked hopefully at him. "I would say there were hundreds by now. Ghazel prefer uneven battles, the more one-sided, the better, as long as it is in their favor. Those horns and drums are calling all goblins within earshot. Yeah, I would say a couple hundred at least are gathering."

Alric stared at him, shocked. "But...how are we going to get out, then?"

No one replied.

Even Gaunt gave up his taunting and lay back down. "And I was going to be emperor."

"The imperial hunts were massive." They heard Myron's voice echo as Royce led him back. "You can see by that tapestry. Hundreds participated—thousands of animals must have been killed, and did you see the chariots?"

"He was looking at the art," Royce told them.

"They were master bronze craftsmen, did you see?" the monk asked. "And this building, this is the guildhall, the knights' guildhall. This is the very place mentioned in hundreds of books of lore, often thought to be a myth—the Hall of Techylor—and isn't that amazing—not Teshlor at all.

"It's astounding, really, in all the years of reading about the Old Empire I never found anything about it, but clearly it was true. Techylor is not a combat discipline or martial art any more than Cenzlyor is a discipline of mystical arts. They're names. Names! Techylor and Cenzlyor were the names of people who were with Novron at the first battle of the Great

Elven War. The Teshlor Knights were literally the knights trained by Teshlor, or actually Techylor."

"This is hardly the time for studying history!" Alric snapped. "We need to find a way out, before they find a way in!"

"I see a light," Mauvin announced. "There's a fire, or a torch, or some— Uh-oh."

"What?" Gaunt asked.

"Well, two things, really," the young count Pickering began. "Hadrian was right. I can only see silhouettes but—oh yeah—there's a lot out there now—a whole lot."

"Second?" Hadrian asked.

"Second, it looks like they're setting up for flaming arrows."

"What good is that?" Alric asked. "This place is stone. There's nothing to burn."

"Smoke," Hadrian replied. "They'll smoke us out."

"That doesn't sound good," Gaunt said.

"Another locked room," Hadrian said to Royce. "How many is this? I've lost track."

"Too many, really."

"Ideas?"

"Only one," the thief said, and then looked directly at Arista.

She watched Hadrian nod.

"No," she said instantly. She stood up and backed away from them. "I can't."

"You have to," Royce told her.

She was shaking her head so that her hair whipped her face, her breath short and rapid and her stomach tightening, starting to churn. "I can't," she insisted.

Hadrian moved toward her slowly, as if he were trying to catch a spooked horse.

Her hands were starting to shake. "You saw—you know what happened last time. I can't control it."

"Maybe," Hadrian told her, "but outside that door are anywhere from, I'm guessing, fifty to a few hundred Ba Ran Ghazel. All the bedtime stories, legends, and fables are true. I know firsthand, and actually, they don't tell even half the story—no one would dare tell the real stories to children.

"I served as a mercenary for several years in Calis. I fought for warlords in the Gur Em Dal—the jungle on the eastern end of the peninsula that the goblins took back. I've never spoken about what happened there, and I won't now—honestly, I work very hard not to think about it. Those days that I lived under the jungle canopy were a nightmare.

"The Ghazel are stronger than men, faster too, and they can see in the dark. They have sharp teeth and, if they get the chance, will hold you down and rip into the flesh of your throat or stomach. The Ghazel want nothing better than a meal of human meat. Not only are we a delicacy to them, but they also use their victims as part of their religious ceremonies. They will make a ritual out of killing us, take us alive if they can—eat us while we still breathe. They'll drink their black cups of gurlin bog and smoke tulan leaves while we scream.

"That door is the only way out of here. We can't sneak out, we can't create a diversion and hope to catch them off guard, we can't hope for a rescue. Either you do something or we all die. It's as simple as that."

"You don't know what you're asking me to do. You don't know what it's like. I can't control it. I—I don't know what will happen. The power is—it's—I don't know how to describe it, but I could kill everyone. It just gets out of control, it just runs away."

"You can handle it."

"I can't. I can't."

"You can. It caught you off guard before. You know what to expect now."

"Hadrian, if I go too far—" She tried to imagine and realized she did not want to. There was an excitement in the thought of the power, a thrill like standing on the edge of a cliff, or playing with a sharp knife; the exhilaration came from the risk, the very real fear that she could step too far. It lured her like the still beauty of a deep lake. Even as she spoke about it, she remembered how it felt, the desire, the hunger. It called to her. "If I reach beyond—if I go too far—I might not come back." She looked at Hadrian. "I'm scared what would happen. I don't think I would be human anymore. I'd be lost forever."

He took her hands. Until he touched her, she had not realized she was shaking. His hands felt warm, strong. "You can do it," he told her firmly. He stared into her eyes and she could not help looking back. There was peace there, a gentle understanding familiar to her now, comforting, reassuring.

*How does he do it?*

Her hands stopped shaking.

An arrow whizzed through Mauvin's window, just missing him. It streaked a thick dark smoke that stank of sulfur. It flew to the far wall and bounced off the stone, continuing to smolder and burn. Two more managed to find their way into the narrow slits while outside it sounded as if it were raining. Then a line of smoke began to leak in through the cracks of the door.

"You have to try," Hadrian told her.

She nodded. "But I want you with me. Don't leave me...no matter what happens."

"I swear I will not leave you." His voice and the look in his eyes were so sincere, so resolute.

Degan began to cough, and Mauvin and Alric climbed down from the stairs.

"Everyone gather," she told them in a soft voice, trying to keep her eyes on Hadrian. "I don't know exactly what's going to happen. Just try and stay as close as you can, and don't you let go of me, Hadrian."

# CHAPTER 18

# DUST AND STONE

The smoke was growing thick and it was becoming hard to breathe as Arista remained standing still, muttering, her eyes closed, her hands twitching.

"Is she going to do something?" Gaunt asked, and followed this with a series of coughs.

"Give her a second," Hadrian told him.

As if in response, a light breeze moved within the room. Where it came from Hadrian could not tell, but it moved around the chamber, swirling and stealing away the smoke. The wind grew stronger and soon it ruffled the edges of their cloaks, slapping their hoods and spinning the dust into little whirlwinds that twirled, dancing about. All at once, the flames in the lanterns went out and the wind stopped. Everything was deathly still for a heartbeat.

Then the front wall of the guildhall exploded.

Arista's robe flared brilliantly as from beyond the missing wall, Hadrian heard the cries of goblins, like a million squealing rats. The square cast in darkness for a thousand years lay revealed, illuminated as if the sun had returned to the Grand Mar. They could finally see the beauty that once had been, the city of Novron, the city of Percepliquis, the city of light.

"Gather your things," Arista shouted, opening her eyes, but Hadrian could tell she was not fully with them. She was breathing deep and slow, her eyes never focusing, as if blind to what was around her. She was not seeing with her eyes anymore.

Mauvin and Alric hoisted Gaunt between them. He grunted but said nothing as he hopped on his good leg.

"Come," she told them, and began to walk toward the collapsed pile that had once been a palace.

"You're doing great," Hadrian told her. She showed no sign of hearing him.

The goblins stayed back. Whether they retreated from the explosion of stone, the harsh light, or some invisible sorcery that Arista was manifesting, all Hadrian could tell was that they refused to approach.

The party walked as a group clustered around Arista.

"This is crazy," Gaunt said, his voice quavering. "They'll kill us."

"Don't leave the group," Hadrian told them.

"They're fitting arrows," Mauvin announced.

"Stay together."

Struggling to shield their eyes as they bent their bows, the Ghazel launched a barrage. All of the party flinched except Arista. A hundred dark shafts flew into the air, burst into flame, and vanished into streaks of smoke. More howls arose from the Ghazels' ranks, but no more arrows flew, and now more than ever, the goblins showed no willingness to advance.

"Find the opening!" she shouted, sounding out of breath, her tone impatient, like someone holding up heavy furniture.

"Magnus, try and find the hollow corridor," Hadrian barked.

"To the left, up there, a gap. No over farther—there!"

Royce was on it, throwing rocks back. "He's right—there's an opening here."

"Of course I'm right!" Magnus shouted.

"Something…" Arista said dreamily.

"What was that, Arista?" Hadrian asked. She mumbled and he did not catch the last few words. He kept his hands on her shoulders, squeezing slightly, although he was not certain if by doing so he was reassuring her or himself.

"Something…I feel something—something fighting me."

Hadrian looked up and stared out over the Grand Mar at the colony of goblins, a writhing mass of insidiously twisted bodies, with dripping teeth and brilliant claws clacking along the length of spears and swords. He spotted what he looked for beyond them, moving in a ring around the Ulurium Fountain. The small, slim figure of the oberdaza, dressed in a skirt and headdress of feathers, shaking a tulan staff and dancing his methodic steps. He spotted two more joining the first.

"We need to get in now!" Hadrian shouted.

Royce threw Myron and a lantern inside the dark hole and then shoved Magnus after him before following them inside. Gaunt, Mauvin, and Alric followed.

"We need to go," Hadrian told Arista.

Across the span of the square, he could hear chanting as two more witch doctors joined in the dance.

"Something," Arista muttered again. "Something taking shape, something growing."

"That's why we need to get moving."

A light appeared in the center of the square. No more than a candle flame, it wavered, hovering in midair; then it began to grow. The light swirled, flared, popped, and grew to the size of an apple. The host of the Ghazel army joined in the chant of the three oberdaza as the hovering ball of fire continued to grow and take shape. Hadrian began to see what looked like limbs and a head emerging from the withering fire.

"Okay, we *really* have to go," Hadrian said, and grabbed

hold of the princess. The moment he did, she staggered back, looking shocked and frightened. The glow of her robe went out.

"What's happening?" Arista asked.

He did not answer but merely grabbed her tightly by the wrist and drew her up the rubble to the opening, where he shoved her headfirst into the hole. Behind him he heard the thrum of a hundred arrows taking to the air and dove into the hole after her.

"Go! Crawl!" he shouted to Arista as he did his best to shove rocks up against the opening. She obeyed and somewhere in the darkness he heard her scream.

"Arista!" He turned and scrambled forward, only to fall.

Dropping ten feet, he landed next to her, and the two found themselves lying in a corridor illuminated by a lantern in Myron's hand.

"You two all right?" Royce asked. "That drop is a bit of a surprise."

"I'm sorry," Arista was saying, rubbing her back. "I couldn't hold them. There was something fighting me, something I've never felt before, another power."

"It's okay," Hadrian told her. "You did great. We're in."

"We are?" the princess asked, looking around, surprised.

"What about getting back out?" Gaunt asked.

"I'd be more concerned about them following us right now," Hadrian told him. "The narrow passage will slow their progress, but they'll be coming."

"Talk as you walk," Royce said. "Or run if you're up to it. Give me the lantern, Myron. I don't want to fall into any more holes."

"Maybe we should stay behind and kill them as they come down," Mauvin said to Hadrian.

"You'll run out of strength before they run out of goblins,"

Hadrian told him. "And then there's that—that thing the oberdaza were making."

"*Thing?*" Arista asked.

They jogged down the corridor with Royce out front holding the lantern high. To either side were white marble walls, and beneath them, a dark polished floor of beautiful mosaic design.

"I don't suppose you saw a map of this place," Royce said to Myron.

"Actually, yes, but it was very old, and parts were missing."

"Better than nothing. Any idea where we are?"

"Not yet."

At first Hadrian thought they stumbled into a room—a great hall, by the size of it—but soon it became clear that it was a corridor, but far larger than any Hadrian had ever before seen. Suits of armor, each similar to the one he had found in Jerish's room, stood on either side. The walls were sculptured relief images of men, scenes of battles, scenes of remembrance; they flashed, frame by frame, as the party raced past.

Hadrian saw a long succession of men being crowned, with the cityscape in the background; in each one the city was smaller, the crowning ceremony less lavish. Two things caught his notice as they ran. The first was that in every instance, the head of the man being crowned was scratched out, deliberately chipped away. The second was that in each depiction, although the crowd always appeared different, Hadrian could swear the artist used the same model for one figure—a tall, slender man—who appeared in the forefront in each scene. And while in the dim fluttering lantern light it was difficult to tell, Hadrian was certain he had seen the man before.

They came to a four-way intersection. To the left was an

incredible door, five stories tall, made completely of gold and inlaid with stunning geometric designs of such artistry each of them expelled a sound of awe.

"The imperial throne room," Myron said. "In there once sat the ruler of the world."

"You know where we are, then?" Royce asked.

Myron nodded, looking at the walls. "Yes...I think so."

"Which way to the crypts?"

The monk hesitated, closing his eyes for a second. "This way." He pointed forward. "Down two doors, then we take a stair down on the left."

They quickly reached the stair and Royce led them down. Gaunt grunted, limping along with one arm around Myron's shoulders, his fist holding on to the monk's rope belt.

"Oberdaza?" Arista said to Hadrian as they chased the end of the line. "You mentioned them before, when we were in Hintindar, didn't you? You said they were witch doctors who used Ghazel magic."

"Scary little buggers."

"What was that *thing* they were making?"

"No idea, but it was on fire and growing."

"I could sense something, something disrupting the rhythm, breaking my pattern, my connection. I've never encountered anything like that before. I didn't know what to do."

"I think you did great," he told her. "You controlled it real well too—didn't even get close to losing you this time."

In the dim light he managed to catch a little smile on her face. "I did control it better, didn't I? You helped. I could sense you near me, this warm light I could cling to, an anchor to keep me grounded."

"You were probably just afraid I'd hit you again." Behind them, down the corridor, echoed a tremendous *boom!* The ground shook under them and dust blew off the walls. "Uh-oh."

They reached another stair.

"We keep going down, right?" he heard Royce ask. "This tomb-thing is at the bottom?"

"Yes," Myron replied. "The imperial crypt is on the lowest level. The palace was actually built over the tomb of Novron as a shrine to glorify his memory. It became a ruling palace long after."

They came to still another stair and raced down it, Magnus grunting with each drop. At the bottom lay corridors smaller and narrower, with shorter ceilings. They moved single file now, Gaunt struggling, hopping. A three-way intersection stopped them. Three statues of long-bearded men holding shields stood before them, staring back.

"Well?" Royce asked the monk.

"This is where the map was torn," he replied apologetically. "The rest is just white space."

"Great," Royce said.

"But we should be close. There wasn't much room left, so it has to be— Look!" The monk pointed at the wall on the right corridor, where an *EH* was scratched.

"Let's hope the Ghazel can't read," Royce said, pushing on.

"They don't need to; they can smell," Hadrian explained.

They ran as best they could, chasing the bobbing lantern. Behind them, the sounds of pursuit grew as the Ghazel gained on them. They passed doors on either side of the corridor, which Royce ignored as he rushed forward. Some were partially open. Hadrian tried to look inside, yet the interior of each was too dark to see anything.

Drums echoed, and the blast of a horn rang down the stone corridors. Gaunt was bleeding again. Hadrian could see dark drops on the floor behind them. If the Ghazel had had any trouble tracking them before, they would have none now.

Again they stopped, this time at a T-intersection at the

center of which stood a large stone door beside a stone table. They all saw letters above it, carved deep into the arch.

"Myron, translate," Royce ordered.

"This is it," he said excitedly. " *'Tread lightly, with fear and reverence, all ye who enter these halls, for this is the eternal resting place of the emperors of Elan, rulers of the world.'* "

Before Myron finished reading, Hadrian heard the chilling sound of claws on stone. "They're coming!"

Royce pulled on the door and struggled with it. Hadrian and Mauvin pushed forward. Together they grabbed hold of the edge and pulled to the sound of heavy stone grinding.

The sharp clacking of hundreds of three-inch nails grew louder as behind them a fiery red light appeared and grew. They all passed through the opening and together pulled the door shut. As they did, as the door closed, Hadrian peered out the closing crack and glimpsed the sight of a giant, stooping figure made of flame striding down the corridor at them.

"There's no way to lock it!" Alric shouted.

"Outta my way!" The dwarf fell to his knees and, drawing his hammer, pounded on the hinges. There was an immediate crack. "That will slow them."

Ahead was another, very narrow downward stair. Here the stone was different. It cast a bluish hue and was carved in fluid curving lines.

*Boom!*

The Ghazel reached the door and struck it hard.

"Run!" Hadrian called forward, and Royce reached the bottom of the stairs in seconds, waiting for the rest to join him.

*Boom!*

Hadrian glanced over his shoulder, watching Myron help Gaunt down. There was a loathsome clicking on the far side of the door, and he imagined all those claws scratching. Magnus remained on his knees, picking up wedges of broken stone and hammering them into cracks to hold the door tight.

*Boom!*

A red glow was visible, seeping in around the edges. Licks of flame curled through like long fingers reaching, searching.

"The door won't stop them," Arista said. She too remained on the landing, standing before the door, and Hadrian could see tension in her face. "And we can't keep running. They will eventually catch us. I have to stop them. Go on ahead."

"You tried that," Hadrian told her sternly.

"I didn't understand then. I'll do better this time." Her little body was breathing fast as she stared unblinking at the door, her hands clenching and unclenching.

"There's three of them and only one of you, and there's this fire thing. You—"

"Go!" she shouted. "It's the only way!"

*Boom!*

Cracks appeared across the face of the door. Bits of stone chipped off and fell on the dwarf's head.

"Go on, all of you!" She closed her eyes and began to mutter. Myron and Gaunt were finally at the bottom. Magnus followed quickly, vaulting down the steps. Mauvin and Alric hesitated partway down, but Hadrian remained—reluctant to leave her.

*Boom!*

The door fractured, the hands of flames bending around, gripping tight, ripping at the stone.

Arista's robe burst forth a brilliant white light, the stairs illuminated so harshly everyone shielded their eyes.

*Boom!*

The door buckled.

"No, you don't!" Arista shouted above the thunder of the stone.

White light rushed to the door, circling it and forcing back the red fire, filling the gaps. The flaming fingers recoiled and fought. Writhing and twisting, sparks erupted where the two met. From the far side they all heard an unnatural howl of pain that shook the bowels of the stone. A loud crack shuddered through the walls and, like a candle she blew on, the fiery light went out with a snap.

Arista remained on the landing, her face slick with sweat, her arms up, her fingers weaving in the air as if she were playing an invisible harp. The stone of the doors glowed with a blue light, brightening and ebbing like a luminous heartbeat. Her movements became faster, her hands jerking. She grunted and cried out as if in alarm.

"No!" she shouted.

A wind filled the space around her; Arista's hair whirled and snapped, her robe blowing, billowing out, shimmering like the surface of a moonstruck lake.

"Arista?" he called to her.

"They're—they're—" She was clearly struggling, fighting something. The pulsing light on the door sped up, growing faster and faster. She screamed and this time her head dodged to one side. She took a step backward and with another grunt struggled to throw her weight forward. "They're fighting me!"

She cried out again and Hadrian felt a powerful gust of wind burst through the door. It staggered both of them. Hadrian placed a hand on the wall to keep from falling.

"More than three!" she said. "Oh dear Maribor! I can't—"

Her face was straining, her jaw clenched; her eyes watered and tears fell down her cheeks. "I can't hold them. Run! *Run!*"

The door exploded. Bits of stone flew cracking across the walls, splitting and whizzing. Dust blossomed in a cloud. Arista flew back, crumpling to the floor—her light all but out. The robe managed only a quivering purple glow.

"No!" Hadrian shouted. He grabbed hold of her and lifted just as through the door the goblin horde charged.

They broke through the fog of dust with snarling teeth and glowing eyes. They attacked with sachels held high, fanged mouths spitting curses and dripping with anticipation.

Alric drew forth the sword of Tolin Essendon. "In the name of Novron and Maribor!" he shouted fiercely as he charged up the steps with Mauvin close behind. The shimmering blade of Count Pickering slid free of its sheath. "Back!" the king cried. "Back to Oberlin, you mangy beasts!"

Hadrian ran down the steps, clutching the princess to his chest. Behind him, he could still hear Alric's cursing the goblins, the blades' ringing, and the Ghazels' screams.

As Hadrian reached the bottom, Arista was stirring, her eyes fluttering open. He handed her to Myron. "Keep her safe!"

He turned, drew his swords, and ran back up the steps with Royce right behind. Above him, Mauvin and Alric fought as dark blood splattered the walls and spilled down the steps. Already a mound of bodies lay on the landing. He was still three steps away when Alric cried out and fell.

"*Alric!*" Mauvin shouted. He turned to his fallen king just as a sachel blade stabbed out.

Mauvin cried out in pain but managed to cleave the head from the goblin's shoulders.

"Fall back, Mauvin!" Hadrian shouted, stepping over Alric.

Standing shoulder to shoulder, the two filled the width of the corridor and fought like a single man with four arms. The whirl of their blades was daunting, and after three attempts the goblins hesitated. The goblins paused their assault and stood beyond the broken door, staring at them across a pile of Ghazel bodies.

"Mauvin, take Alric and go!" Hadrian ordered, breathing hard.

"You can't hold them yourself," Mauvin replied.

"You're bleeding, and I can hold them long enough. Get your king away."

Mauvin glared at the grinning teeth across from him.

Hadrian could see at least two of the oberdaza lying face-down on the stone table and thought, *She gave as good as she got.*

"Take him, Mauvin. Your duty is to him. Alric may yet live. Take him to Arista."

Mauvin sheathed his sword, and stooping, he lifted Alric and retreated down the steps. The goblins moved a step forward, then hesitated once more as Royce appeared beside Hadrian.

"Ugly little buggers." He appraised the faces across the threshold.

Pressure from the back was pushing the goblins reluctantly forward.

"How long before they remember they have bows?" Royce whispered.

"They aren't the brightest, particularly when scared," Hadrian explained. "In many respects they are like a pack of herd animals. If one panics, they all follow suit, but yeah, they'll figure it out. I'm guessing we got maybe a minute or two. Looks like we should have been winemakers after all, huh?"

"Oh, now you think of it," Royce chided.

"We'd be in our cottage around a warm fire right now. You'd be sampling our wares and complaining it wasn't good enough. I'd be making lists for the spring."

"No," Royce said. "It's five in the morning. I'd still be in bed with Gwen. She'd be curled up in a ball, and I'd be watching her sleep and marveling at how her hair lay upon her cheek as if Maribor himself had placed it there in just that way for me. And in the crib my son, Elias, and my daughter, Mercedes, would be just waking up." Hadrian saw him smile then for the first time since Gwen's death.

"Why don't you go down with the others and leave me here?" Royce said. "You might be able to get a little farther—a little closer to the tomb. Maybe there's another door—a door with a lock. You've spent enough time with me already."

"I'm not going to leave you here," Hadrian told him.

"Why not?"

"There are better ways to die."

"Maybe this is my fate, my reward for the life I lived. I wish these bastards had been at the bridge that night, or at least that Merrick had fought better. I regret it now—killing him, I mean. He was telling the truth. He didn't kill Gwen. I guess I'll just tack that on to all the other regrets of my life. Go on. Leave me."

"Royce! Hadrian!" Myron called to them from the bottom. "Run!"

"We can't—" Hadrian said when he noticed a white light growing below them and felt a rising wind. "Oh son of—!"

The stairs trembled and rock cracked. Bits of stone shattered and flew in all directions, hitting them like stinging bees. Hadrian grabbed hold of Royce and leapt headlong down the steps. A loud roar issued from above them as goblins screamed and the ceiling collapsed.

∽

"Hadrian!" Arista cried out. Her robe brightened, and Myron held his lantern high, but she could not see through the cloud of dust. She staggered on her feet, light-headed and dizzy. Her legs were weak and her thoughts muddy. Swaying with her arms reaching out for balance, she stared into the gloom of swirling dirt, her heart pounding. "Oh god, don't let them be dead!"

"Cut that a little close, didn't you?" She heard Hadrian's voice emerging out of the murk.

The fighter and the thief crawled out of the haze covered in what looked to be a fine coating of gray chalk. They waved their hands before their faces and coughed repeatedly as they climbed over the rubble to join the others in the narrow corridor. Behind them, the way was sealed.

Royce looked back. "Well, that's one way to lock them out. Not a good way—but a way."

"I didn't know what else to do. I didn't know what else to do!" she said while her hands opened and closed nervously. Arista felt on the edge of losing control; she was exhausted and terrified.

"You did great," Hadrian told her, taking her hands and holding them gently. Then, looking past her, he asked Mauvin, "How is he?"

"Not good," the count replied with a quavering voice. "Still alive, though."

The new Count Pickering was on his knees, holding Alric and brushing the king's hair from his face. Alric was unconscious. A large amount of dark blood pooled on the ground around him.

"The fool," Mauvin said. "He put his arm up to block, like he had a shield—'cause he always practiced with a shield. The blade cut his arm open from the shoulder to the elbow. When he tried to turn, they sliced open his stomach." Mauvin wiped tears from his eyes. "He fought well, though—really well. Better than I've ever seen—better than I thought he could. It was almost like...like I was fighting beside Fanen again." The tears continued to run down Mauvin's cheeks, faster than he could brush them away.

Alric's chest was moving, struggling up and down. A terrible gurgle bubbled up his throat with each raspy breath.

"Give me the lantern." Hadrian rapidly bent down over the king. He tore open his shirt, revealing the wound. The moment Hadrian saw it, he stopped. "Oh dear Novron," he said.

"Do something," Arista told him.

"There's nothing I can do," he told her. "The sword—it went through. I've seen this before—there's just nothing—The bleeding won't stop, not the way he's—I can't— Damn, I'm so sorry."

His lips sealed together and his eyes closed.

"No," Arista said, shaking her head. "No!" She fell and crawled to Alric's side. Placing her hand on his head, she felt he was hot and drenched in sweat. "No," she repeated. "I won't allow it."

"Arista?" She heard Hadrian, but she had already closed her eyes and began to hum. She sensed the dull solid forms of the old walls, the dirt and the stone, the air between them, their bodies, and the flow of Alric's blood as it spilled on the ground. She could see it in her mind as a glowing river of silver and the glow was fading.

"Arista?" The sound of Hadrian's voice echoed, but it was faint, as if coming from a distance.

She saw a sliver of darkness that appeared as a tear, a dark rip in the fabric of the world. She reached out and felt the edges, pulling them wider until she was able to pass through.

Inside it was dark—darker than night, darker than a room after blowing out a candle—it was the darkness of nothing. She peered deep into the void, searching. Alric was there, ahead of her, and drifting away, pulled by a current, like some dark river. She chased after him.

"Alric!" she called.

"Arista?" she heard him say. "Arista, help me!"

Ahead she saw a light, a single point that glimmered white.

"I'm trying. Stop and wait for me."

"I can't."

"Then I'll come and get you," she said, and pushed forward.

"I don't want to die," Alric told her.

"I won't let you. I can save you."

Arista struggled forward, but progress was hard. The river that pulled Alric away pushed her backward and confounded her legs. She fought, driving against the wash even as Alric glided across the surface.

Despite the difficulty, she was getting closer. Her brother looked back at her, his face frightened. "I'm sorry," he said. "I'm sorry I wasn't a better brother, a better king. Arista, you should have ruled instead of me. You were always smarter, stronger, more courageous. I was jealous. I'm sorry. Please forgive me."

She reached out and almost caught hold of him, their fingertips touched briefly, then he slipped away. She watched as he picked up speed. The current grew stronger, pulling him away, rushing him forward, stealing him from her.

Ahead the light was closer, brighter, and in it, she thought she saw figures moving. "Alric, you have to try and slow down, you're moving too fast, I can't get—I can't grab you. Alric, you're speeding up! Alric, reach out to me! Alric! *Alric!*"

She dove forward but her brother rushed away, washing toward the light at a speed she could not match. She watched as he grew smaller and smaller until he was lost in the brilliance of the light.

"No! *No!*" she cried, staring forward, blinded by the whiteness.

"*Arista.*" She heard a voice call—not Alric's, but familiar. "Arista. Your brother is here with us now. It's okay."

"Daddy?"

*"Yes, dear, it's me. I'm sorry I have no hairbrush to give you at this meeting, but there is so much more, so much more than a hairbrush waiting. Come join us."*

"I—I shouldn't," she told him, although she was not certain why.

The light did not hurt to look at, but it made it impossible to see more than vague shapes, all blurred and hazy, as if they moved on the far side of a frosted glass.

*"It's all right, honey,"* her father said. *"And it's not just us waiting. You have other friends here, others who love you."*

*"My burns are gone,"* Hilfred told her. *"Come see."*

She saw their wispy outlines before her; they were growing clearer and more defined. The current was no longer fighting against her and she was starting to pick up speed. She needed to stop, she needed to go back, there was something that—

*"Arista my love."* This was a voice she had not heard for a long, long time and her heart leapt at the sound.

"Mother?"

*"Come to me, honey, come home. I'm waiting for you."*

There was music playing, soft and gentle. The light was growing all around her such that the dark of the void was fading. She let herself go, let herself drift on the current that carried her forward faster and faster.

"Arista," another voice called. This one was faint and distant, coming from somewhere behind her.

She could almost make out the faces in the light. There were so many and they were smiling with outstretched arms.

"Arista, come back." The voice was not in the light; it was calling to her from the darkness. "Arista, don't leave!"

It came as a cry, a desperate plea, and she knew the voice.

"Arista, please, please don't leave. Please come back. Let him go and come back!"

It was Hadrian.

"*Arista*," her mother called, "*come home.*"

"Home," Arista said, and as she said it, she stopped. "Home," she repeated, and felt a pulling in her stomach as the light diminished.

"*I'll be waiting for you always.*" She heard her mother's voice as it drifted away.

"*Good luck,*" Alric called, his voice almost too faint to hear.

She felt herself flying backward, then—

Her eyes snapped open.

Arista lay on the stone, gasping and struggling to breathe. She inhaled long and hard but still could not manage to get enough air. The world was whirling above her, dark except for a faint purple glow. In this dim haze, she saw Hadrian crouched over her and felt him squeezing her hands. His own were shaking. Suddenly his strained look was replaced with a burst of joy.

"She's okay! See! She's looking around!" Mauvin shouted.

"Can you hear me?" Hadrian asked.

She tried but could not speak. All she could manage was a slight nod and her eye caught sight of Alric.

"He's gone," Hadrian told her sadly.

Again she managed a shallow nod.

"Are you sure you're all right?" Hadrian asked.

"Very...tired," she whispered as her eyes closed, and she fell asleep.

❧

As both Arista and Gaunt slept, Hadrian worked on Mauvin. The count's side was drenched in blood. A stab wound cut through the meat of his arm behind the upper bone. He had been holding it shut with his hand without complaint such that Hadrian had not noticed until Mauvin staggered.

Together, Hadrian and Magnus, with Myron holding the lantern, sewed Mauvin's wound. Hadrian was forced to push muscle back in as he stitched, yet Mauvin made no cry and soon passed out. When they finished, Hadrian wrapped his arm. It was a good, clean job and they had stopped the bleeding. Mauvin would be fine even if his left arm would never be as strong as it once had been. Hadrian checked Gaunt's leg and changed that bandage as well. Then, in the utter silence of the tombs, in the dim light of the lantern, they all slept.

When he woke, Hadrian felt every bruise, cut, scratch, and strained muscle. A lantern burned beside him, and with its light, he found his water skin. They all lay together in the narrow corridor, flopped haphazardly in dirt and blood like a pile of dead after a battle. He took a small sip to clear his mouth and noticed Royce was not with them.

He lifted the lantern and glanced at the pile of rubble where the stairs had once been. The way was blocked by several tons of stone.

"Well, I'm guessing you didn't go that way," he whispered to himself.

Turning, he noticed the corridor bent sharply to the left. Along the walls, he discerned faint, ghostly images etched in the polished stone like burnished details on glass. The images told a story. At the start of the hall was a strange scene: a group of men traveling to a great gathering in a forest where a ruler sat upon a throne that appeared to be part of a tree, yet none of the men had heads. In each instance, they were scraped away. In the next scene, the king of the tree throne fought one of the men in single combat—again no heads.

Hadrian raised the lantern and wiped the dust with his hands, looking closer at the images of the men fighting. He let his fingertips trace the weapons in their hands, strange twisted poles with multiple blades. He had never seen their like before and yet he knew them. He could imagine their weight, how his hands would grasp, and how to scoop the lower blade in order to make the upper two slice the air. His father had taught him to use this weapon, the polearm for which he had no name.

In the next scene, the king was victorious and all bowed to him save one. He stood aside with the rest of the men who had traveled together in the first scene, and in his arms, he held the body of the fallen combatant. Still no heads—each one carefully scratched out. On the ground lay bits of chipped stone and white dust.

Hadrian found Royce at the end of the hall before a closed and formidable-looking stone door.

"Locked?" Hadrian asked.

Royce nodded as his hands played over the door's surface.

"How long you been here?"

The thief shrugged. "A few hours."

"No keyhole?"

"Locked from the inside."

"Inside? That's creepy. Since when do dead men lock themselves into their own graves?"

"Something is alive in there," Royce said. "I can hear it."

Hadrian felt a chill run down his back as his mind ran through all the possibilities of what might lie beyond the door. Who knew what the ancients could have placed in their tombs to protect their kings: ghosts, wraiths, zombie guards, stone golems?

"And you can't open the door?"

"Haven't found a way yet."

"Tried knocking?"

Royce looked over his shoulder incredulously.

"What would it hurt?"

Royce's expression eased. He thought a moment and

shrugged. He stepped back and waved toward the door. "Be my guest."

Hadrian drew his short sword and, using the butt, tapped three times on the stone. They waited. Nothing happened. He tapped three more times.

"It was worth a—"

Stone scraped as a bolt moved. Silence. A snap, then another bolt was drawn. The stone slab shuddered and shook.

Royce and Hadrian glanced nervously at each other. Hadrian handed the lantern to Royce and drew his bastard sword. Royce pushed on the door and it swung inward.

Inside, it was dark and Hadrian held up the lantern with his left hand, probing forward with his sword. The light revealed a small square room with a vaulted ceiling. At the center was a great headless statue. The walls were filled with holes filled with piles of rolled scrolls, several of which lay ripped to pieces, their remains scattered across the floor. On the far side was another stone door, closed tight. Hadrian could see large bolts holding it fast. The ground also contained clay pots, clothes, blankets, and the melted remains of burned candles. Not far away the room's only occupant was in the process of sitting back down on his blanket. When the man turned, Hadrian recognized him immediately.

"Thranic?" Hadrian said, stunned.

Sentinel Dovin Thranic moved slowly, painfully. He was very thin. His normally pale face was drawn and ghostly white. His dark hair, which had always been so neatly combed back, hung loose in his face. His once-narrow mustache and short goatee were now a full ragged beard. He still wore his black and red silks, which were now mere shades of their former glory, torn and filthy.

The sentinel managed a strained smile as he recognized them through squinting eyes. "How loathsome that it is *you* that finds me." He focused on Royce. "Come for your revenge at last, elf?"

Royce stepped forward. He looked down at Thranic and then around the room. "How could I possibly top this? Sealed alive in a tomb of rock. My only regret is that I had nothing to do with it."

"What happened?" Hadrian asked.

Thranic coughed; it was a bad sound, as if the sentinel's chest was ripping apart from the inside. He reclined, trying to breathe, for a moment. "Bulard went lame — the old man was a nuisance and we left him at the library. Levy — Levy was killed. Bernie ran out on me — deserted." Thranic shifted uneasily; as he did, Hadrian noticed a bloodstained cloth wrapped his left thigh.

"How long have you been here?"

"Months," he replied. He glanced across the room at a pile of small humanoid bones and grimaced. "I did what I must to survive."

"Until the wound," Hadrian added.

The sentinel nodded. "I couldn't sneak up on them well enough anymore."

Royce continued to stare.

"Go ahead," Thranic told Royce. "Kill me. It doesn't matter anymore. It's over and you'll fare no better. No one can get the horn. It's what you came for, isn't it? The Horn of Novron? The Horn of Gylindora? It lies through there." He pointed at the far door. "On the other side is a large hall, the Vault of Days, which leads to the tomb of Novron itself, but you will never reach it. No one has...and no one will. Look there." He pointed to the wall across from him, where words lay scratched. "See the *EH*? This is as far as Edmund Hall ever got. He turned back and escaped this vile pit, because he was smart. I stayed, thinking I could somehow solve the riddle, somehow find a way to cross the Vault of Days, but it can't be done. We tried. Levy was the slowest—not even his body remains. Bernie wouldn't go back in after that."

"You stabbed him," Royce stated.

"He refused orders. He refused to make another attempt. You found him?"

"Dead."

Thranic showed no sign of pleasure or remorse; he merely nodded.

"What is it about this Vault of Days?" Hadrian asked. "Why can't you cross it?"

"Look for yourself."

Hadrian started across the room and Thranic stopped him. "Let the elf do it. What can you hope to see in there with your human eyes?"

Royce stared at the sentinel. "So what kind of trick is this?"

"I don't like it," Hadrian said.

Royce stepped to the door and studied it. "Looks okay."

"It is. What's on the other side, however, is not."

Royce touched the door and closely inspected the sides.

"So distrusting," Thranic said. "It won't bite if you open the door, only if you enter the room."

Slowly he drew the bolts away.

"Careful, Royce," Hadrian said.

Very slowly Royce pushed the door inward, peering through the gap. He looked left and right, then closed it once more and replaced the bolts.

"What is it?" Hadrian asked.

"He's right," Royce said dismally. "No one is getting through."

Thranic smiled and nodded until he was beset by another series of coughs that bent him over in pain.

"What is it?" Hadrian repeated.

"You're not going to believe it."

"What?"

"There's a—a thingy."

"A what?"

"You know, a thingy thing."

Hadrian looked at him, puzzled.

"A Gilarabrywn," Thranic said.

# CHAPTER 19

# SEALING OF THE GATE

Renwick stood on the fourth floor of the imperial palace. In front of him the registrar shuffled and rolled parchments, occasionally muttering to himself and scratching his neck with long slender fingers dyed black at the tips. A little rabbit-faced man with precise eyes and a large gap between his front teeth, he sat behind his formidable desk, scribbling. The sound of his quill on parchment reminded Renwick of a mouse gnawing at wood.

Members of the palace staff hurried by, entering the many doors around him. Some faces turned his way, but only briefly. At least the administration wing of the fourth floor was free of refugees. Every other inch of the castle seemed to be full of them. People lined the hallways, sitting with knees up to allow people passage, or sleeping on their sides with bundles under their heads, their arms wrapped tight around their bodies. Renwick guessed the bundles contained what little was left of their lives. Dirty, frightened faces looked up whenever anyone entered the corridors. Families mostly—farmers with sets of children who all looked alike—had come from the countryside, where homes lay abandoned.

He tapped his toes together, noticing that the numbness

was finally leaving. The sound caused the scribe to look up in irritation. Renwick smiled, but the scribe scowled and returned to his work. The squire's face still felt hot, burned from the cold wind. He had ridden nonstop from Amberton Lee to Aquesta and delivered his message directly to Captain Everton, commander of the southern gate. Afterward, starved and cold, he went to the kitchen, where Ibis was kind enough to let him have some leftover soup. Returning to the dormitories, he found a family of three from Fallon Mire sleeping in his bed— a mother and two boys, whose father had drowned in the Galewyr a year earlier trying to cross the Wicend Ford during the spring runoff.

Renwick had just curled up in a vacant corner of the hallway to sleep when Bennington, one of the main hall guards, grabbed him. All he said was that Renwick was to report to the chancellor's office immediately, and he berated the boy about how half the castle had been looking for him for hours. Bennington gave him the impression that he was in trouble, and when Renwick realized that he had left Amberton Lee without orders, his heart sank. Of course the empress and the imperial staff already knew about the elven advance. An army of scouts watched every road and passage. It had been arrogant and shortsighted.

They would punish him. At the very least, Renwick was certain to remain no more than a page, forced back to mucking out the stable and splitting the firewood. Dreams of being a real squire vanished. At the age of seventeen, he had already peaked with his one week of serving Hadrian—the false squire and the false knight. His sad and miserable life was over, and he could hope for no better fortune to befall him now.

No doubt he would also get a whipping, but that would be the worst of it. If Saldur and Ethelred were still in charge, the punishment would be more severe. Chancellor Nimbus and the imperial secretary were good, kind people, which only made his failure that much harder to bear. His palms began to sweat as he imagined—

The door to the chancellor's office opened. Lord Nimbus poked his head out. "Has no one found—" His eyes landed on Renwick. "Oh dash it all, man! Why didn't you let us know he was out here?"

The scribe blinked innocently. "I—I—"

"Never mind. Come in here, Renwick."

Inside the office, Renwick was shocked to see Empress Modina herself. She sat on the window ledge, her knees bent, her body curled up so that her gown sprayed out. Her hair was down, lying on her shoulders, and she appeared so oddly human—so strangely girlish. Captain Everton stood to one side, straight as an elm, his helm under one arm, water droplets from melted snow still visible on the steel of his armor. Another man in lighter, rougher dress stood in the opposite corner. He was tall, slender, and unkempt. This man wore leather, wool, and a thick ratty beard.

Lord Nimbus took a seat at the desk and motioned to Renwick. "You are a hard man to find," he said. "Please, tell us exactly what happened?"

"Well, like I told Captain Everton here, Mince—that's one of the boys with me—he saw a troop of elves crossing the Bernum."

"Yes, Captain Everton told us that, but—"

"Tell us everything," the empress said. Her voice was beautiful and Renwick was astounded that she had actually spoken to him. He felt flustered, his tongue stiff. He could not think, much less talk. He opened his mouth and words fell out. "I—ah—every—um…"

"Start at the beginning, from the moment you left here," she said. "Tell us everything that has happened."

"We must know the progress of the mission," Nimbus clarified.

"Oh—ah—okay, well, we rode south to Ratibor," he began, trying to think of as much detail as he could, but it was difficult to concentrate under her gaze. Somehow, he managed to recount the trip to Amberton Lee, the descent of the party into the shaft, and the days he and the boys had spent in the snow. He told them of Mince and the sighting, and of his long, hard trip north, racing to stay ahead of the elven vanguard. "I'm sorry I didn't stay at my post. I have no excuse for abandoning it and willingly accept whatever punishment you see fit to deliver."

"Punishment?" the empress said with a tone of humor in her voice as she climbed down from her perch. "You will be rewarded. The news your daring ride has brought is the hope I've looked for."

"Indeed, my boy," Nimbus added. "This news of the mission's progress is very reassuring."

"*Very* reassuring," the empress repeated, then let out a sigh of relief, as if it allowed her to take one more breath. "At least we know they made it in safely."

She crossed the room to him. He stood locked in place, every muscle frozen, as she reached out. She took his face in her hands and kissed him, first on one cheek, and then the other. "Thank you," she whispered, and he thought he saw her eyes glisten.

He could not breathe or look away and thought he might die. The very idea that he would collapse right there at her feet and pass away did not trouble him in the least.

"The lad is going to fall," Everton said.

"I—I just—I haven't—"

"He hasn't had a chance to rest," Nimbus said, saving him. Renwick shut his mouth and nodded.

"Then see to his needs," she said. "For today he is my hero."

✦

Modina left the office feeling better than she had in days. *They found the way in!* Nimbus was right—there was still hope. It was a mere sliver, a tiny drop, but that was the way with hope. She had lived without it for so long that she was unaccustomed to the feeling, which made her giddy. It was the first time in what felt a century that she looked to the future without dread. Yes, the elves were coming. Yes, they were not in winter quarters. Yes, they would attack the city within the week—but the party was safe and she knew where the enemy would strike. There was hope.

She reached the stair and sighed. People filled the entire length of the steps. Families clustered together along the sides, gathering like twigs on a riverbank until they created a dam. They had to stop doing that.

"Sergeant," she called down to a castle guard on the main floor who was having a dispute with a man holding a goat. Apparently the man insisted on keeping it in the palace.

"Your Eminence?" he replied, looking up.

Upon hearing this, the crowd went silent and heads turned. There were whispers, gasps, and fingers pointed toward her. Modina did not roam the castle. Since her edict to grant shelter to the refugees—to quarter them anywhere possible—she had returned to her old habit of being a recluse. She lived in her chambers, visiting the fourth-floor offices and the throne room only once a day, and even then by back stairways. Her appearance in the halls was an uncommon sight.

"Keep these stairs clear," she told him, her voice sounding loud in the open chamber. "I don't want people falling down them. Find these good people room somewhere else. Surely there are more suitable quarters than here."

"Yes, Your Eminence. I'm trying, but they—well, they are afraid of getting lost in the palace, so they gather within sight of the doors."

"And why is that goat in here? All livestock was to be turned over to the quartermaster and recorded by the minister of city defense. We can't afford to have families keeping pigs and cows in the palace courtyard."

"Yes, Your Eminence, but this fellow, he says this goat is part of his family."

The man looked up at her, terrified, clutching the goat around its neck. "She's all the family I 'ave, Yer Greatness. Please don't take 'er."

"Of course not, but you and…your family…will have to stay in the stable. Find him room there."

"Right away, Your Eminence."

"And get these steps clear."

"Thrace?" The word rose out of the sea of faces. The faint voice was nearly swallowed by the din.

"Who said that?" she asked sharply.

The room went silent.

Someone coughed, another sneezed, someone shuffled his feet, and the goat clicked its hooves, but no one spoke for a full minute. Then she saw a hand rising above the crowd and waving slightly side to side.

"Who are you? Come forward," she commanded.

A woman stepped through the throng of bodies, moving across the floor of the entry hall below. Modina could not tell anything from looking down at the top of her head. A handful of others followed her, pushing through the pack, stepping around the blankets and bundles.

"Come up here," she ordered.

As the woman reached the stairs, those squatting on the steps rose and moved aside, granting her passage. She was thin, with light brown hair, cut straight across the bottom at the level of her earlobes, giving her a boyish look. She wore a pathetic rag of a dress made of poor rough wool. It was stained, hanging shapelessly from her shoulders, and tied at the waist with a bit of twine.

She was familiar.

Something in her walk, in the way she hung her head, in the weak sag of her shoulders, and the way she dragged her feet. She knew this woman.

"Lena?" Modina muttered.

The woman stopped and raised her head at the sound. She had the same sharp pointed nose speckled with freckles and brown eyes with no visible brows. The woman looked across at Modina with a mixture of hope and fear.

"Lena Bothwick?" the empress shouted.

Lena nodded and took a step back as Modina rushed toward her.

"Lena!" Modina threw her arms around the woman and hugged her tight. Lena was shaking as tears ran down her cheeks.

"What's wrong?"

"Nothing," Lena said. "It's just I—I didn't know if you'd remember us."

Behind her were Russell and Tad. "Where are the twins?"

Lena frowned. "They died last winter."

"I'm so sorry."

She nodded and they hugged once more.

Russell stood beside his wife. Like Lena, he was thin, dressed in a frayed and flimsy shirt that hung to his knees and was tied about the waist with a length of rope. His face was older, cut with more lines, and his hair was grayer than she remembered. Tad was taller and broader. No longer the boy she remembered, he was a man, but just as haggard and gaunt as the rest.

"Empress!" Russell stated. "Oh, you're your father's daughter, all right. Stubborn as a mule and strong as an ox! The elves are foolish to even think about crossing paths with one of the Woods of Dahlgren."

"Welcome to *my* house," she said, and hugged him.

❧

"Dillon McDern had come here with us during Wintertide just a few months ago. We watched Hadrian joust," Russell told her.

She had brought them back to her bedroom, where she sat on the bed with Lena while Russell—who was never one to sit while telling a story—stood before her. Tad was at the window, admiring the view.

"It was a great day," he went on, but there was regret in his voice. "We tried to see you, but they turned us away at the gate, a'course. Who's gonna let the likes of us in to see the empress? So we went back to Alburn.

"After Dahlgren, Vince found us all plots on Lord Kimble's land. We was grateful to get it at the time but it turned out not to be such a good idea. Kimble took most of the yield and charged us for seed and tools. He took Dillon's sons for his army and they was both killed. When he came to take Tad here, well, I didn't see no reason to stay for that.

"Dillon and I were drinking one night and he told me, he says, 'Rus, if I had it to do over again, I'd run.' I knew what he was getting at, and we said goodbye to each other like tomorrow would never come. We packed that night and we ran out. Thing is we was only running 'cause we didn't want

Tad to be pressed into Kimble's army. We got as far as Stock-
ton Bridge when we heard the elves had invaded Alburn. We
heard they torched the place. Dillon, Vince, even Lord Kimble
are all dead now, I suppose. We come here 'cause we didn't
know where else to go. We hoped, but we never expected to
see you."

The door to the bedroom burst open and the girls and Mr.
Rings came bounding in, all three halting short when they
saw the Bothwicks. They stood still and silent. Modina held
out an inviting arm and the girls shifted uneasily toward her,
the raccoon climbing to the safety of Mercy's shoulder.

"This is Mercy and Allie," Modina told them.

Lena smiled at the two curiously, then stared at Allie's
pointed ears. "Is she—"

Modina cut her off. "They're as dear to me as daughters.
Allie's father is on a very important mission and I promised I
would watch over her until his return. Mercy is—" She hesitated briefly. She had never said it in the girl's presence before.
"She is an orphan, from the north, and one of the first to see
the elves attack."

"Speaking of elves..." Russell continued where his wife
had left off.

"Yes, Allie is of elvish descent. Her father saved her from a
slave ship bound for Calis."

"And you've got no problem with that?" Russell asked.

"Why would I? Allie is a sweet little girl. We've grown
quite fond of each other. Haven't we?" Modina brushed a
loose strand of hair behind a pointed ear.

The girl nodded and smiled.

"Her father may have to fight me for her when he gets
back." Modina smiled at them both. "And where have you
two mischief-makers been?"

"In the kitchen, playing with Red."

Modina raised an eyebrow. "With Mr. Rings?"

"They get along fine," Mercy said. "Although…"

"What?"

Mercy hesitated to speak, so Allie stepped forward. "Mercy is trying to get Red to let Mr. Rings ride on his back. It's not going so well. Mr. Thinly chased us out after Red knocked over a stack of pans."

Modina rolled her eyes. "You are a pair of monsters, aren't you?"

Lena began to cry and put her arms around Russell, who held her.

"What?" Modina asked, going to Lena.

"Oh, it's nothing." Russell spoke for her. "The girls—you know—she misses the twins. We almost lost Tad too, didn't we, boy?"

Tad, who was still looking out the window, turned and nodded. He had not said a word, and the Thaddeus Bothwick Modina remembered had never been quiet.

"We survived all those terrible nights in Dahlgren," Lena said, sobbing. "But living in Alburn killed my little girls and now—and now…"

"You're going to be all right," Modina told her. "I'll see to that."

Russell looked at her, nodding appraisingly. "Damned if you ain't your father's daughter. Theron would be real proud of you, Thrace. Real proud."

❧

Renwick had no idea what to do. For the third day in a row, he was confused and uncomfortable. He wanted to return to Amberton Lee, but the empress forbade him. The elven army would be between them now. He tried to resume his castle page duties only to discover he was not wanted, once more due to an edict from the empress. Apparently he had no assigned duties.

He wore a new tunic, far nicer than any he had ever had before. He ate wonderful meals and slept right under Sir Elgar and across from Sir Gilbert of Lyle, in a berth in the knights' dormitories.

"You'll get work plenty soon enough, lad," Elgar told him. He and Sir Gilbert were at the table, engaged in a game of chess that Gilbert was winning easily. "When those elves arrive, you'll be earning your keep."

"Hauling buckets of water to the gate for the soldiers," Renwick said dismally.

"Hauling water?" Elgar questioned. "That's page work."

"I am a page."

"Hah! Is that a page's bed you sleep in? Is that a page's tunic? Are you eating page meals? Slopping out the stables? You *were* a page, but the empress has her eye on you now."

"What does that mean?"

"It means you are in her favor, and you won't be hauling no water."

"But what—"

"Can you handle a blade, boy?" Gilbert asked while sliding a pawn forward and making Elgar shift uneasily in his seat.

"I think so."

"You *think* so?"

"Sir Malness never let me—"

"Malness? Malness was an idiot," Elgar growled.

"Probably why he broke his neck falling off his horse," Gilbert said.

"He was drinking," Renwick pointed out.

"He was an idiot," Elgar repeated.

"It doesn't matter," Gilbert said. "When the fight begins, we'll need every man who can hold a blade. You might have been a page yesterday, but tomorrow you will be a soldier. And with the eye of the empress on you—fight well, and you may find yourself a knight."

"Don't fill his head with too much nonsense," Elgar said. "He's not even a squire."

"I squired for Sir Hadrian."

"Hadrian isn't a knight."

A horn sounded and all three scrambled out of the dormitory and raced past the droves of refugees to the front hall. They pushed out into the courtyard, looking to the guards at the towers.

"What is it?" Elgar called to Benton.

The tower guard heard his voice and turned. "Sir Breckton and the army have returned. The empress has gone to welcome them home."

"Breckton," Gilbert said miserably. "Com'on, Elgar, we have a game to finish."

The two turned their backs on the courtyard and returned inside, but Renwick ran out past the courtyard and through the city toward the southern gate. The portcullis was already up by the time he arrived, and the legion bearing Breckton's blue-and-gold-checkered standard entered.

Drums sounded, keeping beat with the footfalls of men. As the knight-marshal rode at the head of his army, the sun shone off his brilliant armor. At his side rode the lady Amilia, wrapped in a heavy fur cloak, which draped across the side and back of her mount. Renwick recognized other faces: King Armand, Queen Adeline, Prince Rudolf and his younger brother Hector, along with Leo, Duke of Rochelle, and his wife,

Genevieve, who composed the last of the Alburn nobility. With their arrival it was official—the eastern provinces were lost. Sir Murthas, Sir Brent, Sir Andiers, and several others he knew from the rosters formed ranks in the armored cavalry. Behind them, neat rows of foot soldiers marched. These were followed by wagons of supplies and people—more refugees.

Modina ran to embrace Amilia the moment she climbed off her horse. "You made it!" she said, squeezing her. "And your family?"

"They are on the wagons," Amilia told her.

"Bring them to the great hall. Are you hungry?"

She nodded, smiling.

"Then I will meet them and we will eat. I have people for you to meet as well. Nimbus!" Modina called.

"Your Eminence." The chancellor trotted to her side and Amilia hugged the beanpole of a man.

Renwick could not see anymore as the army filled the street. He moved to the wall and climbed steps to the top of the gate, where Captain Everton was once more on duty, watching the progress of the army's return below him.

"Impressive, isn't he?" Everton said to him as they watched the column from the battlements. "I for one will sleep easier tonight knowing Sir Breckton is here, and none too soon, I suspect."

"How do you mean?"

"I don't like the sky."

Renwick looked up. Overhead a dark haze swirled a strange mix of brown and yellow, a sickly soup of dense clouds that churned and folded like the contents of some witch's brew.

"That doesn't look natural to me."

"It's warmer too," Renwick said, having just realized that

he was outside without a cloak and not shivering. He breathed out and could not see his breath.

He rushed to the edge of the battlement and looked southeast. In the distance, the clouds were darker still and he noticed an eerie green hue to the sky. "They are coming."

"Blow the horn," Everton ordered as the last of the troops and wagons passed through. "Seal the gate."

# Chapter 20

# The Vault of Days

*R*unning *through the corridors, she heard the clash of steel
and the cries of men. She had done her duty, her obligations complete. Descending to the tombs, she entered the
Vault of Days. The emperor lay on the floor as the last of his
knights died on the swords of those loyal to Venlin. A rage
boiled in her as she spoke. The room shuddered at the sound
of her words and the would-be killers of her emperor—ten
Teshlor Knights—screamed as their bodies ripped apart.*

*She fell to her knees.*

*"Emperor!" she cried. "I am here!"*

*Nareion wept as in his arms he clutched the dead bodies of
his wife, Amethes, and Fanquila, their daughter.*

*"We must go," she urged.*

*The emperor shook his head. "The horn?"*

*"I placed it in the tomb."*

*"My son?"*

*"He is with Jerish. They have left the city."*

*"Then we will end this here." Nareion drew his sword.
"Enchant it with the weaving-letters."*

*She knew what he meant to do. She wanted to tell him not
to. She wanted to assure him there was another way, but even*

*as she shook her head, she placed her hand on the blade and spoke the words, making the blade shimmer and causing letters to appear. They moved and shifted as if uncertain where they should settle.*

*"Now go, meet him. I will see to it that he never enters the tomb." The emperor looked down at his dead family and the shimmering sword. "I will make certain no one else will."*

*She nodded and stood. Looking back just once at the sad scene of the emperor crying over the loss of his family, she left the Vault of Days. She no longer rushed. Time was unimportant now. The emperor was dead, but Venlin had not killed him. He had missed his chance. Venlin would win the battle but lose the war.*

*"He is dead, then." She heard the voice—so familiar. "And you are here to kill me?"*

*"Yes," she replied.*

*She was in the corridor just outside the throne room. He was inside, his voice seeping out.*

*"And you think you can? Such is the folly of youth. Even old Yolric is not so foolish as to challenge me. And you—you are the youngest of the council, a pup—you dare bring your inexperience and meager knowledge of the Art against me? I am the Art—my family invented it. My brother taught Cenzlyor. The entire council flows from the skills and knowledge of the Miralyith. You have ruined much. I did not suspect you. Jerish was obvious, but you! You wanted power, you always wanted power; all of you did. You hated the Teshlor more than anyone. Above all, I thought I could count on your support."*

*"That was before Avempartha, before I discovered who you are—murderer. You will not succeed."*

*"I already have. The emperor is dead; I know this. I have just one loose end to tie up. Tell me, where is Nevrik?"*

*"I will die before telling you that."*

"*There are worse things than dying.*"

"*I know,*" she told him. "*That's why I choose death. Death for me, death for you…*" She looked down the corridor to where the sunlight was streaming in. She could still hear the parade marching past the cheering crowds. "*Death for everyone. It ends here, and Nevrik will return to his throne. It is time to bury the dead at last.*"

She looked out at the sun one more time and thought of Elinya. "*Maribor take us both,*" she said, and closing her eyes, began the weave.

❧

"He did it."

Arista woke up sweating, her heart pounding.

She lay in a small dark room lit by a single lantern. A thin blanket separated her from the cold floor, another was placed over her, and a bag supported her head. The room was not much bigger than her old bedroom in the tower. It was a perfect square with a vaulted ceiling, the arches forming a star shape as they joined overhead. On either side of the room, two doors faced each other. One opened to the corridor; the other was shut tight and locked from their side. Nooks with brass lattice doors covered the walls, each alcove filled with piles of neatly placed scrolls, round tubes of yellowed parchment. Many of the little grates were open; several scrolls lay spilled on the floor, some of them torn to pieces. In the center of the room was a statue. She recognized it as a version of those she had seen in churches and chapels throughout her life. It was a depiction of Novron, only this one was missing the head. Its remains lay shattered and beaten to powder on the floor.

Hadrian's was the first face she saw, as he sat beside her. "You're awake at last," he said. "I was getting worried."

Myron was just to her left. He was the closest to the light, sitting in a mound of scrolls. The monk looked up, smiled, and waved.

"You're all right?" Hadrian asked with concern in his voice.

"Just exhausted." She wiped her eyes and sighed. "How long have I been asleep?"

"Five hours," Royce said. She only heard his voice, as he was somewhere just outside the ring of light.

"Five? Really? I feel like I could sleep another ten," she said, yawning.

Arista noticed in the corner an unpleasant-looking man— pale and withered—like a sickly molting crow. He sat hunched over, watching them, his dark marble eyes glaring.

"Who's he?"

"Sentinel Thranic," Hadrian told her. "The last living member of the previous team. I'd introduce you, but we sort of hate each other, seeing as how he shot Royce with a crossbow last fall—nearly killed him."

"And he's still alive?" Arista asked.

"Don't look at me. I haven't stopped him," Hadrian told her. "Hungry?"

"I hate to say it, given the circumstances, but I'm famished."

"We thought you died," Mauvin told her. "You stopped moving and even stopped breathing for such a long time. Hadrian slapped you a few times, but it did nothing."

"You hit me again?" She rubbed her cheek, feeling the soreness.

He looked guilty. "I was scared. And it worked last time."

She noticed the bandage on Mauvin's arm. "You're wounded?"

"More embarrassed than anything. But that's bound to

happen when you're a Pickering fighting beside Hadrian. Doesn't really hurt that much, honest."

"Hmm, let's see." She heard Hadrian rummaging around in a pack. "Would you like salt pork...or perhaps...let's see now...how about salt pork?" he asked with a smile, handing a ration to her. She tore it open with shaking hands.

"You sure you're all right?" he asked, and she was surprised at the concern in his voice.

"Just weak—like a fever broke, you know?" Hadrian did not indicate whether he knew, but sat watching her as if she might drop over dead any minute. "I'm fine—really."

Arista took a bite of the meat. The heavily salted and miserably dry pork was a joy to swallow, which she did almost without chewing.

"Alric?" she asked.

"He's in the corridor," Hadrian told her.

"You haven't buried him yet, have you?"

"No, not yet."

"Good, I would like to take him back to Melengar to be laid in the tomb of his fathers."

The others looked away, each noticeably silent, and she saw a disturbing grin stretch across Thranic's face. The sentinel appeared ghoulish in the lantern light; his malevolence chilled her.

"What is it?" she asked.

"It doesn't look like we will be getting back to Melengar," Hadrian told her.

"The horn isn't here?"

"Apparently it's through that door, but we haven't—"

"Through that door is death," Thranic told her. He spoke for the first time, his voice a hissing rasp. "Death for all the children of Maribor. The last emperor's guardian watches the Vault of Days and will not suffer anyone's passage."

"Guardian?" she asked.

"A Gilarabrywn," Hadrian told her. "A big one."

"Well, of course it's big, if it's a Gilarabrywn."

Hadrian smiled. "You don't understand. This one is *really* big."

"Is there a sword? There has to be a sword to slay it, right?"

Hadrian sighed. "Royce says there's another door on the far side. Maybe it's over there. We don't know. Besides, you realize there's no reason for the sword to be down here at all."

"We have to look. We have to..."

*The sword.*

"What is it?" Hadrian asked.

"Is the Gilarabrywn bigger than the one in Avempartha?"

"A lot bigger."

"It would be," she said, remembering her dream. "And the sword is there, on the far side of the room."

"How do you know?"

"I saw it... or at least, Esrahaddon did. Emperor Nareion created the Gilarabrywn himself. Esrahaddon enchanted the blade of the king's sword with the name and Nareion conjured the beast. Only he did it with his own blood. He sacrificed himself in the making, adding power to the Gilarabrywn and assigning it the task of guarding the tombs where Esrahaddon hid the horn."

The sentinel eyed her curiously. "The Patriarch was not aware of its existence, nor did *we* realize it was there until we opened that door. No spell, no stealth, no army, no wishful thinking will grant anyone access to the room beyond. The quest for the horn ends here."

"And *someone* sealed the way out," Gaunt reminded her. He reclined on his pack. His fur-lined houppelande, pulled tight to his chin, was torn and stained. His chaperon hat was a rumpled mess, the folds ripped and pulled down over his ears.

The liripipe was missing altogether and Arista only then realized the same black cloth of Gaunt's headdress wrapped Mauvin's arm. "Which means we're trapped in this room until we die of thirst or starvation. At least this bugger was able to live off goblins. What are we going to do, carve up each other?"

"Don't be so optimistic, Mr. Sunshine," Mauvin told him. "You might just get our hopes too high, and then we'll be disappointed in the end."

"We have to try something," she said.

"We will," Hadrian assured her. "Royce and I don't give up that easily—you know that—but you should rest more before we do anything. We might need you. By the way, what did you mean by 'he did it'?"

"What?"

"When you woke up, you said, 'He did it.' It sounded important. Another one of your dreams?"

"Oh, that, yeah," she said, confused for a moment, trying to remember. Already the memory was fogged and blowing away. "It was Esrahaddon, he did this."

"Did what?"

"All this," she said, pointing up and whirling her hand around. "He destroyed the city—just like they said he did. You remember what I did at the stairs? Well, he was a bit more powerful. He collapsed the entire city, sunk and buried it."

"So he wasn't kidding when he said he was better with hands," Royce observed.

"And the people?" Mauvin asked.

"They were having a Founder's Day celebration. The city was packed with people, all the dignitaries, all the knights and Cenzars, and...yes, he killed everyone."

"Of course he did!" Thranic shouted as best he could. "Did you think the church lied? Esrahaddon destroyed the empire!"

"No," she said. "He tried to save it. It was Patriarch Venlin who betrayed the emperor. He was behind it all. Somehow, he convinced the Teshlor and the Cenzar to join him. He wanted to overthrow the emperor, kill him and wipe out his entire family. I think it was his intention to become the new ruler. But Esrahaddon stopped him. He got the emperor's son, Nevrik, out, then destroyed the city. I think he was trying to kill everyone associated with the rebellion, literally crushing all the enemies of Nevrik in one stroke. He expected to die along with them."

"But Esrahaddon survived," Hadrian said.

"So did Venlin," she added. "I don't know how. Maybe Yolric, or no—Venlin may have done something—cast some spell."

"The Patriarch was a wizard?" Hadrian asked.

She nodded. "A very powerful one, I think. More powerful than Esrahaddon."

"That's blasphemy!" Thranic said accusingly, and then fell into a coughing fit that left him exhausted.

"He was so powerful that Esrahaddon never even considered fighting him. He knew he'd lose and Esra was capable of destroying this entire city and nearly everyone in it."

Arista paused and turned her head back the way they had come. "They were all out there, lining the streets. I think they were having a parade. Each of them singing, cheering, eating sweets, dancing, drinking Trembles, enjoying the spring weather—then it all ended.

"I can still feel the chords Esrahaddon used. The deep chords, like the ones I touched on the ship just before you hit me. I barely touched those strings, but Esrahaddon played them loudly. His heart broke as he did it. A woman he loved lived in the city, a woman he planned to marry. He didn't have time to get her out."

*"This is larger than your loss! It is larger than the loss of a hundred kings and a thousand fathers. Do you think I enjoyed it? Any of it? You forget—I lost my life as well. I had parents of my own, friends, and—"*

Arista finally knew the unspoken words from their last meeting in the Ratibor mayoral office. Her hand touched the material of the robe as she remembered the way she had treated him. She had had no idea.

*As a wizard, you must understand personal vengeance and gain are barred to you. We are obligated to seek no recognition, fame, nor fortune. A wizard must work for the betterment of all—and sacrifices are always necessary.*

She stared at the floor, recalling the memory of the dream and the memories of the past, feeling sadness and loss. Beside her, Hadrian began humming a simple tune and then sang softly the words to the old song:

> *Gala halted, city's doom*
> *Spring warmth chilled with dust and gloom*
> *Darkness sealed, blankets all*
> *Death upon them, fall the wall.*
>
> *Ancient stones upon the Lee*
> *Dusts of memories gone we see*
> *Once the center, once the all*
> *Lost forever, fall the wall.*

"I grew up believing it was all just nonsense, something kids made up. We used to join hands, forming lines, and sing that while someone tried to pull the others down or break the line. If they did, they could take their place. We had no idea what any of it meant."

"Lies! All of it, lies!" Thranic shouted at them, straining to his knees. He was shaking, but Arista couldn't tell if it was from weakness or rage—perhaps both.

"I don't think so," Myron said from within a pile of scrolls.

"You shouldn't be reading those," the sentinel snapped. "The church placed a ban on all literature found here. It is forbidden!"

"I can see why," Myron replied.

"You are defying the Church of Nyphron by even touching them!"

"Luckily, I am not a member of the Church of Nyphron. The Monks of Maribor have no such canon."

"You're the one who ripped up these other scrolls," Hadrian said accusingly.

"They are evil."

"What was on them? What was so terrible? You were the one that burned the library. What are you trying to hide?" Hadrian thought a moment, then gestured toward the statue. "And what's with the heads? You did that too. Not just this one, but all throughout the city. Why?"

When Thranic remained silent, Hadrian turned to Myron. "What did you find out?"

"Many things. The most significant is that elves were never enslaved by the empire."

"What?" Royce asked.

"According to everything I've read since we've entered, elves were never enslaved. There's overwhelming evidence that the elves were equal citizens—even revered."

"I demand that you stop!" Thranic shouted. "You will bring down the judgment of Novron upon us all!"

"Careful, Myron," Mauvin said. "We wouldn't want matters to take a bad turn."

"Blasphemers! Wretched fools! This is why it was wrong to allow those outside the church to learn the Old Speech. This is why the Patriarch locked up Edmund Hall and sealed off the entrance, because he knew what could happen. This is why the heir had to die, because one day you would come down here. I failed to reach the horn, but I can still serve my faith!"

Thranic moved with a speed unexpected from his withered appearance; he reached out and grabbed the lantern. Before even Royce could react, he threw it at Myron, smashing it. The glass burst with a popping sound. Oil splashed across the parchments, across the floor, across Myron. Flames rushed forth, low blue tongues licking along the glistening oil pool. Fire blazed over the scrolls and raced up Myron's legs, chest, and face.

Then vanished.

With an audible crack, the room went black.

"That wasn't very nice," Arista said in the dark. Her robe began to glow, revealing the room in a cold bluish radiance. She was glaring at Thranic. The pulsating light shining up from underneath lent her a fearful image. "Are you all right, Myron?"

The monk nodded as he sat wiping the oil from his face. "Just a little warm," he replied. "And I think my eyebrows are gone."

"You bastard!" Mauvin shouted at Thranic, getting to his feet and reaching for his sword. "You could have killed him! You could have killed all of us!"

Even Gaunt was on his feet, but Thranic took no notice. The sentinel did not move. He slouched backward, resting against the wall in an odd twisted position. Thranic's eyes were open, staring at the ceiling, but he was not breathing.

"What's wrong with him?" Gaunt asked.

Mauvin reached out. "He's...dead."

Heads turned.

"I only extinguished the flames," Arista told them.

Heads turned again.

Royce was sitting in a different place than he had been before the fire. Arista looked back at Thranic's body. Blood dripped from a thin red line at the neck.

Mauvin let go of his sword and sat back down. "You sure you're all right, Myron?"

"I'm fine, thank you." Myron stood up. He walked to the sentinel's side and knelt down. He took a moment to close Thranic's eyes, and taking the sentinel's hand, he bowed his head and softly sang:

> *Unto Maribor, I beseech thee*
> *Into the hands of god, I send thee*
> *Grant him peace, I beg thee*
> *Give him rest, I ask thee*
> *May the god of men watch over your journey.*

"How can you do that?" Gaunt asked. "He tried to kill you. He tried to burn you alive. Are you so ignorant that you don't see that?"

Myron ignored Gaunt and remained beside Thranic, his head bowed, his eyes closed. A silence passed; then Myron folded Thranic's hands over his chest and stood up. He paused before Gaunt. " 'More valuable than gold, more precious than life, is mercy bestowed upon he who hast not known its soft kiss' — Girard Hily, *Proverbs of the Soul*."

The monk took another lantern out of Mauvin's pack. "Starting to run low on these," he said, opening it and reaching for the tinder kit.

"Better let me," Hadrian said. "A stray spark could light you up instead."

The monk handed the lantern over and looked at the rest of them. "Will anyone help me bury him?"

Degan made a sound like a laugh and limped away.

"I will." Magnus spoke up from where he still sat on the far side of the room. "We can use the stones from the cave-in."

Without a word, Hadrian got up and lifted Thranic's body, which folded in the middle like a thick blanket. His arms splayed out to either side, white and limp. Arista watched as he left a trail of dark droplets on the dusty stone. She looked back at the space behind, at the clutter in the corner where Thranic had lain. Pots, cups, torn cloth, soiled blankets, trash—it reminded her of a mouse's den. *How long was he here? How long did he lie in this room alone waiting to die? How long will we?*

Arista stood up and, turning away from the trash and the puddle of blood, moved to the sealed door. She touched the stone and the metal rods that held it closed. The door was cold. She pressed her palms flat against the surface and laid her head close. She heard nothing. She reminded herself that it was *not a living creature* and did not grow restless. She could feel it, a power radiating, pushing against her like the opposite pole of a magnet. Her encounter with the oberdaza made her sensitive to magic. The new smell that had confused her before the palace was no longer a mystery. Beyond the door lay magic, but not the vague, shifting sort that defined the oberdaza. The Ghazel witch doctors appeared in her mind as shadows that darted and whirled, pulsating irregularly, but this...this was greater. The power on the other side was clear, intense, and amazing. In it, she could detect elements of the weave. She could see it with her feelings, for there was more than magic that formed the pattern. An underlying sadness dominated and endowed the spell with incredible strength. An incomprehensible grief and the strength of self-sacrifice were bound together by a single strand of hope. It frightened her, yet at the same time, she found it beautiful.

Outside in the hallway, she could hear the clack of stones being stacked. Hadrian returned, wiping his hands against his clothes as if trying to wipe off a disease. He sat beside Royce in the shadows, away from the others.

She crossed the room, knelt down before them, and sat on her legs with the robe pooling out around her.

"Any ideas?" she asked, nodding toward the sealed door.

Royce and Hadrian exchanged glances.

"A few," Royce said.

"I knew I could count on you." She brightened. "You've always been there for us, Alric's miracle workers."

Hadrian grimaced. "Don't get your hopes up."

"You stole the treasure from the Crown Tower and put it back the next night. You broke into Avempartha, Gutaria Prison, and Drumindor—*twice*. How much harder can this be?"

"You only know about the successes," Royce said.

"There've been failures?"

They looked at each other and smiled painfully. Then they both nodded.

"But you're still alive. I should have thought a failure—"

"Not all failures end in death. Take our mission to steal DeWitt's sword from Essendon Castle. You can hardly call that a success."

"But there was no sword. It was a trap. And in the end it all worked out. I hardly call that a failure."

"Alburn was," Royce said, and Hadrian nodded dramatically.

"Alburn?"

"We spent more than a year in King Armand's dungeon," Hadrian told her. "What was that, about six years ago? Seven? Right after that bad winter. You might remember it, real cold spell. The Galewyr froze for the first time in memory."

"I remember that. My father wanted to hold a big party for my twentieth birthday, only no one could come."

"We stayed the whole season in Medford," Royce said. "Safe and comfortable—it was nice, actually, but we got soft and out of practice. We were just plain sloppy."

"We'd still be in that dungeon right now if it wasn't for Leo and Genny," Hadrian said.

"Leo and Genny?" Arista asked. "Not the Duke and Duchess of Rochelle?"

"Yep."

"They're friends of yours?"

"They are now," Royce said.

"We got the job through Albert, who took the assignment from another middleman. A typical double-blind operation, where we don't know the client and they don't know us. Turns out it was the duke and duchess. Albert broke the rules in telling them who we were and they convinced Armand to let us out. I'm still not certain how."

"They were scared we'd talk," Royce added.

Hadrian scowled at him, then rolled his eyes. "About what? We didn't know who hired us at the time."

Royce shrugged and Hadrian looked back at Arista.

"Anyway, we were just lucky Armand never bothered to execute us. But yeah, we don't always win. Even that Crown Tower job was a disaster."

"You were an idiot for coming back," Royce told him.

"What happened?" Arista asked.

"Two of the Patriarch's personal guards caught Royce when we were putting the treasure back."

"Like the two at the meeting?"

"Exactly—maybe the same two."

"He could have gotten away," Royce explained. "He had a clear exit, but instead the idiot came back for me. It was the first time I'd ever seen him fight, and I have to say it was impressive—and the two guards were good."

"Very good," Hadrian added gravely. "They nearly killed us. Royce had been beaten pretty badly and took a blade to the shoulder, while I was stabbed in the thigh and cut across the chest—still have the scar."

"Really?" Arista asked, astounded. She could not imagine anyone getting the better of Hadrian in a fight.

"We just barely got away, but by that time the alarm was up. We managed to hide in a tinker's cart heading south. The whole countryside was looking for us and we were bleeding badly. We ended up in Medford. Neither of us had been there before.

"It was the middle of the night in this pouring rain when we crawled out, nearly dead. We just staggered down the street into the Lower Quarter looking for help—a place to hide. News hit the city about the Crown Tower thieves and soldiers found the cart. They knew we were there. Your father turned out the city guard to search for us. We didn't know anyone. Soldiers were everywhere. We were so desperate that we banged on doors at random, hoping someone would let us in—that was the night we met Gwen DeLancy."

"I still can't understand why you came back," Royce said. "We weren't even friends. We were practically enemies. You knew I hated you."

"Same reason why I took the DeWitt job," Hadrian replied. "Same reason I went looking for Gaunt." He looked across the room at Degan and shook his head. "I've always had that dream of doing what's right, of saving the kingdom, winning the girl, and being the hero of the realm. Then I'd ride back home to Hintindar, where my father would be proud of me and Lord Baldwin would ask me to dine with him at his table, but..."

"But what?" Arista asked.

"It's just a boy's dream," he said sadly. "I became a champion in Calis. I fought in arenas where hundreds of people would come to cheer me. They chanted my name—or at least the one they gave me—but I never felt like a hero. I felt dirty, evil. I guess since then I just wanted to wipe that blood off me, clean myself of the dirt, and I was tired of running. That's what it came down to that day in the tower. I ran from my father, from Avryn, even from Calis. I was tired of running—I still am."

They sat in silence for a minute; then Arista asked, "So what *is* the plan?"

"We send Gaunt in," Royce replied.

"What?" She looked over at Degan, who was lying down on his blankets, curled up in a ball.

"You yourself said that he needed to be here, but why?" Hadrian asked. "He's been nothing but a pain. Everyone on this trip has had a purpose except him. You said he was absolutely necessary to the success of this mission. Why?"

"Because he's the heir."

"Exactly, but how does that help?"

"I think because he needs to use this horn thing."

"That's obvious, but that doesn't explain why we need him *here*. We could just have brought it to him. Why does he have to come with us?"

"We think that, being the heir, he can cross that room," Hadrian told her.

"What if you're wrong?" she asked. "We also need him to blow the horn. If he dies—"

"He can't blow it if he doesn't have it," Royce interjected.

"But that's where you come in," Hadrian said. "You need to shield him, just in case. Can you do that?"

"Maybe," she said without the slightest hint of confidence.

"Everything with me is try-and-see. What are your other ideas?"

"Only have one other," Royce said. "Someone walks in and diverts its attention while the rest make a mad dash for the far side in the hopes that at least one of us makes it. Hopefully blowing the horn can somehow stop the beast."

"Seriously?"

They nodded.

She glanced over her shoulder. "I guess I'll break the bad news to him."

∽

"Absolutely not!" Degan Gaunt declared, rising to his feet, his hat tilted askew and flat on one side from his lying on it.

When Myron and Magnus had returned, Arista had gathered the group in a circle around the lantern. While they ate sparingly from their remaining provisions, she explained the plan.

"You have to," Arista told him.

"Even if I do, even if I succeed, what good is that? We're still trapped!"

"We don't know that. No one has ever crossed this room. There could be a means to escape on the far side, another exit, or the power of the horn could be such that we could escape with it. We don't know, but an unknown is far better than a certainty of death."

"It's stupid! That's what it is—stupid!"

"Think of it this way," Hadrian told him. "If you fail and that thing eats you, it will be over like that." He snapped his fingers. "Don't do it, and you linger here starving to death for days."

"Or smother," Royce put in. Everyone looked at him. He

rolled his eyes. "The air is getting stale. We have a limited amount."

"If you're going to die, why not die doing something noble?" Hadrian told him.

Gaunt just shook his head miserably.

"That's just it," Mauvin said, disgusted. He held his wound, a pained look on his face. "Hadrian, you've got it right there. Gaunt is not noble. He doesn't even know what it means. You want to know the real difference between you and Alric? You made fun and lurid speeches about nobility, about blue blood and incompetence, but while you might have the blood of the emperor in you, it must be diluted until it is practically non-existent. Your lineage has long forgotten its greatness—your base side is firmly in control. Your wanton desire is unchecked by purpose or honor.

"Alric might not have been the best king, but he was courageous and honorable. The idea of walking through that door, of facing death, must terrify you. How terrible it must be to give up your life when you've never taken the chance to live it. How cheated you must feel, like losing a coin before spending it. To what can you hang on to and feel pride? Nothing! Alric could have walked through that door, not because he was king, not even because he was noble-born, but because of who he was. He wasn't perfect. He made mistakes, but never on purpose, never with an intent to do harm. He lived his life the best way he knew how. He always did what he felt was right. Can you say that?"

Gaunt remained silent.

"We can't force you to do this," Arista told him. "But if you don't, Hadrian is right—we will all die, because there is no going back, and there is no going forward without you."

"Can I at least finish my meal before I answer?"

"Of course," she told him.

She ran a hand through her hair and took a deep breath. She was still so tired—so exhausted—and everything was so hard now. She knew it would be difficult to convince Gaunt, but worse than that, she had no idea what to do if he tried and failed.

Gaunt raised a bite to his lips, then stopped and frowned. "I've lost my appetite." He looked up at the ceiling, his eyes drooping, his lip quivering, his breathing coming loudly through his nose. "I knew this would happen." His hand rose absently to his neck as if searching for something. "Ever since I lost it, ever since they took it, nothing's been the same."

"Took what?" she asked.

"The good luck charm my mother gave me when I was a boy, a beautiful silver medallion. It warded off evil and brought me the most marvelous luck. It was wonderful. When I had it, I could get away with anything. My sister always said I lived a charmed life, and I did, but he took it."

"Who did—Guy?" Arista asked.

"No, another man. Lord Marius, he called himself. I knew nothing would be the same after that. I never had to worry—now it's all falling on me." He looked at the door to the Vault of Days. "If I go in there, I'll die. I know it."

Hadrian reached into his shirt and pulled a chain over his head. Gaunt's eyes widened as the fighter held it up. "Esrahaddon made the medallion you wore, just as he made this one. Just as you received yours from your mother, my father left me this. I am certain they are the same. If you agree to go in—to try and cross the room—I will give it to you."

"Let me see it!"

Hadrian handed the necklace to him. Gaunt fell to his knees next to the lantern and studied the amulet's face. "It *is* the same."

"Well?" Hadrian asked.

"Okay," Gaunt replied. "With this I'll do it...but I'll keep it afterward, right? It's mine for good now, yes? I won't do it otherwise."

"I will let you keep it, but on one more condition. Modina keeps the crown."

Gaunt glared at him.

"Tear up the contract you had with her. If you agree to let her remain empress, then you can keep it."

Gaunt felt the medallion between his fingers. He rubbed it, his eyes shifting in thought. He looked back at the door to the vault and sighed. "Okay," he said, and slipped the chain over his head, smiling.

"The agreement?"

Gaunt scowled, then pulled the parchment from his clothes and gave it to Hadrian, who tore it up, adding the scraps to the pile on the floor.

"How about you?" Hadrian asked Arista.

"Still a bit tired, but I won't get any sleep now."

Hadrian stood up and walked to the door. "Myron, you might want to start praying."

The monk nodded.

"Degan?" Arista called. "Degan?"

Gaunt looked up from his new necklace with an annoyed expression.

"When you get across," Arista told him, "look for the horn in the tomb. I don't know where it will be. I don't even know what it will look like, but it *is* there."

"If you can't find it," Hadrian said, "look for a sword with writing on the blade. You can kill the Gilarabrywn with it. You just have to stab it. It doesn't matter where. Just drive the word written on the blade into its body."

"If something goes wrong, run back and I will try to protect you," Arista said.

Hadrian handed Gaunt the lantern. "Good luck."

Gaunt stood before them, clutching his new medallion and the light. His long cloak was discarded in tatters on the floor, his hat disheveled, his face sick. Hadrian and Royce slid the latches and drew back the bolts. The metal made a disturbing squeal; then the door came free. Hadrian raised his foot and kicked the door open. It swung back with a groan, a large hollow sound that suggested the vast volume of the chamber beyond.

Gaunt took a step, raised the lantern, and peered in. "I can't see anything."

"It's there," Royce whispered to him. The thief stood behind Gaunt. "Right in the middle of the room. It looks like it's sleeping."

"Go on, Degan," Arista said. "Maybe you can sneak by."

"Yeah—sneak," he said, and stepped forward, leaving Arista and Royce standing side by side in the doorway with Hadrian looking over their shoulders.

"Stop breathing so hard," Royce snapped. "Breathe through your mouth, at least."

"Right," he said, and took another step. "Is it moving?"

"No," Royce told him.

Gaunt took three more steps. The lantern in his hand began to jingle a bit as his arm shook.

"Why doesn't he just scream, 'Come eat me!'?" Royce hissed in frustration.

Arista watched as the lantern bobbed. The light revealed nothing of the walls or ceiling and illuminated only one side of Gaunt as he appeared to walk into a void of nothingness.

"How big *is* this room?" she asked.

"Huge," Royce told her.

She tried to remember the dream. She vaguely recalled the emperor on the floor of a large chamber with painted walls and a series of statues—statues that represented all the past emperors—a memorial hall.

"He seems to be doing pretty good," Hadrian observed.

"He's halfway to it," Royce reported. "Walking real slow."

"I think I can see it," Arista said. Something ahead of Gaunt was finally illuminated by his light. It was big. "Is that it? Is that— Oh my god, that's just its foot?"

"I said it was big," Royce told her.

As Gaunt approached, his lantern revealed a mammoth creature. A clawed foot lay no more than ten feet away, yet its tail stretched too far into the darkness to see. Its two great leathery wings were folded at its sides as towering tents of skin stretched out on talon-endowed poles. Its huge head, with a long snout, raised ears, and fanged teeth, lay between its forefeet, making it seem as innocent as a sleeping dog—only it was not sleeping. Two eyes, each one larger than a wagon wheel, watched him, unblinking.

The moment it raised its head, Degan stopped moving. Even across the distance, they heard his labored, rapid breath.

"Don't run," Arista called, stepping forward into the room. "Tell it who you are. Tell it you are the heir. Order it to let you pass."

The Gilarabrywn rose to its feet. As it did, its massive wings expanded. They sounded like distant thunder rolling and Arista felt a gust of air.

"Gaunt, tell it!"

"I—I—I am—I am Degan Ga—Gaunt, the Heir of Novron, and I—"

"Damn it!" Royce rushed forward.

Arista saw it too—the beast lifted its head and opened its mouth. Closing her eyes, she pushed out with her senses. There it was—the beast. In her mind's eye, she could see its massive size, its overwhelming power, and it was pure magic.

She could see it as such, hear its music, feel its vibration, and everything she sensed told her it was about to kill Degan.

"Run!" Hadrian shouted.

In that same instant, panic gripped her. The creature was not a force she could act upon; it was like smoke. She could not grasp, push, burn, or harm it. It *was* magic and acting upon it with magic would have no more effect than blowing at the wind or spitting in a lake.

She opened her eyes. "I can't stop it!"

The beast arched its back to strike.

In one tremendous burst, Arista's robe exploded with the brilliance of a star. Light filled the room, flooding every corner of the great vault. Gold and silver reflected the light, creating dazzling effects that blinded and bewildered. Even Arista could not see, but she heard the beast groan and sensed it recoil. The light went out as quickly as it had appeared, but still she could not see.

She heard footfalls running toward her. They brushed by and she was pulled through the doorway. Still blinking, her eyes still adjusting, she could barely make out Hadrian throwing back the bolts, sealing it out and them in. From the other side they heard a roar that shook the walls, then silence.

Royce and Gaunt lay on the floor panting. Hadrian collapsed near the door, and Arista found herself sliding down a wall to her knees. Tears filled her eyes.

It was over. Thranic had been right. No one was going to cross that room...ever.

# CHAPTER 21

# THE SACRIFICE

Hadrian raised the lantern and looked up at the collapse. Shattered rock and broken stone crushed into a solid wall blocked the corridor and obliterated the stair. He looked at Magnus at his side. "Well?"

The dwarf shook his head with a scowl. "If I had a month, perhaps two, I could tunnel it."

"We have six, maybe seven, days' worth of food and perhaps three days of water," Hadrian told him. "And who knows how much air? I'm also guessing Wyatt and Elden won't wait much beyond five days before setting sail home."

"And don't forget the Ghazel," Magnus reminded him. "By now, how many do you think there might be? Five hundred? A thousand? Two thousand? How many more oberdaza have they brought up to deal with the princess? They will be watching the other end of this for some time, I think."

Hadrian sighed. "It's not looking good, is it?"

"No," Magnus replied sadly. "I'm sorry."

When they returned to the room, Arista was still sitting in the corner by herself. Since the attempt to cross the Vault of Days, she slept a lot and he wondered if she was looking for answers in her dreams. Mauvin lay on the floor, not bothering to use a blanket to cover the stone. He stared up at the ceiling blankly. Gaunt lay curled in the opposite corner from Arista, holding the amulet with both hands, his eyes closed.

By contrast, Royce and Myron sat chatting next to the last remaining lantern. To Hadrian the two appeared surreal. Myron spoke excitedly, sitting cross-legged on the floor, sifting through the piles of parchments he gathered around him. Each one had been carefully wiped clean of oil. Royce leaned comfortably against the wall, his feet up on Gaunt's pack, his boots off as he flexed his toes. They could have been in the Dark Room at The Rose and Thorn or any cozy pub.

"The Ghazel conquered Calis," Myron was saying. "They came out of the east on ships and attacked. Neither the men nor dwarves had ever seen them before. The men called them the spawn of Uberlin, but it was the dwarves that named them the Ba Ran Ghazel—sea goblins. They overran Calis and drove the clans of men west into Avryn while the dwarves returned underground. The elves warned men not to cross the Bernum River and when they did, the elves declared war."

Myron stopped speaking as Hadrian and Magnus approached, both of them looking up expectantly. "No luck, then?" Royce asked, reading his face, which Hadrian was certain was no great feat.

"No," he replied with a sigh. He was aware his shoulders were slumped, his head hanging. He felt beaten, defeated by stone, dust, and dirt. Exhausted, he lay down and, like Mauvin, stared at the ceiling. "There's no way out of here."

Magnus nodded. "The stone they used is solid and the princess did an excellent job as well. The collapse is hundreds of feet deep. I think she took out the entire stair and a good deal of the corridor beyond. Perhaps with a crew of twenty dwarves and a month to work with, I could clear the wreckage, build supports and reinforcements, and form a new stair, but as it is, we'll be dead before I could tunnel a foot-wide hole."

The dwarf sat down amidst the scrolls and, picking one up, glanced at it.

"Can you read Old Speech?" Myron asked.

"Not likely," Magnus replied. "Dwarves aren't even scholars in our own language. Are you finishing that story? The one about how the dwarves saved mankind?"

"Ah—well, yes, I suppose."

"Well, go on. I liked that one."

"Um, I was just saying that when the goblins arrived, it drove men west. They had little choice, and those who crossed the river were mostly women and children, refugees of the goblin push. According to what I read, the elves knew this and some argued to allow the humans to stay, but there was more to consider.

"Elves had already entered into agreements with men that had proved disastrous. The problem was that humans only live for a few decades. A treaty made with one chieftain would be forgotten in just a few hundred years. More than this, though, was the rate of reproduction. Elves had only one child over the course of their long lives, spanning hundreds, sometimes thousands of years. But humans reproduced like rabbits and the king, a chieftain of the Miralyith at that time, thought that men would choke the world with their number and be more plentiful than ants. It was decided to wipe mankind out to the last woman and child before they grew too numerous to be stopped. At that time the Ghazel were attacking the eastern coast of Avryn and the southern coast of Erivan, taking control of what we know as the Goblin Sea."

"Were did you get all this?" Hadrian asked.

Myron pulled out a red leather-bound book. "It's called *Migration of Peoples* by Princess Farilane, daughter, incidentally, to Emperor Nyrian, who reigned from 1912 to 1989 of imperial reckoning. It has wonderful charts and maps showing how the various clans of man shifted out of Calis and into Avryn. There were originally three main clans. Bulard theorized that these distinct groups, both in tradition and linguistic foundations—temporarily homogenized by the empire—created the ethnic divisions and the basis for the three kingdoms after the fall of the empire."

"Nothing in those books about the horn, then?"

Myron shook his head. "But I'm still reading."

"Speaking of linguistics..." Royce began. "The names you found in the Teshlor guildhall, Techylor and, ah—What was it?"

"Cenzlyor?"

"Yeah, him. I knew a man once—a very smart man—who told me words like that and others, like Avryn, and Galewyr, were elven in origin."

"Oh absolutely," Myron replied. "*Techylor* is actually *swift of hand* in elvish, and *Cenzlyor* is *swift of mind.*"

"Is it possible that Techylor and Cenzlyor were actually elves?" Royce asked.

"Hmm." The monk thought for a bit. "I don't know. Until we got here, I never even knew they were people." Myron looked at Magnus. "Is there really no way of digging out? I would so much like to get back to that library again. If Mr. Bulard found these, there may be other books that survived the fire."

"*That's* why you want to get out?" Gaunt exclaimed, sitting up and casting his blanket back. "We're dying here! You know that, right? Your little bookish brain isn't so dense as to not realize that, is it? We will be dead bodies lying on this stone floor soon, and all you can think of are books? You're crazy!"

"This is going to sound really strange," Mauvin began,

"but I have to agree with His Heir-ness on this one. How can you just sit there yapping about ancient history at a time like this?"

"Like what?" Myron asked.

Even Arista was taken aback. "Myron, we are going to die here—you understand that, don't you?"

The monk considered it a moment, then shrugged. "Perhaps."

"You don't find that disturbing?"

Myron looked around. "Why? Should I?"

"Why?" Gaunt laughed. "He is nuts!"

"I just mean—well, how is this different from any other day?" They all looked at him incredulously. Myron sighed. "The morning before the Imperialists arrived and burned the abbey was a lovely fall day. The sky was blue and the weather surprisingly warm. On the other hand, it was a horribly cold and wet night when I met the King of Melengar, Royce, and Hadrian, who opened my eyes to untold wonders. When I traveled south through the snow with the awful news about Miss DeLancy, I had no idea that journey would save my life from the elven invasion. So you see, it is impossible to tell what Maribor has in store for us. A beautiful day might bring disaster, while a day that begins trapped inside an ancient tomb might be the best one of your life. If you don't abandon hope on pleasant days, why do so on those that begin poorly?"

"The odds of death are a bit better than usual, Myron," Magnus pointed out.

The monk nodded. "We may indeed die here, that's true. But we will all die anyway—is there any denying that? When you think of all the possible ways you might go, this is as fine a place as any, isn't it? I mean, to end one's life surrounded by friends, in a comfortable, dry room with plenty to read... that doesn't sound too awful, does it?

"What is the advantage of fear, or the benefit of regret, or the bonus of granting misery a foothold even if death is embracing you? My old abbot used to say, 'Life is only precious if you wish it to be.' I look at it like the last bite of a wonderful meal— do you enjoy it, or does the knowledge that there is no more to follow make it so bitter that you would ruin the experience?" The monk looked around, but no one answered him. "If Maribor wishes for me to die, who am I to argue? After all, it is he who gave me life to begin with. Until he decides I am done, each day is a gift granted me, and it would be wasted if spent poorly. Besides, for me, I've learned that the last bite is often the sweetest."

"That's very beautiful," Arista said. "I've never had much use for religion, but perhaps if I had you as a teacher rather than Saldur—"

"I should never have come," Gaunt complained. "How did I ever get involved in this? I can't believe this is happening. Is anyone else finding it hard to breathe?" He lay back down, pulled his blanket over his head, and moaned.

In the silence that followed, Myron got up and looked around for more unopened scrolls still resting in the many holes.

"Who was he?" Magnus asked Royce. "The one who taught you elvish?"

"What's that?"

"A bit ago you mentioned a man taught you about elvish words. Who was he?"

"Oh," Royce said, wriggling his toes again. "I met him in prison. He was perhaps the first real friend I ever had."

This caught Hadrian's attention. Royce had never spoken of his time in Manzant before, and because he knew everyone Royce had ever called a friend, except one, he took a guess. "He was the one who gave you Alverstone."

"Yes," Royce said.

"Who was he?" the dwarf asked. "How did he come by it? Was he a guard?"

"No, an inmate like me."

"How did he smuggle a dagger in?"

"I asked him the same thing," Royce said. "He told me he didn't."

"What? He found it? Digging in the salt mine? He uncovered that treasure down there?"

"Maybe, but that's not what he told me, and he wasn't the type to lie. He said he made it himself—made it for me. He told me I would need it." Royce looked off thoughtfully. "When I was locked away, I swore to myself never to trust anyone again. Then I met him. I would have died in my first month if I hadn't. He kept me alive. He had absolutely no reason—no reason at all—but he did. He taught me things: how to survive in the mine, where to dig and where not to, when to sleep and when to pretend to. He taught me some mathematics, reading, history, and even a bit of elvish. He never once asked for anything in return.

"One day I was hauled out before Ambrose Moor, to meet an old man named Arcadius who called himself a wizard. He offered to buy my freedom if I did a special job for him—the Crown Tower robbery, as it turned out." Royce looked at Hadrian. "I said I would do it if he also paid for the release of my friend. Arcadius refused. So I pretended to go along just to get out. I told my friend that when I got clear of the prison, I would slit the old man's throat, steal his money, and return to buy his freedom."

"What changed your mind?" Hadrian asked.

"He did. He made me promise not to kill Arcadius or Ambrose Moor—it was the only thing he ever asked of me. It was then that he gave me Alverstone and said goodbye."

"You never went back?"

"I did. A year later I had plenty of coin and planned to buy him, but Ambrose told me he died. They threw his body in the sea like all the others." Royce flexed his hands. "I never had the chance to thank him."

~

Hours went by. Like the others, Hadrian lay on the floor drifting into and out of sleep. He dreamed he fought beside his father against shadowy creatures who were trying to kill the emperor—who looked vaguely like Alric. In another dream, he sat in the burned-out shell of The Rose and Thorn with Gwen and Albert, waiting for Royce, but Royce was late— very late. Gwen was frightened something awful had happened, and he assured her Royce could take care of himself. "Nothing," he told her, "absolutely nothing, can keep Royce from your side, not even death."

He woke up groggy and tired, as if he had not slept at all. The cold floor punished his muscles, leaving him stiff and sore. The air grew thin, or at least Hadrian thought so. It was not hard to breathe, but it did feel as if he were sleeping with his head under a blanket.

*How much is real and how much imagination? Is the flame in the lantern dwindling?*

Everyone was sleeping, Gaunt in his corner, Magnus against the wall—even Myron was asleep, surrounded by scrolls. The princess lay curled up on her side, near the center of the room. She too was asleep, her eyes closed, head on hands, her face revealed by the lantern light. She was not as young as she once had been and no longer looked like a girl. Her face was longer, her cheeks less round, and there were small lines around her mouth and eyes. Smudges of dirt

streaked her face. Her lips were chapped and dark circles
formed under her eyes. Her hair was a mess. The lack of a
brush left her with snarls and mats. She was beautiful, he
thought, not despite these things, but because of them. Looking at her made him feel terrible. She believed in him—
counted on him—and he had failed her. He had also failed
Thrace and even her father. Hadrian had promised Theron
that he would watch after his daughter and keep her safe. He
had even failed his own father, who had left him this one last
chance to bring meaning to his life.

He sighed, and as he did, he noticed Royce was not among
the sleeping. The thief was not even in the room. Getting up,
Hadrian stepped into the hallway and found him sitting in the
dark a few feet from the mound of stones piled over Thranic's
body. He could barely see Royce, as so little of the lantern
light spilled into the corridor.

Hadrian let his back slap against the corridor wall and slid
down to the floor to sit beside his friend.

"I've finally figured it out," Royce said.

"What, the perfect career for us? Not spelunking, I hope?"

Royce looked at him and smirked. Hadrian could see his
friend only by the single shaft of light that crossed the bridge
of his nose and splashed his left cheek.

"No. I realized that the key is *you*—you can't die."

"I'm liking this so far—I have no idea what you're talking
about, but it's starting out good."

"Well, think about it. This can't be the end because you
can't die. That's the whole thing right there."

"Are you planning on making sense anytime soon?"

"It's Gwen, remember? She said I had to save your life,
right? She was adamant about it. Only I haven't. Ever since she
sent us out to search for Merrick, I've never once saved your
life. So either she was wrong or we're missing something. And

as you know, Gwen has never been wrong. We must be missing something and now I know what it is. *This* is it. This is where I save your life."

"That's wonderful, only how are you going to do that, pray tell?"

"Our second plan—I'm the diversion."

"What?" Hadrian said, feeling like Royce had just hit him.

"I'll draw the beast's attention just like Millie did in Dahlgren and you run, get the sword, and slay it. I don't know why I didn't think of it sooner. It makes perfect sense."

"You do remember what happened to Millie, right?"

"Yes," he said simply. The single word issuing out of the darkness sounded like a verdict. "But don't you see? This is what I'm supposed to do. I've even considered if this was why she died. Maybe Gwen knew *everything*. She knew we could not go off and make a life together because I needed to be here to sacrifice myself. Maybe that's why she was on the bridge that night, maybe she went to her death for me—or rather for you and everyone else, but at least so that I could have the strength to die for you."

"That's a whole lot of ifs and maybes, Royce."

"Maybe," he said.

There was a pause.

"But it has to be," Royce went on. "We know she had the sight. We know she knew the future. We know she planned for it, and that she said I would save your life. She knew that without me you would die, and from your death a horrible thing would occur. So if I save you now, we still have a chance to get the horn."

"But what if the future changed? What if we did something in the meantime to alter it?"

"I don't think it works that way. I don't think you can alter the future. If you could, she would have seen that."

"I don't know," Hadrian replied, finding it hard to discuss rationally the virtues of Royce's killing himself.

"Okay, let me put it this way," Royce said. "Can you think of any other way out of here?"

Hadrian was starting to feel a little sick, the air harder to breathe than before.

"So your plan is to draw it away and keep it occupied while I run for the sword?"

"Yep, you get the sword and kill it. I think I can buy you at least two minutes, but I'm hoping for as much as five. More than that I think is dreaming. After five minutes of dodging it, I will get tired and it will get frustrated to the point of using fire. I can't dodge that. Still, even two minutes should be plenty of time to cross that room and find the sword."

"What if it's locked?"

"It's not. I saw it when I was in there getting Gaunt. It's standing open. Hadrian, you know I'm right. Besides, it's not just you I'm thinking about. There are five other people who will die unless I do this—granted their lives don't mean as much to me, but I know it matters to you."

"And you're sure you want to do this?"

"I want to do it for Gwen. Hadrian, what else do I have to live for? The only thing I have is to fulfill her last request. That's all. After I do that…"

Hadrian closed his eyes and rapped his skull against the wall behind him, creating a dull thud. There was a pressure behind his eyes, a throbbing in his head.

"You know I'm right," Royce said.

"What do you want? You want me to say, 'Hooray, thanks, pal, for saving us'?"

"I don't want anything, except for you to live—you and the rest of them—even Magnus and Gaunt. It's what I can give you and the only thing I can give her. If I manage to save you, and you do get this stupid horn and it saves everyone, it will make her death mean something—mine too, I suppose. That's more than either of us could have hoped for. A prostitute and a no-good thief saving the world—it's not a bad epitaph. You can see I'm right, can't you?"

Hadrian let his head rest and stared out at the black. "Don't you get tired of always being right?"

"We made a good team, didn't we?" Royce replied. "Arcadius wasn't such a fool putting us together after all."

"Speak for yourself."

"Watch it. I'm about to die to save your ass, so be nice."

"Thanks for that, by the way."

"Yeah, well, you'll be happy to be rid of me. You can go back to blacksmithing in Hintindar and live a quiet happy life. Do me a favor and marry some pretty farm girl and train your son to beat the crap out of imperial knights."

"Sure," Hadrian told him. "And with any luck he'll make friends with a cynical burglar who'll do nothing but torment him."

"With any luck."

"Yeah," Hadrian said. "With any luck."

The two sat in silence for a moment. In the room, Hadrian could hear Gaunt snoring.

"We should do this sooner than later," Royce told him. "Just in case the air is running out and while you still have plenty of water and food to escape with, right?"

"I suppose."

"You know, when I'm dead, and it's dead—assuming there's anything left of me, it wouldn't be such a bad thing if you laid me to rest in the tomb of Novron. Can't ask for better accommodations, really, and tell Myron to say something nice, something poetic, something about Gwen and me."

❧

"What? No!" Arista shouted.

She was standing against the wall, a blanket pulled around her shoulders, her fingers white where they clutched the dark wool. Her head was shaking from side to side in a slow constant motion, like the ticking of a pendulum clock.

Magnus and Mauvin flanked her. Neither said a word as Royce explained the plan. In their eyes, Hadrian could see concern, but also resignation. Gaunt was up and looking hopeful, his eyes bright for the first time since they had entered the room.

"It's the only way," Royce assured her as he sat down on his pack, where he had left his boots. "And it will work. I know it will."

"You'll die!" she shouted. "You'll die and I won't be able to save you."

Royce pulled his boots on. "Of course I will, and I don't want you to," he said, and paused a moment before adding, "It will all be over—finally."

"No, you'll both die, I know it." Arista looked up at Hadrian with the same expression of terror on her face. "Don't do this. Please."

Hadrian turned away and unbuckled his belt, dropping his swords. He would be able to run faster without them. "Which way you gonna go, Royce?"

"Right, I think," he said, throwing off his cloak. "That will put me on its left; maybe it's right-handed. I'll try to keep it busy as long as possible, but we'll see how fast it is. I'm going to try to sneak to the right corner and get as far in as possible before I draw its attention, so wait for me to yell. With luck, you'll have an open field to run across."

"You're doing it now?" The princess's head was shaking even faster.

Hadrian leaned against the wall and stretched his legs, then jogged in place for a few seconds. "No sense putting it off."

"Please," Arista begged in little more than a whisper. Taking a step toward Hadrian, she reached out and then stopped.

Royce approached Magnus, who took a step back. The thief reached into his cloak and pulled out Alverstone, still in its sheath. He held it out to the dwarf. "I was wondering if you could watch after this for me."

"Are you serious?" the dwarf asked.

Royce nodded.

Slowly, warily, Magnus touched the weapon gingerly with both hands, cradling it like a newborn.

"You're really going to do this?" the dwarf asked, nodding at the Vault of Days.

"It's all that's left to try."

"I—I could go," Magnus said, still looking at the dagger. "I could take a lantern—"

"With your little legs?" Royce laughed. "You'd just get Hadrian killed."

Magnus looked up, his brows running together, his lips shifting as if he were chewing something. "I should be the last person..." The dwarf stopped.

"Let's just say recent events have made me realize I've done a number of things I shouldn't have. Bad things. Worse, I suppose, than what you've done. Right now, hating you seems... stupid." Royce smiled.

The dwarf nodded. "I'll—I'll hold on to it for you, take good care of it, but just until you need it again."

Royce nodded and moved to the door. He reached up and drew back the seals. "Shall we, partner?"

"See you on the other side, pal."

Hadrian threw his arms around the thief and, surprisingly, felt Royce hug him back. With one final smile, Royce pushed open the door and disappeared into the darkness of the Vault of Days.

Hadrian waited at the doorway. He could not see anything, nor could he hear a sound, but he did not expect to.

"Do you want the lantern?" Myron whispered.

"No," Hadrian replied. "I'll run faster without it, but maybe the princess could stand here and make her robe bright when I start to run." He said this without turning, without looking at her.

"Of…course," he heard her say, her voice strained, stalling in her throat.

They all waited, staring into the black room, listening carefully. Hadrian peered into the dark, trying to guess where it was, where either of them was.

"Hadrian, I—" Arista began in a whisper and he felt a light hand on the small of his back.

"Over here, monster!" Royce shouted, his voice booming across the great darkened expanse, echoing off the distant walls. "Come get me before I find the sword with your name on it and drive it through your foul excuse for a heart!"

❧

Royce watched as Arista's robe lit up, throwing white light in the room, at the sound of his voice. It was not nearly as bright as before, but enough to reveal the far wall, the open door, and the great beast in the middle of the room.

The Gilarabrywn was looking right at him. Royce braced himself, trying to decide whether it would strike with its mouth or a taloned foot.

*How fast is it? How quickly can it cover the distance between us?* Royce was far enough away that even as big as it was, the beast would have to take at least ten steps to reach him. He wondered if it would lumber due to its size. He reminded himself it was not a real creature; it was magic and perhaps the same rules might not apply. It was possible that it could sprint like a tiny lizard or lash out like a snake. He stayed on the balls of his feet, shifting his weight back and forth, waiting for the lunge.

"Come on," he shouted. "I'm in your lousy room. You know you want me."

The beast took a slow step toward him, then another.

"Go!" Royce shouted.

Hadrian ran out the door. He had cleared only five strides when the monster whirled on him. Hadrian dug in his heels and slid to the ground as the giant head snapped around with amazing speed.

"Get back!" Arista screamed.

Royce ran forward. "Over here! You stupid thing," he shouted, waving his hands over his head.

The Gilarabrywn ignored Royce and charged Hadrian, who scrambled back toward the light of Arista's robe, which once more brightened.

"Gilarabrywn!" Royce called. The beast stopped its pursuit. "Over here, you stupid thing! What? Don't you like me? Am I too thin?" The beast looked toward Royce but did not move away from the door.

"By Mar!" Royce exclaimed in frustration.

"*Minith Dar,*" the Gilarabrywn said, and its voice rumbled the chamber like thunder.

"It spoke," Royce said, stunned.

"That's right. They talk in Old Speech." He heard Arista.

"What did it say?"

"I'm not sure. I don't know the language well. I think he said, '*Comprehension is missing*,' but I don't know," she shouted.

"I do." It was Myron's voice coming into the darkness. "It said, '*I don't understand*.'"

"It doesn't understand what?"

"Royce can't hear a shrug, Myron," Hadrian said.

"I don't know," the monk replied.

"Ask it," Arista suggested.

There was a pause; then Myron spoke again. "*Binith mon erie, minith dar?*"

The creature ignored Myron and continued to stare at Royce.

"Maybe he didn't hear you."

Myron shouted louder. Still the beast ignored him, his eyes fixed on Royce.

"By Mar," Royce said again.

"*Minith Dar*," the Gilarabrywn replied.

"That's it!" Myron shouted. "*Bimar! Bimar* means *hungry* in Old Speech."

"Yeah, that's right," Arista confirmed. "But it only seems to hear Royce."

"He's elvish," Hadrian said. "Maybe—"

"Of course!" the princess shouted. "It's just like Avempartha! Say something to it in Old Speech, ask it a question. Say, '*Ere en kir abeniteeh?*'"

"*Ere en kir abeniteeh?*" Royce repeated.

"*Mon bir istanirth por bon de havin er main*," the Gilarabrywn replied.

"What'd I say—and what did it say?"

"You asked its name, and it said..." Arista hesitated.

"It said," Myron started, taking over, "'My name is written upon the sword of my making.'"

"You can talk to it, Royce!" Arista told him.

"Wonderful, but why isn't it eating me?"

"Good question," the princess replied. "But let's not ask that. No sense giving it any ideas."

Royce stepped forward. The Gilarabrywn did not move. He took another step, then another, staying on the balls of his feet. He knew the beast was clever and this was just the sort of ploy it might use to get him off his guard. Another step and then another. He was within striking distance; still the Gilarabrywn did not move.

"Careful, Royce," Hadrian told him.

Another step, then another and the Gilarabrywn's tail was just inches away.

"I wonder how it feels about having its tail pulled." Royce reached out and touched it. Still the Gilarabrywn did not move. "What's wrong with it? Myron, how do you say *move away*?"

"*Vanith donel.*"

Royce stood before the giant creature and in a strong voice ordered, "*Vanith donel!*"

The Gilarabrywn backed up.

"Interesting," Royce said. He closed the distance between them. "*Vanith donel!*"

Again the Gilarabrywn retreated.

"Try coming out," Royce said.

The moment Hadrian set foot outside the door, the Gilarabrywn advanced once again. Hadrian retreated into the room.

"How do you say *stop*?"

"*Ibith!*"

Royce ordered it to halt and it froze.

"Myron, how do you say *do not harm anyone*?"

Myron told him and Royce repeated the phrase.

"And how do you say *allow their passage through this room*?"

"*Melentanaria, en venau brenith dar vensinti.*"

"Really?" Royce said, surprised.

"Yes, why?"

"I know that one." Esrahaddon had taught him *Melentanaria, en venau* in Avempartha. Once more Royce repeated Myron's words, and for a third time Hadrian stepped out of the room into the Vault of Days. This time, the Gilarabrywn did not move.

"*Vanith donel!*" Royce shouted, and the Gilarabrywn stepped back, granting them passage.

"This is amazing," Arista said, entering the room with Hadrian. "It's obeying you."

"I wish I had known I could do this back in Avempartha," Royce said. "It would have been real handy."

Royce herded the Gilarabrywn back against the far wall, the great beast stepping backward before the tiny figure of the thief, its head glaring down at him, but showing no signs of violence.

"*Alminule* means *stay*," Myron said.

"*Alminule*," Royce said, and backed up. The Gilarabrywn remained where it was. "Everybody cross. Just stay spread out a bit—just in case."

One by one, they ran the expanse. Arista waited in the open beside Royce to provide light until Gaunt—the last to leave—made the crossing.

# CHAPTER 22

# NOVRON THE GREAT

The stone door on the far side of the Vault of Days was partially open, and taking the lantern from Myron, Hadrian was the first to enter. Inside, tall columns held up a high ceiling. The room was musty and stale. Large painted pots, urns, chests, and bowls lined the walls, as did life-sized statues, braziers, and figures of various animals, some easily identified, others he had never seen before. A colonnade lined both sides with arches framing openings, chambers within which lay stone sarcophagi. Above the arches words were carved and above them paintings of people.

Hadrian heard Arista gasp behind him as the lantern revealed the floor at the center of the room, where three skeletons lay—two adults and a child. Beside them rested two crowns and a sword.

"Nareion," she whispered, "and his wife and daughter. He must have pulled them in here after Esrahaddon went to meet Venlin."

Hadrian wiped the blade with his thumb, revealing a fine script. "This is the sword, isn't it?"

Arista nodded.

"Which one is Novron's coffin?" Mauvin asked.

"The largest," Gaunt guessed. "And it would be on the end, wouldn't it?"

Arista shrugged.

Myron had his head back reading the inscriptions on the walls above the arches, his lips moving slightly as he did.

"Can you tell which it is?" Gaunt asked.

Myron shook his head. "Up there." He pointed at text on the ceiling. "It says this is the tomb of all the emperors."

"We know that, but which is Novron?"

"The tomb of all the emperors, but..." Myron looked at the coffins, counting them with his index finger. "There're only twelve coffins here. The empire lasted for two thousand one hundred and twenty-four years. There should be hundreds."

Hadrian moved around the room, looking at the sarcophagi. They were made of limestone and beautifully carved, each one different. A few had details of hunting and battle scenes, but one depicted nothing but a beautiful lake surrounded by trees and mountains. Another showed a cityscape and buildings being raised. Several of the archways were empty.

"Could they have been moved?" Hadrian asked Myron.

"Perhaps. Still, there are only twenty alcoves allotted here. Why so few?"

"The rest are probably behind this door," Magnus suggested. He was at the far end of the crypt, appearing even smaller than normal against the backdrop of the great pillars and statues. "There's an inscription."

The rest of them moved to the rear of the tomb to a plain wall with a single door and, over it, a single line of words.

"What does it say, Myron?" Royce asked.

"'HERE LIES NYPHRON THE GREAT, FIRST EMPEROR OF ELAN, SAVIOR OF THE WORLD OF MAN.'"

"There you are," Magnus said. "The first emperor is inside."

Royce moved forward. The door was cut from rock. A set of stone pins held it fast and a lever hung recessed in the wall beside it. Royce took hold of the arm and rotated it, drawing out the pins, which ground loudly, until at last they came clear.

With a gentle push, Royce opened the tomb of Novron.

Hadrian held the lantern high as everyone stood behind Royce, who was the first to enter. Hadrian followed directly behind, along with Arista, whose robe helped illuminate the chamber. The first thing Hadrian saw was a pair of giant elephant tusks standing to either side of the door. They were arranged such that the points arched toward each other. Black marble pillars supported the four corners of the crypt, and within the space between them, treasure filled the tomb.

There were golden chairs and tables, great chests, and cabinets. To one side stood a chariot made entirely of gold, to the other an elaborately carved boat. Spears lined one wall, and a group of shields another. Statues of men and animals cast of gold and silver, draped with jewelry, stood like silent guards. In the center of the room, raised high on a dais, rested a great alabaster sarcophagus. On the sides were divided frames similar to those etched on the walls—the story of a council, a battle, and a war. Nowhere was there the scene of Maribor bestowing the crown, which Hadrian thought odd, as it was the quintessential image found in every church.

"This is it," Mauvin muttered in awe. "We've found it, the crypt of Novron himself." The count touched the chariot, grinning. "Do you think this was his? Was this what he rode into battle?"

"Doubt it," Hadrian said. "Gold is a bit heavy for horses to pull."

Arista moved around the room, her eyes searching.

"What is the horn supposed to look like?" Royce asked.

"I don't know exactly," she said. "But I think it is in the coffin. In fact, I know it is. Esrahaddon placed it there for Nevrik. We need to open it."

Magnus wedged his chisel under the stone lid and Hadrian, Gaunt, and Mauvin took up positions around the lid. Myron held the lantern high as the dwarf struck his hammer to the spike. The men heaved the lid off.

Inside lay the coffin. Wrought of solid gold, it was body-shaped and sculpted to depict a face, hands, and clothing. They all stared at the image of a small slender man with angled eyes and prominent cheekbones wearing an elaborate helm.

"I don't understand," Gaunt said. "What—what are we seeing?"

"It's only a case," Mauvin said. "Just decoration. We need to open this one too."

The nimble fingers of the dwarf found latches and popped them, and everyone helped lift the lid. Once more, they all peered in. Before them lay the remains of Novron the Great.

Hadrian had expected a pile of brittle decaying bones, perhaps even dust, but instead they found a body complete with skin, hair, and clothes. The cloth was gray and rotted such that their breath caused it to flake. The skin was still intact but dry and dark like smoked beef. The eyes were gone, only cavities remaining, but the corpse was remarkably preserved.

"How is this possible?" Gaunt asked.

"Amazing," Myron said.

"Indeed," Magnus put in.

"It can't be," Mauvin declared.

Hadrian looked at the face in fascination. Like the outer lid, it was sharp and delicate in feature, with angled eyes and unmistakably pointed ears. The hands were elegant, with long thin fingers still graced with three rings, one of gold, another silver, and one of black stone. They were neatly folded over a metal box on which were scraped the words

## To Nevrik
## From Esrahaddon

"Careful," Royce said, studying the hands.

"There's something there," Arista told him. "I sense magic."

"You should if it's the horn, right?" Hadrian asked.

"It's not the horn. It's something on the box—a charm of some kind."

"It will likely strike dead anyone but the heir," Magnus guessed.

They all looked to Gaunt.

"Can't I just poke it with a stick or something?" he asked.

"Esrahaddon wouldn't have done anything that could hurt you," Arista told him. "Go on, take it. He left it for you, more or less."

Gaunt took hold of his medallion and rubbed, then reached out and grabbed hold of the box, pulling it free of Novron's hands.

Sconces around the walls burst into blue flame. A cold breeze coursed around the tomb and Gaunt dropped the box.

"Welcome, Nevrik, mine old friend," a voice said, and they all spun to see the image of Esrahaddon standing before them. He was dressed in the same robe Arista wore, except it was perfectly white. He looked the same as when Hadrian had last seen him in Ratibor.

"If thine ears to these words attest, then terror's shadow hast fled and thou art emperor. Wish I but knew if Jerish stood at thy side. On chance that dreams abide in mortal spheres, I offer to him that which I withheld in life—my gratitude, my admiration, and my love.

"Stained upon my hands, the blood of innocents brands my soul with such a crime forgiveness gapes appalled. 'Tis my sin that shattered stone and rent flesh. 'Twas I who laid waste to our beloved home. Though to speak of it now feels like folly, for yet hath spark been struck. Still, committed am I. For not a breath nor heartbeat flutter can be granted onto a single Cenzar or Teshlor when the morrow comes. Their evil with me shall I take, the threat resolved, the night consumed, that thou may walk beneath the sun of a better day.

"Convinced stand I, here within these hallowed halls of thy father's reckoning and their solemn rest, certain that Mawyndulë yet lives. Their whispers become a wail as mine eyes focus upon a murder left two thousand years unavenged. Foul is the spirit that haunts these walls, for beyond imaginings are the depths to which his depravity strains. We knew but half! Banned by horn and god alike, 'tis my belief the fiend aims with intent to outlast the law. A crevice hath he found and stretched to slip, for no restriction blocks his way should after a trio of a thousand years he survive. I go now to ensure he does not. While master beyond my art, my art will end him. To slay a fiend, a fiend I must become. Murderer of thousands, I will be stained and accept this as price paid for extinguishing this flame that seeks consumption of all.

"The horn be thine. Render it safe. Deliver it unto thine children with warning against the day of challenge to present same at Avempartha. Look to Jerish as champion—the secrets of the Instarya remain the thread upon which all hope dangles.

"Fare thee well, emperor's son, mine emperor, my student, my friend. Know that I go now to face Mawyndulë honored to die that you might live. Make me proud—be a good ruler."

Esrahaddon's image vanished as quickly as it had appeared and the fires in the sconces died, leaving them once more with only the light of the lantern between them and the darkness.

"Did everyone catch that? I wish I had something to write it down with," Hadrian said. Then, noticing Myron, he smiled. "Even better."

Royce knelt down and examined the box. There was no lock and he carefully lifted the lid. Inside was a ram's horn. It was plain, without gold, silver, gems, or velvet. The only adornment it possessed were numerous markings that ringed the surface, letters in a language he could not read but that he recognized.

"Not much to look at, is it?" Magnus observed.

Royce placed the horn back in the box.

"What does this all mean?" Mauvin asked. Looking doleful, he sat down on a gold chair in the pile of treasure. His eyes moved from one to another, searching.

"Novron was an elf," Royce said. "A pure-blooded elf."

"The first true emperor, the savior of mankind, wasn't even a man?" Magnus muttered.

"How can that be?" Mauvin asked. "He led the war *against* the elves. Novron *defeated* the elves!"

"Legends tell of Novron falling in love with Persephone. Perhaps he did it out of love," Myron offered as he wandered around the room, looking at the objects.

"Techylor and Cenzlyor were elves, then?" Hadrian said. "They may even have been Novron's actual brothers."

"That explains the small number of sarcophagi," Myron pointed out. "The generations were longer. Oh! And Old Speech isn't old speech at all—it's elvish. The native language of the first emperor. Imagine that. The language of the church is not similar to elvish . . . it *is* elvish."

"That's why Thranic was lopping heads off statues," Royce

said. "They were accurate depictions of the emperors, and perhaps Cenzlyor and Techylor."

"But how could it have happened?" Mauvin asked. "How could an elf be the emperor? This has to be a mistake! Novron is the son of Maribor, sent to save us from the elves—the elves are—"

"Yes?" Royce asked.

"Oh, I don't know," Mauvin said, shaking his head. "But this isn't how it's supposed to be."

"It isn't what the church wanted to be known," Royce said. "That's why they locked up Edmund Hall. They knew. Saldur knew, Ethelred knew, Braga knew—"

"Braga!" Arista exclaimed. "That's what he meant! Before he died, he said something about Alric and me not being human—about letting filth rule. He thought we were elves! Or that we had retained at least some elven blood. If the Essendons were heirs to Novron, then we would have. That's the secret—that's why they have hunted the heir. The church has been trying to wipe out the line of Novron so that elves would no longer rule mankind. That's what Venlin was trying to do. That's how he persuaded the Teshlor Guild and the Cenzar Council to unite against the emperor—for the greater good of mankind—to rid them of *elven* rule."

"Instarya," Myron muttered from the corner, where he looked at a worn and battered shield that hung in a place of prominence.

"What's that?" Hadrian asked.

"The markings on the shield here," he said. "They are of the elven tribe Instarya, the warriors. Novron was from the Instarya clan."

Arista asked, "Why was it that Novron fought his own people?"

"None of this matters," Gaunt told them. "We're still

trapped. Unless one of you spotted a door I didn't see. This treasure-filled tomb is a dead end unless, of course, blowing on this does something." Gaunt looked down at the horn.

"No, wait!" Arista shouted, but it was too late.

Everyone cringed as Gaunt lifted the horn to his lips and blew.

৵

Nothing happened.

Not even a sound emanated from the instrument. Gaunt merely turned red-faced, his cheeks puffed out silently as if he were performing a pantomime of a trumpeter. He looked down at it, frustrated. He put his eye to the mouthpiece and peered inside. He stuck his pinky finger in and wiggled it around, then tried to blow it again. Nothing. He blew again and again and then finally threw it to the floor, disgusted. Without a word, he walked to the chariot and sat down, putting his back against a golden spoked wheel.

Arista picked up the instrument and turned it over in her hands. It was just a simple horn, a bit over a foot in length, with a pleasant arc. It was dark, almost black, near the point and faded rapidly to near white at the wide end. Several rings of finely etched markings circled it. There was nothing special about it. The horn just looked old.

"Myron?" she called, and the monk looked up from the treasures. "Can you read any of this?"

Myron took the horn near the lantern and peered at it. "It's Old Speech—or elvish, I suppose, now isn't it?" He looked at the horn and squinted, his mouth and nose crinkled up as his eyes worked and his fingers rotated the horn. "Ah!"

"What?"

"It says 'Sound me, 'O son of Ferrol, spake argument with thine lord, by mine voice wilt thee challenge, no longer by the sword.'"

"What does that mean?" Mauvin asked.

Myron shrugged.

"Is that all?" Arista asked.

"No there's more. It also says:

> Gift am I, of Ferrol's hand
> these laws to halt the chaos be,
> No king shall die, no tyrant cleaved
> save by the perilous sound of me.

> Cursed the silent hand that strikes
> forever to his brethren lost,
> Doomed of darkness and of light
> so be the tally and the cost.

> Breath upon my lips announce
> the gauntlet loud so all may hear,
> Thine challenge for the kingly seat
> so all may gather none need fear.

> But once upon a thousand three
> unless by death I shall cry,
> No challenge, no dispute proceed
> a generation left to die.

> Upon the sound, the sun shall pass
> and with the rising of the new,
> Combat will begin and last
> until there be but one of two.

*A bond formed betwixt opponents*
*protected by Ferrol's hand,*
*From all save the blade, the bone,*
*and skill of the other's hand.*

*Should champion be called to fight*
*evoked is the Hand of Ferrol,*
*Which protects the championed from all*
*and champion from all — save one — from peril.*

*Battle is the end for one*
*for the other all shall sing.*
*For when the struggle at last is done*
*the victor shall be king.*

"It's not a weapon at all," Hadrian said. "It's just a horn. It's used to announce a ceremonial challenge for the right of leadership, like throwing down a gauntlet or slapping some-one's face. Myron, remember you told us that the elves had troubles in the old days with infighting between the clans? This must have been the solution. How the elves decide who rules them. It said that they are only allowed to challenge once — What did you say? A thousand and three years?"

"I actually think that means once every three thousand years."

"Right, well, Novron must have used it to challenge the king of the elves to combat and won, ending the war and mak-ing himself king of both the elves and men."

"I don't see how this helps us," Gaunt said. "Why did we bother coming down here? How is this supposed to stop the elven army?"

"By blowing it, Gaunt just announced his challenge for the right to rule them," Arista said. " '*So all may gather none need fear.*' My guess is they have to stop fighting now and await the outcome of the one-on-one combat between Gaunt and their king."

"What?" Gaunt looked up, concerned.

"Only Gaunt didn't blow it," Hadrian said. "It's like it's busted or something."

So the horn isn't getting us out of here?" Gaunt asked.

"No," Arista said sadly. "No, it's not."

"Well, let's see what a dwarf can do, then," Magnus said, and taking out his hammer, began examining the walls, tapping here and there, placing his ear to them, even licking the stone. He circled Novron's tomb and then moved out into the larger crypt of kings. The rest of them wandered around, looking at the contents of the tomb, while Hadrian looked through the packs.

"There's probably thousands of pounds of gold here," Gaunt said, picking up a vase and staring at it miserably, as if it were mocking him by its mere existence. "What good is it?"

"I'd trade it all for a nice plate of Ella's apple pie right now," Mauvin said. "I wouldn't even mind her stew—and I never really liked her stew."

"I never had her stew, but I remember her pie," Myron said. He was crouched against the wall, still studying the horn. "It was very nice."

They all listened quietly for a time to the tapping of the dwarf's hammer in the other room. Its faint *tink!* jarred Arista's nerves.

"I pretended to *be* Ella when I worked at the palace," Arista said. "But I just scrubbed floors. I didn't cook. She did make great apple pie. Did she—"

Mauvin shook his head. "She was killed during the flight."

"Oh." Arista nodded.

"What do you think this is?" Gaunt asked, holding up a statuette that looked to be a cross between a bull and a raven.

Arista shrugged. "Pretty, though."

"How much?" Mauvin asked as Hadrian sat down on the wheel of the chariot.

"Three days," he said, "if we conserve."

The sound of the dwarf's hammer stopped and Magnus returned. His long face said everything. He entered and sat on a pile of gold coins, which jingled gaily. "There are worse places to be buried, I suppose."

"Alric," Arista said suddenly. "I suppose we should put him to rest properly, then."

"He'll be well buried," Myron told her. "And in a king's tomb."

She nodded, trying to appear comforted.

"Royce and I will get him," Hadrian said.

"I think I should be one of his pallbearers as well," Mauvin said, and followed them out.

They returned with his body and gently laid it on a golden table. Arista draped a blanket over him, and they gathered around it in a circle.

"Dear Maribor, our eternal father," Myron began, "we are gathered here to say farewell to our brother Alric Essendon. We ask that you remember him and see him across the river to the land of the dawn." He looked to Arista, whose eyes were already tearing again.

"Alric was my broth—" She stopped short as tears overtook her. Hadrian put his arm around her shoulders.

"Alric was my best friend," Mauvin continued. "My third brother, I always said. He was my rival for women, my fellow conspirator in plans of adventure, my prince, and my king. He was crowned before his time, but we did not know then how little time he had left. He ruled in an era of terror and he ruled well. He showed valor and courage befitting a king right to the end." He paused and looked down at the blanketed form and laid a hand on Alric's chest. "The crown is off now, Alric. You are free of it at last." Mauvin wiped the tears from his face.

"Does anyone else—" Myron began when Gaunt stepped forward, and all eyes turned cautiously toward him.

"I just wanted to say"—he paused a moment—"I was wrong about you." He hesitated for several seconds, as if he might say more, and then glanced awkwardly at the others before stepping back. "That's all."

Myron looked to Arista again.

"He's fine," she said simply while nodding. "At least I know that."

"And so, Lord," Myron continued with a bowed head, "we say farewell to our king, our brother, and our good friend. May the light of a new dawn rise upon his soul."

Myron then began the song of final blessing, and all of them, even Magnus, joined in.

> *Unto Maribor, I beseech thee*
> *Into the hands of god, I send thee*
> *Grant him peace, I beg thee*
> *Give him rest, I ask thee*
> *May the god of men watch over your journey.*

Mauvin stepped out of the tomb into the crypt and returned with a dusty crown, which he lay upon Alric's chest. "Sometimes the price of dreams is achieving them."

Arista could not stay any longer. She felt like she was suffocating and walked out into the crypt. Entering one of the alcoves, she crouched down and hid behind one of the sarcophagi. She sat with her back in the crux of the corner. Her knees were up, and once settled, she let herself cry. She shook so hard that her back bounced against the wall. Tears ran down her face. She let them run unabated, dripping onto the robe, which dimmed until it went out.

She wanted to believe that when Gaunt blew the horn it had stopped the elves, that perhaps they had heard and were coming to dig them out, but it felt like a lie. She was deluding herself because there was nothing else to hope for, nothing to expect beyond despair. In the darkness, she laid her head down on her arms and cried until she fell asleep.

# CHAPTER 23

# THE SKY SWIRLS

The booming thunder continued shaking the walls and the floors beneath their feet as the metalsmith hammered the last rivet into the helm. The old man's face was etched with deep lines partially hidden behind a mass of gray bristles, a beard he had no time to shave away. "There you are, lad. As fine a helm as you'll find. It will take care of you. Protect that noggin of yours right well. War is upon us, my boy, but don't worry—that's only thunder yer hearing."

"It's *their* thunder," Renwick replied.

The metalsmith looked at him curiously for a moment; then Renwick saw fear cross the man's face as he put the pieces together.

"Yer the boy, aren't you? The one who warned us? The one who rode up ahead of the elven army. You've seen 'em, haven't you?"

Renwick shook his head. "Not me, but yes, my friend did."

"Did he tell you what the devils look like? Rumor has it anyone seeing an elf turns to stone."

"No, but I wouldn't turn an ear to their music."

"You're Breckton's squire now, eh? Aide-de-camp to the marshal-at-arms?"

Renwick shrugged. "I don't even know what an aide-de-camp is."

The old smith chuckled, wiping the sweat from his face with a filthy cloth as overhead an especially loud roll of thunder boomed. Renwick felt it in his chest.

"An adjutant," the smith told him. Renwick shrugged again. "You're like his butler, messenger, and squire all rolled into one, except you're more like an assistant than a servant, which means you'll get some respect."

"But what am I supposed to do?"

"Whatever he says, lad—whatever he says."

Renwick placed the helm on his head. It fit snug around the forehead and the thick batten felt soft and cushioning. He banged his head with the heel of his fist. The helm absorbed the blow. He felt almost nothing.

"It's good."

"You'll be all right. Now get back to Breckton. I have more work to do, as I suspect you do too."

Outside, the streets were wet; warmer air had melted some of the snow. Icicles dripped, sounding like rain, as overhead the sky swirled and thunder crashed.

He jumped a large puddle but did not account for the added weight of the armor. He had never worn any before. It was only a breastplate and helm, but with the shield and sword added, it was enough to throw off his balance. He came up short and splashed in the middle, soaking his foot with ice-cold water. He felt foolish holding the shield as if he expected to be attacked at any moment. The other soldiers wore shields slung on their backs. He paused in the street, examining the straps and trying to determine how to do that, when a flash of lightning arced across the sky and he heard a terrible crack. People on the street ducked into doorways, their eyes skyward. This got him moving again and he jogged the rest of the way to Imperial Square.

Men filled the open area. Soldiers and knights sat on the dry sections of cobblestone or stood in puddles. He worked his way in, trying not to hit anyone with either his shield or his sword. Renwick felt conspicuous. Men with missing teeth and scarred faces glared at him as he picked his way through the crowd. He felt a heat building on his skin, his face flushing with embarrassment as he realized how ridiculous he must look. Renwick knew he did not belong there and so did they.

"Renwick! Over here, lad!" He heard a familiar voice and saw Sir Elgar waving from the center of the square. Never before had he been happy to see him.

"Make room!" Elgar bellowed, and kicked Sir Gilbert and Sir Murthas until they shifted over. Renwick quickly sat down, trying to become invisible.

"Here, lad." Elgar took the shield from him. "Carry it like this." He pulled his arm out roughly and slipped the long strap over his shoulder. "A lot easier that way."

"Thanks," he said, making sure his sword lay flat behind him and was not in anyone's way. Suddenly he felt a jolt as Elgar struck him hard in the chest with his fist like a hammer. Renwick rocked back and looked up, stunned.

"Good armor!" The knight grinned at him and nodded.

A moment later Murthas drew his dagger and hit him hard with the pommel. The sound rang and again Renwick rocked back, shocked, but unharmed. "Excellent."

"Stop!" Renwick shouted, looking at them fearfully.

The two laughed.

"Tradition, boy," Elgar told him. "It is good luck to have new armor tested by friends before enemies. Just praise Novron we're sitting down!"

"Aye!" Sir Gilbert said. "When I got my first helm, Sir Biffard rang it so hard I passed out, but I woke up in the care of Lady Bethany, so I can attest to the good luck of a sound beating on new armor!"

The knights all laughed again.

"Who is this pup?" the man seated across from Renwick asked. His blond hair came nearly to his shoulders, his blue eyes as bright as sapphires. He wore ornate armor inlaid with gold designs of ivy and roses. Over his shoulders he wore a purple velvet cape, held by a solid-gold broach.

"This is Renwick, Your Highness," Murthas replied. "I don't know if he has any other name. He was a page in the palace until recently. Now he is aide-de-camp to Sir Breckton."

"Ah!" the man said. "The fearless rider!"

"Indeed, Your Highness—the same."

"You've done a great service for us, Renwick. I shall be pleased to fight beside you."

"Ah—thank you—ah—"

"You have no idea who I am, do you?" he chuckled, and the rest followed him.

"This is Prince Rudolf of Alburn, son of King Armand," Murthas told him.

"Oh!" Renwick said. "I am honored, Your Highness."

"And well you should be," Murthas said. "There are precious few princes willing to fight beside their knights these days, much less sit with us before the battle."

"Ha!" Rudolf laughed. "Don't flatter me, Murthas. I'm here only to get away from the smothering chatter of women and children. There's a stuffiness to the castle these days. She has them filling the corridors, packed like sausage. You can't piss without a child or woman passing by. And they don't appreciate fine liquor!"

The prince drew forth a crystal decanter of amber liquid,

which he sloshed about merrily. He took the first swallow, smacked his lips loudly, then passed it to Sir Elgar on his right. "From the empress's private stash," the prince told them in an exaggerated whisper. "But I hear she doesn't drink and I'm certain she will not begrudge her knights a bit of warmth on *this* day."

Elgar took a mouthful and handed Renwick the bottle, which he held but did not drink from.

"Ha-ha!" Elgar said, looking at him. "The lad is afraid of getting drunk before his first fight! Drink up, lad, I guarantee that won't be a problem. You could down two such bottles and the fire in your belly would burn up that liquor before it ever reached your head."

Renwick tipped the bottle, swallowed, and felt the liquor burn its way down his throat.

"That-a-boy!" Elgar cheered. "We'll make a man of you today, that's for sure!"

He passed the bottle on to Murthas as overhead huge black clouds swirled and the sky grew dark until it appeared as if dusk had fallen at midday. What light remained cast an eerie green radiance. Lightning continued to flash and thunder cracked. Yet sitting shoulder to shoulder among the stable of men, smelling their sweat, listening to their carefree laughter and the sounds of their belches, curses, and dirty jokes, Renwick felt safe. The liquor warmed him, relaxed him. He placed his hand on the grip of his new sword and squeezed. He thought they could win this battle. He felt that they *would* win, and he would stand among the victors.

"Hide the bottle!" the prince shouted, and Sir Gilbert guiltily stowed it under his shield with a comical look on his face just as Sir Breckton arrived and walked into the center of the circle.

"So there you are!" he said, spotting Renwick. "Got your

armor and sword, I see. Good." He raised his hands to quiet the crowd. "Men! I have called you together here on behalf of the empress. Everyone take a knee!"

The soldiers made a loud shuffling of feet and swords. Renwick saw the small, slender figure of the empress Modina dressed all in white enter the mass of men like a flake of snow amidst a mound of mud and ash. She stepped up on a box placed at the center and looked around her, smiling. Several of the men bowed their heads, but Renwick could not; it was impossible to take his eyes off her. She was the most beautiful thing he had ever beheld and he still felt the kiss she had left on his cheeks. Before that day, he had seen her only once, when she had addressed the city from the balcony. That day he had stood in awe like the rest, marveling at her—so impressive, so powerful. Now, like in the fourth-floor office, what he saw before him was a woman. The picture of innocence wrapped in a pristine white dress that hung from her as if she were bathed in light. Modina wore no coat or cloak. Her unbound hair, glimmering like gold, fell to her shoulders. She appeared so young, not much older than him, and yet in her eyes was the aging from years of pain and hard-won wisdom.

"The elves are coming," she began, her voice soft and faint against the wind. "Reports tell of a host moving up the road from the south. No one has yet provided an accurate number or assessment of troops." She looked to the sky and took a breath. "We are the last stronghold of mankind. You are the last army, the last warriors, the last defenders of our race. If they should take this city..." She hesitated and a few bowed heads looked up.

She looked back as if taking in each face.

"None of you know me," she said, her voice changing, losing its formal tone. "Some have seen me on a balcony or in a corridor. Some have heard stories about me, of me being a goddess and the daughter of Novron—your savior. But you don't know me." She raised her arms out at her sides and slowly turned around. "I am Thrace Wood of Dahlgren Village, daughter of Theron and Addie. I was but a poor peasant from a family of farmers. My brother Thaddeus—Thad— was going to be a cooper until one night I left the door to my home open when I went to find my father. The light…" She hesitated and the pause gripped Renwick's heart. "The light through the open door attracted an elven monster. It ripped my home apart and killed my family. It killed the boy I hoped that I might one day marry. It killed my best friends, their parents, even the livestock. Then it killed my father—the last reason I had to live. But it did not kill me. I survived. I did not want to. My family—my life—was gone."

She looked out at them and he watched as her soft chin hardened as she gritted her teeth.

"But then I found a new family—a new life." She held her hands out to them and tears glistened in her eyes even as her voice grew stronger, louder. "You are my family now, my fathers, my brothers, my sons, and I will never leave the door open again. I will *not* let the beast in. I will never let it win again! It has taken too much from me, from you, from all of us! It has destroyed Dunmore, Ghent, Melengar, Trent, and Alburn. Many of you have lost your homes, your land, your families and now it comes here, but it shall go no farther! Here we stop it! Here we fight! Here we face our enemy without running, without flinching, without bending. Here we stand our ground and here we kill it!"

The knights cheered; the soldiers rose to their feet and beat their swords on their shields.

"The enemy comes, Sir Breckton," she shouted over the clamor. "Sound the alarm."

Breckton waved a hand and men on the roofs of shops

stood up and blared fanfares of long brass horns. The sound was repeated throughout the city as other horns echoed the call. Soon Renwick could hear the bells of the churches ringing. People in the streets quickly heeded the signal and headed for the shelters.

"To the walls, men!" Breckton ordered, and they all rose.

Lightning cracked again; this time Renwick saw the crooked finger of light strike the grain silo on Coswall Avenue. There were a flash and then flame as the roof exploded in fire.

❧

"Everyone into the dungeon!" Amilia shouted, standing on top of the wagon in the center of the courtyard as, overhead, lightning flashed and tower roofs exploded.

Only minutes before, a strike had hit something not too far behind her in the city. She felt a strange tingle on her skin and her hair rose as if lifted by dozens of invisible fingers. There was the taste of metal in her mouth; then a blinding light was followed instantly by a deafening crack. Something exploded and nearly threw her from the cart. Shaking, like a bird on a rock in the middle of a surging river, she remained on the wagon, shouting to the throng of people exiting the castle. She pointed them toward the north tower and the entrance to the old dungeon. They all had the same expression, terror imprinted over bewilderment. Poor and rich, peasant and noble, they filed out pushing and crowding, heads tilted toward the sky, cringing with each flash, screaming with each boom of thunder.

"Inside the tower! Move to your left! Don't push!" She swept her arms to the side in frustration, as if this would somehow move the crowd where she wanted them to go.

The attack came all too suddenly. They had expected horns. They had expected drums. They had expected to see an army coming up the road. They had expected plenty of time to move the population of the city underground—they had never expected this.

At least Amilia's family was already in the dungeon. They had all been lingering in the courtyard, having just seen Modina off to her troop address, when the storm began and the alarm sounded. But now she worried about Modina and Breckton. The empress would be gone only a short time, she knew, but Breckton would be going to the fight. She ached the moment he had left her side, and she worried for his safety all the time. Even while they were together, even when he had stood before her father asking for her hand in marriage, there was a shadow, a fear. It hovered and spoke to her of dangers that awaited him—dangers she would not be allowed to share. Fate had a way of making men like him into heroes, and heroes did not die quietly in bed while holding their wife's hand after a long and happy life.

*Crack!*

She cringed as a flash blinded her. The silver necklace—an engagement gift from Sir Breckton—buzzed around her throat like a living thing and then the roof of the south tower exploded. Chips of slate rained on the ward, the tower became a flaming torch. A sea of screams surrounded her as people scattered or fell to their knees, throwing hands over their heads and wailing at the sky. Amilia watched a young boy collapse under the push of the crowd. A woman, struck in the face with a slate shingle, fell in a burst of blood.

All around the city, lightning struck as if the gods themselves made war upon them. Smoke rose and flames terrified people who struggled to reach the safety of the shelters.

"Amilia! It's no good!" Nimbus called to her as he forced his way with a pair of soldiers against the human current, pushing out of the tower toward her. "The dungeon is filled!"

"How can that be? Are you sure?"

"Yes, yes, all those refugees, we didn't account for them. The cells and corridors are packed solid. We have to send the rest back inside."

"Oh dear Novron," she said, and began waving her arms over her head. "Listen to me! Listen to me. Stop and listen. You need to go back inside!"

No one responded. Maybe they could not hear her, or maybe it did not matter as they continued to be swept forward by the current. Another loud boom of thunder sounded and the people pushed all that much harder. A thick forest of bodies pressed up against the tower and the stables. She could see women and old men being crushed against the stone.

"Stop! *Stop!*" she cried, but the mob was deaf. Like a herd of mindless sheep, they pushed and shoved. A man tried to climb over the woman in front of him in an attempt to get past the mass of people. He was thrown down and did not come up again.

Bodies pressed against the sides of the cart and shook it. Amilia staggered and gripped the side in fear. A hand grabbed her wrist. "Help me!" an elderly woman with bloody scratch marks down the side of her face screamed at her.

A trumpet blared and a drum rolled. Amilia spun to look back at the courtyard's gate. There she saw a white horse and on it was Modina in her equally white dress. She was a vision, riding straight and tall. Her hair and dress billowed behind her. Arms reached out of the swarm of bodies with fingers pointing and Amilia heard shouts of "The empress! The empress!"

"There is no more room in the dungeon," Amilia shouted

to her, and saw Modina nod calmly as she urged her mount forward, parting the crowd.

She raised a hand. "Those of you who can hear my voice, do not fear, do not despair," she shouted. "Return quietly to the castle. Go to the great hall and await me there."

Amilia watched in amazement at the magical effect her words had on the mob. She could feel a collective sigh, a relief pass across the courtyard. The tide changed and the herd reversed direction, moving back into the palace, moving slower, some pausing to help others.

"You should come inside too," Modina told Amilia, and soldiers helped the empress dismount and Amilia climb down from the wagon.

"Breckton? Is he…"

"He's doing his job," she said, handing her reins over to a young boy. "And we need to do ours."

"And what is our job?"

"Right now it is to get everyone inside and keep them as calm as possible. After that, we'll see."

"How do you do it?" Amilia slapped her sides in frustration. "How?"

"What?" Modina asked.

"How can you remain so calm, so unaffected, when the world is coming to an end?"

Modina smirked. "I've already seen the world end once. Nothing is ever as impressive the second time around."

"Do you really think it is coming to an end?" Nimbus asked as the three of them moved—far too slowly for Amilia—toward the palace doors, where the last of the crowd disappeared.

"For us, perhaps," Amilia replied. "And just look at that sky! Have you ever seen clouds swirl like that? If they can control the weather, call down lightning, and freeze rivers, how can we hope to survive?"

"We can always hope," Nimbus told her. "I never give up hope, and I've seen that spark perform miracles."

༅

The lightning storm that ripped through the city stopped. Even the wind paused, as if holding its breath. Renwick stood on the battlement of the southern gate between Captain Everton and Sir Breckton at the center of a line of men with armor glinting in shafts of light that moved across the wall. They stood bravely with grim faces, holding shields and swords, waiting.

"Look at them, lad," Sir Breckton told him, nodding down the length of the wall. "They are all here because of you. Every man on this wall is prepared because of your warning." His hand came down on Renwick's shoulder. "No matter what else you do today, remember that—remember you are already a hero who has given us a fighting chance."

Renwick looked beyond the battlements to the hills and fields. In his left hand, he held on to a bit of wax he picked off a candle at breakfast, which at that moment felt like a month earlier. He played with it between his fingers, squeezing it, molding it. He could still taste the liquor on his tongue, still smell it, but the warmth was gone.

Outside the city the world was melting. The road was dark brown even though the hills remained white. In the stillness, he could hear the drizzle of water. Streaks of wetness teared down the face of the stone and soaked into the earth. Water streamed in the low places, gurgling in a friendly, playful manner. On the trees, buds grew large on the tips of branches. Spring was coming, warmer days, grass, flowers, rain. In another month or so, they would welcome the first caravans to visit the city bringing fresh faces and new stories. A few weeks after that, vendors would open their street stands in the squares and farmers would plow the fields. The smell of manure would blow in, pungent and earthy. Girls would cast aside their heavy cloaks and walk the streets once more in bright-colored dresses. People would speak of coming fairs, the new fashions, and the need for more workers to clear the remains of winter's debris. Renwick found it strange that he had not realized until that moment just how much he loved spring.

He did not want to die that day, not while the promise of so much lay before him. He looked at the line of men again.

*Are we all thinking the same thing?*

He felt comfort in their numbers, a consolation in knowing he was not alone. If they failed, farmers would not plow their fields, girls would not sing in the streets, and there would be no more fairs. Spring might still come but only for the flowers and trees. Everything else, all that he loved, would be gone.

He thought of Elbright, Brand, Mince, and Kine back under the holly tree in the Hovel.

*Do they wonder what happened to me? What will they do once Aquesta is gone? When I'm gone with it? Will they remember me?*

Movement to the south broke his thoughts and Renwick looked out along the road. A column of riders approached slowly like a parade—no, a funeral procession. He spotted only glimpses of them through the shutter of dark trees and gray stones, blue and gold on white horses. Accompanying them was the sound of music.

"Wax your ears!" Breckton shouted.

The command relayed down the line and everyone, including Renwick, stuffed the soft substance in his ears. Breckton turned to him, nodded, and smiled, sharing their secret.

Renwick smiled back.

The troop of elves came into full view and fanned out in the field before the southern wall. Mince had been right about them. The elves were dazzling. Each rider wore a golden helm in the shape of a wolf's head and carried a golden spear. The foremost riders bore streaming silver banners. They wore strange armor—shirts of leafed metal that looked light and flexible and greaves that seemed no more than soft satin, all of which shone brilliantly beneath a column of sunlight that followed them.

They sat on animals that Renwick called horses because he had no other word, but they were unlike any he had seen before. These noble creatures pranced rather than walked. They moved in unison with such grace as to mesmerize and bewitch. They wore bridles and caparisons of gold and silk that glistened as if made of water and ice. They formed up and waited with only their banners moving in the breeze and Renwick wondered if they made the wind for just that purpose.

Renwick counted a hundred, no more. A hundred in light armor could be defeated.

*Perhaps they won all their other battles by putting their enemies to sleep.*

Renwick's heart leapt at the possibility, but as he watched, trying to look into their eyes, he saw more movement on the road. Another column was coming, foot soldiers with heavier banded mail, large curved shields as bright as mirrors, and long spears with strange hooked blades. Their helms were the faces of bears. These troops moved in perfect unison. Like a school of fish or a flock of birds, they banked and turned. Their movements were graceful beyond anything Renwick had ever seen of men. They formed up in rows, and once in position, not one shifted or so much as adjusted a helm or coughed. Three deep they stood in a line that ran the length of the wall, and still more came. These new troops, in light armor like the cavalry's, wore bows with tips that swirled like the tendrils of ivy, and strings that glimmered blue when the sunlight touched them. Their helms were in the shape of hawks' faces.

Still more issued into sight, and even with waxed ears, Renwick could feel the march of these new elements drum against his chest. Great beasts the likes of which he had never seen approached. Powerful animals twice the size of any bull or ox, with horns on their heads. They hauled great devices two and three stories tall, built of poles and levers of white, silver, and green. Ten such devices emerged from the brown bristle tops of barren trees to take position at the rear.

When the last troop was in place, there were at least two thousand elves waiting before the wall. Then more riders appeared. There were no more than twenty and yet to Renwick they were the most frightening yet. They rode black horses, wore no armor, and were dressed only in shimmering robes that appeared to change color. On their heads were masks of spiders. Behind them came twenty more riders. These wore chest plates of gold and long sweeping capes of rich purple. Their helms were the heads of lions.

As Renwick watched, those on the black horses raised their arms in unison and all made identical motions of a complicated pattern that seemed like a dance of arms and hands. He stood fascinated by the fluid gestures. The dance abruptly ended as the twenty clapped their hands, and even through the wax Renwick heard the *boom*.

The ground quaked, and a tremor shook the wall. He felt it sway and saw the men beside him stagger. Cracks formed, fissures opened, chips of stone splintered and fell. Beyond the wall, trees shook as if alive and the earth broke apart. Hills separated from each other, one rising, the other lowering. Great gulfs appeared, ravines forming, jagged cracks that sundered the land and raced at them.

Another jolt struck the wall. Renwick felt the stone snap, the shudder shooting up his legs, making his teeth click. More cracking, more tremors, and then, between the fourth and fifth towers, the curtain wall collapsed. Men screamed as they fell along with thousand-pound blocks of stone into a cloud of exploding dust. The tower to the left of the southern gate slipped its footing, wavered, and toppled, raining stone on a dozen men. The tremor, having passed through the wall, continued through the city like a wave. Buildings collapsed. Streets broke apart and trees fell. Imperial Square divided itself in two—the platform the empress had recently stood on was swallowed by a jagged crevasse. In the distance, the imperial cathedral's tower cracked and fell.

The shaking of the earth stopped but the elves did not move. They did not advance.

"We need reinforcements on that shattered wall now!" Sir Breckton shouted down the line as he reached for his horn, his voice muffled, sounding like Renwick was hearing it underwater. "Wave the red flag!"

Renwick turned to see Captain Everton lying dead, crushed by a block of stone. He did not think. He took up the flag dropped on the stone and waved it above his head. Beside him, Breckton blew on his trumpet until another flag responded.

The mist of dust had only just begun to settle when Renwick heard a cry that no amount of wax could block out. The screech came from overhead and he felt a burst of air as a great shadow flashed across the ground. Looking up, he caught sight of a horror that seized him with fear. A great serpent beast with a long tail and leathery wings flew above him. Clearing the wall, the creature dove with claws that cleaved roofs and walls; then, like a barn swallow, the monster swooped upward, hovered for just a moment, and as Renwick watched, let loose a torrent of flame that bathed the homes and shops below. The creature was not alone. Renwick spotted others; dozens of winged serpents swept out of the swirling clouds and descended on the city. Like a swarm of bats, they swooped, banked, and dove, crushing, clawing, and burning. Within minutes, the whole city was ablaze.

Renwick felt tears on his cheeks. Smoke filled his nostrils, and even through the wax, he could hear the screams. Breckton's hand grabbed him roughly and shoved him back hard. He cried out, but it was too late. Renwick lost his balance and fell off the battlement, plummeting and crashing through the thatch roof of the guardhouse stable. He hit the soft, manure-warmed ground on his back, and every bit of air was driven from him. He could not move or breathe. The wax was out of his ears and sounds flooded his head. The hammering of hooves and the cries of horses were the loudest. Farther away—screaming, snapping, splintering wood, cracking fire, and always the screeching shrieks from the flying beasts.

Renwick managed short shallow breaths as he worked to fill his lungs again. His arms and legs moved once more, and he rolled carefully to his side. It hurt. His head throbbed, his neck ached, and his back was sore. Just as he got to his knees, the stable's roof was ripped away and three horses were stolen from their stalls. They were pulled into the air by two great talons.

He ran, his feet struggling to stay out ahead of him. Fire was everywhere. He was looking toward the gate, searching for Sir Breckton and his post, but everything was gone—the entire southern gate was missing. Only rubble and a shattered bit of slivered wood remained. Under the pile, he saw hands and feet.

The massive stone wall that had ringed the city was gone. Renwick stood on the street, looking out at the elven forces, feeling naked. Then the front row of hawk-helmed archers bent their bows and the sky darkened with a flight of arrows.

It felt like someone else controlled his body as his hands reached behind him and pulled his shield free of his shoulder. He slid one arm through the straps and raised it over his head. The sound was like hail as the arrows peppered the ground, glinting off the cobblestone around him and lodging in the wood of buildings. Three punched through his shield, safely caught, but one went through the back of his hand. He saw it before feeling the pain. Blood sprayed his face. He stared at the shaft protruding through his palm as if it were another person's hand.

"You're alive!" Sir Elgar shouted, his hulking frame casting a shadow over him. "That-a-boy! But get your ass up. This is no time to rest."

"My hand!" Renwick screamed.

Sir Elgar looked under the shield and grinned. Without a word he snapped off the arrow's point and pulled the shaft out. The pain made Renwick's legs weak and his breath shudder. He fell to his knees.

"Up, boy!" Elgar shouted at him. "It's only a scratch."

As absurd as it seemed, Renwick nodded, knowing Elgar was right, and marveled at how little it hurt. Pushing off the ground with the edge of his shield, still ornamented with the four white-feathered shafts, he got to his feet.

Elgar's own shield held two similar decorations. Another arrow was embedded in the knight's shoulder and Renwick grimaced when he saw it.

"Ha-ha! A bee sting is all." The knight laughed. His right cheek bled from a deep gash along the bone. "Murthas, Rudolf, Gilbert—all dead. The wall is gone. There's nothing for it. It's back to the palace for us. We have but one task remaining, one defense left to make."

"Breckton?"

"Alive."

"Where? I must go—"

"His orders are to defend the empress." Elgar grinned and drew his blade. "Break that stick off me, will ya?"

～

Everyone in the great hall sat looking up, watching the progress of the crack that formed along the ceiling of the room. It started at the eastern side and rapidly traced a jagged path to the west. Bits of plaster fell, flakes and chips; then whole clumps dropped and people dove aside as the pieces shattered on the marble floor, scattering white chalk in all directions. The robin's egg–blue sky was falling.

Modina ignored the ceiling. She moved slowly through the crowd, taking note of each person, each face, making eye contact and offering a reassuring smile. Mostly women and children were there. A few peasant families, like the Bothwicks, sat on the floor in small packed groups. They rocked and prayed, whispered and wept. All those who did not find room in the dungeon gathered around the great chamber, where only a few months earlier knights and ladies had dined on their Wintertide meals. Tables that had once served venison and duck for kings now provided protection from falling debris for cobblers, midwives, and charwomen. Even the man and his goat found a space under one of the oak tables. The castle guards, servants, and kitchen staff also came when the tremors began.

Knights and soldiers entered the hall torn and bloody, blackened from fire, telling tales of destruction and flight. Duke Leo of Rochelle was carried in on a stretcher by the viscount Albert Winslow and a man called Brice the Barker. They set him down before the duchess, who took her husband's hand and kissed his bald forehead, saying, "You've had your fun, now stay with me. Do you hear me, old man? It's not over. Not yet."

Brice pushed through the crowd to his family, huddled near the statue of Novron, and joined them with tears filling his eyes. His wife looked up, searching the crowd. Her eyes met Modina's but she was not who the woman looked for.

The Pickerings, Belinda, Lenare, and Denek, sat with Alenda and her maid Emily as well as Julian, the chamberlain of Melengar. Not far away, Cosmos DeLur and his father, Cornelius, sat against the east wall under the tapestry of ships returning from a voyage. The two fat men sprawled in their fine clothes and jeweled rings. A group of thin gangly men circled them, crouching like nervous dogs at the foot of their master's feet during a thunderstorm.

Modina walked by a cluster of women in low-cut gowns. Their tears left dark trails through heavy makeup. One looked up with curious eyes and nudged another, who scowled and shook her head. It was not until Modina was several steps past the group that she recalled the faces of Clarisse and Maggie from Colnora's Bawdy Bottom Brothel.

She returned to Allie and Mercy, who sat with Amilia, Nimbus, Ibis, Cora, Gerald, and Anna. They formed a ring within which the two girls sat. Mr. Rings was taking shelter on Mercy's shoulder, while Red, the elkhound, sat beside Ibis, the big cook holding him close.

"Will they kill me too?" Allie asked.

"I don't know," Anna told her.

"I don't want to be left," the little girl said, burying her head in Anna's lap. Sir Elgar and Renwick entered, both bleeding. Amilia spotted them and stood up, looking beyond them toward the door.

"Sir Breckton?" Amilia asked as they approached. "Is he…"

"Alive the last I saw him, milady," Elgar replied. "The wall is gone, the line broken, Your Eminence," he said to Modina. "A whirlwind ripped apart the flanking cavalry Breckton had hidden to the north. I watched it throw a two-ton stone around like a feather. Then the elves came. They moved like deer and struck like snakes, blades swinging faster than the eye could follow. The encounter lasted just minutes. They even killed the horses.

"Then the flying beasts came, and the arrows. Our troops are mostly dead. Those that live are scattered, wounded, blinded by smoke, and blocked by fire. The elves already have the city. They will be coming here next."

Modina did not respond. She wanted to sit—to fall down—but she remained standing. She had to stand. Around her, everyone was watching, checking to see if she was still with them, still unafraid.

She was afraid.

Not for herself—not a thought of her own welfare crossed her mind. She could not recall the last time she worried for her own safety. She worried for them. The scene was all too familiar. She had been here before, with a family to protect and no means to do so. A weight in her chest made it difficult to breathe.

A loud boom thundered outside, followed by screams. Heads turned toward the windows in fear. Then, from across the room, near the glowing hearth, an elderly woman with gray hair and a torn dress began to sing. The song was soft—a lilting lullaby—and Modina recognized the tune immediately, although she had not heard it in many years. It was a common tune among the poor, a mother's lament often sung to children. She remembered every word, and like the others in the hall, she found herself joining in as a hundred whispered voices offered up the prayer.

*In the dark, when night's chill cuts*
*Cold as death they climb the hill*
*Breaking door and windowpane*
*They come to burn, slash, and kill.*

*Shadows pounding on the door*
*They beat the drums of fear*
*Place your faith in Maribor*
*And loudly, so he hears.*

*Waves they crash upon the bow*
*Of withered ship at sea*
*Wind and weather rip the sails*
*There's little hope for thee.*

*Shadows pounding on the hull*
*They beat the drums of fear*
*Place your faith in Maribor*
*And loudly, so he hears.*

*Within darkling wood you walk*
*So foolish after all*
*Footsteps follow, catching up*
*You run until you fall.*

*Shadows pounding on the path*
*They beat the drums of fear*
*Place your faith in Maribor*
*And loudly, so he hears.*

*When man stood upon the brink*
*Novron saved us all*

*Sent by god above he was*
*In answer to our call.*

*Shadows pounding on the gate*
*They beat the drums so near*
*If your faith's in Maribor*
*He's with you, never fear.*

Another tremor shook the room. The marble floor snapped like a thin cracker splitting as one side rose sharply and the other fell. The room exploded with screams. The maid, Emily of Glouston, fell over the side of the forming chasm and was caught at the last moment by Lenare Pickering and Alenda Lanaklin, who each managed to grasp a wrist. Another shudder rocked the hall and all three slid toward the edge. Tad and Russell Bothwick lunged out, grabbing ankles and pulling back, hauling the ladies to higher ground.

"Hang on to each other, for Novron's sake!" the Duchess of Rochelle shouted. Cold air was blowing. Modina could feel it against her cheek. A great fissure had ripped apart the windowed side of the hall. The wall wavered like a drunken man.

"Get away!" Modina ordered, motioning with her hands.

Bodies scurried as the partition collapsed amidst cries and screams cut horribly short. Stone and ceiling came down, exploding in bursts that cracked the floor. Modina staggered as she watched thirty people die, crushed to death.

Those nearby pulled the wounded from the debris. Modina saw a hand and moved forward, digging into the rubble, scraping at the stone, hurling rocks aside. She recognized him by his ink-stained fingers. She lifted the scribe's limp head to her chest, wondering painfully why it was by his hand and not by his face she knew him. He was not breathing and blood dripped from his nose and eyes.

"Your Eminence." Nimbus spoke to her.

"Modina?" Amilia called, her voice shaking.

Modina turned and saw everyone watching her, the room silent. Every face frightened, every pair of eyes pleading. She stood up slowly, as she might within a flock of birds. Panic was a moment away. She could hear the frantic breathing all around her, the cry of children, the tears of mothers, the hum of men who rocked back and forth.

She took a deep breath and wiped the scribe's blood on her gown, leaving a streaked handprint. She faced the open air of the missing wall and walked the way Nimbus and Amilia had once taught her to, her head up and shoulders back. Modina waded through the room of stares, like a pond of murky water. Only the sight of her checked their fear. She was the last remaining pillar that held up the sky, the last hope in a place that hope no longer called home.

When she reached the courtyard, she stopped. Half the great hall was gone, but the courtyard was in ruins. The towers and front gate lay on the ground like so many scattered children's blocks. The bake house and chapel collapsed along with one side of the granary — barley spilling across the dirt. Oddly, the woodpile near the kitchen was still stacked.

Without the outer wall enclosing the ward, she could see the city. Columns of fire rose from every quarter. Black smoke and ash billowed like ghosts across the rendered landscape. Men lay dead or dying. She could see bodies of soldiers, knights, merchants, and laborers lying in the streets. Missing buildings formed gaps across a vista she knew so well, old friends once framed by her window — gone. Others stood askew, tilted, missing pieces. In the dark air, familiar shapes flew, circling. She saw them turn, wheeling in arcs, banking like hawks, coming around toward her. A thunderous shriek screamed from above the courtyard and a great winged Gilarabrywn landed where once there had been a vegetable garden.

She looked behind her.

"Do you believe in me?" she asked simply. "Do you believe I can save you?"

Silence, but a few heads nodded, Amilia's and Nimbus's among them.

"I am the daughter of the last emperor," she said with a loud clear voice. "I am the daughter of Novron, the Daughter of Maribor. I am Empress Modina Novronian! This is my city, my land, and you are my people. The elves will not have you!"

At the sound of her voice, the Gilarabrywn turned and focused on her.

Modina looked back at those in the great hall. Russell Bothwick had his arms around Lena and Tad, and Nimbus had his arms around Amilia, who looked back at her and began to cry.

# CHAPTER 24

# THE GIFT

*It is as silent as a tomb*, Hadrian thought as he sat in the darkness. The last lantern had died some time ago, as had the last conversation. Royce had been quizzing Myron on linguistics, but even that stopped.

He was in the tomb of Novron, the resting place of the savior of mankind. This place was thought to be mythical, a fable, a legend, yet here he was. Hadrian was one of the first to reach it in a thousand years. Truly a feat—an astounding achievement.

Hadrian rested against a wall, his right arm on what was most likely an urn worth ten thousand gold tenents. His feet were up on a solid-gold statue of a ram. He would die a very rich man, at least.

*Look what you have come to.* He heard his father's voice ringing in his head, deep and powerful, the way he always remembered it being when he was a boy. He could almost see his old man towering above him covered in sweat, wearing his leather apron, and holding his tongs.

*You took all that I taught you and squandered it for money and fame. What has it bought you? You have more riches at your feet than any king and they still chant* Galenti *in the east, but was your life worth living now that it has come to its end? Is this what you sought when you left Hintindar? Is this the greatness you desired?*

Hadrian took his hand off the urn and pulled his feet off the ram.

*You told me you were going to be a great hero. Show me, then. Show me one thing worth the life you spent. One thing wrought. One thing won. One thing earned. One thing learned. Does such a thing exist? Is there anything to show?*

Hadrian tilted his head and looked out toward the crypt. There, in the distance, he saw the dim blue glow.

He stared at it for some time. In the darkness he could not tell how long. The light grew and fell slightly—with her breathing, he guessed. He had no real idea how it worked, whether the shift was of her making or the robe's.

*Is there anything to show?* he asked himself.

Hadrian stood up and, reaching out with his hands, moved along the wall to the opening into the crypt. There was no one out here but her. She was in one of the alcoves, sitting behind a sarcophagus, the one with the scenes of natural landscapes carved on the sides. Her head was resting on her knees, her arms wrapped around her legs.

He sat beside her, and as he did, the light from her robe brightened slightly and her head lifted. Her cheeks were streaked from tears. She blinked at him and wiped her eyes.

"Hi," she said.

"Hello," he replied. "Dream?"

Arista paused, then shook her head sadly. "No—no, I didn't. What does that mean, I wonder."

"I think it means we're done."

Arista nodded. "I suppose so."

"Everyone is in the tomb. Why did you come over here?"

"I dunno," she said. "I wanted to be alone, I guess. I was

reviewing my life—all the things I regret. What I never did. What I should have. What I did that I wished I hadn't. You know, fun, entertaining stuff like that. That kind of thinking is best done alone, you know? What about you? What were you thinking?"

"Same sort of thing."

"Oh yeah? What did you come up with?"

"Well," he said, clearing his throat. "Funny you should ask. There's a whole lot of things I wished I hadn't done, but... as turns out, there's really only one thing I wished I had done but didn't."

She raised her eyebrows. "Really? You're a fortunate man—almost as good as Myron."

"Heh, yeah," he said uncomfortably.

"What is it, this thing you haven't done?"

"Well, it's like this. I'm—I'm actually envious of Royce right now. I never thought I'd say that, but it's true. Royce had the kind of life that mothers warn their children they will have if they don't behave. It was like the gods had it out for him the day he was born. It's little wonder he turned out as he did. When I first met him, he was quite scary."

"Was?"

"Oh yeah, not like he is now—*real* scary—the never-turn-your-back brand of scary. But Arcadius saw something in him that no one else did. I suppose that's something wizards can do, see into men's souls. Notice what the rest of the world can't about a person."

Hadrian shifted uneasily, feeling the cold stone of the floor through a thick layer of fine dust. He crossed his legs and leaned slightly forward.

"It took Royce a long time to trust anyone. To be honest, I'm not even sure he fully trusts me yet, but he did trust her. Gwen changed Royce. She did the impossible by making him happy. Even now, the idea of Royce smiling—in a good way—is—I dunno, like snow falling in summer, or sheep curling up with wolves. You don't get that kind of thing from just liking a girl. There was something special there, something profound. He only had her briefly, but at least he knows what that feels like. You know what I mean?"

"Yes," she said. "I do."

"That's what I regret."

"You can't regret that," she said, nearly laughing. "How can you regret never having found true love? That's like saying you regret not being born a genius. People don't have control over such things. It either happens or it doesn't. It's a gift—a present that most never get. It's more like a miracle, really, when you think of it. I mean, first you have to find that person, and then you have to get to know them to realize just what they mean to you—that right there is ridiculously difficult. Then..." She paused a moment, looking far away. "Then that person has to feel the same way about you. It's like searching for a specific snowflake, and even if you manage to find it, that's not good enough. You still have to find its matching pair. What are the odds? Hilfred found it, I think. He loved me."

"Did you love him?"

"Yes, but not the way he wanted me to. Not the way he loved me. I wish I had. I feel I should have. It was the same with Emery. I actually feel guilty that I didn't. Maybe with time I could have loved Emery, but I hardly knew him."

"And Hilfred?"

"I don't know. He was more like a brother to me, I suppose. I wanted to make him happy, the way I wanted to see Alric happy. But you see, that's just what I'm talking about. Most people never come near their true love, or if they do, it's one sided. That is perhaps more tragic than never finding love at all. To know joy lies forever just beyond your reach—in a way, it's a kind of torture. So you see, if you don't have control, if it's not a choice, then not finding the one you love is really nothing to regret, is it?"

"Well, that's just the thing. I did find her and I never told her how I feel."

"Oh—that *is* awful," she said, then caught herself and raised a hand to cover her mouth. "I'm so sorry. That was terrible of me. No wonder I was such a lousy ambassador. I'm just the embodiment of tact, aren't I? Here your— Oh!" she suddenly exclaimed as a look of revelation came over her face. "I know who she is."

Hadrian suddenly felt very warm; his skin prickled uncomfortably under his shirt.

"She's very pretty, by the way."

"Ah—" Hadrian stared at her, confused.

"Her name isn't actually Emerald, is it? I heard someone call her that."

"Emerald? You think I'm talking about—"

"Aren't you?" She appeared embarrassed and cautiously said, "I saw her kissing you when we left."

Hadrian chuckled. "Her real name is Falina and she is a nice girl, but no, I'm not speaking of her. No, the woman I'm talking about is *nothing* like her."

"Oh," the princess said softly. "So why have you never told her how you feel?"

"I have a list somewhere." He patted his shirt with his hands, trying to be funny, but he just felt stupid.

She smiled at him. He liked seeing her smile.

"No really—why?"

"I'm not kidding. I really do have a list. It's just not written down. I keep adding items to it. There's so many reasons on it now."

"Give me a few."

"Well, the big one is that she's noble."

"Oh, I see," she said gravely, "but that's not impossible. It depends on the girl, of course, but noble ladies have married common men before. It's not unheard of."

"Rich merchants, perhaps, but how many ladies do you know of that ran off with a common thief?"

"You're hardly a common thief," she chided him sternly. "But I suppose I can see your point. You're right that there aren't many noblewomen who could see past both a common background and a disreputable career. Lenare Lanaklin, for one—it's not her, is it?" She cringed slightly.

"No, it's not Lenare."

"Oh, good." She sighed, pretending to wipe sweat from her brow. "Don't get me wrong, I love Lenare like a sister, but she's not right for you."

"I know."

"Still, some women, even noblewomen, can be attracted to outlaws. They hear tales of daring and they can get swept away by the intrigue—I've seen it."

"But what about obligations? Even if she wanted to, she couldn't turn her back on her responsibilities. There are titles and land holdings at stake."

"Another good point."

"Is that what kept *you* from getting married?" he asked.

"Me? Oh dear Maribor, no." She smiled bitterly. "I'm sure Alric wanted to marry me off to a number of prominent allies for that very reason. If my father hadn't been killed, I'm sure I would be married to Prince Rudolf of Alburn right now." She shivered dramatically for effect. "Thankfully, Alric was a kind man—I never would have expected it from him when we were younger, but he never would force me. I don't know of too many others who would have done the same."

"So why didn't you?"

"Marry, you mean?" She laughed a little uneasily. "You might find this hard to believe, Hadrian—given my immense beauty and all—but Emery was the first man to show an interest. At least, he was the first to actually say anything to me. I'm not like Lenare or Alenda. Men aren't attracted to me and the whole witch thing doesn't help. No, Emery was the first, and I honestly believe that if he'd gotten to know me better, he would have changed his mind. He didn't live long enough to figure out it was just infatuation. It was the same with Hilfred." She paused and looked away from him, a sadness overtaking her. "I suppose I should be happy that so few have ever showed an interest in me, or I might have more blood on my hands."

"I don't follow."

"Only Emery and Hilfred expressed feelings for me." She hesitated a moment. "And each time, within something less than a week, they died."

"It wasn't your fault."

"It was my idea to stage the revolt that killed Emery, and it was my plan to save Gaunt that killed Hilfred. My plans—always my plans."

"Emery would have died in the square if it wasn't for you."

"And Hilfred?" she taunted.

"Hilfred made his own choice, just as you did. I'm sure he knew the risks. It wasn't your fault."

"I still feel cursed, like I'm not supposed to be happy—that way."

He thought she might speak again and waited. They sat in silence for several minutes. He watched her close her eyes and he took another breath. This was harder than he had expected.

"The real reason I never told her," Hadrian went on, his

own voice sounding awkward to him, odd and off key, "if I am honest with myself, is that I'm scared."

She rolled her head to look at him with a sidelong glance. "Scared? You? Really?"

"I guess I was afraid she'd laugh at me. Or worse, become angry and hate me. That's the worst thing I can think of— that she would hate me. I'm not sure I could live with that. You see, I'm very much in love with her, and I'd rather be drawn and quartered than have her hate me."

He watched as Arista's shoulders sank. Her eyes drifted from his face, and her mouth tightened. "Sounds like a lucky woman. It's a shame she's not here now. There's not much to lose at this point. It could give you the courage to tell her, knowing that if she hates you, you'll not have to endure the pain for long."

Hadrian smiled and nodded.

Arista took a breath and sat up. "Do I know her?" She cringed again, as if expecting to be struck.

Hadrian sighed heavily.

"What?" she asked. "I do know her, don't I? You would have told me her name by now if I didn't. Oh come on. It hardly seems worth keeping the secret at this point."

"That's it exactly," he said. "The reason I was thinking all this is because..." He paused, looking into her eyes. They were like pools he was preparing to jump into without knowing the temperature of the water. He braced himself for the shock. "The one thing I regret the most in my life is the one thing I can still change before it's too late."

Arista narrowed her eyes at him. She tilted her head slightly the way a dog might when it heard an odd sound. "But how are you going to—" She stopped.

Her mouth closed and she stared at him without speaking,

without moving. Hadrian was not certain she was still breathing.

Slowly her lower lip began to tremble. It started there and he watched as the tremor worked its way down her neck to her shoulders, shaking her body so that her hair quivered. Without warning tears spilled down her cheeks. Still she did not speak, she did not move, but the robe changed from blue to bright purple, surrounding both of them with light.

*What does that mean?*

"Arista?" he whispered fearfully. The look on her face was unfathomable.

*Fear? Shock? Remorse? What is it?*

He desperately needed to know. He had just thrown himself off a cliff and could not see the bottom.

"Are you upset?" he asked. "Please don't be mad—don't hate me. I don't want to die with you hating me. This is exactly why I never said anything. I was afraid that—"

Her fingers came up to his lips and gently pressed them shut.

"Shh," she managed to utter as she continued to cry, her eyes never leaving his face.

She took his hands in hers and squeezed. "I don't hate you," she whispered. "I just—I—" She bit her lip.

"What!" Hadrian said in desperation, his eyes wide, trying to see everything, searching for any clue. She was torturing him on purpose—he knew it.

"This is going to sound really stupid," she told him, shaking her head slowly.

"I don't care—say it. Whatever it is, just say it!"

"I—" She laughed a little. "I don't think I've ever been happier in my entire life than I am right now."

It was his turn to stare. His mouth opened but his mind

could not supply words. He was lost in her eyes and realized he could breathe once more.

"If you knew that I—how much I hoped—" She tilted her head down so that her hair hid her face. "I never thought that you saw me as anything more than a—a job." She raised her head and sniffled. "And the way you and Royce talked about nobles…"

Hadrian noticed his heart was beating again. It pounded in his chest, and despite the chill in the crypt, his shirt was soaked with sweat, his hands trembling.

"We're gonna die here," she told him, and abruptly started laughing. "But suddenly I don't care anymore. I never thought I could be so happy."

This got him laughing too. Somewhere inside him, relief and joy were mixing together to create an intoxicant more powerful than any liquor. He felt drunk, dizzy, and—more than ever before—alive.

"I feel—I feel so…" She laughed once and looked embarrassed.

"What?" he asked, reaching up and wiping the tears from her cheeks.

"It's like I'm not buried alive in a crypt anymore. It's like—like I just came home."

"For the first time," he added.

"Yes," she said, and tears began anew.

He reached out. She fell into him, and he closed his arms around her. She felt so small. She had always been such a force that he had never imagined she could feel so delicate—so fragile. He could die now. He laid his head back on the stone, taking in a breath and feeling the wonderful sensation of her head riding up and down on his chest.

Then they heard the rock begin to shatter.

⚜

No one could see anything and they gathered around the light of Arista's robe as she and Hadrian came out of the alcove. The bright purple light shifted to white, revealing everyone's faces, making them look pale and ghostly.

"What's going on?" Hadrian asked as another round of thunderous ripping occurred. The noise came from the direction of the Vault of Days, the sound bouncing around the stone walls.

"I don't know. Maybe the Ghazel are tunneling in," Mauvin replied; then he narrowed his eyes at Arista. "Are you all right?"

"Me?" Arista said, smiling. "Yeah, I'm great."

Mauvin looked confused but shrugged. "Should we barricade?"

"What's the point?" Hadrian replied. "If they can cut through that rubble, a few golden chairs aren't going to stop them."

"So what are we going to do?" Gaunt asked.

Hadrian looked around, mentally tallying the faces. "Where's Royce?"

Around the circle of light of Arista's robe were Myron, Magnus, Gaunt, Mauvin, Arista, and Hadrian. Royce was nowhere to be seen. Hadrian turned toward the sound and began walking. Behind him, the others followed. When he reached the Vault of Days, he paused, and together with Arista he carefully entered the room.

"Where is it?" Hadrian asked no one in particular.

"Where's what?" Mauvin said.

"The creature, it's not in the corner anymore."

"It's not?" Gaunt said fearfully. "It ate him!"

"I don't think so," Hadrian said, and taking Arista by the

hand, he led them all across the open room. Partway there the air grew foul with dust. A cloud obscured the door ahead like a fog; the grinding and breaking sounds grew louder.

When they reached the far side, they found the door to the scroll room was missing—along with a good portion of the wall separating the two. The scroll room itself had also been destroyed. The far wall was down and stones lay scattered across the floor. Ahead, where there had once been a corridor leading to the collapsed stairs, was a giant tunnel from which came the thunderous noise and the clouds of dust.

They found Royce sitting on his pack, his feet outstretched, his back against the wall.

"I was wondering how long it would take," he greeted them.

Hadrian looked at him for a moment, then started to move past him toward the tunnel.

"Don't go in there," Royce warned. "The thing isn't careful about where he tosses the stones."

"Maribor's beard!" Hadrian exclaimed, and started to laugh.

"By Drome!" Magnus muttered.

"We thought the Ghazel were coming through," Mauvin said, waving a hand before his face, trying to clear the air.

"I'm sure they will be," Royce replied.

"That's right!" Mauvin said. "There's armor in the tomb— shields. We should—"

"I wouldn't worry about it," Royce told him. "I told Gilly to deal with them too."

Hadrian started to laugh, which brought a smile to Royce's lips.

"Aren't they going to be surprised to see what comes out?" the thief chuckled.

"We're going to get out of here?" Arista said, shocked.

"It's a distinct possibility." Royce nodded. "It took a while to master the right phrases, but once I got him going, old Gilly—boy—he took to it like a knife to a soft back."

"Gilly?" Hadrian asked, laughing.

"A pet has to have a name, doesn't it? Later I'm planning to teach it *fetch* and *roll over*, but for now, *dig* and *sic 'em* will do."

Another loud collision of stone rattled the floor and shook dirt from the ceiling, causing all of them to flinch. A thick cloud billowed out of the tunnel.

"Loosens the teeth when he really gets going like that," Royce said. "Wait here while I check on his progress."

The thief stood, wrapped his scarf around his face, and walked into the dark cloud. The ground continued to shudder and the sound was frightening, as if gods were holding a war in the next room.

"How is it fitting through the corridor?" Myron asked.

"I'm pretty sure it's making a whole new one," Magnus replied.

"Better pack up," Royce told them when he emerged. "Gilly has got a rhythm going, so it won't be long."

They gathered their things and returned to the tomb, where Arista placed the horn in her pack. They replaced the lids on Novron's coffin and Gaunt, Mauvin, and Magnus picked up a few small treasures, which they called souvenirs. Royce, much to Hadrian's surprise, did not touch a thing, not even a handful of gold coins. He merely waited for the rest of them. They all bid one last farewell to Alric before heading back to the tunnel.

Hadrian was the last out of the tomb, and as he was leaving, he caught sight of something small lying on the floor just before Arista's light faded. Picking it up, he stuffed it into his pack before trotting out to join the others.

The dust had settled by the time Royce led them through the tunnel. It was no longer a corridor, but a gaping passage like something a monstrous rabbit might burrow. It was round and at least fifty feet in width. The walls were compact rock and stone held together by weight and pressure. The passage ran level for several feet, then angled upward. There was no sign of the Gilarabrywn, but ahead they heard the familiar beat of drums.

"Ghazel—how nice," Hadrian said miserably. "They waited."

The tunnel ended at the great wide hallway with suits of armor and sculptured walls that they had passed through on the way in. While large enough for the Gilarabrywn to walk through, there was no sign of it.

"Where's your pet, Royce?"

He shrugged. "Perhaps I need to get him a leash."

"What did you tell him to do?" Mauvin asked.

"Well, that's the thing...I don't know exactly. I hope I told it to clear the way of all debris and danger up to the square outside the palace, but who knows what I really said? I might have told it to clear the world of all decency and rangers up to the lair outside the ballast."

Magnus and Mauvin both chuckled; even Hadrian smiled. Then Myron spoke up. "He's not joking. That's actually what he said the first time he repeated the phrase back to me. And of course we're assuming I got it right to begin with."

The sounds of yelps and cries cut through the empty hallway. Hadrian and Mauvin drew their swords. They waited a moment but there was only silence.

Royce shrugged and led them onward, always several dozen feet in front. His head turned from side to side. Royce always reminded Hadrian of a squirrel when he had his ears up. He had the same twitchy behavior.

They passed by the doorway to the throne room, the ornate entrance still closed. Royce halted, raising a hand and tilting his head. The rest of them heard it too. A horn, drums, shouts, cries, it all came from ahead of them—faint and muffled.

"Blood," Royce mentioned, pointing up ahead.

As Arista approached, they could see a disturbing splatter that sprayed across the far wall, creating a ghastly painting that still dripped. A dozen arrows lay widely scattered like fallen branches after a storm.

They proceeded until they reached the end of the corridor, where another Gilarabrywn-sized tunnel ran upward. Through it, they felt fresh salt air and began climbing. They reached the end and Royce poked his head out first before waving for the rest to follow. They stood in the square between the Cenzarium and what Arista had left of the Teshlor guild-hall. In the center, where the fountain used to be, the Gilar-abrywn lay on a shallow lake of blood, its tail shifting lazily from side to side, hitting the ground with moist slaps. Bodies of Ghazel littered the square, forming mounds like shadowy snowdrifts running out beyond the range of Arista's light. Swords, bows, headdresses, arms, clawed hands, and heads speckled the stone in a macabre collage of death.

"There must be hundreds of bodies," Mauvin whispered.

"And those are the ones it didn't eat," Magnus added.

"Is it safe?" Hadrian asked Royce, looking at the Gilar-abrywn.

"Should be."

"Should be?"

Royce gave him a sinister grin.

"If it wasn't, we'd already be dead," Arista pointed out.

"What she said," Royce told him.

They stepped out onto the square, their shoes making wet noises as they walked across the bloody puddle. They made a slow circle around the beast, which remained quiet and still except for the ever-slapping tail.

"I think it got all of them," Hadrian announced. "Ghazel always take their dead if they can."

"I wish I had a sugar cube or something to give him," Royce said, looking at the Gilarabrywn with a sympathetic expression. "He's been such a good boy."

—ᶳ—

They reached the sea quicker than Hadrian would have expected. They followed a more direct route, not needing to dodge the Ghazel, and of course, return trips always seemed shorter. No one stopped to stare at the city. No one had any desire to explore. Their feet were no longer weighted by the dread of the unknown. A sense of urgency filled the party and drove them forward without pause.

Despite a lengthy series of language lessons with Myron, Royce was unable to persuade Gilly to leave the city. It refused to pass the lions and Royce had no choice but to abandon his newfound pet. He sent it back to resume its old duties in the Vault of Days but did not mention why.

"Look at that!" Hadrian exclaimed when they came in sight of the *Harbinger* once again. The ship was where they had left it in the sheltered cove, but not how they had left it. A new mast was set and a beautiful sail furled across a new yard. New boards and caulking were visible along the hull near the glowing green waterline, and parts of the cabin were touched up with new boards as well. "Wyatt and Elden have been busy."

"Amazing!" Magnus said, clearly impressed. "And just the two of them."

"With Elden it is more like three and a half," Hadrian corrected.

"And look," the dwarf said, trotting forward to where a series of planks were supported by floating barrels and linked by rope. "They built a gangway. Excellent craftsmanship, especially for the time given."

Magnus was the first on board, followed by Mauvin, with
Hadrian and Arista coming up behind. Royce lingered on the
rocks, eyeing the rocking ship with a sour look.

"Wyatt, Elden?" Hadrian called.

The ship was in fine shape. The mast, rail, and wheel block
had a new whitewash and the deck was nicely scoured.

"Where did they get the paint?" Arista asked.

Hadrian was looking up. "I'm still impressed by this mast.
Even with Elden, how did they set it?"

Not finding them on deck, they headed for the cabin. In the
timeless world of the underground, it was possible they were
both sleeping. Magnus was the first one through the door and
the dwarf abruptly stopped, making an odd sound like a
belch.

"Magnus?" Mauvin asked.

The dwarf did not answer. He collapsed as more than a
half dozen goblins burst out of the hold, shrieking and skittering like crabs. Mauvin retreated, pulling his sword, and in the
same motion cut the head off a charging Ghazel. Hadrian
pushed Arista behind him and stood next to Mauvin, who
had moved beside him.

Five Ghazel advanced across the deck holding their curved
blades and small round shields adorned with finger-painted
triangle symbols and tassels of seabird feathers and bone.
They hissed as they approached in a line. Four more emerged
from behind the cabin; three had bows and one, far smaller
than the rest, was decorated in dozens of multicolored feathers. This one danced and hummed. There was one missing.
Hadrian was sure he had seen another exit the cabin, not a
warrior, not an oberdaza.

"Gaunt, Myron, Arista, get off the ship," he told them as
he and Mauvin spread out to block the Ghazels' advance.
Mauvin stroked his blade through the air, warming up, and

Hadrian could see he was off tempo. His wounded arm would not allow him to move as he needed to.

Myron backed up but Arista and Gaunt refused.

"No," Gaunt said. "Give me that big sword of yours."

"Do you know how to fight?"

"Ha! I was the leader of the Nationalist Army, remember?"

Hadrian lunged forward, but it was a feint and he dodged left, spinning in a full circle. One of the goblins took the bait, rushed forward, and was in just the right spot when Hadrian came around with his swords. The goblin died with two blades in his body. Hadrian drew them out dramatically and shouted a roar at the others, causing them all to hesitate. While they did, he stepped on the dead goblin's fallen sachel and slid it behind him to Gaunt. He roared again and kicked the shield back as well.

"*Galenti!*" he heard one of the Ghazel say, and the others immediately began to chatter.

"*Yes!*" he said in Tenkin. "*Get off my ship, or you will all die!*"

Arista and Mauvin looked at him, surprised. No one moved on either side except Gaunt, who picked up the shield and sword.

"*Known are you, but leave not. Our ship, borrowed for a time—but ours again. Leave it. Fight no more, you and we. I—Drash of the Klune—I too fight in arena. We all fight.*" He pointed at the ground at the dead. "*Not them. Those young fish, not sharks.*" He pointed at Gaunt, Myron, and Arista. "*Young fish and breeder. Like ones we find here— young fish too—good eating. You not want to fight. You leave.*"

Hadrian brought his swords together and let them clash loudly. He held them high above his head in an X and glared at the goblin chieftain, which caused them all to step back.

"*You saw me in the arena,*" Hadrian said. "*You know these swords. I come from old city, where no Ghazel drum beats—no horn blows—all dead. I did this.*" He gestured behind him. "*We do this. You leave my ship now.*"

The chieftain hesitated and Hadrian realized the ploy too late. The focus of his opponent's eyes shifted to something behind Hadrian. At that moment, he realized his mistake. He had given the finisher enough time to move into position. The missing Ghazel, the assassin, was behind him. *No*, he thought, not behind him. The finisher would not kill the chief of a clan; he would seek the oberdaza, the witch doctor—Arista!

From behind him she screamed.

Hadrian spun, knowing before he did that he was too late. The poisoned blade would already be through her back. Like Esrahaddon, Arista was helpless to a blow she had never seen coming. As soon as he turned, the chief launched his attack. It was a sound plan and Hadrian knew it.

All three ranges had targeted him and let loose the moment they heard Arista scream. Three arrows struck Hadrian in the back and he felt the missiles—soft muffled hits. Two landed between his shoulders and one near the kidneys, but there was no pain. Turning back, he saw the arrows lying on the deck, the tips blunted.

The chieftain stared at him, shocked, and for a moment, Hadrian was equally bewildered, until he felt the weight as he moved. Slung on his back was Jerish's shield, which was so light Hadrian had forgotten about it. The thin metal had stopped the arrows like a block of stone.

They had killed Arista. They had killed Wyatt and Elden. Hadrian felt the blood pound in his ears and his swords moved on their own. Three Ghazel died in seconds, including the chieftain. Somewhere beside him Mauvin was fighting, but he hardly noticed as he cast caution aside and fought forward, dashing madly, wildly through the ranks, killing as he went. Another round of arrows flew at Hadrian as he charged. Without a shield to protect him, with no time to turn, he was dead. He expected to feel the shafts pierce his chest and throat. They never reached him. Instead the arrows exploded in flame and burst into ash an instant after leaving their bows.

Hadrian cleaved the archers aside.

Only the oberdaza remained.

A wall of fire erupted between the two of them and flared up whenever Hadrian tried to move toward him. The song and dance of the Ghazel witch doctor changed to a scream of terror as his own wall rushed back at him. The flames attacked their master like dogs too often beaten and the oberdaza was consumed in a pillar of fire that left no more than a charred black spot in the deck and a foul smell in the air.

*Arista?*

Hadrian turned and saw her standing unharmed in her glowing robe. The finisher lay dead on the deck with a length of rope around his neck. Royce stood beside her. Mauvin and even Gaunt waited with blood-covered blades. There were smears on Degan's face and a dark stain on his chest, and his arms and hands were dripping.

"Are you all right?" Hadrian asked.

Gaunt nodded with a surprised expression. "They still fight with one arm," he replied, sounding a little dazed.

"Magnus!" Arista shouted as she rushed forward.

The dwarf lay facedown in a pool of dark blood.

They carefully rolled him over. The wound was in his stomach and spewed rich, dark blood. Magnus was still awake, still alert, his eyes rolling around as he looked at each of their faces.

His hand shook as the dwarf fumbled at his belt. He managed to knock Alverstone loose and it fell to the deck. "Give to—Royce—won—der—ful blade."

His eyes closed.

"No!" Arista shouted at him. She sat down, laid a hand on his chest, and started humming.

"Arista, what are you doing?" Hadrian asked.

"I'm pulling him back," she replied.

"No! You can't! Last time you—"

She grabbed his hand. "Just hold on to me and don't let go."

"No! Arista!" he shouted, but it was too late. He could tell she was already gone. "Arista!"

She knelt with her eyes closed, her breathing quick. A soft, gentle humming came from her, as if she were a mother cat. Hadrian cradled her small hand in both of his, trying not to squeeze too hard but making certain to keep a tight hold. He had no idea what good it did, but because she had told him not to let go, he swore that only death would break his grip.

"Nothing else around," Hadrian heard Royce say. "There's a Ghazel ship down the coast, but it's about a mile away and I didn't see any activity. Is he dead?"

"I think so," Mauvin replied. "Arista is trying to save him."

"Not again," Royce said dismally. "Didn't that almost kill her last—"

"Shut up, okay?" Hadrian snapped. "Both of you, just shut up!"

Hadrian stared at her face, watching her head droop lower and lower, as if she were falling asleep.

*What does that mean? Is she losing? Slipping away? Dying?*

Frustration gripped him. His stomach twisted and every muscle tensed.

Her shoulders slumped and she tilted. He caught her with

his free hand and pulled her to him, pressing her limp head to his chest.

*Still humming—is that a good sign?*

He thought it was. He cradled her with his left hand while still holding tight with his right, his palm growing slick with sweat.

Arista jerked her head as if she were having a dream. She did it again and her humming stopped and she mumbled something.

"What is it?" he asked. "I didn't hear you. What did you say?"

Another mumble, too soft, too slurred.

She jerked again and appeared to cry out. He held tight as her body went limp against him, her head hanging.

"Arista?" he said.

She stopped breathing.

"Arista!"

He shook her. *"Arista!"*

Her head flopped, her hair whipping back and forth.

"Arista, come back! Come back to me! Goddamn it! Come back!"

Nothing.

She lay like a dead weight against him, as loose as a doll.

He pulled her tight. "Please," he whispered. "Please come back to me. Please. I can't lose you—not now."

He lifted her head. She appeared to be sleeping, the way he had seen her dozens of times. There was a beauty about her face when she slept that he could never explain, a calm softness—only she was not sleeping now. There was no reassuring rise of her chest, no breath on his face. He pressed his lips against hers. He kissed her, but her lips did not move. They remained slack, lifeless, and when he pulled back, she still hung in his arms. He hoped that maybe some power from within him could awaken her, like in a fairy tale. That the kiss—their first—could somehow call her back, awaken her.

But nothing happened. Their first kiss—their last—and she never felt it.

"Please," he muttered as tears began running down his cheeks. "Oh dear Maribor, please, don't do this."

His own breath shortened, his chest too tight. It felt as if a blade had sliced through his stomach and he was falling to his own death. He held tight to her, pressing her body against his, her cheek against his face, as if holding her could keep him—

Her hand jerked.

Hadrian held his breath.

He felt a squeeze.

He squeezed back, harder than he had planned.

Her body stiffened. Her head flew back. Her eyes and mouth opened wide and she inhaled. Arista sucked in a loud breath, as if she just surfaced from a deep dive.

She could not speak and drew in breath after breath, her body rocking with the effort. Slowly she turned to look at him and her expression filled with sadness. "You're crying," she said as her hand came up and wiped his cheek.

"Am I?" he replied, blinking several times. "Must be the sea air."

"Are you all right?"

Hadrian laughed. "Me? How are you?"

"I'm fine—tired as usual." She grinned. "But fine."

"He's alive!" Mauvin shouted, stunned.

They simultaneously turned their heads just in time to see the dwarf rising groggily. Magnus looked at Arista and immediately began to weep.

"The wound," Mauvin said, shaking his head in disbelief. "It's healed."

"Told you I could do it," she whispered.

❧

Arista woke to the gentle motion and creaking of the ship at sea. She felt physically drained again, her body weighted. Both arms shook when she lifted them, her hands quivering. She found her pack left beside the bed and reached in, feeling around for food. She pulled out a travel meal and silently thanked Ibis Thinly as if he were the god of food. Just as before, she devoured the salt pork, hard bread, and pickle. She swallowed three mouthfuls of water and leaned back against the wall for a moment. Eating exhausted her.

In the dark, she listened to the ship. It creaked and groaned—verse and chorus—riding up and down. She let the movement rock her head, feeling the food work its magic.

She thought of Alric and in the darkness saw his face. Young and yet strangely lined, with that silly beard that had never looked right on him—his kingly beard—meant to make him appear older. It had never fully filled in. She thought of her father and the hairbrushes he had brought her—his way of saying he loved her. She remembered her mother's swan mirror, lost when the tower collapsed. It was *all* gone now, certainly all of Medford, perhaps all of Melengar as well. She could still hear the sound of her mother's voice and remembered how it had come to her from out of the light.

*What is that place?*

She had come close to it twice now. It had been easier with Magnus; she had not seen her loved ones, only his. They spoke to him in dwarvish. She did not know the words, but the meaning was clear—kindness, forgiveness, love.

*What is that place? What is it like inside?*

She sensed peace and comfort and knew it would be a good place to rest. Arista needed rest, but not there, not yet. Taking the remaining walnuts from her meal, she climbed out to the deck. The length of the ship lay before her, illuminated by the green sea. Royce was in the rigging with an unpleasant, sickly look on his face. Hadrian was at the stern, both hands on the wheel, his teeth clenched as he focused intently on the rising and falling waves. Myron and Degan worked together near the bow, tying off a loose rope that was allowing the jib to flap. Gaunt pulled and Myron tied. Magnus sat at the waist coiling a length of rope, looking like a bearded child left to play on the floor.

"The sleeping princess awakes!" It was Mauvin calling down from the yard above. She smiled at him and he waved back.

"Forget her," the thief barked. "Get to the end of that yard!"

Arista walked across the deck, pausing once reaching the dwarf. She popped another walnut into her mouth. "Feeling all right?" she asked.

The dwarf nodded without looking at her.

"Oh good." She sat down beside him. A warm wind came off the sea and blew through her hair, clearing her face. She looked up and spotted Hadrian taking a precious moment away from steering to look at her and wave with a smile. She waved back, but by then his eyes had turned back to the problems of the sea.

She looked around the deck again; then her head tilted up and she scanned the rigging. Everything was illuminated eerily from below by the glowing sea, which gave the whole ship a ghostly appearance.

"Where're Wyatt and Elden?" she asked Magnus.

"Dead," the dwarf said coldly.

"Oh," she replied, unsettled by the blunt response. She leaned back on her hands, forgetting to chew the walnut as she remembered the two sailors. She had liked them both and regretted now that she had never spoken to either very much, but then, she guessed no one but Myron had spoken much to Elden. She slipped her hand in her pocket and withdrew the little figurine Elden had carved of her and rubbed it with her thumb.

"Poor Allie," she said, shaking her head sadly. Then a thought came to her. "Are you sure they're dead? Or did the goblins just take them? Did anyone actually see—"

"Found them partially eaten," Magnus growled. "Wyatt's legs and arms were gone, his chest torn open—gnawed out like a turkey ready for stuffing. Only half of Elden's face was there, the skin hung off one side and bite marks on his—"

"That's enough!" She stopped him, raising her hands up before her face. "I understand! You don't have to be so—so graphic!"

"You asked," he said tartly.

She stared at him.

He ignored her.

Magnus huffed, stood up, and began to walk away.

"Magnus," she said, stopping him. "What's wrong?"

"Whatcha mean?" he said, but did not turn. He looked out over the side of the ship, watching the luminous waves roll.

"You act as if you're angry with me."

He grumbled to himself, something in dwarvish, still refusing to face her.

Overhead the wind was still ruffling the jib. Myron and Gaunt had paused in their work, both staring at them. Royce was yelling at Mauvin about mainstays and yards.

"Magnus?" she asked.

"Why did you do it?" the dwarf blurted out.

"Do what?"

He whirled at last to face her. His eyes were harsh and accusing. "Why did you save my life?"

She did not know what to say.

"What do you care if I die!" he snapped at her, his eyes fiery. "What difference does it make—you're a princess, I'm just a dwarf! You forced me on this trip. I never wanted to come. You took half my beard. Do you know what a beard means to a dwarf? Of course you don't, I can see it in your eyes. You don't know anything about dwarves!" He flicked the bottom of his severed whiskers at her. "You got what you wanted out of me— you have the blasted horn! And you can find your own way back out. You don't need me anymore. So why, then? Why'd ya do it? Why did you—why did you—" He clenched his teeth, squeezed his eyes shut, and turned his head away.

She sat back, shocked.

"Why did you risk your life to save mine?" he said, his voice now little more than a whisper. "Hadrian said you almost *died*—you stopped breathing like you did with Alric. He said he thought for sure you were dead this time. *He* was your brother!" Magnus shouted. "But me...I murdered your father! Have you forgotten that? I was the one who locked you in the tower. I closed the door on you and Royce and sealed you all in the dungeon under Aquesta, leaving you to starve to death. Did all that just slip your mind? Now Alric is dead. Your family is gone. Your kingdom is gone—you have nothing, and Royce..."

He pulled out the glistening dagger. "Why did he give me this? I wanted to see it, yes! I would have been his slave for the chance to study it for a week. And then he just gave it to me. He hasn't taken it back or even said a word. This—this—this is the most beautiful thing I have ever seen—worth more than a mountain of gold, more than all that back in the tomb. He just gave it to me. After what I did...he should have killed me with it! He should still kill me. So should you. Both of you should have laughed and sang when I..." A hand went to his stomach and he bit his lower lip, making the remains of his beard stand up. "So why did you do it? *Why?*"

He stared at her now with a desperate look on his face—a pained expression, as if somehow she were torturing him.

"I didn't want you to die," she said simply. "I didn't really think beyond that. You were dying and I could save you, so I did."

"But you could have died—couldn't you?"

She shrugged.

Magnus continued to glare at her as if he might either attack her or burst into tears.

"Why is this such a problem for you? Aren't you happy to be alive?"

"*No!*" he shouted.

Over his shoulder, she saw Myron and Gaunt still staring, but now with concerned faces.

"You should have let me die—you should have let me die. Everything would have been fine if you had just let me die."

"Why?" she asked. "Why would it have been better?"

"I don't deserve to live, that's why. I don't and now..." A dark expression came over him and he looked back out at the sea.

"What? What happens now?"

"That's just it, I don't know. I don't know what to do anymore. I've hated you for so long."

"Me?" she asked, shocked. "What did I—"

"All of you—humans. The water flooded the caverns, so we came to you for help—not a handout, but a fair trade, work for payment. You agreed and to a fair price. Then you herded us into the Barak Ghetto in Trent. We mined the Dithmar Range and you paid us all right, then came the taxes. Taxes for living in your filthy shacks, taxes on what we bought and sold, taxes on crops we raised, taxes for not being members of the Nyphron Church—taxes for being dwarves. Taxes so high a number of us turned their backs on Drome to worship your god, but still you did not accept us. You denied us the privilege to carry weapons, to ride horses. We worked night and day and still did not make enough to feed ourselves. We fell into your debt and you made slaves of us. Your kind whipped my kin to make us work, and killed us when we tried to leave. They called us thieves, just for trying to be free." He shook his head miserably. "My whole family—Clan Derin—slaves to humans." He spat the words. "The elves never treated us that badly. And it wasn't just my family, it was all the dwarves."

He hooked a thumb at Myron. "He knows. He told you how centuries ago the dwarves helped you, saved you when you were desperate. And how did you repay us? Tell me, Princess, can a dwarf be a citizen in Melengar?" He did not wait for her answer. "Dwarves are never granted citizenship anywhere. Without it you can't practice a trade. You can't join a guild or open a business. You can't legally work at all. And even in Melengar you put us in the most vile corners, the downhill alleys where all the sewage runs, where the shacks are rotting, and where on a warm day you can't breathe. That's what you've done to us—to dwarves. My great grandfather worked on Drumindor!" He straightened up as he spoke the name of the ancient dwarven fortress. "Now humans defile it."

"Not anymore," she reminded him.

"Good for them, you deserve what you got."

He placed his hands on the rail and stared down the side of the ship.

Myron left Gaunt alone with the rope to listen.

"I'm the last of Clan Derin—the only one to escape—a fugitive, an outlaw because I chose to be free. They hunted me for years. I got good at disappearing. You found that out too, didn't you?

"Your people disgraced and killed mine. Your kind never did anything unless it was for profit—and you call us greedy! I've heard your tales of evil dwarves kidnapping, killing, imprisoning—but that was all your doing. Why would a dwarf kidnap a princess or anyone? That was you using us as an excuse for your own sins.

"Every few years, knights would come into the ghettos and burn them. Those so-called defenders of the law and decency would come in the middle of the night and set fire to our miserable shacks in the dark—and always in winter."

He turned and faced her once more. "But you…" He sighed, his eyes losing their fire, fogging instead with bewilderment and weariness. "You risked yourself and saved my life. It doesn't make sense."

He sat down, looking exhausted. "I've hated you for so long and you go and do this." He put his face in his hands and began to rock forward and back.

"Maybe," Myron said, coming behind the dwarf and placing a hand on his back. "Maybe Magnus did die."

The dwarf looked up and scowled.

"Maybe you should let him die," the monk added. "Let the hate, fear, and anger die with him. This is a chance to start over. The princess has given you a new life. You can choose to live it any way you want starting right now."

The dwarf lost his scowl.

"It's scary, isn't it?" Myron said. "Imagining a different life? I was scared too, but you can do it."

"He's right," Arista said. "This could be a new start."

"That all depends," Magnus replied, "and we'll find out soon enough."

The dwarf stood up.

"Royce!" he shouted. "Come down a second."

The thief looked irritated but grabbed a line and slid down, touching the deck lightly.

"What is it? I can't leave Mauvin up there alone, and I'm not feeling very well as it is."

Magnus held out Alverstone. "Take it back."

Royce narrowed his eyes. "I thought you wanted it."

"Take it. You might need it—sooner than you think."

Royce took the dagger suspiciously. "What's going on?"

Magnus glanced at Arista, and Myron, and lastly at Gaunt, who had finally secured the jib and walked over.

"Before we left Aquesta, I made a bargain with the Patriarch."

"What *kind* of bargain?" Royce asked.

"I was supposed to kill Degan after we found the horn, but before we left the caves. I was hired to kill him and return the horn to His Grace."

"You planned to betray us—again?" Royce asked.

"Yes."

"You were going to kill me?" Gaunt asked.

Royce stared at Magnus and looked down at the dagger.

Myron and Arista watched him closely, tense, waiting.

"Why are you telling me this?"

The dwarf hesitated briefly. "Because...Magnus died before he could go through with it."

Royce stared at the dwarf, turning Alverstone over and over in his hands and pursing his lips. He glanced at Arista and at Myron, then nodded. "You know, I never did like that short son of a bitch." He held out the dagger. "Here, I don't think I'll be needing it."

Magnus did nothing for several minutes but stare at the dagger. He seemed to have trouble breathing. He finally stood up straight. "No." The dwarf shook his head. "Magnus thought—when you gave him that dagger—it was the most valuable gift he could ever receive. He was wrong."

Royce nodded and slipped Alverstone back into the folds of his cloak. He gripped the rope and began to climb.

Magnus stood looking lost for a moment.

"Are you all right?" Myron asked.

"I don't know." He looked down at the deck. "If Magnus died, then who am I?"

"Whoever you want to be," the monk said. "It's a pretty wonderful gift."

⁘

"How far are we?" Arista asked Hadrian, sitting down on the wheel box beside him. The fighter was still grappling with the ship, still struggling to keep its sails balanced.

"Not sure, but judging from the last crossing, we should see land in the next hour, unless Royce and I messed up really bad on the course or I wreck us. Too far this way and the sails collapse and we lose headway, which means we can't steer. Too far the other way and the wind will flip us. Wyatt made this look so easy."

"Is it true what Magnus told me? Did you really find them?"

Hadrian nodded sadly. "He was a good man—they both were. I keep thinking of Allie. They were the only family she had. Now what's going to happen to her?"

She nodded. So much death, so much sadness there were times she felt she might drown. Overhead the canvas fluttered, like the sheet of a maid making up a bed. The rings rattled against the poles and the waves crashed into the hull.

She watched Hadrian standing at the wheel, his chin up, his back straight, and his eyes watching the water. The breeze blew back his hair, showing a worn face, but not hard or broken. He had his sleeves rolled up to his elbows and the muscles of his forearms stood out. She noted several scars on his arms. Two looked new—red and raised. His hands were broad and large, and his skin so tanned that his fingernails stood out lighter. He was a handsome man, but this was the first time she had really noticed. His looks were not what attracted her. It was his warmth, his kindness, his humor, and how safe it felt to sit beside him on a cold, dark night. Still, she had to admit that he was a handsome man in his tattered, coarse cloth and raw leather. She wondered how many women had noticed, and how many he had known. She glanced back across the sea behind them; the crypt of emperors seemed very far away.

"You know, we really haven't had a chance to talk since getting out." She looked at the waves breaking at the bow. "I mean—you said some things in there that—well, maybe they were only meant for in there. We both thought we were dying and people can—"

"I meant every word," he told her firmly. "How about you, do you regret it?"

She smiled and shook her head. "When I woke up, I thought it might have been a beautiful dream. I never really considered myself the kind of woman men wanted. I'm pushy, controlling, I butt into places I shouldn't, and I have far too many opinions on far too many subjects—subjects women aren't supposed to be interested in. I never even bothered to try to make myself more appealing. I avoided dances and never presented myself with my hair up and neckline down. I don't have a clue about flirting." She sighed and ran a hand over her matted hair. "I never cared how I looked before, but now… for the first time I'd like to be pretty…for you."

"I think you're beautiful."

"It's dark."

"Oh, wait." Hadrian reached over to his backpack. "Close your eyes."

"Why?"

"Just do it and hold out your hands."

She did as instructed, feeling a bit silly as she heard him rummaging through his pack, then silence. A moment later she felt something in her hands. Her fingers closed and she knew what it was before she opened her eyes. She began to cry.

"What's wrong?" Hadrian asked in a sudden panic.

"Nothing," she said, wiping the tears away and feeling foolish. She had to stop this. He was going to think she cried all the time.

"Then why are you crying?"

"It's okay. I'm happy."

"You are?" Hadrian asked skeptically.

She nodded, smiling at him as tears continued to run down her cheeks.

"It's not worth getting all that excited over, you know. Everything else in that place was gold and encrusted in jewels. I'm not even sure this is real silver. I was actually so disappointed that I considered not giving it to you, but after what you said—"

"It's the most wonderful gift you could have given me."

Hadrian shrugged. "It's just a hairbrush."

"Yes, it is," she said. "It really is."

## Chapter 25

# The Arrival

Modina faced the Gilarabrywn. She waited for it to attack, to kill her and the rest of her family. But the beast did none of those things. The monster stared at her for a moment, then spread its wings and lifted off, flying away.

They all waited, staring out through the missing wall.

"Horses," someone said, and soon Modina also heard the sound of trotting hooves.

Twelve elves rode on white mounts. They wore lion helms and long purple capes that draped over the back of their mounts. Drawing off their helms in unison, they revealed long white hair, sharp pointed ears, angled brows, and luminous eyes of green, as if a magical fire burned within.

The lead rider looked about the shattered ruins of the castle; the mere turning of his head revealed a startling, unworldly grace and it was easy to understand how they were once thought to be gods. His eyes settled on Modina, and Amilia wondered how she could manage to stand beneath his stare.

"*Er un don Irawondona fey Asendwayr. Susyen vie eyurian Novron fey Instayria?*" he said. His voice sounded like the ringing of fine crystal.

Modina continued to stare back at the elf.

Nimbus rose and, moving to Modina's side, replied, *"Er un don Modina vie eyurian Novron fey Instayria."*

The elf stared at Modina for a long moment, then dismounted, his movements as fluid as silk blowing in the wind. Amilia thought his expression was filled with contempt, but she knew nothing about elves.

"What did you two say?" Modina asked.

"He introduced himself as Lord Irawondona of the Asendwayr tribe. He said the Gilarabrywn heard your claim and came to ask if you were in fact the daughter of Novron. I told him yes."

*"Vie eyurian Novron un Persephone, cy mor guyernian fi hyliclor Gylindora dur Avempartha sen youri? Uli Vermar fie veriden ves uyeria! Ves Ferrol boryeten."*

"He asks, if you are the daughter of Novron and Persephone, why have you not presented the horn for challenge at Avempartha? He says that the *Uli Vermar* ended some time ago and by failing to present the horn you stand in violation before Ferrol."

*"Vie hillin jes lineia hes filhari fi ish tylor baliyan. Sein lori es runyor ahit eston."*

"He says that by not producing the horn, your violation releases them from all treaties, agreements, and requirements to abide your commands."

"Tell him I'm in the process of retrieving the horn."

Nimbus spoke in the musical language and the elven lord replied.

"He insists that you must present it at once."

Nimbus spoke again, and the elf turned and consulted with one of the mounted riders.

"I explained that it was in the ancient city of Percepliquis and would be brought here soon. I hope that I did not overstep my—"

Modina took Nimbus's face in her hands and kissed him on the mouth. "I love you, Nimbus."

The chancellor looked befuddled and, stepping back, checked to see if his wig was on straight.

"He is coming back," Amilia told them.

Once more Nimbus did the talking. There appeared to be some kind of minor dispute and once the elven lord looked over Nimbus's shoulder at the girls sitting on the floor, then nodded. With the tone of general agreement, the elf remounted his horse and rode back out of the courtyard with the others.

"What?" Modina asked.

"They have decided not to wait and will go to Percepliquis to meet the horn. Should you be telling the truth, they will hold the challenge ceremony there. If you are lying, Irawondona will claim his right to rule through default. I presume that will mean they will continue in their march to rid the world of mankind. Either way you must go with them."

"When?"

"You have just enough time to grab a change of clothes, I think. I tried to arrange a small retinue, but they refused. I did manage to gain agreement for the girls to go. Allie deserves to be with her father when he returns and Mercy will comfort her if he does not. I told him they were your daughters."

"Thank you, Nimbus, you may very well have saved all our lives."

"I fear it may only be a stay of execution."

"Not if Arista succeeds, and every day granted to us is another day to hope."

❦

Mince climbed out of the Hovel, pulling his hood up and yawning. The others had kicked him awake, as it was his turn to check the horses. The rule in their group had always been that those who worked ate. It was a simple rule, with little room for interpretation, but early on a cold winter's morning, when he was bundled in blankets and half-asleep, the thought of going outside in the wind and snow made forgetting even simple rules easy. Finally he had relented, knowing they would just kick him harder.

He stood up and stretched his back as he did every morning, thinking about how old he was getting. It was still early, and the sun was only now breaching the tree line, casting sharp angles of golden light in slants, making the snow crystals glimmer. It was warmer, but the night's chill still lingered. He decided it was the wetness that made it feel worse; at least when it was cold, the air and even snow were dry.

Mince walked to the line of horses waiting for him. He knew them all by name and they knew him. Each of their heads turned, their ears rotating his way. They were lucky. The bitter cold had ended abruptly and none of the horses had died. Even the one Mince was certain had stopped breathing survived.

"Morning, ladies and gents," he greeted them as he did each day, with a nod of his head and a wave of his hand. "How are we this miserable excuse of a day, huh? What's that, Simpleton? You don't agree? You think it is a fine day, you say? Much warmer than yesterday morn? Well, I don't know if I can agree with you, sir. What's that, Mouse? You agree with Simpleton? Hmm, I don't know. It just seems...too quiet—far too quiet."

It did. Mince stood still with his feet in the slush and listened. There were no wind or sound. It was a strange sort of stillness, as if the world were dead.

*Perhaps it is.*

Who knew what had happened up north, or to the south, for that matter.

*What if they are all dead now? What if the four of us are all that are left?*

A crow cawed in a nearby tree; the stark call made the silence desolate. A sense of emptiness and loss hung in the air. Mince felt the line tethering the horses, making sure it was still secure, then pulled open the feed bags. Normally they jostled each other, trying to stick their noses in, but this morning something drew their attention. The horse's heads turned, their ears twitching to the left, their big eyes peering.

"Someone's coming?" Mince whispered to Princess. Her head bounced up and down, which shocked him, but then she quickly followed that with a shaking as well.

A few moments later, he heard hooves and he ran to the Hovel to wake the others.

"Who is it?" Brand whispered.

"How should I know?" Mince replied, pulling himself fully inside.

"It's certainly not Hadrian and the rest," Elbright pointed out. "They left their horses with us."

"Maybe it's Renwick coming back?" Kine suggested hopefully, and this returned several positive looks and nods.

"One of us should look," Elbright said commandingly, getting to his knees and pulling on his cloak.

"Not me," Mince said. "Let Brand do it. He's the bold one."

"Hush," Elbright snapped, "I'm going."

He pulled a bit of the tarp aside and looked out.

"Do you see 'em?" Kine asked.

"No."

"Maybe they—"

"Shh!" Elbright held up his hand. "Listen."

Faint voices carried across the stillness of the winter morning.

"*They went down here*," a voice said.

*"Oh my! That does look rather unpleasant. Is Your Grace certain?"*

*"Absolutely."*

"They don't sound like elves," Kine whispered.

"Like you know how elves talk," Mince said.

"It doesn't sound like Renwick either," Brand added.

"Will you all shut up!" Elbright hissed, slapping Kine on the head.

*"It's so deep you can't see the bottom."* The faint voice spoke again.

*"It's very deep indeed."*

*"There are no tracks near it."*

*"They are still inside, still down there, still dredging up secrets and stirring old memories, but they are coming. Already they are quite near and they have the horn."*

*"How do you know that?"*

*"Call it…an old man's intuition."*

*"That's good, isn't it? That they have the horn?"*

*"Oh yes, that is very good."*

The sound of crunching snow could be heard, growing louder.

"They're coming this way," Elbright said.

"Can you see them yet?" Kine asked.

"There are four of them. One looks like a priest in a black frock, two are soldiers, and there's an old man in bright-colored robes with long white hair. The soldiers are kind of strange-looking."

"What are they doing here?" Brand asked.

*"Their horses,"* a voice outside said. They were much closer now. The boys could hear the squishing of the slushy ground. *"You can come out, young men."*

They looked at each other nervously.

"Renwick, Elbright, Brand, Kine, Mince, come, we are going to have breakfast."

Elbright was the first one out, emerging from the tarp carefully. His head turned from side to side. They each followed him slowly, squinting in the sunlight, and just as Elbright had described, four men stood before them in the small clearing. They looked terribly out of place. The man with the long white hair was wearing purple, red, and gold robes and he leaned on a staff. To either side stood the soldiers, in gold breastplates, helms, and sleeves. They also wore colorful pants of red, purple, and yellow. Each held a spear and wore a sword. The priest was the only normal-looking fellow, standing with his weight on one leg in the traditionally drab black habit of a Nyphron priest.

"Who are you?" Elbright asked.

"This is His Grace the Patriarch of the Nyphron Church," the priest told him.

"Oh," Elbright said, nodding. Mince could tell he was trying to sound like he knew who that was, but his friend knew better. Elbright was always doing that, making out like he was more worldly than he was.

"These are his bodyguards and I am Monsignor Merton of Ghent."

"Guess you already know us," Elbright said. "What are you doing here?"

"Just waiting," the Patriarch replied. "Like you—waiting for them to climb back out of that hole and change the nature of the world forever. Certainly you can't begrudge us the desire of a front-row seat."

The old man looked at his guards and they trudged off.

"How's Renwick?" Mince asked. "Did he make it to Aquesta?"

"I'm sorry," Monsignor Merton replied kindly. "We traveled by sea around the horn to Vernes and then by coach. We left quite some time ago, so it is entirely possible that he arrived after we left. Was he a friend?"

Mince nodded.

"He rode to Aquesta with news that the elves were attacking from the southeast," Brand said. "They came right by here, they did."

"I'm sorry I can't tell you more," the priest said.

"Pleasant little place you have here," the old man mentioned, looking around. "It's nice that you put your camp under the holly tree. I like the splash of green on such a day as this, when it seems as if all the color has been stolen. It has been a long, cold winter, but it will soon be over. A new world is about to bloom."

Mince heard the distant sound of music and instantly he threw his hands to his ears.

"Is that...?" Elbright asked, alarmed, raising his own hands as Mince bobbed his head.

"Relax, boys," the Patriarch said. "That melody is not enchanted. It is the "Ibyn Ryn," the Ervian anthem."

"But it's the elves!" Elbright said. "They're coming!"

"Yes." The Patriarch glanced up the hill and then down at the hole. "It's a race now."

# CHAPTER 26

# THE RETURN

"I love this chamber," Arista said as they spread out blankets on the same flat rock. Overhead the glowworms glimmered and winked, and she noticed for the first time how much she missed seeing the sky.

Magnus gathered his rocks in the center once more. "This is nothing compared to the wonders that I have seen in the deep. My grandfather once took me into the mountains of the Dithmar Range of Trent to a place only he knew. He told me that I needed to know where I came from. He took me deep into a crevasse to where a river went underground. We disappeared inside for weeks. My mother and father were furious when we finally returned. They didn't want me to *get ideas*. They had already given up, but my grandfather—he knew."

Magnus sparked a stone against another. "The things he showed me were amazing. Chambers hundreds of times the size of this one made of shimmering crystal so that a single glow stone could make it bright as day. Stone cathedrals with pillars and teeth, and waterfalls that dropped so far you could not hear the roar. Everything down there was so vast, so wide, so big—we felt immeasurably small. It is sometimes hard to believe in Drome, seeing what has become of his people, but in places like this, and certainly in halls like the ones my grand-father showed me, it's like seeing the face of god firsthand."

Arista spread her blanket next to Hadrian.

"What are you trying to do there, Magnus?" Hadrian asked.

"Provide a little light. There are lots of this kind of stone here. My grandfather showed me how to make them burn— smolder, really."

"Let me help." Arista made a modest motion and the trio of rocks ignited and burned as a perfect campfire.

The dwarf frowned. "No, no. Stop it. I can get it."

Arista clapped and the fire vanished. "I just wanted to help."

"Yeah, well, that's not natural."

"And making rocks glow by slamming them together is?" Hadrian asked.

"Yes—if you're a dwarf."

Magnus got his rocks glowing and the rest gathered around them to eat. They were each down to their last meals and hoped to emerge aboveground the following day, or the last leg of the trip would be a hungry one.

"Aha!" Myron said. He had laid his books out near the rocks, giddy that there was enough light to read by.

"Discover the proper pronunciation to another name?" Hadrian asked. "Is Degan's real name Gwyant?"

"Hum? Oh, no, I found Mawyndulë—the one Antun Bulard and Esrahaddon spoke of."

"You *found* him?"

"Yes, in this book. Ever since I read Mr. Bulard's last scribbled words, I've been trying to find information on him. I reasoned that he must have read something shortly before he died. As these were the only books he had with him in the library, it stood to reason that Mawyndulë was mentioned somewhere in one of them. Wouldn't you know it would be in the last book I read? *Migration of Peoples* by Princess Farilane.

It is really a very biased accounting of how the Instarya clan took control of the elven empire. But it mentions Nyphron, the horn, and Mawyndulë."

"What does it say?" Arista asked.

"It says the elves were constantly warring between the various tribes, and quite a bloody and violent people until they obtained the horn."

"I mean, what does it say about Mawyndulë?"

"Oh." Myron looked embarrassed. "I don't know. I haven't read that yet. I just saw his name."

"Then let's be quiet and let the man read."

Everyone remained silent, staring at the monk as he scanned the pages. Arista wondered if all the glaring distracted Myron, but as he rapidly turned page after page of dense script, she realized that the monk was unflappable with a book before him.

"Oh," Myron finally said.

"'Oh' what?" Arista asked.

"I know why the horn didn't make a sound when Degan blew it."

"Well?" Hadrian asked.

The monk looked up. "You were right. Like you said in the tomb, it's a horn of challenge."

"And?"

"Degan's already king. He can't challenge himself, so it made no sound."

"What does all this have to do with Mawyndulë?" Arista asked.

Myron shrugged. "Still reading."

The monk returned his attention to the book.

"We should be out tomorrow, right?" Arista asked Hadrian, who nodded. "How long have we been down here?"

Hadrian shrugged and looked to Royce.

The thief, having completed his survey of the perimeter, took a seat around the glow of the rocks with the rest of them and fished in his pack for his meal. "At least a week."

"What will we find up there?" she asked herself as much as anyone else. "What if we're too late?"

"So the *Uli Vermar* is the reign of a king," Myron said. "Usually three thousand years—the average life span of an elf, apparently."

"Really?" Mauvin asked, and glanced at Royce. "How old are you?"

"Not that old."

"Remember the emperors in the tomb?" Arista said. "Mixing elven blood with human reduces the life span."

"Yeah, but he'll still outlive everyone here, except maybe Gaunt, right?"

"Why me?" Gaunt, who had been miserably picking at the remains of his meal, looked up.

"You're an elf too."

Gaunt grimaced. "I'm an elf?"

"You're related to Novron, right?"

"But...I don't want to be an elf."

"You'll get used to it." Royce smirked.

"Ah, here it is," Myron said. "Mawyndulë was a member of the Miralyith, and during the time before Novron, they were the ruling tribe." He paused and, looking up, added, "Unlike us, elves don't have consistent nobility. Whichever tribe the king is from becomes the ruling one and holds power over the rest, but only for one generation, or the length of the *Uli Vermar*. Then they face the challenge and if a new king wins the throne, his tribe becomes the new ruling elite."

"But not anyone in the tribe can challenge for the chance to be king, I'll bet," Gaunt said. "There is still a hereditary nobility in the tribes, right? There always is."

"For once I have to side with him," Royce said. "People might like to give the appearance of giving up power, but actually giving it up—that doesn't happen."

"Technically, I think anyone can challenge," Myron explained. "But true, traditionally it is the leader of a given tribe. However, he is elected by the clan leaders."

"Interesting," Mauvin said. "A society without nobility, where leaders are elected. See, Gaunt? You really are an elf."

"So someone blows the horn, fights, wins the challenge, and becomes king," Arista stated. "He's expected to rule for three thousand years, but what if he doesn't? If he dies in an accident, then the crown goes to his next of kin. That part I get. But what happens if the king dies and doesn't have any blood relatives? Then what?"

"That would also end the *Uli Vermar*," Myron said. "And the first person to blow the horn then becomes the new king, and he then presents it to anyone else to challenge him. And that's exactly what appears to have happened." Myron tapped the page in the book. "After the battle of Avempartha, as Nyphron was poised to invade his homeland—"

"Wait a second," Mauvin said. "Are Nyphron and Novron the same person?"

"Yes," Myron, Arista, and Hadrian all said together.

"Just as *Teshlor* is the bastardized pronunciation of the elf warrior Techylor, *Novron* is the bastardized form of Nyphron. So as I was saying, Nyphron was poised to invade his homeland when the *Uli Vermar* ended, and the elven high council presented the horn to Novron, making him king and ending the war."

"The *Uli Vermar* ended just then? That sounds awfully convenient," Royce said. "I'm guessing the elven king didn't die of natural causes."

Myron looked back down and read aloud. " 'And so it came to pass that in the night of the day of the third turn, thus was sent Mawyndulë of the tribe Miralyith. And by the council he was thus charged with the...' " Myron stopped speaking, but his eyes raced across the page.

"What is it?" Arista asked, but Myron raised a finger to stall her.

They all watched as Myron reached up and turned another page, his eyes widening, his eyebrows rising.

"By Mar, monk!" Magnus erupted. "Stop reading and tell us."

Myron looked up with a startled expression. "Mawyndulë murdered the elven king."

"And if he had any children, they were also murdered, weren't they?"

"No," Myron said, surprising Royce. "His only son survived."

"But that doesn't make sense," Arista said. "If his son was alive, why didn't he become king? Why did the *Uli Vermar* end?"

"Because," Myron replied, "Mawyndulë was his son."

It took a moment for this to register. The timing was different for each of them as around the circle of flickering light, they each made a sound of understanding.

"So Mawyndulë couldn't become king because he had committed murder?" Hadrian asked.

"Regicide," Myron corrected. "Significantly more deplorable in elvish society, for it places at risk the very foundation of their civilization and the peace that Ferrol granted them with the gift of the horn. As a result Mawyndulë was banished—stricken from elvish society and cursed by Ferrol, thereby barred from Alysin, the elvish afterlife."

"So why did he do it?" Arista asked.

"Princess Farilane doesn't actually say. Perhaps no one knows."

"So Novron blew the horn and became king and that ended the war." Hadrian finished the last of his meal and folded up his pack.

"That was certainly the plan," Myron said. "No one was supposed to blow the horn after Novron did. No one was supposed to challenge his rule. According to the laws of the horn, if it is presented but no challenger blows the horn within the course of a day, then the king retains his crown."

"But someone challenged?"

"Mawyndulë," Myron said. "As it happens there are no restrictions on who can blow the horn other than they must be of elven blood. Even an outcast, even one cursed by Ferrol, can still challenge. And if he wins—"

"If he wins, he's back in," Royce finished.

"Yes."

"But he lost, right?" Mauvin asked.

"Novron was a battle-hardened veteran of a lengthy war," Hadrian concluded. "And Myron said Mawyndulë was just a kid?"

"Yes." The monk nodded. "It was a quick and humiliating defeat."

"But this doesn't make sense," Arista said. "Esrahaddon told us he was convinced that Mawyndulë was still alive."

"Nyphron did not kill Mawyndulë. While the challenge is usually a fight to the death, Nyphron let him live. Perhaps because he was so young, or maybe because as an outcast he was no threat. What is known is that Mawyndulë was exiled, never allowed in Erivan again."

"So how did Novron die?" Mauvin asked.

"He was murdered."

"By who?"

"No one knows."

"I would wager on Mawyndulë," Royce said.

"Hmm..." Arista pulled on her lower lip, deep in thought.

"What?" Royce asked.

"I was just thinking about what Esrahaddon said when he was dying. He warned that the *Uli Vermar* was ending and that I had to take the heir to Percepliquis to get the horn. But his very last words were 'Patriarch...is the same...' I always assumed that he was never able to finish the sentence before he died, but what if he said all he meant to? Myron, how many patriarchs have there been?"

"Twenty-two including Patriarch Nilnev."

"Yes, and how old is he?"

"I don't recall reading about his birth, but he's been patriarch for sixty years."

"Myron, what are some of the other patriarchs' names?"

"Before Patriarch Nilnev was Patriarch Evlinn. Before him was Patriarch Lenvin. Before that—"

Arista's eyes widened. "Is it possible?"

"Is what possible?" Royce asked.

Arista got to her knees. "Does anyone have anything to write with?"

"I have a bit of chalk." Myron produced a white nib from a pouch.

"Nilnev, Evlin, Lenvin, Venlin..." Arista scrawled the words on the flat rock.

"There are two *n*'s on *Evlinn*," the monk corrected.

She looked up and smiled. "Of course there are. There would have to be. Don't you see? Esrahaddon was right. He changed his name, his appearance. He must have found a position in the Cenzar Council of Emperor Nareion, which would have been easy given his mastery of the Art. Esrahaddon knew that Venlin and Nilnev were the same. In fact, every patriarch since the first has been the same person—Mawyndulë."

"It would explain why the church was so intent on finding the heir," Hadrian said. "If they killed the bloodline of Novron, the *Uli Vermar* would end early."

"Which would be fine, if Mawyndulë had the horn. The fact that he didn't was probably the only thing keeping Gaunt alive when they had him locked up. This explains why the Patriarch has sent so many teams down here. What he didn't realize, though, is you actually needed the heir to succeed. Esrahaddon took precautions. That's why he told me that the heir had to come. I'm not sure exactly what he did, but I venture to say that anyone other than Gaunt touching the horn's box would have been killed."

"That also explains why the Patriarch hired Magnus to kill Gaunt. With the heir dead, a single toot of the horn would make Nilnev king by default, just as it was supposed to do with Novron," Hadrian said.

"Yes, but if the Patriarch blows the horn and Gaunt is still alive, then he's not claiming an empty throne but rather announcing his right to challenge, right?" Arista looked to Myron, who nodded. "So if Gaunt wins, he becomes king of the elves and they have to do whatever he says. And if he tells them to go back across the Nidwalden and leave us alone, they will."

"Theoretically," Mryon said.

"So all we have to do is make the Patriarch think he succeeded. We'll tell him Gaunt is dead and keep him hidden until the horn is blown. Then we'll spring the trap."

"Are you forgetting about this fight-to-the-death thing?" Gaunt asked.

"That won't be a problem," Arista reassured him. "He's old, even for an elf. A breath of wind could kill him. He doesn't want to fight you. He's terrified of a fight. That's why he wants you dead."

Gaunt sat silent, his eyes working.

"So what do you say, Degan?" Arista asked. "You wanted to be emperor. How does king of the elves sound to you?"

⁂

Arista reached the surface and lay on the wet ground, exhausted. The dazzling morning light shone in her eyes and played across her skin. She had so missed the sun that she lay with arms outstretched, bathing in its warmth. The fresh air was so wonderful that she drank it in as if it were cool water discovered after crossing an arid desert.

For a time she had thought she might not make it out of the hole and back to Amberton Lee. Even with the rope around her, she clung to rocks, shaking from both exhaustion and fear. Hadrian was always there offering encouragement, calling to her, pushing her to try harder. There were a few places where Royce and Hadrian had to pull her up a particularly difficult section and her progress was often slow. Even with his wounded arm Mauvin climbed faster. Still, now that it was over, she was proud of her accomplishment and the sun on her face was the reward.

She was awakened from her reverie when she heard Magnus quietly say, "He's here."

Getting up, she saw four men walking swiftly toward them. The Patriarch was flanked by two guards and behind them was Monsignor Merton, whom Arista had met once in Ervanon. They appeared out of place, descending the ragged slope with the bottoms of their robes wet from being dragged across the melting snow.

Accompanied by Hadrian, Mauvin, Magnus, and Myron,

Arista moved away from the open maw of the shaft and pushed through a large copse of forsythia, threatening to bloom. Hadrian took her hand and pulled her close.

"Give me the horn, quickly," the Patriarch said, extending his hand. Glancing over his shoulder toward the hilltop, he added, "The elves have arrived."

Arista pulled off her pack and took out the box. "Gaunt died before he could blow it."

The Patriarch smirked at her as he took the box. His eyes were transfixed as he drew out the horn and held it up.

"At last," the old man said, and placed it to his lips. He blew into the horn and a long clear note of ominous tone cut through the air. It lacked any musical quality, sounding instead like a cry—a scream of hate and loathing. Each of them instinctively took a few steps backward until Arista felt the little branches of the forsythia jabbing her. The old man lowered his arms, a smile on his face. "You did very well."

Horses thundered over the top of the hill. Arista was amazed by the elegance and grace of the elven lords, dressed in gold and blue with lion helms. With them was Modina, accompanied by Mercy and Allie, who looked exhausted.

One of the riders dismounted, removed his helm, and approached the group. He pointed to the horn and spoke quickly in elvish. Arista could not decipher every word but caught the gist of his introduction as Irawondona of the Asendwayr, who had been the acting Steward of Erivan. He inquired who had blown the horn.

The Patriarch stood before the elven lord and raised his arms. As he did, his features changed. His face grew longer, his nose narrowed, his brows slanted, his ears sharpened, and his eyes sparkled with a luminous green. His frame became slighter, his fingers longer, thinner. The only thing that remained unchanged was the white, near-purple hair. "*Behold*

*Mawyndulë of the Miralyith, soon to be King of Erivan, Emperor of Elan, Lord of the World.*" The words were spoken slowly, deliberately, such that even Arista understood each one.

He threw his head back, cast his arms straight out to his sides, and slowly rotated, giving them all a fair view. Everyone, including the elves, stared, stunned by the transformation.

Mawyndulë and the elven lord spoke quickly to each other. Irawondona pointed toward Modina during the exchange. Arista was catching only bits and pieces but her heart sank when she heard Myron mutter, "Uh-oh."

He added, "Mawyndulë knows about Gaunt."

"What?" Arista asked.

"He just told Irawondona that he blew the horn, and the elven lord said he has brought his opponent. But Mawyndulë said Modina is not the heir, that Degan is, and that Degan is hiding in the hole behind us."

Mawyndulë turned to face them. "I know all about your plan. Your guardian should have paid more attention to Esrahaddon's warnings. Or did you merely forget what he told you the last time you met?"

Arista looked at Hadrian quizzically.

"He said a lot of things."

"He explained," Mawyndulë said, "that he couldn't tell you anything because all his conversations were being overheard."

"You've been listening?" Arista asked.

"I paid close attention to Esrahaddon until he died, but he rarely said anything of importance. Listening to him was easy, as I knew him so well. While you were on your little trip, I monitored the dwarf. The Art did not work as well with him, but it was enough." He looked at Magnus. "I'll deal with you after I'm crowned. In the meantime, you might as well signal to Royce to bring Gaunt up. He's quite safe. No one can harm him or me now that the blessing of Ferrol is upon us. We are protected from everyone. It's only during the competition that we can be harmed and only by each other. So the last of Novron's line is safe until dawn tomorrow. There are rules to this ritual and we must observe them."

A rustle in the thickets announced the approach of two figures from the mouth of the hole. Degan shuffled forward with Royce behind him. Gaunt looked sick, pale and sweaty such that his bangs stuck to his forehead.

Mawyndulë turned to Lord Irawondona and announced in elvish, "*This is the heir of Nyphron.*" He then motioned toward Gaunt.

The elven lords and an old owl-helmed elf looked skeptically at Gaunt. They appraised him for several minutes, then spoke at length with Mawyndulë. When they were finished, the elves, along with Mawyndulë, returned up the hillside, leaving the party in the snow.

"What happened?" Hadrian asked.

"The challenge will begin at sunrise tomorrow," Myron explained.

⍦

The elves made camp on the crest of the hill. The rest of them gathered outside the Hovel, which hid in the shelter of holly trees partway up the slope. Hadrian built a fire and asked the boys to gather more wood, which they did, restricting their search toward the bottom of the hill. The process was slow, as the boys continued to look over their shoulders toward the top of the hill.

Modina and the girls were permitted to *join their own kind* and she found a place for the girls near the fire before approaching Arista. She was dressed in a dark lavish gown and raised the hem to pick her way around the others.

"What's going on?" the empress asked.

Arista reached out and took her hand the moment she was near. "It will be fine. Degan, as Novron's last descendant, will fight tomorrow. If he wins, he'll become ruler of the elves and they must obey him."

Modina's face was creased with worry. She looked at those circled around the fire. "If Degan loses, we have no hope. You have no idea what the elves are capable of. Aquesta was destroyed in just a few minutes. The walls fell and every building not made of stone has been burned. I'm afraid to even consider the number of dead. I tried, I tried everything, but... they walked through us with so little effort. If Degan fails..."

"He won't fail," Hadrian said. "Arista has a plan."

"I can't take the credit," she said. "It was Esrahaddon's idea. I think this was his intent from the moment he escaped Gutaria."

"What is it?" the empress asked.

Arista and Hadrian exchanged looks before Arista said, "I can't tell you."

Modina raised her eyebrows.

"The Patriarch is really an elf and a very powerful wizard. He's the one who challenged Degan. Apparently he has the ability to eavesdrop on conversations like this one."

Modina nodded. "Then don't say a word. I trust you. You haven't let me down yet."

"How are the girls?" Arista asked.

"Frightened. Allie has been asking about her father and Elden. I assume they are..."

"Yes, they were killed. As was my brother."

Modina nodded. "I'm sorry. If there is anything I..." The empress choked up and paused. She wiped her eyes. "Dear, sweet Maribor, I swear Gaunt can have the throne and I will go back to farming for the rest of my life and be content with an empty stomach if only he can win. I want you to know that we are all in your debt for what you have done, for the sacrifices of Alric, Wyatt, and Elden. Whatever happens tomorrow, you are all heroes today."

Hadrian, Royce, and Mauvin took Gaunt aside for some last-minute sparring tips. Arista focused her attention on the hilltop, where multicolored tents rose to the sounds of alien voices singing ancient songs. The tension around the fire was palpable. Out of everyone, except perhaps Gaunt, Monsignor Merton showed the greatest anxiety. He sat on an upturned bucket, staring into the fire. Before long Myron sat beside him and the two had a lengthy talk.

Myron was the only one who showed no signs of concern. After speaking to Merton, he spent his time with the boys, discovering how they had built the Hovel and asking numerous questions about how the horses had fared while they were gone. They told him how the cold cracked their spit and the monk marveled at their tales. He helped them cook a fine dinner and generally kept the boys busy with chores both in preparation and cleanup.

The sun set and darkness enveloped them save for the light of the campfire. It was not unlike the one Arista had sat beside less than a year earlier and very close to the same spot. A little farther up the slope, perhaps. So much had happened, so much had changed since the night she had ridden with Etcher. Amberton Lee was a different place now. With him she had felt lost in the wilderness. Now she was at the center of the world.

> *Ancient stones upon the Lee*
> *Dusts of memories gone we see*
> *Once the center, once the all*
> *Lost forever, fall the wall.*

She too was different. Perhaps they all were.

"Why don't you and the girls bed down in the shelter there?" Hadrian said to Modina, seeing the girls yawning. "You don't mind, do you, boys?"

They all shook their heads, staring, as they had been for some time, at the empress.

"Where will Degan sleep?" Modina asked, looking across the fire to where Degan was repeating the girls' yawns.

"Near the fire with the rest of us, I suppose," Hadrian responded.

The empress lifted her voice and said, "Degan, you will sleep with me in the shelter tonight."

Degan rolled his eyes. "I appreciate the offer—I do—but really this isn't the night for—"

"I need you rested. The fate of our race depends on your victory tomorrow. The shelter is the most comfortable place. You will *sleep* there, do you understand?"

He nodded with an expression that showed no will to argue.

Modina stood, looked at Arista, and then embraced and kissed her. "Again, thank you."

She went around the fire, thanking, embracing, and kissing each. Then, wiping her face, Modina returned to the shelter of the Hovel.

"Do you think it will work?" Arista asked Hadrian, who smirked. "Sorry. I'm just nervous. This was my idea, after all."

"And a damn fine one at that. Have I mentioned how smart you are?"

She scowled at him. "I'm not that smart—you're just blinded by love."

"Is that a bad thing?"

Her expression softened. "No."

He sat propped against one of the trees and she lay down in his arms. When he squeezed her, she felt a weight lifted and she reveled in the warmth and safety of his embrace. Her eyes drifted to the stars. She wanted to tell them not to leave, to order the sun never to rise, because for this one moment everything was perfect. She could stay as she was, stay in Hadrian's arms, and forget about what was to come.

"One of the great disappointments about living so long is that when the moment of triumph comes, there is no one to share it with," Mawyndulë said as he stepped into the ring of firelight, looking at them with a pleasant smile. His guards followed and placed his chair for him. Mawyndulë sat, showing no disappointment with their glares.

Arista closed her eyes and reached out delicately. She sensed Mawyndulë's power. In her mind, magic appeared as a light in darkness. The oberdaza flickered like torches but Mawyndulë burned like the sun. She avoided him and focused on his guards. They were not men or even elves. They were the same as the Gilarabrywn—pure magic.

"It's a bit chilly, isn't it?" the old elf said. "And what a pitiful excuse for a fire."

Mawyndulë clapped his hands and the flames grew tall and bright. The boys jerked back in fear. Monsignor Merton got up and took several steps back, his eyes wide.

The old man held his hands out to the licking flames and rubbed them together. "Ah, much better. My old bones can't take the cold like they used to."

"Magic," Merton whispered, "is forbidden by the church."

"Of course it is. I don't want mongrels practicing my Art; it's insulting. Would you like it if I wore your clothes? Took them out, got them all dirty, and made fun of them in public? Of course not, and I won't allow humans to defile what is mine."

"How is magic...yours?" Royce asked.

"Inheritance. My family invented the Art, so it is mine.

Wretched thieves stole it, so I took it back. Esrahaddon was the last of the thieves. He used my Art to destroy Percepliquis." The old man's eyes drifted off, looking at something unseen. "He killed all of them—did it to stop me, but he failed. Not only did I survive, but I was able to keep him alive as well. I needed to know where the boy was, you see. I thought in time he would relent and eventually he did, although unknowingly." The old man smirked and looked back at them. "Is anyone else hungry?"

Mawyndulë spoke words unknown to Arista and made a gesture with his fingers, and before them a banquet of food appeared. A tableful of hams, ducks, and quails were roasted to bronze perfection and wreathed in vegetables, candied walnuts, and berries.

"What's wrong, Merton?" Mawyndulë asked without bothering to look at the priest, who had an expression of horror across his face. "Are you shocked? Of course you are, and with good reason, but please eat. The food is delicious and I do so hate to dine alone. Go ahead, everyone, dig in."

Mawyndulë did not wait for them and began tearing off chucks of ham. Glass goblets appeared on the table and filled themselves with a deep-red liquid. The Patriarch picked up one and drained it to wash down the ham. The goblet was full again before he set it back onto the table.

No one else touched the food.

"Where is he?" Mawyndulë asked. "Where is my worthy adversary? Hasn't run off, has he? The rules clearly state that if he fails to show, I win by default."

"He's sleeping," Hadrian said.

"Ah, getting a good night's rest. Very wise. Personally I can never sleep before these things. Gaunt takes after his ancestor. Nyphron slept the night before too. I knew him, you know, your beloved Novron. Ah, but yes, you already discovered that little fact. Here's something the books won't tell you. He was an ass. All those tales about him saving humanity for the love of a farmer's daughter are absolute rubbish. He was no different than anyone else, and like everyone, he sought power. His tribe was small and weak, so he harnessed all of you as fodder for his battles. The Instarya are the best warriors, of course. I will grant them that. There's no point in denying it. That is *their* art, and he taught it to your knights. Still, humans would not have won if not for Cenzlyor, who taught them my Art as well.

"Novron was so arrogant, so sure of himself. He played the wise, forgiving conqueror at Avempartha and those in power were more than willing to bow before him. They were all frightened children at his feet—the boy from the inferior clan. Your great god was just a vindictive brat bent on revenge."

The old man bit into a leg of duck and sat back with a glass of wine in his other hand. He leaned on one arm of the chair and looked up toward the stars. He followed the duck with a fresh strawberry and swooned. "Oh, you've *got* to try one of these. They're perfect. That's the problem with the real thing—you can never find them at their peak. Or they're too big or too small, too tart or sweet. No, I must admit, I pride myself on creating a good strawberry."

He licked his fingers and looked at them. No one moved.

"It was *you*," Merton said at last. "The one you spoke of at the cathedral, the ancient enemy controlling everything."

"Of course," the old man said. "I told you that if you thought hard enough, you'd figure it out, didn't I?" He picked a grape this time but grimaced as he chewed. "See, I'm not nearly as good at these. Far too sour."

"You *are* evil."

"What do you know of evil?" Mawyndulë's tone turned harsh. "You know nothing about it."

"I do," Royce said.

Mawyndulë peered at the thief and nodded. "Then you know that evil is not born, but created. I was turned into what I have become. The council did that to me. They made me believe what they said. They put the dagger in my hand and sent me out with words of blessing. Elders who I revered, who I respected and trusted as the wisest of my people, told me what needed to be done. I believed them when they said the fate of our race was upon me. Back then, we were as you are now, a flickering flame in a growing wind. Nyphron had taken Avempartha. The council convinced me that I was our nation's last hope. They told me my father was too stubborn to make peace and that he would see us all die. As long as he breathed, as long as he was king, we were doomed. No one dared move against him, as the murderer would pay first in this life and then in the next."

Mawyndulë plucked another strawberry but hesitated to eat. He held it between his fingers, rolling it.

"Ten priests of Ferrol swore I would be absolved. Because the existence of the elven race was at stake, they convinced me that Ferrol would see me as a savior, not a murderer. The council agreed to support me, to waive the law. They were so sincere and I was...so young. As my father died, I saw him cry, not for himself but for me, because he knew what they had done, and what my fate would be."

"Why are you here?" Arista asked.

Mawyndulë seemed to have just become aware of them around him. "What?"

"I asked why you were here. Won't they allow you in the elven camp? Are you still an outcast?"

Mawyndulë glanced over his shoulder. "After I am king, they will accept me. They will do whatever I say."

He shifted in his seat and stroked one of the long arms of

the chair. It was of unusual design but strangely familiar in shape. It was not until he moved that Arista realized she had seen similar ones in Avempartha. The Patriarch had brought his own chair with him—not from Aquesta, not from Ervanon, but from home.

*He hasn't touched anything but that chair.*

She imagined Mawyndulë sealed in the Crown Tower, living in isolation, surrounded by elven furnishing, doing what he could to separate himself.

Mawyndulë looked over to where Magnus sat. "I would have honored our agreement, dwarf. Your people could have had Delgos once more. I have no use for that rock. Of course, now I will have to kill you. As for the rest, you've done me a great service by retrieving the horn and for that I am tempted to let you all live. I could make you court slaves. You will be wonderful novelties—the last humans! A shame you die so quickly, but I suppose I could breed you. The princess looks healthy enough. I could raise a small domestic herd. You could perform at feasts. Oh, don't look so distraught. It's better than dying."

Mauvin's expression hardened and Arista noticed the muscles on his sword arm tighten. She threw him a stern look. He glared back but relaxed.

"Why bother to create the New Empire," Arista asked quickly, "just to destroy it?"

"I broke Esrahaddon's spell and released the Gilarabrywn from Avempartha to show my brothers how weak the human world is, to encourage them to march the moment the *Uli Vermar* ended. Others took it upon themselves to use the occasion to their advantage. Still, I took advantage of Saldur, Galien, and Ethelred's blundering to press for the eradication of the half-breeds. While my word will be undisputed as king, killing any who bear even a small amount of elven blood might not be popular with my kin once I assume the throne. And I cannot abide having their abomination survive. I was the one who started the idea that elves were slaves in the Old Empire. It made it easier, you see—it is so simple to hate those you feel are inferior."

"You're so sure of yourself," Mauvin said. "This protection of Ferrol is some sort of religious blessing. Placed on you by your god. It's supposed to prevent anyone—other than Gaunt—from harming you, right? Thing is, a week ago Novron was a god too. Turns out that was just a lie. A story invented to control us. So what if this is too? What if Ferrol, Drome, and Maribor are all just stories? If it is, I could draw my sword and cut through that miserable throat of yours and save everyone here a lot of trouble."

"Mauvin, don't," Arista said.

Mawyndulë chuckled. "Ever the Pickering, aren't you? Go on, dear count. Swing away."

"Don't," Arista told him firmly.

Mauvin's eyes showed that he was considering it, but the count did not move.

"You are wise to listen to your princess." He paused. "Oh, but I forget, you're his queen, aren't you? King Alric is dead. You left him down there, didn't you? Abandoned him to rot. What poor help you turned out to be."

"Mauvin, please. Let it go. He'll be dead tomorrow."

"Do you really think so?" Mawyndulë snapped his fingers and a huge block of stone making up a portion of the ruins exploded, throwing up a cloud of dust. Everyone jumped.

The old man laughed and said, "I don't agree with your assessment. I think the odds are decidedly in my favor. It's a shame, though, that there will be so few of you left." He paused to look them over. "Is this all that survived? A queen, a count, a thief, the Teshlor, and..." He looked at Myron. "Who exactly would you be?"

"Myron," he said with his characteristic smile. "I'm a Monk of Maribor."

"A Monk of Maribor, indeed—the heretical cult. How dare you worship something other than an elf?" He smirked. "Didn't you just hear your friend? Maribor is a myth, a fairy tale to make you think that life is fair or to provide the illusion of hope. Man created him out of fear, and ambitious men took advantage of that fear—I know of what I speak. I created an entire church—I created the god Novron out of the traitor Nyphron and a religion out of ignorance and intolerance."

Myron did not look concerned. He listened carefully, thoughtfully, then recited: " *'Erebus, father unto all that be, creator of Elan, divider of the seas and sky, brought forth the four: Ferrol, the eldest, the wise and clever; Drome, the stalwart and crafty; Maribor, the bold and adventurous; Muriel, the serene and beautiful—gods unto the world.'* "

"Do not quote me text from your cultish scriptures," Mawyndulë said.

"I'm not," Myron said. "It's yours—section one, paragraph eight of the Book of Ferrol. I found it in the tomb of Nyphron. I apologize if I did not get all the words correct. I am not entirely fluent in elvish."

Mawyndulë's grin faded. "Oh yes, I recall your name now. You are Myron Lanaklin from the Winds Abbey. You were the one left as a witness while the other monks were burned alive, is that right? That incident was Saldur's doing—he had a fetish for burning things—but you are as much to blame, aren't you? You forced him by refusing to reveal what you knew. How do you live with all that guilt?"

"Seemingly better than you live with your hatred," Myron replied.

"You think so?" Mawyndulë asked, and leaned forward.

"You're about to become a slave while I am about to be crowned king of the world."

His attempt at intimidation had no effect on the monk, who, to Arista's astonishment, leaned forward and asked, "But for how long? You are ancient, even by elven standards. How short-lived will your victory be? And at what cost will you have achieved that which you *think* is so great? What have you had to endure to reach this moment? You wasted your long life to obtain a goal you can't possibly live to appreciate. If you hadn't allowed hatred to rule you, you might have spent all those years in contentment and love. You could have—"

"I'm already enjoying it!" Mawyndulë shouted.

"You have forgotten so much." Myron sighed with obvious pity. " *'Revenge is a bittersweet fruit that leaves the foul aftertaste of regret.'* —Patriarch Venlin, The Perdith Address to the Dolimins, circa twenty-one thirty-one."

"You are clever, aren't you?" Mawyndulë said.

" *'Clever are the Children of Ferrol, quick, certain, and dark their fate.'* —Nyphron of the Instarya."

"Shut up, Myron," Hadrian growled.

Arista also saw the flare in the elf's eyes but Myron appeared oblivious. To her relief, Mawyndulë did not strike out. Instead he stood and walked away. His two guards followed with the chair. The banquet vanished and the fire's flames dwindled to mere embers.

"Are you insane?" Hadrian asked Myron.

"I'm sorry," the monk said.

"I'm not." Mauvin clapped the monk on the back, grinning. "You're my new hero."

# CHAPTER 27

# THE CHALLENGE

Trumpets announced the gray light of the predawn.

The elves had transformed the top of Amberton Lee overnight. Where once only the desolate remains of ancient walls and half-buried pillars stood, the crest of the hill now displayed seven great tents marked by shimmering banners. In the misty haze of melting snow, a low wall of intertwined brambles created an arena marked by torches that burned blue flames. Drums followed a loud fanfare and beat to an ominous rhythm—the heartbeat of an ancient people.

Degan shivered in the cold, looking even worse than the night before. Hadrian, Royce, and Mauvin fed him coffee that steamed like some magical draft. Gaunt clutched the mug with both hands and still the liquid threatened to spill from his shaking. Arista stood with her feet in the cold dew, every muscle in her body tense as she waited. Everyone waited. Aside from the three whispering last-minute instructions into Gaunt's ear, no one else spoke. They all stood like stones on the Lee, unwilling witnesses.

Modina waited with the girls, prepared to face what could be their last sunrise. The boys stood only a few feet from her with Magnus and Myron. The lot of them formed a straight line, uniformly standing with their arms folded across their chests—all eyes on Degan.

Mawyndulë appeared relaxed as he sat in his chair, his legs outstretched and crossed, his eyes closed as if sleeping. The rest of the elves milled about in small groups, speaking in hushed, reverent tones. Arista guessed this was a sacred religious event for them. For those in her party, it was just terrifying.

She turned when she heard Monsignor Merton say, "I know you have a good reason." At first, she thought he was speaking to her, but when she saw him, his eyes were looking up. "But you have to understand I'm but the ignorant fool you made. I don't mean that as an insult, of course. Perish the thought. Who am I to pass judgment on your creation? Still, I hope you have enjoyed our talks. I am entertaining at least, aren't I, Lord? You wouldn't want to lose that, would you? Many of us are entertaining and it would be a shame if we disappeared altogether. Have you considered how you might miss us?" He paused as if listening, then nodded.

"What did he say?" Arista asked.

Merton looked up, startled. "Oh? What he always says."

She waited, but the monsignor never explained further.

The drums grew louder, the rhythm faster. The sky began to lighten and birds, newly returned to the north, began to sing. The faces of the men and elves grew more serious as the priest of Ferrol entered the ring with a thurible burning Agarwood incense. He began singing softly in elvish.

Gaunt placed a hand to his chest, rubbed his shirt, and whispered to himself. Arista cringed and Hadrian said something sharply but quietly and Gaunt pulled his hand away. Arista glanced at Mawyndulë and suspected the damage was done. The old elf narrowed his gaze at his opponent.

Mawyndulë rose from his seat and walked toward Gaunt.

He glanced to the eastern horizon. "Not long now," he said. "I just wanted to wish you good luck."

The once Patriarch held out his hand. Gaunt looked at it hesitantly but reached out to shake. Mawyndulë was quick and nimble and he tore Gaunt's collar wide, revealing the medallion hanging there. He staggered backward as Hadrian and Royce quickly pulled Gaunt away. Mawyndulë sneered and glanced at Arista, then Hadrian, and lastly Myron. He looked about quickly, nervously.

"Not long now," Royce reminded him. "And how will you fare when your magic is useless?"

Mawyndulë smiled and with clenched teeth he began to laugh.

"*Muer wir ahran dulwyer!*" Mawyndulë shouted suddenly. All the elves turned to face him. Everyone else looked at Myron.

"He evokes the Right of Champion," Myron said.

"What does that mean?" Royce asked.

"It means he asks for someone else to fight in his stead."

"Can he do that?" Arista asked.

"Yes," Myron replied. "Remember the inscription on the horn:

> *Should champion be called to fight*
> *evoked is the Hand of Ferrol,*
> *Which protects the championed from all,*
> *and champion from all—save one—from peril.*

"If the champion wins, Mawyndulë will be king."

"*Byrinith con duylar ben lar Irawondona!*" Mawyndulë shouted and there was a loud murmur among the elves as they all turned to face the elven lord.

"Oh damn," Hadrian said. "He had to pick the big guy. I'm pretty sure he knows how to fight."

Lord Irawondona stepped forward in his shimmering armor. He said something that none of them could hear. Mawyndulë replied by nodding and Lord Irawondona raised his hands and shouted, *"Duylar e finis dan iskabareth ben Mawyndulë!"*

"He just accepted," Myron reported.

Gaunt, who had been shaking his head, erupted, "I'm not fighting him. I'm supposed to fight the old guy, not this guy."

"Myron." Arista spun the monk to face her. "Can Gaunt do the same? Can he pick a champion?"

"Ah—yes. I believe so. It would only make sense, as the entire competition is designed for a fair contest between the opponents."

She watched Lord Irawondona remove his cloak. The elf looked imposing even from across the field. "Hadrian is the only one who has any chance of winning. Name him your champion. Myron, tell Gaunt the words he needs to say."

"They weren't on the horn."

"You just heard him," Royce reminded him. "Just repeat what you heard Mawyndulë say, and quickly."

"Oh, right. *Muer wir ahran dulwyer,*" Myron said.

"Degan, say it! Say it loud!"

"*Muer wir*—ah—*ahran*—ah—" Gaunt stumbled and hesitated.

"*Dulwyer,*" Myron whispered.

"*Dulwyer!*" Gaunt shouted.

The heads of the elves turned.

"Now the next line and substitute my name for Irawondona," Hadrian said.

Myron fed him the words and Gaunt recited them. The

elves looked confused for a moment, until Gaunt pointed at Hadrian. Myron gave Hadrian the next line and Arista stood shaking as she heard him recite it aloud, accepting the role of Gaunt's champion.

"Degan," she said, "give Hadrian the medallion back."

"But he said—"

"I know what he said, and he'll let you have it after the fight, but right now he needs all the help he can get. Give it to him now!" Degan tore the chain off his neck and handed it to her.

"Boys!" Hadrian shouted. "Fetch me that bundle near my blanket and the shield!"

The four boys sprinted down the slope to the camp.

"You *can* beat him, can't you?" Arista asked while slipping the chain over his head. She was trembling. "You will beat him for me, won't you? You can't leave me like Emery and Hilfred. You know I couldn't take that, right? You know that—you *have* to win."

"For you? Anything," he said, and kissed her hard, pulling her to him.

The boys returned and threw open the bundle, revealing the brilliant armor of Jerish Grelad. "Help me on with this," Hadrian said, and everyone, including Degan and Myron, looked for ways to assist.

An elf appeared before them, holding one of the strange halberd weapons they had seen images of in Percepliquis. He held it out to Hadrian.

"You know how to use this?" Arista asked.

"Never touched one before."

"Something tells me *he* has," she said as across the field Lord Irawondona lifted his own halberd with both hands spread apart, holding it like a double-bladed quarterstaff. He spun it with remarkable speed such that the blades hummed.

"Yeah, I think you're right."

Hadrian took a breath and turned to her. Their eyes met just at the moment the sun broke over the trees and shone on their faces. Hadrian looked beautiful, glimmering in his golden armor. He appeared like an ancient god reborn onto the world of man.

The priest of Ferrol shouted something and neither needed Myron to translate.

It was time.

Arista found it hard to breathe and her legs grew weak as she watched Hadrian enter the ring of torches. He stepped to the center and waited, planting his feet in the packed snow and shifting his grip on the strange weapon.

She looked at Mawyndulë and saw he was no longer smiling; his face showed concern as Irawondona entered the ring. The blue torches flared with his passing and the elven lord strode about the space casually, confidently.

"Hadrian's the best in the world, Arista," Mauvin whispered to her. "Better than any Pickering, better than Braga, better than—"

"Better than an *elven lord*?" she asked sharply. "He's probably played with that weapon since he was a child—some fifteen hundred years ago!"

The drums rolled and the horns blared once more in a sharply definitive sound that hurt her ears. She tried to swallow but found her throat tight. In her chest, her heart hammered, and her hands rose to her breast in an attempt to contain it.

Hadrian waited awkwardly as if uncertain whether the fight had begun. Irawondona walked around the circle of blue burning torches, spinning his spear, rolling it across his shoulders, down his arm, and around his wrist, grinning at the crowd. He threw the weapon up, where it rotated above his head, and whirled it such that it made the sound of birds in flight. He caught it again and laughed.

"How good is he?" Arista asked Mauvin. "Can you tell by the way he moves?"

"Oh, he's good."

"How good? You've fought Hadrian. Can he beat him?"

"He's real good."

"Stop saying that and answer the damn question!"

"I don't know, okay?" Mauvin admitted. "I can only say that he's really fast, faster than Hadrian, I think."

"What about all the whirling? What can you tell from that?"

"That's nothing, he's just trying to intimidate."

"Well, it's working on me."

Hadrian stood still, waiting.

Irawondona continued to spin the spear with his hands. "I must commend you on at least knowing how to hold the *ule-da-var*," Irawondona told him.

"Yeah, but I don't know how to do all that fancy spinning stuff," Hadrian replied. "Does that help? Or is it just needlessly tiring your muscles?"

Irawondona closed the distance between them with brilliant speed and slashed at Hadrian. One stroke aimed down and across with the top blade and another up with the bottom blade. Hadrian dodged the first strike and parried the second with a last-minute swing.

"That was good," Mauvin whispered. "I'd be dead right now."

"In the first exchange?" Arista asked.

"Yeah, contrary to popular belief, sword fights don't last long, a few minutes at best. I watched his feet and they fooled me—he's *very* good."

Irawondona jabbed—Hadrian slapped the blade aside. He jabbed again, and again; each time Hadrian caught the stroke.

"Very nice," Irawondona said. "Now let's see how good you really are."

The elf slapped the shaft of his spear, causing it to hum and the blade to quiver. He jabbed again, this time too fast for Arista to see. Hadrian blocked, caught, and slapped but then Irawondona swung.

"Duck!" Mauvin shouted. "Oh no!"

Hadrian did duck, stabbing his lower blade into the snow. Irawondona's first stroke passed over Hadrian's head, but then the second came down. Before it landed, Hadrian pulled on his planted pole and slid himself across the snow on his knees, leaving Irawondona to strike nothing but the bare ground.

Both combatants paused, breathing hard.

"Whoa!" Mauvin said. "That was really good."

"You don't move like a human," Irawondona said.

"And you fight surprisingly well for a talking *brideeth*."

The reaction on Irawondona's face was immediate. His happy grin vanished.

Arista looked to Myron.

"I don't know that word," the monk replied.

"I wouldn't think you would," Royce said. "I taught him that one."

Irawondona lashed out again. He moved with blinding speed, spinning forward so that the dual blades flashed in the growing sunlight, their movement visible only by the streaks of light they left. She could hear the sound of the humming knives vibrating the air.

Hadrian leapt back, looking uncertain how to deal with the oncoming whirlwind of metal. He dodged and dodged again as the blades swept close to his head and legs equally. The elf lord drove him back to the edge of the thicket wall. Once there, he flicked the bottom blade, slashing out at Hadrian's chest. With an agile spin, Hadrian traded places and slammed the elf lord with his elbow while tripping him with the pole. Lord Irawondona quickly somersaulted to his feet with a look of shock on his face.

"You fight like..." Lord Irawondona stopped. He was breathing hard and eyeing Hadrian with concern.

Hadrian now advanced.

This time the blades collided. Staccato strikes sounded across the hilltop. Poles spun up against each other, striking, crossing, clipping. Again there were the hum of bees and then more strikes. Irawondona pushed Hadrian back, jamming him, driving him off balance, his whirling pole streaking in the golden light. Hadrian stumbled and staggered off balance, and the elf lord flashed a grin. He pressed his attack but then Hadrian made an unexpected twist and raked Irawondona across the side with his long blade. A clean stroke—Hadrian's blade sliced from neck to leg.

The elven lord fell back, shocked. He felt along his side with fear on his face, at the same time Hadrian looked at his weapon—neither found blood. They looked bewildered for a moment; then Irawondona shook it off and regained his stance. He no longer made an effort at exhibitionism.

They circled each other, more hesitant than before, each feinting and falling back, reaching, searching for a weakness in the other. Irawondona charged again; once more the blades clamored, ringing with a sound horrible to hear. One blow after another the metal collided edge to edge, razors striking razors. Just listening to the noise made Arista weak.

Once more Hadrian fell and again Irawondona stabbed, this time faster, forcing Hadrian to log roll away. Irawondona chased but was not fast enough and Hadrian was able to get back on his feet and caught the elf in mid-stride. The elf lord was too late to pull back and Hadrian's short blade sliced down the back of Irawondona's exposed calf.

"Ha-ha!" Hadrian laughed. "Not fast enough! Now you're—"

No blood.

Once more the two looked at the clean blade and the unscarred flesh and slowly Irawondona began to smile.

"Oh dear Maribor!" Arista cried. "Not again, oh please god, not again."

"What is it?" Mauvin asked. "What's wrong?"

"Hadrian can't harm him. I don't understand. Did we make a mistake when naming him as champion?"

The elf lord, grinning with confidence, attacked again, this time more openly. Hadrian dodged and counterattacked and his strike found Irawondona's neck. The long blade came slicing across from under the exposed throat from the bottom up. Irawondona's head jerked up, but once more, the blade did not bite.

The elf lord laughed. "I am a god," he said, and began to strike out at Hadrian without fear.

"No!" Arista screamed. She looked to the others desperately, tears filling her eyes. "Oh god, Royce, do something. Save him! Please, you have to save him!"

⋙

Royce looked at Hadrian as he retreated under the constant bombardment from Irawondona. The elven lord was not letting him rest. It was all Hadrian could do to dodge or glance aside the blows. It would not be long now.

He pulled Alverstone from its sheath. He had never found anything that the blade could not cut. Hadrian had even used it to blind the Gilarabrywn and that was supposed to be impervious to all weapons except the one bearing its name.

In the ring, Irawondona struck wildly from high over his head. Hadrian lifted his pole to block and the long blade struck it. The crack was tremendous as the pole broke in two. The blade struck Hadrian in the chest. The armor prevented the blade from penetrating, but Royce heard something snap and Hadrian cried out. Still, he managed to trip Irawondona to the ground. Hadrian was breathing hard, his face clenched in pain. He spat blood and staggered. "I'm sorry, Arista—I'm so sorry."

"Say goodbye to your champion, Gaunt," Mawyndulë declared. "I will be king now, as it was meant to be."

Royce sprinted for the old elf.

Mawyndulë looked amused for a moment, then shocked. His guard stepped out but at the last minute Royce sidestepped and dove for Mawyndulë. He drove the dagger at the old man's chest. The chair toppled, with both of them falling over and sprawling across the snow.

They got to their feet simultaneously.

Mawyndulë remained unharmed.

"The blessing of Ferrol is upon me, fool! You can't harm me—but no such protection defends you!"

With a wave of his hand, a column of flame formed around Royce. Fire coursed up his body and engulfed him.

"*Royce!*" Arista shouted. She raised her hands to counter the spell, but before she could, the thief stepped out of the flames.

Everyone stopped.

Even Irawondona paused.

When the flames abated and died away, Royce remained unharmed.

"That can't be," Mawyndulë said.

Then the old elf's eyes widened. "Irawondona!" he shouted. "Forget that one! Kill this one. Kill Royce Melborn!"

The elf lord looked puzzled, glancing back at Hadrian, who had collapsed to his knees and was struggling to breathe, his arm and legs drenched in blood.

"Gaunt isn't the heir; Hadrian is worthless," Mawyndulë shouted. "It's this one. Royce Melborn is the Heir of Novron. Kill him. Kill him now!"

⸙

Royce looked as stunned as anyone.

Irawondona left Hadrian and walked toward Royce and Mawyndulë.

"Myron! Mauvin!" Arista shouted. "Water—bandages—now!"

She entered the ring and threw her arms around Hadrian, lying him down. "Royce?" Hadrian asked. "*Royce* is the heir?"

"Yes!" Arista told him as she poured water over his wounds and began binding them tightly with linen. "Why didn't I see it? Arcadius didn't just happen to bring you two together. Somehow he knew. He was reuniting the heir and the guardian. Esrahaddon must have known too. Gaunt was just a diversion. When he begged me to help find the heir, he never said *Degan Gaunt*, he just said *the heir*! He's why we were able to reach the horn. Esrahaddon knew that only the *true* heir could get past the Gilarabrywn. All this time the heir and the guardian *were* together."

"But why didn't Esrahaddon tell us?"

"To keep him safe. That's why he led everyone to Gaunt. Can Royce defeat Irawondona?"

Hadrian shook his head. "Not a chance."

"Then we have to hurry. You still have a fight to win."

"But I can't hurt him."

"Only because the true heir never named you as champion. Once Royce does, you'll be able to hurt him. You'll have to fight and this time you *must* win."

She stood up and shouted, "Royce! Don't fight. Just give me some time and then name Hadrian as your champion." She knelt back down to tend to his wounds.

"Arista, I can't." Hadrian lay on his back, his chest heaving for air, blood smeared on his cheek and pooling around him.

"You *can* beat him," Myron said as he tore more bandages.

"No, I can't—"

"You don't understand," the monk interrupted. "I speak not from faith in you, but from fact. You are a Teshlor Knight. Techylor was the best warrior in the world and the leader of the Instarya warrior tribe. Irawondona is from the hunters' tribe, he doesn't know how to fight."

"Believe me, he does."

"Not like you do."

"Okay, fine, but you fail to take into account that I can't move. My ribs are broken. I can't even stand up."

"Leave that to me," Arista told him, and began to hum.

✍

Irawondona spoke briefly to Mawyndulë in elvish as Royce slowly retreated from them, backing away between the tents and down the snowy hill.

"*Just kill him!*" Mawyndulë demanded as his guards helped right his chair.

Royce stopped his retreat and crouched, digging his feet in the snow and feeling the weight of Alverstone in his hand. He had heard what Arista had shouted and he looked over to where Hadrian lay. His friend was in bad shape, but Arista was going into one of her trances.

"Come here, little prince," Irawondona jeered, walking toward him. Royce was surprised that the elf could speak Apelanese. "It is our turn to dance." He waved the halberd, spinning it like he had when fighting Hadrian.

Royce looked at Arista once more, then tossed Alverstone away.

Irawondona smiled. "So you're going to make this easy for me, are you?"

"Not really," Royce replied. "I just don't want to accidentally hurt you."

"I don't think you understand how this works, little prince."

"On the contrary, I think it's you who is confused."

"Just kill him and get it over with, you idiot!" Mawyndulë ordered.

Irawondona advanced, racing down the slope, and lunged. Royce dodged, backing farther away.

"You're quick," Irawondona told him. "But then, you are the descendant of one of us."

The elf lord spun his pole once more and advanced. Irawondona attacked and with each swipe Royce dodged and withdrew farther down the slope on the east side of the Lee, nearing the place where Arista had killed two Seret Knights.

"Stop running, little prince, accept your fate. We are done with human rule. I would prefer to wear the crown, of course, but even a Miralyith is better than a mixed blood. It is time that mankind left Elan for good."

"And then you'll live happily ever after?"

"Indeed we will. We will roam the world as we once did. We will destroy the goblins and then it will be just the dwarves and us again, and eventually...just us. Then Erivan will rule Elan again. When that day comes, Ferrol will walk among us once more."

"Do you really think Mawyndulë will honor any agreement he made with you? He hates you more than he does us. It was *your* people that betrayed him. They convinced him to kill his own father. He wants to be your king so he can enact his revenge on those who hurt him the most."

"You're lying."

"Am I? For three thousand years he's sought his revenge. Kill me and you will place a tyrant on your throne and his first order will be your death."

"He is still an elf. Better that he rule than a half-breed like you."

"Whatever bonds of kinship he had, he lost long ago."

"Even so, even if he kills me, if my death and the death of every clan leader is the cost, so be it. We will be rid of your kind—of your blood."

He struck out and once more Royce dodged. But this time he realized too late his own mistake. Irawondona had anticipated the move; he saw the feint and compensated, swinging around with the long blade. Royce was caught. The metal entered him with a surprisingly quiet hiss. Looking down, he saw the blood-coated tip as Irawondona pulled the blade free.

Royce collapsed.

"Royce!" he heard Hadrian cry. "Do it, do it now!"

The elf lord raised his blade once more. "Farewell, Son of Nyphron."

Royce took a breath. "*Byrinith con—duylar ben—Hadrian Blackwater,*" he said as loud as he could manage.

"*Duylar e finis dan iskabareth ben Royce Melborn!*" Hadrian replied quickly even as Irawondona's stroke came down.

The tip of the long blade slammed against Royce's chest but

he barely felt it. A bright spark flashed and a loud crack echoed as the blade shattered and sent bits of metal skipping down the hillside.

Irawondona stood above him, stunned.

Royce muttered and coughed. "My friend is going to kill you."

Irawondona looked down at him, confused, but Royce took little notice now. He lay staring up at the blue sky. "You *were* right, Gwen. You were right."

∽

The elven lord looked over his shoulder and saw Hadrian, bandaged and standing in the ringed arena. With what sounded like an elvish curse, Irawondona spat on Royce, glared at Mawyndulë, and walked back toward the ring.

Irawondona entered. "Your weapon is destroyed," the elf said in a pitying voice as he gestured at the halberd, lying in two pieces.

"No, it's not." Hadrian reached behind him and drew out the great spadone blade.

Irawondona hesitated but then threw aside his broken pole and drew his own sword, which gleamed much the same way as Mauvin's. The two moved to the center of the ring.

Irawondona attacked first, spinning and swinging. Hadrian took hold of the advance guard of his sword with his off hand, gripping his blade up to the flanges, and caught the attack with two hands much the same as if he had still wielded the pole. He pivoted and spun the sword around but the elf slipped away. He riposted instantly, but Hadrian was there with the hilt guard again. There was a spark and the two separated once more; this time they both panted for breath.

Irawondona attacked again and feinted. Hadrian saw the

ruse and moved to cut—but then the elf leapt in the air and spun. Irawondona flew from the ground so nimbly that he appeared to fly, leaving Hadrian's sword nothing but air. Irawondona flipped, and as he touched down, he struck Hadrian across the back with a hammer punch from his sword's pommel. The blow drove Hadrian to the dirt once more.

Hadrian was down as Irawondona attacked. Once more, reflex saved him. Hadrian rolled aside and kicked Irawondona in the knee, causing the elf to stagger back long enough for Hadrian to gain his footing.

❧

Arista, Mauvin, Magnus, and Myron rushed to Royce where he lay on the hillside, struggling to breathe. Arista was not a doctor, but Royce looked bad. Already the earth around him was dark with blood. His chest and sides were slick and shiny, violently thrusting to breathe; both eyes were rolled up, exposing only whites.

"Stay alive, Royce," Arista told him. "Do you hear me? You need to stay alive!"

Royce muttered something and drew in air with a horrid gurgle. "I saved—I saved him."

"Not yet you haven't. It's not over! Royce, listen to me." Arista took his hands. "You can't die, do you understand? Do you hear me?"

He jerked, his head twitching.

"Damn it!" she said, and placing her hands on his chest, she closed her eyes and began the chant. Immediately she felt the resistance, a solid separation, as if a wall stood between them. The Hand of Ferrol left no cracks or seams. The shield was perfect and impervious.

She opened her eyes. "I can't help him," she told the others. "Hadrian! Hurry! He's dying!"

⋙

At the sound of her voice Irawondona smiled. "I don't even have to fight to win. I'm faster than you are. I can avoid you until he dies. Then Mawyndulë will be king. But rest assured I will kill you then. You will be the first; then I will kill your woman, and that empress of yours, then every last man, woman, and child on the face of Elan."

Hadrian nodded. "You could do that. And when your son and grandson ask about this day, you can tell them how in the fight that decided everything, you did nothing. You chose to run until time ran out, because you were afraid of being killed in a fair fight by a human—a fight ordained by your god, Ferrol. Then they will know that your race gained their dominance through cowardice and that mankind was truly the greater race."

Irawondona glared.

"Go on, you can admit it. You're afraid of me." Hadrian raised his voice. "You're afraid of me, and I'm only a human. I'm not even a noble or a knight. Do you know what I am? I'm a thief. Both of us are, Royce and I." Hadrian pointed down the hill. "We're nothing but a pair of common thieves. My father was a lowly blacksmith. He worked in a pathetic village not far from here." Hadrian let himself laugh. "An orphan and a blacksmith's son—two human thieves who terrify the invincible elven lords. It's so pathetic."

"I'm afraid of no human."

"Then prove it. Don't wait for him to die. Don't be a coward. Have at me."

Irawondona did not move.

"I thought as much," Hadrian said, and turned his back on the elf.

There was no sound. Hadrian knew there would not be. Years with Royce had taught him so. It was the look on the faces of those who watched that let him know Irawondona had moved.

Hadrian had already shifted his grip on the two-handed pommel of the spadone. His fingers spread in the fashion his father had taught him. His knees bent as his back bowed and his arm moved. One minute he was on the hill at Amberton Lee and the next he was in Hintindar behind the forge as his father shouted instructions.

*Don't look!* Danbury ordered, tying on the blindfold. *Trust your instincts. Don't guess; know what he is doing. Believe it. Act on it!*

Hadrian swung outward to his right. The great sword of Jerish Grelad caught the morning sun on its worn blade and glinted, shining for one brief moment.

*It's more than fighting, Haddy*, Danbury said. *It's what you are. It's what you will be—what you must be. Trust in it.*

Hadrian's knees hit the snow, sending up a burst of ice crystals. He could see the shadow now, the rushing darkness of Irawondona running at him from behind. Pulling against the weight of the spadone, he started the pivot, the collapsing rotation.

It was a blind attack.

*You don't have to see your opponent to kill him*, his father had explained. *You just have to know where he will be. That's the key to everything. And if you know, what good are eyes? What good is seeing? Trust in what I've taught you and you'll hit him.*

Hadrian continued the spin, one knee coming up, his shoulder twisting his waist as he put his full weight into the arc. He did not look. He did not need to. He knew. He knew exactly where Irawondona was and where he would be.

He felt metal kiss metal as Irawondona tried to parry. The force of the spadone, the weight behind it, was too much to deflect. The metal sang, but there was hardly a quiver to the stroke as it carried through the weak defense, driving the sword from Irawondona's grip. The spadone continued in its stroke and Hadrian hardly felt the impact as it cut into the elf's side. Irawondona's body offered even less resistance than his blade, and Hadrian completed the swing as if he were performing it alone behind the blacksmith's shop. The only difference was the splash of blood.

The blue torches flared brilliantly white, then went out with a loud snap.

"*Ir a wondon*," the priest of Ferrol announced, and then, looking at Hadrian, added, "It is done."

"*No!*" Mawyndulë cried, raising his arms. He looked as if he was trying to speak when he coughed and blood sprayed the front of his robes. To either side, his guards started to draw their weapons but disappeared with a loud *pop*.

Mawyndulë collapsed face-first. Behind him, Monsignor Merton stood holding the bloodstained Alverstone in both hands.

The elves did not move or react. Instead they stood silently, their faces solemn, their eyes downcast. No one looked at Irawondona and none bothered with Mawyndulë; instead they started down the hill toward Royce.

"*Hadrian!*" Arista screamed.

He pushed his way through the elves, then finally past Modina, the girls, and the boys to find Arista kneeling on the ground clutching Royce. The ground was soaked and his friend's eyes were closed.

"Help him!" Hadrian told her.

"I can't! I tried!" she cried, her eyes frightened.

"But I won," he said, and looked to Myron. "The blessing is gone now, right?"

The monk nodded.

"There—see? Do it, do it now! Pull him back!"

"I tried!" she shouted at him. "Don't you think I tried! I was waiting, and the second the wall was gone, I went in. But I still can't reach him. Hadrian...he doesn't want to be saved. I think he wants to die."

Hadrian felt the strength at last go out of his legs and he collapsed to his knees.

"He sees her, Hadrian," Arista cried, cradling Royce's head on her lap. "He sees her in the light. He doesn't even hear me. All he sees is her and he keeps saying he did it, he saved you."

Hadrian nodded. Tears filled his eyes and he reached out and brushed the hair away from Royce's face. "Damn it, Royce! Don't leave me, pal. Com'on, buddy, you have to come back. I finally did it. I killed the bad guy, saved the kingdom, won the girl, and you're ruining it all for me. You don't want to do that, do you? Please, we still need you."

"What happens if he dies?" Gaunt asked from above him.

"The elves will be without a king," Myron said in a shaking voice. "The next elf to blow the horn will be king, unless there is another challenger and a fight. But either way, an elf will be crowned."

"Do you hear that, Royce? It isn't over. You have to live or we all die. You won't have saved me after all. Com'on, pal." He lifted him, cradling Royce in his arms. "You can't leave now."

Hadrian studied his face—no change.

"There's just nothing keeping you here anymore, is there?" Tears ran down Hadrian's cheeks. "I love you, buddy," he said, and laid him back down.

Those watching fell silent as they listened to Royce's breathing. It grew shallower and slower, fainter with each rasping in and out. Somewhere a bird sang, and the wind blew across the hilltop.

"Who is he?"

Hadrian heard a small voice disturb the silence.

"Mercy, shush," the empress Modina said. "His name is Royce, now be quiet."

Hadrian looked up suddenly.

"What?" Arista asked.

"Gwen," he said.

"Huh?"

"Gwen told me how to save him."

"She did?"

"Yes, something about…It was the last time I saw her—one of the last things she ever told me. I—I didn't realize…"

"Realize what?" Arista asked.

"She knew."

"Knew what?"

"She knew everything," Hadrian replied. "I remember she told me what to do to save him but at the time I didn't understand. Damn, I wish I had Myron's brain!"

Hadrian took a breath and tried to calm down. "I was with her in The Rose and Thorn, at the table. Royce was there—no—no, he wasn't—he was in the kitchen doing something. He was happy—happy about…about…*the wedding*! Yes, we were talking about the wedding and about how Royce had changed over the years. I felt bad taking him away from her and she said that he had to go or I would die." He looked back toward the arena, where Irawondona's body still lay. "She meant this. She saw this! But then she said something else. She said…Oh, what did she say?"

He struggled to remember her voice, her words: *He's seen*

*too much cruelty and betrayal. He's never known mercy.* That was what she had said but then there was something else, something she wanted him to do. *You have to do this, Hadrian. You have to be the one to show him mercy. If you can do that, I know it will save him.*

"No," he said, stunned. "Not show him mercy—oh god! She wanted me to show him Mercy!"

He leapt to his feet and grabbed the little girl standing beside Modina. She pulled back, frightened.

"Relax, honey. Don't be afraid," he said softly. "Just tell me your name."

The girl looked at Modina, who nodded.

"Mercy."

"No—no, what's your *full* name?"

"Mercedes, but no one calls me that except my mother—at least, she used to."

"What's your mother's name, honey?" Hadrian asked, his hands trembling as he held her.

"My mother is dead."

"Yes, dear, but what was her name?"

The little girl smiled. "Gwendolyn DeLancy."

"Did you hear that, Royce!" Hadrian shouted. "Her name is Mercedes."

He kept shouting at him. "Elias or Sterling if a boy, right? But there was only one name for the girl, *Mercedes*. There was only one name because Gwen had already named her! This is your daughter, Royce! This is your and Gwen's daughter! How old are you, sweetie? Five? Six?"

"Six," she said proudly.

"She's six, Royce. That would have been the year we spent locked up in Alburn, remember? Gwen took her baby to Arcadius. She probably didn't want you to feel trapped, or maybe she didn't want her growing up in a whorehouse. In any case, she knew she would die before introducing you to your daughter. That's why she told me to. Royce, you have a daughter, you old bastard!" He reached out and took hold of Royce's face. "Part of Gwen is still here! Do you hear me?"

"Is he my father?" Mercy asked, drawing closer. "My mother told me that one day I would meet my father and that he would take me to live in a beautiful place and I would become a fairy princess and a queen of the forest."

Royce's eyelids twitched.

"Now!" Hadrian told Arista, but it was not necessary. She was already chanting. The chanting quieted to a hum and then Arista went silent. She jerked abruptly and violently. Hadrian took hold of her. He had one hand on each of them as he prayed to Maribor. Every muscle in Arista's body was taut and her head hitched as if she were being slapped. Then suddenly she shook and her breath shortened to gasps. The time between gasps grew until she stopped breathing entirely.

All around them the crowd stopped breathing as well.

"Royce!" Hadrian screamed at him. "She's your daughter, and if you die, she'll be an orphan, just like you! Are you going to abandon her and leave her alone like your parents did? *Royce!*"

Both bodies lurched in unison and they gasped for air. Arista, damp with sweat, laid her head against Hadrian. Royce breathed deeply, and slowly his eyes fluttered open. He did not speak, but his eyes focused on the little girl.

# CHAPTER 28

# FULL CIRCLE

The rear wheel of the wagon fell into another hole and bounced so hard that Arista woke. She pulled back the blanket and squinted at the sky. The sun was low on the horizon and the movement of the wagon made the forest on a hill to their right look as if it were marching in the opposite direction. Her neck and back were sore, her muscles stiff, and she was still groggy. She realized that despite the bouncing buckboard, she had slept the day away. Now her stomach ached from hunger. Her teeth felt fuzzy, almost sandy, and her left hand was numb from her lying on it. She rode in the back of the wagon that Magnus and Degan drove. Hadrian had made her the best bed he could, laying down all their blankets as padding in the space left by the consumed supplies.

Modina and the girls rode with her. Allie and Mercy were asleep between her and the empress. The two curled up in tight balls, their knees pulled to their chests. Modina sat with a blanket around her shoulders, staring off at the landscape. The sled runners had been replaced by wheels and they traveled on a rutted, muddy road that formed a dark line between two fields of snow that occasionally showed a patch of matted, tangled weeds. Seeing them got her thinking. She wiped her face with the blanket and, digging her brush out of a nearby pack, began the arduous process of clearing the snarls from her hair.

She pulled, grunted, and then sighed. Modina looked over with a questioning expression, and Arista explained by letting go of the brush and leaving it to hang.

Modina smiled and crawled over to her. "Turn around," she said, and taking the brush, the empress began working the back of Arista's head. "You have quite the rat's nest here."

"Be careful one doesn't bite you," Arista replied. "Do you know where we are?"

"I have no idea. I'm not really much of a world traveler, you know."

"This doesn't look like the road to Aquesta."

"No," Modina said as she worked on a particularly tough snarl. "It's too late to travel that far today, and neither you, Royce, nor Hadrian were up for a long trip. After all, you three had a pretty big day."

"But the people in—"

Modina patted her shoulder. "It's all right. I sent Merton back with instructions for Nimbus and Amilia, and Royce sent the elves with him—well, most of them. A few insisted on staying with their new king. There's nothing left in Aquesta to go back to. The city was destroyed. I ordered the remaining stores to be divided between those who survived. The people will be sent to Colnora, Ratibor, Kilnar, and Vernes, but organized into equal groups so no one city is too overwhelmed."

Arista laughed and shook her head, making it hard for Modina to work. "Are you sure you're the same Thrace Wood I once knew?"

"No, I don't suppose I am," Modina replied. "Thrace was a wonderful girl, naive, starry-eyed, bursting with life. For a long time I thought she was dead and gone, but I think—no, I know—some part of her still exists, but I'm Modina now."

"Well, whoever you are, you're amazing. You truly are the empress worthy of ruling all of mankind."

Modina lowered her voice and said, "I'll tell you a secret—it's not me at all, really. Sure, on occasion, I come up with something intelligent—and I am usually surprised by it myself—but the real genius behind my throne is Nimbus. Amilia deserves everything this empire can give her for hiring him. The man is a wonder: quiet, unassuming, but utterly brilliant. If he had a mind to, he could replace me in a heartbeat. I am convinced he could organize a perfectly lovely coup, but he has no aspirations for power at all. I haven't been in politics long, but even I can see that a man as capable as he and yet so absent of greed is a rare thing. Do you know he still sleeps in his cubicle? Or at least he did until the castle was destroyed. Even though he was chancellor of the empire, he lived in a tiny stone cell. He, Amilia, and Breckton are my jewels, my treasures. I don't know how I could have survived without them."

"Don't forget Hadrian," Arista reminded her.

"Hadrian? No, he's not a treasure of *mine* and neither are you." She paused in her brushing and Arista felt Modina kiss her head. "There's not a word that can describe how I feel about the two of you, except perhaps...miracle workers."

❦

The center of the village clustered along the main road. Wood, stone, and wattle-and-daub buildings with grass-thatched roofs lined either side, beginning at the little wooden bridge and ending before the slope that climbed a hill to the manor house. They consisted of a ramshackle assortment of shops, homes, and hovels, casting long shadows. Beyond them,

Hadrian could see people in the fields working in the strips closest to the village. Down in the valley, near the river, the fields were nearly clear of snow and villeins worked to spread manure from large carts. Hooded in wool cowls, the workers labored. Long curved rakes rose and fell in the faltering light. In the village, smoke rose from a few of the buildings and shops, but none came from the smithy.

As they approached, their horses announced their arrival with a loud hollow *clop clip clop* as they crossed the bridge. A pair of dogs lifted their heads, the sign above the shoemaker's shop squeaked as it swayed, and farther down the road a stable door clapped absently against its frame. The intermittent warbling wail of lambs called out from hidden pens.

Hadrian and Royce led the procession through the village. Behind them rode three elves—Royce's new shadows. Now that Royce was their king, and given what happened to Novron, and his predecessor, they were adamant about his protection.

The change in the elves' demeanor had been dramatic. The moment Royce got to his feet, they all knelt. The sneering looks of contempt were replaced instantly with reverence. If they were acting, Hadrian thought they were all remarkable performers. Perhaps it was seeing Royce come back from the dead, or some magic of the horn, but the elven lords could not appear to be more devoted to him.

Royce did not protest his new protectors. He said little on the subject and rode as if they were not there. Hadrian guessed he was humoring them—for now. Everyone, especially Royce, was too exhausted to think, much less argue, and Hadrian had just a single thought—to find shelter before dark. With that in mind, he headed south, following the little tributary of the Bernum River he knew simply as the South Fork, which brought them to his boyhood home of Hintindar.

A man sitting in front of the stable was filing the edges of the coulter on a moul board plow when he caught sight of them. He had a bristling black beard and a dirty, pockmarked face. He was dressed in the usual hooded cowl and knee-length tunic of a villein. The man stared, shocked, for a handful of seconds, then emitted a brief utterance that might have been a squeak. He ran to the bell mounted on the pole in the middle of the street and rang it five times, then bolted up the main street toward the manor house.

"Peculiar man," Hadrian remarked, stopping his horse at the well and, in turn, halting the whole party.

"I think you scared him," Royce said.

Hadrian glanced back at the elves sitting in a perfect line on their great white stallions in their gleaming gold armor, the center one holding aloft a ten-foot pole with a long blue and gold streamer flapping from it. "Yeah, it was probably me."

The two continued to watch the man run. He appeared only as tall as an outstretched thumb, but Hadrian could still hear his feet slapping the dirt.

"Know him?" Royce asked.

Hadrian shook his head.

"What's the bell for?" Royce asked.

"Emergencies, fires, the hue and cry—that sort of thing."

"I'm guessing he didn't see a fire."

"Are we stopping here?" Myron asked. He and Mauvin sat on their mounts just behind the elves and just before the wagon. "The ladies want to know."

"Might as well. I sort of planned to ride up to the manor to announce ourselves but...I think that's being taken care of."

He dismounted, letting his horse drink from the trough. The others got down as well, including Arista and Modina—the empress still wrapped in her blanket. They left the sleeping girls wrapped up in their covers.

Hadrian was just about to rap on the bakery's door when a crowd of people began filing into the village, following the cow path from the fields. They carried rakes over their heads and trotted into the street, stopping the moment they saw them. Hadrian recognized most of the faces: Osgar the reeve, Harbert the tailor, Algar the woodworker, and Wilfred the carter.

"Haddy!" Armigil shouted. The old brew mistress pushed her way through. Her broad hips cut a swath through the crowd. "How did ya—What aire ya doin' 'ere, lad? And what 'ave you brought with ya?"

"I—" was all he got out before she went on.

"Never ya mind answering. Ya needs to be gone. Take the lot of ya and go!"

"You need to work on your manners, dear," Hadrian told her. "The last time I came to town, you hit me, and now—"

"Ya don't understand, lad. Things have changed. There's no time to explain. You need to get out of here. His lairdship caught the storm after you left last time."

"Haddy?" Dunstan the baker and his wife approached, staring at him in disbelief. They were both dressed in worn wool, covered in speckles of mud, and their bare feet and legs were caked with drying earth.

"How are you, Dun?" Hadrian asked. "What are you doing in the field?"

"Plowing," he replied dully as he stared at the strangers on his street. "Well, trying to. Things have warmed up a lot, but the ground's still not quite soft enough."

"Plowing? You're a baker."

"We bake at night."

"When do you sleep, then?"

"Quit yer yammering and go, shoo! Away with ya!" Armigil shouted, waving at him as if he were a cow in her vegetable garden. "Haddy, you don't understand. If they find you here—"

"That's right!" Dunstan agreed, as if he suddenly woke from a dream. "You need to go. If Luret sees you—"

"Luret? The envoy? He's still here?"

"He never left," Osgar said.

"He charged Lord Baldwin with disloyalty," Wilfred the carter put in.

"Siward died in the fightin'," Armigil said sadly. "Luret locked up poor old Baldwin in his own dungeon, and that's why you and yer friends need to get!"

"Too late," Royce said, looking down the road toward the manor house. "A line of men are marching down the hill."

"Who are they? Imperial troops?" Hadrian asked.

"Looks like it. They're wearing uniforms," Royce said.

"What's going on?" Arista asked, coming forward. She beamed a smile at Dunstan and Arbor.

"Oh, Emma!" Arbor spoke to her with a fearful tone but said nothing more. Arista appeared puzzled for a moment and then laughed.

"Oh dear," Armigil went on when she noticed the wagon, where Allie and Mercedes were stretching and yawning. A sorrowful expression came over the brew mistress. "Ye got wee ones with ya too?"

"Is it too late to hide them?" Arbor asked.

"They can see us from there," Osgar answered.

Mauvin stepped up near Royce, peering up the road at the small figures coming down the hill. "How many do you count?"

"Twelve," Royce replied, "including Luret."

"Twelve?" Mauvin said, surprised. "Seriously?"

Royce shrugged. "Maybe the fella that ran up there mentioned we had women and children."

"But twelve?"

"Eleven, really."

Mauvin rolled his eyes and folded his arms across his chest in disgust as he watched them approach.

"So Luret has you all working in the fields?" Hadrian asked as he dismounted and tied up his horse.

"Are you daft man?" Armigil shouted. "What ere you makin' conversation fer? They're coming to arrest ya—if you're lucky, that is! They'll haul you to the dungeon, beat you, starve you, and likely torture you. That Luret is not right in the head."

Mince and the boys took it upon themselves to gather the horses and tie them to the wagon, taking time to pause and nod politely to the townspeople.

They soon heard the stomp of feet as the soldiers from the manor house marched at them in an even rhythm. They moved in a two-line formation of six men in back and five in front. They wore chain mail and flat helms. Those in front carried spears, those in the rear, crossbows. Luret rode behind them on a pale speckled mare with a black face and one white-circled eye. Luret looked much the same as he had the last time Hadrian had seen him. The man still had hawkish features and brutal eyes. His attire, however, had improved. He wore a thick brocade tunic along with a velvet cape and handsome long gloves neatly embroidered with chevrons that ran up his wrists. His legs were covered in opaque hose, and his feet covered by leather shoes with brass buckles, which caught what remained of the setting sun.

"Aha! The blacksmith's son!" Luret exclaimed the moment he saw Hadrian's face clearly. "Back to claim your inheritance? Or have you run out of places to hide? And who is this rabble?" He smirked, and waved his hand in the air. "Outlaws the lot of you, I'm sure." He paused a moment as he took notice of the elves, but his sight fell back to Hadrian again. "You've brought them here to roost, eh? Think you can hide out amongst your old friends?" He pointed at Royce. "Oh yes, I remember you, and you too." He looked at Arista. "I don't think they will be quite so quick to take you in this time, not after the beating I gave them." He looked at Dunstan, who stared down at his own feet. "They learned their lesson about harboring fugitives. Now it's time for you to learn a lesson too. Arrest the lot of them. I want chains on these two." He pointed at Hadrian and Royce.

The soldiers managed only one step forward before Hadrian drew his swords. The rest followed his lead. To his left, Degan stepped up, and beside him Magnus held his hammer. To his right the elves advanced to stand in front of Royce, causing him to sigh. Even the boys drew daggers, except for Kine and Mince, who did not have any, but they put up their fists, nonetheless.

The soldiers hesitated. Luret drummed his fingers on his saddle horn. "I said arrest them!"

One of the soldiers near Royce jabbed forward with his spear. The nearest elf severed the metal tip from the shaft. The guard backed up, holding the wooden staff.

None of the others moved.

Luret's face reddened. "You are defying arrest! You are challenging an imperial envoy and duly appointed magistrate and executor of this estate. I demand you surrender at once! Surrender or by the power invested in me by the empress herself I will have you shot where you stand!"

No one moved.

"I don't recall investing anything in you, much less the power to kill members of my personal entourage," Modina said as she walked forward from the rear of the party.

Luret put a hand to shield his eyes from the setting sun and squinted in her direction. "Who is this now?"

"You don't recognize me?" Modina asked in a light and lilting voice. "And yet you are so quick to evoke my name. Allow me to introduce myself. Perhaps it will jog your memory. I am the slayer of Rufus's Bane, the high priestess of the Church of Nyphron, Her Most Serene and Royal Grand Imperial Majesty, Empress Modina Novronian."

She cast off the blanket.

Several people in the crowd gasped. Arbor staggered backward, causing Dunstan to catch hold of her, and Hadrian was certain he heard Armigil mutter, "I'll be buggered."

The empress stood in her lavish gown. She was also adorned in the long black velvet mantle embroidered with the imperial crest, which she'd put on before presenting herself.

"This— No, it's not possible!" Luret muttered. "It's a trick. A trick, I say! I won't be hoodwinked. Look at this child. She is an impostor. A fake. All of you lay down your arms and come peacefully and I will only execute the blacksmith's son and his companion. Defy me and all of you will die!"

At that moment, the six soldiers with the crossbows began to sniffle. They blinked hard, their eyes watered, and they crinkled their noses. One by one, they began to sneeze, and then the thick sinewy skein of the crossbows snapped in loud pops, the metal bolts dropping helplessly to the dirt.

Hadrian glanced at Arista, who smiled mischievously at him.

"Before you get yourself into any more trouble," Modina said, addressing Luret, who was now clearly concerned, "allow me to introduce the rest of my contingent. This is the princess—or rather now Queen Arista of Melengar, conqueror of Ratibor, and sorceress extraordinaire."

"I think she prefers *wizardess*," Myron whispered.

"Pardon me, *wizardess*. This is Royce Melborn, newly crowned king of the ancient realm of Erivan. With him, as you may have noticed, are three of his elven lords. This short gentleman is Magnus of the Children of Drome, a master of stone and earth. Beside him is Degan Gaunt, leader and hero of the Nationalists. Over here is the legendary sword master Count Pickering of Galilin. This is the Marquis of Glouston, the famed and learned monk of Maribor. And while he shouldn't require any introduction, before you stands Hadrian Blackwater, Teshlor Knight, Guardian of the Heir of Novron, champion of the empire, and hero of the realm.

"These defenders of the empire have passed through the underworld, fought armies of goblins, crossed treacherous seas, entered and returned from the lost city of Percepliquis, and this very day halted the advance of an unstoppable army and defeated the being who long ago murdered our savior Novron the Great. They saved not only the empire but all of you as well. You owe them your lives, your respect, and your eternal gratitude."

She paused to stare at the wide-eyed Luret. "Well, envoy, magistrate, and executor, what say you?"

Luret looked at the faces around him. He saw his men laying down their weapons. He glanced at the faces of the villagers, then kicked his horse and bolted. He did not head back up the road to the manor but rather fled out to the open fields.

"I could make him fall off the horse," Arista mentioned, but Modina shook her head.

"Let him go." She looked at the soldiers. "The rest of you can go as well."

"Wait," Hadrian said. "Lord Baldwin is imprisoned at the manor, is that right?"

The soldiers slowly nodded, their faces coated in concern.

"Go free him at once," Modina said. "Tell him what you have seen and that I will be visiting him and his household tomorrow. In fact, tell him he will have the honor of hosting me and my court until such time as I arrange more permanent accommodations."

They nodded, bowed, and walked backward for a dozen steps before giving up, turning, and running up the street.

"I think you made an impression," Hadrian told her, then looked at the villagers.

They all stood like posts, staring at Modina, their mouths agape.

"Armigil, you do still brew beer, right?" Hadrian asked.

"What, Haddy?" she said, dazed, still staring at the empress.

"Beer, you know…barley, hops…It's a drink. We could really do with a barrel about now, don't you think?" He waved a hand in front of Dunstan. "Maybe a warm place to rest. Perhaps a bite of food?" He snapped his fingers three times. "Hello?"

"Is that really *the* empress?" Armigil asked.

"Yeah, so she's gonna be able to pay you if that's what you're worried about."

This snapped her out of her daze. The old woman scowled at him and shook a finger. "Ya know better than that, ya overgrown skunk! 'Ow dare ya be callin' me inhospitable! Whether she's the empress or a tart dragged from the gutter, ya know they both would be equally welcome to a pint and a plate in Hintindar—at least now that Uberlin 'imself is gone." She looked at Dunstan and Arbor. "And what are ya doing standing there and gawking fer? Throw some dough in the oven. Osgar, Harbert, get over 'ere and lend a 'and with a barrel. Algar, see if'n yer wife has any more of that mince pie and tell Clipper to cut a side of salt pork from—"

"No!" Hadrian, Arista, Mauvin, and Degan shouted all at once, startling everyone. They all began to laugh.

"Please, anything but salt pork," Hadrian added.

"Is—is mutton okay?" Abelard asked, concerned. Abelard the shearer and his wife, Gerty, had lived across the street from the Blackwaters for years. He was a thin, toothless, balding man who reminded Hadrian of a turtle, the way his head poked out of his cowl.

They all nodded enthusiastically.

"Mutton would be wonderful."

Abelard smiled and started off.

"And bring your fiddle and tell Danny to bring his pipe!" Dunstan shouted after him. "Looks like spring came a bit early this year, eh?"

♰

Arista was being careful, having learned her lesson before. This time she limited herself to just one mug of Armigil's brew; even then, she felt a tad light-headed. She sat next to Hadrian on top of flour sacks piled on the wide pine of the bakery floor. The floor itself was slippery from the thin coating of flour that the girls loved playing on. Allie and Mercy slid across the floor as if it were a frozen pond, at least until enough people arrived to make a good slide impossible. Arista thought about offering to help Arbor, but she already had half a dozen women working in her cramped kitchen, and after everything, it felt too good just sitting there leaning against him, feeling Hadrian's arm curled around her back. She smelled the sweet aroma of baking bread and roasting lamb. She listened to the gentle chatter of friendly conversations all around her and drank in the warmth and comfort. It made her wonder if this was what Alric had found within the light. She wondered if it smelled of baking bread, and remembering, she was almost certain it had.

"What are you thinking?" Hadrian asked.

"Hmm? Oh, I was hoping Alric was happy."

"I'm sure he is."

She nodded and Hadrian raised his mug. "To Alric," he said.

"To Alric," Mauvin agreed.

Everyone in the room with a glass, mug, or cup—even those who had never heard of Alric—raised drinks. Her eyes landed on Allie, who now sat between Modina and Mercy nibbling like a bird on a hunk of brown bread.

"To Wyatt and Elden," she whispered, too quietly even for Hadrian to hear, and downed the last of her cup.

"I wanted to say how sorry I am, Dun," Hadrian told his friend as he handed out another helping of food. "Was it bad, what happened after we left?"

Dunstan glanced up to see where his wife was. "It was hard on Arbor," he said. "I think I looked worse than I was. She had to do most of the work around here for close to six weeks, but all that is over. I'm used to getting my head cracked now and again." Dunstan grinned, then stared curiously at Hadrian and Arista, sitting arm in arm. Royce had just entered and Dunstan glanced nervously over at him. "You better watch yourself. He doesn't look the type to be understanding about such things."

Dunstan moved away, leaving Arista and Hadrian looking at each other, puzzled.

Royce hesitated at the door, his eyes on the girls as they sat at Modina's feet. The empress was one of the few in the room to sit on a chair. It was not her idea, but the Bakers insisted. He walked over and sat beside Hadrian.

"Where are your shadows?" Hadrian asked.

"You look concerned."

"Just that if you've started another war, I'd like a heads-up is all."

"The level of confidence you have in my diplomatic skills is overwhelming."

"What diplomatic skills?"

Royce frowned. "They're outside. I talked with them about space," Royce said.

"You did?"

"They speak Apelanese. And I do know some elvish, remember."

Royce sat back against the table leg, his eyes on Mercy as she giggled at something Allie whispered in her ear.

"Why don't you go talk to her?" Hadrian asked.

Royce shrugged, his brow creased with worry.

"What is it?"

"Nothing." Royce stood up. "It's a little warm in here for me."

They watched him gingerly step around those on the floor and slip back out. Hadrian looked at Arista.

"Go ahead," she told him.

"You sure?"

"Of course I am. Go."

He smiled, gave her a kiss, and then stood to chase after Royce.

Arista sat for a moment looking around her at all the friendly, rosy faces, talking, laughing, smiling. The bowls of steaming pottage were coming off the open hearth and making their rounds. Abelard, seated on an overturned bucket, was rosining his bow and plucking strings on his fiddle while he waited for Danny, who sat beside him finishing up a plate of lamb. The place was filling up and sitting room was getting scarce. Despite the crowd, a wide berth was maintained around Modina, who planted herself in the corner across from the door, smiling more brightly than Arista had ever seen her. Only the girls dared come within an arm's length, but every eye in the room repeatedly glanced her way.

Arista stood up and found Arbor throwing a round loaf in the oven. She leaned against the counter and wiped her head with the back of her flour-covered hands. "That's the last of it," she said, and smiled at her. "I was worried about you," she told Arista. "We both were."

"Really?"

"Oh yes! The way you left that night, and then when the soldiers came—we were afraid for you. The village was in turmoil that whole week. Men came through here four times spilling the flour and searching. I didn't know what they wanted you for—I still don't."

"It doesn't matter anymore," Arista said. "That's all over and everything is going to be different from now on."

Arbor's expression showed she did not know what to make of that.

"Say, do you still have that dress I gave you?"

"Oh yes!" She looked down at Arista's robe. "You'll be wanting it back, of course." She started to leave and Arista took her hand.

"No, that's not why I was asking."

"But it's okay. I took real fine care with it—never wore it once. I just looked at it a few times, you know."

"I was just thinking you should try it on, because I think you're going to be needing it."

"Oh no, I'll never need a dress that fine. Like I told you before, there's no chance of me going to a fancy ball or anything like that."

"That's just it," Arista told her. "I think you will—that is, if you accept."

"Accept what?"

"I'd like you to be the maid of honor at my wedding."

Arbor looked back at her, confused. "But, Erma, you're already married to Vince."

It was Arista's turn to look puzzled and then she laughed aloud.

✦

Hadrian caught up with Royce at the footbridge. It was dark, but the moon was bright and he spotted his friend's dark figure leaning over the rail, staring into the dark waters trickling below.

"Crowd getting to you?" Hadrian asked. Royce did not reply. He did not even look up. "So what will you do now?"

"I don't know," Royce said softly.

"You realize that being the real descendant of Novron makes you not only the King of Erivan but Emperor of Apeladorn as well. Have you spoken with Modina?"

"She already told me she would step down."

"Emperor Royce?" Hadrian said.

"Doesn't really sound right, does it?"

Hadrian shrugged and leaned against the same rail. "It could in time."

Except for the bakery, the street was dark, although there were some lights on at the manor house. They were tiny dots from where they stood, like bright yellow stars at the top of the hill.

"I hear you're going to marry Arista."

"Where'd you hear that?"

"Myron mentioned something about doing the honors."

"Ah—right. Well, I thought he'd do a good job, and nei-

ther of us are real thrilled with the idea of a Church of Nyphron ceremony."

"I think it's a good idea." Royce looked back at the water
below. "And don't wait. Marry her right away and start being
happy."

The breeze rustled the bare limbs of the nearby trees and
blew a faint hiss as it passed under the bridge. Hadrian pulled
his collar tight and looked over the edge. He stared down at
the dark waters below.

"So are you going to look for who killed her?" Hadrian
asked. "You know, don't you? Do you want me to come?"

"No," Royce replied. "He's already dead."

"Really? How do you feel about that?"

Royce shrugged.

"I knew it wasn't Merrick," Royce said, tearing a leaf and
throwing it over the edge of the bridge. "I still remember his
face, looking up at me. Telling me it wasn't him. Explaining
how it couldn't have been him. He was confounded by it. Merrick confounded—that was my first clue. Today I got the final
clue."

"What clue?"

"Emperor Royce—he was terrified of that possibility. Royce
Melborn on the throne—could there be a more frightening
thing? That's why he never told us. He brought us together hoping you would change me, but he couldn't fix me. I'd spent too
many years learning to hate. I'd lost the value of life. Then he
learned about Mercedes. I'd lost my humanity, but she was
clean. He could educate her, make her into the perfect ruler."

"Arcadius? But why would he kill Gwen?"

"That's my fault as well. I told him that she had agreed
to marry me. He knew we would come for Mercedes and all
that he invested in her would be lost. He never thought in his

wildest dreams that I would ever take that step with Gwen, and when he found out, he had to kill her before she had the chance to tell me about my daughter."

He looked up at the stars and ran a hand across his face. When he spoke, his voice quavered. "I told Arcadius she was at the Winds Abbey. He hired Merrick to take her and bring her to Colnora. He was there before the meeting, hiding with a crossbow."

Royce turned to Hadrian and his eyes were moist. "But what I can't understand is that he loved her too. So how could he pull that trigger? How could he watch her scream and fall? How frightened must he have been to do that? How much of a horror am I?"

"Royce." Hadrian placed a hand on his shoulder. "You're not like that anymore. You've changed. I've seen it. Arista and Myron, they've mentioned it as well."

Royce laughed at him. "I killed Merrick, didn't I? I never even gave him a chance. And if it wasn't for Arista, Modina would have died in the fire I set. I can't be a father, Hadrian. I can't raise... I'm evil."

"You didn't kill Magnus. Even after he told you his plans to double-cross you again, you let him go—you *forgave* him. The old Royce didn't know what forgiveness was. You aren't him anymore. It's as if—I don't know—it's like some part of Gwen came to you when she died. She's still alive in there somewhere, still literally your better half."

Royce wiped his eyes. "I loved her so much—I miss her so much. I can't help feeling it's my fault, my punishment for the life I've led."

"And Mercedes?"

"What about her?"

"Is she a punishment? She's your daughter. A part of Gwen that still lives. She has her eyes, you know... and that smile.

The gods don't give a gift that precious to someone so undeserving."

"Are you my priest now?"

Hadrian stared at him.

Royce looked back down at the stream below. "She doesn't even know me. What if she doesn't like me? Few people do."

"She might not at first. Maribor knows I didn't. But you have a way of growing on a person." He smiled. "You know, like lichen or mold."

Royce looked up and scowled. "Okay, forget what I said. Definitely steer clear of the priesthood." He paused, then said, "She does look like Gwen, though, doesn't she? And her laugh—have you heard it?"

"She told me that her mother said her father would make her a fairy princess and that they would live in a beautiful place where she would be a queen of the forest."

"Did she?"

Hadrian nodded. "Seems a shame to disappoint her, and if Gwen told her that, it must be true."

Royce sighed.

"So will you take the throne from Modina?"

"Emperor Royce? I don't think so. But I'm stuck with the job of elven king, aren't I?"

"How's that going, by the way?"

"Funny as it sounds, I think they're terrified of me."

"A lot of people are terrified of you, Royce."

He laughed. "I feel like one of those guys in the circus that train bears with just a chair and a whip. They destroyed half of Apeladorn without a single loss of life on their side and the only thing stopping them from finishing the job is me and their crazy religion. They really hate humans but are convinced I was chosen by Ferrol to be their ruler. To disobey me is to disobey their god. To kill me is unthinkable. So here they are, ruled by a human who they must obey and can't kill. You know they've got to be panicking."

"Only you aren't human."

"No—I'm neither."

"Maybe that will help."

"Perhaps."

"So you still haven't told me. What do you plan to do?"

Royce shrugged. "I don't know yet. How could I? I don't know anything about them, really. I do know that I've seen cruelty from both sides. After seeing how Saldur's empire treated people like me, I can understand the elves' hatred. The old me certainly remembers that feeling, the certitude of justice, the purity of unquestioned purpose."

"And the new you?"

Royce shook his head. "I forgave Magnus, for Maribor's sake."

"Why did you?"

"Tired, I guess. Tired of killing—no, that's not really it. The real reason, I think, is that part of me wondered what Gwen would think. I can't imagine her wanting me to kill Magnus any more than she would want me to punish the elves for what they did. She was such a better person than I am, and now that she's gone, I..."

Hadrian squeezed his shoulder. "Trust me—she's proud of you, pal." He gave him a second, then in a bright tone said, "How is it we never had *king* and *emperor* on our list of potential careers? When you think about it, it beats the heck out of winemakers, actors, and fishermen."

"You always think everything is so easy," Royce replied, wiping his eyes.

"I'm just a glass-half-full kinda guy. How's your glass looking these days?"

"I have no idea. I'm still trying to get over the sheer size of it."

Hadrian nodded. "Speaking of glasses..." He lifted his head when he heard the sound of a fiddle and pipe. He put his arm around Royce's shoulder and led him off the bridge. "How about a nice pint of Armigil's brew?"

"You know I hate beer."

"Well, I'm not sure you can really call what she brews beer. Think of it more as...an experience."

# CHAPTER 29

# FROM OUT OF A CLEAR BLUE SKY

A surprising number of people survived the attack on Aquesta and came out of their underground bunkers to find a different world. The elves were gone and so was the city. All that remained were the bodies of the dead and the shattered rubble of the once-strong walls. In the weeks that followed, the weather grew warm, the snow melted, and people took to the roads. Many dispersed south or east to Colnora, which had managed to survive unscathed. Some, those originally from there, ventured north to find a ravaged land, which they vowed to rebuild. A few remained in Aquesta, picking up the stones and brushing away the dirt.

The empress took up residence at the unlikely estate of Lord Baldwin. It took several weeks before the full contingent of the imperial government was reestablished, but soon messengers in imperial uniforms were racing across the roads bearing news and orders from the empress.

Much to the dismay of the Aquestians, the empress decided not to return. She announced plans to build a new city at Amberton Lee, which would be named New Percepliquis, after the ancient imperial capital. She called on all artisans, engineers, mapmakers, stone workers, wood carvers, road layers, and a host of others to come. With many out of work and, in many cases, homeless, they came in droves. Among this assortment of workers came a surprisingly large number of dwarves, the largest assembly of little folk seen in centuries. No one knew from where they came, but once they arrived, the work began in earnest and those passing near the Lee remarked at the sounds of hammers in the dark of night.

Rumors spread along with the people. One story maintained that it was not the elves who had destroyed Aquesta, but Nationalists who invented the lies about them to strike fear across the countryside. These stories told that Degan Gaunt fought in single combat against the empress's champion, Sir Hadrian, to decide the fate of the empire. Another bit of gossip held that Rufus's Bane had risen from the dead and laid waste to the countryside, hunting the empress. When it found her in Aquesta, she led it away to save her people and single-handedly slew it once again on a hilltop. They said it remained there in a secret place guarded by priests, who watched over it to make certain that it did not rise again.

The most outlandishly incredible—and therefore most popular—tale was one replete with amazing adventures, monsters, heroes, and villains. It was a story about how the elves invaded, and nothing could stand against them. In this version the empress in her wisdom sent ten heroes into the bowels of Elan to seek the Rhelacan from the tomb of Novron. Among them were the Teshlor Sir Hadrian, a dwarven prince who they befriended in the depths, a pious monk, the last giant to walk the world, and the good wizardess Arista— whose evil twin sister was the Witch of Melengar. The story told of how this courageous band fought through caves, sailed across underground seas of glowing water, battled hordes of goblins, and slew a Gilarabrywn. It told how three of them fell in battle, but the remainder emerged victorious.

According to this story, Sir Hadrian, armed with the Rhelacan, defeated the king of the elves and saved the empire. The tale grew with each passing tinker and new characters were added, including a thief, a sailor, and a master swordsman.

All that really mattered was that the empress was alive and well and that Amilia the Beloved was with her. Not all the news was welcome, however, as edicts declared dwarves and half-elves were to be recognized as full citizens of the empire. This touched off the Spring Riots in Colnora and Vernes, which Sir Breckton squelched with a contingent of imperial troops.

In the north, the realm of Melengar all but vanished. What the imperial invasion had not destroyed, the elves had. The young king Alric, who never married and had no heirs, did not return, nor did his sister. After more than seven hundred years, the line of Essendon ended, and it was Count Mauvin Pickering, now Imperial Governor Pickering, who returned to administrate the province of Melengar. By all accounts, he was a good and just man, and before long rumors of his marriage to Lady Alenda Lanaklin circulated.

The death of Archibald Ballentyne left the province of Chadwick vacant of a lord. The seat was replaced when the empress appointed Degan Gaunt earl. In her announcement speech, she said that the appointment was not only deserved but appropriate.

By Summersrule, heralds were crossing the empire shouting in every village about the news from New Percepliquis. The first buildings were standing on the mount at Amberton Lee, just enough to allow the empress to move her court, and she was using the holiday to celebrate the move and commemorate those who had given their lives to save the empire.

The games where held in the newborn city, which was little more than chalk and string outlines. Thousands came hoping to glimpse Sir Hadrian or Sir Breckton on the field, but neither entered the competition. Sir Renwick won top honors, un-horsing Sir Elgar in the final tilt.

The highlight of the celebration, however, was the marriage of Sir Breckton to Lady Amilia in a moonlight ceremony performed by Patriarch Merton. On the last day of the celebrations, Empress Modina made the startling announcement that she had adopted, as daughter and heir, the half-elf child Allie, henceforth to be known as the imperial crown princess Alliena Novronian.

The celebration lasted a full two weeks, and when it was over, the roads were filled with carts and wagons of soon-to-be-footsore travelers on their long journeys home. The hilltop at Amberton Lee, now officially renamed New Percepliquis, was once more filled with the sounds of hammers, chisels, and saws. Sheep grazed on the southern slope, and milk cows on the north.

As the sun began to set, lights appeared in the windows of the "palace"—a simple thirty-room blockhouse. It was the first of the dwarven constructions and designed to be servants' quarters for stable hands and groundskeepers. For now it housed the whole of the imperial government.

On the front steps, which were broad and afforded a fine view from the hilltop, a small group gathered to watch the sunset and the approach of the imperial carriage.

"It really is coming along nicely," Hadrian told the dwarf as he sat with his arm around Arista. He was dressed in a soft tunic and she in a comfortable blue linen dress. "It's hard to imagine this is where I fought only four months ago."

The now leveled land revealed tiers where buildings would be constructed partially into the sides of the hill. Huge blocks of stone marked corners that anchored string lines held in place with stakes that designated future walls, roads, and pathways. Most were rectangular, but some were octagonal or completely circular. Still others defied any description, looking haphazard and bewildering from their footprints in string.

"It's beautiful," Arista said.

"Bah! You can't tell a thing yet!" Magnus scoffed. He tapped his temple. "If you could see what's in here, then you could really appreciate it. This city will make the old one below us an embarrassment." He looked out across the hill. "But it will take time—years—decades, really—but yes, it *will be* beautiful."

The laughter of children blew in with the evening summer breeze as down the slope Allie and Mercy chased fireflies, where a holly tree stood and five boys once spent days in a tent they called the Hovel.

The carriage pulled to a stop, and when the door opened, the white-wigged chancellor Nimbus stepped out. He was dressed in his usual outlandish colors, and on his chest was the massive gold chain of his office. He smiled at Modina and Amilia and greeted them all with a sweep of his hand and a lavish bow.

"It's about time you arrived," Modina said, rising to meet him.

"Forgive me, Your Eminence," he said, dusting himself off. "But there was a great deal to be done before blowing out the last candle in Aquesta."

"How long will you be staying?" Amilia asked.

"I'm afraid not long. I've really only come to see what you've started here and to say goodbye."

"I can't believe you won't stay. I don't know how I will get along without you."

"Alas, as I told Your Eminence in our correspondence, it really is time for me to move on. You have matters well in hand. New Percepliquis is coming along nicely. When I accepted this chain of office, we both knew it was temporary. I will be leaving in the morning."

"Really?" Amilia asked. "So soon? I thought we'd have a few days at least."

"I am afraid so, my lady. I've had many farewells and found that they are best kept short."

"You've been wonderful," Modina told him, squeezing his hand. "This empire wouldn't have survived without you. Every citizen owes you a debt of gratitude."

Nimbus addressed Amilia while gesturing toward the empress. "We did all right with her, didn't we? I think that board really helped."

"Yes," Amilia agreed, and raced down the steps and hugged him tight. She kissed his cheek, startling the chancellor. "Thank you—thank you for everything."

Modina motioned for Nimbus to come closer and briefly whispered in his ear.

"Oh yes, the new couple," Nimbus said, looking at Hadrian and Arista. "Congratulations on your wedding. What will you do now?"

"Yes," Modina said. "Now that the honeymoon is over and you've been duly knighted, Sir Hadrian, what are your plans?"

"Don't look at me. Arista is running this show. I thought we'd be back in Medford by now."

"Oh right." She rolled her eyes. "I could just see you as king in the royal court, listening to the earls and barons griping about who has the right to water cattle on the north bank of the Galewyr, or settling a dispute with the clergy over their refusal to pay a tax on the vast tracks of church-owned land. No, I know how it would turn out. I would be the one left alone in the throne room sorting through the tangled string of a dozen petitions while you're off hunting or jousting. I'm sorry but I've had more than my share of ruling and it would only make us both miserable. That's why I gave Melengar to Mauvin. It also made it easier to admit Melengar to the empire, as he didn't have any problem with accepting a governorship as opposed to a crown.

"Do you know what our good knight here has actually been doing with his time? During our honeymoon?" Arista bumped Hadrian with her shoulder. "Why he was too busy to take part in the joust?"

Everyone looked slightly uneasy, wondering what she might say next.

Arista paused a suitable moment to let their minds wander, then said, "He's been working as the smithy in Hintindar."

Magnus chuckled, Modina modestly smiled, but Russell Bothwick roared. He slapped his thigh until his wife, Lena, laid a calming hand on his leg. "You're a romantic, you are," he said through laughter-invoked tears. "Stoking a forge instead of—"

"*Russell!*" Lena burst out.

"What?" he asked, looking at his wife, bewildered. "I'm just saying that the man has got his priorities all wrong."

"Well, it's not like I'm there *all* day and night," Hadrian said, defending himself. "The fact is they don't have one. Grimbald left over a year ago and they have all this work. They're desperate. I hate seeing my father's forge lying cold. It was taking twice as long to till the fields with dull hoes and spades."

"But it hardly seems the best use of time for the last living Teshlor Knight," Nimbus remarked. "And you." He looked at Arista. "The last master of the Art...what have *you* been doing?"

"I learned to bake bread really well." She too received many surprised looks, not the least of which came from Modina, Amilia, and Lena. "No, seriously, I've gotten good. Arbor says I'm ready to marble rye and wheat together."

Nimbus glanced at Modina, who nodded.

The empress leaned forward. "I would like to ask you both something. The lord chancellor and I have been corresponding on this matter and I think he is right. There is so much that needs to be done. There will be warlords, more uprisings like the riots this spring. With the elves back across the river, goblins have begun raiding again. And of course something must be done about Tur Del Fur."

"I'll second that," Magnus grumbled. "It was bad enough when humans controlled Drumindor; now there's Ghazel wandering its halls."

"The empire needs people of good character to guide and protect the people, good arms, strong arms, wise arms. I can only do so much." She gestured at those in her court. "We can only do so much. The realm is vast and we can't be everywhere. Plus, there is the matter of stability. While I am alive, the empire will be strong, but even small kingdoms have fractured at the passing of a monarch. The larger the empire, the greater the threat. With no structure in place, no solid tradition to hold us together, the empire could break into civil wars."

"Two of the things that made the Old Empire so strong—so cohesive," Nimbus told them, "were the Cenzarium and Teshlor Guild. The Grand Council was created from the best and brightest of both. They maintained order and could govern in the absence of a ruler. Until these institutions are restored—until wizards and knights of the old order patrol the roads and visit the courts of distant governors to ensure they are upholding the law—until they guard the borders of Calis and Estrendor, the empire will not be safe or whole."

"Imagine what a hundred Hadrians and a hundred Aristas could do," Modina told them. "And you." She glanced at Myron. "We need a new university. Sheridan is gone. We can think of no one better to lead such a project."

"But I—" the monk began.

"Think of it as a bigger monastery," Nimbus interrupted. "Administering to a larger flock. You will teach them of lore, philosophy, engineering, languages—including elvish—and of course about Maribor. Teams can be sent into the old city to retrieve any volumes that still remain there. They can be the seeds that can help you spread knowledge to all who are willing to learn."

"We will collect all the works and place them under a huge dome of the greatest library ever constructed," Modina added.

"That does sound nice, but my brother monks…"

"There will be plenty of work for all."

"I've already started laying the foundation for the scriptorium," Magnus told him. "It's five times the size of what we had at the Winds Abbey."

"And the Cenzarium?" Arista looked at the dwarf.

Magnus smiled sheepishly. "The walls are already going up. If you look out there, to the left, you can see them."

"So this has already been settled on?" she asked, pretending to sound indignant.

"While certainly no one," Nimbus replied deftly, "least of all those present here—would ever ask any more of you two, and while you have earned a long and well-deserved rest, I was confident you would not abandon your empress, or the empire you fought so hard to establish."

"Where's the guildhall to be?" Hadrian asked.

Magnus pointed. "Across the square from the Cenzarium, of course. Just like in the old city."

"At least we will be close neighbors," Hadrian said.

"We can have lunches together." Arista grinned at him.

"And in between them will be a fountain and statue of Alric, Wyatt, and Elden," Modina explained.

"Well?" Hadrian asked her.

Arista narrowed her eyes and pursed her lips. "You're replacing yourself with us, aren't you?" she asked Nimbus.

"Yes, you are to be the seeds of a new grand council."

"At least you're honest. All right," she said, and then glared at Magnus. "But *I* will be the one to decorate the interior of the Cenzarium. I've seen dwarven tastes and it isn't conducive to the Art."

Magnus scoffed and grumbled something under his breath.

The door to the palace opened and Royce stepped out. "Hadrian, do you know where—" Royce stopped the instant he saw Nimbus, a look of shock on his face.

"Royce?" Hadrian asked.

Royce said nothing but continued to stare at the wigged chancellor.

"Oh, that's right," Modina said. "You've never met Nimbus, have you?"

"Yes—yes, I have," Royce said. He stepped forward, approaching the chancellor. "I thought you were dead."

"No," Nimbus replied. "I'm still alive, my dear friend."

Everyone looked at them, confused.

"But how?"

"Does it matter?"

"I came back," Royce told him. "I tried to free you. I tried to save you, but Ambrose told me..."

"I know, but I wasn't the one who needed to be freed, and I wasn't the one you needed to save."

❦

The morning arrived bright and clear. Golden sunlight slanted across Amberton Lee, casting shadows marking the growing city that spread out like a newly planted field of hope. In the valley, a low mist, like a white cloud, shrouded the twisting Bernum River and the air was still and quiet even on the hilltop.

Modina was already up. She wrapped a cape over her shoulders and headed out to the porch. She found Royce sitting there, his feet dangling from the side, watching the girls as they raced down the dewy hillside, chasing after Mr. Rings.

"You realize you're taking one of my favorite girls from me," she said.

He nodded. "I made Lord Wymarlin of the Eilywin tribe steward and gave him orders to set Erivan on a peaceful footing. I've left them alone too long and need to check on his progress." Royce looked out at the girls. "Besides, I don't want her growing up only knowing half the story. I need to learn it too. I have to cross the Nidwalden where no man has ever set foot, see Estramnadon and the First Tree. Three thousand years seems impossibly long now, but one day...It will be better if both sides became friendlier neighbors, I think. They aren't ready to embrace men, and men aren't prepared to welcome them yet, but in time...maybe.

"I've asked a number of those with mixed blood to pack their belongings and meet me at Avempartha. There aren't many of us left now—a shame, as they could make perfect ambassadors—a foot in each world, as it were. They can be bridges for the future. We'll start there, and then I'll send them back here. Perhaps one day we'll see an actual bridge across the Nidwalden with carts going both ways." He pointed at the two girls. "That is the start of it, the heir of one throne and the heir of the other chasing an overgrown rodent together."

Hadrian and Arista came out to the porch. They took up seats beside Royce and nodded good-morning greetings.

"Just make sure you take good care of her," Modina said.

"Believe me—no harm will come to that little girl so long as I live."

Hadrian laughed suddenly and Modina and Arista turned to him.

"What?" Arista asked.

"Sorry, but I just got a vision in my mind of Mercedes's poor would-be suitors. Can you imagine the courage of the lad capable of asking *him* for her hand?"

They all laughed except Royce, whose face darkened as he muttered, "Suitors? I never really thought—"

Hadrian slapped Royce on his shoulder. "Come on, I'll help you with your gear."

⌁

Royce finished loading the last saddlebag onto a packhorse the grooms had brought out. He once again checked the cinches of the pony Mercedes would ride. He was not about to trust the security of her saddle to anyone.

Myron was there, petting the horses' noses and saying a blessing over them. When he caught Royce watching, he smiled and said one over the new king as well. "Goodbye, Royce. I'm so pleased to have met you. Do you remember what we talked about at the Winds Abbey the last time we were there?"

A smile tugged at the corners of Royce's mouth. "Everyone deserves a little happiness."

"Yes, never forget that. Oh, and if you find any books across the Nidwalden, bring them the next time you visit. I'd love to learn more about the elves."

"So this is goodbye," Hadrian said as he and Arista came down the palace steps hand in hand.

"You'll finally be rid of me," Royce told him.

"You'll be visiting again soon, won't you?" Arista asked.

He nodded and smiled. "I doubt they have Montemorcey on the other side of the river. I only have room to bring a few bottles."

"Then I will be sure to always have it on hand," Arista told him. In her hands, she held out the Horn of Gylindora. "It's supposed to go with the ruler of the elves."

"Thanks."

"No escort for the king?" Hadrian asked, looking around.

"They are meeting us at the crossroads at the bottom of the hill beyond the forest. I didn't want them staring at me while we said goodbye."

He took Arista's hand and placed Hadrian's on top of it. "I am officially turning him over to you. He's your problem now. You'll have to watch out for him and that won't be easy. He's naive, gullible, immature, horribly unsophisticated, ignorant about anything worth knowing, and idealistic to a fault." He paused to make a show of thinking harder. "He's also indecisive, pathetically honest, a horrible liar, and too virtuous for words. He gets up twice each night to relieve himself, wads his clothes rather than folds them, chews with his mouth open, and talks with his mouth full. He has a nasty habit of cracking his knuckles every morning at breakfast, and, of course, he snores. To remedy that, just put a rock under his blanket."

"That was you? All those nights when we camped?" Hadrian looked shocked.

Arista put her arms around the thief and hugged him tight. Royce squeezed her back, then looked into her eyes for a long moment. "He's a very lucky man."

She smiled and kissed him goodbye.

Hadrian grabbed him next, hugging him and clapping him on the back. "Be careful out there, pal."

"I'm always careful. Oh, and do me a favor. See that Magnus gets this." Royce handed him Alverstone. "Wait until I'm gone, and tell him—tell him the maker said he should have it."

Modina, Amilia, and Nimbus came out of the palace with the two girls and Mr. Rings, who Amilia held awkwardly in her arms. The empress was wiping tears from her cheeks and struggling to keep her lips from shaking. When she got to the steps, she bent down and hugged Mercedes, holding her for several minutes before letting her go. When she did, the little girl ran down the steps and pointed. "Is that my pony?"

Royce nodded and Hadrian threw her up onto it.

"Bye-bye, Allie!" she shouted, petting the pony's mane. "I am off to become a fairy princess." Amilia handed up the raccoon.

Nimbus was dressed in traveling clothes, a small pack on his back and his familiar leather satchel at his side.

"You're leaving now as well?" Amilia hugged Nimbus.

"I regret to say I must be off, Your Ladyship. It is time to go."

"I am sure your family in Vernes will be happy to see you return."

He smiled and, dipping his head, removed his chain of office and placed it in her hands.

"Where's your horse?" Hadrian asked.

"I don't need one," Nimbus replied.

"I think the empire can spare at least that much," Modina told him.

"I am certain it can, Your Eminence, but I honestly prefer walking."

It took another round of hugs, kisses, waves, and wishes of safe travels before Royce, Mercedes, and Nimbus actually started down the slope. Allie ran alongside all the way to the trees and then waved madly before turning and running back to Modina.

Nimbus walked with them and Royce was careful to keep a slow, even pace.

They entered the forest and soon lost all sight of the palace, the city, and the hill. They traveled in silence, listening to the morning symphony of birdsongs and honeybees. Mercedes was mesmerized by her new pet.

"What's my pony's name?" she asked.

"I don't think it has one yet. Would you like to name it?"

"Oh yes...Let me see...What's yours called, Daddy?"

"Mine is Mouse. The empress gave her that name."

Mercedes crinkled her nose. "I don't like that. Is mine a boy or a girl?"

"Boy," Royce told her.

"Boy...okay, hmm." She tapped her lips with a perplexed expression, then furrowed her brow in serious thought.

"How about Elias?" Nimbus suggested. "Or perhaps Sterling."

Royce stared at the ex-chancellor, who smiled pleasantly in return.

"Sterling is nice," Mercedes said.

The forest thinned and they reached the open field where the old road crossed the new ones, freshly pressed by holiday travelers, leading west to Ratibor and north to Colnora. A short distance away a group of riders in gold and blue on white mounts waited.

"This is where we part," Nimbus told them.

Royce stared at the thin man in the wig. "Who are you really?"

Nimbus smiled. "You already know that."

"If it hadn't been for you..." Royce paused. "I've always regretted that I never said thank you."

"And I wish to thank you as well, Royce."

He was puzzled. "For what?"

"For reminding me that anyone, no matter what they've done, can find redemption if they seek it."

The thin man turned and walked down the road toward Ratibor. Royce watched him go, then turned to his daughter. "Let's go visit the elves, shall we?" he asked. Just then, thunder cracked from overhead, shaking the ground and rustling the leaves on the trees.

Royce looked up at the clear blue sky, confused.

"Look!" Mercedes said, pointing down the road.

Royce turned to see Nimbus standing still, his head bent back, his eyes looking up.

A white feather drifted downward. It swirled, blowing on a gentle breeze until it was close enough that the tall spindly man in the white powdered wig reached up and caught it between his fingers. He kissed it gently, then slipped it into his leather pouch. He pulled the bag closed and continued on his way, whistling a merry tune, until he passed behind a hill and was gone.

# GLOSSARY OF TERMS AND NAMES

ABNER GALLSWORTH: Aquesta city administrator

ADAM: Wheeler from Ratibor

ADDIE WOOD: Mother of Thrace/Modina, wife of Theron, killed in Dahlgren

ADELINE: Queen of Alburn, married to Armand, sons: Rudolf and Hector, daughter: Beatrice

ADWHITE, SIR: Knight and poet, wrote *The Song of Beringer*

ALBERT WINSLOW: Landless viscount used by Riyria to arrange assignments from the gentry

ALBURN: Kingdom of Avryn ruled by King Armand and Queen Adeline, member of the New Empire

ALENDA LANAKLIN: Daughter of the marquis Victor Lanaklin and sister of Myron the monk

ALGAR: Woodworker in Hintindar

ALLIE: Daughter of Wyatt Deminthal, half-elf, once held hostage by Merrick Marius

ALRIC ESSENDON, KING: Ruler of Melengar, brother of Arista, son of Amrath

ALVERSTONE: \al-ver-stone\ Dagger used by Royce

ALYSIN: Elven afterlife

AMBERTON LEE: Hill with old ruins not far from Hintindar, site where Arista killed two seret

AMBROSE MOOR: Administrator of the Manzant Prison and Salt Mine

AMILIA: Secretary to the empress, carriage maker's daughter, born in Tarin Vale

**AMITER, QUEEN:** Second wife of King Urith, sister of Androus, killed by Imperialists

**AMRATH ESSENDON, KING:** \am-wrath\ Former ruler of Melengar, father of Alric and Arista, killed by the Nyphron Church

**AMRIL:** \am-rill\ Countess that Arista cursed with boils

**ANDROUS BILLET:** Viceroy of Ratibor, murdered King Urith, Queen Amiter, and their children

**ANKOR:** Tribe of Ghazel

**ANNA:** Chambermaid of Empress Modina

**ANTUN BULARD:** Historian and author of *The History of Apeladorn*, passenger on the *Emerald Storm*, hired to find the Horn of Gylindora

**APELADORN:** \ah-pell-ah-dorn\ The four nations of man, consisting of Trent, Avryn, Delgos, and Calis

**APELANESE:** Language spoken by the four kingdoms of men

**AQUESTA:** \ah-quest-ah\ Capital city of the kingdom of Warric, seat of power for the New Empire

**ARBOR:** Baker in Hintindar, married to Dunstan, shoemaker's daughter, first love of Hadrian

**ARCADIUS VINTARUS LATIMER:** Professor of lore at Sheridan University, caretaker of Allie

**ARCHIBALD BALLENTYNE:** Earl of Chadwick, commander of Sir Breckton, promised providence of Melengar for service to the New Empire, infatuated with Empress Modina, nickname: Archie

**ARISTA ESSENDON, PRINCESS:** Sister of Alric, daughter of Amrath, Princess of Melengar, leader of rebel victory in Ratibor, former mayor pro tem of Ratibor, former regent of Rhenydd, Witch of Melengar, imprisoned in Aquesta after trying to free Degan Gaunt

ARMAND, KING: Ruler of Alburn, married to Adeline, sons: Rudolf and Hector, daughter: Beatrice

ARMIGIL: Brew mistress of Hintindar, family friend of the Blackwaters

ART, THE: Magic, generally feared due to superstition

ARVID MCDERN: Son of Dillon McDern of Dahlgren

ASENDWAYR: Tribe of elves, hunters

AVEMPARTHA: Ancient elven tower, home of Gilarabrywn that attacked Dahlgren

AVRYN: \ave-rin\ The central and most powerful of the four nations of Apeladorn, located between Trent and Delgos

AYERS: Proprietor of The Laughing Gnome in Ratibor

BA RAN ARCHIPELAGO: Island of the goblins

BA RAN GHAZEL: Goblins of the sea

BACKING: Rigging a sail such that it catches the wind from its forward side, having both backed and regular rigged sails can render a ship motionless

BAILEY INN, THE: Boardinghouse routinely used by Riyria when in Aquesta

BAILIFF: Officer who is employed to make arrests and administer punishments

BALDWIN: Lord whose landholdings include Hintindar

BALLENTYNE: \bal-in-tine\ The ruling family of the earldom of Chadwick

BANNER: Crew member of the *Emerald Storm*, one of the few survivors

BARAK: Ghetto in Trent inhabited by dwarves

BARKERS: Refugee family living in Brisbane Alley of Aquesta, father Brice, mother Lynnette, sons Finis, Hingus, and Wery

BARTHOLOMEW: Carriage maker of Tarin Vale, father of Amilia

BARTHOLOMEW: Priest in Ratibor

BASIL: Officers' cook on the *Emerald Storm*, died at sea

BASTION: Servant in the imperial palace

BATTLE OF MEDFORD: Skirmish that occurred during Arista's witch trial

BATTLE OF RAMAR: Bloody fight that Hadrian once fought in

BATTLE OF RATIBOR: Rebellion against Imperialists, led by Emery Dorn and Arista

BEATRICE, PRINCESS: Daughter of King Armand, Princess of Alburn, sister to Rudolf and Hector

BELINDA PICKERING: Extremely attractive wife of Count Pickering, mother of Lenare, Mauvin, Fanen, and Denek

BELLA: Cook at The Laughing Gnome in Ratibor

BELSTRADS: \bell-straads\ Noble family from Chadwick, including Sir Breckton and Wesley

BENDLTON, BROTHER: Cook at the rebuilt Winds Abbey

BENNINGTON: Guard in Aquesta

BENTLY: Sergeant in the Nationalist army, promoted by Hadrian to adjunct general

BERNARD: Lord Chamberlain of the imperial palace

BERNARD GREEN: Candlemaker from Alburn, living in Aquesta

BERNICE: Former handmaid of Arista, killed in Dahlgren

BERNIE DEFOE: Topsail crew member of the *Emerald Storm*, former member of the Black Diamond thieves' guild, hired to find the Horn of Gylindora

BERNUM HEIGHTS: Wealthiest residential district in Colnora

BERNUM RIVER: Waterway that bisects the city of Colnora

BERYL: Senior midshipman on the *Emerald Storm*, died at sea

BETHAMY, KING: Ruler reputed to have had his horse buried with him

*BETRAYAL IN MEDFORD*: Imperialist version of the play *The Crown Conspiracy*

BIDDINGS: Chancellor of the imperial palace

BISHOP: Lieutenant aboard the *Emerald Storm*, died at sea

BLACK DIAMOND: International thieves' guild centered in Colnora

BLACKWATER: Last name of Hadrian and his father, Danbury

BLINDEN: Quartermaster's mate on the *Emerald Storm*, died at sea

BLOOD WEEK: Time of the year when stock that won't be able to be fed during the winter is butchered

BLYTHIN CASTLE: Castle in Alburn

BOATSWAIN: Petty officer on a ship who controls the work of other seamen

BOCANT: Family who built a lucrative industry from pork, second-wealthiest merchants in Colnora

BOTHWICKS: Family of peasant farmers of Dahlgren, father: Russell, mother: Lena

BRAGA, PERCY: Former Archduke and Lord Chancellor of Melengar, expert swordsman, uncle-in-law to Alric and Arista, killed by Count Pickering, commissioned the murder of Amrath

BRAND: Street urchin, reputed to have killed a kid in a fight to win a tunic, nickname: Brand the Bold

BRECKTON: Sir Breckton Belstrad, son of Lord Belstrad, brother of Wesley, commander of the Northern Imperial Army, knight of Chadwick, considered by many to be the best knight of Avryn

*BRIDEETH*: Elven swear word, highest insult

*BRIGHT STAR*: Ship sunk by Dacca

BRISTOL BENNET: Boatswain on the *Emerald Storm*, died at sea

BRODRIC ESSENDON: Founder of the Essendon dynasty

BUCKET MAN: Term for assassin in the Black Diamond thieves' guild

BULARD, ANTUN: See Antun Bulard

BURANDU: \bur-and-dew\ Lord of the Tenkin village of Oudorro

BYRNIE: Long (usually sleeveless) tunic of chain mail formerly worn as defensive armor

CALIAN: \cal-lay-in\ Pertaining to the nation of Calis

CALIANS: Residents of the nation of Calis, with dark skin tone and almond-shaped eyes

"CALIDE PORTMORE": Folk song often sung while drinking

CALIS: \cal-lay\ Southern- and easternmost of the four nations of Apeladorn, considered exotic, in constant conflict with the Ba Ran Ghazel

CAPSTAN: Spoked wheel on a ship that turns to raise the anchor

CARAT: Young member of Black Diamond thieves' guild

CARREL: Small individual study area in a library

CASWELL: Family of peasant farmers from Dahlgren

CENZAR: \sen-zhar\ Wizards of the Old Novronian Empire

CENZARIUM: Home of the Cenzar Council in Percepliquis

CHAMBERLAIN: Someone who manages the household of a king or nobleman

CHANFRON: A piece of plate armor used to protect a horse's head

CODE OF CHIVALRY: Eight virtues each knight should aspire to

COLNORA: \call-nor-ah\ Largest, wealthiest city in Avryn, merchant-based city, grew from a rest stop at a central crossroads of various major trade routes

CONSTANCE, LADY: Noblewoman, fifth imperial secretary to Empress Modina

CORA: Dairymaid at the imperial palace

CORNELIUS DELUR: Rich businessman, rumored to finance Nationalists and involved in illegal trade good markets, father of Cosmos

COSMOS SEBASTIAN DELUR: Son of Cornelius, also known as the Jewel, head of the Black Diamond thieves' guild

COXSWAIN: Helmsman of a racing ship

CRANSTON: Professor at Sheridan University, tried and burned for heresy

CRIMSON HAND: Thieves' guild operating out of Melengar

*THE CROWN CONSPIRACY*: Play reputed to be based on the murder of King Amrath, follows the exploits of two thieves and the Prince of Melengar

CROWN TOWER: Home of the Patriarch and center of the Nyphron Church

CUTTER: Moniker used by Merrick Marius when a member of the Black Diamond thieves' guild

DACCA: A fierce seafaring people who live on the island of Dacca, south of Delgos

DAGASTAN: Major and easternmost trade port of Calis

DAHLGREN: \dall-grin\ Remote village on the bank of the Nidwalden River, site of Gilarabrywn attack

DANBURY BLACKWATER: Father of Hadrian

DANTHEN: Woodsman from Dahlgren

DAREF, LORD: Noble of Warric, associate of Albert Winslow

DARIUS SERET: Founder of the Seret Knights

DAVENS: Squire who Arista had a youthful crush on

DAVIS: Crew member of the *Emerald Storm*, died at sea

DEACON TOMAS: Priest of Dahlgren, witnessed destruction of Gilarabrywn, proclaimed Thrace Wood as the Heir of Novron

DEFOE, BERNIE: See Bernie Defoe

DEGAN GAUNT: Leader of the Nationalists, sister of Miranda, Heir of Novron, imprisoned in Aquesta by Imperialists

DeLancy, Gwen: Calian prostitute and proprietor of Medford House and The Rose and Thorn Tavern in Medford, girlfriend of Royce Melborn

Delano DeWitt: Alias used by Wyatt Deminthal when he framed Hadrian and Royce for King Amrath's death

Delgos: One of the four nations of Apeladorn. The only republic in a world of monarchies, Delgos revolted against the Steward's Empire after Glenmorgan III was murdered and after surviving an attack by the Ba Ran Ghazel with no aid from the empire

DeLorkan, Duke: Nobleman from Calis

DeLunden, Bishop: Head of the Nyphron Church in Aquesta

DeLur: Family of wealthy merchants, father: Cornelius, son: Cosmos

Deminthal, Wyatt: Quartermaster and helmsman of the *Emerald Storm*, father of Allie, blackmailed by Merrick Marius to ensure Riyria disabled defenses of Drumindor

Denek Pickering: Youngest son of Count Pickering

Denny: Worker at The Rose and Thorn

Derin: Clan of dwarves

Dermont, Lord: General of the Southern Imperial Army, killed in the Battle of Ratibor

Derning, Jacob: Maintop captain on the *Emerald Storm*, member of Black Diamond, rescued Royce and Hadrian from Tur Del Fur jail

Destrier: Unusually large warhorse used by knights

Devon: Monk of Tarin Vale, taught Amilia to read and write

DeWitt, Delano: See Delano DeWitt

Digby: Guard at Essendon Castle

Dilladrum: Erbonese guide, hired to take crew of the *Emerald Storm* to the Palace of the Four Winds, killed during escape

DIME: Crew member of the *Emerald Storm*, died at sea

DIOYLION: \die-e-leon\ *The Accumulated Letters of Dioylion*, a very rare scroll

DIXON TAFT: Bartender and manager of The Rose and Thorn Tavern, lost an arm in the Battle of Medford

DOBBS: Servant in the employ of Merrick Marius

DOGGER: Type of small ship, often used by Tenkin

DOVIN THRANIC: Sentinel of the Nyphron Church, half-elf, hired to find the Horn of Gylindora

DR. GERAND: Physician in Ratibor

DR. LEVY: Physician, hired to find the Horn of Gylindora

DRASH: Ghazel chieftain, arena fighter, known as Drash of the Klune

DREW, EDGAR: Old seaman

DROME: God of the dwarves

DRONDIL FIELDS: Count Pickering's castle, once the fortress of Brodric Essendon, the original seat of power in Melengar

DRUMINDOR: Dwarven-built fortress located at the entrance to Terlando Bay in Tur Del Fur, can utilize lava from the nearby volcano for its defense, overrun by goblins after the defenses were disabled by Royce and Hadrian

DRUNDEL: Peasant family from Dahlgren consisting of Mae, Went, Davie, and Firth

DUBRION ASH: Author of *The Forgotten Race*, a history of the dwarves

DULNAR, SIR: Knight who lost a hand in the Wintertide games

DUNLAP, PAUL: Former carriage driver of King Urith, dead

DUNMORE: Youngest and least sophisticated kingdom of Avryn, ruled by King Roswort, member of the New Empire

DUNSTAN: Baker in Hintindar, childhood friend of Hadrian, married to Arbor

DUR GURON: Easternmost portion of Calis

DURBO: Tenkin dwelling

DUSTER: Moniker used by Royce while a member of the Black Diamond

ECTON, SIR: Chief knight of Count Pickering, military general of Melengar

EDGAR DREW: See Drew, Edgar

EDITH MON: Head maid in charge of the scullery and chamber servants in the imperial palace

EDMUND HALL: Professor of geometry at Sheridan University, found Percepliquis, declared a heretic by the Nyphron Church, imprisoned in the Crown Tower, husband of Sadie, father of Ebot and Dram

EDMUND HALL'S JOURNAL: Heretical document of journey into Percepliquis, one of the treasures kept in the Crown Tower

EILYWIN: Tribe of elves, builders

ELAN: The world

ELBRIGHT: Street urchin, leader of a small band consisting of Mince, Brand, and Kine, nickname: the Old Man

ELDEN: Large man, friend of Wyatt Deminthal

ELGAR, SIR: Knight of Galeannon, friend of Gilbert and Murthas

ELINYA: Esrahaddon's lover

ELLA: Cook at Drondil Fields

ELLA: Alias used by Arista while masquerading as a maid in the imperial palace

ELLIS FAR: Melengarian ship used to send envoy to Nationalists, captured by Imperialists

ELQUIN: Masterwork of Orintine Fallon, poet

ELVEN: Pertaining to elves

*EMERALD STORM*: Ship of the New Empire, captained by Seward

EMERY DORN: Young revolutionary from Ratibor, in love with Arista, killed in the Battle of Ratibor

EMPRESS MODINA: Previously Thrace Wood of Dahlgren, locked in a near catatonic state after loss of family and village, appointed empress of the New Empire

ENDEN, SIR: Knight of Chadwick, considered second best to Breckton, killed in Dahlgren

ENILD, BARON: \in-illed\ Nobleman of Galien of Melengar

ERANDABON GILE: Panther of Dur Guron, Tenkin warlord, madman

ERBON: Region of Calis northwest from Mandalin

EREBUS: Father of the gods, also known as Kile when in human form

ERIVAN: \ear-ah-van\ Elven empire

ERLIC, SIR : A knight who survived the destruction of Dahlgren

ERMA EVERTON: Alias used by Arista while in Hintindar

ERVANON: \err-vah-non\ City in northern Ghent, seat of the Nyphron Church, once the capital of the Steward's Empire as established by Glenmorgan I

ESRAHADDON: \ez-rah-hod-in\ Wizard, former member of the Cenzar, convicted of destroying the Old Empire, sentenced to imprisonment, held in Gutaria, killed by Merrick

ESSENDON: \ez-in-don\ Royal family of Melengar

ESSENDON CASTLE: Home of the ruling monarchs of Melengar

ESTRAMNADON: \es-tram-nah-don\ Believed to be the capital or at least a very sacred place in the Erivan Empire

ESTRENDOR: \es-tren-door\ The northern wastes

ETCHER: Member of the Black Diamond thieves' guild, traitor who turns Arista over to seret

ETHELRED, LANIS: \eth-el-red\ Former King of Warric, co-regent of the New Empire, Imperialist

EVERTON: Alias used by Arista, Hadrian, and later Royce

EVERTON, CAPTAIN: Commander of Aquesta's southern gate

EVLIN: City along the banks of the Bernum River

EXETER: Family name of the rulers of Hanlin

FALINA BROCKTON: Real name of Emerald, waitress at The Rose and Thorn

FALLON MIRE: City where Merton prevented the spread of a terrible disease

FALLON, ORINTINE: Poet who wrote about how patterns in nature relate to patterns in life

FALL-THE-WALL: Children's game

FALQUIN: Professor at Sheridan University

FAN IRLANU: Visionary of Oudorro, seer, fortune-teller, predicted Royce's future, including the death of someone near to him

FANEN PICKERING: \fan-in\ Middle son of Count Pickering, killed by Luis Guy

FAQUIN: Inept magician who uses alchemy rather than channeling the Art

FARILANE, PRINCESS: Wrote *Migration of Peoples*

FAULD, THE ORDER OF: \fall-ed\ A post-imperial order of knights dedicated to preserving the skill and discipline of the Teshlor Knights

FENITILIAN: Monk of Maribor, made warm shoes

FERROL: God of the elves

*FESTIVIOUS FOUNDEREIONUS*: Celebration to commemorate the founding of Percepliquis

FINILESS: Noted author

FINISHER: Stealthy Ghazel fighter

FINLIN, ETHAN: Member of the Black Diamond, stores smuggled goods, owns a windmill

FLETCHER: Maker of arrows

FORECASTLE: Raised portion in the bow of a ship containing living quarters of senior crew members

FORREST: Ratibor citizen with fighting experience, son of a silversmith

FREDA, QUEEN: Queen of Dunmore, wife of Roswort

FREDRICK, KING: Ruler of Galeannon, husband of Josephine

GAFTON: Imperial admiral

GALEANNON: \gale-e-an-on\ A kingdom of Avryn, ruled by Fredrick and Josephine, member of the New Empire

GALENTI: \ga-lehn'-tay\ Calian nickname attributed to Hadrian, Calian word for *killer*

GALEWYR RIVER: \gale-wahar\ Marks the southern border of Melengar and the northern border of Warric and reaches the sea near the fishing village of Roe

GALIEN: \gal-e-in\ Former archbishop of the Nyphron Church

GALILIN: \gal-ah-lin\ Province of Melengar ruled by Count Pickering

GARNACHE: Loose outer garment

GAUNT, DEGAN: See Degan Gaunt

GEMKEY: Gem that opens a gemlock

GEMLOCK: Dwarven invention that seals a container, can be opened only with a precious gem of the right type and cut

GENEVIEVE HARGRAVE: Duchess of Rochelle, wife of Leopold, patron of Riyria, nickname: Genny

GENTRY SQUARE: Affluent district of Melengar

GERALD BANIFF: Primary bodyguard of Empress Modina, family friend of the Belstrads

GERTY: Midwife in Hintindar who delivered Hadrian, married to Abelard

GHAZEL: \gehz-ell\ Ba Ran Ghazel, the dwarven name for goblins, literally: sea goblins

GHAZEL SEA: Southern body of water east of the Sharon Sea

Ghent: Ecclesiastical holding of the Nyphron Church, member of the New Empire

Gilarabrywn: \gill-lar-ah-bren\ Elven beast of war; once escaped Avempartha, destroyed the village of Dahlgren, and was killed by Thrace

Gilbert, Sir: Knight of Maranon, friend of Murthas and Elgar

Gill: Sentry in the Nationalist Army

Ginlin: \gin-lin\ A Monk of Maribor, winemaker, refused to touch a knife

Glamrendor: \glam-ren-door\ Capital of Dunmore

Glenmorgan: 326 years after the fall of the Novronian Empire, this native of Ghent reunited the four nations of Apeladorn; founder of Sheridan University; creator of the great north-south road; builder of the Ervanon palace (of which only the Crown Tower remains)

Glenmorgan II: Son of Glenmorgan. When his father died young, the new and inexperienced emperor relied on church officials to assist him in managing his empire. They in turn took the opportunity to manipulate the emperor into granting sweeping powers to the church and nobles loyal to the church. These leaders opposed defending Delgos against the invading Ba Ran Ghazel in Calis and the Dacca in Delgos, arguing the threat would increase dependency on the empire.

Glenmorgan III: Grandson of Glenmorgan. Shortly after assuming the stewardship, he attempted to reassert control over the realm his grandfather had created by leading an army against the invading Ghazel that had reached southeastern Avryn. He defeated the Ghazel at the First Battle of Vilan Hills and announced plans to ride to the aid of Tur Del Fur. Fearing his rise in power, in the sixth year of his reign, his nobles betrayed and imprisoned him in Blythin Castle. Jealous of his popularity and growing strength, and resentful of his policy of stripping the nobles and clergy of their power, the church charged him with heresy. He was found guilty and executed. This began the rapid collapse of what many called the Steward's Empire. The church later claimed the nobles had tricked them, and condemned many, most of whom reputedly ended their lives badly.

GLOUSTON: Province of northern Warric bordering on the Galewyr River, ruled by the marquis Lanaklin, invaded and taken over by the New Empire

GNOME, THE: Nickname of The Laughing Gnome Tavern

GRADY: Seaman on the *Emerald Storm*, died in the arena fight in the Palace of the Four Winds

GRAND MAR: Main avenue of Percepliquis, leads to the imperial palace

GRAVIN DENT, SIR: Well-respected knight from Delgos

GRAVIS: Dwarf who sabotaged Drumindor

GREAT SWORD: Long sword designed to be held with both hands

GREEN: Lieutenant on the *Emerald Storm*, died at sea

GREIG: Carpenter aboard the *Emerald Storm*, one of the few survivors

GRELAD, JERISH: Teshlor Knight, first Guardian of the Heir, protector of Nevrik

GRIBBON: The flag of Mandalin, Calis

GRIGOLES: \gry-holes\ Author of *Grigoles Treatise on Imperial Common Law*

GRIMBALD: Blacksmith in Hintindar, had taken over the shop from Danbury Blackwater

GRONBACH: Dwarf, fairy tale villain

GRUMON, MASON: \grum-on\ Blacksmith in Medford, worked for Riyria, died in the Battle of Medford

GUARDIAN OF THE HEIR: Teshlor, protector of the Heir of Novron

GUNGUAN: Vintu pack ponies

GUR EM: Thickest part of the jungle in Calis, as it butts up against the eastern tip of Calis

GUTARIA: \goo-tar-ah\ Secret Nyphron prison, designed to hold Esrahaddon

GUY, LUIS: Sentinel of the Nyphron Church, killed Fanen Pickering, son of Evone and Jarred

GWEN DELANCY: See DeLancy, Gwen

GWYDRY: Tribe of elves, farmers

HADDY: Childhood nickname of Hadrian

HADRIAN BLACKWATER: Mercenary, one-half of Riyria, Guardian of the Heir, known throughout Calis as Galenti, renowned arena fighter

HALBERD: Two-handed pole used as a weapon

HANDEL: Master at Sheridan University, originally from Roe, proponent to have Delgos's republic officially recognized

HARBERT: Tailor in Hintindar, husband of Hester

*HARBINGER*: Ship used by Dovin Thranic, Antun Bulard, Bernie Defoe, and Dr. Levy

HARKON, ABBOT: Abbot of the rebuilt Winds Abbey

HARTENFORD: Author of *Genealogy of Warric Monarchs*

HARVEST MOON: The full moon nearest the fall equinox

HEIR OF NOVRON: Direct descendant of demigod Novron, destined to rule all of Avryn

HELDABERRY: Wild-growing fruit often used to make wine

HERCLOR MATH: Dwarven mason

HESLON: A Monk of Maribor, great cook

HESTLE: Family name of rulers of Bernum

HIGHCOURT FIELDS: Once the site of the supreme noble judicial court of law in Avryn, location of the Wintertide games

HILFRED, REUBEN: Bodyguard and lover of Arista, severely burned in Dahlgren, killed in Aquesta while trying to free Degan Gaunt

HILL DISTRICT: Affluent neighborhood in Colnora

HILL McDAVIN: Author of books on maritime commerce

HIMBOLT, BARON: Nobleman of Melengar

HINGARA: Calian guide, died in the jungles of Gur Em

HINKLE, BROTHER: Monk who cleans the stable in the new Winds Abbey

HINTINDAR: Small manorial village in Rhenydd, home of Hadrian Blackwater

HIVENLYN: Ryn's horse, name means *unexpected gift* in elvish

HOBBIE: Stableboy in Hintindar

HORN OF DELGOS: Landmark used by sailors to determine the southernmost tip of Delgos

HORN OF GYLINDORA: Item Esrahaddon indicates is buried in Percepliquis; Dovin Thranic, Dr. Levy, Bernie Defoe, and Antun Bulard were hired to retrieve it

HOUSE, THE: Nickname used for Medford House

HOVEL, THE: Nickname of snow fort used by Renwick, Mince, Elbright, Brand, and Kine

HOYTE: Onetime First Officer of the Black Diamond, set up Royce to kill Jade, sent Royce to Manzant Prison, killed by Royce

IBIS THINLY: Head cook at the imperial palace

IMP: Slang for *Imperialist*

IMPERIAL PALACE: Seat of power of the New Empire, originally named Warric Castle

IMPERIAL SECRETARY: Caretaker of Empress Modina

IMPERIALISTS: Political party that desires to unite all the kingdoms of men under a single leader who is the direct descendant of the demigod Novron

INSTARYA: Tribe of elves, warriors

IRAWONDONA, LORD: Elf, member of the hunter tribe

JACOB DERNING: See Derning, Jacob

JADE: Assassin in the Black Diamond, girlfriend of Merrick, mistakenly killed by Royce

JASPER: Rat in the imperial palace dungeons

JENKINS: Merrick Marius's head servant

JENKINS TALBERT: Squire in Tarin Vale

JEREMY: Guard at Essendon Castle

JERISH GRELAD: See Grelad, Jerish

JERL, LORD: Nobleman, neighbor of the Pickerings, known for his prizewinning hunting dogs

JERVIS, SIR: Killed during a Wintertide joust with the Earl of Harborn

JEWEL, THE: Head of the international Black Diamond thieves' guild, also known as Cosmos DeLur

JIMMY: Tavern worker at The Laughing Gnome

JOQDAN: \jok-dan\ Warlord of the Tenkin village of Oudorro

JOSEPHINE, QUEEN: Queen of Galeannon, married to Fredrick

JULIAN TEMPEST: Elderly chamberlain of the kingdom of Melengar

*Kaz*: Calian term for anyone with mixed elven and human blood

KENDELL, EARL: Nobleman of Melengar, loyal to Alric Essendon

KENG: Form of currency used by the Old Empire

KHAROLL: Long dagger

KILE: Name used by Erebus when sent to Elan, performs good deeds in the form of a man

KILNAR: City in the south of Rhenydd

KINE: Youngest of Elbright's street urchins, best friend of Mince

KNOB: Baker at the imperial palace

KRINDEL: Prelate of the Nyphron Church and historian

KRIS DAGGER: Weapon with a wavy blade, sometimes used in magic rituals

"LADIES OF ENGENALL": Lively popular tune played on a fiddle

LAMBERT, IGNATIUS: Chancellor of Sheridan University

LANAKLIN: Once ruling family of Glouston, in exile in Melengar, opposes the New Empire

LANDONER: Professor at Sheridan University, tried and burned for heresy

LANGDON BRIDGE: Swan-decorated bridge in the warehouse district of Colnora that spans the Bernum River

LANKSTEER: Capital city of the Lordium kingdom of Trent

LAUGHING GNOME, THE: Inn in Ratibor, run by Ayers

LAVEN: Citizen of Ratibor, turned rebel Emery Dorn in to the Imperialists

LEIF: Butcher and assistant cook at the imperial palace

LENA BOTHWICK: Wife of Russell, mother of Tad, from a poor family in Dahlgren

LENARE PICKERING: Daughter of Count Pickering and Belinda, sister of Mauvin, Fanen, and Denek

LEOPOLD HARGRAVE, DUKE: Duke of Rochelle, husband of Genevieve, patron of Riyria, nickname: Leo

LINDER, BARON: Nobleman killed by Gilbert in a Wintertide joust

LINGARD: Capital city of Relison, kingdom of Trent

LINROY, DILLNARD: Royal financier of Melengar

LIVET GLIM: Port controller at Tur Del Fur

LONGWOOD: Forest in Melengar

LOTHOMAD THE BALD, KING: Ruler of Lordium, Trent, expanded territory following the collapse of the Steward's Reign, pushing south through Ghent into Melengar, where Brodric Essendon defeated him in the Battle of Drondil Fields in 2545

LOUDEN, SIR: One of several knights defeated by Sir Hadrian in the Wintertide joust

LOWER QUARTER: Impoverished section of the city of Melengar

LOZENGE SHIELD: Shield decorated with alternating colors of diamonds

LUGGER: Small fishing boat rigged with one or more lugsails

LUIS GUY: See Guy, Luis

LURET: Imperial envoy to Hintindar, arrested Royce and Hadrian

MAE, LADY: Love interest of Albert Winslow

MAGNUS: Dwarf, killed King Amrath, sabotaged Arista's tower, discovered entry into Avempartha, rebuilding the Winds Abbey, obsessed with Royce's dagger

MALEVOLENT: Sir Hadrian's horse

MALNESS, SIR: Former knight to squire Renwick

MANDALIN: \man-dah-lynn\ Capital of Calis

MANZANT: \man-zahnt\ Infamous prison and salt mine, located in Manzar, Maranon, Royce Melborn is only prisoner to have been released from it

MARANON: \mar-ah-non\ Kingdom in Avryn, ruled by Vincent and Regina, member of the New Empire, rich in farmland

MARES CATHEDRAL: Center of the Nyphron Church in Melengar, formerly run by Bishop Saldur

MARIBOR: \mar-eh-bore\ God of men

MARIUS, MERRICK: Former member of the Black Diamond, alias: Cutter, master thief and assassin, former best friend of Royce, known for his strategic thinking, boyfriend of Jade, murderer of Esrahaddon, planned destruction of Tur Del Fur, blackmailed Wyatt to betray Royce and Hadrian

MAUVIN PICKERING: \maw-vin\ Eldest of Count Pickering's sons, friends since childhood with Essendon royal family, bodyguard to King Alric

MAWYNDULË: A powerful wizard

McDERN, DILLON: Blacksmith of Dahlgren

MEDFORD: Capital of Melengar

MEDFORD HOUSE: Brothel run by Gwen DeLancy and attached to The Rose and Thorn

MELENGAR: \mel-in-gar\ Kingdom in Avryn ruled by the Essendon royal family, the only Avryn kingdom independent of the New Empire

MELENGARIANS: Residents of Melengar

MELISSA: Head servant of Arista, nickname Missy

MERCS: Mercenaries

MERCY: Young girl under the care of Arcadius Latimer and Miranda Gaunt

MERLON: Solid section between two crenels in a crenellated battlement

MERRICK MARIUS: See Marius, Merrick

MERTON: Monsignor of Ghent, savior of Fallon Mire, speaks aloud to Novron

MESSKID: Container used to transport meals aboard a ship, resembles a bucket

MILBOROUGH: Melengarian Baron, died in battle

MILFORD: Sergeant in the Nationalist army

MILLIE: Formerly Hadrian's horse, died in Dahlgren

MINCE: Orphan living on the streets of Aquesta, best friend to Kine

*MIR*: Person with both elven and human blood

MIRALYITH: Tribe of elves, mages

MIRANDA GAUNT: Sister of Degan Gaunt, helping Arcadias raise Mercy

MIZZENMAST: Third mast from the bow in a vessel having three or more masts

MODINA: See Empress Modina

MON, EDITH: See Edith Mon

MONTEMORCEY: \mont-eh-more-ah-sea\ Excellent wine imported through the Vandon Spice Company

MOTTE: A man-made hill

MOUSE: Royce's horse, named by Thrace, gray mare

MR. RINGS: Baby raccoon, pet of Mercy

MURDERESS: Lady Genevieve's prize hunting bird

MURIEL: Goddess of nature, daughter of Erebus, mother of Uberlin

MURTHAS, SIR: Knight of Alburn, son of the Earl of Fentin, friend of Gilbert and Elgar

MYRON LANAKLIN: Sheltered Monk of Maribor, indelible memory, son of Victor, brother of Alenda

MYSTIC: Name of Arista's horse when traveling to Ratibor

NAREION: \nare-e-on\ Last emperor of the Novronian Empire, father of Nevrik

NARON: Heir of Novron who died in Ratibor in 2992

NATIONALISTS: Political party led by Degan Gaunt that desires rule by the will of the people

NATS: Nickname of the Nationalists

NEST, THE: Nickname of both the Rat's Nest, home to the Ratibor Black Diamond thieves, and the adopted home of four street orphans in Aquesta

NEVRIK: \nehv-rick\ Son of Nareion, the heir who went into hiding, protected by Jerish Grelad, nickname Nary

NEW EMPIRE: Second empire uniting most of the kingdoms of man, ruled by Empress Modina, administered by co-regents Ethelred and Saldur

NIDWALDEN RIVER: Marks the eastern border of Avryn and the start of the Erivan realm

NILYNDD: Tribe of elves, crafters

NIMBUS: Tutor to the empress, assistant to the imperial secretary, originally from Vernes

NIPPER: Young servant assigned primarily to the kitchen of the imperial palace

NOVRON: Savior of mankind, demigod, son of Maribor, defeated the elven army in the Great Elven Wars, founder of the Novronian Empire, builder of Percepliquis, husband of Persephone

NOVRONIAN: \nov-ron-e-on\ Pertaining to Novron

NYPHRON CHURCH: The worshipers of Novron and Maribor

NYPHRONS: \nef-rons\ Devout members of the Nyphron Church

OBERDAZA: \oh-ber-daz-ah\ Tenkin or Ghazel witch doctor

OLD EMPIRE: Original united kingdoms of man, destroyed one thousand years in the past after the murder of Emperor Nareion

ORRIN FLATLY: Ratibor city scribe, assistant of Arista

OSGAR: Reeve of Hintindar

*OSTRIUM*: Tenkin communal hall where meals are served

OUDORRO: Friendly Tenkin Village in Calis

PALACE OF THE FOUR WINDS: Home of Erandabon Gile in Dur Guron

PARKER: Quartermaster and later commander of Nationalist army, killed in Battle of Ratibor

PARTHALOREN FALLS: \path-ah-lore-e-on\ The great cataracts on the Nidwalden near Avempartha

PATRIARCH: Head of the Nyphron Church, lives in the Crown Tower of Ervanon

PAULDRON: Piece of armor covering the shoulder

PERCEPLIQUIS: \per-sep-lah-kwiss\ Ancient city and capital of the Novronian Empire, named for the wife of Novron, destroyed and lost during the collapse of the Old Empire

PERCY BRAGA: See Braga, Percy

PERIN: Grocer from Ratibor

PERSEPHONE: Wife of Novron, Percepliquis was named after her

PICKERING: Noble family of Melengar and rulers of Galilin, Count Pickering is known to be the best swordsman in Avryn and believed to use a magic sword

PICKILERINON: Seadric, who shortened the family name to Pickering

PITH: Small-value coin of the Old Empire

PLANCHETTE: Footrest for a woman's sidesaddle

PLESIEANTIC INCANTATION: \plass-e-an-tic\ A method used in the Art to draw power from nature

POE: Cook's assistant aboard the *Emerald Storm*, Merrick's assistant

POLISH: Head of the Black Diamond thieves' guild in Ratibor

PRALEON GUARDS: \pray-lee-on\ Bodyguards to the king in Ratibor

PRICE: First Officer of the Black Diamond thieves' guild

PRINCESS: Name of Arista's horse on the ride to Percepliquis

QUARTZ: Member of the Ratibor thieves' guild

QUEEN'S GAMBIT: Series of moves used to open a chess game

QUINTAIN: Used in training for the joust; when hit, it will spin and can knock the rider off his saddle

RATIBOR: Capital of the kingdom of Rhenydd, home of Royce Melborn

RAT'S NEST, THE: Hideout of the Black Diamond thieves' guild in Ratibor

RED: Old elkhound, large dog frequently found in the kitchen of the imperial palace

REEVE: Official who supervises serfs and oversees the lands for a lord

REGAL FOX INN, THE: Least expensive tavern in the affluent Hill District in Colnora

REGENT: Someone who administers a kingdom during the absence or incapacity of the ruler

REGINA, QUEEN: Wife of Vincent, Queen of Maranon

RENDON, BARON: Nobleman of Melengar

RENIAN: \rhen-e-ahn\ Childhood friend of Myron the monk, died at a young age

RENKIN POOL: Citizen of Ratibor with fighting experience

RENQUIST: Commander of the Nationalist army, promoted to the position by Hadrian

RENTINUAL, TOBIS: History professor at Sheridan University, built a catapult to fight the Gilarabrywn

RENWICK: Imperial page, assigned to act as Sir Hadrian's squire

RHELACAN: \rell-ah-khan\ Great sword given to Novron by Maribor, forged by Drome, enchanted by Ferrol, used to defeat and subdue the elves

RHENYDD: \ren-yaed\ Poor kingdom of Avryn, ruled by King Urith, now part of the New Empire

RILAN VALLEY: Fertile land that separates Glouston and Chadwick

RIONILLION: \ri-on-ill-lon\ Name of the city that first stood on the site of Aquesta, destroyed during the civil wars that occurred after the fall of the Novronian Empire

RIYRIA: \rye-ear-ah\ Elvish for *two*, a team or a bond, name used to refer collectively to Royce Melborn and Hadrian Blackwater

RONDEL: Common type of stiff-bladed dagger with a round handgrip

ROSE AND THORN, THE: Tavern in Medford run by Gwen DeLancy, used as a base by Riyria

ROSWORT, KING: Ruler of Dunmore, husband of Freda

ROYALISTS: Political party that favors rule by independent monarchs

ROYCE MELBORN: Thief, one-half of Riyria, half-elf

RUDOLF, PRINCE: Son of King Armand, Prince of Alburn, brother to Beatrice and Hector

RUFUS, LORD: Ruthless northern warlord, intended emperor for the New Empire, killed by a Gilarabrywn in Dahlgren

RUFUS'S BANE: Name given to the Gilarabrywn slain by Thrace/Modina

RUPERT, KING: Unmarried king of Rhenydd

RUSSELL BOTHWICK: Farmer in Dahlgren, married to Lena, father of Tad

RYN: Half-elf who helped save Alric from Baron Trumbul

SALDUR, MAURICE: Former bishop of Medford, former friend and advisor to the Essendon family, co-regent of the New Empire, nickname: Sauly

SALIFAN: \sal-eh-fan\ Fragrant wild plant used in incense

SALTY MACKEREL, THE: Tavern in the shipping district of Aquesta

*SARAP*: Meeting place or talking place in the Tenkin language

SAULY: Nickname of Maurice Saldur, used by those closest to him

SENON UPLAND: Highland plateau overlooking Chadwick

SENTINEL: Inquisitor generals of the Nyphron Church, charged with rooting out heresy and finding the lost Heir of Novron

SERET: \sir-ett\ The Knights of Nyphron. The military arm of the church, first formed by Lord Darius Seret, commanded by sentinels

SET: Ratibor member of the Black Diamond thieves' guild

SEWARD: Captain of the *Emerald Storm*, died at sea

SHARON SEA: Southern body of water west of the Ghazel Sea

SHERIDAN UNIVERSITY: Prestigious institution of learning, located in Ghent, Arista studied there

SHIP'S MASTER: Highest non-officer, in charge of running the daily workings of the ship

*SHIRLUM-KATH*: Small parasitic worm found in Calis, can infect untreated wounds

SIWARD: Bailiff of Hintindar

SKILLYGALEE: \skil`li-ga-lee\ Oatmeal porridge served to sailors for breakfast

SPADONE: Long two-handed sword with a tapering blade and an extended flange ahead of the hilt allowing for an extended variety of fighting maneuvers. Due to the length of the handgrip and the flange, which provides its own barbed hilt, the sword provides a number of additional hand placements, permitting the sword to be used similarly to a quarterstaff and as a powerful cleaving weapon. The spadone is the traditional weapon of a skilled knight.

STANLEY, EARL FRANCIS: Nobleman of Harborn, killed in a Wintertide joust with Sir Jervis

STAUL: Tenkin warrior aboard the *Emerald Storm*, hired to find the Horn of Gylindora, killed by Royce in jungles of Calis

SUMMERSRULE: Popular midsummer holiday, celebrated with picnics, dances, feasts, and jousting tournaments

TABARD: Tunic worn over armor, usually emblazoned with a coat of arms

TAD BOTHWICK: Son of Lena and Russell, from a poor farming family of Dahlgren

TALBERT, BISHOP: Head of the Nyphron Church in Ratibor

TARIN VALE: Hometown of Amilia

TARTANE: Small ship used for fishing and coastal trading; single mast, large sail

TEK'CHIN: One of the fighting disciplines of the Teshlor Knights, preserved by the Knights of the Fauld, handed down to the Pickerings

TEMPLE: Ship's master of the *Emerald Storm*, second in command

TENENT: The most common form of semi-standard international currency. Coins of gold, silver, and copper stamped with the likeness of the king of the realm where the coin was minted

TENKIN: Community of humans living in the manner of Ghazel and suspected of having Ghazel blood

TERLANDO BAY: Harbor of Tur Del Fur

TESHLOR: Legendary knights of the Novronian Empire, greatest warriors ever to have lived

HALL OF TESHLOR: Building in Percepliquis were Teshlors trained and lived

THEOREM ELDERSHIP: Secret society formed to protect the heir

THERON WOOD: Father of Thrace, farmer of Dahlgren, killed by the Gilarabrywn

THRACE WOOD: Daughter of Theron and Addie, name changed to Modina by the regents, crowned Empress of the New Empire, killed the Gilarabrywn in Dahlgren

THRANIC, DOVIN: See Dovin Thranic

TIBITH: Friend of Mince and Kine who died

TIGER OF MANDALIN: Moniker given to Hadrian while in Calis

TILINER: Superior side sword, used frequently by mercenaries in Avryn

TOLIN ESSENDON: Son of Brodric, moved the Melengar capital to Medford, built Essendon Castle, also known as Tolin the Great

TOPE ENTWISTLE: Northern scout, signaled the elven advance

TOPMEN: Members of a ship's crew who work high up in the rigging and sails

TORSONIC: Torque-producing, as in the cable used in crossbows

TRAMUS DAN: Guardian of Naron, later changed his name to Danbury Blackwater

TREMBLES: Fermented sweet drink made from flowers

TRENCHON: City bailiff of Ratibor

TRENT: Northern mountainous kingdoms not yet controlled by the New Empire

TRILON: Small, fast bow used by Ghazel

TRUMBUL, BARON: Mercenary, hired by Percy Braga to kill Prince Alric

TULAN: Tropical plant, found in southeastern Calis, used in religious ceremonies, leaves are dried and burned as offerings to the god Uberlin, smoke of the leaves produces visions when inhaled

Tur: Legendary village believed to have once been in Delgos, site of the first recorded visit of Kile, mythical source of great weapons

Tur Del Fur: Coastal city in Delgos, on Terlando Bay, originally built by dwarves, was overrun by goblins when the city's volcanic defenses were disabled by Royce and Hadrian

Uberlin: God of the Dacca and the Ghazel, son of Erebus and his daughter, Muriel

*Uli Vermar*: Obscure reference used by Esrahaddon

Ulurium Fountain: Great sculptured fountain at the end of the Grand Mar, before the palace in Percepliquis

Umalyn: Tribe of elves, priests of Ferrol

Urith, King: Former ruler of Ratibor, died in a fire

Urlineus: Last of the Novronian Empire cities to fall, located in eastern Calis, constantly attacked by Ghazel. After its collapse, it became the gateway for the Ghazel into Calis

Uzla Bar: Ghazel chieftain, challenging Erandabon Gile for control of Ghazel

Valin, Lord: Elderly knight of Melengar, known for his valor and courage, no strategic skills

Vandon: Port city of Delgos, home to the Vandon Spice Company, pirate haven, grew into a legitimate business center when Delgos became a republic

Vault of Days: Large hall outside Novron's tomb

Vella: Kitchen servant in the imperial palace

Venden pox: Poison, impervious to magic remedies

Venlin: Patriarch of the Nyphron Church during the fall of the Novronian Empire

Vernes: Port city at the mouth of the Bernum River

VIGAN: Sheriff of Ratibor

VILLEIN: Person who is bound to the land and owned by the feudal lord

VINCE EVERTON: Alias used by Royce Melborn while in Hintindar

VINCE GRIFFIN: Founder of Dahlgren Village

VINCENT, KING: Ruler of Maranon, married to Queen Regina

VINTU: Native tribe of Calis

WANDERING DEACON OF DAHLGREN: Name that refers to Deacon Tomas

WARRIC: A kingdom of Avryn, once ruled by Ethelred, now part of the New Empire

WATCH OFFICER: Officer of the watch, in charge during a particular shift, responsible for everything that transpires during this time

WESBADEN: Major trade port city of Calis

WESLEY: Son of Lord Belstrad, brother of Sir Breckton, junior midshipman on the *Emerald Storm*, killed in the arena fight in the Palace of the Four Winds

WESTBANK: Newly formed province of Dunmore

WESTERLINS: Unknown frontier to the west

WHERRY: Light rowboat, used for racing or transporting goods and passengers on inland waters and harbors

WICEND: \why-send\ Farmer in Melengar, name of the ford that crosses the Galewyr into Glouston

WIDLEY: Professor at Sheridan University, tried and burned for heresy

WILBUR: Armor smith in Aquesta

WILFRED: Carter in Hintindar

WINDS ABBEY: Monastery of the Monks of Maribor, rebuilt by Myron Lanaklin with the help of Magnus the dwarf after being burned

WINSLOW, ALBERT: See Albert Winslow

WINTERTIDE: Chief holiday, held in midwinter, celebrated with feasts and games of skill

WITCH OF MELENGAR: Derogatory title attributed to Arista

WYATT DEMINTHAL: See Deminthal, Wyatt

WYLIN: \why-lynn\ Master-at-arms at Essendon Castle

WYMAR, MARQUIS: Nobleman of Melengar, member of Alric's council

YOLRIC: Teacher of Esrahaddon

ZEPHYR, BROTHER: Monk at rebuilt Winds Abbey, illustrator

ZULRON: Deformed *oberdaza* of Oudorro

# extras

www.orbitbooks.net

# about the author

After finding a manual typewriter in the basement of a friend's house, **Michael J. Sullivan** inserted a blank piece of paper and typed *It was a dark and stormy night, and a shot rang out*. He was just eight. Still, the desire to fill the blank page and see where the keys would take him next wouldn't let go. As an adult, Michael spent ten years developing his craft by reading and studying authors such as Stephen King, Ayn Rand, and John Steinbeck, to name just a few. He wrote ten novels, and after finding no traction in publishing, he quit, vowing never to write creatively again.

Michael discovered forever is a very long time and ended his writing hiatus ten years later. The itch returned when he decided to write books for his then thirteen-year-old daughter, who was struggling in school because of dyslexia. Intrigued by the idea of a series with an overarching story line, yet told through individual, self-contained episodes, he created the Riyria Revelations. He wrote the series with no intention of publishing it. After presenting his book in manuscript form to his daughter, she declared that it had to be a "real book," in order for her to be able to read it.

So began his second adventure on the road to publication, which included drafting his wife to be his business manager, signing with a small independent press, and creating a publishing company. He sold more than sixty thousand books as a self-published author and leveraged this success to achieve mainstream publication through Orbit (the fantasy imprint of Hachette Book Group) as well as foreign translation rights including French, Spanish, Russian, German, Polish, and Czech.

Born in Detroit, Michigan, Michael presently lives in Fair-fax, Virginia, with his wife and three children. He continues to fill the blank pages with three projects under development: a modern fantasy, which explores the relationship between good and evil; a literary fiction piece, profiling a man's descent into madness; and a medieval fantasy, which will be prequel to his best-selling Riyria Revelations series.

Find out more about Michael J. Sullivan and other Orbit authors by registering for the free monthly newsletter at www.orbitbooks.net

**if you enjoyed**
**HEIR OF NOVRON**

look out for

# SEVEN PRINCES

by

## John R. Fultz

1

## City of Men and Giants

In the twenty-sixth year of his reign madness came to the King of New Udurum. It did not fall upon him like a flood, but grew like a creeping fungus in the hollows of his mind. At first he hid the madness from his Queen, his children, and his subjects, but eventually he could no longer steady his shaking hands or hold the gaze of his advisors during council.

Udurum was a city of both Men and Giants. The power of

King Vod had fostered an era of peace between the two races for almost three decades. Vod himself was both Man *and* Giant, and therefore the city's perfect monarch. He was born as a Giant, grew into a sorcerer, and became a man to marry a human girl. He slew Omagh the Serpent-Father and rebuilt the fallen city of Giant-kind. Now, twenty-five years after he forged a path through the mountains and began the reconstruction of New Udurum, his children were grown and he felt the call of an old curse. This was the source of his madness.

The children of King Vod and Queen Shaira were neither Giant nor human, but a new breed all their own. His first son Fangodrel was pale of skin, with sable hair and the anguished soul of a poet. These were altogether human qualities. His second and third sons likewise stood no taller than average Men, but they carried the strength of Giants in their modest frames, and their skins were the color of tempered bronze. These were Tadarus and Vireon, whom many called his "true sons". His daughter, youngest of the brood, was named Sharadza. She took after Queen Shaira, almost a mirror image of her mother, yet in her fifteenth year was already as tall as her brothers.

When Vod began ignoring his royal duties, his court began to grumble. Both Men and Giants feared his dissolution as an effective monarch. His uncle, the Giant called Fangodrim the Gray, tried to quell the fears of the court as best he could. But even he knew that Vod's rule sat in peril.

When the chill of early fall began to invade the warmth of late summer, Vod called for his children. "Bring them all before me," he told Fangodrim. A cadre of servants ran along the gigantic corridors of the palace in search of Vod's offspring.

Sharadza sat beneath the spreading arms of a great oak, listening to the Storyteller. The leaves had turned from green to orange and red; the rest of the courtyard's lush foliage was following suit. All the colors of the rainbow revealed themselves in this miniature version of the deep forest beyond the city walls. She was not permitted to exit the gates of New Udurum, not without the escort of her father, and he had not taken her into the forest since last season. Here, beneath trees grown safely within the palace grounds, she got a taste of those wild autumn colors, but in her heart she longed to walk among the colossal Uyga trees once again. The sun shone brightly through the turning leaves, but had lost its heat. The faintest breath of winter blew on the wind today. She sat on a stone bench as the old man finished his tale.

"So the God of the Sky had no choice but to recognize the Sea God as his equal. But still sometimes the Sky and Sea fight one another, and these battles Men call hurricanes. Doomed is the ship that ventures across the waves while these two deities are in dispute." The old man turned his head to better meet the eyes of the Princess. "Are you troubled, Majesty?" he asked.

Sharadza had been distracted by the varicolored leaves blown upon the wind. Beyond the tops of the palace walls, gray clouds poured across the sky. Soon the season of storms would be upon them, and then the crystal purity of winter. She did not mind that chilliest of seasons, but fall was her favorite. Each tree seemed hung with fabulous jewels. She smiled at the old man. It really was not fair to invite him here and pay less than full attention to his stories.

"Forgive me, Fellow," she said. "I am somewhat distracted these days."

The old man smiled. He ran a hand through his short white beard and nodded. "You are growing up," he sighed. "Mayhap you do not care for my stories any longer."

"No, don't think that," she said, taking his wrinkled hand in hers. "I treasure your visits, I really do. You know so many tales that I could never find in the library."

Old Fellow grinned. "Would you have another?" he asked.

Sharadza rose and walked about the oak tree, trailing her fingers along its rough bark. "Tell me what you know of my father," she said. "Tell me about Old Udurum. Before I was born."

"Ah," said the Storyteller. "You had better ask the King for stories of his youth. He would tell them better than I."

"But you know he won't talk to me," she said, blinking her green eyes at him. "I hardly see him . . . He's always in a meeting, or in council, or off brooding in the forest with his Giant cousins. He forgets I even exist."

"Nonsense, Majesty," said Fellow, rising from his stone seat. His back was slightly bent, and he supported himself with a tall, roughly carved cane. His robes were a patchwork of motley, as if he wore all the shades of the fall leaves, a myriad of colors spread across the fabric of his flowing raiment. Yet Fellow wore such colors all year round. He had very little taste when it came to matters of style. She had given him gifts of silken tunics, delicate scarves woven in Shar Dni, and other garments worthy of a nobleman's closet, but he refused to wear any of them. He would, however, accept whatever jewels or coins she managed to wheedle from her parents. Even Storytellers had to eat, and Fellow was little more than a vagabond. Yet he was so much more.

"Your father cherishes you, as does your kind mother," said Fellow in the tone of an encouraging schoolmaster, which he was not. Sharadza's tutors were never so informal with her, nor did she relish spending time with them the way she savored her every rendezvous with the Storyteller. He wandered the streets of the city between visits, telling his stories on street corners and in wine shops, earning his daily bread by weaving tales for the weary Men and Giants of Udurum.

"What do you know of him?" she asked, challenging Fellow to spill any secrets he might possess.

The old man licked his dry lips. "I know that he built New Udurum on the ruins of the old city, after the Lord of Serpents destroyed it."

"Everyone knows that."

"Yes, but did you know the young Vod was born a Giant but was raised by human parents?"

Sharadza nodded, sitting back down on the cold bench. Thunder rolled low in the distance, like the pounding of great breakers at the edge of a distant sea. She had heard rumors of her father's human parents, but he never spoke of them to her.

"Oh, they did not know he was a Giant at first, just a very large baby," said the Storyteller. "But they soon found out when he grew too fast." His voice sank to a whisper. "They say his human father abandoned him, but his mother never did. She died not long after the building of the new city."

"She would have been my grandmother," said Sharadza.

"Not entirely," said Fellow, "for she was never related to your father by blood."

"What about the Serpent Lord? Is it true my father slew him?"

"Yes," said the Storyteller. "By virtue of his sorcery, the same powers that make him both Giant and Man, your father destroyed the oldest enemy of Giant-kind. His magic made him tall as the Grim Mountains, and he wrestled with the Great Wyrm, his flesh burned by the great fires that it spit in his face. Their battle took place right here, among the ruins of Old Udurum. Nearly all the Giants had been slain and their city toppled. When young Vod crushed the life out of the monster, he vowed to rebuild the city. That is why we have this capital of Giants and Men. Your father brought peace to the Great Ones and the Small Ones. He is a hero. Never forget that."

Sharadza nodded. How could she ever forget the legacy of her father? But there was much she still did not understand. The wind caught up her long black curls, and she brushed them away from her face.

"Is it true the Giants are dying?" she asked.

The Storyteller frowned at her. "Since the destruction of Old Udurum, no Giantess has borne a child. Some say the dying Serpent Lord put a curse on his enemies, and that is the reason why the she-Giants are barren. If your father had not fallen in love with your mother, a human, you and your brothers might never have been born at all! The Giants who live among us now are old. Yes, they are a dying breed, and they know it. Little more than a thousand still walk the world, and by the time your own children are grown someday, they may all be gone."

"Is there nothing we can do?" Sharadza asked. Such finality made her want to cry. Her cousins were Giants, so if they died a part of her died with them. Her father's best friend was his uncle Fangodrim, who was uncle to her as well.

"Likely not," said Fellow. "These things are decided by higher powers than you or I. But remember that it is not death that counts in the end, but a life lived well."

Sharadza smiled through her brimming tears. Fellow was always saying things like that. "Jewels of wisdom" he sometimes called them. It was one of the things she loved about him.

"Fellow," she said, "I have another question for you."

"Of course, Majesty."

"How did my father learn sorcery? Was he born with it?"

Fellow sat quietly for a moment. Sharadza heard the moaning wind and a peal of approaching thunder.

"I'd best tell that story another time," said the old man.

"Why?"

"Because your mother is coming."

"Oh! You must hide. I'm not supposed to be listening to your tales. She says you're a liar and not to be trusted."

Fellow smiled at her, the skin about his gray eyes wrinkling. "Do you believe that, Princess?"

She kissed his cheek. "Of course not. Now go. I hear her steps along the walk."

Fellow turned toward the tall hedge and disappeared into the leaves. He would find his way back out onto the streets of New Udurum by a hidden path she had shown him months ago. She could not explain her mother's distrust of the Storyteller, but she knew in her heart it was baseless, so she smuggled him into the royal gardens whenever she could, at least once a week. She began to think of him as her grandfather, albeit a grandfather she could never publicly acknowledge. She had learned much from his stories, and there was much more to discover.

Queen Shaira rounded the corner of the hedge maze with two palace guards in tow. Shaira was not a tall woman, but her presence loomed as that of a Giantess. Her hair was dark and her eyes bright as emeralds, both like her daughter's. Looking at her mother, standing there in her gown of purple silk and white brocade, a crown of silver and diamond circling her brow, Sharadza knew exactly what she would look like when she was grown. There could be no doubt that she would be the spitting image of her beautiful and regal mother. At the age of forty-five, Shaira retained every bit of her beauty, and this gave Sharadza no small comfort.

Her mother called her name, and smiled at her in that loving way that nobody else could ever smile. In the warmth of that smile, the day felt a bit less cool. The blaze of summer lived in her mother's green eyes. Maybe it was the fact that Shaira had grown up in a desert kingdom, or maybe her love itself was the source of the heat.

Sharadza ran to embrace the Queen.

"What are you doing out here, Little One?" asked Shaira. Even though Sharadza stood taller than her mother already, Shaira still called her by that nickname. She felt comfortably small in her mother's arms. It had always been so.

"Admiring the leaves," she answered. "Aren't they beautiful?" She cast her gaze upward at the splendid fall colors.

Her mother gave her a quizzical look, as if suspecting that she told only part of the truth. "Your father summons you before the throne," she said, running her hands along Sharadza's hair, smoothing the dark curls.

"Me?" Sharadza asked, stunned by the news.

"You and your brothers," said her mother, and the Princess saw a worried look pass across her face like a shadow passing across the face of the sun.

"What is the matter?" Sharadza asked.

"Come," said the Queen. "We shall soon know."

She followed her mother across the grand courtyard as big wet drops of rain began to fall. The sound of the drops hitting the leaves was a chorus of whispers. Then a blast of thunder split the sky, and she entered the palace proper.

Mother and daughter walked toward the King's hall as the storm broke against monolithic walls built by the hands of Giants.

Not far from Udurum's gates, beneath the branches of enormous trees, a gathering of Giants stood in a circle about two struggling figures. By the purple cloaks and blackened bronze they wore, these Uduru were known to all as the King's Warriors. They howled and leaped and shouted curses, but their great axes, swords, and hammers hung sheathed on their backs. Their eyes focused on the two man-sized combatants at their center.

Among the brown leaves lying big as shields on the forest floor, two sinewy, broad-chested youths rolled in a contest of power and stamina. Straining muscles gleamed with sweat, and the wrestlers breathed through gritted teeth. A pulp of leaves and mud smeared their bodies. The Giants, each standing three times the height of the wrestlers, shouted and waved bags of gold above the peaks of black war helms.

"Tadarus!" some shouted.

"Vireon!" cried others.

On the ground, Vireon stared up into his brother's face, feeling the weight of him like a boulder against his chest. Their arms locked together like the trunks of young oaks. Vireon's legs shot upward, his heels dug into Tadarus' abdomen, and his brother went flying. The giants roared. Now both brothers stood on their feet, coiled in the manner of crouching tigers. Tadarus laughed. Vireon smiled back at him.

"My little brother!" roared Tadarus. "You know I will beat you. I always do."

Now Vireon laughed to show his defiance. "You are but one year my senior. And youth has its advantages."

Shoulders slammed together and the Giants reeled from the sheer force of their collision. Once more the brothers stood locked in stalemate.

Vireon wondered who would tire first. If he could simply outlast his brother, he would win. The Giants would never underestimate him again.

They might have been twins, these two, but for Vireon's more narrow face and slightly lesser height. They shared the same jet-black hair, the same sky-blue eyes, and the strength of raging Uduru.

Tadarus slammed Vireon's back against a tree trunk. The monolithic Uyga trunk trembled, bark exploded, and the last of the tree's faded leaves fell in a slow rain about the brothers as they wrestled. The Giants howled at this display of strength, and Vireon leapt forward, flipping over his brother's head. They rolled together longwise through a debris of branch, bark, and leaf. Dead wood cracked beneath their bodies.

At the end of the roll, Vireon arose first, his arms still locked on his brother's shoulders. He took advantage of Tadarus' split second of disorientation and hurled him through the air, screaming after him. Tadarus crashed through a pine tree as thick as his waist, shearing it in half. Both he and the upper half of the tree fell with a double crash into the forest beyond the ring of bewildered Giants.

Vireon stood panting in the center of the chattering Uduru. The thrill of victory was a momentary sensation, replaced by instant worry for his brother, who lay somewhere in the shadows of the great trees.

"What excellence!" growled Boroldun the Bear-Fang. "The younger triumphs at last!"

"Hail, Vireon the Younger!" bellowed Danthus the Sharp-Tooth. "I knew your day would come!"

The Giants exchanged bags of gold, precious jewels, and other baubles as the supporters of Vireon claimed their winnings. Vireon payed them no attention, but leaped across the stump of the felled tree to find his brother. Tadarus lay among a knot of big ferns growing about a wedge-shaped boulder. Vireon feared the big rock had brained his brother.

*Gods of Earth and Sky, let him be well.*

Vireon bent low over his brother. "Tadarus?"

Without opening his eyes, Tadarus sprang up and knocked Vireon off his feet with the force of his shoulder. Vireon's posterior met the ground, and he stared up into the grinning face of his brother.

"Did you think you had actually *hurt* me?" Tadarus said. A few

Giants came tromping near, flattening the undergrowth with their every step. Some of them shouted to their fellows that Tadarus was fine – of course. The elder brother offered his hand, and Vireon took it. Now they stood together as the Giants looked upon them with admiration.

"I beat you," said Vireon.

"So you did," said Tadarus, smiling. "And you killed a tree."

The Giants laughed, thunder among the redwoods.

"I say your next bout should be fought on the plains of the Stormlands, or perhaps the top of a mountain!" said the Sharp-Tooth. "To avoid more casualties of nature!"

The Giants and Tadarus laughed. Vireon saw no humor. He regretted the felling of the pine. He would carry it back to the palace for the woodcarvers, or at the least to stoke the fires of the kitchens. Even a tree's death must serve a purpose.

"I am proud of you, brother," said Tadarus. Once more he placed his hands on Vireon's shoulders, warmly this time. His white teeth showed in the forest gloom as he looked his brother in the eye. "You have proven yourself my equal this day. And won a ton of loot for old Sharp-Tooth!"

Vireon at last smiled. His beefy chest swelled. He loved his brother. Only praise from his father could find more currency in his heart.

"I stand amazed, yet again," said the Sharp-Tooth to his fellows. Most of the Giants wandered toward the city gates as drops of rain began to fall, but three of the Sharp-Tooth's fellows lingered, his steadfast drinking companions, Dabruz the Flame-Heart, Grodulum the Hammer, and Hrolgar the Iron-Foot. "These whelps are sturdy as Uduru, though they could pass for Men in any kingdom south of the Grim."

"The True Sons of Vod!" said the Iron-Foot. "They are both men and giants."

"Perhaps we're neither," said Tadarus, sharing a gourd of cool water with Vireon. "Perhaps we are something new. Mother said we carry the best of both races in our blood. Perhaps there is no name for what we are."

"Aye," said Danthus. "You speak with your father's wisdom. But here, Vireon, take you this hammer won from Ohlung the Bear-Slayer." He held the great weapon out to Vireon. The length of it was greater than half the youth's body, but he grabbed its haft and lifted it above his head, testing its balance. It was a Giant's weapon, forged in the smithies of Old Udurum, before the coming of the Serpent Father. Its pitted head was carved into the likeness of a grinning demon, and a band of beaten bronze wound about the dark stone.

"It is a good hammer," said Vireon, admiring the ancient signs of the Uduru carved into the back of the demon-head. "But too unsubtle for me. I think my brother should have it."

Vireon passed the hammer to Tadarus, who grinned at him again and took the war hammer, swinging it about him a few times playfully. "A fine weapon," said Tadarus. "But you won. It should be yours!" He offered it back to Vireon.

"And as mine, it is also mine to give!" Vireon rammed his elbow into Tadarus' tight stomach. Tadarus grunted, then laughed. He nodded, and the argument was done.

The rain fell now in pleasant sheets, so the brothers washed the earth from their bodies while cold winds blew through the upper leaves. The Giants stood counting their loot, heedless of the rising storm.

"Now," said Tadarus, banging his fists together with fresh vigor. "Which one of you Uduru will challenge me and my brother? Let's have a *real* wrestling match!"

The Giants roared their mirth at him, and Vireon went to fetch the felled tree. "None will wrestle you, Prince," said the Sharp-

Tooth. "For there is the off chance that you might win. And no Giant could stand being bested by such a small thing."

Tadarus laughed. "Then flee, Giants! Or face my wrath!" He lunged at the Uduru, and they scattered among the trees, laughing at his temerity, dropping coins and jewels in their wake. Vireon joined his brother, the slain tree slung over one shoulder. Tadarus took up his hammer.

"Thank you, Brother," said Tadarus. "For the hammer."

Vireon grinned. "It was the least I could do after humiliating you in front of the Uduru."

Tadarus looked at his brother with a semblance of anger on his handsome face.

"Do you imply that you could best me twice?" he asked.

Vireon grinned. "Three times, even."

Tadarus threw down his hammer, and Vireon his tree trunk. Again they faced each other, crouching ready to spring. The rain pelted them and thunder rolled among the deeps of the forest.

A different thunder, that of a horse's hooves pounding the wet earth, met Vireon's ears. He turned his head just as Tadarus slammed into him. They rolled through the mud for a short while until the voice calling them rose above the sound of the storm.

"Prince Tadarus! Prince Vireon! The King commands your presence!" The hooded cloak of the King's Messenger shone brightly violet during a brief flare of lightning. A black steed, caparisoned in jewels and silk, had carried the rider to them. His name was Tumond, a good man. And he only carried important messages for the King of New Udurum. For Father to summon them in such a manner, the matter must be of great urgency.

Tadarus knew these things as well as Vireon. The brothers rose from their mud-fight, took up hammer and tree, and ran beside the horse as it galloped across the field toward the black towers of the city.

Lightning bolts hurtled madly across the black sky as the brothers ran. Orange watch-fires burned along the city wall in gigantic braziers. The Princes followed the herald onto the wide street called Giant's Way. All eyes large and small turned to catch a glimpse as they jogged toward the spires of jet and basalt that marked the palace of Vod, living heart of the City of Men and Giants.

The eldest Prince of New Udurum stood near a north-facing window high in a tower of the gargantuan palace. Fangodrel watched the thunderheads rolling in and casting their shadows across the great forest. The rolling landscape was a panoply of colors as far as the eye could see, an ocean of autumn leaves in every shade of the rainbow save one. All the green had bled away from the world, and the myriad hues of autumn stood triumphant. A chill wind stole through the open window and raked his chest with icy fingers.

The wide chamber lay shrouded in the gloom of a small brazier topped with low-burning flames. On the bed behind him the servant girl Yazmilla lay senseless among the silken pillows. Her flesh had not been enough to quench his restless hunger. At least her ceaseless yammering had stopped, now that she was unconscious. Now he might have chance for concentration.

He turned his attention to the parchment on his writing table. The poem was almost finished. A few more lines would bring the piece to a transcendent climax. Forty-two lines were ideal. The first thirty had taken a month of agonizing introspection . . . long walks beneath the cold moon . . . a hundred meditations in the moldy air of the city graveyard. Every line was a piece of his soul, a shard of truth, jagged and dangerous to the touch. The splinters of his essential self. This would be his greatest work, a poem that would shame all the hundreds that came before it. His crowning achievement in the realm of verse. If he could only finish it.

He took up a white-feathered quill and dipped its point into a cup of black ink. The point hovered over his parchment. His mind reeled with blank frustration. He hesitated. A drop of ink fell onto the page, blotting like black blood. His left fist clenched, fingernails digging into his palm, and he bit his lip until it bled. His red eyes watered, and he threw the quill across the room like a dart. He stuffed the unfinished poem into the drawer of the table, slamming it shut.

*Inspiration is a fickle whore.*

The sleeping girl would wake soon, whimpering and crying, begging for more of the bloodflower. He lifted to his lips the long pipe, carved from white oak into the shape of a many-legged Serpent of legend. Touching a candle's flame to the round bowl in the back of the Serpent's skull, he inhaled the sweet crimson vapor. It sang in his veins and sent sparks flying behind his eyes, so that he imagined it was his skull, not the Serpent's, to which he touched the flame. Leaning his head back, he slumped onto a divan of burgundy velvet. From his reclining position he watched the stormclouds moving toward the window. A few wet drops blew in to kiss his naked skin.

The lights of the city were kindled below as the day turned to night; a million tiny jewels spread in secret patterns far below the tower chamber. He drew another lungful of the bloodflower smoke into his lungs, and watched lightning caper among the thunderheads. He enjoyed the advent of a storm, the casting of light into darkness, the warm air growing cold, the faint stench of fear that rose from the streets as the commoners fled for shelter. He brought the Serpent's tail to his lips once more. Now thunder rang inside his skull, shaking his very bones with its violence. He fell prone on the divan, trembling, moaning his pleasure to the corners of the dim chamber.